BETWEEN TWO WORLDS

A MULTICULTURAL AND MULTILINGUAL ANTHOLOGY

THIRD EDITION

ALAN HIDALGO

BETWEEN TWO WORLDS
A MULTICULTURAL AND MULTILINGUAL ANTHOLOGY
THIRD EDITION

iUniverse books may be ordered through booksellers or by contacting:

iUniverse
1663 Liberty Drive
Bloomington, IN 47403
www.iuniverse.com
1-800-Authors (1-800-288-4677)

ISBN: 978-1-4917-8112-8 (sc)
ISBN: 978-1-4917-8113-5 (e)

Print information available on the last page.

iUniverse rev. date: 11/24/2015

Dedication

THIS BOOK IS dedicated to the many students who have touched our lives with their sincerity, their search for the truth, their unbridled joy, and their nobility in overcoming hardships. They continue to challenge and inspire us.

This book is dedicated to the many friendships we have made throughout the world. These special people have shown us the depth and beauty of their countries and their cultures.

This book is dedicated to our families, both physical and spiritual.

Acknowledgments

THE ALAN HIDALGO Team would personally like to thank so many people who have shared their lives with us. From a compilation of student upon student, friend upon friend, and colleague upon colleague, the inspiration to create the Between Two Worlds series became a reality. It is our sincere desire that this literary work and the supplementary educational resources will inspire young people to make good decisions, lead virtuous lives, find fulfillment as they reach their potential, and in the process, bless others as well.

Preface

═══

To the Reader:

The characters and events in the ten novels that compose the *Between Two Worlds Anthology* are purely fictional. Even so, you may find that you relate with the struggles, failures, and triumphs of the main characters found within each novel.

For the Educational Instructor:

There are three textbooks in the series: The *Between Two Worlds Anthology*, the *Between Two Worlds Student Workbook*, and the *Between Two Worlds Instructor Manual*. Teachers and professors will notice that there are ten words that have been placed in bold print in each of the ten novels of the anthology. These words were chosen for the vocabulary lessons in the student workbook due to their academic and thematic qualities. Each of the three texts is designed to correlate to the other; for instructional purposes, all three must be incorporated for maximum results in a classroom setting. The *Between Two Worlds Student Workbook* may be used at various secondary and post-secondary educational levels e.g. courses in English, ESL, character building, multiculturalism, and diversity training.

Contents and Synopsis

NOVELS

- Manuel De La Rosa grew up in a small agricultural town in southern California near the Mexico border. Adapting to a new culture is difficult as he transitions from elementary school, to junior high school, and to high school. His parents treat him well enough, but they continue to live their lives as if they are still in Mexico. Watching his older brothers choose different paths in life, Manuel struggles to find his own way. By the time he is seventeen, he is at a crossroads, and a possible prison sentence forces him to reflect on his decisions.

- Lorena Olorsisimo is the youngest child of a very traditional Filipino family. Entering high school, she has her sights on achieving perfect grades, making the varsity basketball team, and earning a scholarship to UCLA. Then she meets Greg, a handsome, wealthy senior in high school who will challenge her most cherished beliefs.

- Mike Nathan was a star the moment he set foot on his high school campus. As a freshman who stands six feet eight inches and weighs a solid 220 pounds, he is a recognized superstar in both football and basketball. Mike, partly due to his size, and partly due to his personality, is also a natural leader. Other students follow him and most teachers fear him. He is known throughout the school as a young man who speaks his mind. When his science teacher, Mrs. Larson, dares to confront him, she introduces the concept of people skills and effective communication. What begins as an experiment for Mike becomes an entirely new way of relating to people and the many challenges that social interaction often present.

- Diane Davis is a poor white girl who grows up in a predominantly Hispanic community. Misjudged by her peers and abused by her family, she revels in her independence and freedom upon being accepted by New Mexico University. But after experiencing popularity for the first time in her life, she struggles to find inner peace. Not finding what she is looking for in alcohol and drugs, Diane reflects on the lives of two girls, one a Christian and the other, a Muslim. Slowly, she finds her way...

- Doctor Marc Wilson is a leading medical expert in the field of cancer research. During a clinic, he is asked about the key to his success. After careful consideration, he answers that it all comes down to perspective. When a young intern is not satisfied with this answer, Marc begins to reminisce about the parents who abandoned him and his many childhood struggles. If it were not for the love of his grandmother and the inspiration of a studious college student who had emigrated from Guatemala, Marc may not have survived his long and perilous journey.

- William "Billy" Dean is a Hoosier from head to foot. Basketball is his main love in life though he is not a standout player. In fact, Billy does not stand out in anything. He is a well-liked young man who does not fight to reach his full potential due to his fear of failure, or worse, rejection. Instead of taking risks, Billy prefers to settle for mediocrity. Fortunately for him, he meets people that edge him to realize his capabilities. From Brett, his childhood friend; to Fan, a Chinese student who studies at Indiana University; to Marcelo, the Italian owner of a pizza restaurant; and to Maria, a young lady from Nicaragua: William is inspired to believe in himself and to not be afraid to face the difficulties of life.

- Miranda Frondizi is an Argentine beauty. Intelligent and cultured, she led a sheltered life of privilege until her family was forced to move to southern California due to financial hardship. Once in the United States, she attends a junior college entirely against her wishes. Miranda is not accustomed to her new setting, which is much more representative of various nationalities and economic classes than the previous places she frequented in her native Argentina. In her first encounter with American students, she lets her perceived superiority be known, leading to instant social dilemmas. It is not until she meets Ben, a highly intellectual student, that she begins to reconsider her worldview.

- John Kim is the second born. He does not feel second, however, but last. His father constantly belittles him while openly favoring his older brother, Paul, who is the more handsome and stronger of the two. As if this is not enough, Paul is also a celebrated black belt in Tae Kwon Do. Paul is everything that John is not. Tired of being rejected, John decides to give up entirely. He stops training and avoids both his father and his brother. As he does so, his resentment for them grows. Struggling with loneliness, John meets Robson Da Silva, a new student who trains in Brazilian Jiu Jitsu under his uncle, Mario Da Silva. A new friend, a new martial art, and a new teacher open the way toward the true meaning of being a champion.

- Betania struggles when her family moves from Veracruz, Mexico, to Brownsville, Texas. Not only does she have to adapt to a new culture, but she is belittled for not speaking English at her new school. In her loneliness, she turns to her older sister and other Mexican immigrants in her neighborhood for comfort. Unfortunately, when she attends what she thought to be an innocent party, she quickly finds out that the music and laughter are all part of a recruiting ploy for a powerful gang. Before she realizes the danger, Betania is in. Getting out will not be so easy.

- Aaron Holmes and Terry Washington are more than cousins; they are like brothers. Both of them live with their grandparents and both of them are star athletes. As they prepare for the next football season, they are well aware that their coach believes that a state title is within their grasp. Aaron, optimistic and intuitive by nature, feels more than ready for such a challenge. Terry, a highly intellectual and introspective young man, struggles with issues he considers far deeper than football. He dwells on his difficult upbringing and the many injustices of the world. This deep introspection makes him vulnerable to a radical new political organization, known as The Standard, which is led by the mysterious genius, Doctor Timothy Ajala.

THE DECISION

1

IT WAS A decision that had to be made.

"*Te digo que no tenemos remedio!*" said Carlos. He was a small man, with thick black hair that grew disheveled in all directions across his somewhat dark, square reddish face. Elena, his wife, sat in resigned silence. Her brown eyes filled with tears as she pressed the little child in her arms tightly against her breast.

Carlos and Elena De La Rosa, along with their son, Carlitos, lived in the outskirts of Tijuana, Mexico. People referred to the area as *El Niño*. It was arid and dusty, and so remote that it could not be considered a town, but a mere *colonia*. The streets were nothing more than dirt paths filled with rocks and broken glass, and houses were composed of anything people could find. Discarded wood. Cardboard. Thin sheets of metal. A few homes had electricity, the result of flimsy wires tied to the main lines that were anchored by large wooden posts, but most did not.

For the people who lived in *El Niño*, choices were limited: move out and risk living in the violence of Tijuana, get involved in the drug trade, or work from time to time and hope not to starve to death.

Carlos turned from his wife. "*Pues, lo siento, pero me voy mañana con mi tío, Roberto,*" he said quietly. "*Es mejor que me vaya. Si no, pues, tú y el bebé se mueren de hambre. Te prometo que un día voy a volver. Mientras tanto, quédate con tus papás en Mexicali.*"

Elena rocked their small child in her arms. At times her long black hair brushed against his face. As there was no other place to go in the one room home, Carlos left for the little *tienda de abarrotes*. There, he would buy nothing, but at least he could spend some time talking with other men from the *colonia*.

2

No clouds, no trees, no shade. The heat was intense. Carlos used his forearm to wipe the sweat from the sides of his of his forehead as he loaded several pillow cases that had been converted into traveling bags inside the trunk of an old rusted car. He then assisted Elena into the back seat and quickly placed Carlitos next to her. Greeting the driver, he sat in the front seat and closed the final door. Within twenty minutes, they would arrive at the *La Central Camionera de Autobuses de Tijuana.*

"*Dos boletos para Mexicali, por favor,*" said Carlos, paying the fare of the autobus that would take his wife and son to Mexicali, where they would stay with his *suegros.*

Carlos held his little boy one last time, wrapping his thick right hand and forearm around him. Little Carlitos blinked a few times, his large eyes full of innocence. Kissing Elena, Carlos embraced her tightly with his one free hand. He stroked her hair that fell to her waist and whispered, "*Todo va a estar bien. Vas a ver. No hago esto para mí, pero para ustedes.*" Then, turning his attention to his baby boy, he added, "*Y tú, pórtate bien.*"

A few minutes later, the large bus had pulled away, so Carlos waited. And waited. And waited.

Day turned to night, and the revelers began to appear in the many *cantinas* and *tiendas.* Carlos walked down the *avenida Revolución.* There was a mixture of people. Merchants, *tijuanos, turistas.* After several blocks, he turned away from the noise and lights and headed down a smaller side street. There, in the emptiness of the curb, softly idling, was a familiar light blue truck with a custom made working bench that extended the full width of the bed. Without saying a word, Carlos knocked on the window. His uncle lowered it slightly, greeted him, and motioned for him to enter. Carlos then slowly made his way through a cramped space. Once there, his uncle placed the folding seat back into place. In the morning, Carlos would be in San Ysidro, on the other side of the border.

3

Tío Roberto had made Carlos a simple offer: a couch to sleep on and work to wake up to each day. Besides that, his uncle guaranteed him nothing. For the next several months, Carlos would accompany tío Roberto and several cousins whom he had never met to the many houses on their route. Some of the homes were modest, whereas others belonged to the finest neighborhoods of San Diego. Carlos often stood with his mouth agape as he stood in front of the palaces before him. The men mowed lawns, trimmed bushes, and dumped piles of grass and leaves into large dumpsters day in and day out.

"*Qué te pasa, primo?*"

Drinking a large plastic bottle of water, Carlos wiped his mouth and replied, "*Nada. Es que yo pienso en mi mujer y mi hijo.*"

The other man nodded, took a drink of his own water, and then reached into his pocket. He pulled out a picture of a pretty young woman. She was wearing a blue dress. Her thick black hair reached her shoulders. "*Mi novia*," he said.

Carlos nodded. "*Es muy guapa.*"

"*Gracias.*"

Most of these men had made great sacrifices to live in the United States.

4

Several years passed, and the De La Rosa family settled into the Imperial Valley. In the blazing hot summers, Carlos picked carrots, cantaloupe, and watermelon. During the more pleasant climate of the winter, he harvested alfalfa. There was always something to do, whether it was picking, harvesting, or transporting irrigation pipes.

It did not take long for the De La Rosa family to grow. After Carlitos came Juan, the first child to be born in the United States. Two years later, a third son was born, named Manuel. Finally, after the three boys, came two lovely daughters, Cecilia and Yolanda.

Carlos De La Rosa had a family. He had work. He had a small farm of his own. He was content at last.

5

CARLITOS AND JUAN, the eldest of the three boys, loved to play games with their friends and ride their bikes on the dirt roads that dominated the outskirts of Holtville. Cecilia and Yolanda, the two youngest children, preferred to stay inside the house where they played with their dolls. Manuel, however, often went unnoticed. He spent most of his time alone, preferring the company of his many animals. The other boys shook their heads and smiled when they saw little Manuel carrying a chicken while being trailed by two stray dogs.

"Your little brother's funny," said one, stopping on his bike to stare.

"Naw, he just likes to take care of them," said Carlitos, the oldest of the group.

"Man, he's got his own zoo!" said another boy. "Ducks, chickens, dogs, cats."

"Yeah, all right, let's go!" said Juan.

The other boys turned to Carlitos, who nodded in approval. Each of them then mounted their bicycles and disappeared down the road. Manuel, meanwhile, placed a large brown hen in a chicken coop, completely unaware that he was being observed.

6

AS A CHILD, Manuel grew up in two different worlds. The first one was the De La Rosa home. There, Manuel's parents only spoke Spanish. This world was simple and reflected life in Mexico. Home was where Manuel enjoyed his mother's sweet demeanor and delicious cooking. Home was where his father arrived after work so tired that he did not wish to talk to anyone. Instead, upon entering the house, he would grab a large bottle of *cerveza* and turn on the television to watch a game of *fútbol*.

But Manuel was quickly discovering another world, a world called school. School was where Manuel learned English. School was where Manuel learned about the Presidents of the United States, such as George Washington and Abraham Lincoln. And school was where Manuel felt a different type of culture, one that had more of an Anglo, or white American, influence. School was also a place that offered Manuel more structure in his life. There were rules that he and the other children had to follow, such as raising their hands before they spoke, or learning how to form a straight line when they went to the cafeteria. School was where Manuel tried new kinds of foods, such as macaroni and cheese, or peanut butter and jelly sandwiches, or his new favorite, apple sauce. This was Manuel's second world.

Each year he studied diligently to earn good grades and please his teachers. They noticed him and often recognized his efforts with special awards. Despite this, however, his parents never came to his school to visit. Neither his father nor his mother had ever had a conversation with any of his teachers.

"*Mamá! Mamá!*" said Manuel. "*Mi maestra quiere conocerte esta noche.*"

Manuel's mother let out a deep sigh. "*Esta noche? Pa' qué?*" she replied, her eyes glued to the *telenovela* playing on the television.

"*Ya te dije!* It's 'Back to School Night'! *Todos los padres van a la escuela para hablar con los maestros. Mi maestra me dijo que me van a dar un premio en frente de todos!*" said Manuel, hopping up and down.

"*No sé, hijo,*" she replied. "*Tu papá siempre viene muy cansado y quiere que tenga la comida lista.*"

Manuel lowered his head, somewhat **sheepishly**. He did not want to argue with his mother, but he could not hide his disappointment.

7

THE SIMPLE LIFE was vanishing. Carlitos was having trouble in school, and Juan began acting strangely. Conflict had entered the De La Rosa home.

"*Ni vas a la escuela,*" said Manuel's mother to Carlitos. "*Estás trabajando mucho, hijo, y eso no es bueno!*"

"*Quiero dinero, mamá,*" replied Carlitos, "*y la escuela no me paga nada.*" Manuel smiled at his brother's comment.

Juan, too, received a scolding from his mother. As he ironed his black shirt and oversized khaki pants, she wagged her head at him. Then, entering his closet, she grabbed a red dress shirt with long sleeves and a striped silk tie. "*No me gusta la ropa que estás escogiendo. Por qué no te pones esta?*" she asked, holding up the shirt in one hand. "*Se ve muy linda con la corbata.*"

Juan shook his head and laughed. "*Chale, Ma! No soy un pinche niño y jamás me voy a poner una camisa roja!*"

Carlitos winced. Manuel struggled to refrain the laughter that was bubbling from within him.

"*No le hables así!*" said Carlitos. "Show some respect, man!"

"*Cállate, pinche méxicano!*" said Juan, sticking out his chin. "You don't tell me what to do!"

Carlitos and Juan stood face to face. Carlitos was the taller of the two, but Juan was much more thickly built. His head was blocky, and looked as if it could be used as a battering ram. Manuel's eyes widened. His mother cringed. After a brief silence, Carlitos slowly shook his head and walked away, muttering, "*Qué huevón!*"

8

MANUEL WAS NOT ready to face the many challenges of junior high school. He had to switch classes every hour. This was hard. He had to adapt to a different teacher and a different group of kids. Many of his classmates, the same children he had known since kindergarten, no longer seemed to like their teachers. Suddenly, it was not popular to pass out paper or volunteer to read.

"Who would like to read the first paragraph?" asked Mrs. Jacobs, an older teacher who had very tanned skin and short gray hair.

Manuel quickly raised his hand.

"Man, that's embarrassing!" said the boy next to him.

Manuel quickly lowered his hand. It was the last time he volunteered for anything. His friends were changing. Many of them no longer spoke to each other. In elementary school, everyone used to play and eat lunch together, but in junior high, they all seemed to belong to a particular group made just for them. Some played sports. Others preferred music. A few liked to study and took great pride in their grades, but they were not very popular. And finally, there were the ones who had been **labeled** the bad kids; they did not care about school and rarely came at all. As Manuel watched the many circles of boys and girls huddled together during lunch, he did not know where he belonged.

9

WHILE MANUEL STRUGGLED to find his place, his brothers made some clear decisions of their own. Carlitos dropped out of school to work in the fields with his father. He calmly explained to his mother that he probably was not going to graduate, and since he was not a legal citizen…

"I'm not going back to Mexico," he announced. "I mean, I like visiting, but I don't want to live there. And it's not like I'm gonna go to college, so I might as well work in the fields like Pa."

Manuel's father accepted Carlitos' decision, happily taking him to work with him each day. His relationship with Juan, however, was becoming increasingly filled with tension. Each week the two could be heard fighting. El señor De La Rosa's face lit up as he shouted so loudly that his voice echoed throughout the neighborhood.

"*No sirves para nada!*" he bellowed as Juan walked out the front door.

It was anyone's guess when he would return. Manuel's mother appealed to Juan to listen to his father, but he did not seem to care.

"*Ya, mamá, déjame!*" he said, gently slapping her hand off his arm.

"*Estoy rezando por ti, hijo,*" she replied. "*Te quiero mucho.*"

Whenever she said this, Juan would stop for a moment. For a split second, his scowl faded…but then it returned just as fast. Juan refused to listen to his parents. He also refused to listen to his teachers at school. It did not take long before he was transferred to the community school in El Centro for a **litany** of offenses: stealing, gang violence, and using profanity with anyone who dared oppose him.

10

TOWARD THE END of junior high, Manuel was as undecided as ever. He felt lost and without direction in life. Nobody said anything that truly interested him, and his grades suffered as a result. Whereas once he was considered a top student by his teachers, he had since fallen into mediocrity, being content merely to pass his classes with minimal effort. Each day he trudged through the same tired routine. One afternoon, however, as he entered his very last class, he was surprised to see a young man standing at the door.

"Hello," greeted the young man with a warm smile.

Manuel looked at him. He reminded Manuel of his older brother, Carlitos. They both had the same clean cut image. No facial hair on their smooth brown skin, dress slacks and collared shirts; yet there was something noticeably different about this young man. Something in his eyes told Manuel that he was not as carefree as his older brother. There was a certain intensity about him.

"What's up," replied Manuel. He did not bother to stop as he made his way to a desk that was located in the back of the room.

Slowly, other students made their way into the classroom. As the bell sounded, Mr. Thomas, Manuel's eighth grade history teacher, stood up behind his desk. He was a large man with a wide face and short brown hair. For the most part, students appreciated his well prepared lessons and pleasant personality. "I would like to introduce a former student," said Mr. Thomas. "His name is Pablo Ruiz. His family still lives here in Holtville, but Pablo's actually in Santa Barbara now where he attends classes at the university." Then, motioning to Pablo, he continued, "They're all yours."

The young man smiled and walked from the corner of the room to the wooden podium that was positioned front and center. "Thank you, Mr. Thomas. *Hola, me llamo Pablo y estoy aquí para animarles a tener éxito en la vida y hablarles un poco de mi experiencia en la Universidad de Santa Bárbara.*"

Many of the students' eyes perked up as Pablo addressed them in Spanish.

"My message to you today is to feel proud of who you are," he continued, "and I'm not just talking to the Mexicans, so don't think I'm here to try to pump up my race because I'm not. I'm Mexican American. My parents were born in Mexico, but I was born here; so yeah, I cherish my heritage, but I'm proud to call myself a first generation American. So whether you're Hispanic or white—I think I see a few other **nationalities** here, too—I'm here to encourage you. It doesn't matter where you come from or who you are, you have the freedom to make something of your life. That's the beauty of living in the United States.

"Anyway, I bet a lot of you are just like me. Born in Mexico or the Imperial Valley, going to school here in little Holtville, eating barbecue at the Carrot festival and celebrating el *Día de la Familia*."

Manuel smiled as did several other students.

"I bet another thing we have in common is that some of you come from a poor family. Maybe your life's been kind of hard. Maybe your dad skipped out on you. Maybe you have an older brother in jail. Maybe some of you girls have been told that you can't go to college. Well, I'm here to tell you to forget all that! The truth is that you can do whatever you put your mind to. If you want to be a doctor, then be a doctor! If you want to be a nurse, then be a nurse! If you want to be a police officer, then be a police officer! And if you want to start your own business, then go for it! Don't let anything hold you back!"

Students whispered to each other as Pablo extended his index finger at them, pointing slowly at each row of desks. Many nodded their heads whereas others appeared startled by his authoritative tone and posturing.

"Now, I know what some of you are thinking…'Yeah, here's this guy from college talking to us about how great school is and how we need to choose a career…' Look, that's really not why I'm here. I just want to help you succeed in life, no matter what you decide. College may not be the right thing for all of you, but that doesn't mean you don't have to come to school right now and do your best. Trust me; school has a lot more to offer than just a bunch of books. School gets you ready for the real world. School is where you learn to respect your teachers, follow the rules, and get along with others. Later, that's going to help you when you get a job. No matter what you decide, though, you're going to have to do something. I mean, you're not going to be a kid forever."

A few students who earlier were fidgeting in their desks suddenly became quite still. Mr. Thomas seemed to notice this. A smile broke upon his face.

"Take my family," continued Pablo. "I have three brothers and no sisters. Believe me; my parents had their hands full with us growing up because we're all so different. The oldest one, Pedro, is in jail. He ruined his life by selling drugs. While I was hanging out at the Memorial Library, he was kicking it with drug dealers. He never took school seriously and always got in trouble. My other older brother, Tomás, kind of like your teacher, Mr. Thomas, also struggled in school. In fact, he wasn't as smart as the one who was locked up for messing with drugs!"

Many of the students laughed.

"Anyway," said Pablo, "Tomás is driving a truck in San Diego for a beverage company—one of those vitamin waters—I think. He knew he was never going to go to college, but he made sure he got his high school diploma. Do you know why you need a high school diploma even if you don't plan on going to college?"

A few students raised their hands. Pablo called on one young man.

"To get a job?" he offered.

"That's right!" replied Pablo. "If you don't graduate from high school, you're not going to be able to do anything except maybe work in the fields or some packing shed. Even the Army won't take you."

Pablo paused. He then frowned and wagged his head.

"Well, like I was saying, my brother Tomás didn't go to college, but he did finish high school. He's a cool dude and has a steady job. He was never a good student, and he usually took the easiest classes, but he always got along with his teachers. In fact, I would say they really tried to help him out because they liked him so much. In other words, getting bad grades doesn't mean you have to act like an asshole!"

A few students cocked their heads back. Others laughed nervously. Most of them turned toward Mr. Thomas, but he remained with the same, relaxed expression.

Pablo reached into one of the shelves of the podium where he was standing and withdrew a sports bottle. He took a few drinks before continuing. "Now, my youngest brother is still in high school. He's only a few years older than all of you. You might know him, Ignacio Ruiz."

Immediately, several students began to whisper.

"Hey, uh, excuse me," said one boy, raising his hand.

"Yes?" asked Pablo.

"Do they call your brother 'Nacho'?" he asked.

"Yeah, that's him," replied Pablo.

Students began to chat in obvious recognition of the name.

One boy said to another, "That dude's bad! My brother said that he abuses people in wrestling practice. He's hella strong!"

"He's really cute, too!" said a girl to two of her friends.

"It looks like some of you have heard of him," interrupted Pablo. "Well, Ignacio doesn't take all the hardest classes like I did. He's too busy being buff and playing sports, but he does all right. In fact, I would say that football and wrestling have really helped him stay focused in school. He's either going to join the military or go to college. It may be a junior college and not a university, but he's going somewhere. Knowing him, he'll probably end up being a cop or some type of law enforcement officer."

Pablo folded his hands together and took a deep breath. "Now, like I said, college may not be for all of you, but I know it's the right path for a lot of you guys, so if you're planning on going to college, man, then start now! All you have to do is put the same energy into school that you put into other things that you like. If you like cars and read Hot Rod magazines all the time, do the same thing with your class assignments. If you like rap music, then memorize the vocabulary words in your English class. If you like talking to girls, then pay attention when your teachers talk about poetry. Anybody can do it." Pablo shrugged and extended his palms upward. "We're all the same, guys, so no excuses. My parents don't even speak English and here I am about to graduate from the University of Santa Barbara. I still remember when I was your age, sat in..."

Pablo paused as he walked around the podium to the front row in the middle of the room. He touched one of the desks where a petite girl with long black hair and a white blouse sat quietly.

"...this desk right here. I learned a lot in this class. Anyway, right now I'm studying politics and international studies. I either want to run for office someday or become a professor at the university level."

"I hope you become a politician. I know I'd vote for you," interrupted a deep voice.

"Thanks, Mr. Thomas," replied Pablo. "So, in order to reach my goals, I have to get my **doctorate.**"

One of the students raised her hand.

"Go ahead," said Pablo.

"I don't get it," she said. "You want to be a doctor?"

"No, no," said Pablo. "Like I said, I'm into politics. You know, like a congressman or a senator. At the university level, you can earn different degrees. The first one is a bachelor's degree; that takes four years. Then, you can go for a master's degree, which is six years of school. And if you want a doctorate, it usually takes at least eight years."

Some of the students shook their heads.

"You want to go to college for eight years?" asked the same girl with a rising shrillness in her voice.

"Of course!" replied Pablo, laughing at her astonishment. "College life is awesome! Anyway, when I get my doctorate, I want to help people, especially people that aren't aware of their rights. I don't know about you, but I want to make our communities around here better and in order to do that, it's going to take leadership. I guess that's really why I'm studying… to be a leader."

"Doesn't it cost a lot?" asked a boy sitting in the front area, just a little to the left of Pablo.

"Yeah, it does," said Pablo. "That's why you need good grades. But don't worry too much. I'm a poor kid and most of my education is being paid through Cal Grants and scholarships. Like I said, anybody can do it." Pablo turned toward the clock, took a quick drink, and concluded, "Well, that's about all. Thank you for letting me come to your class. Remember, guys, life is all about choices, so make the right ones and go on to be a big success!"

A few students began to clap when Mr. Thomas began clearing his throat rather loudly.

"Oh, one more thing!" said Pablo. "Don't be fooled by all the gang talk either 'cause it's a dead end. Most of those wannabe gangsters that I knew when I was your age are in prison, dead, or picking food out of a dumpster behind McDonald's™ or something like that."

Laughter was heard throughout the classroom. A few boys who were sitting in the back, however, folded their arms in front of their chests and slumped in their desks.

"Hey, everyone, we only have a few minutes until the bell rings," said Mr. Thomas. "Let's show Pablo that we appreciate him coming to our class. Remember, he just got you out of an assignment!"

As boys and girls began to applaud and whistle, Pablo shook hands with Mr. Thomas. Afterwards, he was instantly surrounded by a throng of students.

"Do you have a girlfriend?" asked one girl, a flirtatious smile across her face.

Pablo laughed. "Well, not at the moment. I'm trying to concentrate on my studies right now."

"That's a nice way of shutting you down, Elsa," said the boy next to her.

"*Cállate!*" she replied. "I'm just asking!"

Rolling his eyes, the boy smiled and continued, "I bet there's a lot of fine girls at your college."

Nodding his head, Pablo replied, "You have no idea, bro! There are so many beautiful girls in Santa Barbara that you can't even keep track! And you know what? They're not just pretty, they're smart, too! That's just one more reason to pursue your education, man!"

Another boy approached Pablo. He had long dark hair that was slicked back with gel. In a very serious tone, he asked, "Were you ever in a gang?"

"No, man, never!" replied Pablo. "My brother hung around those losers and look where it got him! He's serving time right now!"

The boy frowned and walked away.

Next, a student with short hair and a nice collared shirt approached Pablo. He asked, "I really like to draw and design things. Some people have told me I should become an architect, but it sounds kind of hard."

"Of course it's hard!" said Pablo. He patted the boy hard on the back, causing him to stumble slightly. "First, you have to get really good grades just to be accepted into a university. Second, you have to be really good at geometry and all that stuff. That's not really my field, but talk to your math teachers and research it for yourself. If that's what you want to do, then do it! *Todo en la vida cuesta!* That's just the way it is, man."

The boy thanked Pablo and slowly returned to his seat. Manuel, too, slowly made his way over and shook Pablo's hand. He **lingered** a while and listened as Pablo interacted with his classmates, but he did not ask any personal questions of his own.

11

IN HIGH SCHOOL, Manuel continued to feel disconnected. Some of his friends joined the football team, but Manuel was not very athletic. Other friends became involved in various school activities, but Manuel preferred to stay to himself. He did not have any **tangible** goals and nothing really interested him. For Manuel, each day was basically the same. Go to school, eat lunch, talk to a few friends, and return home. By the time he reached his sophomore year, he had begun to drift.

"Excuse me, but could you please be quiet!" said Manuel's English teacher, a short man with a shaved white head.

Manuel was not the least bit interested in *A Midsummer Night's Dream*. He knew William Shakespeare was somebody famous, but he did not understand why he was so important. Manuel could barely understand the words, let alone feel that people with such strange names could ever mean anything to him. He was much more interested in talking about a very pretty girl who had just recently arrived at the school. Moving toward one of his friends, he asked, *"Cómo se llama esa muchacha nueva?"*

"Diana."

"Sabes si ella tiene novio?" Manuel asked.

His friend shook his head. "I don't think so."

Manuel smiled. He then felt his teacher staring down on him. As he looked up, their eyes locked. Manuel took the encounter personally. "Relax, man!" said Manuel. "I wasn't talking about you."

"I didn't say you were," replied his teacher, "but you're talking when you should be listening, and you're not in your seat."

"Just 'cause you don't understand, you don't have to get all mad," said Manuel.

A few students laughed.

Manuel's teacher put his book down. "Okay, that's enough. Come here!" He motioned to Manuel with a rigorous flip of the wrist. "You need to learn how to speak to adults!"

Manuel stared at his teacher as he wrote him a disciplinary referral and told him to leave the room. Surveying the class, he noticed that some students appeared nervous. A few were smiling. A couple of girls frowned and slowly wagged their heads. Manuel accepted the paper from his teacher and slowly left the classroom. From there, he walked down a hallway and entered the disciplinary office. After waiting alongside a few other boys, Manuel was summoned by the secretary to speak to Mr. Jones, the vice-principal. Walking into a small, cramped room, he slumped into one of the two chairs in front of the large wooden desk and set his eyes downward.

"So, why were you smarting off to your teacher?"

Manuel observed Mr. Jones. His arms were tanned, freckled, and hairy. The comb over which sought in vain to cover his white, slightly pinkish scalp made Manuel smirk. In his mind, this middle-aged white man dressed in a fancy shirt and tie would never understand him. Manuel saw no reason to defend himself. Instead, he continued to look at the carpet, saying nothing. His silence only seemed to further upset Mr. Jones.

"Well, if you're just going to sit there, you can leave for the day! And when you come back you'll have detention waiting for you!" Picking up his phone, Mr. Jones continued, "Let me just look up your file. Ah, there it is. I'm sure your parents will be happy to see you."

"They don't speak English," interrupted Manuel, his head still bowed.

Mr. Jones put the phone down. "No problem," he said with a scowl. "I'll ask Mrs. González to call them."

12

MANUEL'S MOTHER WAS not very happy to hear that he had been suspended. When his father returned from work and heard the news, he began comparing Manuel to Juan.

The next day at school, Manuel knew he was to report to the detention room, but he decided not to do so. He figured nobody would even notice.

"Where you going?" asked Freddy, who was Manuel's closest friend. He was a dark skinned boy with short black hair and mischievous eyes.

"Home or the park," replied Manuel as the two walked through the hallway. "Where do you want to go?"

"I thought you had detention," said Freddy.

"I do, but I ain't going," Manuel said proudly.

Freddy laughed as he patted Manuel on the back.

13

MANUEL WAS WRONG. People did notice. It did not take more than five minutes before he was called out of class to see Mr. Jones.

"Mr. *Deelahroosuh*, why didn't you serve your detention yesterday?" asked the vice-principal.

Manuel did not like the way Mr. Jones mispronounced his name. He said it entirely wrong.

"'Cause I didn't feel like it," said Manuel.

The light pinkish face of Mr. Jones turned a deep red. "Look, don't act stupid!" he said. "After you left the other day I figured out that I've already dealt with your family! I remember your brother, Juan, and now I see you're just like him!" Mr. Jones leaned forward. "I'm going to expel you the next time I see your face in this office, Mr. *Deelahroosuh*. Is that clear?"

Manuel curled his lips but said nothing in response.

"One more incident is all it will take to transfer you out of here," mumbled Mr. Jones as he handed Manuel a small white slip of paper. "Okay, that ought to do it! You will come next Saturday, and if you fail to show up, then you'll have a new school." He then extended his arm and pointed his index finger. "I'll be watching you *Deelahroosuh*!"

"Fine, whatever," grumbled Manuel as he got up to leave.

Passing once more through the main office, he saw Freddy sitting where he had been only ten minutes earlier, a bright yellow colored referral crumpled up in his hand. Manuel approached him, shook his hand and asked him, "*Qué pasó?*"

"Too many lates, man," replied Freddy. "*Y tú?*"

"*Nada, buey, ese pendejo no me agarró—*"

"Hey! *Cállate!*" called out a voice from the corner of the room.

It was the office secretary, Mrs. González. Though quite rotund, she was able to quickly get up from her desk and enter the vice-principal's office. When she returned, Mr. Jones was following her. Pointing at Manuel, she began somewhat hesitantly, "Mr. Jones, this boy just insulted you. He called you a bad word. He…"

Mr. Jones nudged her gently on the elbow. "Go ahead, Mrs. González. Tell me exactly what he said."

Mrs. González inclined her head. She bit her lower lip, and then proceeded to say, "Well, he said that you are really, um, dumb—like stupid dumb."

Mr. Jones nodded his head in small quick movements. His nostrils began to flare. "Mr. *Deelahroosuh!* You can forget about what I told you before about a *next time.* I'm transferring you to El Centro!" He turned and walked toward his office. Then, just as he approached his door, he turned and in a more measured tone, said to Manuel, "You're not my problem anymore."

14

MANUEL DID NOT want to admit it, but he was scared. He never imagined that he could get expelled from school. His mother told him how disappointed she was with his conduct. Carlitos told Manuel that he needed to be more respectful. His younger sisters whispered that Manuel was becoming *malo.* The only one who seemed pleased was his brother, Juan.

As the two stood outside near the large tamarisk tree in their front yard, Juan lit a cigarette and then grabbed Manuel affectionately by the back of the neck. "*No te preocupes, buey!* It's no big deal! School is for losers, *hermano!* You're better off without it!"

Manuel was quiet. "I don't know, Juan. I think I messed up. You should'v seen the look on Pa's face. He wouldn't even talk to me."

Juan scowled. He furrowed his brow and his eyes narrowed. "*Me vale chingada!*" he shouted. "*Ese viejo no entiende nada, buey! Sabes qué?* I haven't been to school in over a year." Juan then reached into his pocket and pulled out a wad of cash. "And I'm doing just fine, bro!"

15

THE BUS DROPPED Manuel and a few other students in front of a small, very plain looking building that was divided into two wings. Hesitantly, Manuel crossed the large cement sidewalk. He looked at the large white letters on the outside wall: Alternative Education. Manuel was not sure what that meant, but he knew what this school was. It was a place to put all of the worst kids so that they would not cause trouble for the students and teachers at the real schools.

Manuel checked his schedule. As he did so, his hand shook. He took a few steps past the office, a place he would avoid. Then, several doors later, he found his classroom. Number seven. He looked up and down the lonely cement hallway. There were only a few students. He glanced toward the parking lot. His eyes stopped for a moment on the sight of the white bus that had dropped him off. It did not look like a typical school bus.

Taking a deep breath, Manuel opened the door. His heart pounded loudly, but he maintained a calm exterior. Most of the students were reading quietly, and some were whispering and writing on some sort of worksheet. Manuel took a quick look around, his eyes being met by several boys. They seemed to be studying him. To his dismay, there were only two girls in the room. One of them was pregnant.

Manuel approached the teacher, who was seated at an old wooden desk in the corner near the door. He was much older than any teacher Manuel had seen. His thinning hair was completely gray and his white skin was wrinkled and dry, even chalky. Standing only inches away, Manuel could see the long black and gray hairs protruding from his ear lobes.

Manuel handed him his schedule. With a motion that lacked both energy and interest, the man pointed to an empty desk without saying a word or making eye contact. As Manuel slipped into his seat, he looked at the many gang signs etched into the small flat desktop. He then noticed the old gum which was stuck to the bottom.

A large boy with a shaved head sat across from Manuel. He whispered quietly, "Hey man, what are you here for?"

Manuel did not respond. He refused to look at the boy. But it did not take long for him to realize that trouble would be hard to avoid in his new school.

"Dealing? Fighting?" the boy continued.

"Hey, fool," whispered another boy. "Do you bang?"

The boy then showed Manuel a small tattoo on his forearm that showed the Roman numeral XIV in red ink. Manuel swallowed deeply. He had never claimed **affiliation** with a gang, but he knew enough. He looked at the boy but said nothing. These kids could smell fear, and Manuel knew that if they did, he would be easy prey.

To his surprise, someone from the other side of the room shouted, "Hey, I've seen that *vato* before! Check it out! It's Juan's little brother! What's up, *carnal*? Yo, Mr. Spriggs, you sat that homey in the wrong place! He belongs with the Brothers!"

Manuel was confused. He looked at the teacher, who, with an expression that lacked even the smallest hint of emotion, pointed to an empty desk on the other side of the room. Manuel quickly got up and moved places.

"Yo, check it out," continued the same boy. "This little fool is Juan's brother!"

Kids whom Manuel had never met welcomed him, smiling and nodding in approval. Though still confused, Manuel shook every hand that was offered him.

"What's your name, *carnal*?" asked the boy, who though small in stature appeared to be the established leader of the classroom.

After Manuel responded, the boy waved his hands excitedly and snapped his fingers. "Check it out, fool," he said to Manuel. "From now on, you hang with us. It's good to have you, *carnal*." He then frowned. "Damn, why didn't Juan tell us you were coming?"

16

ASSEMBLED AROUND A table in the park were several young men. A few of them were smoking. Others had bottles of liquor in their hands. In the far distance the sounds of small children could be heard, playing on the slides and swings. It was early, but the sun shone brightly and Manuel could feel the heat on his dark brown face.

"You sure you're up to this, *hermano?*" asked Juan.

Manuel nodded. "Yeah," he replied.

"Okay, take this bag and don't talk to nobody," Juan continued. "*Ponte águila, hermano*! What you gonna do if you sense trouble?"

Manuel put the small bag into his pant pocket. "Get rid of it and then go back and get it when no one's around."

"*Simón!*" said Juan. He smiled and then turned to face the others. "My little brother's finally grown up!"

"*Orale!*" replied one of the boys as he shook Manuel's hand.

Manuel left the group and began the long walk to his bus stop. Every once in a while he would dig his hand in his pocket and feel the small plastic bag. When his bus finally arrived, he entered and sat alone. The trip from Holtville to El Centro seemed longer than usual.

Once on the little campus of the community school, Manuel was more subdued than usual. He avoided people and headed straight for his classroom. The hours passed slowly. Manuel's eyes darted back and forth constantly from the clock to his desk. It seemed as if the day would never end. But it did, and at the sound of the bell, Manuel quickly left the school premises.

"Hey, man, where you going?" called out a boy heading in the opposite direction.

With a slight hesitation, Manuel replied, "I'm gonna buy something real fast."

"You better hurry!" the boy shouted. "The bus don't wait long!"

Manuel nodded. He continued down the sidewalk, taking mental notes of each street name he passed. He turned a corner and then entered a small store. Grabbing a drink and some chips, he nervously reached into his pocket, and as he did so, his fingers caressed the small plastic bag.

Manuel removed his hand and tried the other pocket. There, he felt several bills. He grabbed all of them and placed them on the counter.

"Here, you gave me too much," said the man behind the register.

"Huh?" Manuel grunted.

"You gave me four dollars. It's only two ninety-five."

"Oh, yeah. Thanks," said Manuel, taking back his dollar and receiving a nickel. As he walked out, he saw a man standing outside wearing dark sunglasses. He had a tattoo of a jaguar on his right arm that broke through his black short sleeve shirt.

"You Chuy?" asked Manuel.

"Yeah."

"Juan told me to give you something."

"Then give it to me and get the hell out of here."

Manuel reached into his pocket, grabbed the small rolled up bag, and handed it to the man. Without saying a word, he quickly put it inside his pants and walked away.

Manuel decided to head straight for the bus stop, but when he arrived, he found that it was empty. His only thought was to find a phone and to call his parents to pick him up. He quickly turned around and headed for downtown. As he made his way past a park, he noticed a car slowing down. It had a long hood and trunk, tinted windows, and was covered with several dents and scratches among the faded brown paint.

A side window lowered slightly. *"Oye! Qué haces en nuestro barrio?"*

"Nada," replied Manuel, not bothering to look at the car.

"What's your name?"

Manuel remained silent, but quickened his pace.

The window continued to lower. "Come here!"

Manuel turned to see a boy who may have been a few years older than himself. He had a brown shaved head and dark menacing eyes. Manuel stared at him for a moment, and then turned away to continue toward downtown El Centro.

"I said get over here!" shouted the boy.

Manuel ignored him, but then he heard a deeper voice, the voice of a man. "Get that fool and bring him here!"

Manuel began to run. As he did so, he heard the squeal of tires and the full throttle of an engine.

"We're gonna kill you!" called out the boy.

Seeing a small alley, Manuel cut through the front lawn of a corner house. He looked over his shoulder to see the car in fast pursuit. He continued running until he saw an old gray wooden gate. He shook it until it opened. Once on the other side, he slumped down, breathing heavily. As he caught his breath, he peeked through a hole in the fence. The car drove by slowly. The same boy he had seen earlier had his head out of the window, scowling menacingly as he waved a pistol. Manuel waited over an hour before he attempted to move.

17

WHENEVER MANUEL WAS with his older brother, he felt safe. But Juan could not protect him forever. He could not even protect himself. One late night, while driving on the wrong side of one of the country roads of Holtville, Juan was pulled over by a police officer.

Responding to the flashlight knocking on the window, Juan shouted, "Broderick! *Qué tal, amigo?*"

"You're swerving all over the road, Juan," replied Officer Broderick.

Juan smiled widely. "*Y qué?* It's late. Ain't nobody around."

"You want to get out of the car and open the trunk?" said officer Broderick. Then, turning away, he added, "Tell your, uh, friend, to stand over there."

"*Orale, cómo no!*" said Juan, still smiling. "Whatever you say, *jefe.*"

Juan turned to the young lady sitting next to him and motioned for her to get out of the car. She frowned. Juan then put a large bottle of beer up to his mouth and swallowed deeply. With keys in one hand and a beer in the other, he opened the trunk of his car. "There you go, *jefe!*"

The young lady accompanying Juan folded her arms in front of her. She was wearing a thin black blouse that tightly clung to her cleavage. "Hey! How long do I have to stay here? It's cold!"

Officer Broderick swiveled his head quickly, paused, and then faced Juan's car once again. He poked around with his flashlight. Finally, he knocked it against a small brown box. "So what do we have here?"

Juan shrugged innocently before taking another gulp of his beer as the officer opened the box. Inside were several bags of white powder.

"Sheesh," huffed Officer Broderick, "you didn't even try to hide it."

With a childish grin on his face, Juan stuttered, "Yeah, yeah, *jefe*. Can we speed it up, *la vieja tiene frío*!"

"Huh?"

"She's cold, *chapa*!" said Juan, raising his arms demonstrably.

Officer Broderick shook his head. "Okay, that's enough. Turn around, Juan. You've had more than your fair share of chances."

"Don't you want me to walk in a straight line, *jefe*?" asked Juan, moving his beer through the air in tiny steps.

The officer remained still with his lips pressed firmly together.

"What, Broderick? You're not gonna lecture me?" asked Juan. He then laughed and took one more gulp from his bottle.

Drawing his handcuffs, the officer replied somberly, "Not this time."

"Yeah, yeah, here we go," said Juan, still smiling.

18

MANUEL WAS SEVENTEEN. His life had changed completely. Though he was the lone remaining son, his father rarely spoke to him. Carlitos had moved to Seeley, a small town nearby. He was married with a little girl of his own. Juan had been transferred from Centinela State Prison to a facility in Avenal. Manuel had not seen him in over a year. Cecilia and Yolanda spent most of their time at school. They kept a certain distance from Manuel. Deep down, he knew they disapproved of him, but secretly he cared for them and hoped that they would never change.

"Anybody home?" asked Carlitos, opening the front door of the De La Rosa home.

"Carlitos!" called out Yolanda.

She quickly ran to him and gave him a hug.

"Where's Manuel?" asked Carlitos.

"He's in his room," Yolanda replied. "He's always in there."

"Yeah, I heard," said Carlitos. He placed his hands around the long black hair that covered Yolanda's slightly wide symmetrical face. "Hey, if you get any prettier, Pa's going to have to lock you up in your room, too!"

Yolanda smiled as Carlitos made his way to Manuel's room. He knocked lightly and opened the door. Inside, Manuel was sprawled on his bed, listening to music.

"Hey," said Carlitos.

"What's up," replied Manuel indifferently.

"You doing okay?" asked Carlitos, closing the door behind him. He took a few steps and sat in the one piece of furniture found within the room, an old sofa chair that was situated next to Manuel's bed.

"Yeah," replied Manuel, "I guess."

"I came here to talk to you."

"So talk."

Taking a deep breath, Carlitos began, "Look, Manuel, you and I both know you're just going to end up locked up somewhere like Juan. Why don't you quit messing around and come work with me in the fields? I'm in charge of my own crew, now, so I can hook you up. We need some extra help with the lettuce harvest. My boss is a relative of the family. He's a cool *gabacho*. I know he'll let me hire you. Do your part, and you'll have a permanent job."

Manuel looked at his brother without saying a word.

"You can have a decent life, start making some money," continued Carlitos. "Come on, it's time to change. You're not a kid anymore."

Manuel inclined his head, breaking off eye contact.

"Man, we've had this old chair forever," said Carlitos, touching the worn out armrests with his palms. He began to rub an old stain with his thumb as if to remove it.

"That's because it's so ugly nobody else wants it," said Manuel, after which Carlitos began to laugh. Sitting up on his bed, Manuel nodded several times before saying, "Maybe you're right."

19

Manuel had made his decision. He would accept his brother's offer to work in the fields. As far as he was concerned, school had little more to offer.

"I haven't seen you here for a while," said the secretary at the front counter. She had straight black hair that fell to her shoulders. Her eyeliner, dark blue shadow, and long lashes made her brown eyes sparkle. Manuel thought she was very pretty.

"Yeah," said Manuel. "I need a work permit."

"So you want to go into the independent studies program?" she asked.

Manuel furrowed his brow. "Yeah, I guess."

"Go in that room over there and see Mrs. Grines," she said, pointing toward the back.

She walked over to the side of the long counter and opened a small, swinging door, allowing Manuel to pass. He smiled slightly before passing a few other ladies who were working at their desks. Manuel then entered a small office. Inside, he saw an older white woman with a stout, somewhat wrinkled face and shoulder length blonde hair.

"Excuse me," he began, "are you the counselor?"

"Yes, I'm Mrs. Grines. May I help you?" she replied, revealing a slight Midwestern accent.

"I haven't been to school much," said Manuel. "I need to work. The lady over there said I could study in some program."

"You want me to put you on independent studies?" she asked.

"Yeah, I guess," said Manuel. "I just want to work."

"Son, do you really think that is what's best for you?"

Manuel was surprised that she actually seemed to care. "Yeah, it will keep me out of trouble," he replied. "My brother can get me a job in the fields."

"But you could do so much more," said Mrs. Grines. "I mean, you only have a little ways to go. Your attendance hasn't been so good, but it looks like you've passed quite a few classes. You seem like a smart boy."

Manuel shrugged.

Mrs. Grines paused for a minute before adding, "I think you could do more with your life. I'm not saying you'll be able to graduate this year with your lack of credits, but who knows? Whatever you decide, don't just give up to work in the fields."

Suddenly, Manuel became **defensive**. "What's wrong with working in the fields?" he shouted. His entire body became tense as his eyes narrowed. "My father did it and my brother does it now! Your people don't do it because they're too lazy! We're the ones who do all the work!"

"I'm sorry," said Mrs. Grines, fidgeting in her chair. "I wasn't trying to say that what you're doing is bad. Any job that is an honest one is a good one. Don't make this an issue of race, son. I grew up on a little farm in Oklahoma. If we weren't baling hay, we had to feed and clean the animals. In fact, that was the main reason I chose to go college. It's hard work and I respect the people who do it. I'm just saying that you could finish your studies, graduate, and get a better paying job, that's all. I didn't mean to offend you."

Manuel had never heard an adult apologize to him before. He took a breath of air and allowed his muscles to relax.

"With a high school diploma," continued Mrs. Grines, "you could even join the military and learn all kinds of new things, get paid, and save up money for college. I'm just saying you have a lot of options. Believe it or not, we've had students leave here and go on to college."

"I'll think about it," Manuel replied softly. "I'll take a few classes, maybe, but right now I just want to work." Then, after looking down for a moment, he added, "Thanks anyway, though."

"Okay, it's your decision," she said. Then, with a sigh, she added, "I'll help you fill out the papers."

20

MANUEL SLEEPILY TURNED off his alarm. It was still dark. He glanced at his clock. The bright red numbers displayed a four, a three, and a zero. He slowly got out of bed and took a shower. After getting dressed, he groggily entered the kitchen where he was startled by the sight of his mother standing in front of the stove.

"*Qué hace, mamá?*" asked Manuel.

"*Buenos días, mijo,*" she replied.

"Oh, yeah, *lo siento, buenos días, mamá,*" said Manuel, smiling slightly.

"*Tu desayuno, por supuesto,*" said his mother, handing Manuel a plate. "*Chorizo, frijoles, y huevos.*" Then, holding a bundle of tortillas wrapped in paper towels, she added, "*Y toma unas de estas.*"

"*Gracias, mamá!*" said Manuel, eagerly accepting the food.

"*De nada,*" she replied. "*Cómetelo porque tu hermano viene pronto.*"

"*Sí, mamá,*" said Manuel between large bites.

Not long afterwards, Manuel heard the sound of a truck engine outside of the house.

Pointing to a brown bag on the table, Manuel's mother said, "*Es tu almuerzo. Llévatelo.*"

Wiping his face, Manuel got up from his seat and walked over to his mother. He kissed her on the cheek. "*Te quiero mucho, mamá,*" he said to her with a large smile on his face.

"*Yo sé, mijo,*" she replied, quickly turning her attention to the table where Manuel had left his plate and glass. With a tinge of sadness in her voice, she shouted, "*Qué te vaya bien!*"

Once outside, Manuel slowly hoisted himself into his brother's truck. Carlitos was wearing a blue cap that covered his short black hair. Unlike Manuel, his face was recently shaved and the pleasant smell of his cologne filled was easily noted. Carlitos immediately greeted Manuel in a loud, cheerful tone. "*Buenos días!*"

"Man, it's too early to be so happy!" said Manuel, yawning. "This is worse than getting ready for school!"

Carlitos laughed. "Yeah, but they don't pay you for going to school, *hermano,*" he replied as the two drove away. "Got some stuff for you in the back."

Manuel glanced at his brother, then turned to look behind him. On the back seat he saw a large gray hat, a white scarf, a pair of old gloves, and a spade knife.

"Thanks, Carlitos," said Manuel.

"No problem, bro," he replied, ruffling Manuel's thick unkempt hair. "This is exciting! It's your first day! I'm just doing for you what *Pa* did for me."

"Yeah, he actually talked to me last night," said Manuel.

"Cool," said Carlitos.

After several miles, they turned down a dirt road toward a private gate. Once there, Carlitos greeted two men who were sitting in a small guard house. After exchanging a few pleasantries, they waved him in.

"This is it," said Carlitos, "one of the many fields owned by the family."

"Man, those *gabachos* must be loaded!" exclaimed Manuel.

"Yeah, they own a lot of land," said Carlitos. "They're rich, all right."

"Yeah, rich because of us," added Manuel. "All they do is watch while we do all the work."

"*Aguas!*" said Carlitos, briefly losing his smile. "Careful what you say, man. The family has had these farms for a long, long time, and they work it, too. Trust me, man, I've done stuff for a lot of white people, and some of them treat you like dirt. But here, it's different. There's a lot of people wanting to work for the family because they know how good we got it here. We got our own patio for lunch, refrigerators, indoor bathrooms. But best of all, if you work hard, they notice."

Manuel was not expecting his brother's rebuke. He said nothing in reply. As Carlitos pulled up to a large green field, he introduced Manuel to several other men who were dressed in jeans, long sleeved collared shirts, and an array of caps and *sombreros*.

"*Buenos días, compas!*" greeted Carlitos.

"*Buenos días!*" they replied in unison.

Carlitos turned to an older man who stood to the side. "*Oiga! Este muchacho es mi hermano, Manuel! Dígale lo que él tiene que hacer y me lo cuida*, eh?"

The man nodded. "*Por supuesto, jefe.*"

Carlitos then turned to Manuel. "Okay, bro, I'll pick you up about three."

"You're leaving?" asked Manuel, startled by his brother's departure.

"Yeah, I have to work with the irrigation pipes and then talk to Glen about production."

"Who's he?" asked Manuel.

"Come on, man, get out already!" said Carlitos, pushing Manuel toward the door. "I don't have time to explain everything to you. I work all over the place, all right? Now, don't worry! These men will take care of you and teach you everything you need to know. I'll see you at three. Grab your stuff and don't forget your lunch."

Manuel nodded. He left his brother and joined the others who led him into a lettuce field that seemed to stretch for miles. As one man climbed into a large green tractor with a conveyer belt, others signaled to Manuel that he was to follow. He watched as they stooped down and with a slash of their blades removed the lettuce and placed it onto a large belt. From there, the various heads were carried into a huge bed that was attached to the back of the tractor. Manuel slowly tried to mimic their movements.

"*Así, joven,*" called out a voice.

It was the older man with whom Carlitos had spoken earlier. Manuel watched as he deftly reached down and quickly cut the lettuce stem without damaging the leafy outer section. He then carved out the core and threw the lettuce head onto the conveyer belt.

"*Gracias,*" replied Manuel.

As the hours wore on, the temperature began to rise. The cool morning air was replaced by a dry heat, reminding Manuel that he lived in a desert. His forearms began to throb from the constant grip he maintained, and soon his back ached as well.

"*Vámanos!*" said a man to Manuel.

Manuel squinted his eyes. "*A dónde?*"

"*A almorzar,*" he replied.

The men walked out of the fields and made their way to an enormous outside cement patio that had a white tin cover overhead. Underneath were a large shed and two rectangular tables made of hard white plastic. Manuel followed the others inside. To his surprise, the shed was divided into one large bathroom area and another room composed of several wooden cabinets. The older man who had spoken to Carlitos earlier handed Manuel a brown paper bag. "*Es tuyo,*" he said.

Manuel paused for a moment. He then figured his brother must have left it there for him. "Gracias," replied Manuel as he reached for the lunch his mother had prepared.

After washing his hands, Manuel walked slowly toward the outside tables. On each was a large igloo™ water container. Manuel watched the older men sit at one table and the younger men at another. Joining a group of men who appeared in their late teens and early twenties, he sat gingerly, his body reacting to the hard wooden bench. Some of the older men laughed.

"*Ya andas como un viejito, joven!*" said one of them.

"*Sí, y apenas le están saliendo unos pelitos en la barbilla!*"

Laughter broke out at both tables. Manuel smiled as he rubbed the small patch of hair on his chin.

"*No tienes cantimplora?*" asked one young man with long black hair.

Manuel furrowed his brow. Confused, he replied, "*Qué es eso?*"

"*Cantimplora—tu propia botella de agua,*" said another, raising a large canteen. He then proceeded to unscrew the black top and take a drink.

The young man with long black hair handed Manuel a plastic cup full of water. "*Toma.*"

Manuel thanked him. He then glanced at the other table. Some of the men looked almost as old as his father. They spoke entirely in Spanish whereas at his table the younger ones scattered phrases in English throughout their conversations. Manuel listened with curiosity as the older men began discussing the difficulties of married life.

"*Es porque tú la dejas hacer lo que quiera!*" said a pudgy man with a thick black mustache. "*El hombre tiene que enseñarle a la mujer quién manda!*"

"*Ella es terca, hombre!*" said another in response. "*No me hace caso!*"

"*Pues, en mi casa, yo le digo a mi mujer 'aquí, solo mis chicharones truenan'!*"

Manuel smiled as he turned his attention to the the younger men seated next to him. They were arguing about which state of Mexico had the prettiest girls.

"*Aracely es de Chihuahua!*" said one young man with very short hair and a handsome face.

"*Ana Brenda es de Tamaulipas,*" said another.

"*Anabel es de Yucatán!*" said the young man with long black hair. He blew kisses into the air, which prompted a response of laughter and loud whistles from the others.

As more comments flowed, the men nodded each time with wide eyes and eager smiles.

"*Siempre las famosas son de México! Chicas como Thalia, Lucero, Paulina!*" shouted one of the older men from the other table.

Several of the young men nodded and in a chorus replied, "*Cierto!*"

"Pues, yo siempre he pensado que Sofía era la más bella de todas!" said one tall boy who appeared even younger than Manuel.

One of the older men scowled. *"Ella es de Colombia, buey!"* he shouted.

Manuel joined the others as they burst into laughter.

21

AS THE HEAT of the summer burned into Manuel's skin, he began to detest the fields. Long hours and hard work left him with little energy to do anything more than lie in bed after a long shower. He had earned money, but found no time to spend it. School had become a fading memory; even one day a week of independent studies seemed too much for him. After one particularly long day, Manuel was surprised to see one of his friends waiting for him under the shade of the tree in his front yard.

"So this is the sad life of a high school dropout!" said Freddy, pointing to Manuel's dirty boots and hands.

"Later!" shouted Manuel to his brother as he drove off. He then wearily removed his hat and placed his gloves inside. "Very funny, man."

"Dude, I never see you anymore!"

"Yeah, I know," said Manuel. "It's sad, fool. All I do is work. It's like I'm an old man, now."

"Yeah, I can tell," said Freddy, shaking his head. "You look even skinnier than you usually do. But don't worry 'cause that's exactly why I'm here!"

Manuel turned on the garden hose. He touched the water until it became cold, and then washed his hands and splashed his face as Freddy continued.

"I've got two words for you. Party and San Diego."

"Those are three words, man," said Manuel, still holding the hose.

"I'm impressed," said Freddy. "You still remember how to count!"

Manuel frowned. "I'm not stupid, Freddy!"

"I know, I know!" said Freddy, laughing. "Damn, man, take it easy! I'm just messing with you! Anyway, check this out! I got a cousin in San Diego who has his own place!"

"So?" interrupted Manuel. He then took several gulps of water from the hose.

"So he said we could kick it with him!" replied Freddy. "The dude's loaded!"

"Is that right?" asked Manuel.

"Yeah, that's right! It's all going down this weekend!" Freddy smiled widely. "Trust me, fool, we don't have parties like they do over there!"

Manuel stared at Freddy.

"We leave tomorrow night!" said Freddy, slapping Manuel on the shoulder. "Come on, fool, show a little excitement! Damn, *es verdad! Eres un viejito!*"

Manuel frowned. "Freddy, I can't. My brother said we have to work late tomorrow."

Freddy cocked his head back. "On a Saturday?"

"Yeah," said Manuel. "Right now everyone's working non-stop—twelve hour shifts seven days a week."

"Come on, man," said Freddy, waving his arms in the air. "This ain't just another party. This is San Diego! Beach—cool breeze—the only thing hot over there is the girls!"

Manuel laughed. He could not remember the last time he had done so.

"The fields aren't going anywhere, dude!" continued Freddy, shaking his head.

"I want to go, Freddy, but what do I tell my brother?"

"That you're taking a day off! Don't worry! He'll get over it! That's the cool part of having your brother as your boss, right?"

Manuel smiled. He put the hose down, walked to the edge of the house, and turned off the water. He then dried his hands on his white T-shirt. "All right, I'm in. See you tomorrow."

"*Hasta mañana*, fool!" said Freddy. "We'll pick you up around five. Jaime's driving and Mario's coming, too."

"Cool," said Manuel. "I haven't seen those guys for a while."

"Yeah, yeah, you can thank me later!" said Freddy, waving behind him as he walked away. Suddenly, he stopped and turned to face Manuel. With a large, mischievous smile, he added, "Oh, and take a shower! I don't know if that's dirt on your chin or what! And do something with your hair!"

"What's wrong with it?" asked Manuel.

"It looks like a dirty mop, man!"

Manuel scowled. "What are you talking about?"

"Chop it off, man! That fro of yours is out of control!"

"Shut up!" said Manuel.

"I'm serious, dude, you're gonna make us all look bad!" Freddy ran his hand over his cropped black hair and pulled on his checkered shirt. "And put on some nice jeans and a collared shirt! You can't be wearing stuff like that tomorrow!"

"Yeah, yeah," said Manuel.

Freddy's laughter echoed in Manuel's ears as he disappeared down the street.

22

AFTER DRIVING DOWN the Interstate, the boys entered San Diego with cheers and whistles.

"Put the windows down, Jaime," said Freddy. "Time to breathe that ocean air!"

Manuel stuck his face halfway out of the car. "Man, that feels good!"

"What's that smell?" asked Jaime.

"Forget the ocean! I'm just breathing in Manuel!" said Mario.

"Smells like onions!" said Jaime. He took one hand off the wheel and waved it in front of his nose.

"Or garlic," added Mario.

"That's still better than the way you guys smell!" said Freddy. "And I don't know why you're talking, Mario. You used to work in the fields, too!"

"That was a long time ago!" said Mario.

"I've never worked in the fields," said Jaime.

"So what are you trying to say?" asked Manuel.

"That my parents went to college."

"*Pinche* Jaime, *se cree un* rich *gabacho*," said Manuel, shaking his head.

"That has nothing to do with it!" said Jaime.

"Hey! Hey! Turn off here!" interrupted Freddy. "Now keep going straight till I tell you to stop."

After passing several streets, the boys pulled into the parking lot of a large apartment complex. They got out and stretched their legs, and then followed Freddy up a flight of stairs.

"This is it," said Freddy, pointing to a door.

"Looks pretty nice," said Jaime.

As they got closer, the sound of music and several voices grew louder. Freddy then rang the doorbell. After a slight pause, the door swung open and a young man greeted them with an inviting smile.

"*Primo*, you made it!" His dark pants and shirt, as well as his dark skin, contrasted with his bright green eyes.

"Hell, yeah!" said Freddy as the two quickly embraced. "We wouldn't miss one of your parties, *Gato*! Yo, fool, these are some of my boys. Manuel, Jaime, and Mario."

"Hey, *cómo andan*?" said the young man. "I'm Ernesto. *Pásale, pásale!*" As the boys crossed the living room, Ernesto introduced Manuel and his friends to others at the party. "*Muchachos, mi casa es tu casa.* Grab some beers, have fun, *allí hay hielo,*" he continued, motioning toward a kitchen counter full of food and drinks.

Manuel was impressed by the nice furniture, the modern appliances and the overall spaciousness of the apartment. He grabbed a bottle of cold beer, took a few sips, and observed two separate crowds that were divided by a kitchen in the center. As he did so, a girl approached with an empty plate.

"Hey," said Manuel, looking at her deeply. He could not help but notice the long lashes that accentuated her large brown eyes.

"Hi," she replied, and then released a pleasant smile.

Exchanging introductions, Manuel learned that her name was Alina. She had a firm jawline, long hair, and a petite, but curvaceous figure. Manuel could not help but stare. "Are you with someone?" he asked.

"I am now," she replied, smiling once more.

Manuel lost his seriousness. He, too, smiled softly. "You want to sit down?"

"Yeah," said Alina. She pointed to the corner of the room. "There's nobody at that couch."

It did not take long for Manuel to completely forget about his friends. The only person he did see was Ernesto, who continually passed by to open the front door. The apartment, though quite large, was becoming crowded. As Manuel sat sprawled on an exquisite leather couch talking to Alina, a few boys hovered over him. Manuel stared back at them and they eventually went away. One boy, however, remained standing next to him.

"Hey dawg, can you and your girl move over?" he asked.

Manuel looked up to see a tall thin boy who was wearing a large black cap that covered his slender face. "We were here first, man," said Manuel. "Go find some place else."

"That ain't right, dawg. You got space," said the boy, flashing hard eyes at Manuel.

Manuel began to stand up, but Alina grabbed him by the shoulder.

"It's okay," she said. "Come on, sit closer to me."

Manuel stared at the boy, and then along with Alina, scooted to the far side of the couch.

"*Gato!*" called a voice from the other side of the kitchen. "Get over here! We got business!"

"Hey, 'living *la vida loca*,' right?" shouted Ernesto to Manuel. He smiled, raised the beer in his hand high into the air, and then promptly disappeared into one of the bedrooms located toward the back of the apartment.

Turning toward Alina, Manuel practically had to shout due to the noise, a combination of loud music, people talking, and the sound of video games. "I'll be right back! I gotta take a piss!"

Alina frowned, crinkling her forehead. Manuel did not seem to notice her displeasure as he got up and walked through a small hallway that led to the bathroom. Afterwards, he began to make his way back when something caught his attention. It was the faint sound of voices. Walking to the end of the hallway, he saw a partially closed door. Carefully opening it, Manuel saw Ernesto exchanging drugs for bills of cash with two other young men.

"Now I know how this *vato* affords all this," Manuel muttered to himself.

Quietly closing the door, he continued to the living room. When he returned, Alina was no longer there. Several other people were leaving as Manuel searched for her.

"Hey," said Manuel to a couple who were quickly heading toward the front door, "did you guys see a girl sitting over here? I was just talking to her."

The young man to whom he had spoken shook his head in response. He then pointed beyond the kitchen. "Looks like trouble over there. This party's over. We're gonna bounce."

"Damn!" shouted Manuel, frowning.

A few people quickly passed by. Confused, Manuel crossed through the kitchen to a second, almost identical living room; the only exception being a large television screen mounted into the far wall. Amidst the crowd, Manuel spotted Freddy talking away and smiling. Mario and Jaime, as well as a few others, were standing next to him, laughing and patting Freddy on the back.

"Oh, hell no!" exclaimed Ernesto, suddenly appearing next to Manuel. "What's Freddy doing?"

Manuel looked at him and replied casually, "You know, Freddy—always joking, trying to steal the show."

"Yeah, but that's Gordo," replied Ernesto with a flash of panic in his eyes. "Quick, man, tell him to back off because that *carnal* is bad news. Look at that big ol' Charlie Brown head he's got!" Ernesto placed his hands up next to his head. Manuel laughed. "He's a total thug. To be honest, I didn't invite him; he just came. He's not like Freddy—all talk—you know what I mean?" Then, turning in the other direction, he suddenly said, "Damn! Everyone's leaving because of those two! *Ya vengo, ya vengo!*"

Manuel nodded as Ernesto disappeared to the other side of the apartment, appealing to people that it was much too early to leave. In front of him was Freddy, a beer in one hand and a girl wrapped around the other. He continued to entertain the small group that remained by outwitting the much larger Gordo.

"I mean, come on, fool, they shouldn't just call you *Gordo*," said Freddy. "That's too nice. They should call you *feo también* or *te apellidas así*? Yo, everybody, *les presento al señor Gordo Feo!*"

Freddy laughed and laughed. People around him were laughing as well. But Gordo and a few others standing next to him were not laughing. Manuel quickly made his way through the crowd and tapped Freddy on the shoulder. "Hey, man, it's getting late. I think we should go."

"Hey! Where've you been, man?" asked Freddy. "Have you met my new *amigo*? *Te presento al señor Gordo Feo!*"

Freddy raised his beer as if giving a toast. Mario and Jaime laughed as he did so and raised their beers, touching bottles.

"I'm not your *amigo, pendejo!*" growled Gordo.

"Come on, man, let's get out of here," said Manuel, grabbing Freddy by the shoulder.

"*Espérate!*" said Freddy. His eyes had a glazed look about them. Turning to Gordo and pointed his finger in his face, he continued, "*Tú no tienes buenos modales, amigo.*"

Gordo quickly slapped Freddy's hand out of his face and shoved him hard in the chest. Freddy stumbled awkwardly toward a girl standing next to him, causing her to fall to the ground. Manuel grabbed her gently and helped her to her feet. "Are you okay?" he asked.

"Yeah, I think so," she replied.

Manuel then grabbed Freddy by the arm to steady him. "Come on, man, I'm telling you it's time to leave." He then turned to Jaime and Mario. "Come on, let's go."

Freddy blinked several times. Only a few feet away, Gordo and a few others were laughing.

"Hold on, *compa*," replied Freddy, pausing to get his bearings.

"No, Freddy!" pleaded Manuel.

"Yo! *Gordo Feo!*" said Freddy, walking straight up to him. "You can mess with me but you need to apologize to this girl!"

"I've had enough of this little *payaso!*" said Gordo to his friends. Then, without warning, he grabbed Freddy by the neck and threw him to the floor. He then knelt down on the carpet next to Freddy and began slapping him hard in the face.

"*Dale! Dale!*" said one of Gordo's friends.

Freddy began to gasp for air as Gordo leaned his forearm into his throat.

"Hey, where's Ernesto?" Manuel asked two people standing next to him. "Ernesto? Gato?"

"What?" said one boy, raising his palms upwardly.

"We got to do something!" said Manuel to the people standing next to him.

They returned his plea with blank faces.

"I'm out of here," said a girl with long black hair that reached down to her waist. As she walked by, she turned to Manuel. "You better hope Gordo goes easy on your friend."

Manuel decided it was time to act. Pushing his way through a small circle of people, he grabbed Gordo by the shoulder. "Okay, man, he's had enough! Just let him go, all right!"

"Shut the hell up!" growled Gordo. "Or your next!"

"Get back, man!" said another boy. He placed both hands on Manuel's chest and shoved him. Manuel fell back a few steps.

"*Mira! Mira!*" said Gordo, playing to the small crowd that had gathered around him. Squeezing Freddy's cheeks and lips, he made it appear as if Freddy was speaking. "*Mande?*" said Gordo, cupping his hand to his ear. "I can't hear you, *maricón*! Where's your big mouth, now, huh *pendejo*? C'mon! Say something!"

Gordo smiled at the people cheering him on. As he continued to humiliate Freddy, Mario and Jaime approached Manuel. "Do something, man!" said Mario.

"Okay," replied Manuel. He looked at them both. "Will you guys back me up?"

Both of them quickly nodded.

"Look! Look!" said Gordo. "I'm gonna do an experiment! I'm like a *pinche* scientist!" He then pointed to one of the young men close by. "*Mira el reloj, buey*! We're gonna time this fool!"

People around Gordo began to laugh.

Then, inclining his head, Gordo shouted at Freddy, "*Oye, idiota*, let's see how long you can hold your breath!"

"Come on, man! That's enough!" said Manuel. "Get off of him!"

Gordo laughed. Swiveling his head, he seemed to be basking in the approval of the crowd. After a moment of gloating, he redirected his attention to Freddy, pinching his nose and closing his lips together. Manuel looked in horror as Freddy remained motionless underneath the weight of Gordo's body. There were no signs of breathing. With eyes darting back and forth, Manuel spotted a discarded bottle lying on the floor only inches away from Freddy's limp hand.

"I said that's enough, *cabrón!*" His hand came down quickly. A loud, popping noise was heard as Gordo slumped to the ground in the midst of shattered glass, a small stream of blood oozing from the top of his head.

23

"Is this the one?" asked the police officer.

"Yeah," said a young lady as she pointed toward Manuel.

"Everyone says it was him," said a second officer.

"All right, go ahead and take him. Once we sort things out I'll meet you at the station."

"Can I go now?" the young lady asked.

"Afraid not," said the officer. "Nobody's going anywhere. We still have a lot of questions, so take a seat."

"But I didn't do anything!" she screamed. "It was only him!"

"You heard her," added Ernesto. "Why don't you let these people go and let me go back to sleep?"

The officer shook his head and then pointed to an empty chair. "You," he said, pointing to the young lady, "sit down." Then, pointing to Ernesto, he added, "And you, shut up!"

Both of Manuel's arms were jerked behind his back. He felt a slight pinch as the cold metal dug into his skin and rubbed against his wrist bones. "You have the right to remain silent," began the officer as he led Manuel toward the door.

Manuel glanced at Mario and Jaime, who were sitting together on the same leather couch where he had been earlier along with Alina. Both of them sat with their faces buried in their hands.

"Anything you say can and will be used against you in a court of law," continued the officer.

As Manuel was led outside the door, he turned toward Ernesto. His bright green eyes practically glowed in the darkened room.

"You have the right to speak to an attorney, and to have an attorney present during any questioning. If you cannot afford a lawyer, one will be provided for you at government expense. Do you understand?"

Manuel nodded without saying a word.

"I said 'do you understand'?"

"Yes," said Manuel.

Manuel shuffled down the cement steps, almost stumbling as he was pushed by the officer behind him. Once they reached the parking lot, the officer lowered Manuel's head and shoved him into the back of the car. He then joined his partner who was seated behind the wheel.

"Well, the paramedics did their job. Right on time," began the officer who was driving.

"They're always on time," replied the other. "It still doesn't look good, though. They both have serious injuries. One kid was totally drunk." Then, looking back at Manuel, he added, "And the other one—the one you hit—he has a serious **laceration**."

Manuel looked down, avoiding eye contact.

"Yeah, it looks like even two against one wasn't enough," goaded the driver.

Manuel's jaw tightened. He remained silent. When they arrived at the police station, Manuel was taken into custody and ordered to empty his possessions. He then had his picture taken and afterwards, his fingerprints.

"It's pretty late," began the police officer standing in front of him. "Anybody you want to call before we situate you?"

"I'm staying here?" asked Manuel.

"For now," replied the officer. "We have a holding cell."

"I want to call my parents," said Manuel.

The officer pointed to a phone. Manuel slowly picked up the receiver and marked his number. After several rings, Manuel heard the voice of his father.

"*Pa! Pa! Habla* Manuel!"

"Manuel?" replied his father slowly. "*Es la una de la mañana, hijo.*"

"*Yo sé, Pa, yo sé…*"

Manuel hesitated as he slowly explained what had happened. When he finished, he was greeted with an awkward silence. Then, finally, his father spoke, scolding him harshly. "*Qué muchacho más necio! Qué recibas lo que mereces!*"

They were the last words Manuel heard before a steady dial tone took over. Looking up at the officer, he felt completely alone.

"No driver's license, no real identification," mumbled the officer. "How old are you?"

"Seventeen," replied Manuel.

"Where do you live?" he continued.

"Holtville," replied Manuel.

"Nobody here has ever seen you," he continued. "Well, follow Officer López over there. You're going to stay the night until we figure this out." Then, turning away from Manuel, the man called out to another officer, "Try getting ahold of probation. The kid says he's seventeen."

"Come with me," said Officer López, a short stocky man with cropped black hair and a thick black mustache. .

As Manuel followed him down a hallway, the officer seemed to take pity on him. "Assault with a deadly weapon," he said aloud, "that's a pretty serious charge."

Manuel made eye contact but said nothing in reply. Suddenly, Officer López stopped in front of a small cell. He motioned for Manuel to enter. "So how'd you get into this mess?" he asked.

After careful thought, Manuel replied, "When I didn't go to detention."

Officer López cocked his head back suddenly. His mouth fell open. "What? What did you say?"

"When I was in school, I—I got detention," said Manuel. "It was just an hour, but I decided not to go." Manuel inclined his head. "That's really when it all started."

Officer López shook his head in disbelief. "Sheesh," he muttered, "that's a first. I've done border patrol, narcotics—yeah, no way—I've never heard that one before. Well, you're gonna have a lot of time to think about it. It's not too late, you know. Maybe the judge will go easy on you.... Of course, if that guy doesn't come out of the hospital things could get rough."

Manuel nodded. He understood. His thoughts were then interrupted by the sound of the thick iron door clanging shut. As the officer walked away, Manuel felt as if he were in the middle of a bad dream. He sat there, alone in his cell, trying to recall the past events that had led him there. Then, for some strange reason, his mind wandered to a face he had not seen for some time. It was Pablo. He was looking directly at Manuel.

"Remember, guys, life is all about choices, so make the right ones and go on to be a big success!"

The memory made Manuel warm and happy inside. But just as he began to feel comforted, the vision of Pablo began to vanish, slowly transforming into something else—a colder, harsher presence. Pablo then disappeared completely, replaced by a man dressed in a blue prison uniform. His thick, bony head was shaved and his body was covered with tattoos. Manuel felt a shiver from deep within as Juan smiled at him approvingly.

"Nos vemos, hermano, nos vemos…"

Novel 2

MORE THAN TRADITION

1

PEEKING THROUGH THE fingers that covered her tear stained face, Lorena observed the countenance of each family member that had assembled around her. Her father was clearly upset. His brown eyes were dull, and he sat as rigid as a large stone with his chin propped up in his palm. Her mother's tan roundish face, though somewhat covered by the long bangs of her black hair, appeared tired, and the creases around her eyes revealed that she, too, had been crying. Samuel and Mary, the eldest of her siblings, inclined their heads, making eye contact impossible. Her brother, Raymond, whose handsome visage was usually accompanied by a pleasant smile, instead scowled in anger; and Ruth, the sister with whom she was closest, appeared lost in thought. Lorena's grandmother bore the same calm demeanor that perpetually marked her. Her gray hair, which was tightly pulled back into a bun, and the wrinkled skin that surrounded her forehead and mouth, seemed frozen in time. Lorena found her moods impossible to interpret. The only person in the room that offered a tinge of hope was her grandfather. There was always an aspect of light that emanated from his eyes—even in the worst of circumstances

Being part of an extended family whose members took great pride in their heritage and traditions, the Olorsisimos could trace their baptismal records to the Philippines and beyond to Spain. From such a family Lorena inherited a **uniquely** attractive countenance, the result of a rich blend of Chinese, Filipino, Japanese, and Spanish nationalities. Lorena was aware of her family's traditions, but she never understood their depths until she became the very reason for the family gathering that fateful night.

2

As a small child, Lorena spoke a mixture of English and Tagalog. But though she spoke her mother tongue quite well, it was not enough for her grandfather. He continually teased her, telling her that she was not really Filipino. As Lorena munched on a slice of pepperoni pizza, her grandfather sat next to her, eating a more traditional Filipino dish of rice and *lumpia*.

"You're only Filipino on the outside. On the inside, you are American," said Lorena's grandfather.

"*Hindi po, Lolo*," replied Lorena in Tagalog.

"Okay, then what do you like best? *Pancit? Arroz caldo? Talbos ng kamote*? No, you would much rather eat this," said her grandfather, pointing to her slice of pizza. "Or a cheeseburger!"

Lorena looked at her grandfather and smiled.

"Well?" he asked.

"Everyone likes pizza, *Lolo*," replied Lorena.

3

The history of the Olorsisimo family could be traced back to her grandfather's journey from the Philippines to the United States. Lorena had heard him tell the story often, yet each time it seemed that he would reveal something new. She would sit on the family couch, a black and red plush ensemble consisting of two connecting sections, while her grandfather whisked her back in time to a mysterious island that was far removed from her suburban life in Anaheim.

"We were poor when I first came to America," he began with a twinkle in his eye, "but nobody knew it! Most of us were young. Being new immigrants, we were just grateful to be here in this great country. Besides, in Quezon City, things were much worse! My family could not afford to send me to school, so I ended up selling candy in the streets!"

"What kind of candy, *Lolo*?" asked Lorena.

"All kinds!" replied her grandfather. "Candies that you could suck on, chewing gum, stuff like that."

"And you sold enough to come here?" asked Lorena.

Her grandfather laughed. "Well, it helped," he replied, "but when I got older, I started working in construction." Lorena's grandfather then flexed his arms. They were slender and his brown skin was dry with age. Even so, he still had some muscle tone and his hair was surprisingly thick and dark for a man his age. "There were a lot of new roads and buildings at that time, so many of my friends did this, too. But I was not like them. Instead of spending my money, I saved it. They would tell me, 'Quentin, come join us!' But I refused. Then, finally, one day I had enough for my trip. My trip to America!"

Lorena clapped her tiny hands together as her grandfather took a bow.

"I arrived in San Diego, where my cousins gave me work and a place to stay. I did so well that I brought the business to Los Angeles."

"And it was hard, right, *Lolo*?"

"Of course it was!" he replied, furrowing his brow and frowning before breaking into a wide grin. "We didn't just clean or dust or vacuum carpets. We also had to dispose of trash and scrub toilets. And another thing, *maliit na batang babae,* the girls' bathrooms were always the worst!"

Lorena laughed as her grandfather tickled her. "Were people nice to you, *Lolo*?" she asked.

"Most of them were, but some people looked down on me," he recalled, "but only until they got to know me! If they were grumpy, then I told them one of my jokes or a funny story until I saw a smile on their face! And, you know what, after a while, they liked me! Pretty soon, I had a lot of loyal customers. Everyone wanted me to clean their office. They even gave me gifts!"

Lorena never tired of hearing her grandfather's story. Whenever he spoke about coming to America, it seemed as if she were hearing it for the very first time. "And that's when you met *Lola*!" exclaimed Lorena.

"Oh, yes!" replied her grandfather. "That's the best part of the story! Your grandmother wasn't here and poor little me, surrounded by so many young beautiful girls…" He paused and shook his head while a mischievous grin spread across his bronze face. "They were all after me, you know."

Lorena laughed. Mock anger radiated from her grandfather. "But my heart remained in the Philippines," he continued. "I never forgot about your grandmother, so I traveled back to the island to ask her to marry me! But when I returned, she was studying at one of the best schools in Quezon

City. It was called Ateneo de Manila University. I was afraid. I thought that maybe she was too good for me and would reject me."

"Why, *Lolo?*" asked Lorena innocently.

"Well, despite the fact that I was so very handsome and charming, I thought she might want to marry a doctor or something like that."

"Ngunit ang kanyang sinabi ay oo!" said Lorena.

"She did!" Lorena's grandfather continued. "Her parents were not so happy at first. They did not want us to marry, and they did not want me to take her away from them."

"What did you do, *Lolo?*" asked Lorena.

"I told them that even though I had no education and not much money, I would always love her and take care of her, so they reluctantly gave us their blessing."

"And then you had *Ama*!" said Lorena.

"How do you know about these things?" her grandfather asked, tickling her again. "Yes, your daddy was born first. And then came your uncles and aunts. Your grandmother helped me run my business. We worked very hard, but we didn't want that for your daddy or the rest of them. We wanted them all to go to college and study!"

"That's why *Ama* is a dentist!" said Lorena with a tinge of joy and pride.

"Yes, and because your daddy is a dentist, I don't think you should eat this," said her grandfather as he disappeared through the swinging white hinged doors that led to the kitchen. When he returned, he showed Lorena a chocolate bar.

"*Lolo*, where did you find that?" asked Lorena.

"I have my special hiding place," replied her grandfather with a playful wink of the eye.

"Please, *Lolo*, please!" begged Lorena.

"Okay, okay, but don't tell your father!" he said, breaking off a large piece of chocolate for Lorena.

"I will go to college, too, *Lolo*," said Lorena between small bites of chocolate.

"Yes, *ang aking maliit na prinsesa*, of course," replied her grandfather, stroking her hair which fell well past her shoulders in long black strands.

4

As LORENA GREW older, it was made clear that her family had high expectations. Everyone was expected to do well in school. Each of Lorena's brothers and sisters were involved in a variety of activities. Lorena, being the youngest, felt the pressure to succeed at a very young age.

Upon embarking on her freshman year of high school, Lorena was happy that she would not be alone. Her brother, Raymond, was a senior; and her sister, Ruth, was a junior. Both of them stood out for excellence in their own unique way. Raymond was the Associated Student Body President and the top ranked tennis player in the school. Ruth, not to be outdone, was known for her beautiful singing voice. Not only was she the lead vocalist of the school choir, she had also performed at several Christmas concerts at Disneyland.

Lorena was determined to continue her family's tradition of achievement and excellence. High school meant greater expectations, and she was not about to disappoint her family. In her first year, Lorena was the starting shooting guard on the junior varsity basketball team, a club officer in both the Interact Club and the Spanish Club, and was able to attain a perfect 4.0 GPA. Her goals were set from the very beginning and she made it known to everyone. She was going to earn both scholastic and athletic scholarships in order to attend UCLA. There, she would be the starting point guard on the women's basketball team.

The life of Lorena Olorsisimo had been predestined. Her family had shown her the path to success, so all she had to do was follow in their footsteps. Her life was the **epitome** of discipline, structure, and focus, and no one thing nor any single person would be allowed to disrupt it. She lived in a bubble. An impenetrable bubble. Or so she thought.

5

HER SECOND YEAR of high school brought more ambition and higher goals to achieve. Lorena was ecstatic when she learned that she had made the varsity basketball team, and equally proud to be elected an officer in the Interact club. She was carving her own path and nothing else seemed to matter. That is, until someone new entered her life. His name was Greg Johnson.

Lorena had seen him before, but she really took notice when the varsity teams were forced to share the gym for an hour. Greg was a forward on the boys varsity basketball team, and with each practice Lorena found herself looking over to the other side of the court more and more to watch him. She had heard of love at first sight but had never taken such a trite cliché very seriously.

At fifteen years of age, she was blossoming into a pretty young lady. With shoulder length black hair; a round, symmetrical face; bright eyes and sparkling teeth; it was inevitable that boys would take notice. Some of them openly flirted with her, but no one truly interested Lorena until she saw Greg. In her eyes, he was the perfect boy: tall, handsome, and a varsity basketball player. Culturally, they shared common roots as well. Though Greg's father was white, his mother was Filipino.

Their relationship started simply enough. A ball had bounced over to the girls' side of the gym, and Greg finally made eye contact with her, greeting Lorena with a simple "hello." She smiled. And though they did not exchange another word, she felt something she had never felt before. Her entire body became soft and still...

Greg offered Lorena a ride home after basketball practice that night. She was hesitant to accept, but to her own surprise, she did. This slowly became a pattern until Lorena felt very comfortable with Greg. She began to linger in his car each night in front of her home. Sometimes, they talked for hours.

Lorena could not pinpoint it exactly, but she had the strange sense that Greg was missing something. Outwardly, he appeared to have everything an adolescent could wish for. His face was not only handsome, but somewhat exotic and angularly unique as he had gotten the best of the Anglo and Filipino features due to his mixed heritage. Besides his physical attributes, Greg came from a very wealthy and prominent family. At the age of sixteen, his parents had given him a sports car that was the envy of every other high school student. And if this were not enough, he was an extremely polished and cultured person. Upon meeting Greg, people quickly became **enamored** of him. Lorena could not think of a single person who did not like Greg, including her older sister, Ruth, who spoke of him often. But despite this, Lorena could see that Greg was restless. He gave her the impression of a person who was constantly on his way to a new destination without ever having arrived.

"...then my grandfather said, 'One day I'll take you to the Ati-Atihan festival!' I love my *Lolo*. He's so special. I haven't been to the Philippines since I was a little girl."

"That's nice," replied Greg, a somewhat distracted look on his face.

"What about you?" asked Lorena.

"What do you mean?" said Greg, furrowing his brow.

"Tell me something about your parents or your grandparents."

"There's not much to tell," replied Greg. "My dad's a surgeon and my mom's into politics."

Lorena crinkled her forehead. "How can you say it like that?" she asked. "They must have really interesting lives! Tell me something! Tell me a story!"

"Like what?"

Lorena smiled. "Oh, I don't know. A special moment. A time where you felt especially loved."

Greg instantly smirked. He then rubbed the short dark hair on the back of his head. "A special moment? Every night when I drop you off. And a time when I felt especially loved?" Suddenly, Greg paused. He then broke off eye contact.

Lorena stared at Greg's cheek. She wanted to kiss him.

"When I'm with you," Greg began, "I feel so.... Oh, never mind."

"What?"

"No, it's getting late. The last time we talked so long your brother came out, remember?"

"Okay," said Lorena, unbuckling her seatbelt, "but before I go, just tell me what you were thinking. Really, I want to know."

"No, you don't," said Greg.

"I do," insisted Lorena.

"It's embarrassing."

"Tell me," Lorena whispered. She reached out and turned Greg's head so that he faced her.

His eyes began to soften. "Okay, I'll tell you." Slowly unbuckling his seatbelt, Greg said, "When I'm with you, I don't feel lonely."

Lorena tilted her head back. She raised her eyebrows. "But you have so many friends. In fact, when are you ever alone?"

"You wouldn't understand, Lorena," said Greg, "because you have a big family. I'm an only child."

"But look at how your parents spoil you. You're constantly the center of attention."

Greg's face suddenly changed. His jaw tightened as he pressed his lips together. A slight moisture could be seen in the corner of his eyes. "Do we have to keep talking about my parents?"

Taken aback by the question, Lorena fell silent. After a brief silence, she began to gently stroke Greg's shoulder. He quickly embraced her and pulled her closer to him. Then, before she fully realized what was happening, he kissed her on the lips. Nervously, she returned his kiss. His face felt warm and Lorena could smell the pleasing scent of his cologne.

Suddenly, interrupting their tight embrace, a light appeared from Lorena's porch. Greg and Lorena quickly released each other.

"Don't worry," said Greg, "my windows are tinted. Nobody saw anything."

Lorena nodded, gathered her gym bag, and opened the car door. As she walked toward her house, the two lights mounted on both sides of the garage allowed her to see a figure standing on the cement walkway that led to the front door. It was her older sister, Ruth, who possessed the same dark hair and white teeth. Unlike Lorena, however, her eyes were dull and serious and her body was pear shaped. Her face displayed a curious expression.

"How long have you two been out there?" asked Ruth.

"Uh, I don't know," said Lorena, sidestepping her sister on her way inside. She then turned and smiled as Greg's car left the curb of the sidewalk.

"Lorena, I don't think it's right for you to stay in another boy's car like that. It's late."

But Lorena did not answer. She was thinking about Greg and her first kiss, and she could still smell the scent of his cologne.

6

THE NEXT DAY at school Greg asked Lorena to be his girlfriend. She knew that her parents would not approve, so she informed Greg that they would have to keep their relationship a secret. As the two began to openly spend more time together, however, a few of Lorena's friends began asking her questions. Lorena's older sister, Ruth, also became more inquisitive.

While Lorena and Greg sat together during lunch on one of the green metal benches positioned against the outside wall of a classroom, Ruth walked directly up to them. They were entirely unaware of her presence, fully absorbed in their own conversation and laughter. Behind them, on both ends of the bench, were paper plates with a few slices of pizza and large styrofoam cups with transparent straws poking out.

"Hey, Greg. Hey, Lorena."

Greg turned to her. He smiled easily. "Oh, hey, Ruth. Would you like to join us?"

"May I?" replied Ruth, her voice dripping of sarcasm. "Are you sure it's okay?"

"What do you mean?" asked Greg.

"There's not a lot of room on that bench," said Ruth, "and you're sitting very close to my sister."

Lorena glanced at Greg and then at her sister. "Ruth, why are you being so rude?"

"Am I being rude?" Ruth retorted. "I'm just worried, Lorena. You're my little sister and I'm trying to look out for you, that's all."

Lorena frowned slightly. "We're just having lunch together, Ruth. We're not doing anything wrong."

Ruth took a few more steps toward them. "Greg, why are you spending so much time with my sister? You're a senior and she's only a sophomore."

Greg shrugged his shoulders and raised his palms upward. "Ruth, we're friends. I really like Lorena. I don't understand. Aren't we all friends?"

"Yeah, Ruth, aren't you and Greg friends, too?" added Lorena.

Ruth bit her lip. "Well, just because we have some classes together doesn't mean we're friends." She turned toward Greg and added, "Besides, I've seen you with a lot of girls, Greg, so I don't think you need my sister as another one of your '*friends*.'"

"Ruth, stop!" said Lorena.

Frowning deeply, Ruth stared at Lorena. Her eyes remained fixed in position, so much so that she did not even blink. "Just be careful," she said before walking away.

After a brief silence, Greg shook his head and laughed. He got up from the bench and began to stretch his athletic six foot frame.

"Greg, it's not funny!" said Lorena. "She may tell my parents."

"No, no," replied Greg. "It's not that. It's just...well, I was afraid this might happen, so I never told you."

Lorena stood up and approached him. "Tell me what?"

"Well, it's your sister. I mean, you know why she's acting like this, right?"

"Greg, what do you mean?" asked Lorena. "She's just concerned. I'm the baby of the family. My brothers and sisters are very protective of me."

"I'm sure that's true," said Greg, "but come on, you saw how personal she's taking all of this."

Lorena lowered her brow. Noticing this, Greg smiled. He reached over and caressed her forehead. "You're so cute when you're angry. It's like looking at an upset kitten."

Lorena paused for a moment. She closed her eyes.

"Don't you get it?" whispered Greg. "Gosh, I didn't want to say anything, but come on, it's so obvious."

"What is?" asked Lorena, slowly opening her eyes.

"Your sister...she's jealous!"

"Jealous?" repeated Lorena, quizzically.

"Oh, yeah!" said Greg. "Look, I've had to keep a little distance from your sister because she can come on pretty strong." He stepped away from Lorena. "Every year we have a few classes together." Greg paused. Moving two of his fingers with each hand, he continuedand, "And she has asked me to *study* with her on more than one occasion. She's a smart girl. I mean, believe me, I wish we could study together and hang out a little, but I've always told her that I was too busy because she's a little, well, needy."

"Ruth? That doesn't sound like her."

"Lorena, Lorena," said Greg, placing both of his hands on her shoulders. "Do you want to talk to some of my friends? There are at least five guys that barely even look at your sister because they know how much she wants a boyfriend!"

Lorena gave Greg a look of incredulity, raising her eyebrows as her eyes slightly protruded.

"See?" continued Greg. "That's why I didn't want to say anything. Don't get me wrong. Your sister has a lot of nice qualities, but I think she's having a hard time seeing us happy together, especially after I turned her down."

"Wow," replied Lorena, "I never knew."

"I told you I didn't want to tell you!"

"Well, I don't want to hurt her," said Lorena.

"Neither do I! I keep telling you that's why I never brought it up." Greg paused. He then shook his head. "Well, I guess you can't blame her for being jealous." He gently began to caress Lorena's cheek with the back of his hand. "Ruth doesn't have your pretty face." He stroked her bangs. "She doesn't have your pretty hair." He then gripped her biceps with both hands, slowly bringing them down her arms until he touched her fingertips. "And she definitely doesn't have your body."

Lorena stared at Greg. She could feel her heartbeat. Her head was becoming light.

"I'm sorry, Lorena. I really care about you—more than you'll ever know. But I don't want to get between you and your sister. If you want to break up, I'll do my best to leave you alone. But I have to be honest, it's not going to be easy."

Lorena pulled Greg closer to her. "No, that's the last thing I want. Don't worry about Ruth. We just have to be careful."

7

As EACH DAY passed, Lorena spent more time with Greg. She was both amazed and thrilled to be with him. It appeared that there was nothing he could not do, and though Lorena had lived in Orange County her entire life, he took her places that she had never seen before.

Money was never an issue, and Southern California provided anything two young people could ask for. Greg and Lorena often took trips down

Beach Boulevard. She loved the blue skies and the ocean breeze. From there, they made their way to the pier, holding hands as they talked about their future goals in life.

"My oldest brother, Samuel, is a dentist like my father. And my sister, Mary, actually works with my mother at the Children's Hospital. She inspired her to be a nurse. As for me, I'm going to be a veterinarian."

"I think that's wonderful," said Greg, "but personally, I don't want anything to do with the medical field even if that means having animals as patients."

Lorena laughed. "But why?"

"Because I'm just not into it. I'm more like my mom. She's the one who's helped me the most. Last summer she even got me an internship at D.C."

"Wow," said Lorena, "so someday am I going to call you Senator Johnson?"

"Yeah, you probably will," said Greg. He tilted his head up toward the blue sky. "Or maybe even President Johnson."

Lorena smiled and began to laugh again, but then she looked at Greg's face. He had made the statement in earnest.

8

BESIDES THE BEAUTIFUL beaches and parks, Orange County also boasted some of the most exquisite restaurants in the entire state. Their personal favorite included a certain Italian restaurant located in San Juan Capistrano. The two usually chose to eat outside, reveling in the beautiful weather and the site of the historic Mission. As people passed them by, Greg gave each one a psychological profile.

"Hmmmm. Bald, short and fat," he began, "I'd say he's an accountant based on the nerdy clothes. Prefers to work alone. Definitely single. And lives in an apartment where his idea of culture is a microwave dinner."

Laughing, Lorena hit him on the shoulder. "You're so mean!"

"Okay, check these guys out," said Greg, pointing to a family of five. A man and a woman were both pushing a stroller while one small child struggled to keep pace in the middle.

"Super square. Thick glasses. Two little munchkins and another kid with a Mickey Mouse hat. Tourists, for sure," stated Greg matter-of-factly.

"Where are they from?" asked Lorena. She looked first at the man. He had dark hair and glasses. She then turned toward the woman. She had thick brown hair that flowed over her shoulders. They were both wearing shorts and thin, cotton shirts.

"They have to be from, like, Alaska or Seattle or somewhere," said Greg.

"Why do you say that?"

"Did you see those white legs?" said Greg, shaking his head. "The mom was actually kind of cute but you could see she was the typical worn-out housewife. She lost whatever sex appeal she had a long time ago."

Lorena broke into laughter but then quickly scolded Greg. "Mean, Greg Johnson! So mean!"

Greg released a mischievous grin. He then turned his left wrist, exposing a large, classically designed watch composed of a round white face and a black leather band. Pulling out a hundred dollar bill, he placed it on the table and stood up. "It's late. We better go. Remember, if anyone asks, this is my mother's number. She'll tell your parents that we were at the house studying all night."

Lorena winced slightly. "I don't know, Greg. I don't want to lie to them. I don't even know if I can."

"Lorena, you don't have to! If they ask where you were, you just tell them to call Mrs. Johnson." He raised both hands and extended his forefingers directly at Lorena. "That way, it's not a lie."

"Hmmmm," replied Lorena, "I guess I never thought about it like that."

9

INSIDE THE SUNLIT living room, Lorena sat on a black leather couch. Seated next to her was Greg's mother, Mrs. Johnson, who was a striking woman with long black hair, dark eyes accentuated by long lashes, and a curvaceous figure that most women of twenty would envy.

"Wow! Greg is so cute here!" said Lorena while pointing to an old photograph of little Gregory dressed in a traditional black and white tuxedo.

"This was at a fundraiser for the governor. Greg was in kindergarten at the time," said Mrs. Johnson.

"Oh," said Lorena. Then, looking at another, she asked, "Where are you guys in this picture?"

"That was at a restaurant in Sacramento."

"Gosh, I didn't know Doctor Johnson was so handsome!" exclaimed Lorena.

Mrs. Johnson promptly closed the photo album. "That's not my husband," she replied dryly. "He's a—a colleague of mine." Mrs. Johnson stood up and promptly put the thick, blue photo album atop a wooden shelf.

Entering the living room, Greg shouted, "Mom, you're not boring her with old pictures, are you?"

"Can't a mother be proud of a future President?" replied Mrs. Johnson. She walked over to Greg and embraced him tightly. She then caressed his handsome, angular face with her delicate manicured hands. "What do you think, Lorena? President Gregory Johnson?"

Lorena swallowed before smiling somewhat nervously. After having turned page upon page of the many photographs, it struck her that Greg had immediately been thrust into the adult world of galas and banquets. His social training was evident. When he was with adults, he charmed them with his **cordial** manners and conservative appearance. When he was with his peers, however, Lorena was beginning to see a young man who could be quite **hedonistic**.

"Well, we should be going," said Greg.

"Have fun, dear," said Mrs. Johnson.

As they walked outside, Greg held the door open for Lorena. "When will I meet your father?" she asked.

Letting out a puff of air, Greg rolled his eyes and replied, "Probably never. I barely see him myself."

Heading toward the 405 freeway, Greg began, "Listen Lorena, you're going to meet some really cool people. Some of them go to UCLA and might be able to help you when you get there."

Lorena smiled, her face emanating the appreciation she felt.

"But don't act like a child, and whatever you do, don't embarrass me!" Lorena's smile immediately vanished.

"Remember, you should feel honored to even be at this party," continued Greg.

"You'll be the youngest one there, but no one needs to know that. Just pretend you're older and follow my lead." Then, stroking her shoulder, he added, "Trust me! You're going to have a great time!"

After exiting the freeway, Greg passed several streets until he pulled up to a large gate. He slowed down to a stop in front of a black and silver panel, where he began to push several buttons until a large black metal gate opened, allowing them to enter an exclusive, **affluent** neighborhood located in Beverly Hills. Lorena marveled as they passed several large, beautiful homes with impeccable landscaping.

Finally, Greg stopped in front of a particularly large, distinguished home. The front lawns boasted the most artistic design that Lorena had ever beheld. There were a myriad of green bushes and trees, water fountains, cement patterns of various block designs, and statues of lions throughout. Two large, separate garages were surrounded on both sides with extended parking space. Several cars were parked on both sides, crowding each driveway. The large domicile was divided into two ninety degree angles, creating two separate buildings connected by a huge, outside porch. For one unfamiliar with the neighborhood, the single residence appeared to be two houses that stood closely next to each other. Lorena was in awe.

Upon entering, they immediately stepped into a large living room. Lorena estimated that it would have taken up at least half of the entire first floor if placed within her own house. At the end of the room, she observed a kitchen complete with a bar counter where several young people were being served by a young man wearing a white uniform. To her right, she stopped to stare at four different luxury couches and a dozen chairs. To her left was a large jacuzzi with several people inside, laughing as they held on to their drinks.

"They have a built in hot tub in their living room!" gushed Lorena.

Greg smiled slightly. Grabbing Lorena by the hand, he replied, "Yeah, yeah, let's go outside."

Making their way across the crowded living room, Greg greeted several people. As they crossed over to an outside patio area, Lorena observed a circular swimming pool. Scattered around it were several folding chairs and tables, and to the side, a cement barbecue pit.

"Lorena, meet Geoff," said Greg, introducing her to the host of the party. "Geoff attends Pepperdine, and this humble abode is his."

Geoff was somewhat on the short side, handsome and refined. He had thick, wavy black hair, olive colored skin, and seemed very relaxed in his polo shirt, shorts, and Birkenstock sandals. Geoff put his arm around Lorena very comfortably and kissed her on the cheek. She did not resist though the gesture took her by surprise.

"Well, it really isn't my home," said Geoff. "It belongs to my parents. I do have one in Colorado under my name, though. Great skiing in Aspen, you know."

Lorena laughed. He reminded her a little bit of Greg in that he spoke with great polish and culture, literally projecting an air of the upper class.

"What's so funny?" asked Geoff.

"Oh, nothing," interrupted Greg. "Lorena's just the type of girl that smiles and laughs easily. Hey, Geoff, we'll catch up with you later. I want to show Lorena around if that's okay with you."

"Sure thing," said Geoff. "See you soon."

Greg quickly led Lorena to a corner near the stairway. "What was that childish laughter all about?"

"Sorry," replied Lorena, **perplexed**. "I thought he was joking. How many college students have their own home?"

"Have you seen this house?" Greg asked. "His dad is a major stockbroker. He has some of the richest clients in the world. Geoff's dad actually has lunch regularly with Warren Buffet!"

Lorena stared at Greg, then asked, "Is that where his parents are?"

Greg shook his head and frowned deeply. "Oh, never mind. Look, just follow my lead and remember, whatever I do, you do, got it? I'm not going to have my girl embarrass me in front of the crème de la crème!"

Even though Lorena delighted in the beautiful surroundings as well as the delicious food being served, she felt uneasy surrounded by so many older people. She tried to limit her conversation to agreeing with others and doing nothing more than releasing a quick smile. Whereas Greg was in his element, Lorena felt completely lost. Then, to her surprise, he handed her an alcoholic beverage. She hesitated, which caused Greg to hold the glass in his hand longer than he anticipated.

"Greg, I don't think…"

Greg scowled at her. It was a deep, menacing scowl. Still, it was not his facial expression that bothered Lorena. It was the contempt in his eyes. Lorena could literally hear his voice inside her head, shouting, *"Don't embarrass me!"*

Finally, she accepted the drink that was offered her. "What is it?"

"It's called a Cosmo," Greg replied with a marked tinge of superiority in his voice.

Lorena stared nervously at the red colored cocktail, afraid to venture a taste.

"Don't worry!" said Greg. "It's actually good for you. It has cranberry juice!"

Lorena began with little sips. She attempted to will herself to like it, but was disgusted by the foreign taste. This did not seem to bother Greg, however. He continued to mingle, introducing her to more people. As he did so, the drinks kept coming, and Lorena found it harder to concentrate. Soon, she felt a mixture of dizziness and nausea as faces and voices blended into an indecipherable collage. The next thing Lorena remembered was Greg leading her to a private room upstairs. On the way there, she could faintly recall the site and sound of several couples kissing while their arms and legs were tightly wrapped around each other.

10

WITHOUT REALIZING IT, Lorena had become involved in an **exclusive** relationship. She rarely had time for her family or friends. As this became apparent to her, she felt odd, as if she were losing her identity. The reflection in the mirror was no longer her own, but one of a complete stranger.

Lorena did everything with Greg. Together, they frequented restaurants, visited stadiums, and often attended house parties. Lorena thought she was having fun, yet deep down she knew that something was wrong. Greg had become the center of her life.

"Greg, I don't know. Maybe we should take a break this weekend," said Lorena, seated at a table in her favorite Italian restaurant. She waited impatiently for the main course to arrive.

"And do what?" asked Greg.

"I don't know," replied Lorena, meekly. "Just spend time with our families."

"What are you suggesting, Lorena?" scoffed Greg, visibly annoyed. "Are you trying to punish me?" Wagging his head, he dipped his breadstick into a small metal cup full of melted butter. In the background, beyond the noise of people talking at each table, the sound of live jazz music could be heard. "Anyway, you'll change your mind once you find out what I have planned," said Greg, sparking up the conversation once again.

Lorena waited while Greg inserted a thick breadstick into his mouth.

"Well?" she asked.

"Well what?"

"Tell me what you have planned this weekend!" said Lorena, perking up a bit.

Greg reached into his blue blazer and took out two tickets. He conspicuously laid them on the table.

"What's this?" she asked.

"Only the best magic show in Vegas!" replied Greg.

But instead of delight, Lorena was struck by disappointment. "Las Vegas? You're taking me to Las Vegas?"

"Yes! Vegas!" replied Greg with great excitement emanating from his voice. "And there's more…" He paused for emphasis as he leaned closer to Lorena. "I reserved two nights for us at the Bellagio!"

Lorena opened her mouth, but then looked down as their waiter arrived with two plates of fettucini alfredo. As soon as he had left, Greg waved his hands in the air and shouted, "Well, don't thank me all at once!"

"Las Vegas, a hotel…. It just doesn't make any sense," whispered Lorena. Her eyes had a trancelike quality to them.

"It makes complete sense," said Greg.

"But we're still teenagers!" blurted Lorena.

Greg raised his brow. He curled some noodles around his fork which he promptly pointed at Lorena. "And?"

"And we're not allowed to go to Las Vegas. We're not old enough!"

"Lorena, we can do anything we want. You're just blinded by your family traditions."

"That's not true, Greg."

"Sure it is!" said Greg, a familiar scowl spreading across his face. "Society establishes these archaic laws to try to stop young people like us from enjoying life!" He paused to take another bite from his plate. "And then gullible people like you, Lorena, just bow down without ever questioning the status quo! We can't gamble. We can't stay in a hotel. We can't drink alcohol. The whole thing is ridiculous! In most countries you and I would be considered adults! I swear! The United States is so backward in its thinking!"

Lorena stared at Greg.

"Don't you agree?" he asked.

Lorena continued to think, and then said quietly, "I don't know. Like I said, we're still so young to do..." Her voice trailed off.

"We're still so young to do what?" asked Greg, exhaling loudly. "I'm almost eighteen and you're almost sixteen, right? I don't know about you, but I'm an adult. My parents understand that. My friends in Europe understand that. The problem with you, Lorena, is that your family still treats you like a child, and so naturally you act like one."

Lorena pressed her lips together. After a prolonged silence, Greg muttered, "Maybe I should ask some other girl to go with me."

Lorena flinched suddenly. "Greg, you know I want to be with you, but I feel so uncomfortable with the lies. What am I supposed to tell my parents?"

"Don't worry!" said Greg. "My mom's got it covered. She's going to tell them that we're going as a family!"

Lorena furrowed her brow. "Wait! What? I'm confused. Your parents are coming with us?"

"Of course not!" huffed Greg. "Don't be absurd!"

"So your mom doesn't care that we'll be alone, in a hotel, in Las Vegas, for an entire weekend?" asked Lorena. "And she's willing to lie for us?"

Greg laughed somewhat derisively. "Lorena, you're so funny sometimes! Come on, you know my mom's cool like that! You should be grateful I have such an understanding and supportive mother!"

Lorena did not answer at first, but instead rolled the noodles on her plate around her fork. After further pause, she meekly stated, "My parents would never do something like that."

Greg twisted his lips into a snarl. "Yeah, that's exactly right! If it were up to your parents, we wouldn't even be together!"

A few people sitting at a table nearby turned their heads. Greg leaned forward and proceeded in a forced whisper, "Lorena, I love you and I thought you loved me, so of course I want to share special moments with you. Visiting the most exciting cities, staying in the most beautiful hotels…. How can that be a bad thing?"

Greg touched Lorena's forehead gently, moving her dark hair out of the way of her brown eyes. This gentle caress prompted her to look directly at the mixture of Asian American features that made Greg so handsome. The angular face, the almond shaped eyes…

"Don't you love me as much as I love you?" asked Greg.

Lorena smiled. "You know I do, but maybe we should set boundaries."

Greg's gentle face suddenly turned hard as his fist came heavily down on the table, causing the silverware to rattle noisily. "Damn it, Lorena! What's wrong with you?"

A waiter standing nearby stopped. "Is everything okay?" he asked.

"Yes, thank you," said Greg, smiling quickly. The man lingered a moment before attending an adjoining table. Greg then leaned more closely toward Lorena. "Really, Lorena? Really? Are you that immature? Don't you realize that even junior high girls are having sex? I just don't understand you. In fact, I'm starting to feel like giving up. You just make everything so damn complicated! I give you everything, I take you everywhere, and yet all you do is complain, complain, complain! I'm not good enough, my mother's not good enough…." Greg paused. His eyes darted downward. He reached for his glass of water and took a forced drink. Wiping his upper lip with his cloth napkin, he continued, "I need a grown woman, Lorena, not a little girl who still needs her mommy and daddy telling her what to do!"

Lorena swallowed deeply. A surge of panic entered her body. "Greg, it's not like that."

"Then what? Does your family have a rule against fun, too?"

"No, of course not. It's just that they have always taught me to wait…"

"To wait?" interrupted Greg. "Wait for what?"

"You know...to get married first..."

Greg scoffed loudly and then shook his head from side to side. "Look, you're going to have to either choose me and the new millenium or your family and the Stone Age!"

Lorena bowed her head. A melancholy frown took over her face. "Okay, okay! Just forget I ever brought it up! I guess my family doesn't matter."

11

LORENA WAS TRAPPED. She felt powerless. Slowly, her outings with Greg became less frequent. It was becoming painfully obvious that he was losing interest, and doubts had popped into her head that could no longer be ignored.

Each day Lorena passed through her classes without speaking a word. Her mind had already exhausted all possibilities. She was in a daze, a stupor. Her body felt lifeless and limp. The change in her demeanor was apparent, yet few people intervened. As the pattern continued, however, someone finally called out to her. As Lorena sat in her desk, staring at her Spanish book, she felt a hand on her shoulder.

"Lorena," said Mrs. García, "may I have a word with you after class?"

She looked up at her teacher. She was an attractive woman with long black hair and dark eyes. With her lips firmly pressed together, Lorena nodded affirmatively.

"I promise it won't be long," said Mrs. García.

As the school bell rang and students poured out of their seats, Lorena remained seated. Her teacher motioned for her to come to her desk. "Lorena, I've noticed a change in you. So have some of your other teachers. Are you okay?" began Mrs. García.

Once again, Lorena nodded without saying a word.

"Well, you used to be one of my top students, but now, well, you're failing my class and you never attend our club meetings. This is no way to end the school year."

Tears welled up in Lorena's eyes.

"Are you sure you're okay?" asked Mrs. García.

Lorena moved her head from left to right.

"What is it, Lorena?"

"I haven't been feeling very well lately."

"Are you ill?"

"I don't know."

"You just don't seem happy anymore, Lorena. You used to be so cheerful and bubbly."

After a long silence, Lorena asked, "May I be excused?"

Mrs. García nodded, and Lorena quickly left the room.

12

LORENA PRACTICALLY BUMPED into her diminutive grandmother. She had begun to push open the swinging hinged doors to the kitchen when her grandmother came through from the other side.

"Helo, Lola," said Lorena, greeting her grandmother in Tagalog.

"Hi. Kamusta ka? Bakit mukha kang malungkot? Masama ba ang pakiramdam mo?" her grandmother replied.

Lorena paused. She considered telling her grandmother the truth but instead replied, *"Maayos naman ako. Salamat."*

Smiling, the elderly woman slowly walked away. Lorena watched her for a moment and then entered the kitchen. She opened the refrigerator, took out a cold can of soda, and assembled the necessary ingredients for a ham sandwich on the long dark granite counter. As she placed two slices of bread down, the kitchen doors swung open.

"Hey," said Ruth.

"Hey," said Lorena dryly.

"Any more sodas?"

"Yes."

"Mind if I grab some of that?" asked Ruth.

"Of course not," said Lorena.

The two girls proceeded to make their sandwiches in complete silence, reaching around each other without a single utterance. The situation felt awkward for Lorena and was a far cry from their normal mode of active conversation.

Finally, Ruth asked, "Everything okay?"

Lorena shrugged. "Yes…why?"

"No reason."

Taking turns with the mayonnaise jar, the two sisters continued the finishing touches on their respective ham sandwiches. Each one added some pickles and lettuce.

"I haven't seen much of Greg, lately," said Ruth.

Lorena took a few bites of her sandwich, swallowed hard, and then replied, "He's been really busy. You know, looking at different schools for next year."

"Oh, where is he going?"

"He isn't sure, yet."

"Is he going to attend a school close by?"

"Ruth, I said he's not sure!"

Ruth lowered her brow and frowned. "You don't have to get angry." Then, after taking a bite of her sandwich, she added, "What are you going to do if he goes off to some school far away? Do you know if he's even going to stay in California? With his parents, he could easily get into one of the Ivy League schools."

"Gosh, Ruth, you seem to know everything about Greg," said Lorena, staring directly into her sister's eyes.

"He talks about it in class," said Ruth. She then grabbed the cold can of soda next to her and took a drink.

Lorena continued to stare at her. Once Ruth had finished swallowing, Lorena asked, "To you?"

"To everybody."

"Why don't you just say how you really feel?" asked Lorena.

Crinkling her forehead, Ruth replied, "What are you talking about?"

"Greg told me how much you like him," said Lorena. "I know you're jealous."

Ruth cocked her head back. "Is that what you think?"

"That's what I know!"

"Look, Lorena, maybe I did like him, or at least I've always thought he was cute, but that has nothing to do with it. The truth is that I don't

trust him and I'm just worried about you. I know he's your boyfriend…
and all the other stuff."

Lorena's mouth dropped open. She put down her sandwich..

"Who are you trying to fool, Lorena?" said Ruth. "I'm your sister.
Nobody knows you as well as I do."

A chill ran down Lorena's spine. "Does anybody else know?"

"I think Raymond knows, but he's too busy studying to do much. The
rest, well, I guess they trust you too much."

Lorena began to bite her lower lip. "So you know about…?"

"I know everything," interrupted Ruth before pausing to take the last
few bites of her sandwich. "I know you two go off on dates and then tell
everyone that you were studying!" She let out a puff of air and shook her
head. "I can't believe mom and dad fall for that! Anyway, I'm just trying
to protect you, but if you don't tell the truth soon, you're going to get hurt.
Greg may seem like a good guy, but I'm not so sure."

Lorena bit her lower lip nervously. "Are you going to tell them?"

"No," said Ruth, "but you should."

"You know, I think I'll eat the rest of my sandwich in my room," said
Lorena. She quickly wrapped it in a paper towel, gathered her drink, and
passed through the wooden swinging doors that separated the kitchen
from the living room.

13

LORENA WALKED GLUMLY down one of the many hallways of her school
when she suddenly spotted Greg about to enter a classroom. She quickly
ran toward him.

"Greg!" said Lorena. "Where have you been?" I've been looking all
over for you!"

"Sorry, I've been really occupied," he replied flatly.

"Huh?"

"Busy, Lorena, busy," replied Greg with a condescendent tone that had
become all too familiar.

"Busy?" repeated Lorena. "I must have texted you a thousand times!
You haven't been at school for three days!"

"Lorena, calm down!" said Greg. "I was away looking at a university I may attend. I was going to call you."

"Greg, I need to talk to you!"

"Okay, okay," said Greg, rubbing Lorena's shoulders. "I guess you really missed me."

"I did miss you," said Lorena, "but I guess you didn't miss me."

"Lorena, don't start."

"Well, what do you expect? You disappear without telling me. You don't answer your phone. Even your friends didn't know where you were!"

Greg scowled in anger. "This is exactly why I didn't talk to you! I needed some time to focus!"

"Greg, I need you!" said Lorena.

Greg quickly turned away, not appearing to look at anything in particular. "Well, maybe you need to learn to be more independent," he replied coldly.

Bursting into tears, Lorena cried, "How can you say that? I've given up everything for you!"

Swallowing deeply, Greg replied, "Lorena, I didn't want to do this now, but maybe it's for the best. I think we should go our separate ways. I mean, I'm about to graduate..."

"Greg, I'm pregnant."

Greg's mouth slowly dropped open. He waited for a few students who were nearby to pass them. Once he and Lorena were alone, he asked, "What did you say?"

"I said I'm pregnant," replied Lorena.

Greg's jaw tightened. He pressed his lips together tightly. Grabbing Lorena by the arm, he led her away from the classroom to a grassy area nearby.

"Well, what are we going to do?" asked Lorena, wiping the corners of her eyes.

"What are *we* going to do?" repeated Greg.

"Yes, I need your help."

"Well, what do you want from me?"

"Greg!" said Lorena. "I'm fifteen years old and I'm pregnant! I—I don't know what to do. I'm afraid."

"Lorena, it's okay," said Greg. "It's not a big deal. Just get an abortion and forget about it."

"I can't do that!"

"Why not?"

"Because I'm Catholic!"

"So?" said Greg, shrugging his shoulders.

"So?" repeated Lorena, glaring at him. "So the Catholic church does not believe in abortion! We believe that all life is sacred. To get an abortion would be…"

As Lorena's voice trailed off, Greg interrupted, "What?"

"Well," said Lorena quietly, "it would be murder."

"Oh, here we go!" said Greg, rolling his eyes.

Lorena was about to say something when Greg's cell phone rang.

"Don't answer it," said Lorena firmly. A tear slowly fell down her cheek. "Greg, please."

Furrowing his brow, Greg slid the phone to his ear. "Yeah? Oh, hey! What's going on, man? No, I'm not busy. Got a couple minutes before class starts."

Greg took a few steps away from Lorena. Finally, after suffering through a lengthy coversation, she took a few steps toward him, grabbed the phone out of his hand, and ended the call.

Greg scowled. "What do you think you're doing?"

"Greg! This is serious! I'm scared!" cried Lorena, waving the phone in his face. Wiping her cheeks with her free hand, she continued, "Nobody knows that I'm pregnant!"

"Lower your voice or everyone is going to know!" hissed Greg. "Look, I already told you what you need to do. I can't deal with this right now. I've got too many things on my plate with college applications and all. May I have my phone back, please?"

Lorena looked at Greg. She shook her head. Reluctantly, she held his phone up in her open palm.

As Greg snatched it from her hand, he shouted, "Thank you!" Then, without another word, he strode off down the hall and disappeared into a classroom.

Lorena stood silently. She felt numb. Slowly, her eyes moved toward a familiar green bench. She stumbled over to it and sat down. There, she put her head into her hands and wept.

14

"*SUSMARYOSEP!* HOW CAN this be?" shouted Lorena's father. "You have always had pride in your studies! What is happening to you?"

"*Ama*, please, I…" Lorena feebly protested.

"Yes?"

"Alex, please, let her explain," interrupted Lorena's mother.

"Okay, fine," he mumbled. Then, turning toward Lorena, he continued, "Could you please tell me why I received a phone call from one of your teachers?" He held a white paper with official lettering in front of Lorena's face. "And this letter?"

Lorena looked at it half-heartedly. "*Ama*, I'm struggling, but I'll do better."

"Struggling?" huffed Lorena's father, exasperation in his voice. "I don't understand. Struggling with what?"

Lorena looked at him, and then at her mother. "I—I can't tell you."

Her father lowered his eyebrows. "I don't know what to say to you, Lorena, none of your brothers or sisters have ever had failing grades in school or unexcused absences. Do you understand how serious this is? Do you? Do you?"

Lorena backed away as her father raised his voice, then instinctively reached out to embrace her mother.

"Please don't protect her, Ana. If she continues like this, no university will accept her."

"Wait!" a voice called out.

Lorena turned to see her sister, Ruth, standing a small distance away in the living room.

"*Ama*, I can tell you why Lorena is failing in school."

Lorena flinched, and then her entire body began to tremble. "Ruth, please," she begged. "This is my problem."

"What is going on, here?" asked Lorena's mother. "Lorena, you're shaking."

"She's been lying to you," said Ruth.

"Ruth, stop!" cried Lorena, still clinging to her mother.

"No, Lorena, they need to know your secret," replied Ruth.

Lorena's face crumbled, displaying her deep fear.

"*Ama, Nanay,*" began Ruth, "Lorena has been seeing a boy without your permission."

"Lorena, is this true?" asked her father.

Lorena looked at her father. She opened her mouth to respond, but then her legs began to buckle. Her arms slipped off her mother's body as she collapsed to the floor.

"Lorena! Lorena! Are you okay?" gasped her mother, kneeling down on the floor.

But Lorena did not answer. Her eyes appeared hollow.

"She looks like she's in a state of shock! Alex, see what you've done! You've frightened her!"

Lorena's father arched his brow. He raised his hands in the air. "This is my fault?" He then shouted downward. "Lorena, what's wrong? Lorena, answer me!"

"Now is not the time!" said Lorena's mother. She then turned to Ruth. "Quick, get some towels and cold water. Alex, help me lift her to the couch."

15

As LORENA WALKED past the main parking lot of her school, she happened to see Greg standing next to his car, accompanied by several friends. She looked up, attempting to make eye contact. He continued speaking, oblivious to her presence. Lorena hesitated briefly, then quickened her pace. As she reached the end of the walkway, she heard Greg's voice echo in the hall.

"Lorena, Lorena! Wait up!"

Lorena slowed down, thought better of it, and continued on her way. Behind her, she could hear the sound of footsteps quickly approaching.

"Hey! Where are you running off to?" asked Greg.

Lorena continued walking. Finally, Greg put both hands on her shoulders, forcing her to stop. "Lorena, talk to me," he said gently.

Instead of speaking, Lorena looked at him with eyes that screamed of sadness.

"Wow, someone needs a hug," said Greg, putting his arms around her.

At first, Lorena stood rigidly, but then her body slumped.

"Hey, hey, it's okay," whispered Greg, holding her tightly as she collapsed into his arms. Lorena buried her head into his chest, moistening his collared shirt. "Lorena, let me give you a ride home," said Greg, leading her back to the parking lot. "I'm sorry I haven't been around much lately. My parents have really been pressuring me about choosing a school. They want me to attend an Ivy league university—on the East coast—but that's not really what I want."

A glimmer of hope gently flashed before Lorena. "Do you want to attend a school nearby?"

"I'm not sure," replied Greg. "Hey, do you really want me to drop you off at your house? You look like you need something to eat."

"Yes, that would be nice," Lorena replied. As they drove off, Lorena began to have second thoughts. "Wait. Greg, what about my situation—our situation?"

Greg turned to her and said, "Yes, yes, I'm sorry I haven't been there for you, Lorena, but it's been hard with everything happening right now. I did talk to my mom and you have her support. She knows some people at the abortion clinic—"

"Abortion?" interrupted Lorena. "Greg, I already told you how I feel about that! And wait a minute! Did you just say that you told your mother?"

"Lorena!" said Greg, raising his voice. "Now's not the time to get emotional! I'm trying to help you! In fact, right now I'd say I'm the only one! Yes, I did tell my mother, but she's not like your parents. She's a problem solver."

"I don't know, Greg," said Lorena. "Abortion is—"

"Come on, Lorena, it's your only option," interrupted Greg.

"But I've always believed—"

"Who cares what you believe!" interrupted Greg once again. "Sorry, Lorena, but enough is enough! If you have a baby everyone is going to—"

"Look where you're going!" screamed Lorena.

Passing through a red light, Greg turned to Lorena and scowled.

"Take me home!" said Lorena. "I want to go home!"

"Fine," said Greg, "I'll take you home, but hear me out on this. What is your plan, Lorena? Are you really going to tell your parents that you're pregnant?"

Lorena opened her mouth to respond, then promptly closed it.

With an air of conceit in his voice, Greg continued, "Think about it, Lorena. Do you really think your parents are going to approve of this? You think they're going to give you a kiss and a hug and tell you that they're proud of you?" After a brief pause, he added, "Yeah, we both know that's never going to happen. More likely, they will be ashamed of you! In fact, knowing them, I wouldn't be surprised if they completely disowned you!"

Lorena looked outside the window. She stared at the familiar houses that quickly passed by as they approached her neighborhood.

"Besides, like you said, we both did this, so you can't say it's your decision," continued Greg. "It's my decision too, and I say get the abortion! We both know we're not ready to be parents! Having a baby would ruin our lives!"

"But what about the baby's life?" replied Lorena, still staring out the window. "Did you ever stop and think about what the baby wants?"

Uncharacteristically, Greg hesitated. Then, after a long, awkward pause, he reached out and touched Lorena on the shoulder. "Lorena, calm down. Be reasonable. Please, I'm begging you."

Lorena continued to stare out the window. Greg's face began to contort, revealing his anger. Pounding the steering wheel with his right hand, he continued, "Damn it, Lorena! Look at me when I'm talking to you!"

Lorena turned, a forlorn expression on her face.

Greg, unmoved, continued, "Number one, it isn't a baby yet! Number two, people get abortions all the time!"

"Not in my family," whispered Lorena.

"Then do it for religious reasons!" said Greg.

Lorena furrowed her brow as she curled her upper lip. "What are you talking about?"

"Well, you believe that abortion is like murder, right?"

"Yes!" said Lorena emphatically.

"Well, I agree. When the baby is fully developed, having an abortion would be murder. But right now it's not a human being, it's just a bunch of cells that are forming…and that's exactly why you need to do this before it's too late."

Lorena shook her head in frustration.

"Lorena, trust me. It's the only solution."

"Killing our baby is a solution?" she asked.

As the words fell off her lips, Lorena fell limp against the leather chair, closed her eyes, and took a deep breath. Greg attempted in vain to moisten his lips. He swallowed several times, making short, gurgling sounds. Then, his entire face tightened. His expression of panic was replaced by a look of cold determination.

"Lorena, I'm telling you for the last time! Get the abortion!"

Tears began to roll down Lorena's cheeks. "No, Greg, no!" she cried. "I'll talk to my family! They'll help us!"

"No, they won't!" Greg shouted with a ferocity Lorena had never heard before. "And there is no way in hell that my mom is going to allow this! Nobody can know about this, Lorena! Nobody! An abortion is the only way out! Do you understand? I'm not asking you, I'm telling you!" Then, after a brief pause, he added, "If you have a baby, I swear—I swear I will fight you every step of the way! I'll deny it's mine! And—and you will be completely alone!"

Greg demonstrably slammed on his breaks as the car screeched to a halt in front of Lorena's home.

"Okay," whispered Lorena.

Greg remained motionless.

"I said *okay*," Lorena repeated, slightly louder. "Tell me what I need to do and I'll do it."

16

As LORENA WAITED in the lobby, she tried in vain to wipe the moisture that continued to form in her eyes. Next to her sat Mrs. Johnson, and a few chairs down from them sat a young couple in complete silence.

"Don't worry, dear," said Mrs. Johnson. She thumbed through the various celebrity magazines that lay on a nearby coffee table. "Everything is going to be okay. I know the doctor very well. The entire staff here is very professional. Trust me, now is the time to act."

Lorena nodded as she reached for a box of tissue paper. Mrs. Johnson smiled at her and then began to peruse through her magazine. Soon, a nurse dressed in blue scrubs approached. She motioned to Lorena to follow her. Lorena looked at Mrs. Johnson, but she had buried her face into a fashion magazine.

"Come this way, sweetie," said the nurse.

Lorena nodded as she was guided away behind two large brown doors. She continued down a hallway and then entered a small room. There, she was told to lie down on a bed.

"We have to do an ultrasound. How long has it been since your last regular period?" asked the nurse.

Lorena looked downward. "About eight weeks," she mumbled.

"Yes, you're definitely pregnant," said the nurse as she stared into a digital monitor.

At that moment, a tall man in a green uniform walked into the room. He began to examine Lorena, touching her with a white plastic device that looked like a dulled toy hammer that a child would use. As he did so, she jerked suddenly.

"Don't worry," he admonished, "I know it's cold. Just try to relax. Trust me, I've done this many times. In fact, Mrs. Johnson is a personal client of mine."

The nurse huffed suddenly. "Yeah, to hide those little indiscretions from her husband."

"Shush!" he replied, grinning. "I haven't given her the sedatives yet." Then, turning his attention back to Lorena, he continued, "You'll be awake during the procedure. Normally, we do this on the second visit, but I was told we were to do everything today, so I'm assuming you've been counseled. I'm going to dilate your cervix so you're going to feel some discomfort. From there, I'm going to suction everything out."

"Don't worry, honey," said the nurse, "you'll be done before you know it. We have plenty of nitrous oxide if you need it."

Lorena burst into tears, but her sobs were quickly drowned out by the noise of a large metallic device. It was rectangular in shape and contained two plastic cylinders in the center. Above them was a long tube. The image of the machine and the constant whirring sound burned its way into Lorena's mind.

17

"KUMUSTA?"

"Hindi masyadong maganda," replied Lorena, lying flat in her bed.

Her mother stood by the doorway, allowing a tint of white light to enter the dark room. "Do you have a fever?"

"Hindi, Nanay," replied Lorena. She gently rubbed her stomach. *"Masama ang pakiramdám ko.*

"Pagkakalason?"

Lorena looked at her mother, confused.

"Naintindihan mo ba ang sinabi ko?"

"Hindi, Nanay," replied Lorena.

"I asked if you have food poisoning," said her mother. She took a few steps closer, stopping at the edge of Lorena's bed. "Do you have nausea?"

"I think so," said Lorena, rolling away from her mother.

"Let me touch you."

Lorena held on to her covers tightly. *"Paki,* Mommy, I want to sleep."

Lorena's mother remained standing. She hovered above Lorena before slowly walking away and closing the door behind her.

Alone in the darkness of her bedroom, Lorena quietly began to weep. The weight of her secret seemed unbearable. She felt weak and exhausted. Closing her eyes, she slipped into unconsciousness and began to dream.

Lorena was holding a tiny baby girl. She rocked her gently in her arms. The infant smiled. Lorena felt a stream of joy pass through her entire body. She observed the small round head, the little patches of dark hair, the deep brown eyes, and the small button nose. "There, there..." whispered Lorena.

Suddenly, she awoke. Lorena slowly made out vague shapes. Furniture, pictures, her favorite stuffed bear. She looked groggily at her arms and then her hands. She had clasped one hand above the other, palms up, forming the shape of a cradle.

18

SUMMER ARRIVED. RUTH had graduated but Lorena did not attend the ceremony, electing to stay home with her grandparents. Lorena's friends were busy at play. At times they would call to invite her to the beach, but she was not allowed to leave the house. The Olorsisimo household had become divided. Lorena was upset with Ruth. Raymond was upset with Greg. Lorena's parents were upset with each other. Lorena's grandfather wanted to take her out to cheer her up, but her father discouraged this.

Lorena passed most of her time alone and dejected in her room. She found it difficult to concentrate and conversation was impossible. Accompanied only be the monotone sound of her clock, she watched television on the flat screen monitor that was positioned on the top shelf of her desk. When Ruth knocked on the door, Lorena completely ignored her. The pattern had become familiar to both sisters. This time, however, Ruth opened the door and entered.

"Lorena, when are you going to forgive me?" she asked.

Lorena maintained her eyes intently on the television screen.

"Please! Talk to me! I did it for your own good, you know," continued Ruth.

After a brief silence, Ruth grabbed the remote control and turned off the television program. "Lorena, I know you think you're in love, but trust me, it's just **infatuation**! You'll get over him."

Nodding, Lorena began to slowly rock in her desk chair.

"I know he broke your heart," continued Ruth. "A couple of my friends said that he's leaving for Cornell University. Did you know that?"

Lorena finally made eye contact with her sister, opened her mouth as if to speak, but then closed it, saying nothing.

"Has he tried to contact you?" asked Ruth.

Suddenly, Lorena burst into heavy sobs. Her chest began to heave, followed by deep moans that left her gasping for breath.

Ruth's eyes widened. Her mouth fell agape. She stood still for a moment, seemingly confused by Lorena's sudden display of emotion. Recovering her composure, Ruth knelt next to Lorena's chair, grasping her hands. "Lorena, Lorena, it's okay. Stop crying! I told you he would hurt you. You should have listened to me!"

"You don't understand," replied Lorena between sobs.

"Just because I don't have a boyfriend doesn't mean I can't understand what you're going through. Forget him, Lorena. You don't need him."

Wiping her eyes, Lorena replied, "No, Ruth, it's not that. He didn't just break up with me. There's more."

"What do you mean?"

"Before he left me…"

"What?"

Lorena remained silent.

"Tell me!" said Ruth.

"He got me pregnant!" blurted Lorena.

Ruth gasped. Her face then seemed to fall. "Lorena, how could you?"

Lorena inclined her head, then whispered, "Please don't be angry with me."

"No, it's okay," said Ruth, leaning on Lorena and hugging her. "I'm sorry. I shouldn't have spoken to you that way. it's just that—I—you—why didn't you tell me? I would have helped you!"

"I know! I know!" cried Lorena. "I thought he loved me! I didn't want to do it, but he kept saying that I had to!"

"It's okay, it's okay," said Ruth as she gently stroked Lorena's forehead. "Right now everything seems impossible, but we'll help you get through this. Everyone will help you. How long have you known?"

Looking up at her sister through wet eyes and tangled hair, Lorena replied, "It doesn't matter."

"Don't say that, Lorena. I told you we'll help you get through this. I'm not saying it's going to be easy. I mean, you're so young, and mom and dad are going to be furious. Well, I mean even more than furious, but we'll all take turns watching her—or him. I bet even Mary will want to."

Lorena shook her head. "Ruth, stop."

"No, Lorena. I mean it. We will help you."

"Ruth, you can't."

"Yes, I can. We all can! A baby is a lot of responsibility, Lorena. You're going to need our help, trust me."

"Ruth!" shouted Lorena. "There is no baby!" Lorena slowly turned away. "Not any more."

19

"YOU ARE ALL here because we are one, united family," began Lorena's father. "Everyone knows what happened, so what do you have to say?"

Lorena sat in a chair with her face staring vacantly at the brown carpet of the Olorsisimo living room. On the large family couch sat Lorena's parents and grandparents. Assembled in another smaller couch sat Raymond and Ruth, and in two other chairs were her older siblings, Samuel and Mary.

"All I have to say is that if I ever see Greg again, I'm going to smash his face!" said Raymond, breaking the silence.

"That's not going to solve anything," said Ruth.

"Lorena, how did this happen?" asked Mary. "You have always been so focused. You know the difference between right and wrong."

Lorena inclined her head. Then, while still staring at the floor, she said, "I thought he loved me. He made me feel special, and I loved him."

Lorena's father quickly adjusted his seated position. "And what do you know about this?" he asked. "What do you know of love?"

"I...I..." stuttered Lorena.

"Is a high school boy mature enough to handle life's problems?" he continued. "What can he do? Tell me, Lorena, is he able to take care of you? Is he ready to be a husband? Or a father?"

Patting Lorena's father on the knee, her mother interjected, "Lorena, when you are young, it is easy to fall in love, but as you get older you learn that just because a boy tells you that he loves you.... Well, it doesn't make it true."

Lorena nodded slowly.

"I'm sorry, but what I don't understand is how nobody knew about any of this until now," said Samuel.

"She lied to us," said her father sternly.

"Opo, Ama, ngunit bakit?" said Mary.

"I was afraid," Lorena whispered.

"Afraid of what?" asked her mother.

"Afraid of disappointing you," said Lorena. "Afraid of being a failure. I thought you would disown me."

"Disown you?" repeated Lorena's mother. She walked over to Lorena and knelt beside her. "Lorena, I am heartbroken by what you have done, but disown you? That would be like disowning myself."

"You're not alone, Lorena," said Ruth. "We're a family and nothing can come between us, okay?"

"Lorena, you should have come to us," said Mary. "We would have taken care of you...and your baby."

Lorena nodded. She scanned the room, looking at each one of her family members. Then, she buried her face once more into her hands and began to cry. At that moment, her grandfather walked over to Lorena. He then placed her hands into his own, raised her to her feet, and wrapped his arms around her. "Look at your family," he said.

Lorena slowly rubbed her eyes, and then looked at each face in the room.

"Is there anyone here who condemns my granddaughter?"

There was nothing but deep silence.

"There, you see."

Her grandfather had brought **serenity** to the moment. Then, one by one, each member of the Olorsisimo family approached Lorena, tenderly embracing her.

PEOPLE SKILLS

1

WHEN MIKE NATHAN first stepped on campus, he was announced! From day one, he was a celebrity, with nicknames ranging from *Supersize* to *Big Dog* to the *Jolly White Giant*. Boston High School had had its share of top athletes, but no one like Mike. Although he was only a freshman, he stood six feet eight inches tall and possessed a body that was lean and muscular. His short blonde military style haircut, perpendicular jaw, and clear blue eyes gave him a mythical aspect, as though he were a different human being altogether. Mike could not be referred to as *tall* or *big* because his body was perfectly proportional. At a distance, he looked like any other boy. But up close, it was only too recognizable that Mike was an entirely different size.

The high school varsity basketball coach, Mr. Reynolds, had been watching Mike since he was in the sixth grade. The football coach, Mr. Jackson, had also salivated over him for some time. Mike was the first freshman to ever start on both the varsity football team and the varsity basketball team. Normally, seniors resented upstart freshmen, but in Mike's case they were in awe. He had a combination of size, strength and coordination that was unmatched by any other student. Nobody challenged Mike Nathan. Not students. Not teachers. Not anyone.

Mike seemed to have it all. He was intelligent, handsome, and highly gifted due to his **pedigree**. His father stood six feet, four inches tall and had played professional football for numerous teams throughout his career. His mother was six feet, two inches tall and had played basketball for Boston College. According to the rumors, Mike had a real chance of breaking seven feet. Everyone said it was just a matter of time before he reached the NBA™. Of course, weighing in at a solid 220 pounds, the

NFL™ was also a real possibility. In every class at school since the fourth grade, Mike had not only been the biggest and the strongest, but the unquestioned leader.

Although he was a good student, most teachers dreaded having Mike in class because he constantly argued with them. He took pride in questioning authority. It was obvious that Mike was very sharp, but unfortunately he seemed to use his intellect sparingly when it came to school, being content to receive mediocre grades when he could easily have been at the top of his class.

Arriving late to his fourth period, Mike smiled at the rest of the students who were listening quietly. "Sorry, Mrs. Larson," he began, talking over his teacher. She was small, blonde, and petite. Mike literally towered over her. "The PE teacher kept me in his office for five minutes making me listen to another boring lecture. I told him to write me a pass, but he wouldn't do it because he said it was my fault for not following directions. Can you believe that guy? Anyway, I know you're cool so you understand, right?"

Mrs. Larson opened her mouth but did not say anything. She seemed to be weighing her options.

"Mrs. Larson?" asked Mike, moving his hand up and down, inches apart from his teacher's face. A few students laughed as he did this.

"Oh, yes, Michael," she replied with eyes that appeared distant.

Mike stared at her a moment, smiled, and shouted, "Great!" He then began to walk away, adding, "I knew you were cool...unlike Mr. Peterson!"

"Just a minute, Michael," said Mrs. Larson, awakening from her stupor. "I need to ask you a question, first."

Mike turned to face his teacher. She hesitated.

"What's your question?" Mike asked.

Mrs. Larson stood still, gaping momentarily. "My question?" she quivered.

"Yes," replied Mike, "You said you needed to ask me a question."

"My question," said Mrs. Larson slowly. "Yes, my question." Then, putting her hand up to her mouth, she cleared her throat and asked, "What did you do to make your PE teacher so upset with you?"

"Well," Mike began, "I don't remember everything, but he said something about me talking during push-ups and giving a half-ass effort."

Students in the classroom broke into laughter. Feigning embarrassment, Mike covered his mouth with his incredibly large hand. "Oh, excuse my language, Mrs. Larson. I don't use words like that but that's how Mr. Peterson talks—not the best role model if you ask me."

Mrs. Larson put her textbook down on the large black table counter that she used to display science experiments. All eyes were on her. One boy actually rubbed his hands together and smiled at the other students throughout the room. They enjoyed the mental **sparring** matches Mike had with the teachers. It was show time!

"Well, as much as I appreciate your **sarcastic** wit, Michael, may I ask you a question?"

"Ask away!" said Mike, smiling down on his teacher.

"Did he just start randomly yelling at you or were there any warnings before that occurred?" continued Mrs. Larson.

"Hmmmmm," replied Mike, placing his hand on his chin. "Let me see. I think it was something like this." He then began walking like a penguin in front of the class as he stuck out his stomach as far as his firm abdominals would allow. Imitating the deep, gravelly voice of his physical education teacher, Mike continued, "Nathan, move your arms more and your mouth less!"

Student laughter could be heard across the room. Mrs. Larson, too, began to giggle. She then shook her head and asked, "Okay, Michael, we now know what Mr. Peterson did. But what about you? Did you obey?"

The class immediately became quiet. Mike stopped smiling and glared at Mrs. Larson. "Obey?" he repeated incredulously. "First of all, I'm not a dog. I don't *obey*. Second of all, if Peterson is going to smart off to me, I have the right to smart off to him. So I told him that since I'm not fat and out of shape like some people, I can talk and do push-ups at the same time. It's not hard if you're in top physical condition—something that he might remember from twenty years ago. Of course, then again, he probably was a chubby little nerd that couldn't even make the team and that's why he became a PE teacher so he could feel better about himself—bossing around *real* athletes!"

"That's for sure!" called out David, one of Mike's closest friends.

"True dat!" said another.

The class began to applaud. Acknowledging their adulation, Mike took a deep bow.

"Well, thank you, Doctor Freud," quipped Mrs. Larson. "But is there something you could do instead of **psychoanalyzing** everyone and telling them what is wrong with them?"

Without missing a beat, Mike replied quickly, "It's not my fault if people can't handle the truth. What can I say? I'm an honest person. What do you want me to do, lie?"

"Michael," Mrs. Larson continued, **unabated**, "this isn't about honesty. It's not even about ability, either. It's about position."

Mike cocked his head back. "Huh?"

"Maybe you are a better athlete than Mr. Peterson, Michael," said Mrs. Larson. "And maybe his class is too easy for you. But that's not the point."

Mike furrowed his brow. "Then what is it?"

"The point is that Mr. Peterson is your teacher. That's his position and that position grants him a certain level of responsibility. Even power. Don't you understand, Michael? If you always talk back to people then you're probably going to get into a confrontation. And if those people you confront are in a position of power, then most likely you are going to lose."

"Lose?" Mike repeated with indignation. "I don't even know the meaning of the word! Look, Mrs. Larson, you're a cool teacher and all, but I'm not going to let you or anyone else boss me around just because they work here. I have the same rights that you do, you know!"

A chorus of students shouted, "Amen, brother!" Others began to applaud loudly and whistle. Mike then raised his huge hands as high as his long arms would allow, blissfully soaking in the admiration and approval of his fellow students.

Mrs. Larson folded her arms in front of her. "The die is cast," she whispered. Taking a deep breath, she continued, "Michael, nobody is trying to take away your individual rights. People are just asking you to respect the rules—same as everybody else. It's not only about you; it's about everyone. Think about it! What if everyone acted like you? What if all sixty students in Mr. Peterson's class talked while he was trying to give instructions? What if everyone in PE decided they would exercise whenever they felt like it? What would happen? Could he even do his job?"

"Everybody wasn't talking," Mike mumbled. Then, not satisfied with his response, he quickly added, "Besides, his pace is too slow. I was getting bored waiting for everyone to catch up."

Mrs. Larson curled her lips. After a brief pause, she asked, "Michael, has it ever occurred to you that there are times when people tell me what to do and I don't like it either?"

Mike arched his eyebrows.

"But who bosses you around, Mrs. Larson? I mean, you're a teacher," stated a girl seated in the front.

"I have people tell me things I don't like all the time!" replied Mrs. Larson. "Or at least I may not agree with the *way* they tell me things. But that is when you have to use people skills—"

"People what?" interrupted Mike.

"People skills," repeated Mrs. Larson. "These are social skills we use to relate to people. It's based on being polite, on knowing what to say and how to say it. It may mean keeping your mouth shut even when you're really angry. It may mean not getting in the last word or remaining calm even when the other person is rude and hostile."

"I'm nice to people if they're nice to me," said Mike, "but if they're mean to me, then we're going to have a problem because my dad taught me not to back down from anyone!" Mike then began waving his fists in the air like a boxer.

"Well, Michael, then I have two words for you. *Loser* and *jail*."

Mike suddenly dropped his hands. In unison, the class broke into a large, "Oooohhhhhhhh."

Tightening his strong, perpendicular jaw, Mike narrowed his blue eyes and gave Mrs. Larson a hard look. "What's that supposed to mean?" he asked.

Mrs. Larson had lost her earlier timidity. In a calm, confident tone, she replied, "It means that if you always react to people according to how they treat you, then they're in control, not you. I, for one, decided a long time ago not to allow others to dictate my emotions. In other words, I want to be in control of my life."

"I don't get it!" said Mike. "Weren't you just saying that we're supposed to follow the rules?"

Mrs. Larson paused for a moment. "Yes, Michael, but you decide the best way to react to those rules."

The class quieted down. Mrs. Larson raised her chin. Her eyes seemed to sparkle. Mike, however, was not ready to wave the white flag.

"Okay, Mrs. Larson, I see your point," he said, looking up at the clock. Observing the time that had elapsed, he could not help but release a knowing smirk in the direction of a few of his friends. "If that works for you, great. But that's not me. I mean, if anybody messes with me I'll take him out!"

"Yeah!" shouted a few of Mike's **sycophants** seated in the back rows.

"Hey, Mrs. Larson!" shouted Ricky, another close friend of Mike's and the established class clown. "Go back to the part where you called Mike a loser and said he's going to jail!"

The class immediately broke into laughter. Even Mrs. Larson joined in. Regaining her composure, she said, "Don't misquote me, please! What I meant to say is that people who believe they have the right to hurt someone whenever they get angry will suffer serious consequences. And yes, eventually that could mean being put in jail."

"I'm not afraid to go to jail!" announced Mike. "I'll rule the thugs!"

"And there you will enjoy a life where you will be told what to do for the rest of your life!" said Mrs. Larson. "You will be told what to wear, what to eat, and where to sleep. You will be told where to go and for how long. And if you even think about rebelling against authority then a corrections officer will throw you in solitary confinement where you will be alone in a dark little room for hours and hours until you won't even know what day it is."

Suddenly, the room became very quiet. Even Mike stood there, all six foot eight inches of him, staring at his teacher in silence.

Mrs. Larson took full advantage of this unexpected opening. Turning away from Mike, she pointed her index finger at the class. "If any of you thinks school is too difficult because you have an assigned seat, or you have to raise your hand to talk, then you are clueless! You think you can do whatever you feel like? Get real!"

Nobody said a word. Nobody even moved. Then, an awkward silence was interrupted by the sound of the bell. Everyone bolted for the door and headed straight for the cafeteria. Everyone except for Mike, that is.

Strangely enough, he stayed next to Mrs. Larson, staring at the Bunsen burner attached to the middle of her table counter.

2

"SOMETHING THE MATTER, Michael?" asked Mrs. Larson. "It's not like you to miss lunch."

Nodding, Mike replied, "Well, I hate to say it, but what you said makes a lot of sense. It's just that it doesn't seem fair to me, that's all. I mean, why should I be nice to someone who doesn't deserve it?"

"Because that's the Golden Rule, Michael. It's not about being *fair*, it's about treating others the way you wish to be treated."

Mike rubbed his forehead. "I don't know," he said.

"I think you do." Mrs. Larson folded her hands in front of her. "You're a smart boy, Michael, maybe too smart. You're so good at pointing out what's not fair, or why a teacher is wrong, but is that really so important?"

"Well, maybe not," murmured Mike, looking down at his teacher. "But this people skills stuff. It sounds so hard."

Mrs. Larson laughed. "Well, you're right about that. It is hard. But if anyone is up to the challenge, it's you! It takes a really big man to have this type of self-control. People skills are not for the weak." Then, after a brief pause, she asked, "So, do you think you have what it takes to be 'nice to someone who doesn't deserve it'?"

Mike leaned against the table counter. He was so tall that he actually sat on it though his feet were firmly planted on the floor. "I guess I can give it a try. It seems a little weird, though. Especially the part of having to obey everyone."

"I never said everyone, Michael. There is a time to make a stand, a time to rebel. It's just that teenagers can be so **egocentric** sometimes. They think the world revolves around them and don't seem to realize that we share this planet with a lot of people, and they're just as important as we are. We're not always going to get our way. Sometimes, we have to let go of what we want in order to get along with others." Mrs. Larson twitched her lips for a moment. Then, a familiar sparkle came to her eyes. "Michael, did you know that we have department meetings every two weeks?"

Mike shook his head and shrugged his shoulders.

"Anyway," Mrs. Larson continued, "in the science department I have to follow an agenda that Mr. Randolph gives us. He's the chairman, so he's in charge. To be really honest with you, I usually don't want to go because I'm so busy. I have to pick up my kids after school, and because my husband works late, I'm the one who usually has to make dinner, so the last thing I want to do is attend a department meeting where half the time the agenda doesn't even concern me!"

In a very sympathetic tone, Mike replied, "Wow, you have a pretty tough life, Mrs. Larson."

"Oh, I haven't finished! Besides my department meetings, Ms. Woodward calls meetings for the entire staff every Friday morning. She can talk quite a long time, so we have to arrive early. Do you think everything she says is pertinent to me?"

"I'm guessing 'no,' " said Mike.

"That would be a good guess. Trust me, it's not. But that doesn't mean I can talk in the middle of her meetings, or just ignore her and play with my cell phone. Do you know what would happen if she was speaking and I interrupted her?"

"You'd get fired?" offered Mike.

A large grin broke out onto Mrs. Larson's face. "Well, no, not quite. The first time she would probably just give me a stern look and remind me she was not finished. The second time she would tell me we would need to speak after the meeting—I can tell you right now it wouldn't be much fun. And if it happened a third time, who knows? I'm sure I would get written up. Maybe she would even change my teaching assignment or transfer me to another school. Do you understand what I'm saying, Michael?"

Mike nodded.

"All of us have to obey rules. It's just part of life."

Mike continued to lean against the table. He stared at his teacher and then at the floor. Finally, he stood erect, displaying his full height, and said, "Thanks, Mrs. Larson. You gave me a lot to think about. No other teacher has talked to me like this before."

Mrs. Larson reached up and patted Mike on the shoulder. He smiled at her and then headed for the door. As he did so, Mrs. Larson called out to him. "Just don't forget about me when you're dunking in the Garden!"

3

MIKE HURRIEDLY MADE his way to the lunch line. Nobody objected as he cut in front of them. As he set his tray on the long horizontal metal bars, he looked through the transparent plastic counter that displayed the usual three choices. Hamburgers, chicken patties, or pizza. His friends, who were only slightly ahead of him, were busy making their share of negative comments about the food.

Ralph, a small boy with bright red hair and freckles splattered across his face, muttered, "Man, pick your poison."

Right behind him was David. Athletic and handsome, he had sandy brown hair that was always perfectly groomed back and to the side. "Yeah," he agreed. "Sometimes I think the school gets this stuff from those big dumpsters behind the restaurants and then they just heat it up and feed it to us!"

Mike and his friends laughed loudly. So did a few other students behind them. One of the cafeteria workers frowned as she used the flat edge of her spatula to scoop up a square piece of pizza.

"Do these guys ever cook anything different?" asked Ricky, shaking his wavy black hair. Then, with a blank expression on his face, he repeated over and over again. "Pizza, chicken or hamburgers, pizza, chicken or hamburgers…"

"I don't think they know how!" replied Ralph. "Or at least they haven't been programmed to cook anything else!"

Once again, the boys laughed as Ricky began moving his hands slowly in clumsy, robotic movements. Mike then opened his mouth to join in on the fun when he caught a glimpse of the cafeteria workers. It was as if they had been invisible up to that moment. Mike was not sure why he had never noticed them before. He had no excuse, unlike Ralph who was so short of stature that he was not able to see them. Some of the ladies were older, a few were younger, around his mother's age, but all of them had the same tired, annoyed look on their face.

"Hey!" called out Ricky to an older woman who was dispensing his food. "Is this really pizza or did you guys just dip a piece of wood in some red paint and throw some old cheese on it?"

The entire lunch line began to laugh.

"Just take your food and sit down!" she snapped at him.

"Dang, whatever happened to *the customer is always right?*" whiffed Ricky.

The ladies behind the counter scowled at him.

"Ooohhh! Scary!" said Ralph, raising his hands and shaking his fingers.

"Watch out, Ralph," warned Ricky as he reached the register, "or she might make you take seconds!"

As Mike's friends burst into laughter, **histrionically** staggering and banging the metal counter, Mike uncharacteristically remained quiet. He could not help but picture himself behind the same counter. Hair net, white uniform splatted with food stains, beads of sweat.... These ladies regularly cooked for two thousand kids and were forced to suffer the same old jokes day in and day out.

"Hey, how about an extra chocolate brownie?" asked David as he handed a woman his cafeteria card.

Ignoring him, she quickly scanned it and returned it to him.

"Hello!" David repeated, waving his hands directly in front of her. "I asked you a question."

"No!" she shouted.

"How about some chocolate milk, then?" David continued.

"That's not the plan your parents purchased!" she bellowed. She then began to shake her thumb. "Now move it! You're holding up the line!"

Mike, following David, grabbed a small carton of regular white milk, but before he went to the register, he looked at the woman behind the counter and said awkwardly, "Hey, uh, I know you probably worked real hard to make this, uh, chicken square."

"Chicken fried patty!" shouted the woman.

"Oh, yeah, chicken fried patty," Mike repeated as she scowled at him. "Anyway, I appreciate your hard work and uh, you're a really good cook. I'm sure you've been doing this a long time."

She adjusted the hair net that blended in with her many steaks of gray. "What's that supposed to mean?"

"No, uh, nothing," Mike replied. "I didn't mean it like that!"

Mike's friends, who were waiting for him at the end of the line, began laughing loudly.

"All I meant was that you are a really good cook and thanks for cooking our pizza—and hamburgers—and chicken fried...whatever it is...every day," said Mike. He paused for a moment before adding, "I'm sure you're good at cooking other stuff, too. It's just that this is all you ever give us."

Setting down her spatula, the woman crossed her arms in front of her. "Oh, now our food isn't good enough for you?" She turned to the women to her side as well as those who remained in the back of the kitchen. "Hey, girls, our food isn't good enough for Mr. Super Size here! I guess he wants his own menu!" She then picked up her spatula and pointed it directly in Mike's face. "Look, honey, one more word out of you and I'm calling campus security! You want to see Mr. Willis?"

"Okay, okay, relax already!" said Mike as he hurriedly caught up with his friends.

As they made their way to one of the long blue tables, Ralph shouted, "Way to go, Mike!" He then jumped on top of the bench in order to give Mike a high-five. "Whew! I've never seen that old bag so upset!"

"Yeah! That was awesome!" said David, patting Mike on the back.

"I hope we don't have to call an ambulance because Mike gave her a heart attack!" said Ricky. He proceeded to walk in a circle, mimicking the sound of a police siren, when he stopped suddenly. Grabbing his chest, Ricky collapsed to the floor. A small crowd gathered around to observe him.

"Make way! Make way!" shouted Ralph, pushing through several students. He made the sound of a heart monitor slowly fading until it flatlined. Ralph then pretended to place two imaginary electric paddles on Ricky's chest and called out, "Clear!"

As Ricky convulsed on the floor, kids throughout the cafeteria pointed at him and laughed. Some even cheered, standing on the long table benches to get a better view. Observing the entire episode were the cafeteria workers. A few shook their heads. One puckered her lips and huffed loudly. Mike sat quietly. He really wanted to see if people skills worked.

4

MIKE VISITED MRS. Larson early the next morning to tell her what had happened. Her first reaction was to break into laughter. The expression of total defeat on Mike's face, however, seemed to make her take his agitation more seriously.

"I must say," said Mrs. Larson, wiping away tears, "your freshman class is something special."

"Special like *good* or special like *creepy*?" asked Mike.

"Special like good," replied Mrs. Larson. "You have so many characters in your group." Then, smiling up at him, she continued, "Michael, don't give up. Those ladies have been hearing insults for twenty years, so you're not going to change them with one compliment."

"I'm sorry, Mrs. Larson, but so far, people skills suck!"

"I wouldn't say that."

"Then what would you say?" asked Mike.

"Well, let me put it this way. You're good in basketball, right?"

"Better than good, Mrs. Larson!" Mike replied with his usual overabundance of confidence. "I'm the best!"

Mrs. Larson raised her brow. "Really? The best?" she asked. Then, pressing her thumb against her lips, she added, "So, you're better than the players on the Celtics™?"

"Well, maybe not that good."

"My point is that just because the right principles did not work once doesn't mean they don't work at all," said Mrs. Larson. "When you're playing basketball, you try to do the same things whether you're playing against a weak opponent or a strong one, right? You still pass and dribble and shoot. The only difference is that—"

"It's harder!" interrupted Mike.

Mrs. Larson nodded with a wide grin. Mike, for his part, picked up his backpack and abruptly left for his first period class.

"Uh, okay, bye!" she called out. "No need to thank me!"

5

IT DID NOT take long for Mike's usual group of friends to start joking and laughing in the back of the room while their math teacher, Mr. Franklin, continued his lecture on geometric formulas. He was a very thin, serious man with thick glasses who simply did not relate well to students unless they had made it clear to him that they wished to make mathematics their entire pursuit in life. The athletes in particular teased him mercilessly. They were well aware that Mr. Franklin gave at least three warnings before taking any action.

"Now, who can tell me how many degrees are in Angle X?" asked Mr. Franklin.

A few students raised their hands. Mike watched as the same ones, Roy, Esther and Megan, participated while everyone else either stayed quiet or totally ignored their teacher. While Mr. Franklin called on Megan, David began speaking to Mike in a loud voice. "So check it out, kid; we were walking by when these three girls..."

Mr. Franklin gave the boys a stern look, but David ignored him and continued talking to Mike. "I think they were from Brookline High, but anyway, one girl, I mean, really nice..."

Mr. Franklin shouted from the front of the room, "Mike, if you cannot control your mouth then maybe you should go to the office!"

Mike could feel his face getting warm. David started to laugh. Other students directed their attention to Mike. "Excuse me, sir," Mike announced, clearing his throat. "It wasn't me talking, but just the same, I'm sincerely sorry we interrupted your class. I know you really love math and this is important for our future."

Kids throughout the room burst into laughter.

Cocking his head back, David proclaimed, "That was **ingenious**, man!"

"Are you trying to get smart with me?" interrupted Mr. Franklin, pushing his glasses higher on the ridge of his nose.

"No, sir," Mike said as if responding to a sergeant in the military. "Please continue."

Mr. Franklin hesitated for a minute. He appeared unsure as to how to proceed. Finally, he adjusted his position on his elevated chair, mumbled a low "thank you" and went on with his lecture. Mike looked around the room and displayed a triumphant, if not surprised, smile of satisfaction.

6

AS STUDENTS COMPLETED their assignment on *The Odyssey* in complete silence, Mike began to fidget in his desk. This was partly due to the fact that he could not sit comfortably because it was too small for him, and partly due to the fact that he needed to go to the bathroom. As he struggled against his bladder, Mike decided he simply could not wait any longer. Slowly making his way out of his desk, he got up and walked over to his teacher, who appeared to be deeply focused while grading papers at her desk.

"Miss Tasker," Mike began, "I know you do not allow students to leave the classroom. You are a strict teacher and everyone respects you for that. But even though you're tough, you've always been fair. I promise I won't abuse your niceness if you give me a hall pass to use the bathroom."

Miss Tasker, a young teacher with short auburn hair and freckles across the bridge of her nose, opened her mouth to respond. Before she could speak, however, Mike held up his hand. "I'm sure you've been there before, Miss Tasker! I mean, even teachers use the bathroom, right? But whatever you say, I'll respect your decision because you're in charge."

Miss Tasker turned toward a sign posted on the wall in huge dark letters: No Bathroom Passes So Don't Even Ask!

"Well," began Miss Tasker, "I'm not sure if I'm getting manipulated here, and I'm not so sure if *niceness* is a word. I think the correct usage is *kindness*, but go ahead just this once."

Several students raised their eyebrows in disbelief as Mike left the room. Ricky then got up and walked straight to Miss Tasker's desk.

With a wide grin, he asked, "Hey, Miss Tasker, how's it going?"

She frowned wearily at him. "May I help you?"

Ricky then snapped his fingers several times. "Yeah, I'm kind of thirsty. Can I have a pass?"

Miss Tasker's face quickly soured. Motioning with her hand, she shouted, "Sit down!"

Ricky's eyes widened as he quickly returned to his desk.

"And it's *may* I have a pass? Not *can* I have a pass." shouted Miss Tasker, her voice echoing throughout the room.

When Mike returned, he thanked his teacher and sat down quietly. After briefly studying his assignment, he got up once again and walked over to a bookshelf where he grabbed a dictionary. As he did so, he could feel Miss Tasker's eyes on him. He quickly returned to his desk, took out a piece of paper from his binder, and began to write. When the bell rang and students scurried over to the door, Mike passed by Miss Tasker and handed her a note. She grinned at him quizzically and opened it.

> Dear Miss Tasker,
>
> Thank you for letting me use the bathroom. I'll try to be more responsible in the future and make sure I go during passing periods instead of kicking it with my friends and talking until just before the tardy bell. By the way, "niceness" is a word. It's just not used very often.
>
> Mike Nathan
> Future Superstar (football or basketball—
> I just haven't decided yet)

7

THE TRANSFORMATION OF Boston High's most popular student was the constant topic in the teacher's lounge. Even after several months, however, there were a few staff members who were not convinced.

"I don't know," said Mrs. Hayes. "I won't have Mike as a student until he's an upper classman, but from what all of you have told me about him, the whole things sounds like some kind of scheme to get what he wants."

"Trust me, it's not," said Mrs. Larson. "I've had several personal talks with Michael, and I've had him as a student since the first day of class. He's sincere."

"Yes, it's actually amazing how much more polite he is," said Mr. Dodd, a freshman technology teacher. "In my class, we're constantly conducting research and collecting data for keyboarding skills, but that gets a little old, so I like to find controversial topics that we can breakdown into multimedia projects. Whenever we discuss them, though, Mike intimidates everyone. Even I don't like debating him." He paused to take a bite of his sandwich. "Well, I mean that's how it used to be. All of a sudden, Mike changed. I still remember the first time he said something like 'Mr. Dodd, I know you are more educated than I am, but I still think you should consider what I'm saying.' I was so stunned my jaw dropped!"

A handful of teachers laughed.

"That's a good impression," said Mr. Alajari.

"But how can you be so sure?" asked Miss Hansfield. "He sounds like a smart kid who just learned some manipulative words and phrases. He'll probably become a politician!"

A few of the teachers chuckled. Several nodded. Then, interrupting the chatter, the shyest person in the room spoke up quite assertively. "No, he's the real deal," replied Mr. Franklin.

Upon hearing his words, the teacher's lounge immediately became quiet. Each person sitting at the long table leaned forward. They were not accustomed to hearing him speak.

"Those of us who have him in class know because we've had to deal with him all year," continued Mr. Franklin. "The other day I was going over the parallel postulate, and I guess I was losing some people when all of a sudden Mike yells, 'Guys, come on! Let's quiet down. Maybe this stuff is a little boring, but if it's in the book then we must need it. I don't want to turn into a hobo with a sign that says: Will Work for Food. Let's listen and get educated so we can all graduate and have a decent life, all right?'"

The entire table burst into laughter.

"That is so funny!" said Miss Tasker. "He does things like that in my class, too!"

"What happened next?" asked Mrs. Larson.

"Um, it got quiet," stated Mr. Franklin. "From what I understand, we have you to thank for this."

"I might have played a small part," replied Mrs. Larson.

"Well, you got my gratitude," barked a loud voice from one of the lounge chairs. It was Mr. Peterson, shouting from behind a newspaper. Folding it up loudly, he displayed his stout, stubbled face. "I thought what that kid needed was a good kick in the ass, but with his size—and family and all, everyone was afraid to do it! Not to mention Willis loves the kid because he gets our school in the news every week. Everyone in Boston knows who he is!" Mr. Peterson got up and walked toward Mrs. Larson. "Well, I don't know what you did, Larson, but it worked."

8

FOR THE NEXT several weeks, Mike made it his personal mission to win over the cafeteria workers. He had seen results in the classroom, but in the cafeteria he continually experienced failure. After one more very unsuccessful attempt, the cafeteria manager called campus security.

"All I said was 'keep up the good work' and 'you sure look pretty today'!" Mike complained as he was escorted away.

"Well, why did you do that?" asked one of the security officers.

"It's called people skills, chief!" Mike replied.

"People what?"

"I was using people skills on them," Mike replied to the officer.

"Well, next time just eat your food and keep your mouth shut," he replied as they entered the discipline office.

Mike looked down at the officer and barked, "You know, maybe you ought to learn some yourself!"

As Mike's voice echoed loudly throughout the room, Mr. Willis cringed. A stout man with virtually no neck, a large head, and black cropped hair, he was practically as wide as he was tall. Dressed in one of his typical three piece suits, he stood up from his desk and frowned deeply. "Now what is it, Mr. Nathan?"

Mike tapped a boy on the shoulder who was sitting in front of Mr. Willis. He promptly moved to another chair, allowing Mike to take his place. With a scowl across his chiseled face, Mike shouted, "You tell me, Willis!"

"The cafeteria workers said he was harassing them, calling them names and such," said one of the security officers.

"Mike, why did you call them names?" asked Mr. Willis.

"I didn't!" Mike replied. "I complimented them! I told them how much I like the food!"

Mr. Willis furrowed his brow as he rubbed his clean-shaven face. "Well, why were you making fun of the food?"

"I wasn't!" said Mike. "I was just trying to encourage them, telling them how much I appreciate their hard work!"

Mr. Willis broke into laughter. "Okay, Mike, come on, that's enough! What's the scam?"

"There's no scam, Willis!" replied Mike, raising his hands demonstrably as he kicked Mr. Willis' desk. "Man, why doesn't anyone believe in people skills around here?"

"People what?" asked Mr. Willis. He grabbed a spray bottle that lay next to a potted plant, ripped off a few sheets from a roll of paper towels, and quickly cleaned the large dust mark left by Mike's shoe.

"People skills!" repeated Mike. "It's when you're nice to people. You know, when you speak to them with good manners and all!"

"So now you're saying those ladies got mad at you for being nice and showing them good manners?"

"Well, yeah!" said Mike. "They're totally gonzo! I didn't even do anything wrong!"

"Well, just leave them alone, all right?"

"Excuse me for trying to brighten up their dreary lives," huffed Mike.

"I don't think they want you to do that," said Mr. Willis, frowning. Then, after a brief pause, he rubbed his forehead and added, "I don't think they even like kids."

Mike stared at his vice principal, rolled his eyes, and shook his head. "Well, am I in trouble? Come on, Willis, I didn't even get to eat lunch."

Mr. Willis made a motion to the two security officers. "Oh, you may go. I'll handle it from here."

"Yes, Mr. Willis."

As the two men walked away, Mr. Willis said, "Look, Mike, next time you eat don't even look at those old ladies, okay?"

"Whatever," Mike mumbled.

"If you keep getting in trouble, I'll be forced to suspend you," continued Mr. Willis, "and that would really hurt the team! Hey, speaking of that, what do you think about the Brookline game? My friend, Ted Walker, he's the athletic director over there, and he bet me two front row tickets at the Garden that we're not going to be able to beat them this year. What do you say to that?"

"Are you kidding?" Mike replied, standing up quickly and towering over Mr. Willis. "Their center is weak! He's a senior, but I played against him in summer league and tore him up!" Mike raised his long arms high in the air and spread his fingers as if palming a basketball. "I even dunked on him twice!"

Mr. Willis smiled and rubbed his hands together. After talking to Mike a little longer about the basketball season, he let him go with a warning.

9

MIKE WAS DETERMINED. As he followed his friends through the cafeteria line, he decided that he would not give up, even if it meant another trip to the office.

"Hamburger, chicken, or pizza?" asked the cafeteria worker.

Mike looked at her hesitantly.

"Well, what will it be, honey, I don't got all day!"

"Hey! Don't rush him!" said Ricky. "It's like choosing between the injection and the chair!"

All of Mike's friends burst into laughter. Ralph gave Ricky a high five. Mike, however, ignored them.

"You know," Mike said slowly, studying the three all too familiar choices as if seeing them for the first time, "I think I'll have a hamburger. I mean, it looks as juicy as the ones at Carl's Jr™."

Ralph crinkled his nose and huffed, "Yeah, right."

"Look, if you don't like it then why don't you go there instead?" the cafeteria worker replied, her eyes flashing.

"Hey, that's good advice," interjected Ricky. "You should be a school counselor!"

"Connie!" called out the woman. "Mike Nathan and his friends are doing it again!"

"Watch out, Mike!" said Ricky. "They're calling out the big guns now!"

From deep within the kitchen emerged a short, stocky woman with a round pudgy face and thick bleached hair that was conspicuously the result of too much dye. "What's going on here?" she shouted. "Am I going to have to call campus security again?"

"No!" Mike replied.

"Listen here, Mike Nathan," continued Connie. "Yeah, we all know who you are, Mr. Superstar! If you keep it up, I'll talk to the principal this time, so no more coddling from your biggest fan, Mr. Willis!"

"Okay, Connie, we're leaving, we're leaving," said Mike, "I don't know why Gladys got so upset in the first place!"

"How do you know our names?" snapped Connie.

Mike looked down at the ladies and pointed at their uniforms. "Uh, your name tags."

"Leave!" said Connie, pointing to the many tables inside the cafeteria. "Leave right this instant before I call Ms. Woodward!"

"Way to go, Mike!" said Ralph, jumping as high as he could so that he could pat Mike on the back.

As the boys settled down into their benches at the cafeteria table, Mike brooded over his failure to reach the ladies behind the counter. He watched them for a few moments as they quickly moved other kids down the line. Most of them wore a blank look of resignation while others, quite worse, displayed a menacing scowl.

10

AFTER SEVERAL UNEVENTFUL days, Mike decided to approach Mrs. Larson. He waited until the class ended and then made a beeline for her desk. "Mrs. Larson, I need to talk to you!"

"Sure, Michael, which question?"

"No, I don't mean the homework—that's easy!" said Mike. "I need help with something more important!"

"Hey, Mike, are you coming?" asked Ricky, who was waiting along with David near the door.

"Yeah, I'll be there," said Mike. "I just have to talk to Mrs. Larson first."

"All right. It's not like they're gonna run out of food," said Ricky, smiling.

Mike nodded as his two friends left the room. He then continued with a marked intensity, "Mrs. Larson, it's not working! Well, I mean, it is but not with those cafeteria ladies!"

Mrs. Larson shook her head. "Still can't get through, huh?"

"Yeah, and I've tried everything!"

"Well, Michael, remember our conversation about the playing level?"

Mike nodded his head. "Yeah, and in this case the teachers are like high school players and Connie is like Larry Bird!"

"Huh?"

"You know, Connie, the cafeteria manager!" said Mike.

"Oh, wow, you have been trying," said Mrs. Larson. "Look, people skills do work, but you have to remember that most of those ladies have heard the same wisecracks for twenty years. You've seen a difference in the classroom. I've seen a difference in the classroom. Everyone has! In fact, you're often the main topic in the teacher's lounge."

Mike's face instantly contorted. "You guys talk about me?" he asked.

"Yes," replied Mrs. Larson. "I guess we're not so different than you kids. Just like you talk about teachers, we talk about students." Mrs. Larson ran her hand through her blonde hair. "Pretty lame, I know. Anyway, all I was trying to say is that a lot of the teachers are really impressed with you, Michael, and have noticed a big change."

"Thanks, Mrs. Larson, but that's not what we're talking about," said Mike flatly.

Mrs. Larson smiled. "Michael, people skills are important—really important, but that doesn't mean we can get along with everyone. Some people are just really difficult."

"So you think I should just give up and let them win?" asked Mike incredulously.

"No, I just think, well, that maybe you should give it a rest."

Mike's eyes narrowed. His jaws tightened. "I can't give up! I'm a winner! And as my coach, it's your duty to show me how to win!"

Mrs. Larson opened her mouth as she arched her eyebrows. "Michael, I'm your teacher, not your coach."

"Well," replied Mike, "you taught me this stuff, so it's your responsibility! Now, come on, tell me what I have to do!"

Mrs. Larson shrugged her shoulders. Her eyes then darted to the digital clock mounted on the wall. "Does it really mean that much to you?" she asked. "I was just about to leave."

"You're not leaving till we get this right!" Mike shouted.

Mrs. Larson frowned at him.

Mike inclined his head and inhaled deeply. "Sorry, Mrs. Larson. It's just that I need your help. I'm working my ass off and here you are worrying about food!"

Mrs. Larson let out a broad grin. "Okay, okay," she said. "I understand. Maybe—maybe it's your tone."

"Huh?"

"Your tone of voice," Mrs. Larson repeated.

Mike furrowed his brow. "What's that supposed to mean?"

"That's the new play, Michael," said Mrs. Larson. "In order to reach these ladies, you're going to have to convince them that you're sincere."

"But I am sincere!" Mike shouted.

"But I am sincere," Mrs. Larson whispered softly.

"Huh?" Mike huffed, looking down at her.

Mrs. Larson reached up and touched his shoulder. She repeated once again in a soft whisper, "But I am sincere."

Mike furrowed his brow and turned the palms of his hands upward. He shook his head as his frustration was beginning to boil over.

"Sometimes," continued Mrs. Larson, "it's not only *what* we say, Michael, but *how* we say it."

Mike's serious expression slowly evaporated. He curled his lip and nodded, and then a wide smile broke out onto his face. Without as much as a *goodbye*, he turned around and quickly bolted out the door.

Mrs. Larson muttered, "Sheesh, they're going to start calling me Doctor Frankenstein."

11

AS MIKE ENTERED the cafeteria, his friends waved to him from their usual place at one of the many long tables.

"Hurry up, Mike!" David called out above the noise.

Cutting in front of several students, Mike announced, "Wow! This food is delicious!"

The cafeteria workers sighed. One of them rolled her eyes.

"It's really nourishing, too," continued Mike as he observed the customary choices. Then, in a sad tone that portrayed sincere remorse, he added, "I sure feel sorry for all of those poor children in other countries that are starving when we get more than enough to eat over here."

"That's right," snapped one of the cafeteria ladies, "so you should be grateful."

With a large grin on his face, Mike replied sweetly, "Yes, ma'am."

Frowning deeply, she asked, "Are you on something?"

"Me? Of course not!" said Mike, still smiling. He then looked at the woman's name tag and said pleasantly, "Oh, you have a great sense of humor, Mildred. No, I'm just happy and grateful for all that you're doing here."

"Connie!" bellowed the woman.

Within seconds, a stout woman with very blonde hair waddled out from the back of the kitchen. "Mike Nathan!" she said, pointing her finger in Mike's face. "I warned you! You're going straight to the principal's office!"

Holding both hands in front of his chest, Mike began, "Connie, Connie, please. Before you do anything, may I say something?"

"What?" cackled Connie, showing no attempt to hide her disdain.

In the sweetest voice he could muster, Mike continued, "Look, I know in the past that maybe my buddies and I teased a little too much—"

"That's right!" interrupted Gladys, pointing at him menacingly with her spatula.

"But—but," said Mike, raising the pitch in his voice, "that's all in the past. I've changed. And I'm working on my friends. The truth is that you ladies work very hard and you deserve our respect."

To Mike's surprise, several of the other cafeteria workers approached him. Soon, a small crowd of white uniforms and hair nets had developed.

"Go on!" said Connie, motioning for him to continue.

"Hey! A little service here!" interrupted Ralph from the far side of the food counter. He banged his empty plastic tray noisily against the metal circular tubes that ran across the counter. "I just got out of detention and I'm hungry!"

"Wait your turn!" snarled Mildred. "We're listening to your friend!"

"Well, like I said," Mike continued, nervously looking at the small crowd of ladies, "you all deserve our respect, so on behalf of my friends—and the many other thousands of kids who have mistreated you throughout the years—I'm sorry."

Mike took a deep breath as the eyes of a dozen women were upon him. One of them was holding a large spoon of mashed potatoes. As she faced Mike with her mouth agape, her right hand fell limp. The large utensil she was holding fell downward, causing the thick white glob stuck against it to slowly slip off and fall to the floor with a loud plop.

"Ladies," said Connie, breaking the silence, "serve this young man an extra helping of whatever he wants."

Mike let out a huge sigh of relief. Several ladies then fought to give him everything behind the counter, creating a mountain of food barely sustainable by the light brown plastic tray. Lifting his food in triumph for all to see, Mike displayed three slices of pizza, two hamburgers, two chicken patties, two scoops of mashed potatoes, two servings of tater tots, three cups of chocolate pudding, and four chocolate milks. Mike smiled to the ladies and began his trek to the table where his friends were seated. As he did so, he left a small trail of food on the floor. None of the cafeteria workers said a word, however, as Mike walked away among cheers from his fellow students.

12

TEACHERS NO LONGER felt threatened by Mike Nathan. He was not the same **confrontational** young man who had walked into their classrooms at the beginning of the year. The funny thing for Mike was that what started out as an experiment became something he actually believed in. Mike Nathan, the big superstar who thought he was smarter and more important than everyone else, had not only begun to respect others, but had taken the lead to ensure that his classmates would do the same. This was especially true in Mrs. Larson's class.

Whenever people began talking in the middle of one of her lectures, Mike would shout above their voices, saying, "Listen up, people! Mrs. Larson has a hard life! She has to pick up her kids every day and make dinner for her husband! So shut your mouths for five minutes and pay attention!"

As the room would inevitably quiet down, Mrs. Larson usually gave Michael an awkward smile and mouthed the words, "thank you."

In the hallways, Mike was on the patrol as well. "Yo, chief!" he said to one of the campus security officers. "I just pulled this poor kid out of a trash can! You guys are lucky I got your back!"

"Did you see who did it?" asked the security officer.

"Naw," replied Mike, "they ran off when we started yelling at them."

"Yeah, they knew we meant business!" added Ralph as he stuck his chin out and stood as tall as he possibly could.

The campus security officer frowned at the diminutive Ralph. "Uh, right," he replied slowly before turning to Mike. "I have to be honest. Earlier in the year, you would have been my first suspect, Nathan, but now, well, I'm glad you're on our side."

"No prob,' " said Mike, extending his fist.

The officer reached out and bumped it.

"Uh, hello, anybody care about me?" cried out a voice.

The officer turned toward the boy. He was adjusting his glasses and tucking in his shirt. "Oh, sorry about that, kid," replied the officer. "Come with me and let's find out who did this to you."

"About time. I need to call my mom."

As the officer escorted the boy away, Ricky turned to Mike and said, "Man, talk about ingratitude. No wonder he got thrown in a trash can."

"He probably popped off to someone," said Ralph. "You know, a lack of people skills."

Mike nodded and smiled.

IF THEY ONLY KNEW

1

MISS DAVIS OBSERVED her new student, a large girl with a mass of thick coiled strands of dark hair. Her obesity was compounded by her loose pants and oversized shirt. Several piercings extended beyond her ears to her eye lashes, nose, and lips. Her head remained tilted downward, and the other students seemed to completely ignore her.

A few minutes before the bell was set to ring, Miss Davis walked over to her. "Anabella, I would like to talk to you after class."

Slouching in her desk, Anabella slowly tilted her head upward. With a scowl on her face, she replied, "Why? I haven't done nothing!"

Miss Davis smiled. Her large white front teeth and dimples gave her that adorable aspect that most students found irresistible. It did not seem to work on the newest addition to her class, however. "Yes, I know. You haven't written a single equation on your paper."

"I'll stay after class with you," a voice called out.

Several students laughed.

"That's okay, Darren," replied Miss Davis. "But I could send you to detention hall if you need more time to finish your homework."

"I'm good," he replied with a slight smile.

"Serves you right for flirting," said the young lady sitting beside him.

The bell rang and a flood of students left the room, all save for one.

"What do you want?" asked Anabella as she slouched even lower in her chair.

Miss Davis sat in a nearby desk. As she did so, she ran her hands against the ends of her dark skirt before crossing her shapely, tan legs. "I want to welcome you to our class, Anabella. I want to be your friend."

"My friend?" she replied, furrowing her brow deeply. "Teachers aren't my friends!"

"Why not?"

"Because they're not!" she replied. Then, inclining her head, she asked, "Can I go now?"

"So, where are you from?" asked Miss Davis.

Anabella shifted her weight in her chair and then huffed. "Why? Don't I look like I live in Placitas?"

Miss Davis smiled at her. "So you're not from here?"

Anabella laughed. "Hell, no! I'm from the War Zone."

"What's your background?"

"My what?" snorted Anabella.

"Your background," repeated Miss Davis. "You know, your family, where you're from, how you ended up at our school."

Anabella snarled at Miss Davis. "Why do you want to know?"

"I already told you. I want to be your friend."

Folding her arms in front of her, Anabella said, "Look, I'm a foster kid, okay?"

"Okay," replied Miss Davis calmly. She paused briefly before adding, "It's hard to grow up without loving parents. It's hard when you feel like you don't belong."

Anabella wagged her head. "Are you serious? How would you know? You were probably one of those perfect little cheerleader girls when you were in school."

There followed an awkward silence. Anabella seemed to be waiting for a reaction. Instead, Miss Davis replied softly, "Actually, I wasn't. I wasn't popular, either." She inclined her head. "In fact, I didn't fit in at all."

"You look like you fit in here okay."

"I didn't go to school in this area. I didn't even go to school in Albuquerque."

"Where did you go?"

"Here, let me show you." Miss Davis stood up. She walked over to a bookshelf behind her desk. Returning quickly, she placed a large book in front of Anabella. "This is my high school yearbook."

Anabella took the book into her hands. "Belen? You grew up there? I thought only Mexicans lived there."

106

"No, but I was definitely a minority."

Thumbing through the book, Anabella exclaimed, "Wow, you're like the only white girl in the school!"

"Almost," replied Miss Davis. "There were a few others, but they didn't talk to me much. Actually, hardly anyone talked to me, and if they did, it was usually to give me a hard time."

"Kids messed with you?"

"Sometimes," replied Miss Davis slowly.

"So what was that like?" Anabella's tone had changed. It was sincere—even respectful.

Miss Davis sighed. "Well, it wasn't easy, but my problems had more to do with my family than school..."

2

IN THE LAST several decades, the small towns of Bernalillo County had gone from mostly Caucasian to Hispanic, and Belen was no exception. Households were **comprised** primarily of Mexicans and Mexican Americans. Though many white Americans had lived in Belen for several generations, each year it seemed that more and more of them moved to the larger cities of New Mexico, such as Albuquerque or Rio Rancho.

Ed Hebert and Norma Davis were exceptions to this pattern. They had lived in Belen their entire lives. Ed grew up working in the automotive shop founded by his grandfather, and Norma's father had been a bus driver for the school district for as long as anyone could remember.

The two met when Norma began working at the front desk of the Hebert family business. She was only sixteen. A pretty girl with a ready smile and long, sandy blonde hair, Norma made an instant impression. And though married and her elder by almost ten years, Ed was smitten.

Norma refused his advances at first, but Ed was relentless. He smiled at her constantly. He brought her little gifts. He told her she was the prettiest girl he had ever seen. And though Ed had a reputation as a hellraiser, this meant little to Norma. She found herself attracted to his rugged face, his strong arms that he proudly displayed through his rolled up sleeves, and his ever present confidence. Even his bright red hair added to his mystique. When compared to other boys her age, Ed seemed much more exciting.

Day in and day out, he begged Norma to take a drive with him along the countryside in his vintage Ford Mustang convertible. After scores of rejections, she accepted, and the two of them roared down one of the many country roads together.

Ed drove with one arm dangling out of the window. He puffed continuously on the cigarette in his mouth. With a broad smile on his face, he grabbed a cold can of beer and handed it to Norma. She hesitated. He then rubbed the icy drink on her bare shoulder.

"Oh, I don't know!" replied Norma, shouting at the top of her lungs in order to overcome the noise of the powerful V-6 engine and the roaring of the wind.

"Come on, darling!" Ed insisted. "It's not going to bite you! You want to have fun, right?"

Norma nodded, smiled, and then replied, "Hell, yeah!"

"Just pour it down!" said Ed, deftly shifting his lips to move the cigarette in his mouth. He then raised his beer and downed it thoroughly. Once finished, he smirked confidently and threw the empty can to the road.

With eyes that reflected her admiration, Norma attempted to imitate Ed's actions. Not accustomed to the taste, however, she coughed, spewing a mixture of beer and saliva into the air.

"Damn, girl!" said Ed. "Don't spill nothing! Those are leather seats!"

"Sorry!" said Norma, breaking into a shy grin.

"Don't worry 'bout it none! Just take another drink! You'll get it!"

Norma took his advice and continued drinking. Ed smiled at her. He then reached behind his seat and grabbed another can. Once again, with a touch of noted agility, he took puffs from his cigarette from one side of his mouth while he gulped beer with the other. Norma shot him a wide smile. She then released her seatbelt and poked her head out of the window, screaming joyfully as she waved her beer in the air.

"That's it!" said Ed, nodding with approval at the sight of Norma's long hair blowing in the wind. "Let everyone see how pretty you are!"

3

OVER A YEAR later, Norma found herself a few months shy of her eighteenth birthday and her midsection bulging with a baby girl. Reassuring words did not come from Ed. Instead, he took a few puffs from his cigarette. He then walked over to the refrigerator placed in the corner of the garage and grabbed a bottle of beer.

"Just wait a while, sweetheart," said Ed as he touched his forehead with the cold glass. "I told you that a divorce takes time."

"I'm tired of waiting!" screamed Norma. "Everyone in town knows it's yours!"

"Oh, come on, now," said Ed as he put out his cigarette on the bottom of his steel toe working boots. "You know you're the one I want to be with. It's that bitch of a wife I've got."

"Ed, I'm not going to wait any longer," replied Norma. Her eyes were large and sullen. "You told me that you loved me and that we were going to be together! You promised me a house of my own, too! You think it's easy looking like this? You don't think I hear the whispers? Nobody wants me working here anymore and my parents are ashamed, but at least they'll take care of me."

"All right, darling, all right," said Ed, lowering his head **despondently**. "I'll make it happen. I swear."

4

ED HAD VERY few interests in life. His custom blue Mustang, ice cold beer, women; and generally it was in that order. He had lived life on his own terms, but that was coming to an end. Faced with the possibility of losing Norma, he abandoned his wife. Shortly thereafter, Norma gave birth to a baby girl whom she named Diane.

The bliss of their new life together was shortlived. Between the public spectacle of living with a married man and the pressure of raising a baby, the relationship between Ed and Norma quickly fizzled. This became particularly clear when Norma unexpectedly arrived at the automotive shop. Marching into the garage with little Diane in her arms, she shouted,

"I came to tell you that I'm going to live with my parents! And of course I'm taking Diane with me."

"In Albuquerque?" Ed called out from within the oil changing pit.

"Yeah, that's right!" she replied.

Ed allowed the oil to drain out of the car. He then walked up the ladder, clanging his boots noisily on each step. As he passed two of his employees, they turned, avoiding eye contact. "You can't just get up and leave!" he shouted at Norma. "It ain't no secret you got no brains, but that don't mean I'm gonna let you embarrass me!"

The two of them stood face to face. Ed, with his cool brown eyes and a grisly reddish beard that reflected three to four days growth; and Norma with her moist blue eyes and long sandy blonde hair. Ed paused to wipe the grease off his hands. He bent over and spit his chewing tobacco into a metal jar that lay on his work bench. Norma turned so that none of the saliva would splatter toward Diane.

"Why should I stay?" asked Norma. "All you do is work and drink! You ain't never changed a diaper! You never take us out no more! You don't do nothing for nobody but yourself!"

"Keep it down, woman!" Ed barked. He raised the back of his hand. "You think you can disrespect me in public?"

"I'm leaving, Ed, and don't try to stop me! You know what the police said if I call them again."

Ed shook his head. He then began to laugh. "Go ahead and leave! You ain't putting out anymore anyway! All you do is take care of that baby all day! The trouble with you is that you don't know how to satisfy a man!"

"That's not true, Ed," said Norma. "I try to do things with you—for you—but it's hard when you're drunk half the time or here working! And me, all alone in the house, trying to take care of Diane! What about me?"

"Damn it, woman!" said Ed. "Don't I get you stuff? Don't I get you what you need?"

"Sorry, Ed, but there's more to being together than putting cold beer in the fridge and paying a few bills!" said Norma. "We've been together for two years and you still haven't made an honest woman out of me!"

"My wife's got a lawyer! You know this stuff takes time! I'm with you, aren't I?"

"I don't know, Ed, are you? People all over town don't think so!"

"What's that supposed to mean?" he asked.

"It means that you're doing other women!"

A few of the men in the garage exchanged glances.

"Oh, that's it!" said Ed, grabbing Norma by the neck. He then pulled her along with him. Clutching Diane tightly, Norma fought from stumbling as she was led forcefully outside the garage. Once in the parking lot, Ed pushed Norma aside and continued, "If you want to believe them lies, then go on! Get the hell out of here! You'll be crying and begging me to take you back in a few days. You really think your parents want you back? They're as embarrassed of you as anyone!"

Norma began to cry. Ed, for his part, merely stood there, a large smirk on his face. Shifting Diane to one arm, Norma dried her tears and headed directly to her car.

Ed's smile immediately faded. He followed in quick pursuit. "You know my old man's dying!" he shouted as Norma put Diane in her car seat. "See this place? It'll all be mine soon enough! All mine, you hear? I'll be one of the richest men in town!"

Norma did not bother to turn around and make eye contact. Instead, she drove off with her baby daughter strapped in the back seat among a pile of boxes.

5

IT WAS A warm evening in Albuquerque. As the sun began to set, the sky was full of streaks of red and orange and blue. Parked in front of a pleasant home marked by brown stucco exterior and panels of stone veneer siding was a small beige sedan. In the front seat was Norma, checking her face in the rear view mirror. A sudden knock on the window startled her. As she put the window down, a tiny face appeared, barely clearing the top section of the door.

"Mommy, when will you come home?" asked little Diane as she jumped up and down in order to see her mother. Her long hair, a unique blend of blond and auburn colors, fell upon her shoulders and back and bounced rhythmically in the air.

"Later, baby, but don't wait up. I'll see you tomorrow, okay, and we'll get some ice cream together."

"Oh, thank you, Mommy," said Diane, continuing to hop up and down.

"Okay, baby, now go back to your grandma."

"Mommy."

Norma scowled at Diane. "What is it?"

"I miss you, Mommy."

Norma nodded impatiently. "Yeah, I know, sweetie, now go on! Mommy has to leave."

As Diane disappeared inside the house, a middle-aged woman with shoulder length blonde hair came running out. She waved her arms excitedly at Norma.

Releasing a large moan, Norma asked, "What is it? I'm gonna be late."

"Norma, you can't keep leaving her like this! It just ain't right!"

"Mother, please! Don't start!" said Norma. "I work five days a week, so I deserve a little fun on the weekends!"

"Honey, you chose to have Diane and you chose to live with her father. We're here to help you, but it's time you reconcile or get your own place. I know Ed wants you back. He's been calling a lot lately."

"Of course he wants me back!" said Norma. "He thought he'd have fun chasing other women, but now he knows better. And besides, most of the girls know him and what a rotten son of a bitch he is. They don't want nothing to do with him and I don't neither! You know the way he treated me!"

Norma's mother frowned for a moment. She then continued, "I know, but this has gone on long enough. You can't keep coming home late every weekend, and your father is tired of men coming to the house. I'm sorry, Norma, but we've decided that if you don't want to go back to Ed then you need to get your own place. Make a choice...even if it means doing it alone."

"What are you saying?"

"I'm saying that we could take care of Diane."

Norma narrowed her eyes before slamming her hand on top of the door. "How dare you! How dare you, Mother! Now I know what this is all about. You want to take my daughter from me!"

"I never said that. I'm just saying we could take care of her until you figure some things out."

Norma shook her head derisively. "You just won't let it go, will you? Ever since I got pregnant with Diane, you and Daddy have been ashamed of me!"

"Norma, that's not true."

"It's not my fault Ed turned out to be such a lying good for nothing drunk! He promised me that he would marry me and take care of me! But he didn't! And now you want to throw me out, too!"

"Norma, please! The neighbors will hear you! Now quit feeling sorry for yourself and grow up! You knew what you were getting when you got pregnant and you knew what you were getting when you chose Ed over us!"

Norma puckered her lip. After a brief pause, she blurted, "Fine, Mother, you win! I wouldn't want to hurt your fine reputation here as well! I'm leaving. We'll talk about this when I get home tonight—or tomorrow morning."

6

IT TOOK A lot of pleading and begging, but Ed convinced Norma that he had changed. Within months, the two were married. At first, Ed was a model citizen. It appeared that he had stopped drinking, and he kept his temper in check. His courteous demeanor resulted in the birth of Diane's younger brother, Todd. But history has a way of repeating itself. Just as before, when Ed felt that he was not receiving the attention he deserved, he began spending more time in the bars and less time at home.

As he stumbled into the living room one night, Norma was there waiting for him. "Kind of late, don't you think?" she asked, holding baby Todd on her lap.

"Woman, please don't tell me you've been sitting there all night waiting for me," replied Ed, who was visibly drunk. He struggled to place his keys on the small dinner table.

"What am I supposed to do?" she asked.

"Try going to bed," replied Ed.

Putting baby Todd down on the vanilla colored carpet, Norma stood up and blocked his path. "Don't just walk past me, Ed, like nothing happened!"

"What the hell is your problem?" barked Ed.

Sniffing his shirt, Norma blurted, "Drinking ain't the only thing you've been doing, is it?"

"Well, I ain't getting nothing from you since this kid arrived," replied Ed, his speech slow and slurred.

"So it's okay to knock me up and have me take care of your kids, but then I ain't appreciated no more?" said Norma.

"Hey!" said Ed, raising his hand. "I said that's enough!"

Awoken by the noise, Diane opened her bedroom door just in time to see her father's hand come down against her mother's face. Norma screamed in pain as she fell to the floor. "Diane, get your little brother and lock the door!" she shouted.

Diane quickly grabbed her baby brother. She then went back to her bedroom where she locked the door and huddled with him in her bed. From there, she could hear her father and mother screaming at each other. This was followed by the inevitable crash of her mother being thrown against the furniture, the sound of her cries, and finally, the scariest sound of all—silence.

Finally, a knock was heard on the door. A voice called out to her. Diane promptly unlocked the bolt and opened the door slowly. Her mother's face was red and badly bruised. Her hair was wet and matted with a mixture of tears and blood. Diane knew the routine. It was not the first time.

7

YEARS PASSED. DIANE's father was gone, but the situation at home had not gotten much better. As Diane faced the difficult transition from child to young lady, she felt terribly alone. She was often the one who cleaned the house, attempting in vain to remove the many stains in the carpet caused by everything from chewing tobacco to cigarrete ashes to beer. And it was usually up to her to find something—anything—to eat for her as well as her younger brother.

Late one night, as Diane attempted to study, her mother lingered in front of her.

"I used to be a beautiful girl before you came along," said Norma. She passed her hand through her limp hair that had sprouted premature strands of gray. Her eyes, red and swollen, were full of **contempt**. With a bottle of liquor placed firmly in her hand, she took a few steps toward Diane.

Diane did not bother to look up from the small wooden table. Turning a page from one of her many textbooks, she replied, "Mom, I need to study. And besides, I think you're drunk."

Norma laughed. "Well, look at you. Already sassing me!" She suddenly reached out, clutched a handful of Diane's long auburn hair, and yanked it.

"Ouch!" Diane shrieked. "Mom, Stop! You're hurting me!"

"You think you're better than me, little girl?" asked Norma. "Think you're prettier than me? Think you're smarter than me 'cause you come home every day with those perfect grades? Let me tell you something little girl, you ain't worth shit!"

Todd swiveled from the television to the small kitchen table. "Mommy, no!" he cried out.

"Get!" said Norma, pointing to the hallway.

Todd hesitated, and then turned to Diane. She nodded to him with her lips pressed firmly together. Todd then headed straight for his bedroom. As soon as he left, Norma pulled Diane closer to her. "You know what your problem is, Diane?" she began. "You're too serious. Here, take a little sip. It'll make all your problems go away."

Norma raised her bottle and began to pour its contents into Diane's mouth. As the hard liquor reached her throat, Diane felt a burning sensation and began to choke. She frantically reached for the bottle.

Norma laughed once again. She jerked the bottle out of Diane's reach and continued to pour. "Not so fast, little girl!"

Diane clenched her teeth, causing the honey colored liquid to pour down her chin and spill to the tiled floor.

"Open up your mouth, damn it!" shouted Norma.

Diane refused. In a rage, her mother slapped at the books and papers spread across the table. She then pressed the bottle against Diane's mouth, attempting to wedge it past her lips and teeth. Crying in pain, Diane fell to the ground. Her mother then began an all too familiar tirade. "It's all because of you! I lost my life because of you! Your father started treating me bad because of you! The Hebert family won't even give us a damn penny because of you! You! You! You!"

"Mom!" Diane shrieked. "I had to call the police! He was killing you!"

"Shut your mouth! It wasn't up to you, Diane! Now, look at me! I ain't got a job! I ain't got no husband! We could've gotten some real money out of them but now they won't even look at us!"

Picking herself off the floor, Diane muttered, "Mom, you never had a husband."

"What did you say?" growled Norma.

"What do you want me to say, Mom? You want me to lie? Is that it?"

With nostrils flaring, Norma raised her bottle threateningly.

"Mom, if you hit me with that bottle," said Diane, mouthing the words slowly. "I swear I'll call grandma and grandpa."

Norma slowly lowered the bottle. Then, turning away, she muttered, "You make me sick."

As soon as she had slammed her door shut, Todd poked his head out of his bedroom door. "Are you okay?" he asked.

"Yes," replied Diane, kneeling on all fours below the table. She picked up her books and the scattered papers that lay on the floor. "Go ahead and finish watching your cartoons. I'll fix you some dinner and then you need to brush your teeth and get ready for bed."

8

AS HER MOTHER'S many boyfriends came in and out of the house, Diane felt increasingly **insecure**. She loathed having to face them: the stench of cheap cologne, the lusty eyes, and the inappropriate remarks. Diane never knew how long they would stay, or if she would be left alone with any of them.

"You need to get her out of those baggy jeans and into a tight skirt!" said Rodney, a particular boyfriend of Diane's mother who continually gave her unwanted attention. "A girl like that shouldn't be hiding!"

Diane attempted to ignore him. Picking up her school books, she got up from the kitchen table and walked through the tiny hallway to her bedroom. To her dismay, the man followed her.

"Would you like me to take you shopping, sweetheart?" he asked. "I'll buy you anything you want."

Diane looked at him with a sense of disgust. His ill-conceived white tank top behind an unbuttoned checkered shirt revealed his farmer's tan and pot belly. A mixture of black and gray thinning hair ended in large, bushy sideburns that partly covered his sweaty face.

"Don't waste your time on her, Rod; she's too good for our kind!" Norma called out from the kitchen.

"Too bad," said Rodney, not taking his eyes off of Diane. "How old are you now, honey bunch?"

Diane remained silent. She plopped onto her bed and then buried her nose in a book. To her dismay, Rodney sat down next to her. He pressed her book down and then gently stroked her cheek. "Anybody ever tell you that your skin is as soft as cream?"

Diane frowned and turned away.

"How old are you now, sugar?" he continued.

"She's fourteen," replied Norma, suddenly appearing at the entrance of Diane's room. "Come on, Rod, why don't we go to my bedroom?"

As Diane trembled in fear, Rod turned toward her and smiled before being led off by her mother.

9

DIANE NEVER STYLED her hair or wore makeup, and her clothes were old and did not fit her properly. Most of her classmates considered her a poor, simple girl who focused too much on her studies. Some of them ignored her when she attempted to strike up a conversation. Others, however, openly harassed her.

As she left the high school campus and began her customary walk toward her brother's elementary school, Diane reflected on her life. No father, no friends, and it felt as if she had no mother as well.

"Hey, guys!" a tall, muscular boy named Roy called out to his friends. "Who's that hottie over there?"

Lost in thought, Diane had not even noticed the group of popular football players walking behind her. She quickened her pace in order to avoid them.

"Man, who is that?" replied another boy named Nick. "She must be a freshman because I know all the fine girls in our school!"

It was obvious to Diane that the boys were shouting so that she could hear their every word. In order to avoid them, she cut through the parking lot of a small grocery store. Her strategy did not last long, however. The boys ran up to her and quickly formed a circle around her.

"Going somewhere?" Roy asked.

Diane was quiet. Each of the boys was older than her. She looked up at Roy. He possessed prototypical qualities: tall, dark, muscular, and handsome.

"Hey, don't run away," he continued. "I just want to talk."

Looking up at him, Diane quietly whispered, "What do you want?"

"What's your name?" asked Roy.

Diane remained serious. "Why do you want to know?"

"I've just been watching you, that's all," said Roy in a soft, endearing tone. "You're different. You're not like the other girls." He touched Diane's faded cotton shirt just above the shoulder. Then, he placed his finger around one of the loopholes in Diane's jeans and tugged slightly. "I respect that."

Diane relaxed her stiff stance. Somewhat hesitantly, she introduced herself.

In cavalier manner, Roy extended his hand. "Hello, Diane Davis; I'm Roy Lamas."

Diane grasped his hand and smiled. "I know."

His eyes widened. "You do?"

"Yes, everybody knows you."

"Do you know me?" called out another voice from within the group of boys.

Diane looked at him. He was not nearly as tall or as handsome as Roy, but was strongly built. He had spiky blonde hair and a small pink mouth.

"Yes, you're Nick Miller. You own Old Miller Farms."

"Man, this girl's smart," said Nick, smiling to the surrounding boys. "But I don't really own 'em. My family does."

Roy then slapped Nick on the chest.

"Okay, man, back off already! She's my girl."

Diane smiled quizzically.

"Now, about that question," continued Roy.

"Question?" repeated Diane. Her face softened. Her heartbeat accelerated.

Roy reached back and rubbed his head. He winked at his friends. Then, kneeling on the ground, he asked, "Will you go to the prom with me this year?"

The others burst into laughter. Diane frowned deeply.

"Hey, is it true your dad's a convict?" asked Nick. "Isn't he like some Hell's Angel or something?"

"Yeah, my uncle said he's doing time for murdering somebody!" added another boy.

Nick nodded. He then furrowed his brow. "My little sister's in your brother's class. How come you guys have different last names?"

Diane remained still. The many boys around her pointed and laughed. Then, with a huge smile on his face, Roy extended his index finger and made a circle in the air. Four boys instantly grabbed Diane by the legs and arms. She struggled and began to scream, but one of them covered her mouth. They then carried her several feet until they reached their destination—a large dumpster. There, they dumped her amidst waves of laughter. Diane crashed down against an array of rotten food, cardboard boxes, and discarded bottles.

"Oh yeah," said Roy, peeking into the dumpster. "I forgot to tell you that the prom queen gets to ride on her own float!"

"Don't even think about telling anyone, or something worse might happen to you!" said Nick as the boys walked off.

"If we're lucky, maybe a truck will come and haul her away for good!" added another boy.

"Yeah, that's what they do with white trash!" said Roy. Then, looking at Nick, he added, "No offense, man."

"You're not talking about me," replied Nick. "I might be white but I'm not trash like her!"

Diane waited until she could no longer hear the laughter. She then attempted to climb out of the large dumpster. Reaching for the top ridge, she lost her footing and slipped. Pieces of old cabbage landed on her face. In frustration, she screamed. Waiting several seconds, she clutched at the sides of the dumpster once again, attempting to stand up. Slowly, she hoisted herself over the edge and down awkwardly to the pavement. After several blocks, she reached her brother's elementary school.

"What happened to you?" asked Todd, holding his nose with one hand and waving the air with the other.

"Nothing," said Diane.

"Your butt's wet."

Diane curled her lips and inhaled deeply

"Were you in a food fight?"

"I don't want to talk about it!" replied Diane.

"Come on, tell me!"

"I said I don't want to talk about it!" repeated Diane, wiping her eyes.

"Are you crying?"

"No!"

"What happened to your elbow?" asked Todd.

"I scraped it on a trash can," said Diane, quietly.

"You should be more careful."

Diane glared at her brother and shook her head. "Look, I don't really need the advice of a fourth grader!" Then, after a short pause, she continued, "I didn't just bump into it. I was thrown inside."

"What?" replied Todd, his eyes bulging. "Did you tell the teacher?"

Diane rolled her eyes and shook her head as they crossed a set of railroad tracks and made their way toward their home on an old back road that stretched across several small homes surrounded by acres of dusty brown dirt and dry bushes.

"It wouldn't do any good, Todd," said Diane. "High school is different."

"What do you mean?"

"All of these boys are popular and play football. One of them is Nick Carter," replied Diane.

"So?" said Todd.

"Oh, I don't know why I'm even trying to explain these things to you," said Diane.

The two walked in silence. "Okay, fine!" shouted Diane. "I'll tell you! The school wouldn't do anything about it, Todd. Nick's dad is the richest man in town. And this other boy, Roy, is like the most popular boy in school. They're all seniors and I'm just a nobody freshman."

"Well, we could tell grandpa," said Todd.

Massaging her little brother's short bristled blond hair, Diane replied, "Grandpa's retired…and old. He doesn't even work here anymore. It's all right. Just drop it, okay?"

"We could tell Mom," offered Todd.

Diane smirked at him. "Uh, no," she said, wagging her head vigorously.

"Why not?"

Diane's voice rose considerably. "Because I don't know what's worse, Todd! Mom insulting me for smelling like trash or having her defend me by going to the school drunk out of her mind and embarrassing me even more!"

10

BY THE TIME she was an upperclassman, Diane had naturally blossomed into an intelligent, attractive young lady. She did not have the money to buy pretty clothes or expensive cosmetics, but she still caught the attention of her male classmates. Diane rejected them all, however. Somehow, she still did not feel she belonged.

There was only one person in the entire school that Diane could truly call a friend. She was an Arabic girl named Abra, whose family had moved to the United States from Yemen. Conspicuous by her strong accent and her full length colorful hijab, Abra had piqued Diane's curiosity from the very beginning. Whereas most students moaned when Diane repeatedly raised her hand to participate in class discussions, Abra actually competed with her. The two girls often argued to the point that their teachers were left as mere spectators. Ostensibly, the Diane and Abra formed a somewhat odd pair, but intrinsically they were kindred spirits.

As the two left school one day, Abra faced Diane and protested, "Please, don't take it personally, it's just my father. He doesn't really like foreigners."

"Foreigners?" Diane repeated incredulously. "I'm not a foreigner, Abra! Not to be rude, but you're the foreigner! I was born here, not you!"

"Yes, of course," said Abra. "I understand, but you know what I mean. My father is different. He doesn't really like the American culture. He's very protective. Please try to understand."

"Well, if he doesn't like America then why did he come here?"

"Reasons," muttered Abra.

"I think you're overreacting. He can't be that bad. I'm sure he will like me. Just try, okay?"

Abra shook her head as the two girls continued to walk down the sidewalk.

"Didn't you tell me that you thought he was creepy when you came to our store?" asked Abra, raising her thick dark eyebrows.

"Well, his eyes..." began Diane until her voice trailed off. "I felt like he was staring at me the whole time. And he never smiles. But hey, what about your mom?"

"No, Diane, it's not up to her!" said Abra. "Now stop following me, please! I'm serious! Just go home!"

"I'm going to your house. You already said that you can't come to mine—not that I would want you to..."

"Diane, you're my friend, yeah? Nothing is going to change that. It's okay. I'll see you at school tomorrow!"

"It's a free country, Abra, so I can walk with you if I want. Your father doesn't own the sidewalk, you know!"

"At least let's try it when my Uncle Aamir is here. When he visits, my father takes off to Albuquerque for more supplies and visits some of our relatives there. He will be gone for a week or so and my uncle will take over the store. Aamir loves Americans. In fact, he wants to become an American. He drives my father crazy! They always end up arguing about our beliefs and traditions. Anyway, he's going to college in Las Cruces. I'll tell you when my father is away and Aamir is with us. You'll like him! He's so much fun!"

Diane shook her head from side to side. "Why should I wait when I'm here right now?"

Abra lowered her head. She took a deep breath. "I'm the youngest in my family and the only girl. And I'm the only one left. My oldest brother lives in Yemen and my other brother left for Saudi Arabia. Now do you understand?"

Diane wiped away the auburn hair that naturally fell over her forehead and covered her eyes. "No, Abra, I don't think that has anything to do with our friendship."

"Okay," huffed Abra, "but don't say I didn't warn you."

When the two girls arrived at the house, Abra entered and motioned to Diane to wait outside. After a short silence, Diane put her ear close to the door. She first heard a soft voice, speaking in Arabic, followed by a deeper voice. Suddenly, the door opened. Startled, Diane jumped back at the sight of Abra's father. "What do you want?" he asked in a very sharp tone.

Diane hesitated as she looked into the large dark eyes that seemed to penetrate her thoughts. "Um, hello sir, I just wanted to visit with Abra. I thought—"

"Abra is very busy. I'm sorry. Please leave."

The door abruptly closed in Diane's face.

11

DIANE KEPT HER focus in school and was among the top five students in her graduating class. With a 3.97 accumulative G.P.A., she boasted the highest marks of any senior in mathematics. But despite these achievements, she did not receive any **accolades**, which puzzled her. As the bell rang for lunch, she complained bitterly to Abra.

"I know that some scholarships and awards are subjective, but I should have won something! It's not fair!"

Abra nodded in agreement as the two girls strode through the main outside hallway of their relatively small high school.

"I mean, enough is enough!" said Diane.

"Well, talk to Mr. Payne about it!" said Abra. She pointed to one of the dull brown classroom doors that composed a linear shape alongside the long white building. "Now's your chance, right?"

"You are so right, Abra. Come on, let's do it!" said Diane, her eyes lighting up.

"No, no, no, Diane," replied Abra. "This is your battle. I'll wait for you outside."

"But you didn't win anything, either!" said Diane. "We both know you should have won something!"

"Like what?" asked Abra.

"I don't know," said Diane, shrugging her shoulders. "How about learning English faster than anyone else?"

Abra frowned. "Nice try."

"Okay, fine, but wait for me!"

"Yes, yes, I'll be right here," said Abra, who remained outside the door, her arms folded around her books.

Gathering her courage, Diane entered the room and approached her calculus teacher, Mr. Payne, who was sitting behind his desk. She watched as he pushed back his silver framed glasses that constantly slid down his small angular face.

"Hello, Diane, what can I do for you?" asked Mr. Payne.

"Hello, sir, I was wondering if you could help me."

"Sure, what is it?" he asked as he organized some papers.

"Well, I was a little miffed that I didn't get the scholar-athlete award, but you know, they might have cared more about the actual athletic part..." Diane smiled while her teacher remained quiet. "Uh, any-who, when I wasn't given the prestigious mathematics award, though, I was in shock. I mean, nobody has marks as high as I do and I could really use that scholarship."

Mr. Payne adjusted his glasses and inclined his head. After a brief pause, he replied, "Diane, I'm very sorry, but there was another student, Alejandro Flores, that had marks that were also very high—almost as high as your own—so we thought because of his extraordinary ability to overcome obstacles in his life, that he needed the scholarship the most."

"I still don't understand," Diane replied. "What do you mean by 'almost as good'?"

"Well, in the past, most of the high school achievement awards went to Anglo students and so many minorities were left out," replied Mr. Payne. "Now, we're trying to balance this out. Alejandro moved here from Mexico only a few years ago. His parents work in one of the packing sheds and do not even speak English. Our school felt that he's been such an inspiration that we wanted to **recompense** him and people like him."

"So, you're saying that the reason I didn't get the mathematics award is because I'm white?" Diane asked.

"I never used those words, Diane," replied Mr. Payne very quickly. He swallowed deeply. "It's just that the school board—I mean—our staff—is trying to, well, even the playing field."

"But all you're doing is continuing the pattern!" Diane replied. "This is reverse discrimination!"

"Try to think objectively," said Mr. Payne. "Now, if you will excuse me, I really have to catch up on a few things before my next class."

He then began to rearrange several pens on his already meticulous desk and open and shut drawers. As Diane stood there staring at him, Mr. Payne turned away, **ostensibly** busy.

"Whatever happened to 'may the best man win'?" Diane asked.

Mr. Payne furrowed his brow. A quizzical expression broke out on his face. Slowly, he stuttered, "But you're not a man."

"See?" said Diane, tapping her forehead. "Even that cliché demonstrates discrimination!"

"I'm sorry, Diane," replied her teacher. "You're an excellent student, but there's nothing more I can do. I'm going to have to ask you to leave."

12

HIGH SCHOOL WAS coming to an end, and Diane was beginning to feel nervous. She had been accepted by several universities, yet she still felt that she would struggle due to a lack of financial support. She decided to stop by the career center after school. She was sure that her counselors could guide her through the maze of financial opportunities that existed.

Diane waited in the lobby. And waited. And waited. To her amazement, several students walked directly past her straight into her counselor's office. After her lunch time had completely evaporated, she opened the closed door of the counselor's office and marched inside.

Mrs. Hernández, a woman who prided herself on her formal attire and salon styled raven black hair, faced Diane with narrowed eyes and curled red lips. "Excuse me, but didn't I tell you that I would call you when I was ready?" she asked in a rather **petulant** tone.

"Well, yes, you did," replied Diane, "but this girl here, not to mention a bunch of kids before her, have cut in front of me."

"Excuse me?" asked Mrs. Hernández, demonstrably pointing her pen at Diane.

"I've been waiting for an hour and you keep talking to other students instead of me," said Diane. "I've already missed my lunch and now I'm missing class! You do realize that I'm a senior, don't you?"

Mrs. Hernández scowled. "Well, yes, I am aware of that, but many of these students have appointments. What is your name?"

"Diane Davis."

"Well, Diane, I can't think of anything that would be so important that you would have to rudely interrupt another student's session, but if you remain seated I will be with you as soon as I am able."

"I need to find out more about financial aid," continued Diane.

Mrs. Hernández let out a burst of laughter as she shook her head. Then, facing the student sitting at her desk, she said, "Excuse me a moment, won't you?"

"Sure," said the girl. She quickly got up from her seat and walked past Diane.

"You should have come much earlier and asked me how I could help you!" said Mrs. Hernández. "It's not the counseling department's fault if you fail to be responsible and file your paperwork on time."

"Excuse me," replied Diane, "but isn't that your job, Mrs. Hernández? I see students leaving class with call slips practically every day!"

"Well, that's different!" she replied, her eyes flaring. "Many of those students are in special programs, such as the Migrant Program, and some qualify for more scholarships since they are minorities, such as our Hispanic students or the few African American students who attend our school. Other students are not rich—"

"Who said that I'm rich?" interrupted Diane, "and at this school I am a minority!"

"—or middle class," added Mrs. Hernández.

"Who said that I'm middle class?" asked Diane.

Mrs. Hernández glanced downward at her polished fingernails. "Well, I'm sure your parents make more money than most of our kids. Now if you don't mind, I have a lot of work to do."

Diane stared at the woman. Finally, she turned and walked away, muttering, "It's not just the Mexican students or the black students who need help, you know."

13

HER TAN CHEEKS displayed just a touch of pink blush, and the celestial color of her eye shadow matched the blue dress she was wearing. With a hot curling iron deeply embedded in one side of her shoulder length auburn hair, Diane cringed when her brother banged on the door and called out to her. "Owww!" she screamed. "Todd, you just made me burn my hand!"

"Diane, come quick! It's mom!"

"Todd, I can't! The graduation ceremony begins in an hour!" replied Diane, continuing to make the final touches on her hair.

"Diane, I'm serious! Get out, now! Mom's just lying on her bed and she won't get up!"

"I don't believe this!" said Diane as she took the curling iron out of her hair. "She probably just had one too many!"

Diane began to nudge her mother by lightly shaking her shoulder. "Mom. Mom, get up! You have to take me to school." After her mother failed to respond, Diane continued, "Mom, can you hear me?"

"Is she bad?" asked Todd.

Diane shot him a worried expression. "Stay with her and tilt her head up. I'm going to call for help."

After a few rings, an operator replied. Between sharp breaths, Diane described her mother's condition. "Don't worry, honey, an ambulance is on its way," came the voice from the other end of the phone.

Dipping an old rag in cold water, Diane began wiping her mother's forehead. Then, looking at her brother, she said, "Hey, I just remembered. Grandma and grandpa were going to meet us at school. Why don't you call them and tell them to come here instead."

"Yeah," said Todd, "good idea."

Diane looked at an old black circular plastic clock that hung on the wall. It was large. Very large. Her mind drifted for a moment, remembering that her mother had purchased it to cover up a hole in the thin brown cardboard like wall of their small home. Her eyes then narrowed toward the long silver hands of the clock. Only ten minutes had passed, but it seemed like an eternity. A short while later, Todd returned. "I told them something's wrong with Mom, and they said they're on their way."

"Good," said Diane as she stroked her mother's forehead. This continued for quite some time until she heard the sound of a vehicle pulling up to their entrance of dirt and gravel broke the silence. "That must be them."

"Grandma and grandpa?" asked Todd. "But I just called them!"

"No, the ambulance!" shouted Diane. "Todd, stay here," she ordered. "I'm going to get the door." She briskly walked through the small living room and opened the front door.

A young man in a navy blue uniform greeted Diane. He had short brown hair and a face that showed scattered battles with acne. "Hello, my name is Warren Summers."

Diane nodded. "My mom looks bad. I didn't know what to do."

"It's okay; we're here to help you. Our dispatcher informed us that your mother is lying on her bed, unconscious."

"Yes, that's right, and thank you for coming so quickly!" replied Diane.

"Lead us to her," replied Warren. He then pointed to a smaller man who was also dressed in a blue uniform. "The guy over there taking out the gurney is my partner, Javier Sánchez."

A few people gathered to witness the event.

"Norma probably overdosed and killed herself," said one woman from within the crowd of onlookers.

"*Siempre está borracha,*" said another.

Inside the bedroom, Todd lay in an awkward position behind his mother doing his best to prop her up with his arms.

"Hey there, big guy, mind if we take over?" asked Warren. "I promise we won't hurt your mother."

Todd nodded and slowly scooted out of the way. As Warren approached Diane's mother to check her vital signs, his partner stared at Diane. She made a somewhat peculiar impression. Her face was attractively adorned with make-up, blush, and eye-shadow. Her blue dress fit sveltely on her tanned body, covering her shoulders with thin circular straps and reaching down to her mid-thigh. But only half of her hair had been styled and curled while the other half remained straight, dangling to the side.

"How long has she been like this?" asked Warren.

"Oh, I'm not sure," replied Diane, "Todd?"

"I'm not sure, either."

"Less than twenty minutes?" asked Javier.

"Maybe," said Todd. "It couldn't have been too long because I heard her talking to herself like she always does—then it got quiet. I just thought she fell asleep—that's usually what happens."

"She's breathing very slowly. Pulse is slow, too," said Warren. "You said she was talking to herself? What did she say exactly?"

"The normal stuff about how Diane ruined her life," Todd replied flatly.

"Todd!" shrieked Diane, her cheeks reddening.

"Well, that's what she was saying."

"Let's get her to her side and give her oxygen," said Javier with a restrained smile.

The two paramedics gently moved Norma to the gurney. They then propped her to her side and bended her top knee.

"What are you doing?" asked Todd.

"That's the best position for her to breathe. Especially if she vomits," replied Warren.

Todd crinkled his nose.

"Like you've never seen Mom throw up before," said Diane with a raised brow.

"I'm guessing she was drinking that," said Javier, pointing to a large bottle of Vodka.

"I'm sure she was," replied Diane.

"Do you know if she took anything else with it?" asked Warren.

"Sometimes she pops downers."

"Barbiturates and Vodka—not a good combination," said Javier, wagging his head back and forth.

"She's pretty cold. Let's put a blanket over her," said Warren. Then, turning to Diane, he added, "Excuse me, but could you take your brother out of the room and then come right back?"

"Okay," said Diane slowly, giving both men a quizzical look. Walking to the living room, she said to Todd, "Stay here right by the door. Grandma and grandpa should be here any minute." Diane then quickly returned to her mother's bedroom.

"Young lady, I want to commend you and your brother," said Warren. "I think we've done all we can here. We need to get her to the hospital and pump her stomach. She's not waking up. If she doesn't regain consciousness soon, we run the risk of her falling into a coma."

Diane nodded.

"Are you old enough to drive to the hospital?" asked Warren.

"Yes, but my grandparents are on their way," replied Diane.

"Okay, okay, then we're going to leave," said Warren. "We're taking her directly to the Medical Center."

"Okay," said Diane as she watched the two men wheel her mother out of the house and into the ambulance.

"Excuse me, folks," said Javier, pushing his way through the small crowd.

Diane waited impatiently by the door. A few bystanders lingered close by, but she offered no explanations. When a small blue car pulled up to the house, she let out a sigh of relief.

"What's going on here?" asked her grandfather as he got out of the car.

"Grandpa!" shouted Diane. She quickly ran outside, followed by her brother.

"I think Norma overdosed, Earl," offered a neighbor.

"Could you all go home, please!" replied Diane's grandfather. He rubbed the thin gray hair that fell alongside the edge of his large, stocky tan face. Then, placing his large hairy arm around Todd, he bellowed, "Have a little respect for our daughter and her family, for Pete's sake!"

"Is she going to be all right?"

"Of course she will, now please, go home!" said Diane's grandfather.

"I'm so glad you're here," said Diane. "They took Mom to the Medical Center."

"Don't worry, sweetie," said her grandmother. Then, embracing Diane, she added, "Your mother's going to be okay. Come on, both of you."

Diane gently pushed her brother into the back of the car.

"Make sure you put your seatbelts on!" shouted Diane's grandfather.

Diane nodded. She then began to assist her brother.

"I got it!" shouted Todd.

"Okay, okay. I was just trying to help," said Diane.

Within moments, the car slowly left the dirt lot in front of the house. Diane's grandmother was the first to speak. "When you called, I thought you were going to tell me something about the graduation ceremony. I never dreamed it could be something as awful as this."

Diane's mouth dropped open.

"What's the matter, Diane?" asked her grandmother.

"Nothing," Diane sighed. She then buried her head into her hands.

When they arrived at the Albuquerque Medical Center, the receptionist advised them to wait in the lobby. Diane stared at Todd, who appeared to be glued to the large television screen. She then looked at her grandparents. Her grandfather was reading a magazine. Her grandmother had begun to knit. Diane observed her dress and played with her hair, a look of melancholy on her face. After several hours of waiting within the lobby, a nurse emerged from a hallway. Tall and thin, she stood erect with a small pencil wedged between her ear and her dark thick hair. She released a slight smile and then announced, "Hello everyone. Mrs. Hebert is doing much better now."

"Oh, thank God!" blurted Diane's grandmother.

"Can we see her?" asked Todd.

"We're going to keep her for the night," continued the nurse. "Give her a little more time and we'll let you all come in and speak with her tomorrow."

14

DRESSED CASUALLY IN blue jeans and an oversized red sweatshirt, Diane plopped an old brown suitcase near the door of the small living room.

"Whew! I definitely stuffed in as much as I could!" she said between heavy pants.

Todd followed her with a red and white duffel bag. On the side was an emblem of a wolf and the word *Lobos*.

"Is that everything?" asked Diane's grandmother.

"Yes, I believe so," said Diane.

"Well, then, let's load it up."

"Thank you, Grandma, I don't know what I'd do without you," said Diane.

"I may be an old woman, but this is a special occasion, so don't you worry," she replied.

"Bye, mom, I'm leaving!" said Diane, looking toward the hallway that led to her mother's bedroom.

There was no reply.

"Don't worry, Diane," said her grandmother. "She probably just doesn't want you to see her, um, break down in tears."

"Yeah, I can only imagine how torn up she is," said Diane **caustically**.

As the two drove off, Diane looked back to see if her mother had come out of the house, but only her brother remained. He stood where the car had been only moments ago, waving to them. With a tear in her eye, Diane turned to look forward. An hour later, she had arrived at her destination: the University of New Mexico.

After reviewing her campus map and asking several students for directions, Diane finally was able to locate her dormitory building. "This is it. Coronado Hall. I'm on the second floor."

"Oh, dear me," sighed Diane's grandmother.

The two made their way up the stairs, with Diane leading the charge. Once she was able to find her room, she entered with a large smile. A few moments later, her grandmother joined her. "Well, it's kind of small, especially for two people."

"I don't care," replied Diane. "I'm just happy to be here."

"Have you met your roommate?"

"No, I haven't."

"Well, that one must be yours." Diane's grandmother pointed to an empty bed. She slowly eased herself down upon it. "Any thoughts as to what you want to study?"

"Yes! I'm going to major in mathematics and become a teacher!" replied Diane without a hint of hesitation.

"Wow! You seem so sure of yourself. You might want to wait a little, honey. I mean, come on, you've just arrived. Who knows what the future holds?"

"No, I'm sure of it!" Diane replied confidently. She walked over and sat down next to her grandmother on the bed. Suddenly, she lost her smile. With a grim expression, she added, "I want to help kids so that they won't be treated like I was…" Her voice faded. Tears began to fall down her cheeks.

"There, there, sweetie," said her grandmother, embracing her warmly.

The door opened. A tall young lady dressed in white shorts and a thin cotton blouse walked into the room holding a volleyball under her right arm. "Oh, sorry, maybe I came at a bad time?"

Diane slowly let go of her grandmother and observed her roommate. She possessed a dark complexion, long curly black hair, and deep brown eyes.

"Oh, hello, I'm sorry. First day and all," said Diane, wiping her face.

"No worries. I understand. This is my second year here, but I was a little homesick my first year." She dropped the volleyball on her bed. "I'm Rebecca, but you can call me Becky. Hey, um, I'll be right back. I'm going to grab something from my car."

Diane turned to her grandmother. "Great first impression, huh?"

Her grandmother smiled warmly. "Are you going to be okay?"

"Yes, Grandma, I'm going to be fine."

"Well, your grandfather said he wouldn't take you because he doesn't like 'goodbyes,' but he did want to give you this," she said, handing Diane an envelope.

Diane looked at her curiously. "What is it?"

"Just a little something to show you how proud we are."

Diane slowly opened the envelope. Inside, she saw a card. When she opened it, a check fell to the ground. Quickly picking it up from off the floor, she glanced at the amount given her. Once again, tears began to flow. She grabbed her grandmother and hugged her profusely. "Grandma, I love you!" said Diane.

"We love you too, honey."

"Thank you, Grandma, but are you sure? It's too much! I mean—can you and Grandpa afford it?"

"Yes, Diane," she replied. "We tried to give you money in the past, but your mother always…. Well, never mind. You're an adult now, and that money's been waiting for you."

"Thank you," said Diane, holding her tight. "Thank you so much."

15

THE YOUNG MEN at the university treated Diane very well. There was no hazing or condescending looks or rude giggles as she walked by. This motivated her to look as attractive as possible. She exercised at the student recreation center each day and bought fashionable clothes that fit her tightly. Whether in class, the library, or one of the many student restaurants, Diane was often approached by male students. Though she did her best to contain herself, deep within she gushed whenever someone complimented her or paid her attention.

Diane dated several students, but for the most part, she was not looking for a serious relationship. Then she met Jonathon. More than his perfectly combed blonde hair, his perfect white complection, and his immaculate clothing, he had a certain charisma that captivated Diane. Unlike the others, Jonathon was not merely a student. He had already established himself as a successful real estate agent.

As they shared a pizza one night at Saggios, Jonathon would not break eye contact. "Do you realize that you're the perfect blend of beauty and brains?"

"Well, I'm still working on the 'beauty' part," said Diane, winking at him.

"I'd say you have it down," said Jonathon. After a brief pause, he asked, "So have you decided?"

"I'm still not sure," said Diane.

"I'm not that far away from campus, so it's not like you're going to miss out on your studies. And at my place you won't have to worry about crazy roommates running around the halls!"

"No wonder you sell so many houses!" said Diane, smiling. Then, turning more serious, she continued, "You know I want to, but…"

"What?" said Jonathon, playfully grabbing Diane's hand.

"I don't know," said Diane. "Dating is one thing, but living together… and besides, my roommate is actually very nice."

Jonathon placed a key on the table. "Take it. That way you can live at both places—no commitment."

Diane pulled him toward her and kissed him firmly on the mouth. "You know something? You are impossible to resist!"

Jonathon brought his hand to his face and blew on his knuckles. He smiled widely. "Well, you know what they say. It takes one to know one."

16

DIANE MOVED INTO Jonathon's apartment during the weekend. It was a two bedroom deluxe model, overlooking a beautiful pond with ducks. There was also a club house that offered a weight room, a pool and a Jacuzzi.

Space was also a welcome change. Instead of a very limited desk area, Diane could spread her books and papers on Jonathon's large adjustable coffee table while she listened to music or watched a movie on his large high definition screen. Diane and Jonathon often talked into the wee hours of the night, discussing issues that ranged from politics to the economy to the latest fashion trends.

Living with Jonathon also made Diane realize the full extent of his lifestyle. Throughout the week he was off mixing business with pleasure as he attended upper scale social events or played golf with potential clients. Though Diane often joined him, there were times when her studies would not allow her to do so. This slowly created distance between the two.

"Now what are you studying?" Jonathon asked.

Diane shuffled the many books and papers scattered across the table. "Well, one class is British literature and the other class is psychology," she replied. "And then there's my personal favorite: analytic geometry."

Jonathon frowned. "Hmmmm. Sounds like fun. Well, this is my last attempt. Are you sure you don't want to come?"

Diane curled her lips. "Of course I do, but I can't! My grandparents promised to continue helping me as long as I keep my grades up. Not everyone is making thousands of dollars every week off the housing market, you know!"

"Okay, suit yourself," said Jonathon, smiling as he walked passed her.

"Hey!" Diane called out. "Are there going to be any pretty girls at this *business party?*"

"Of course!" replied Jonathon, not bothering to stop on his way out. "It wouldn't be a party without them!"

17

THE TREND BETWEEN business and work continued to the point that the line between the two began to blur. Night after night Jonathon arrived late. He often seemed tired and uninterested in any form of intimacy. After harboring suspicions for months, Diane decided to act. She searched his computer. She looked at his personal cell phone. The evidence piled up. Flirtatious messages, romantic rendezvous, and pictures of beautiful women; Diane understood. She had never been Jonathon's girl, but simply one of many, albeit perhaps the one with the highest status.

Diane could no longer face the uncertainty. She packed her things and left. Upon reaching her dormitory, she saw her roommate reading at her desk.

"Diane, are you back?" asked Becky.

"Yeah, I guess so," Diane replied. She noticed some clothes on her bed. "What is all of that stuff over there?"

"Oh, sorry, one of my friends from the volleyball team crashes here sometimes. Um, don't worry. I'll get rid of it."

"Yeah, it didn't work out," said Diane, "so I'm afraid you're stuck with me for the rest of the year."

"Diane, I'm sorry, but to be honest with you, I think it's for the best," said Becky. She began to move the clothes off of Diane's bed and into her closet.

Diane inclined her head. "I guess I was pretty stupid to think a guy like that would want to be with me."

"Oh, no, don't say that," said Becky. "It's hard to find a good guy. You have to be patient."

"Becky," began Diane, "I know we don't really know each other very well, but, do you have a boyfriend? I mean, I never see you at any of the parties."

"That's because I don't go to them," said Becky. "I'm too busy with volleyball practice. And besides, I'm a Christian." She raised a large book with a leather cover in the air. It was marked by a large cross.

"Oh, I didn't know you were so religious," said Diane.

"I'm not," replied Becky. "It's not about religion, Diane. It's about a relationship."

Diane shifted her eyes and then put her suitcase on her side of the room.

"Is something wrong?" asked Becky.

Shaking her head, Diane replied, "No, not at all. Well, I better unpack and let you get back to your reading."

18

DIANE DATED SEVERAL young men, but somehow it was not the same. The happiness she felt was fleeting. Even when drinking surrounded by dozens of friends, she felt alone. She decided that the best therapy to combat her loneliness was to throw herself into her studies.

On most nights, Diane would head toward the top floor of the library. The intense focus soothed her pain, yet the inner panic she felt at times began to overwhelm her. When she was invited to a party at the end of the year, Diane found it hard to resist.

"Hey, Diane!"

Standing in front of her was Christy, a petite brunette with a perpetual smile who resided in the same dormitory. Diane looked at her and put her index finger to her lips, which only seemed to make Christy smile all the more.

"I knew I'd find you here," said Christy, placing her arms on Diane's table. "Great news! Dan's having a huge graduation party!"

"Yeah?" replied Diane. She turned away from her mini-computer. "Dan's loaded! I can only imagine what his house looks like!"

"Ssshhhhh!" hissed a young man sitting at a table nearby. He furrowed his brow and scowled at the girls before turning his attention to several books stacked before him.

Diane and Christy exchanged glances and then began to giggle.

"I've never been there," said Christy, "but his girlfriend, Lori, said we're invited. Can you believe it? We can ride with Brad and Lorenzo. Are you in?"

"Wow!" said Diane. "I can't believe it! How'd you pull it off?"

"Easy," said Christy. "Lorenzo and Brad are friends with Dan, and Lorenzo likes me, and Brad likes you!"

Diane smiled, but then suddenly turned to her small computer monitor. "I don't know," she said somewhat despondently. "Brad's really cute, and it does sound fun, but..."

"Oh, come on, Diane! You want to live in the library surrounded by nerds?"

The same young man who had earlier shushed the girls pointed his pencil at them. "I heard that!"

Christy smiled. "Oops! Sorry!"

19

THE RED SPORTS car ascended the hills with ease, only stopping at a large black gate.

"Sandia Heights!" shouted Lorenzo. He smiled widely, revealing white teeth that contrasted nicely with his olive colored skin and dark, thick hair.

"Here's the number Lori gave me," said Christy, handing him a note.

"Thanks, babe," said Lorenzo. He reached out of the car and punched in the code. Slowly, the large metal gate opened, allowing them to pass.

As they searched for addresses, Diane said, "Guys, this must be it! Just look at all the cars!"

They quickly found a place to park and ran to the door as fast as they could. Brad, a thick muscular young man with short light brown hair, led the way. "Looks like the party's started!" he shouted.

Diane felt a flash of excitement upon hearing the sound of loud music and a cacophony of voices. "Wow!" she gushed, pointing to the beautifully furnished rooms throughout the house.

"Did you bring your bikini?" asked Brad.

"I've got it on underneath," said Diane, smiling.

"Well, what are you waiting for? I want to see that killer body of yours!"

"Lead the way!" said Diane.

"All right!" said Brad as he grabbed her by the hand. He then bulled his way through a swarm of people until they exited the house and entered the backyard. Diane's eyes widened. In front of her was a large swimming pool shaped in a figure eight. She quickly took off her clothes, revealing a pink bikini, and jumped into the cool water.

"Man, you're incredible!" shouted Brad as he took off his shirt. He then took a flying leap off the side of the pool and landed with a large splash only inches away from Diane.

"You two don't waste any time, do you?" said Christy, reaching the pool area with Lorenzo.

"No way!" said Diane. "That's for losers!"

Christy smiled and shook her head. "Oh, you are so going to get it."

"Is that right?" asked Diane. She then began to splash Christy. Brad joined in and splashed Lorenzo as well.

"Okay, who's up for a chicken fight?" asked Brad.

Both girls smiled at them and nodded.

"Come on, Diane!" said Brad.

He then dove under the water and put Diane on his shoulders. Lorenzo did the same to Christy.

"Ready?" asked Brad.

"Ready," said Lorenzo.

Brad charged Lorenzo as people around them began to cheer. Diane, laughing hysterically, grabbed Christy and wrestled with her until she pushed her back. Lorenzo, attempting to steady her, swayed back and forth as he clutched Christy's slender thighs.

"One more push, Diane!" shouted Brad through gritted teeth.

Diane complied, pushing Christy until she fell back like a large tree, plunging into the water amidst shrieks and laughter.

"My girl's in shape!" said Brad, smiling triumphantly.

"You know it!" said Diane, flexing her arms to show off her shapely biceps. "Who's next?"

"I'll take that challenge!" said a young man standing nearby. "I need a partner!"

"I'm game!" said another girl.

One by one, Brad and Diane took on all comers until they had defeated everyone in the pool.

"Winners and still champions!" said Brad, smiling broadly.

"No fair, man," said one of the boys who had just lost. "You play football and I see that girl in the gym like, every day!"

"Oh, come on!" said Diane, flashing large puppy eyes and a pouting face. "You're breaking my heart!"

"Yeah, it's not our fault we're studs!" said Brad. He then lowered Diane off his shoulders and together they made their way outside the pool.

"Wow! What a rush!" beamed Diane before sticking her tongue out. She then ran the towel through her wet hair.

"Yeah, you guys were unstoppable," said Christy. She then handed Diane and Brad two bottles of beer.

"You think that's a rush?" asked Lorenzo. "The party's just starting! It's time to dance, boys and girls!"

"I don't know if I'm up to it," said Diane. "I must have thrown down ten girls!"

"Hey, what about me?" asked Brad.

"Yeah, you had a little to do with it," said Diane, winking.

"Well, if you guys need a little more energy," said Lorenzo, "I've got the medicine right here."

He then pulled out several colored pills with smiley faces engraved on them.

"Oh, hell yeah!" said Brad.

"What is it?" asked Diane.

"You're kidding me, right?" said Lorenzo.

Diane looked at him and shrugged her shoulders.

"It's Ecstasy," Christy replied as she plopped two pills in her mouth and then swallowed them with her beer.

Diane started to do the same when Brad grabbed her wrist firmly. "Easy, Diane, if this is your first time, only take one and down it with water, not alcohol."

Looking at her friends somewhat nervously, Diane set aside one of the pills and grabbed a bottle of water. At first, she felt nothing, but as she entered the house and joined the others, a new source of energy surged through her body. She laughed as never before. She danced as never before. She shouted at the top of her lungs. But by the time the evening had ended, Diane was beginning to feel dizzy. On the drive home, she rambled nonsensically, and once they had arrived at the university, she had to be led to her room.

After several failed attempts to open the door, Brad assisted her. "Are you sure you're gonna be okay?" he asked.

Diane looked at him wearily. "Um, yeah. I'm fine. Good night, Brad."

He kissed her on the cheek and disappeared down the hallway.

Upon entering, Diane turned the light on and moaned, "I thought I was in good shape, but what a workout! Whew!" She then stumbled over to her bed. Sitting down slowly, she began rubbing her temples.

"Diane, it's one in the morning," moaned Becky. "Could you please turn the lights off and keep it down."

Diane smiled at her. "Oh, sorry," she said, slowly. Then, suddenly, she said, "Hey! Becky! Have you ever taken Ecstasy to—you know—get energized for a game?"

"Energized?" repeated Becky. She slowly sat up on her bed. "Are you talking about drugs?"

"I guess."

"I'm an athlete on scholarship. I can't fool around like that. And besides, it's wrong."

Diane continued to rub her temples as she plopped into bed fully clothed. "Isn't your season over?"

"That's not the point, Diane."

"Well, it was incredible. That's all I can say."

"Look, I really have to get some sleep. I'm going to a youth conference with my church tomorrow." Then, after a brief pause, Becky added, "But if you want to come with me, we could talk more."

"Church on a Saturday?" asked Diane, incredulously. "No thanks! Besides, isn't it going to be in Spanish?"

"It's bilingual," replied Becky, "and it will be a lot of fun."

"Yeah, I bet. Sorry, but I think I'll take a rain check on that one," said Diane, laughing.

"Are you sure? I would love to introduce you to some of my friends. There will be games and music and dramas…" Becky stopped in mid-sentence as the sound of Diane's profound snoring filled the room. With a short huff, Becky threw off her covers, got to her feet, and pulled down the light switch.

20

DIANE STOOD PROUDLY on the platform. Her diligence had paid off. She was a proud graduate of the University of New Mexico, receiving her Bachelor's degree cum laude in mathematics. After the ceremony, she rushed toward her family members.

"It's so good to see you all!" gushed Diane. "And Todd, you're getting so big and handsome!"

She massaged her brother's cropped light brown hair as she had done throughout his childhood. The only difference was that she had to reach up to do so.

"Thanks," said Todd, releasing a shy grin.

"Well, we are so proud of you, Diane," said her grandfather, embracing her warmly.

"I'll say!" added her grandmother. "Nobody else in our family has graduated from college."

"I couldn't have done it without your help," said Diane.

"Well, we're not done yet," said her grandfather. "We want to take you out to celebrate. Are you hungry?"

Nodding, Diane followed them to their car. Once inside, she began, "So, where's Mom?"

Her grandparents turned to each other simultaneously. After an awkward pause, her grandfather replied, "We don't know, sweetheart.

She's with some guy from Grants. Met him at some bar, I think. Anyway, we haven't seen much of her since they hooked up."

"Oh, well, what else is new," replied Diane, rolling her eyes.

"She was doing pretty well for a while," said her grandfather, "even got off welfare and was working a bit."

"Grandpa, please!" said Diane. "Don't try to defend her! What kind of mother doesn't even attend her daughter's graduation? I mean, come on, two in a row? Someday when I get married she'll probably be off drunk somewhere!" Turning to her brother who was seated next to her, Diane continued, "How are you doing, Todd? Are you okay?"

"Yeah, I'm all right. Mom pretty much leaves me alone."

"I bet she does," said Diane, shaking her head as she rolled her eyes. She then stopped and stared at her brother. "You're looking kind of skinny. Does she ever cook for you?"

"Sometimes."

"Does she ever mention me?"

Todd inclined his head.

"Well?" Diane prodded.

"Now, Diane, there's no reason to spoil such a joyous occasion," said her grandmother. "This day is about you, not your mother."

"Thanks, Grandma, but I would really like my brother to answer my question."

Inhaling sharply, Todd blurted, "She said she doesn't want to talk to you because you think you're better than the rest of us."

"What?" squealed Diane as she curled her lips.

"Once," continued Todd, "when I got some bad grades, I thought she was going to get mad; but instead all she said was that at least she wouldn't have to listen to me brag about how smart I am like you always did."

"That's the craziest thing I ever heard!" said Diane as she fidgeted in her chair. She then grabbed her seatbelt and began pulling on it. "This dang thing! It's too tight! Anyway, I never bragged; I just wanted her to see my grades so she'd be proud of me!"

"Diane, honey, don't worry about it," said her grandmother. "It doesn't make any difference."

"It does to me!" said Diane.

21

HER DAILY SCHEDULE was full from the time she rolled out of bed in the morning to the time she stumbled back into it late at night. Each day, Diane worked as a substitute teacher. Afterwards, she attended classes at the university. In the late evening, she returned to her apartment to quickly change. Though beset with fatigue, Diane was determined to pursue an active social life, frequenting the most popular clubs in Albuquerque and Rio Rancho. With detailed precision, she attempted to categorize work, school, and festivity into equally important divisions that would allow no sacrifice. She was pushing herself to her limits and it was beginning to show.

As Diane stood before the counter of the main office of one of her favorite junior high schools, the secretary hesitated.

"What's the problem?" asked Diane. "Aren't you going to give me a key?"

"Um, just wait here, Miss Davis."

Diane waited impatiently, but the secretary never returned. Instead, the school principal, Mrs. Brown, approached her at the front desk. An elegant woman, with radiant black skin, an attractive symmetrical oval face, and short dark hair, she projected a conspicuous mixture of professionalism and elegance. "Diane, let's talk for a minute," she began. Then, motioning with her hand, she continued, "Please, come to my office."

Nodding, Diane slowly followed her. As she sat down, she crossed her tan legs and smoothed out a few wrinkles in the gray skirt she was wearing. To her surprise, Mrs. Brown took the time to close the blinds to her window. She then closed the door, causing Diane to shuffle uneasily in her chair.

Sitting behind her desk, Mrs. Brown asked, "How are you doing?"

"Oh, I'm fine, thank you."

"Really?"

Diane stroked her eyebrows, careful to not smear her light mascara. "Well, I think I may be coming down with something, that's all. It's not contagious, if that's what you're worried about."

"Are you sure? Because my secretary made a comment to me last week. And your eyes—they're extremely red."

Twitching nervously, Diane replied, "Allergies. I don't think I'll ever overcome the pollen here." After a brief pause, she smiled and added, "People keep telling me I need to move to one of those coastal cities near the beach."

Mrs. Brown frowned, causing a few lines to show around her smooth dark mouth. "Diane, let me make this abundantly clear to you. If you're lying to me and putting my kids in danger, you could be looking at some serious consequences."

Diane brushed aside the light auburn bangs that fell over her eyes. She lifted her face and attempted to appear confident, but then suddenly, she broke into tears. Mrs. Brown pressed the speaker button of her phone. "Marjorie, I'm going to have to speak to Miss Davis for quite some time. Please see which teachers have a first period prep to cover her class, and then see if we can get another substitute. Miss Davis won't be teaching today."

"Yes, Mrs. Brown," echoed the reply.

Passing Diane a box of tissue paper, Mrs. Brown said, "Well?"

"Everything is going wrong in my life!" sobbed Diane. "I've tried my best to work and attend school, but I think the stress is finally getting to me!"

"And?"

"And what?" asked Diane, removing the tissue from her face. "I'm on my own, Mrs. Brown. I pay all the bills, I study—"

"Do you want me to fill out a report to the police department?" interrupted Mrs. Brown. She placed her elbows on her desk. "I'm not going to ask you again. What's going on, Diane? What's *really* going on?"

Diane inclined her head and whispered softly, "Occasionally, I do things to help me with fatigue or stress."

"Things like drugs?"

"Not exactly."

"Diane," continued Mrs. Brown, "I know you're not going to like what I'm about to tell you, but believe me, it's for your own good. I'm going to take you off our substitute teaching list for our school. You need to get your life together."

Diane blinked uncontrollably. She stared at Mrs. Brown sitting behind her desk, with hands folded, her pretty face composed of smooth black skin, her red lipstick, the white pearls around her neck. Everything became a blur as a familiar white weather beaten face scowled at her disapprovingly.

"I'm just never going to be able to please you, will I, Mother?" shouted Diane.

Mrs. Brown jerked her head back. Her eyes widened. Diane, for her part, began to tremble. She slowly began to rub her forehead. "I'm so sorry, Mrs. Brown, I—I don't know what just got into me."

With a deeply furrowed brow and a hint of fear, Mrs. Brown inhaled deeply. "The only reason I'm not calling the police is because you've always done such a great job for us, and, well, I really like you. In fact, this whole incident is sad because I understand you are about to finish the final phase of the credential program. I was prepared to offer you a position next year. My only worry was that you wouldn't accept, but now I see you have other issues."

Diane nodded and slowly got up from her chair.

"Straighten out your life, get some help, and then come back and see me, okay?" said Mrs. Brown. "If not—if I hear you are continuing to work as a substitute teacher in another district—I'm going to tell them everything I know."

22

DIANE WAS A natural. She had never sold anything in her life, but her attractive physical appearance combined with her sunny personality gave her an edge. Also, being one of the few female employees at the automobile center resulted in a larger clientele than the other salesmen.

"Just sold another truck!" said Diane, smiling to one of her co-workers, a nice looking young man dressed in a collared white shirt and a red tie.

"Man! What's your secret?" he asked, smiling as he shook his head.

"Oh, just some tricks that an old boyfriend taught me," said Diane, winking at him.

"Why don't you let me take you to lunch and you can reveal some of your magic to me," commented another of Diane's coworkers.

"Maybe another time," replied Diane. "I'm heading over to the store to buy a few things and I'll probably grab my lunch over there."

Leaving a small group of gawking men, Diane drove off the lot to a large superstore. Once there, she quickly grabbed a few packages of toothpaste and facial creams before heading for the deli.

"Diane Davis? Is that you?"

Diane turned to see a young woman dressed traditionally in a Hijab. Her thick eyebrows and high cheekbones were unmistakable. "Abra!" Lunging forward, Diane wrapped her arms around her. "What are you doing here? It's been so long!"

"I'm actually passing through," said Abra. "I'm leaving New Mexico State for the UCLA Medical Center in California."

"Wow!" exclaimed Diane.

"Yes, I'm so excited! I'm going to be a pediatric surgeon!" replied Abra, her face beaming. "I volunteered at the medical center at Las Cruces and got to know Doctor Goravan. He's a plastic surgeon, and he restores children born with cleft lips. He's amazing!"

Diane nodded, noting the enthusiasm in Abra's voice.

Catching her breath, Abra asked, "I can't wait to help these poor children. But what about you, Diane? You attended UNM, right? Are you teaching or are you continuing your studies?"

"Well, yes, I got my degree in mathematics, but I'm in business now," stuttered Diane. "I work for a car dealership."

"Really?" replied Abra as she arched her brow. "Well, sad to say, but you'll probably make a lot more money in the financial sector than in education. I'm not surprised since you were always so good with numbers in high school." She paused and shook her head. "Wow, that wasn't an easy time for us, was it?"

Diane winced. "Don't remind me!"

"I still remember the cruel comments I got for being Muslim and the kids who called me abracadabra!"

Diane remained silent.

"At least I got out of that dreadful English class!" continued Abra. "Kids who could care less about school, throwing papers at me, and all the teacher did was talk about Mexico!"

With a slight frown, Diane asked, "So your father gave you permission to be a doctor? He doesn't mind you leaving? I thought he was totally against that."

"He was!" replied Abra. "Trust me, it was a huge scandal! I tried to convince him, but he wouldn't bend! He was ready to marry me off to the highest bidder! Uncle Aamir practically had to kidnap me so that I could attend New Mexico State! But UCLA...no...my father won't speak to me anymore." She inclined her head. "I'm leaving in a few days, and I don't know if I'll ever come back."

Diane could see the moisture in Abra's eyes. She reached out and touched her on the shoulder. "I'm so sorry, Abra."

"Yes, it's hard." Abra rubbed her cheeks slightly with her thumb and forefinger. "But sometimes sacrifices are necessary to reach our goals, right?"

Diane nodded.

Suddenly, Abra's face broke into a wide smile. "I'm going to live with two other girls in an apartment just off campus in Los Angeles. I'm determined to be a doctor no matter how hard it gets. I believe it is my destiny. "الخـــيرات نفعـــل أن منـا يـــود الله."

Diane furrowed her brow.

"Allah wishes for us to do good deeds."

"Oh," said Diane.

Abra smiled quizzically. "What's the matter, Diane? Why so glum? We are finally free! Free to pursue our dreams! Isn't it wonderful! We can finally reach our potential without worrying about ignorant people keeping us down!"

Diane was only able to muster a weak smile in response. After a short, awkward silence, Abra opened her arms and embraced her. "Well, I gotta go," said Abra. "It was so good seeing you again. You're still the smartest girl I know! And, well, thanks."

"For what?" asked Diane, furrowing her brow.

"For being my friend," said Abra. "For being such a great example for me. You always had courage, Diane. Courage to stand up for yourself. I admired that. I admired your focus and discipline. You always had the best grades and that motivated me, too."

Diane felt a knot in her throat. With a tear in her eye, she replied, "Oh, Abra, you didn't need me for that. Thank you for being my friend, too. My only friend. And go on to be a great doctor at UCLA!"

23

DIANE RHYTHMICALLY TAPPED a mechanical pencil on her desk calendar. She then paused to draw a few silly caricatures of cats and dogs. Slowly, a figure in the distance caught her eye. She peered through the large window of her office. Alone in the parking lot of the automobile center stood a tall man with dark hair. Promptly rising to her feet, she straightened out her white blouse and gray skirt, and then took a quick look in the mirror. She took out her lipstick. She then gently ran her fingers through her shoulder length auburn hair.

The sky was a clear blue as Diane walked toward a man who stood next to one of the luxury cars. The sound of the clicking of her high heels must have caught his attention. He turned toward her and smiled.

"I see you're looking at the red sports coupe," said Diane.

"Yes."

Diane held out her hand and introduced herself.

"Pleased to meet you," he replied. "I am Ivan."

Arching her brow, Diane released a wide smile. "Wow! I love your accent! Where are you from?"

"I am from Russia."

"Wonderful!" Diane raised her hand and rattled a set of keys. "Like to take me for a ride?"

"Yes, I would," said Ivan.

"You're going to love the smooth ride," said Diane as she entered the car. To her surprise, her charm did not seem to have any visible effect. She played with her hair a bit. After a moment of awkward silence, Diane continued, "Customers are so funny. My last one said that I was as cute as a chipmunk. Should I take that as a compliment?"

Ivan issued no reply, but instead began to tinker with the radio.

"State of the art," said Diane.

Again, he said nothing. Diane watched him carefully. He appeared to be in his late twenties or possibly early thirties. He was well-dressed, clean-shaven, and had short black hair that contrasted with his white skin. Diane was finding it difficult to believe that he had failed to pay her the attention to which she was accustomed.

"Do you mind if I play my own music?" asked Ivan.

"No, go right ahead," said Diane. "The stereo system is incredible. It's as if you're in a live concert!"

Music slowly began to play. It was soft, melodic, and sounded similar to a hymn.

Diane crinkled her nose. "That sounds like the songs an old roommate from college used to listen to. Even when she played them in Spanish, I'd still recognize it."

"Yes, the sound of worship can be heard in all languages," said Ivan. "Do you like it?"

Diane pressed her lips tightly together. "No, not really, it's not my taste."

"It was not mine until I found peace with God."

Diane furrowed her brow.

"I was making much money in the Russian Trading System in Moscow, but I was not happy. I felt so empty inside. Superficial relationships, loneliness, a lack of purpose. I turned to alcohol and drugs to cope."

Diane began to fidget in her seat, shifting her tan legs within her skirt.

"I lost my position in the Exchange, I lost my girlfriend..."

"You better turn here," interrupted Diane.

"But in my darkest hour, I had an **epiphany**. Somehow, I knew. I knew that only the truth could set me free."

Diane turned away to look out the window. She attempted to focus on the familiar buildings.

"That is when I fell to my knees and prayed. It is strange to do this in Russia."

Diane suddenly turned and faced Ivan. "Why is that?"

"Russia is a hard, cold place," he replied. "The people are strong, self-sufficient. It is perceived as weakness to cry out to God. I was not a religious man, but in my desolation, I recalled a childhood friend of mine. He was poor in my eyes, a simple fellow, yet he possessed a joy and peace that I did not. He once asked me, 'Ivan, *ibo kakaya pol'za cheloveku, yesli on priobretet ves' mir, a dushe svoyey povredit?*' In Russian, this means 'for what shall it profit a man, if he gains the whole world, but loses his own soul'?"[1]

Diane ran her tongue around her front teeth. After a brief pause, she said, "Um, I think we better be heading back."

"Yes, of course," said Ivan before making a turn at the light. "I did not know at the time that these were not his own words, but spoken from the Holy Scriptures."

As they returned to the dealership, Diane smiled and said, "Well, I hope you liked the sports coupe, and, um, thank you for sharing."

Ivan clutched the door handle. "You are very welcome. I believe I will purchase this car."

His words did not provoke her normal response. As he opened the door and placed one nicely polished black shoe on the pavement, Diane remained seated. "So, you feel free now?"

Ivan paused. He sat back down in his seat and closed the door. "I do. I no longer build my house on the sand, but on the rock."

Diane hesitated. "I—I don't understand."

"I cannot fully explain this to you. You must seek God to understand. However, before I left Russia to come here, a friend gave me a very special gift. I keep it with me at all times. Perhaps it will help you." Ivan reached into his coat pocket and carefully withdrew an old writing card that was somewhat thick in texture. "It is a prayer. May I share it with you?"

"Is it in English?" asked Diane.

Ivan laughed. "Yes, of course. It is a beloved prayer that has been recited by many world leaders and even by simple men like me."

Ivan then closed his eyes. He inhaled deeply and slowly. A certain peace seemed to engulf his face.

> "Lord, make me an instrument of your peace,
> Where there is hatred, let me sow love;
> Where there is injury, pardon;
> Where there is doubt, faith;
> Where there is despair, hope;
> Where there is darkness, light;
> Where there is sadness, joy.
>
> O, Divine Master,
> Grant that I may not so much seek to be consoled as to console;
> to be understood as to understand; to be loved as to love;

For it is in giving that we receive;
It is in pardoning that we are pardoned;
It is in dying that we are born again to eternal life."[2]

Ivan finished, and tears formed in Diane's eyes.

24

THE LARGE TRUCK barreled across the highway. "The guys are really going to be jealous," said Gary, a large smile on his his rugged face. With short red hair, stubble on his cheeks, chin, and neck, somehow Gary connected Diane to the remote memories she had of her father. He was taller, no doubt, and had a spiked chain tattoo on his firm bicep, something her father never had, but somehow Diane sensed a resemblance.

"Keep your eyes on the wheel, tough guy," said Diane, "and remember, it's not a date."

"Whatever you want to call it is fine with me."

"Gary, I'm serious. Right now, what I really need is a friend."

"Okay, okay. You asked for moral support and you got it."

"Thanks," replied Diane with a slight smile. "And believe me, it has nothing to do with you. You're a great guy. It's just that, well, I'm not ready for a relationship, that's all."

"I'll have to take your word for it," said Gary. "You said just follow this highway, right? I've never been to this tiny little town." Then, after rubbing his red sideburns, he added, "I guess grunge guys don't have a chance against the white shirts on the display floor."

"Being a mechanic has nothing to do with it!" replied Diane. "Gary, trust me, you wouldn't want me as a girlfriend right now."

"Isn't that my decision? Come on, Diane, do you know how many guys at work want to go out with you? It reminds me of the military. There were only so many girls like you. Even in jeans and a T-shirt you look hot. And on top of all that, you're nice, you're smart, got a great personality, and you're—"

"A recovering addict," interrupted Diane.

Gary's eyes widened. "What?"

"Gary, if you only knew," replied Diane. "The reason I'm working as a sales rep is because I had to stop working as a substitute teacher. I reported to a school after smoking marijuana and...a few other things."

His light blue eyes widened. "Wow, I never would have guessed, but you seem like you have everything together now."

"Well, believe it or not, it was a client who got through to me," said Diane. She then pointed to a sign on the road. "Here, turn on this road and pass the railroad tracks. Yeah, he told me all about his life, his struggles, and then he told me how he made things right."

"And how did he do that?" asked Gary.

"By getting peace with God," replied Diane, "and learning to love and forgive."

"So that's what you're doing?" asked Gary.

"Yeah, slowly..." Suddenly, Diane jumped in her seat. "Stop! Over there!"

Pulling up to an old, broken country home, Gary exclaimed, "You lived here?"

"Yeah, believe it or not, this is where I grew up," replied Diane.

"You want me to go with you?"

Diane took a deep breath. "No, I would rather you stay here. It might get a little ugly. I haven't seen my mother in years."

"Is it just your mom?" asked Gary.

"Yeah, I don't even know where my dad is, and my younger brother took off to join the Army."

Gary contorted his face.

"What?" asked Diane. "Your freckles just got a little brighter."

"I was in the Marines for eight years," said Gary.

"Oh yeah, I forgot," said Diane with a wide grin. Then, taking a deep breath, she added, "Okay, say a prayer for me. If it doesn't go well, I'll come right back."

Gary nodded as Diane stepped out of his truck. She walked up the dirt driveway to the little house with trepidation. It was completely dilapidated, even worse than she had remembered. Holes in the roof, broken windows, chipped paint.... It all struck her as a sad type of symbolism. "I'm surprised Todd and I didn't die of pneumonia," she muttered.

Diane knocked on the old wooden door, careful not to get a splinter. She heard the sound of bottles clinking from within. Finally, the door opened. Her mother looked old, small, and weak. Instead of a woman in her late forties, she could have easily passed for sixty due to her wrinkled, sagging skin and stained teeth. She was dressed in old gray sweats. Her long sandy brown hair had turned lifeless and gray.

"Hi mom," said Diane.

Her mother blinked a few times.

"May I come in?"

Silence.

"It's been a long time," said Diane.

Her mother nodded.

"I want to talk to you, Mom. Please, may I come in?"

"Well, the place is kind of messy." Avoiding eye contact, her mother added, "What do you want, anyway?"

"May I come in?"

"I just said that the place is kind of messy!"

Diance winced. The harsh tone of her mother's voice sent memories long forgotten spiraling through her mind.

"Why are you here, Diane? You never visit, you never call, and now you pop up all of a sudden and don't even give me time to get ready. What do you want, anyway?"

"I'm sorry, Mom. I did call a few times, but your phone was disconnected."

Diane's mother slowly shook her head. She then released a tired sigh. "What do you want?"

Diane hesitated.

"Well, speak up, girl!"

"I wanted to tell you that I forgive you!" blurted Diane.

Her mother's mouth dropped open. Then, her entire face contorted, displaying the many deep creases across her eyes and forehead. "Forgive me? You came all the way over here to tell me that?" She slowly began to close the door. "Whatever, Diane. I don't have time for your nonsense."

Diane reached out quickly and grabbed the door handle. "Yeah, Mom, that's right!" she shouted. "You've never had time for me! But now you're going to make time!"

"Diane, who the hell do you think you are? Look at you, just look at you! Wearing them fancy clothes and pretty little earrings."

Diane frowned. "Jeans and a T-shirt are not fancy, mom, and there's nothing wrong with looking nice."

A crooked smile of contempt flashed across the face of Diane's mother. "You always thought you were better than the rest of us! And me in particular!" She paused. "And to think, after all the years of me taking care of you, this is what I get? You're nothing but an ungrateful little—"

"Mom, that's enough!" Diane interrupted. "I don't think I'm better than you! I just, I just want to help you."

"Help me?" repeated her mother with a slight chuckle. "By taking off and abandoning me and your brother so you could live it up in the big city? I don't know what's going on in that silly head of yours, but I don't need your help and I sure as hell never asked for it! Now, I—I want you to leave!"

"Mom, wait a minute! Wait a minute! I know I haven't stayed in touch. I just had to get away, but I'm trying to make it right, now. I've grown. I understand now. It's true. You saved me from…him. But you also have to understand that all the drinking and the drugs and the way you treated me made my life unbearable!"

"That's enough out of you, Diane!" said her mother. Her body began to tremble. "You've always had a fresh mouth! Get out! Get out! I don't want you here! Get out right now before I call the police, you hear?"

"Go ahead, Mom," Diane replied calmly. "We both know that they probably wouldn't even come, and if they do it would take at least an hour!"

"Well, then go away!"

Gary suddenly appeared. "Is everything okay?" he asked.

"Everything is fine," replied Diane.

Diane's mother stood silently, and then quickly left toward the back of the house.

"I'll be all right. Just wait in the truck. I promise I won't be long," said Diane.

"Okay," said Gary. "But if I hear gun shots, I'm coming in. And after all this is over, you owe me dinner!"

"Deal," said Diane, smiling.

Entering the old house, her smile quickly faded. The interior had not changed much. The old green sofa where her mother would lay in a drunken stupor, the empty beer bottles on the kitchen table, and the same torn up, stained carpet…. Then, something new caught her attention. Diane crinkled her nose. She smelled an odd, unpleasant odor. Lying on the kitchen counter were several unopened cans of cat food. A shiver ran up Diane's spine. "Mom, you don't own a cat, do you?"

"Go away!" came a voice from within the bedroom.

"I wasn't done talking to you," said Diane.

"I've had all the talking that I can take for one day," replied her mother as she curled up within the covers of her bed.

"Mom," continued Diane, "I've had to ask God to forgive me, and I also want you to know that I forgive you, too."

"Go away, Diane, just go away," whispered her mother.

"Okay, I'll leave. But I want you to know that I love you. I know you were hurt. I know you've had a hard life, and when you're ready, I'd like to talk. I'd like to be your friend."

Diane's mother hid her face underneath the lone blanket that covered her bed. From within, Diane heard the sound of her weeping. Walking over to the edge, she sat down and gently removed the blanket. Then, Diane stroked the dry skin of her mother's forehead.

"Mom, I have to go," Diane whispered, kissing her on the cheek. Making her way through the little house, she closed the door behind her and headed toward the truck. There, Gary was waiting for her with the door wide open.

"You okay?" he asked.

She placed her hand in his, allowing him to steady her as she moved forward onto the black rubber step and into the raised seat. "Yes," Diane replied quietly. "Let's go. I'm getting hungry and I owe someone dinner."

Smiling, Gary closed her door. He quickly made his way to the other side and nimbly jumped into the driver's seat. Shifting the gear into drive, he had barely pressed the gas pedal when a voice called out, "Diane! Diane!"

"Do I stop?" asked Gary.

"Yes!" said Diane. She lowered her window and turned to see her mother standing in the doorway. "Mom, I'm here!"

"Diane, I'm sorry!"

"I know, Mom! I know! May I come over tomorrow?"

"Yes! Yes, Diane!"

Wiping her eyes, Diane nodded to Gary. The large wheels of the truck began to turn and the sound of smashed dirt and gravel could be heard below. Through the rising trail of dust, Diane stared at the fading image of her mother as they continued down the country road that led back to the highway.

THE KEY

1

DOCTOR MARC WILSON, a leader in treating cancer patients, is a composed gentleman. Although powerfully built due to his commitment to weight training, he is not one to raise his voice or **vie** for attention. Doctor Wilson learned many years ago that life is difficult and emotional outbursts would not be the way for him to reach his goals. Instead, he developed a style that is best characterized in his own words as "quiet determination."

"Sir, how do you deal with the pressure of dealing with life and death on a daily basis?" asked a young man from within the circle of white coats. "I have to be honest. I've always wanted to be a doctor, but sometimes the stress really makes me have second thoughts..."

Doctor Wilson smiled. He was conducting a clinic for medical interns at the University of Chicago Cancer Center. These future doctors wished to be on the cutting edge of new breakthroughs in cancer research.

"Sure, it comes with the territory, but if it is your calling in life, then you will find an inner strength to succeed."

"Doctor Wilson, how do you know if being a physician is your true calling?" asked a female intern.

"You have to ask yourself why you are here," he replied. "Was it your dream to become a doctor? Or are you merely trying to live up to the expectations of your parents...or attempting to impress others with a title?"

A few students inclined their heads.

"Do you love medical research?" he continued. "Do you have a passion to help people? Although one must have intelligence to enter the medical field, it really comes down to having the right **perspective**."

A young man was then called upon to continue the line of questioning. "Excuse me, Doctor Wilson, I don't mean to be contentious, but how do you define the 'right perspective' as you put it? I mean, isn't that extremely **subjective**?"

Doctor Wilson paused to reflect. How did he obtain his perspective on life? How did he become the person that he is today? For the man standing before them was far different than the boy who struggled to find his way in life.

2

RICARDO SÁNCHEZ WAS part of a large family that had emigrated from Puerto Rico. His family, as well as several relatives, had settled into Compton, an area of Los Angeles, California that was marked by both poverty and violence. It did not take much time for Ricardo to get into trouble; he had a knack for finding it.

As a young man, Ricardo was given the nickname *Voz de oro*. It was a gift he took advantage of on more than one occasion, especially since he was an avid gambler. Dice, dominos, pool, cards. Ricardo did them all, and did them all well, but when it came to a game of poker, he was magical. Long after hours, he could be found in a small back room filled only with smoke and a few men seated around a table at a popular night club known as Hard Times.

"Hey, ain't nobody that lucky," said Leon, smirking at the rest of the men at the table.

"That's 'cause you don't know me *Juan del pueblo!*" replied Ricardo with an air of confidence. "Gentlemen, I bid you a good night *y más suerte la próxima vez. Me voy a mimil!*"

Leon appeared confused. After a short pause, he motioned with his cigar to the man standing next to him. After a few whispers were exchanged, he smiled. "Hey man, what ya doing? The night's too young to be leavin' now. It ain't even midnight. Nobody leaves before midnight."

"Sorry amigo, like I said, I have to go to sleep—big day tomorrow. *Tú sabes*," replied Ricardo, stuffing the many bills into his pockets.

"I don't know nothin', *Don Juan*, except for the fact that you stayin' at this table."

José Sánchez, one of Ricardo's cousins, whispered into his ear, "*Oye primo, ese caco tiene conexiones!*"

"*Y qué?*" replied Ricardo.

"Man, I'm telling you to play nice!" said José, prompting the others to face him.

"*Cállate, tonto!*" whispered Ricardo before smiling at everyone seated around him.

Biting his lip, José said in a low voice, "Play one more hand and let him win back some of his money."

"*Como la gatita de Dorita, si se lo sacan llora y si se lo meten grita!*" whispered Ricardo. "Man, you want me to win or what? Anyway, *no te preocupes, pai!*" After an awkward silence, Ricardo grabbed his glass of whiskey and quickly finished what little remained. "Well…okay, it seems my cousin has convinced me to stay a little longer, but I must insist on two things. One, I must relieve myself, and two, I really must limit myself to one hand because I must *atender a mi pobre mamá quien está enferma.*"

"What was that?" asked Leon.

"He said that he must see his mother who is sick," said a man with a thick Spanish accent who was leaning against the dark brown wooden wall located a few feet from the table.

"Yeah, that's fine. I'm a reasonable man. We all have to respect our mommas. One more hand it is, so go ahead and piss, but don't get lost or I might just have to go lookin' for you."

Ricardo bowed to Leon graciously, smiled, and walked to the bathroom. As he left the room, Leon waved to the two African American men who were standing next to the door. They immediately followed Ricardo, rather **conspicuously**.

Before opening the door, Ricardo turned and asked, "You guys want to watch?"

After a brief silence, one of them replied, "It's cool. We'll be right here waiting for you. Ain't no windows in there anyway."

Ricardo smiled and entered the bathroom. Once inside the stall, he locked the door behind him, squatted on the toilet seat fully clothed, and quickly took out all of his cash. Without hesitation, he separated the one dollar bills from the larger ones. Then, he wrapped them inside two single bills, each worth a hundred dollars. With a flush of the toilet, he went to the sink to wash his hands before leaving.

"Did you miss me?" asked Ricardo, a smirk on his face.

While maneuvering a toothpick from one side of his mouth to the other, one of the men nodded his head in the direction of the back room. Ricardo smiled at him contemptuously, and then began walking.

"Well, deal them up!" said Ricardo as he entered. "But as I said, it is very late so this will be my last hand."

Exhaling smoke from his cigar, Leon said, "We'll see. It just all depends."

"We're playing straight up. Nothing wild. No tricks," said the dealer.

Ricardo took his five cards. He had two queens and an ace. Leon, seated on the other side of the table, slowly moved his cards around in his right hand. Both men looked up and their eyes met. Leon immediately flashed a toothy smile, revealing a large gap between his front teeth. He then tapped his cigar in his ash tray.

"*Qué bruto!*" whispered Ricardo to José. "The man knows nothing about poker. He might as well show us his cards…"

José did not respond, but instead furrowed his brow and frowned before turning his attention to his cards.

"*La misma expression de siempre,*" whispered Ricardo. "*Pues, eres bien tonto, primo, pero por lo menos nadie lo sabe, entonces ganas de vez en cuando aunque sea por pura suerte…*"

"*Cállate, hombre!*" José hissed. "I'm trying to concentrate!"

"*Perdón! Perdón!*" said Ricardo. "*Qué mal genio tienes!*" Then, signaling to the dealer, he said, "I'll take three."

"Give me just one," Leon followed quickly. "That's all I need—if that." Facing Ricardo, he added, "Just icing on the cake, you know what I mean?"

Ricardo returned his smile with a sly smile of his own.

"I'll take two," said José.

The other men seated around the table proceeded to request their cards.

"I don't want to scare y'all off, but let's add two hundred to the pot," said Leon.

"I'm in," said the man next to him, "but it's all I got." He then proceeded to push a pile of money into the middle of the table, counting out several one dollar bills until he reached the full amount necessary.

"You going to throw in some pennies, too?" asked Ricardo.

The man sneered at him.

José was next. He appeared reluctant to continue. His eyes moved nervously toward Ricardo, who slowly shook his head from side to side. José promptly folded. "This just isn't my night. I'm out," he said.

Nodding toward José, Ricardo quickly announced to Leon, "I'm in, but two hundred? No, no, no, amigo—me *parece muy poco*. I'll raise you everything you lost…and then some!" Ricardo paused to pull out a stack of bills. He quickly showed both sides, revealing a hundred dollar bill at each end. Shuffling them, he continued, "You hear that, amigos? Yes, fifty, or for those of you who are not so good with math, five thousand dollars."

José's eyes widened. *"Acho men!"*

The man next to Ricardo quickly slumped his shoulders, waved his head back and forth, and withdrew. "I'll see you guys later."

The dealer then shook his head in disgust. "Y'all making this too damn personal!" he said, folding as well.

Ricardo smiled at Leon. "Looks like it's just you and me, amigo. You in or you out?"

Leon hesitated. He then exchanged whispers with one of his men. Clearly irritated, he stood up and walked over to another man who was standing near the door. The two began to argue in the corner of the room.

"That's a lot of cash!"

"You let me worry about that!" Leon shot back.

"Come on, Leon. We got a business to run."

Leon's eyes narrowed as he frowned deeply. He stuck out his thick index finger and poked the man standing in front of him several times on the chest. "Yeah, my business."

"Something wrong, amigo?" **jeered** Ricardo, interrupting the private conversation from his seat at the table. "Is the bank closed? Bad credit?"

Leon smirked at Ricardo and then snapped his fingers. His lackey immediately opened a dark attaché case, revealing several thousands of dollars. Snatching a thick stack of bills, Leon quickly returned to the table with a wide grin that fully displayed the large gap in his front teeth.

"It's cool, Don Juan," said Leon. "I'm calling your bluff." Leaning closer, he added, "Show me what you got."

Ricardo hesitated. "You sure you don't want to raise me?"

Leon shook his head. "Quit stalling! Come on, now, show me what you got!"

Ricardo exhaled deeply before throwing five cards on the table with an expression of disgust.

"Deuces! Deuces!" said Leon, grinning widely. "Nice try, Don Juan, but your luck done run out! This is my time! My time!" Leon turned over his cards, displaying a pair of jacks and a pair of sevens. "Two pairs, Don Juan, and any one of 'em would've beat you!"

"Ya se luce el chayote! Horita!" said Ricardo. *"Vámanos José!"*

He then kicked his chair and quickly left the table. José remained seated, his mouth agape. Leon displayed the large gap in his teeth, smiling widely as he clutched at the bills in the middle of the table. As he quickly inserted the cash into his coat pocket, his flunkies showered him with praise.

"José, I said *vámanos!*" repeated Ricardo.

José rose slowly. He took small steps as if in a trance. Once outside, Ricardo wasted no time in getting into his car.

"Le salió el tiro por la culata!" said José, quickly joining him in the front seat. "I told you to give him back a little, not to bet everything! Why do you have to always let your pride get the best of you, *primo?*"

Ricardo ignored his cousin, and instead pushed down the gas pedal as far as it would go. His eyes moved to the rearview mirror.

"What's the rush? It's bad enough that you lost all our money! You don't have to kill us, too!" José continued.

"Ya, cállate, hombre! Te quejas como una vieja!" said Ricardo. "It wasn't five thousand dollars, *primo!*"

José furrowed his brow as his head suddenly cocked back. "What are you talking about?"

"It was maybe two hundred and fifty—three hundred at the most," said Ricardo.

José continued to furrow his brow.

"Ay, necio!" said Ricardo. "I wrapped a bunch of ones and put some fives between two Benjamins!"

José remained silent, apparently deep in thought. Finally, he shouted, "Oh! I get it! Only the bills at the beginning—"

"—and the end," finished Ricardo, nodding his head and smiling.

The two began laughing.

3

IT DID NOT take long for Leon to know he had been duped. Word traveled quickly that a fast talking Puerto Rican had made him look like a fool. With his reputation at stake, Leon and several of his men let it be known throughout the streets of Compton that Ricardo was a marked man. When this became known to the Sanchez family, Ricardo's father urged him to hide in a small town on the other side of the state.

"*Siempre te metes en problemas, hijo!*" said his father. "*Pero esta vez pones a toda la familia en peligro!*"

"*Ay, Papi, no exagere!*" replied Ricardo.

"*No, esta vez, tú vas a escucharme a mí! Hasta que te diga, te vas a quedar con mi hermano, Octavio.*"

4

LODI WAS VERY different than the fast paced lifestyle of Los Angeles. In fact, Ricardo found the small town to be dull and boring. In search of more excitement, he began to make the acquaintances of several unsavory characters. This resulted in an **ultimatum.**

"*Mira*, Ricardo," said Octavio, a stout man with bushy eyebrows of black and gray. "You've been here for two weeks now and you still have no job. Tomorrow, you work in the fields with the rest of us."

"The what?" replied Ricardo, his eyes widening. Then, wagging his finger in his uncle's face, he continued, "No, no, no *tío*, I don't do that stuff. I didn't cut sugar cane in Puerto Rico, and I'm not doing it here!"

"How about grapes?"

"*Tampoco.* I don't like to get my hands soiled."

"*A mí, plín, acho!* I've honored my oldest brother long enough!" said Octavio in a tone that revealed his exasperation. "Either you work or you find another place to stay!"

5

WHILE THE OTHER men labored vigorously, picking the best clusters of grapes, storing them in large thirty pound crates, and transporting them into gondolas bound for the winery for crushing and pressing, Ricardo merely stood watching them.

"Ricardo, *toma*," ordered Octavio, handing him a sharp curved knife. "And try not to lose a finger!"

Ricardo responded with a blank expression. He then awkwardly gripped the strange looking object which resembled a menacing metal claw. Several workers passed by and laughed, pointing at him. Donning dark slacks, shiny black shoes and a flowing, light collared shirt; he seemed more fit for a dance floor than the vineyards.

"*Por qué él no lleva puesto sombrero?*" asked one man.

"*Porque dice que le despeina el pelo,*" replied Octavio as Ricardo ran his hand lightly over his slicked back hair.

"*Con este calor, su gel se va a derretir!*" said another to the laughter of the entire group.

Suddenly, their playful teasing ceased, followed by a few whistles and finger pointing. Each of the men stopped working. Before them on the paved road just outside the vineyards stood a beautiful, dark colored young woman dressed in a white sleeveless blouse and a tightly fitting white skirt. She was holding a clipboard.

"Hey! Hey! Show some respect!" shouted Octavio. "*Muestrenle un poco de respeto, por favor!*"

Ricardo quickly approached her. "Excuse me, *princesa*, but may I ask who you are and from where you have descended?"

She released a loud giggle before covering her mouth. "I'm Shirley— Shirley Wilson, and I *descended* from that truck."

"No, no, no, I mean, where are you from?" asked Ricardo.

"I'm from here. Never lived anywhere else."

"But where are you *really* from?" continued Ricardo.

"Do you mean my heritage?" asked Shirley.

"Yes, yes," said Ricardo, approaching her even more closely. "These large precious eyes, this soft jawline that descends like a precious curve to these luscious lips—"

"That's enough, Ricardo," interrupted Octavio.

Not willing to concede, Ricardo continued, "But I must understand this mystery. How was such a precious woman conceived?"

Octavio frowned as he wagged his head.

With a wide smile, Shirley began, "Well, my parents are black, but my dad had some Irish in him and my mom's got some Native American, I think."

"I have no idea how that happened," said Ricardo, "but I am so glad it did."

"Why, thank you."

"And what is a beautiful princess doing out here with these unworthy servants?"

"I—I work in the main office," stuttered Shirley. Then, after brushing back the thick fluffy hair that curved over both sides of her face, she added, "You have nice eyes. They're like…"

"Yes?" said Ricardo, stepping closer until the two stood inches apart.

"…like honey." Shirley paused for a moment. She remained very still, as if in a daze. "You're different."

"Am I?" said Ricardo. He took Shirley's hand and kissed it, causing her to giggle. "Maybe if you tell me where I can reach you I can reveal to you just how *different* I am."

"That won't be necessary, Ricardo," said Octavio, brushing Ricardo aside. "I've heard enough—more than enough. The Bergman Family is very prestigious, and they don't need people like you hurting their fine reputation. Now stop bothering Miss Wilson and get back to work—or whatever it was you were doing."

"Well, there must be a way for Ricardo Acevedo de Sánchez to see this vision of loveliness," said Ricardo as he kept his gaze firmly on Shirley's face.

Shirley smiled. She hesitated. "Oh, Octavio, I need you to sign this."

Octavio took the clipboard from her hand. "Of course," he replied, signing the form while glaring at Ricardo.

"Thank you," said Shirley. Then, turning to Ricardo, she added, "Well, maybe I'll see you at the Cinco de Mayo celebration."

Ricardo smiled and bowed as Shirley returned to a small white truck.

6

SHIRLEY LIVED WITH her mother, who was known to everyone as Ms. Donna, and her younger brother, Jackie. Though she appeared to have been placed under a spell, Ricardo was not able to work the same magic with the rest of her family.

Sitting at the kitchen table, Shirley tried in vain to convince her mother that she had found true love. Jackie, laboring away at the pipes below the sink, let out a huff or a chuckle every once in a while.

"I'm sorry, but that man's a dreamer! When are you going to accept that?" asked Ms. Donna as she took another bite of one of her famous oatmeal and chocolate chip cookies. A widow while relatively young, Ms. Donna had just enough wrinkles around her eyes and mouth to show her wisdom while still retaining the unique features that came from her Native American ancestry. And though portly, her high cheekbones and prominent jawline gave her a unique, somewhat exotic aspect that most people found quite attractive. "I've seen plenty of men like that before, Shirley. They always look for the easy way out."

"Oh, come on, Momma, he's doing the best he can! He's even driving back and forth to Los Angeles to find work."

"Yes, and I bet that's not all he's doing," said Ms. Donna, folding her arms.

"Jackie, tell her not to say such things," said Shirley, shouting toward the sink.

Jackie, who had the same blend of African, Irish, and Native American features, appeared to be a male version of Shirley—save the patchy facial hair. "I'm sorry, Shirley, but Momma's right." He backed away from the sink and stood up. Removing an old blue floppy cap from his head, he wiped the sweat from his forehead. He then waved the socket wrench in his hand at Shirley. "Everyone in town knows he's dealing."

Shirley opened her mouth as if to say something but instead inclined her head. She then walked away, plopped herself onto a white sofa located in the living room, and pouted quietly.

7

DESPITE THE MISGIVINGS of Ms. Donna and Jackie, Shirley continued to see Ricardo. Then, to their dismay, he visited so often that before they realized it he was actually living with them. Ms. Donna continually asked Ricardo if he had found steady work. Jackie mostly ignored him.

While lying on a double-sized bed, Ricardo played with Shirley's long dark hair. She did not respond. Instead, she remained on her side, gently massaging her massive belly.

"*Princesa*, talk to me," pleaded Ricardo.

"You're never here!" Shirley shouted. "My mother lets you stay here and eat and you don't even seem grateful! You know she's sick, and she still works—or she's at church—and what about me? I'm all alone, Ricardo, can't you see that?"

"Your brother is here, is he not?" said Ricardo. "He should help more."

"He does help," snapped Shirley, "but he's out a lot. He works! In fact, he's starting to make some good money." She paused before adding, "Besides, he doesn't like you. He says you're a freeloader and I'm starting to believe him!"

"*Princesa*, no, no, no!" Ricardo replied. He began to rub her neck and massage her shoulders.

"That feels good," said Shirley.

"I've told you that things are getting better! Just give me a little more time; you will see! I have a friend in Stockton that started a new business. A few weeks over there and we'll be swimming in *dinero*!"

"That's what you always say!" said Shirley, a deep frown on her face. "Why can't you just get a real job and make an honest living? I don't even care if we're poor, just stay here and be a husband—and a father! I'm about to have a baby if you haven't noticed!"

"Now, now," replied Ricardo. "You're hysterical, *mi princesa*. Look, stop crying. Where is that beautiful smile I long to see?"

"I don't know. I think it's gone."

Ricardo paused. His eyes darted in all directions. "Are we alone?"

"Yes, Jackie's still at work, I guess, and service won't be out for another hour."

"Do you expect them back soon?"

"Look, if we had our own place, then we wouldn't have to worry about—"

"Yes, yes, we will, *princesa*, I promise!" interrupted Ricardo. "But right now we need to find that smile of yours!"

Ricardo dangled a bag of white powder in front of Shirley. "Let me make you a little drink to relax you."

"What is it?"

"Oh, just a little natural remedy from the island." Ricardo got up and disappeared into the kitchen. When he returned, he held in his hand a glass of whirling liquid that had a slight grayish texture. Shirley took a small sip, then a second, and a third. Soon, her body relaxed and she fell asleep with a smile on her face.

8

THERE WAS A long silence on the other end of the phone. Shirley opened the refrigerator door with her free hand and proceeded to pour herself a glass of wine. A few moments passed before she replied, "Yes, I understand—*comprendo*—but can you give him a message? Yes, *mensaje*. Okay. Bye." Turning to her mother, Shirley loudly complained, "Can you believe this? His own mother can't even locate the man!"

"You can't blame her," replied Ms. Donna, wagging her head. "Actually, I know exactly how she feels."

Shirley curled her lips. "What's that supposed to mean?"

Ms. Donna opened the oven door and took out a rectangular metal pan that was filled with chocolate chip cookies. "You know good and well what that means," replied Ms. Donna. "Half the time you're out and about doing God knows what and I'm the one taking care of the kids."

"Not all the time…" said Shirley before sipping her wine.

"And if it's not me, it's Jackie. Or you ship them off to Los Angeles like you're trying to do right now."

"Momma, I don't need this!"

"You mean the truth?" asked Ms. Donna.

Before Shirley could answer, a little boy with dark skin and a large closely shaved head entered the kitchen. His jaw was strong and firm, and his face had a certain seriousness to it, uncommon for a boy so young. "Ms. Donna, will you help me with my homework?" he asked.

"Hey, baby," said Shirley.

"Hi," he replied without emotion.

"Don't you want to give your mother a hug, Marc?" asked Ms. Donna.

"Okay," said Marc, weakly wrapping his arms around Shirley while wearing the same serious expression. "I heard you talking on the phone. Are we going to Los Angeles to stay with *abuelo* and *abuela*?"

"No, no, baby, I was just worried about your father," Shirley replied. "I just wanted to see how he's doing."

"When is he coming back?"

"Oh, you know him…" replied Shirley, posing a nervous smile. "Always trying to make money. Always traveling."

"Actually, that's the problem; he doesn't know him," said Ms. Donna.

"Ms. Donna, I'll be in my room if you can help me," replied Marc.

"What are your brother and sister doing?" asked Ms. Donna.

Marc looked up to his grandmother and said, "Devan's playing with his cars like always, and I think Lisa's fooling with some dolls or something like that."

"Okay, let's get that homework done," said Ms. Donna, putting her arm around Marc and steering him out of the kitchen.

"Hey, Momma, think you could watch the kids for a few days?" asked Shirley. "A friend of mine invited me over to his place in Stockton."

Without bothering to stop, Ms. Donna waved her hand in the air and replied dryly, "No, Shirley. Don't even think about it."

The next morning, Shirley was gone.

9

Ms. Donna washed the dish and then placed it in the deep white porcelain sink. From there, Marc rinsed it and set it inside a faded green plastic tray. This routine continued for several minutes.

"Momma! Momma! I was offered a job in Tracy!" said Shirley, bursting into the kitchen.

"My heavens!" replied Ms. Donna. She jumped, practically dropping the dish in her hands. "Shirley, what has gotten into you? You nearly gave me a heart attack!"

"And it's in sales! I know I can do this, Momma, I know I can!"

Grimacing, Ms. Donna wiped her hands on the blue apron tied around her dress. She turned toward Marc. "You've done well, Marc. Is your homework finished?"

"Yes, ma'am."

"That's a good boy. Why don't you grab a snack and take a break. I need to talk to your mother."

"Can I take it to the living room and watch something?" asked Marc.

"Sure, honey, just don't spill anything on my coffee tables!"

"Yes, Ms. Donna."

Marc poured himself a large glass of milk and took a few cookies out of a large white jar. He then left the room.

"Shirley Wilson!" said Ms. Donna. "Take a breath!"

"Okay, Momma, I will, but you need to listen!"

"I'm listening."

"Okay," continued Shirley, breathing deeply through her nose. "It's a great opportunity! We get to travel, work as a team, and they even pay for our hotels and our food!"

"Hotels and food?" repeated Ms. Donna. "I thought you just said this job was in Tracy."

"Well, their headquarters is in Tracy," said Shirley. "That's where we start and that's where we end."

"So how are you going to travel with three kids? Marc isn't going to adjust to that very well. He's not a little boy anymore, Shirley. And who's going to watch Lisa? You can't leave a young girl in a hotel room and expect two boys to take care of her."

171

Shirley grabbed her mother's arm. "You're right, Momma. I couldn't do it with all my kids hanging on me. That's where you come in. Now stop washing those dishes. I need your full attention. I got it all planned out."

Shirley led Ms. Donna to the small brown table located in a nook within the kitchen.

"Here it comes," sighed Ms. Donna as she sat down.

With eyes that flashed her emotion, Shirley gave a full account of her new career. She would sell vacuum cleaners and other cleaning supplies at various shopping malls and open air markets.

"We're going up and down the state!" said Shirley. "We'll get to see Sacramento, the Golden Gate Bridge, the beaches, everything!"

The more Shirley spoke, the deeper the frown on Ms. Donna's face became. "How much are you getting paid to do all this?"

"Well, it's not exactly set. We get paid on commission."

Ms. Donna wagged her head. She touched the back of her thick dark hair, "Look what's become of you, Shirley! That man changed you from a God fearing, polite young lady to a woman who wastes her life away and has no sense. You even sound like him!"

Shirley furrowed her brow. "This has nothing to do with *him*."

Ms. Donna maintained her eye contact in silence.

"Momma, I don't need a lecture! Besides, Ricardo's in the past. He's not part of our lives anymore. It's been years since I've spoken to him. For all I know he could be in Puerto Rico right now." Biting her lip nervously, she continued, "Don't you see? This is a new beginning for me! Please, Momma, just give me a little time to pull myself back together. I'm not getting any younger. This could be my last chance."

Ms. Donna furrowed her brow. "Stop that! If your father were alive he would put you over his knee and spank you! You are an intelligent, attractive young lady and you still have so many—"

"Momma!" interrupted Shirley. "Look at me!" She touched the skin below her deep brown eyes. She then played with her fluffy dark hair that rested around her shoulders. "I have wrinkles. My hair's always a mess." She placed her hands on her thick thighs. "These old jeans. They're all I've got. I can't even fit into my nice clothes anymore."

Ms. Donna stared at her in silence.

"Please, if I don't do this my life is basically over."

Ms. Donna shook her head in a disparaging manner. "Shirley, Shirley, Shirley. Are you trying to get me to feel sorry for you? How 'bout feeling sorry for the kids? The only thing they've ever received from their parents is lies and empty promises. Just two people that go in and out of their lives. How do you expect them to feel? I'm the one who feeds them. I'm the one who gets them ready for school. Even Jackie takes Marc out and puts him to work and pays him. How do you think he got that motorcycle? He saved up enough money to buy the parts and then Jackie put it together for him."

Shirley lowered her brow. "Marc has a motorcycle?"

"Yeah, Jackie takes him out in the country and they ride together— even Devan goes with them. If you paid more attention to your own kids you'd know that."

Burying her face in her hands, Shirley exclaimed, "Momma, please, I know I haven't been a good mother, but that's why this is so important!"

Ms. Donna remained resolute. She folded her arms in front of her chest. "Why should I believe you? This isn't the first time you promised to make things right. How do I know you're not just going to smoke and drink all day and end up worse than you are now?"

"Because this time I'm not waiting on Ricardo to rescue me," replied Shirley. After taking a deep breath, she raised her head and continued, "I know he's not coming back. It's over between us. I accept that. The only chance I've got—the only chance my kids have—is if I can get back on my feet again. It's up to me, now."

After a long pause, Ms. Donna replied, "I don't know. It sounds like this could take a while." Then, scratching the back of her head, she continued, "You know I live off your father's pension. Most of his life insurance is gone. Marc's a big boy. He eats like a man."

"I'll give you all my food stamps!" said Shirley. "And if I make enough, I'll send you part of my check, too."

"Shirley, please! You're probably going to need what little money you make," replied Ms. Donna. "Besides, if you do start making something that welfare check is gonna stop."

"No, it won't. They pay us in cash."

"Well, that doesn't seem right."

"Momma," said Shirley, scowling, "I don't think my little check and some food stamps are going to break the government."

After a slight pause, Ms. Donna asked, "How long?"

"The first tour is six weeks."

"Hmmmmm," purred Ms. Donna.

"Hey, hey!" interrupted a cheerful voice. Both women turned to face Jackie, who had entered the kitchen directly from the outside patio. He was wearing the usual combination of brown working boots, faded blue jeans, white cotton shirt, and his inseparable blue cap. "What's all this shouting I hear?"

"We weren't shouting," said Shirley.

"Your sister's leaving us again, but this time for six weeks!" said Ms. Donna with a crooked smile.

"You're leaving again?" asked Jackie, arching his brow. "Where to this time? Timbuktu?"

"Very funny," said Shirley. "No, I got a job in sales."

"Really?"

"Yes, really!" said Shirley with pride in her voice. "And when I get back, I'm getting a place of my own!"

Both Ms. Donna and Jackie pressed their lips together and shook their heads in unison.

10

MARC LOOKED AROUND the living room. His sister and brother were seated next to him on a long cream colored couch that could easily seat up to four people. His grandmother was across from him, fidgeting on her old, brown recliner. His uncle remained standing, leaning against the wall close to the only hallway of the house. And standing in the center wearing a snug blue skirt and a white cotton blouse was his mother. She had lost some weight and looked quite attractive.

"I met a man and he's a keeper! His name is Eddy!" said Shirley, a huge smile beaming from her face. Then, flashing a small ring that appeared to be little more than gold plated metal and glass, she continued, "We went to Vegas and made it official!"

But instead of an enthusiastic reaction, she was met with a number of blank expressions from Marc and his siblings, a frown from her Jackie, and a complete look of bewilderment from Ms. Donna.

"Married?" repeated Ms. Donna, her jaw dropping quickly.

"You went to Las Vegas?" asked Jackie with a furrowed brow.

"How old is he?" asked Ms. Donna

"He's in his forties—late forties."

"He got a job?" asked Jackie.

"He works in sales like me. I met him in Tracy. We were on the same team."

"In other words he's not making nothing neither," said Ms. Donna. Then, turning to Jackie, she added, "Or at least she isn't reporting any of that money because the welfare checks keep coming."

"We're making a little," replied Shirley, her smile slowly beginning to fade. Turning to Marc and his siblings, she continued, "But the important thing, children, is that your mom is finally here to stay! And even more than that, you're going to have a father as well!"

"A father?" asked Marc, scowling.

"Yes, baby, a father," said Shirley.

She walked over to Marc and attempted to hug him, but he twisted his body to avoid her.

"Shirley, you're moving too fast for these kids!" said Ms. Donna.

"She's moving too fast for all of us," added Jackie.

"Oh, come on!" said Shirley, crinkling her forehead. "Don't you two understand? This is a special moment! Eddy is a good man! He comes from a small town in Alabama. He's a real southern gentleman and together we can all form a family!"

An awkward silence followed.

"Well, okay then…so, when are we going to meet this Southern gentleman?" asked Jackie.

"Wait right here!" said Shirley, her voice full of excitement. "He's outside in his car!"

"Oh, dear Lord," whispered Ms. Donna as he conspicuously rolled her eyes.

The room became quiet. Within a few moments, Shirley reentered the house with a middle- aged African American man. Of short stature, he was well-dressed, wearing gray slacks, a white collared shirt and a black bow tie that had small white dots sprinkles throughout. Tipping his gray parlor hat, he exposed a full head of salt and pepper hair.

"Good evening ma'am," he stated to Ms. Donna in a thick Southern **drawl.** Extending his hand to Jackie, he added, "and sir. Nice little cap ya got there, by the way." Finally, he turned to the children. "And a fine *howdy do* to all of you as well."

Not a single person uttered a word in response.

"I just want all of you to know that I'm not just passing through," continued Eddy. "I already got us an apartment right here in town."

"Really?" replied Jackie with a raised brow. "And you got that for everyone?"

"Yes, sir!" replied Eddy with great enthusiasm in his voice. He opened his mouth widely, flashing a toothy smile. "It's a three bedroom so there's plenty of room. In fact, this little princess right here will have a room all to herself!"

Eddy began to tickle Lisa's chin, but Marc put his arm around her and pulled her away.

"Kids, we're going to the grocery store to do some shopping," said Shirley, "and then we're going home."

"When are you coming back?" asked Marc.

Shirley smiled awkwardly. "No, baby, I mean we're all going. We—we want to show you the apartment. We fixed it all up."

"That's right!" added Eddy. "And we're all going to celebrate with some barbecue—hamburgers and hot dogs—and some ice cream, too! Y'all like ice cream, don't ya?"

"I love ice cream!" said Lisa.

"Me too!" said Devan.

"Both of you be quiet!" ordered Marc.

"Shirley, may I speak to you for a minute? Alone?" asked Ms. Donna, furrowing her brow.

Shirley nodded. "I'll be right back, Eddy. Why don't you get to know my brother a little better while I talk to my mom in the kitchen?"

Once inside, Ms. Donna whispered forcefully, "Shirley, what in heaven's name do you think you're doing?"

"What does it look like I'm doing?"

"It looks to me like you're trying to force a father—and a mother—on these kids," said Ms. Donna.

Shirley shook her head vigorously. "I should have never come here," she said. "Momma, I'm leaving and I'm taking my children with me."

Ms. Donna frowned deeply.

"Yes, my children," said Shirley, "or do I have to remind you that they're mine?"

"All I'm saying is that you're moving too fast!" said Ms. Donna. "They barely knew Ricardo, and now you're introducing a stranger as their father?"

"I'm their mother and that's all that matters," said Shirley, tightening her jaw.

"It ain't that easy," said Ms. Donna. "These kids don't look at you that way, Shirley, and everyone except you knows why."

"Momma, what is this all about?" asked Shirley. "Are you upset because I'm taking the kids? Isn't that what you always wanted?"

"Of course, Shirley, but not like this."

"Well, I'm doing better now and Eddy's been real good to me. He treats me better than any other man ever did. It's time for me to take my rightful place as their mother."

"Shirley!" said Ms. Donna. "This isn't about you! It's about the kids and what's best for them!"

Shirley took a few steps toward the living room, then quickly did an about face. "I just don't understand you. All my life all you've ever done is tell me how I ruined my life by choosing to stay with Ricardo, or for failing my duties as a mother, and here I am now with a good man, a place of our own, and you're still criticizing me and telling me how I'm doing everything wrong! Well, I'm tired of it! I don't need your help anymore! I can take care of myself, and I can take care of my kids, too. Besides, Eddy said he's always wanted the chance to be a father."

After a slight pause, Ms. Donna asked, "So that's what this is all about? A second chance?"

"I'm leaving, Momma, and I'm taking my children with me," said Shirley. "Oh, and another thing, you won't be getting any more money from my welfare check. Eddy and I will take care of that from now on."

Shirley promptly walked out of the kitchen and returned to the living room. There, Marc was standing next to Jackie as he spoke with Eddy. Devan and Lisa remained seated in their exact same spots on the sofa.

"So you a single man? I don't see no ring," said Eddy.

"Yeah, for now," said Jackie.

"What's that supposed to mean?" asked Eddy.

"It means I got a real nice girl—name's Gloria," said Jackie. "But we're not married."

"And she's fine!" interrupted Marc.

"Now don't be talking like that, boy," said Eddy, wagging his index finger in Marc's face. "That's a lack of respect!"

Marc looked at his uncle curiously. "What did I say?"

"No, it's all right," said Jackie. "She is beautiful."

"So what are you waiting for? You should be tying the knot, young man!" said Eddy.

"I might, soon enough, but I wouldn't want to marry her before I knew I had something to offer," said Jackie, arching his eyebrows. "You know, rushing in and all that."

Shirley cleared her throat.

"What?" asked Jackie, shugging his shoulders and raising his hands.

"Nothing," she huffed.

"Yes, well, I've been looking forward to getting to know y'all," said Eddy as he placed both hands in his pockets. "So, is *Jackie* short for *Jackson?*"

"No, actually, it's a nickname I've had since I was a boy."

"So what's your given name?" asked Eddy.

"Robert," replied Jackie.

Eddy cocked his head back. "Robert? Now how in Sam Hill do you go from Robert to Jackie?"

"'Cause he can fix anything!" said Marc. "Ain't that right, Uncle Jackie?"

Eddy quickly furrowed his brow at Marc. "Excuse me, son, but this is an adult conversation we all got us here."

Marc squinted his eyes. "Huh?"

"You keep interrupting, boy, and that's not something you should do when two men be talking," said Eddy. "You need to learn to stand there politely like your Momma's doing right here."

"What the hell?" exclaimed Marc.

"Marc, you know your grandmother doesn't like that kind of language in her house," said Jackie.

"Sorry, but this guy's getting on my nerves."

Devan and Lisa giggled from their seated position on the couch.

"It stands for Jack of all trades," said Jackie. "Ever since I was a kid I've been good with my hands. Always loved taking things apart and putting them together again. My father died when I was still pretty young, so I had to fix things in the house. Then I started doing odd jobs for people. Now I do it for a living. Not too long ago I went independent and made it official."

Jackie reached into his pocket and handed Eddy a card.

"Is that a fact?" replied Eddy, smiling. He studied the card for a moment. "How much money you be making?"

"That's none of your business!" said Marc.

Rubbing Marc's shoulders, Jackie said, "You'll have to forgive my nephew. I'm probably the only real male role model he's had in his life."

"Well, that explains a lot," said Eddy, frowning. "Based on what I've seen here, it doesn't look like you've been doing enough."

"Now hold on there," said Jackie, crinkling his forehead. He removed his blue cap and ran his hand through his thick dark hair. "You think ten minutes makes you an expert?"

"Ten minutes is more than enough to see this boy needs a firm hand to teach him to respect his elders," replied Eddy.

Shirley nudged Eddy. "Um, honey, we really need to go."

Turning to Devan and Lisa, Eddy rubbed his hands together and said, "Yes, sir! Yes, sir! We're going to buy us some steak and potatoes, some greens, and of course some ice cream for you children!"

Shirley smiled while Jackie frowned.

Eddy bent down slightly and asked Lisa, "You have a favorite flavor, sweetheart?"

Marc looked with disapproval as his siblings smiled and sprung to their feet. Reluctantly, he followed them as they jumped into an old blue Dodge. Jackie took a few steps outside the door as well.

"Please give my regards to your lovely mother," said Eddy, tipping his hat.

"Yeah, I'll do that," replied Jackie.

As Eddy and Shirley ushered the children into the car and slowly pulled away from the house, Jackie stood with his lips pressed tightly together.

11

As they approached the round counter of the register, Marc remained standing. The expression on his face emanated his boredom. He bit his lower lip. Turning to his mother, he said, "Hey, we're gonna check out the magazines and stuff."

"No, Marc, stay here with us and help," said Shirley.

Ignoring his mother's pleas, he began walking down one of the wide corridors of the grocery store. His brother and sister followed him **methodically**.

A moment later, Eddy scooted past a few people to join Shirley at the front of the line. He placed a bag of hot dog buns in the grocery cart. "Where did those kids run off to?" he asked.

"Who knows," replied Shirley.

"Should I go looking for them?"

"No, they're probably keeping an eye on us. They'll catch up."

Eddy frowned. He and Shirley then began putting their items on the counter. After paying the cashier, they pushed the shopping cart outside the sliding windows and headed toward the parking lot. Once at the car, Eddy opened the trunk. He and Shirley inserted several brown paper bags within. Suddenly, Marc appeared with Devan and Lisa.

"You want to help put those groceries in the trunk?" Eddy asked Marc.

"No thanks," Marc replied dryly.

Eddy curled his lips as Marc opened one of the side doors and sat in the back. Devan and Lisa quickly followed.

As they drove down one of the main streets that led to their apartment complex, Lisa suddenly shrieked, "Give it back! They're mine!"

"Come on, just give me a little bit!" said Devan.

"No!"

Devan turned to Marc. "Tell her to give me some!"

"No, she's right. If you wanted candy you should have jacked it!" said Marc.

"What are you kids arguing about?" asked Eddy.

Marc could see his eyes through the rearview mirror. His brother then tried to reach over him, but Marc shoved him back.

"Hey! Hold on there!" said Eddy. Then, turning to Shirley, he asked, "Where did they get those things? Did you buy them that stuff?"

Shirley shook her head and made a humming sound.

"Soda pop, a magazine, and candy..." muttered Eddy. "Did you kids buy those things?" His question was reciprocated with silence. "Uh-huh. I see how it's gonna be."

When they arrived at their new place of residence, a complex of two-story apartments, Shirley entered carrying several bags of groceries while Eddy stood in front of the faded brown door. Across the wall were various patches of missing paint and crumbling stucco. "I can see it will be my job to instill some respect and structure into your lives."

Marc looked away.

"Are you listening to me?" asked Eddy, walking up to Marc. A small man, his eyes were barely above Marc's own.

"Well? You don't got nothing to say?" asked Eddy, standing mere inches away.

"Not really," said Marc, "Now can you back off 'cause your breath smells like old beer."

Eddy frowned, sticking his lips out slightly. "You don't think I have the right to instill values in your life, boy?"

"I don't even know what that means," said Marc.

"You don't know what *values* are?"

"No, that other word."

"What other word?"

"Instill," said Marc.

"Well, now, I see. You know what you kids lack?" asked Eddy. His eyes shifted from Marc to Devan and then to Lisa. Marc took a deep drink from his bottle of soda pop. Devan buried his face in his magazine. Lisa plopped a few candies into her mouth. "A good education, that's what," continued Eddy. "Lucky for you, I'm just the man to teach you kids. The Lord Almighty must have put me in your lives to give y'all proper instruction."

"Are you done yet?" asked Marc, impatiently. "I'm hungry, man. I thought you said we were going to eat some great meal and have some ice cream."

"Okay, okay," replied Eddy. "Fair enough, but I want you to answer me just one question before I let y'all go inside. What kind of grades you be getting in school?"

"Who cares, man, I'm hungry!" said Marc. He motioned to his brother and sister. "I'm going inside. Come on!"

"Not so fast!" said Eddy, putting his hand on Marc's chest. "I asked you what kind of grades you be getting. I'm also wondering if you sass your teachers like you be sassing me."

"Man, first of all, you better get your hands off me before I bust you up. And second, why do you care? I don't even know you. Besides, you talk funny."

Marc bumped Eddy as he walked past him. Devan flashed eyes that expressed his unwavering support for his brother. And even little Lisa curled her lips and narrowed her eyes, creating an expression as threatening as her cute little face was capable of producing. Eddy stood alone in front of the door, his mouth agape.

12

As EDDY SOUGHT more influence over Marc, the wedge between the two widened. It also trickled down to affect the entire family. Marc's primary strategy to combat Eddy's growing influence was to spend as little time in the apartment as possible.

"Where's that boy of yours?" asked Eddy, a large bottle of gin in his hand.

"I don't know," said Shirley. She was dressed in a thinly layered blue nightgown. "He's probably at my mother's house."

"Did he ask you permission?"

Shirley downed a mixture of vodka and orange juice. Her eyes had a glazed look to them. "What was that?" she asked.

"I'm going after him!" said Eddy. "That boy needs to know he can't just come and go as he pleases! This is his home now and he needs to be talking to me, not Ms. Donna and not your brother, Mr. Jack of all trades!"

Eddy jumped into his car. As soon as he arrived at the house, he stormed across the small cement entrance and banged on the door.

"Yes?" asked Ms. Donna, frowning quickly upon seeing Eddy.

"My—oh—my!" blurted Eddy, poking his head forward. "Something sure smells good! Y'all got some chicken and mashed potatoes going on, don't ya? Maybe some dinner rolls and butter?"

"That dinner is for my grandson," said Ms. Donna, her wide girth not giving any ground at the entrance of the door. "Now how may I help you?"

"I'm just here to talk to Marc," replied Eddy. "He disobeyed me by coming over here—say, you got room for one more at the table?"

"No, I don't," said Ms. Donna, "and Marc's busy cleaning the carpet."

"Marc be working over here?"

"Yes, he is, now if you'll excuse us—"

Before Ms. Donna could finish closing the door, Eddy pushed it open and forced his way inside the house. There, Marc was pushing an old black vacuum cleaner in up and down strides.

"Hey, boy!" shouted Eddy. "Why don't you turn that thing off? We need to talk!"

Marc looked at Ms. Donna before responding. She nodded. Marc then promptly turned off the machine, ending the noise.

"Who said you could come over here without reporting to your mother and me?" Eddy continued. "It's late and we didn't even know where you were!"

Marc smirked in response. "Why do you care? All you and my mom ever do is drink all day! At least here I can get something to eat."

"We feed you kids!"

"That's not what I hear," interrupted Ms. Donna. "Devan and Lisa told me all they eat is pizza and candy and drink soda. That is, if there is something."

Eddy scowled deeply. "That's not all they eat," he replied. Then, as a slight pause, he added, "I told Shirley she needs to cook more, but she just ain't much of a cook. And besides, they be getting breakfast and lunch at school."

"We're usually too late for breakfast," said Marc. Then, turning to Ms. Donna, he added, "This dude and my mom are always drunk, and I'm the one who has to get everybody ready for school. They don't even wash our clothes!"

"Now, Marc, she's still your mother and Eddy's married to her," said Ms. Donna. "Mind your manners, son."

"Yes, ma'am," replied Marc.

"'Yes, ma'am'?" repeated Eddy, his eyes widening slightly. "Since when did you learn these manners, boy? Look at you! Showing respect and cleaning over here! Why don't you act like that with us?"

"'Cause it's different over here," said Marc.

"What's that supposed to mean?" asked Eddy.

Marc furrowed his brow. He looked down and then back to Eddy. "It means they aren't hypocrites."

Eddy smiled, exposing his large buckteeth. "Hypocrites? Well, now, we finally got us some educated speech here. Where did you learn that word?"

"From me," interrupted Ms. Donna, "and I think he used it very well."

Eddy frowned. He then turned to Marc. "Well, are you coming home with me or not?"

"Yeah, after I'm done working."

"And after he's eaten," added Ms. Donna.

"How you gonna get home?" asked Eddy.

"I'll have Jackie drop him off," said Ms. Donna. "And I'll send some food over to the children—and only for the children. In fact, I may ask Jackie to go inside and make sure they get it."

"Excuse me?" said Eddy, puffing out his slight chest. "I'm not going to just stand here and listen to you presume you can tell me what is going to happen in my very own house!" He shook his head. "Where I'm from women know how to speak to a man!"

"You can't talk to my grandmother like that!" said Marc, stepping closer to Eddy. "And anyway, you don't even have a house. This is a house. You're just renting an old beat up apartment."

"Boy, shut your mouth!" said Eddy, his eyes flashing.

Ms. Donna raised her arms and stepped between the two, her considerable girth instantly separating them. She took a deep breath. "Eddy, I'm going to ask you to please go home. Jackie will make sure he arrives to your *house* within an hour. Is that acceptable to you?"

Eddy's eyes darted from Marc to Ms. Donna. "Yes, I approve. Just make sure he's not late or there's going to be some real consequences."

"Yes, you have my word," replied Ms. Donna.

Eddy tipped his hat softly and turned to leave. Once gone, Marc erupted. "Ms. Donna, why did you act all nice to him like that?"

"Now, Marc, you need to calm down."

"You should've let me take care of him," said Marc, still breathing heavily. "I could knock that little fool out with one punch!"

"Marc, that's enough!" said Ms. Donna firmly. "I didn't raise you to be some type of hoodlum. Remember that the Lord Jesus said to turn the other cheek."

"Well, maybe he did but if Eddy gets up in my face again I'm gonna sock him in the eye!" Marc clenched his fist and flexed his bicep. "I'm bigger than him and he knows it!"

"Stop talking nonsense, finish your chores, and then have a nice home cooked meal," said Ms. Donna, rubbing Marc's shoulder. "I'll call your uncle. We promised that man that you would be home within an hour."

"Yes, ma'am," replied Marc. He grabbed the vacuum cleaner, quickly finished a spot in the corner by the couch, and promptly washed his hands. Then, he sat down and eagerly downed the meal Ms. Donna had prepared before him.

13

EDDY OPENED THE glass door of the liquor cabinet. He mixed a few drinks and handed a glass to Shirley. "Don't worry, honey, everything's going to be all right."

Shirley nodded as she reached out to take the drink.

"See? I even put a little umbrella in it! Give it a touch of class!"

Shirley nodded.

Entering the door, Marc immediately threw a pair of dark yellow gloves on the sofa.

Eddy scowled at him. "Boy, how many times have I told you not to throw your grubby clothes all over my furniture?"

"*Your* furniture? You bought all this stuff with my mom's welfare checks!" snapped Marc. Then, looking around the living room and the tiny connected kitchen, he asked, "Where is everybody?"

Eddy turned away.

"Have you been crying?" Marc asked his mother. He then noticed her red lipstick and long eye lashes. She was wearing a white dress that reached below the knees. "And why are you all dressed up?"

"Marc, honey," began Shirley, putting down her drink. "Come sit down. I need to tell you something."

"Can it wait? I'm hungry! Uncle Jackie didn't have time to get me anything. He just paid me and dropped me off. I haven't ate nothing since school."

"How much money did he give you?" asked Eddy, his eyes suddenly brightening.

Shirley frowned deeply. "Not now, Eddy, we have to tell him."

Eddy shrugged. He rubbed the back of his thick, unkempt salt and pepper hair. "Well, maybe I should take him out and we can order food for everyone. It might go over better that way."

Marc shook his head at him. "I'm not buying you nothing." Then, looking at his mother, he asked, "What's going on?"

"Marc, honey, we got a call from the child protective service. It seems some teacher poked her nose where it doesn't belong and reported that Lisa was being neglected."

Marc lowered his brow. "What does that mean?"

"It means they took her away from us."

"What? No...no..." Marc backed away from her. "Where's Devan?"

"He's in his room—your room."

"I'm tired of this!" Marc screamed in his mother's face. "It's bad enough you guys waste all your money drinking all day, but now they took my little sister away!"

"Marc, we're going to get her back! Don't worry!" said Shirley. She reached out to touch Marc, but he quickly walked away.

"They took my sister away!" shouted Marc as he paced up and down the tiny living room.

"Your sister is my daughter, you know!" said Shirley.

"She isn't your daughter!" said Marc. "You've never taken care of her!"

"Hey, hey now, that's enough, boy!" said Eddy. "Now you get on back to your room with your brother! We'll take care of this."

"Aw, shut up!" said Marc. "You're nothing but an old lazy drunk!"

Eddy walked up to Marc. "What did you say to me, boy?"

"You heard me!" said Marc, looking at Eddy defiantly.

After a short pause, Eddy continued, "I haven't had a drink all day. I've been busy attending your mother. We both went to the court house sober and looking our Sunday best."

"You're not like Ms. Donna! You don't even go to church, so what do you know about looking your Sunday best?" shouted Marc. He then took a step closer to Eddy, his wide forehead nearly touching Eddy's nose. "Now when is my sister coming back?"

"Don't you get up in my face like that, boy!" said Eddy. He then grabbed Marc by the neck. Without hesitation, Marc pushed him back and then punched him square in the nose. Eddy instantly fell to the ground.

"Marc, no!" screamed Shirley.

"I already told you never to touch me!" said Marc, standing menacingly over Eddy.

Rubbing his temples, Eddy shook his head slowly. He then touched his nose. When he brought his hands in front of his face, his fingertips were covered in blood. He snorted a few times and slowly got back to his feet. "You really done it now, boy! I've had all the disrespect I'm gonna take from you kids! That brother of yours wasting his time looking at those hot rod magazines, your sister complaining about this and that, and you…"

"What? What are you going to do?" asked Marc.

"You're about to find out," said Eddy with a chilling calm in his voice. He then walked toward the bedroom he shared with Marc's mother.

Shirley called out, "Eddy, Eddy, what are you doing, honey?"

"Something I should have done a long time ago!" he shouted from within the other room. "I'm going to teach that boy some respect!"

"I'm right here!" said Marc. "I ain't going no where!"

"Oh, that's good," said Eddy, reappearing from the bedroom, "because then I won't have to go out looking for you!" He lifted a pistol. "Yeah, that's right, who's the bigger man now, huh?" He waved the gun in Marc's face with his finger placed firmly on the trigger. "This is how men settle their differences in the South."

Marc looked at Eddy's eyes. They were practically leaping out of their sockets. The redness gave him a crazed look.

"Now, are you going to respect me, boy?" asked Eddy, placing the gun directly on the very center of Marc's forehead.

A mixture of sweat and tears began to drip from Marc's face. He shifted his eyes toward his mother. She stood stiffly with her mouth agape.

"Hey! I'm talking to you!" said Eddy, poking Marc in the forehead with the barrel of the gun. "If you respect me, you nod your head up and down. And if you don't..."

Marc remained still. Eddy then tightened his finger around the trigger of the pistol until it slowly crept backward. Once again, Marc looked at his mother. She nodded. Marc unconsciously did the same.

"All right. It looks like what we have here finally is an understanding. Boys got to respect men, you see." Eddy spoke slowly between heavy, nervous breaths. "Now, I'm only going to say this once. You get out of my house and don't come back 'cause if you do, I will kill you, boy. You understand me? I will kill you."

Marc remained motionless.

"Well, get going!" said Eddy,

Frozen in his position, Marc slowly moved his neck, then his hands, and finally his legs.

14

INSIDE THE HOME of Ms. Donna, Marc sat on the couch. His head was placed firmly between two hands that were rolled up into fists, almost giving the appearance of a large solid rock lying atop two smaller stones. Ms. Donna sat on her sofa reading a book. Soft music was playing on the radio. Suddenly, a familiar blue cap broke through the entrance. It was Jackie with Devan at his side.

"Well, here he is," said Jackie. "Tried to talk some sense into Shirley, but Eddy kept interrupting. At least they agreed to let Devan come with me."

"You did well, Jackie," said Ms. Donna.

Devan raced to Marc, who smothered him in a warm embrace.

"I still say we need to call the police," said Jackie.

"I say we go over there right now, Uncle Jackie, and give Eddy a hella beat down!" added Marc, waving his fist.

Devan nodded.

"Now, now," said Ms. Donna, wagging her index finger in Marc's face, "none of that language in my house. Vengeance is the Lord's, Marc. You'd be wise to remember that."

"So what do we do, Momma?" asked Jackie.

"We need to fight for custody and get Lisa," replied Ms. Donna. Then, after a deep pause, she added, "And you boys are going to have to go stay with the Sanchez family in Los Angeles."

"Wait a minute!" said Marc. "We can't go there! Come on, Ms. Donna, you have to let us stay here with you!"

"You will, honey, just not right now.

"No way! We're not going back there! I hate it there!"

Ms. Donna laid her hand on Marc's shoulder. "I will send for you and your brother as soon as I'm able."

"You—you don't want us here?" asked Marc, his eyes pleading to her. "But why? You have room."

"Marc, Marc," interrupted Jackie, "come over to the kitchen for a minute. You too, Devan. I need to tell you something." Jackie then turned to Ms. Donna. "Momma, why don't you sit down."

Ms. Donna nodded.

Once inside the kitchen, Jackie took a deep breath. "Look boys, your grandmother didn't want to say anything, but she's about to have surgery."

Marc raised his brow. "Surgery? What for?"

"You know Ms. Donna's been sick for quite a while…. Well, she's been battling breast cancer. She's had treatment, but just when they think she's got it licked, it comes back. Surgery is her only option. I've been looking after her and taking her to treatments, but she told me not to say anything."

"Why didn't she want us to know?" asked Marc.

"I don't know," replied Jackie. "She probably didn't want you all to worry about her. Look, this whole situation has left her weaker than ever. All of this stress isn't good for her. Lisa, your mom, Eddy. Look, as soon as things calm down, I'll go to Los Angeles and get you."

"Uncle Jackie, let us stay with you at least!" begged Marc.

"Marc, you know there's no room in my little apartment, and I'm usually out working."

"They barely speak English and Uncle Braulio is crazy! That's the only reason he's not locked up! He stabbed some dude, remember?"

Rubbing the back of his neck, Jackie replied, "Marc, I know, I know. But that was a long time ago. He's on medication now."

Marc, unconvinced, shook his head vigorously. "Come on, Uncle Jackie, please! Devan and I will work for you—for free! We'll sleep on the floor. I need to help you all get Lisa back!"

Jackie put his arm around Devan, affectionately pulled him up to his chest, and hugged him. "You don't say much but I know you're just as worried as your older brother. I see it in your eyes. You got the same big brown eyes and the soft face of your..." His voice trailed off. He then grabbed Marc around the neck with his free hand. "And you, my big man, strong jawed and tough as nails."

Marc smiled.

"Truth is," continued Jackie. "I just couldn't handle both of you boys right now. To be honest with you, Gloria and I just got engaged. We were talking wedding dates, buying a house—then all this happened." Jackie paused. He took off the blue floppy cap that continually rested on his head and scratched the top of his head. Readjusting his cap, he then rubbed the patches of black, puffy hair on his cheeks that somehow formed a slight beard. "Marc, I'm sorry, but I agree with your grandmother. For now, it's the best solution."

"It's all Eddy's fault!" said Marc.

"That's probably true, but right now he's the one taking care of your mom, and she lets him do as he pleases."

The boys nodded in agreement.

"Marc, you've looked after your brother and sister all your life. I know you care about them. I know you love your grandmother, too, so go to Los Angeles for the summer and I promise you this will all work out in the end."

Marc blew out a long gust of air. He looked up to his uncle, who stood a few inches taller, and nodded slowly.

15

MARC FELT UNCOMFORTABLE attending school in Compton. He found his surroundings very different than the rural settings to which he was accustomed. The classroom was small, crowded, and the desks appeared old and dirty. Urban kids were different. They seemed rough to Marc. They seemed to know so much more.

"Hey, what are you, man?"

Marc turned to see a tall, thin African American boy sitting behind him with black hair that formed a razed shadow on his small, circular face.

"What?" asked Marc.

"Are you black or Latino?" the boy continued, drawing the attention of others in the classroom.

Marc lowered his head.

"You Samoan?" asked a student sitting across from him.

Before Marc could answer, the student sitting directly in front of him, a chubby boy with thick black hair and brown skin, joined the conversation. "*Eres de Centroamérica, verdad?*"

"I'm a little bit of everything," said Marc.

"Cool," said one boy.

"He's going to have to decide what he is sooner or later," replied another.

"You new here?" continued the boy sitting across from Marc.

"Yeah," said Marc.

"You in a clique?" asked the boy behind him.

"No, man," replied Marc.

"Where do you live?" asked the boy in front of him.

Marc looked at them. He then left his desk to speak to the teacher, who was standing in the front center of the room behind a thin wooden podium. "Excuse me, Mister."

The teacher furrowed his brow and frowned. He was African American and had a youthful, yet very professional appearance. His hair was closely clipped. The glasses he wore had very thin lenses. He was dressed in a dark red long sleeved collared shirt with a bright golden silk tie. "That's *Mr. Holloway.*"

"May I move to another side of the room?" asked Marc.

"Well, everyone is seated alphabetically."

"I don't feel comfortable where I'm at."

"And why is that?"

Marc looked back at some of the boys who were seated next to him. Some were black. Some were Hispanic. Most of them were dressed in the same loose fitting blue jeans and oversized T-shirts. To his dismay, all of their eyes were upon him.

"I want to remind everyone that we still have a few minutes before the bell rings," said Mr. Holloway. Directing his attention back to Marc, he continued, "Sit down and at the end of the period, we'll talk."

When Marc walked back to his desk, the boy across from him whispered, "You got a problem, homey?"

Marc ignored him.

"Crying to the teacher like a little bitch," muttered the boy who sat behind him.

As the bell rang, one of the boys next to Marc bumped him as he walked by. Marc looked him directly in the eyes. He was taller, but slenderly built. His facial hair seemed to indicate that he was a few years older.

"Watch it, bro," he said threateningly, giving Marc a menacing look before smiling to his friends.

Marc waited until the classroom was empty before approaching his teacher once again. "Listen, I'm not trying to cause trouble; it's just that you have me next to all the bad kids."

Mr. Holloway removed his glasses and rubbed his eyes. "Perhaps," he said. "It's the first day, so it's going to take a while for me to get to know everyone. But in this class probably most of them are going to be problematic."

"What does that mean?" asked Marc.

"It means that you are in basic math—a freshman course."

"But I'm a sophomore."

"Yes, and so are most of the kids in this class—some are even juniors. That's what happens when you don't pass Pre-Algebra—you repeat it."

"So how do I get out of this class?" asked Marc.

"Hard work. The counselors place students based on their level. What class did you take as a freshman?"

"I don't remember. Most of the stuff seems the same, though. I'm not from here." Then, as an afterthought, Marc added, "Last year was a bad year. I missed a lot of school, but I'm not dumb."

"I'm sure you're not, and really that's true for most of these kids. They're not dumb. In fact, some of them are actually quite sharp. It's just that they use their brains to steal or sell drugs instead of seeing the big picture."

"So this school has a lot of gangs?"

Mr. Holloway paused. "I wouldn't say that, but in certain classes you are going to see kids who are gang affiliated. They may not all be active, but if push comes to shove, they choose sides. Crips, the Piru Bloods, one of the Compton Varrios, the MS. Even the Samoan kids are starting to form gangs. Do your best to stay away from them, but I know that's easier said than done."

Marc nodded.

"We do have some great kids here, and many go on to achieve great things, but you're not going to see a lot of them in this class." Mr. Holloway inclined his head. He seemed to be contemplating his statement. "There's always a few diamonds in the rough. But sadly, they're the exception at this level. Most of these kids won't even make it to their senior year."

Marc hoisted his backpack around his shoulder and started to leave. Suddenly, somewhat unconsciously, he asked, "What's the big picture?"

But before his teacher could answer, a new set of students began to noisily enter the room. Marc stared. There was something different about them. He could not decide what it was. Their clothes were different, but it was more than that; it had something to do with their faces.

"Hey, what's up Mr. Holloway?" said a boy who appeared to be around Marc's age. He had dark skin, a shaved head, and an angular face. A certain friendliness wafted from him. "I brought you this." He then pulled out a large red apple and held it up for all to see. While some of his classmates laughed, others moaned at his antics. He proceeded to blow deep breaths on the piece of fruit and rub it on his shirt before handing it to his teacher. "For my favorite teacher."

Mr. Holloway smiled, showing evenly placed blocky white teeth. "An apple, Kenny? Really? Isn't that a little old school?"

"Yeah, you could have given him a gift card or something!" said a girl from the back. She was wearing shorts and sandals and had a shirt with a USC emblem emblazoned on the front.

"Well, what did you get him?" asked Kenny. As the girl smiled and shrugged her shoulders, he continued, "Yeah, exactly, that's what I thought!"

"All right, all right, you guys, settle down, now," said Mr. Holloway. "It's the first day so you can sit where you want, but you know how it works. After the first test, I'm making a seating chart."

Kenny lingered for a moment before offering his hand to Marc. "Hey, what's up?"

Marc grasped his hand and shook it slowly. He then watched Kenny walk straight toward an attractive girl sitting down in the front row.

"What class is this?" Marc asked Mr. Holloway.

"These guys are sophomores, like you," replied his teacher, "but this class is Algebra Two. It's an Honors class."

"I get it. These are the smart kids."

"Like I said," replied Mr. Holloway, "that's not always the case. Sure, these kids are intelligent, but what separates them from most of the kids in your class is that they know where they want to be in ten years and what it's going to take to get there. That's the big picture."

Marc observed the various faces, loud enthusiastic voices, and laughter that filled the room. "You don't seem so strict with these kids."

"Yes, I give them a little more freedom. Here," said Mr. Holloway, handing Marc a hall pass. "Stay focused, study hard, and then maybe you'll find yourself in a different class."

"All right, thank you."

"And in the meantime, I'll move you to the very front," Mr. Holloway called out as Marc headed for the door.

Throughout the rest of the day, Marc did his best to orient himself with his classes and the school campus. During lunch, he sat next to a few other boys, but did not talk to them. Instead, he ate his food in silence. When his last class had finally ended, he let out a deep breath of relief that he had made it through the day without any major confrontations.

On the way to meet his brother, Marc passed an elementary school. Passing several children, he noticed a group of small boys following him. At first, he ignored them, but as they got closer and closer, he stopped. Turning to face them, he asked brusquely, "What do you want?"

"Hey, you want to buy some crack?" asked one small boy, dangling a little plastic bag in the air.

Marc gave him a hard look before continuing on his way.

"It's cheap!" shouted the boy.

"Come on back, dude!" shouted another.

Ignoring their calls, Marc made his way toward his brother's middle school. After several blocks, he reached the campus. Marc looked around the sea of faces passing him on the sidewalk.

"Hey, you know a kid named Devan?" Marc randomly asked a boy who stood before him.

"Devan who?"

"Devan Wilson."

The boy furrowed his brow and shook his head.

"I don't know any boys named Devan, but what's your name?" called out a girl with long black hair that hung down to her waist. She was leaning against a stone wall that had the letterhead of the school embedded inside it. Next to her were two other girls. All three were wearing blue jeans and cotton blouses with tight sleeves that hugged their arms.

Marc smiled, but then suddenly saw his little brother walking toward him. "Oh, there he is, but thanks anyway."

"You still didn't tell me your name," she continued. "My name's Irma."

"*Me llamo Pilar*," said another.

"Uh, sorry, we gotta go," replied Marc.

As the two boys walked down the sidewalk, Marc asked, "How'd it go?"

"All right. I liked my science class. The teacher said we're going to build stuff."

"Anybody give you trouble?"

"No."

16

MARC'S PLAN TO live quietly was beginning to unravel. He was successful at avoiding trouble at school and rarely walked the streets of Compton, but he found that conflict was inevitable while in his new home. His paternal grandfather was rarely home, working from dawn until dusk; and his grandmother mainly stayed to herself in her bedroom. That left the boys alone with their uncle. Confirming Marc's fears, he found out that Braulio had been diagnosed with schizophrenia and struggled with an addiction to heroin. His constant mood swings and overbearing demeanor kept the boys continually on edge. Because of this, Marc and Devan made a pact to never leave each other while at home.

While Marc watched television, Devan kept his eyes on the pages of a hot rod magazine.

"*Oigan, muchachos*, ask your abuela for some money. I need to buy some *chiva*," said Braulio.

Marc attempted to ignore the wrinkled, gaunt face of his uncle. His black hair was long and dirty and his handle bar mustache gave him a menacing aspect.

"*Oye, baboso*, I'm talking to you," Braulio continued, standing directly over Marc.

Once more, Marc ignored him.

Braulio then grabbed the remote control and turned the television off.

"Hey!" exclaimed Marc. "I was watching that!"

"*Cállate la boca, mocoso!*" replied Braulio. Then, turning to Devan, he continued, "How 'bout you? You got money?"

Devan remained silent. Marc, looking straight at his brother, made circles with his index finger around his temple. Devan laughed but kept his face buried in his magazine.

"Maybe this will help you," said Braulio, ripping the periodical out of his hands.

"Hey! Give it!" said Devan, aggressively grabbing his arm.

Braulio promptly slapped Devan in the face. "Sit down, *mocoso!*

"Hey! Don't touch my brother!" said Marc.

"Nobody tells me what to do in *mi casa!*" replied Braulio.

Before he could say another word, Marc rushed him and tackled him to the floor. As the two boys rolled on the carpet, Braulio shouted threats and obscenities at the top of his lungs. Struggling to gain the upper hand, Marc fought to get on top of his uncle. Once secure in a dominant position, Marc held him there by shoving his forearm into his throat.

"I'm gonna kill you! I'm gonna kill you!" shouted Braulio. "Get off of me!"

"Calm down!" said Marc.

"*Cállate! Te voy a matar! Suéltame!*" screamed Braulio at the top of his lungs. His eyes bulged as the words flung out of his mouth.

As Marc strained to control him, Braulio continued to scream, flailing and thrashing about wildly. Finally, he succeeded in knocking Marc off of him, reversing the position. Marc looked up to see his uncle kneeling over him, gnashing his teeth. Saliva dripped from his mouth. His red eyes were full of rage. Braulio slowly brought his face closer and closer to Marc's own. As Marc felt a singe of panic, a foot came thundering down onto Braulio's head, knocking him to the ground.

"*Oh, Dios mío!*" said the boys' grandmother, rushing out of her room. "What you boys doing to my son?"

"*Abuela!*" said Marc. "No, no, no. It's him! *Es tío!*"

"*Mamá, me quieren matar!*" said Braulio, rolling on the floor.

"You leave him in peace!" said Mrs. Sánchez in her broken English.

Marc, somewhat confused, stared at his grandmother while Braulio quickly stood up and hurried to his room, slamming the door behind him.

"*Oh, por Dios, ahora tengo que tratar con los tres!*" said Mrs. Sánchez. She then returned to her bedroom, slamming the door shut behind her.

Breathing heavily, Marc turned to his brother. "Can you believe that crazy fool?" Then, taking a deep breath, he huffed, "Man, that was scary! I thought he was going to bite me or something!"

Marc stooped down to pick up his brother's magazine that had been tossed to the floor. He then burst into laughter.

"What's so funny?" asked Devan.

"You kicked him in the head!" said Marc, practically choking to get the words out.

At first, Devan smiled shyly, but then he too began to laugh.

"You kicked his head like it was a soccer ball!" said Marc between laughter, wiping the tears from his eyes.

17

"*HOLA, MUCHACHOS*," GREETED Mr. Sánchez. He was an elderly man, with long fleshy cheeks and a notable mixture of gel and thinning black and gray hair that formed an inverted triangle upon his high forehead. A very slim mustache rested above his upper lip. Besides the family albums which hung on the wall, he was the closest resemblance the boys had of their father. Marc possessed only the faintest of memories, and Devan could not recall the man named Ricardo Sánchez.

"*Hola, señor*," replied the boys in unison.

"We go to the store today," he continued. "You boys come? Yes?"

"Do we have to?" asked Marc.

"No," he replied slowly, frowning. "You stay home. *Tu tío se queda con unos amigos.*"

"Uncle Braulio will be with his friends?" asked Marc.

"*Sí, así es.*" He lingered a moment. "*Pues, tu abuela*—she in the car already. I go now."

Marc smiled at Devan, who promptly reciprocated. Having the home to themselves for the first time, they quickly grabbed two cans of sodas from the refrigerator and a few bags of chips. Then, they settled onto an old brown couch in the living room as they searched for something on television to watch. Turning the lights off, the boys leaned against the soft cushions. Their leisure lasted a few hours until their uncle returned. To Marc's surprise, Braulio entered the house and without saying a word, made his way directly to the kitchen and opened the refrigerator.

"I can't believe he didn't yell at us," whispered Marc to his brother.

Watching him curiously, Marc observed Braulio as he cautiously stirred a black sticky substance with a straw onto a small spoon. Getting up from his seat, Marc went to the refrigerator and grabbed another can of soda. "What are you doing?" he asked.

"Agua de chango," replied Braulio. "Now get out of here!"

Marc rolled his eyes and quickly made his way back to the couch next to Devan.

"What did he say to you?" whispered Devan.

"I think he said something about a monkey."

"Huh?"

"I don't know," continued Marc. "He's crazy. He's drinking pancake syrup."

"But he doesn't have any pancakes," said Devan.

Marc shook his head and made the familiar motion of moving his index finger in a circular motion next to his ear. This always brought a smile to Devan's face. As the two boys settled into the couch, the sound of the television show was interrupted by the heavy snorting that came from the adjoining kitchen.

"What the hell?" exclaimed Marc. He turned to see Braulio holding a spoon to his nose.

"What's he doing?" asked Devan.

"I don't know," replied Marc, "but I don't think that's pancake syrup. Just stay cool. Hopefully, *abuelo* will come home soon."

Marc glanced behind his shoulder. There, standing next to the stove, he observed his uncle with a huge smile on his face. Moments later he was kneeling next to Marc with a knife to his throat.

"Don't think I don't know what you're up to!" whispered Braulio.

Marc moved his eyes as far as they would go in an attempt to see his uncle, but all he could make out was his shadow in the darkness, a hand, and a knife shaking quickly. Devan slowly walked toward them.

"Don't!" growled Braulio.

"What—what are you doing?" Marc stuttered.

"Don't act like you don't know! You're trying to take my place!"

"Braulio, stop it," said Devan.

"Cállate!" He pressed the sharp blade of the knife closer to Marc's skin, causing a slight indention on his neck. Then, whispering in Marc's ear, he continued, "I heard you. You want my mother to love you more than me. I heard you say—I heard you say you want to take my place!"

Marc began to breathe heavily through his nose. Devan continued to stand as close as he could.

"That's right," whispered Braulio into Marc's ear. "While you were watching me, I was watching you. I saw you…waiting…"

Marc swallowed. His right arm began to tremble.

"…for me to fall asleep."

"Uncle Braulio," whispered Marc. "No one's trying to replace you. We just want to watch television. Now, please, let me go."

"No! No! No!" shouted Braulio. "I won't let you get rid of me!"

"Okay, okay," said Marc slowly. "Just let me go and me and my brother will leave."

"Leave?" Braulio repeated. He lessened his hold on the handle of the knife.

"Let us get our stuff and we'll walk out that door and never come back."

"Yeah, let him go," said Devan.

Braulio scowled. "No! You're not going to replace me! You're not going to replace me! You're not going to replace me!" He then gripped the knife more firmly.

"No one is going to replace you, *tío*," said Marc. "I don't even want to be here. Really, let me go and I'll leave. I promise."

Braulio stood erect with his eyes fixed straight ahead. After a brief silence, he whispered slowly through his clenched teeth, "Okay, *márchense y no se lleven nada!*"

Marc got up slowly as his uncle withdrew his hand. He continued to point at the boys with the knife.

"Okay, okay, we're leaving," said Marc.

"What about my jacket?" asked Devan.

"*Váyanse!*" said Braulio.

"We just want our jackets," said Marc.

Braulio raised the knife in his hand threateningly. "*Váyanse!*"

Grabbing Devan by the arm, Marc led him quickly out of the house.

18

AFTER ROAMING THE streets for hours, Marc became scared. As the night crept in, he knew that he and his brother were not safe.

"Should we go back?" asked Devan. "I'm getting hungry and it's getting cold."

"Me too, but let's keep walking," replied Marc. "We'll find something on Compton Boulevard—make a phone call—figure out something."

As they continued, they stumbled upon a little restaurant. The aroma of grilled chicken and cheese dripping into the night air caused them to stop.

"Are you thinking what I'm thinking?" asked Marc.

Devan nodded.

"Come on," said Marc, walking inside. He looked at the simple plastic tables that were covered with thin green tablecloths. A few tables were occupied. A little English could be heard, but it was mostly drowned out by the Spanish speakers.

"Hey, uh," started Marc hesitantly, approaching a woman at the counter. She was small, with thick black hair to her waist, and her dark face contrasted with her very bright red lipstick. "My brother and me are lost," continued Marc. "We just need to make a phone call. And we're kind of hungry. Could you help us? We'll work for it. I'll go back there right now and clean dishes if you want."

The woman curled her upper lip, then replied flatly, "Wait here."

A few minutes later, she returned with a man at her side. He had a dark complexion, was small of stature, and below his high cheek bones was a bushy black mustache that seemed to cover half of his face.

"Hi," began Marc, "could we use your phone, please?"

The man blinked a few times.

"Do you speak English?" Marc asked. "*Teléfono?*"

"Looks like you need more than a phone call," replied the man, pointing at Devan, who was shivering due to the cold night air.

Marc looked at his brother but did not reply.

"Do you speak English?" asked the man. "*Por qué te echaron de la casa?*"

"Um, are you asking us where we live?" asked Marc.

"No, I asked you why you were kicked out."

"Sir, please. Honestly, we don't really have a home, but we're not bad kids. We just need to make a phone call. My brother and I will even work for it."

"I tell you what," said the man, tapping his fingers against the front counter. "I'm from Guatemala. I know what it's like to be in the streets. Come in the back with me and wash dishes and anything else my brother tells you to do. After that, you can have your phone call and we'll even throw in some *mole de plátano y unos tamales*."

The woman arched her eyebrows, and then curled her lips once again.

"Come," she said, showing little enthusiasm.

Marc and his brother followed her past the kitchen and into a small back room. There, a young man was washing dishes. He was clean-shaven, but other than that he appeared to be a younger version of the first man the boys had met.

"*Un poco de ayuda por la noche*," she said, frowning. "*Deciles lo que necesitas*."

"*Perdón? No entiendo*," he replied.

She turned to leave. "*Preguntale a tu hermano*."

"Um, okay, *hablan español* or do you guys speak English?"

"English," replied Marc.

"Well, I'm Justo. Hmmmmm. Orders are orders, I suppose. Okay, you, big guy," he began, pointing at Marc, "start washing dishes. Then, pointing at Devan, he continued, "And you, take out any trash you see outside and grab that broom."

19

"No answer," said Marc despondently. He put the phone down. "I don't get it. I called Ms. Donna and Uncle Jackie."

"Maybe we should go home," said Devan.

"Where's that?" asked Marc.

"With *abuelo* and *abuela*—"

"—and Braulio," finished Marc. "I don't think so."

Justo entered the kitchen area of the restaurant. "So is someone going to pick you up?" he asked. "It's getting pretty late."

Marc hesitated, then replied, "We can't get ahold of anybody."

"What are you going to do?"

Marc looked at Devan. He had a car magazine in his hands. "Where'd you get that?"

"It was on one of the tables I cleaned."

Marc shook his head.

"Look," said Justo, "if you need a place to stay, we've got a few extra blankets. I have a room in the back. Danilo set it all up for me."

"Is that the cook?" asked Marc.

"Yeah, and my brother and the owner of this fine establishment," said Justo. "It's just the three of us. Danilo, Fátima—that's his wife—and me."

"So you live here?" asked Marc.

"Yeah, my brother's place is pretty small, and they've got the kids and Fátima's mother. My little room in the back, though, is pretty nice. Got a bathroom, a shower, my own desk. Besides, this way we don't have to invest in security."

"Are you sure he'll let us?" asked Marc.

"Wait here," replied Justo.

He disappeared for a few minutes, and then returned with two blankets in his hands. Smiling, he said, "Danilo said you guys will provide more security. Sorry, no pillows, though. Maybe tomorrow we can find you some."

Marc watched closely as Justo laid a few blankets on the floor next to his mattress. Cautiously, he signaled to his brother to lie down.

"*Buenas noches, muchachos.* I've got some reading to do, so hopefully my desk lamp won't bother you too much."

But there was no answer. Marc and his brother were fast asleep.

20

DANILO, HIS DARK slacks and white collared shirt loosely flowing with each movement of his slight frame, passed by the large metal sink located in a tiny room adjoined to the main cooking area. Suddenly, he stopped. "You're a hard worker, Marc, and you pick things up fast."

Marc turned. Water dripped off his orange rubber gloves. "Thanks, Danilo. Trust me, I can do a lot more than wash dishes and pack stuff. My uncle taught me how to do a lot ever since I was a little kid." He then lowered his head.

"Still no answer?"

"No, I've called my grandmother every night. If we're eating too much…" Marc's voice trailed off.

"*Tranquilo*!" said Danilo, holding up his hands. "You've only been here a few weeks. Besides, the food we give you guys is not much—mostly *las sobras*. Justo will take you and your brother to Goodwill™ on Saturday to get some clothes."

Marc stared at Danilo a moment, and then replied, "Thank you."

Danilo smiled, causing his thick mustache to curve slightly. "I'm sure it won't be long, and if it is, things will work out. You'll see."

21

MARC'S EYES SHIFTED toward his brother, who emanated a silent nervous energy. His lips were pressed closely together and his hands were raised, demonstrably revealing crossed fingers. With a slow nod, Marc began to press buttons. After several ring tones, a voice answered, "Hello?"

"Uncle Jackie!" shouted Marc. "Where have you guys been? We've been calling Ms. Donna but she never answers! We left a ton of messages!"

There was a pause on the other side.

"I know, Marc, I know," replied Jackie. "I actually called you a few times, but Mrs. Sánchez said that you and Devan had disappeared. She said she thought you guys were with me. I—I was confused and then with everything else…"

"Uncle Jackie, what's going on?" asked Marc. "You sound different."

"Yeah," replied Uncle Jackie. Then after a deep breath and yet another long pause, he added, "A lot has happened, and I haven't gotten much sleep lately. I'm just glad you guys are okay. I could never have forgiven myself if something had happened to you. Especially now."

Marc waited for further explanation, but when none came, he proceeded to press his uncle. "Uncle Jackie, tell me."

"Marc, we got Lisa back."

"Cool!" said Marc. "I knew Ms. Donna could do it!" Marc turned to his brother and informed him of the good news.

Devan jumped in the air.

"Marc, there's more," continued Jackie. "Your mother's problems—Lisa—and you boys living over there. The strain was too much for your grandmother."

"What do you mean?" asked Marc. A chill passed through his body.

"Your grandmother took a turn for the worse. She's been in the hospital, and…"

"And what?"

"Ms. Donna passed away last night."

Marc nearly dropped the phone. Devan, standing next to him, furrowed his brow. He silently mouthed, "What?"

"Marc? Marc? Are you there?" sounded Jackie's voice. "Marc!"

"Sorry, Uncle Jackie," replied Marc, grasping the phone more firmly. "I…I…"

"It's okay," said Jackie. "You don't have to say anything. Your grandmother battled as much as she could, but the cancer spread. She was really weak. It was just a matter of time, I'm afraid."

"But why?" asked Marc, his voice cracking.

"What do you mean?"

A few tears formed in Marc's eyes. "The doctors. Why didn't they save her?"

"They tried," said Jackie. Then, after a brief silence, he continued, "Marc, I know how you feel, but there was nothing else they could do."

"Why not?"

"I don't know. I'm not a doctor. Look, we all feel terrible. I promise we'll talk more about your grandmother, but right now I need to know what's going on. Where are you? Your brother's with you, right? You're both safe?"

"Yeah, yeah, we're doing all right," said Marc. "We're living with a guy at a restaurant."

"What?"

"It's a long story, but we're okay."

"So you're both safe?"

"Yeah, we're good," replied Marc quietly.

"That's a relief. Hey, things are moving too fast. I need to take care of…stuff…and then get you boys back over here. Can you hold out a few more days?"

"Yeah, of course," whispered Marc. After a brief pause, he added, "Devan wants to talk to you, but don't tell him."

"I won't. Not now, anyway," replied Jackie. "Marc, it's gonna be okay. Gloria's been helping a lot. She's going to marry me, Marc, and we're going to take care of you all. Momma—Ms. Donna—she made us promise that we would keep you all together."

"That's great, Uncle Jackie," said Marc flatly. "Um, here's Devan."

Handing the phone to his brother, Marc wrote down the address of the restaurant on a piece of paper and showed it to him before leaving it on the counter.

22

WHILE DEVAN LAY still in the little room located in the back of the restaurant, Marc put on a pair of dark shorts and a white cotton shirt. They fit snugly on his thick, muscular frame. Getting down on his knees, he crawled toward two blankets and an old pillow that were spread on top of the cold cement floor. Once there, he sprawled out his body before propping himself up with his elbow. Above him was the familiar light of a small desk lamp.

"Hey, Justo," said Marc. "Sorry to bother you, but I just wanted to thank you for all you've done for me and my brother."

Justo, sitting at his old metal desk, put his book down. "Don't worry about it, Marc."

"I still can't believe it," said Marc, shaking his head.

"Believe what?"

"Everything," said Marc. "You took two kids off the streets that you didn't even know. You fed us, got us clothes, a place to stay."

"*Tranquilo*," replied Justo. "Where we're from, there's a lot of kids in the streets with no food and no clothes…too many."

"Well, it's late, and my uncle said he'll be here tomorrow morning. I guess I better get some sleep."

"Okay, man, *qué descansés!*"

Justo lowered his head toward his book. Silence followed.

"And even though he might not say it, I know Devan's thankful, too," said Marc from his position on the floor. "Someday, I'll make it up to you. I'll ask my uncle if he can pay you guys. If not tomorrow, then real soon."

"Marc, it's okay," said Justo. "And this isn't '*adiós.*' It's only '*hasta luego.*'"

Marc furrowed his brow. "I thought those things meant the same thing."

"Well, '*adiós*' means you are leaving someone; '*hasta luego*' means 'see you later.'"

"Thanks, Justo." After a brief pause, Marc smiled. He then noticed the books underneath the light of the small lamp. He sat up and put his arms around his knees. "You going to study all night?"

"Yes, of course," said Justo flatly.

"Seriously?"

"Yeah, seriously."

"But why?"

"Because I don't want to sleep on a floor all my life."

"How's a book going to change that?"

"These aren't just any books; they're my textbooks."

Marc got up to his feet. Taking a closer look at Justo's desk, he saw titles pertaining to economics and business.

"You're in college?"

"Yes, I am," said Justo. "Well, technically it's a university. I'm finishing my MBA."

"Your what?"

"My MBA," repeated Justo.

Marc laughed. "Aren't you a little short to be playing basketball?"

"MBA stands for Masters in Business Administration. Education is everything, Marc."

"Education?" repeated Marc incredulously.

"Yeah, education," said Justo. "Schools, libraries, the internet..."

Marc frowned deeply, then shook his head. "It can't be that important. I mean, I get by. I read pretty good, and my uncle never even went to college and he owns his own business."

"Really?" said Justo. "What kind of business?"

"He's a handyman. He fixes stuff."

"Like what?"

Marc stuck his chin out proudly. "Anything. Carpet, tile, plumbing, cabinets, even some electrical stuff. He taught me quite a bit, too."

"That's good, Marc, but let me ask you something. Does your uncle make much money doing this?"

"Well, he's not rich, but he does all right."

"How big is his business?"

"You mean, like, how many homes does he fix?" asked Marc.

"More than that. Does he have an office or a store where clients enter and speak to personnel? Does he have affiliates? How many people does he employ? What kind of mechanisms does he have in place to ensure maximum profit?"

Marc looked down for a minute. He rubbed the back of his head. "It's not like that. I mean, he has a few of his buddies, and I help him a lot, but it's mostly him."

"Look, Marc, I'm not trying to put your uncle down. He sounds like Danilo. I'm sure he's a great guy—and a talented one. I'm just saying that maybe he could do better. Does he understand tax deductions? Does he understand payroll? Does he understand advertising? Has he established business credit?"

Marc paused. "Um, I don't know. I've never heard him talk about that stuff. Maybe you could help him with all that."

Justo laughed. "I would love to! First, though, I have to get through to my own brother!"

"Danilo doesn't let you do all that here?"

Justo frowned. He raised his hand, tilting it from left to right. "He allows me do a little, and slowly we're becoming more profitable, but the truth is he's just not very ambitious. He's happy to get by. For him, getting out of Guatemala and taking over this business was enough. But he still struggles. The guy works nonstop, but he doesn't have a whole lot to show for it. It reminds me of what Thoreau said." Justo paused before raising his hands in dramatic fashion. " 'The mass of men lead lives of quiet desperation.' "[3]

Marc raised his brow and shook his head. "I don't even know what that means."

"It means that most people only survive, Marc," said Justo. He shook his head. "They're just living day by day with no real purpose."

"I guess you're right. I wish my family had more money," said Marc. "I probably wouldn't be in this mess right now. I wish I was rich."

Justo pointed his index finger at Marc. "No, no, no! Maybe I'm not explaining myself very well. I'm not studying just to make money. Yeah, it's important, but money is just a means to an end."

Marc shrugged.

"Look, I'll break it down," said Justo. "You've heard of the lottery, right?"

"Yeah, of course."

"Well, did you know that most of the people who win end up losing it all?"

"Yeah?"

"Yes! It's true! They can't handle it! They spend all that money on homes they can't afford long term, or they buy fancy cars, or they open businesses that they don't know how to run. Or worse, they just waste thousands and thousands of dollars on luxurious vacations, jewelry, clothes..."

"Man, that's sad," said Marc.

"It is," said Justo. "It's very sad, and it's all about education. They needed to be empowered, but instead, they simply drowned. All that money was too much for them. Francis Bacon was right."

"Bacon?" asked Marc, crinkling his forehead.

"Yeah, the great philosopher...?"

Marc smiled widely, showing his slightly stained teeth. He then rubbed his temple. "Man, this is embarrassing, but at first I thought you were talking about food!"

Justo let out a loud chuckle, but then quickly covered his mouth.

"Don't worry," said Marc, looking over at his brother. "We could have an earthquake and that guy would keep sleeping."

Justo smiled and nodded. "Anyway, I wasn't referring to a *chancho*! I was alluding to the famous quote 'knowledge is power.' "[4] After a slight pause, Justo continued, "Look, Marc, it's really late, but let me just say this. Take your education seriously, okay? Don't waste it! Enjoy every day you spend in school and make the most of it!"

"Yeah, okay, I'll try, but I'm not going to lie. School is kinda boring."

"Boring?" Justo repeated, his eyes glowing under the light of his desk lamp. "Marc, how can you say that? Is it boring to learn about the most fascinating people in the world? Is it boring to read about the most passionate romances? The greatest battles? The most incredible inventions? No, no, no; I'm sorry, but school is not boring. Maybe you are boring, but school is not boring!"

Marc frowned. He lay down on his blankets that were spread out on the floor. Finally, he muttered, "Well, that sounds pretty nice the way you say it, but my teachers don't teach us like that."

"They probably do," said Justo, "but maybe you're not listening."

23

JACKIE, WEARING HIS trademark blue cap, threw in a small bag full of clothes and closed the back door of his jeep. In the front seat was a woman with short dark hair that curled around her ears. Her high cheek bones and bright eyes made her quite conspicuous. It was Gloria. Sitting behind her was Devan, and next to him, Lisa. Marc, however, remained standing on the pavement of the restaurant parking lot. He lingered behind while Danilo and Justo approached his uncle.

"I can't thank you both enough," said Jackie, extending his hand. "Are you sure I can't offer you something?"

"No, these boys worked hard while they were here," said Danilo. "Besides, they—they kind of remind me of some other boys I used to know."

Danilo turned to face Justo, smiled, and walked away.

"Well, I guess this is it," said Jackie. "Come on, Marc, we better go."

"Sure, Uncle Jackie, I just want to tell Justo something."

"Oh, okay. We'll be waiting for you in the car."

"Thanks," said Marc as his uncle walked away. "Hey, man, I just wanted to tell you that I'm going to work harder in school—and one more thing—*hasta luego.*"

Justo smiled. "Marc, remember you told me that you couldn't believe that Danilo would let you and your brother live with us?"

"Yeah, you said it wasn't a big deal. That where y'all are from a lot of kids are in the streets."

Danillo nodded. "Well, that's true. But there's more to it. The real reason is that you remind him of himself and Devan reminds him of me."

Marc cocked his head back. His brow lowered. "Really? How?"

"We were alone, too, Marc, just two boys a little older than you and your brother. Growing up, we had no father. And then, our mother died. We buried her and decided right then and there that we would save every *lempira* we could get our hands on and leave Guatemala. When our opportunity came, we hiked through the jungle and hopped on top of a train. It took us through the mountains and then to Mexico. I can still see them throwing rocks at us and shouting..." Justo paused. He cupped his hands around his mouth. "*Váyanse! Malditos indios!*" He inclined his head. "It was dangerous. Between the Mexican bandits and the police, many didn't make it. *Guatemaltecos, hondureños, salvadoreños....* They were all looking for a better life. Some were killed. Some were thrown in prison. We were the lucky ones. We made it past Mexico. We made it here."

Marc stared silently.

"Marc, if you could have anything—anything in the world—what would it be?" asked Justo.

"I don't know."

Justo raised his hand and pointed at Marc with his index finger. "Yes, you do!"

"Well, I guess there's something..." said Marc before his voice faded.

"Say it."

"Okay," whispered Marc, hesitantly. "I wish there was a cure for cancer."

Justo swallowed. Then, with a very serious expression, he said, "Find one."

24

"DOCTOR WILSON?" ASKED the young man.

"Yes?"

"Perspective, sir," reminded the student.

"Oh, yes," replied Doctor Wilson, his mind slowly coming back to the reality of the white cement walls of the university hospital. "There are many factors, I suppose," he continued, still somewhat disoriented.

"Sir," interrupted a young woman, "Was it due to your traveling? You said earlier that you have participated for many years in the organization Doctors without Borders."

"Yes," replied Doctor Wilson, "without doubt. We must travel the world to truly understand it, but I don't think that alone brings about the right perspective."

"Was it your personal studies?" asked yet another intern.

"Excuse me?"

"Your personal studies, Doctor Wilson, with the Ronald McDonald houses^{TM}."

"Oh yes," he recalled, "those were invaluable. By speaking with the family members of the patients, I was able to gain real insight into their personal lives, their suffering, their hopes…. Part of the process of developing the correct perspective as a physician is to understand the human element of our patients. We are not merely treating diseases; we are treating people, and these people have real feelings of fear—fear of the unknown, fear of pain, fear of death."

Doctor Wilson paused. He felt in **limbo**. As he looked at the interns who had gathered to hear him, their faces blurred.

"Sir," said the young woman who had earlier questioned him, "You mentioned the words 'calling' and 'passion.'"

Doctor Wilson smiled. This young lady understood. "Please, follow me," he said before walking outside the large staff room and down a hallway. On each side were rooms with closed doors. A chart hung in a plastic tray on the outside of each one. Once at the end of the hallway, Doctor Wilson stopped. The students slowly stopped as well, bunching up against each other to fit within the narrow space provided them.

"You have to have a reason for being a doctor, or a surgeon, or whatever you become, and that reason must burn within you," said Doctor Wilson. "My brother is one of the best, if not the best, formula one auto mechanics in the country, and I'm not saying that just because he's my brother. It's a fact. He's loved cars ever since he was a boy. I can assure you that he would work on those powerful engines for free, but fortunately for him the job pays quite well. And my sister, she's a social worker. She works long hours and in my opinion deserves a much higher salary, but she loves her work. She's a very sweet woman, but when it comes to protecting kids, she's a tiger." Doctor Wilson raised his hand, clawing through the air. Several students laughed. "So, why am I telling you this?"

Faces turned in an array of directions. Some inclined their faces toward the floor. Some turned away. Others remained fixated on Doctor Wilson.

"We were discussing the concept of perspective. How we view the world around us. When we have the right perspective, we begin to understand our purpose in life, our calling. We all have one. A unique mission to fulfill in this world."

Doctor Wilson approached the students more closely. Raising his hands in front of him, he made an outward motion. Slowly, they moved as the parting of a sea. Doctor Wilson walked between the two newly formed lines that clung to the walls. He cupped his hand to his ear. The room became even more silent until only the faint voices of nurses and various medical staff could be heard.

"Listen! There are people on the other side of these doors. They are calling out to you: 'Help me! I need you!' " Doctor Wilson looked directly into the eyes of each intern. "You…are…my…only…hope." He paused. "Will you obey the call?"

The room was filled with a tangible sense of eagerness mixed with a droplet of self-doubt. No other questions were asked.

"You have begun a **heuristic** journey," continued Doctor Wilson. "One that will lead you up the peaks and down through the valleys. Will you fail for lack of knowledge? Will you fail for lack of effort? Life is a gift. Accept this gift and fulfill your life purpose by doing so."

Novel 6

HIDDEN POTENTIAL

1

WILLIAM DEAN, OR *Billy* as he was known, was about as ordinary as a boy could be—or so he thought. He lived in Bloomington, Indiana, known for its beautiful landscapes full of grassy fields and trees, country hospitality, and of course, Indiana University. Billy easily blended in with his community. Growing up, he was always of average height and weight. His short brown hair and brown eyes were typical enough. He was not so handsome that people would instantly notice him, but there was a certain pleasant aspect to him. He did not excel at music or sports, but he did play in the school band and participated each year on the basketball team. Billy was what most people would call *average*. So average, in fact, that he often became lost in the crowd.

Besides the three seasonal sports of football, basketball, and baseball, Billy did venture out once in an attempt to try a different athletic activity. It was more of a whim. He had just finished the eighth grade when his best friend, Brett Dreardon, pushed him to do so.

"You might as well try, man, because you love to swim and you've had lessons from the Rec," said Brett, referring to the Recreation Center. Every child and teenager had been involved in the Rec's many programs at one time or another.

"I don't know," Billy replied. "Those high school guys are total studs. Some of them are even eighteen years old!"

"I'm not talking about them! There are two groups. The club is for everyone. It's the swim team that competes. The Rec club starts with little kids, so anyone can do it! It's just for fun! You'll see kids younger than us and some that are older—like the girls." Brett paused to elbow Billy and smile at him. "Trust me, the club's nothing like the swim team. Those guys compete in private meets. They're serious, but you don't have to compete like them unless you want to. I mean, you know, if you're ready. Besides, most of their meets are during baseball season."

Billy nodded. He understood that in Brett's world everything revolved around baseball. "I don't know..." repeated Billy before his voice trailed off.

"Come on! It'll be fun! You love to swim! Besides, how else are we going to beat the heat?"

Billy paused. He was not so keen on having to swim with smaller children, and he felt intimidated at even the thought of competing against older students. However, he did feel that he would have fun with Brett and he was sure he knew at least a few other kids at the Recreation Department. "Okay, let's do it."

2

THE FIRST DAY did not unfold even remotely in the way Billy had expected. He had dreamt about jumping off the diving boards, having fun with his friends, and watching pretty girls in their bathing suits. Instead, to his dismay, he learned that the club program was merely a funnel for the swim team. Coach Miller was very strict. The practices consisted primarily of drills: practice laps, flip turns at the edge of the pool, dives, stroke relays. Instead of enjoying himself leisurely, Billy was feeling dizzy and slightly nauseated as a result of the many flip turns. Water constantly flowed through his nose and mouth, causing him to choke and gasp for air.

"Let's go, people!" shouted Coach Miller, walking the sidelines of the pool like a drill sergeant. "The only way you're going to graduate from here and make the swim team is if you increase your speed!"

Just when Billy had lost all faith in the possibility of having fun, Coach Miller blew his whistle and said, "Okay! Open pool for thirty minutes!"

Twenty kids of all ages burst into cheers. Some began splashing each other. Others quickly formed games of Marco Polo and a few older kids ran toward the diving boards.

"Now this is more like it," muttered Billy.

"Hi!" rang a high-pitched voice.

Billy looked around but did not see anyone. Then, he spotted a petite girl with middle length blonde hair, bright blue eyes, and a smattering of freckles across her button nose and upper cheeks. She had a huge smile on her face, revealing slightly buck teeth. The water swayed back and forth, touching her shoulders and lower neck at the four foot mark. She had to bobble up and down to keep from swallowing water.

"Oh, hi," said Billy.

"I don't think I've seen you here before," she continued. "Do you want to race?"

Billy released an awkward smile. "Well, um, I don't think that would be very fair. I'm a lot bigger than you and you're..."

"A girl?" she interrupted. "Come on, I don't mind losing."

After some **cajoling**, Billy consented to her challenge. He followed her lead, grabbing the edge of the pool. Then, he set his legs against the cement wall. A few other kids slowly gathered around them.

"I'll give you a three count," announced the little girl with the perpetual smile. "Ready?"

Billy nodded.

"Three...two...one!"

Billy did not exert himself. At the halfway mark, however, he realized that his tiny competitor was ahead of him. With a look of determination, he buried his head in the water, holding his breath as he thrust his arms into the water time after time. But instead of overtaking her, he noticed that even more distance separated the two. When Billy finally reached the other side of the pool, the same enchanting smile that had misled him earlier was waiting for him. "Hey, you're pretty fast. You should go out for the swim team. Bye!"

Billy was **mortified.** He moped around the pool for twenty minutes before being reunited with Brett. "Thanks for a great time," said Billy.

"You're welcome," said Brett, smiling.

Billy glared at him. "I was being sarcastic."

"Oh," said Brett. "Well, don't worry, it will be better tomorrow."

"Tomorrow?" exclaimed Billy. "Uh, no, I don't think so."

"What?" said Brett, raising his brow. He slapped Billy on his naked chest. "Come on, man. You can't quit on the first day!"

"But I just got beat by a girl!"

"That's nothing to be ashamed of! That kid's practically a fish! She's been swimming since she was a baby!" Then, after a brief pause, Brett continued, "That girl's a champ, Billy! She's the youngest member of the swim team! Heck, she'll probably end up in the Olympics someday!"

"Oh," Billy replied, releasing a smile. "That makes me feel a lot better." After a brief pause, he added, "So you mean she can beat you, too?"

"Heck, no!" said Brett with a wide grin on his face. "She's just a little girl for crying out loud!"

3

As with most boys from Indiana, Billy's favorite sport was basketball. It was the one sport that he truly loved. His father had tried to make him a wrestler, but Billy did not like the harsh practices and the constant pushing from his father, who often criticized him for his lack of **aggression**.

Billy's basketball highlights never occurred in a gymnasium in front of large crowds, but rather in the driveway that led to his house. He particularly loved the point guard position, where he could audibly direct the offense and **orchestrate** the flow of the game. Dribbling back and forth, he pointed at imaginary players as he barked instructions.

"Set the screen!" he said. "Post up, man! Use your size!"

"Only ten seconds left," said Billy aloud, imitating the voice of a professional broadcaster. "Everyone seems to be covered. It looks like it's going to be up to Dean to take it himself. He fakes right, goes left and scores with the left hand!"

As the ball swished through the net, Billy raised both of his arms triumphantly, looking around at imaginary foes and awestruck fans. As he turned in a circle, he suddenly put his hands down and frowned. His mind began to wander.

"Why waste your senior year?" Coach Avery had told him in the locker room. "You might as well have a little fun or study a little more so you'll be ready for college. I don't want to hurt your feelings, Billy, but you barely made the team last year. It would be better to give a spot to a junior who might turn out to be something, or even a sophomore. This is varsity, and we have to suit up the best Bloomington High has to offer."

Billy observed the mixture of red and gray hair on the sides of Coach Avery's head. On top he was completely bald. His face was large, but his nose and mouth were small, features that were accentuated by the broad dimpled chin that extended below his lips. Though most of Billy's teammates considered him to be a stern man, Billy found him quite compassionate, especially compared to his father. "Well, if it's all right with you, sir, I would still like to try out for the team. I love basketball... even if I'm not that good."

Coach Avery frowned. He put his hand on Billy's shoulder. "Well, okay, son. You're a good kid, and the other guys like you. Go ahead and try out. I've never had any problems with you and you've always been a good practice player."

4

AFTER SEVERAL WEEKS of grueling practices, Billy did earn his spot. He learned the plays, ran each drill as hard as he could, and yet he did nothing to cause his coach or anyone else to notice him. Once more, he had achieved perfect anonymity. As he walked out of the locker room side by side with Brett, he suddenly stopped.

"Where's your truck?" asked Billy.

"It's broke," said Brett.

"You mean we have to walk?"

"Man, quit crying!"

"Well, how long before it runs?"

Brett removed his baseball cap and scratched his straight black hair. Unlike Billy's, Brett's hair was a little on the long side and somewhat unkempt. "I don't know. I'm working on it. I think it has to do with the fuse box—nothing big. I'll fix it."

As the boys stepped off the school premises, they walked in silence. Billy then looked up to see Brett shaking his head.

"Hey, man, what's wrong with you?"

"Nothing's wrong with me," replied Billy.

"You can fool everyone else, but not me. I've known you since kindergarten!"

"What are you talking about?"

"You! You're so damn **tentative** out there and I'm tired of it!"

Billy crinkled his nose. "You're tired of it," he repeated under his breath.

The boys continued down one of the many country roads that lay on the outskirts of Bloomington. To their left was a large green field, to their right, white wooden houses.

"We play at your house, or my house, and you tear it up," continued Brett, "and then we get together with the team and it looks like you're afraid to do anything."

"I just don't want to mess up."

"Mess up what?" shouted Brett. "You never play!"

Billy curled his lower lip, biting it slightly. "Well, I mean, embarrass myself."

Brett scowled. "You can't think like that! You have to believe in yourself! You have to believe you're gonna win! If you don't think every shot's going in the bucket, then why take it in the first place?"

"Easy for you to say," grumbled Billy. "You're a starter. In fact, you start in every sport."

Brett stuck his chin out, one of the few places on his face not covered with freckles. "Man, you want to know the truth? I was really looking forward to us playing together this year. With your ability to take it to the hole and my smooth stroke, we'd be unstoppable!"

Billy walked silently as Brett made a shooting motion, cocking his left elbow and following through with a snap of the wrist.

"Come on, man, this is our senior year! It's our last chance!" shouted Brett. "Are you telling me you're going to be happy glued to the bench again?"

"No," said Billy, lowering his head, "but I'm just not good enough so you might as well accept it. I have."

Brett stopped walking. He turned away for a moment. Billy followed his eyes toward a man standing in his garage. Brett then turned back to face him, as if satisfied that he could speak openly. "Listen, Billy, back a couple years, maybe that was true, but not anymore. You don't have any excuses, man! I've seen you play, remember? Like last summer, when we went to the gym at IU? You were dominating! Everyone thought you were this all-star being recruited to play there!"

"Well, that was different." Billy replied. "I didn't know any of those guys."

"Exactly! You were free, man! You didn't care what anyone else thought about you. Look, Billy, you need to get over this. I mean, I may not be the best, but when I play, and I mean any sport, it's war, man. I'll do whatever it takes."

"Well, you're a good player, a southpaw and all. If I had your talent things would be different."

Brett scowled deeply. He pointed his index finger in Billy's face. "William, that's a load of crap and you know it!"

Billy stopped. Only on a rare occasion did anyone address him by his formal name. If his father called him *William*, it was usually not a good sign.

"You want to know the truth?" Brett continued. "I'm not better than you anymore."

Billy snorted as he shook his head.

"Naw, man, it's true. You're taller than me, you've got major hops, and you've developed a great jumper. I mean, come on, Billy, you're starting to dunk! No one on the team can dunk besides Hank, and it's only because he's like six-five!"

"Well, it's not a big deal when it's in your driveway," muttered Billy.

"The rim's still ten feet! If you could do it in a driveway, you can do it in the gym."

Billy's eyes widened. He shook his head vigorously. "No, no, no—I could never do that. I'd probably end up losing the ball or clanging it. I'd get laughed off the team."

Brett furrowed his brow. He shook his head. "I don't know what your problem is. When you play at school, it's like you're another person…and to think, your dad's this bad ass cop."

Billy jerked his head up. "What does that have to do with anything?"

"Well, he's your dad, isn't he? How come he's so…?"

"…great while I'm just a nobody?" finished Billy.

"I wasn't going to say that!" said Brett. "I was just gonna say 'tough'…with that flat top and the deep voice…" Brett began taking long strides, tilting his body from side to side. He stuck out his elbows to the sides.

Billy laughed. "He's not King Kong!"

"I know, I know, but wasn't he some champion wrestler?" asked Brett.

"Yeah, we've got trophies with his name on it on top of the fireplace." Billy frowned. "Do we have to talk about this? I get enough of it from our teachers. Some of them went to school with him, and Mr. Murphy's so old he actually taught him!"

Brett flashed a wide grin. "Man, when's Murphy going to retire? Last year, he was in the middle of going over one of our tests and then all of a sudden he forgot what he was talking about!"

Billy laughed for a moment and then suddenly became more serious. "I'm not my dad, all right?" he said, glaring at Brett. "I wish everyone would stop comparing me to him and just accept me for who I am."

"All right, all right," said Brett, smirking. The two boys took several steps in silence. Then Brett added, "Then try to be more like your mom!"

"Huh?"

"Sorry, man, but even your mom's tougher than you!"

Billy crinkled his forehead.

"You're going to look me in the eye and tell me that your mom doesn't have an attitude?"

Billy thought for a moment before answering. "Well, don't compare me to my mom, then!"

Brett laughed and then punched Billy hard on the shoulder. "Man, you're lame!" He whistled loudly. "The whole thing's sad!"

"What is?"

"That you're afraid to be good!" said Brett.

Billy stopped, **stupefied** by his statement.

"Well, you gonna say something or what?" asked Brett.

Billy displayed a shy smile. "You really think I'm good?"

"Don't act dumb!" said Brett. "Of course you're good!"

"As good as you?"

"When you play loose, I'd say you're better."

Billy said nothing in reply, but instead kicked a small rock, causing it to tumble down the road.

"But only in basketball, man," added Brett, grabbing Billy into a headlock. "So don't let it get to your head!"

The two boys began to wrestle. After a short struggle, Billy managed to get loose. He pushed Brett's head and then slipped behind his back. He lifted Brett off the ground and threatened to throw him down.

"Okay, okay," said Brett between laughs. "I guess you learned a little from your dad."

As they got closer to Billy's home, they picked up a few rocks on the side of the road and threw them as far as they could.

"See that tree over there?" asked Brett.

"Yeah, I see it," said Billy.

Brett then cocked back his left arm and threw the rock, sending it whizzing through the air until it made a large thunk on the center of the trunk. Billy nodded approvingly and did the same. His stone, however, curved to the right and landed in the thatch brush surrounding the tree. Brett shook his head and laughed.

When they reached Billy's home, Brett followed him inside and without the slightest hesitation, opened the refrigerator, poked his head inside, and promptly grabbed a carton of fruit punch. "Hand me two glasses, will ya?"

"Sure," said Billy.

His mother, who was seated at a dark round table in the corner of the kitchen, muttered, "Help yourself."

"Oh, thanks, Mrs. Dean," said Brett.

"How was practice?" she continued. With scissors in her right hand, she meticulously cut out letters from one of the many magazines scattered across the table. She then matched them with pictures of various kinds of animals.

"Okay, Mom," replied Billy rather apathetically. He then poured himself some fruit punch as Brett had done.

Brett, filling his empty glass for a second drink, walked over to Billy's mother. "How are those rugrats treating you, Mrs. Dean?"

"They're called first graders, Brett," she replied. "And they don't crawl. They're small children, not babies."

"Oh, yeah, whatever," said Brett. He picked up one of the pictures, arched his eyebrows, and then promptly set it down where he had found it on the table. "It must be fun to play around with those little kids all day."

"Well, yes, it is," said Billy's mother. "You do realize, however, that I'm their teacher and not their playmate, right?"

"Of course!" replied Brett. "But you know what I mean. It's not like your teaching them important stuff like our teachers."

Billy's mother raised her head, showing her youthful tan face. She wiggled her shoulders slightly, causing her wavy brown hair to rub against the table. Billy could see through her deceiving cherubim face.... Her jaw was tightening.

"Well, we're going to study in Jill's old room," said Billy, pushing Brett forward.

"Hey! You almost made me spill my punch!" said Brett, balancing his glass.

"Sorry," said Billy. He then turned to his mother. "Okay, Mom, see ya."

"No, no, no," she replied. "I want to hear the rest of this. What did you mean by that comment, Brett?"

Brett shrugged as Billy continued to nudge him. "What comment?"

"Mom, just drop it, okay?" implored Billy.

"The comment about not teaching my students the way your teachers do," continued his mother.

"Oh, come on, Mrs. Dean," said Brett, "Don't take it the wrong way. It's just that in high school, you have to learn important stuff—like math—or how to write a research paper. We even have physics this year. But in elementary school, you just play around and color all day."

Billy's mother curled her lips to the side. "You know, Brett, teaching elementary school is a very demanding job," she began. "We have a strict curriculum to follow. It's not just fun and games. In case you forgot, I graduated from Indiana University and earned a degree in order to practice my profession. In fact, I was at the top of my class."

Billy rolled his eyes. "Mom, please! We get it! You have a very difficult job and you studied hard in college." He then walked over to his mother and massaged her shoulders. "Okay, now just relax and go back to your difficult task here," he said in a very soothing tone. "Yeah, that's it. Relax. No stress."

"Yeah," said Brett, "and if you need any more coloring books or toys for your classroom, just let me know. My little sister doesn't play with that junk anymore."

Billy's mother slowly began to rise from her chair, but Billy pushed her down gently.

5

THE TIME HAD come; time for all of his hard work to pay off; time to meet the challenge. Billy was six feet tall, strong, and fast. Though not a three point specialist, he had developed a quick midrange jump shot that was practically unstoppable. Along with springy legs and quick feet, he possessed all of the natural attributes to take over a game. Brett was right. Billy decided that it would be better to try his best and fail than settle for being satisfied with a gaffe free performance that offered no risks.

Midway through the team's first full court scrimmage, Billy was outplaying his counterpart, Toby Morris. Though only a junior, Toby was the established starting point guard on the team, and he was not accustomed to seeing Billy play with such intensity. Something had changed, and it became undeniable to the entire team when Billy stole the ball from Toby and dunked it authoritatively at the other end of the court.

"What the…?" shouted the team's starting center, Hank McNamara. He wiped his hand through the sweat that clung to his short blonde hair.

"Henry! Watch your mouth!" bellowed Coach Avery, blowing his whistle in the middle of Hank's expletive. Then, as the gym became silent, he slowly took the whistle out of his mouth. Across from him were ten gaping faces. On the bench were three other boys who were exchanging wide eyed glances. Coach Avery swallowed quickly and stuttered, "Uh, nice work blue team."

"Looks like someone's losing his spot," added Brett, loud enough for all to hear.

"Shut up!" barked Toby. "You know it was luck."

"Jumping like that ain't luck, you idiot!" said Brett.

Once more the shrill sound of a whistle overpowered their banter.

"Guys! Guys!" said Coach Avery. "Come on! Stop gawking and play!"

"But Coach, Billy just dunked!" said Hank.

"I know he did! But there's more to this game than just…jumping high! Now, come on, let's play!"

Hank frowned. Doubt was written all over his face. He then retrieved the ball and inbounded it to Toby, who began dribbling down court.

"You better watch yourself, Dean," Toby snarled. "Make sure you know your place!"

Upon hearing Toby's threatening voice, a sunken feeling overwhelmed Billy. As it did so, he regressed to his normal passivity for the next few plays. When Toby made an uncontested basket from the corner, Billy made eye contact with Brett, who shot him a look of disgust.

"Watch out!" said Brett. "Billy's been sick for a long time, but now that he's healthy you're finally seeing how good he really is!"

Shaking his head, Billy stared quizzically at his friend. Brett punched the air with his fist and scowled at him. Encouraged, Billy nodded and quickly ran up to Toby, squatting inches in front of him. As he did so, he muttered to himself, "I'm bigger than this guy. I'm way better than him. What am I afraid of? Come on, Billy, play your game!"

Responding to Billy's **monologue**, Toby's eyes narrowed. "You talking to me, Dean?"

Billy looked at the snarl on Toby's face. He then looked at the other starting members. They did not seem to know what to make of Billy's new tactics. Doubt entered Billy's mind. As it did so, he slowly loosened his defense and retreated.

"That's it, Dean, let the real players do their stuff," said Toby.

Billy stared at Toby. He became angry. Angry at Toby. Angry at himself. Once again, Billy squatted low in his defensive stance. Toby puffed out a breath of air, then attempted to switch direction and dribble past Billy for a lay-up. It was a move he had done often. This time, however, Billy cut him off by stepping on the dark, thickly painted boundary line. He then completely smothered Toby.

"Dead! Dead! Dead!" Billy called out. A host of blue jerseys responded by playing tighter defense, seemingly inspired to challenge the gold team.

Toby pivoted to his left and to his right. Brett, who could easily have run to his rescue, instead stayed far away on the outer elbow of the court, waving his hands up and down while he shouted for Toby to throw him the ball. Finally, in an attempt to clear space, Toby swung his elbows wildly, hitting Billy hard in the face. Billy responded by shoving Toby in the chest. Stunned by this aggressive reaction, Toby stumbled backward, eventually falling on his behind. A few players smiled. Brett laughed and clapped his hands together in approval.

Toby's head swiveled quickly in all directions. His face then flushed with anger. Rising to his feet, he rushed Billy. "Come on, Dean! You want to start something?"

"Yeah, I do!" Billy replied. He met Toby's charge with one of his own. As he did so, he gave Toby a slight head-butt.

As the two boys stood together, Billy realized for the first time that Toby was quite a bit shorter than he. Billy could see the top of Toby's spiky blonde hair that covered his large round head. He also realized that Toby was not as heavy as he had thought. He had always perceived Toby to be of the same size, or even the more muscular of the two. But observing him up close, it was evident to Billy that though his frame was more streamlined than Toby's, and he possessed longer limbs, Billy also had the wider torso of the two boys.

"Hey! Hey! That's enough!" shouted Coach Avery. "Let's play! Blue ball!"

"Coach, he shoved me!" said Toby. "That's a foul! If this were a real game he would have gotten a technical! Maybe even thrown out!"

"Yeah, but you would have gone first for that elbow," replied Coach Avery. Then, smiling, he added, "I like that defense, Billy. Show me what else you got!"

As Toby shook his head, scowling, Billy received the ball from the half-court line and started dribbling. He distributed the ball to his shooting guard, received a hard screen from Chet, the chubbiest player on the team, and then curled around to the other side of the key. Seeing Billy open, one of his teammates fed him the ball. Billy made one pump fake, causing Hank to sail past him, and then laid the ball in for an easy basket.

Coach Avery nodded with a slight smile. "Let's go, gold team!" he barked. "You're making it too easy on them!"

As the scrimmage continued, Billy's confidence grew. He became more assertive and instead of merely looking for his teammates, he began pulling up for jump shots and driving the ball to the rim. When the final whistle blew, signaling the end of the scrimmage, the blue team had done something that had never been done before. They had beaten the gold team. Coach Avery quickly pulled Billy aside.

"Son, that was amazing!" he gushed. "Why didn't you tell me? I wouldn't have been so hard on you. Now it all makes sense, you being the son of Rick Dean and all."

Billy crinkled his forehead.

"I wouldn't have discouraged you to play this year if I had known," continued Coach Avery. "What is it exactly?"

"Coach?"

"Your sickness."

"Uh," stuttered Billy. "It's a type of…syndrome, sir."

Brett quickly joined the conversation. "It's lupus, Coach, ever hear of it?"

Coach Avery gave both boys a blank look.

"It kind of comes and goes," continued Brett.

Billy furrowed his brow and pressed his lips together. He wiped the sweat from the sides of his face and across his short brown hair.

Coach Avery scratched the freckles on top of his bald head. "Uh, yeah, well, good luck with that, Billy, and great work. I hope it doesn't kick in again because today you were fantastic! I think you're going to have to switch colors for our next scrimmage!"

"Don't worry, Coach," Brett interrupted again. "It's in retention!"

"Remission!" corrected Billy.

"Yeah, remission," repeated Brett.

Coach Avery nodded awkwardly, blew his whistle, and signaled to the rest of the boys to hit the showers. Billy could not help but laugh as many of his teammates came over to congratulate him. All but a very few patted him on the back and expressed their support.

6

DURING THE NEXT few weeks, several students approached Billy to inquire of his illness. Some even apologized for past hazing. Billy never attempted to explain the truth of Brett's silly remark, so the rumor quickly spread that he had bravely battled lupus for years.

On the basketball court, Billy had reached his goal. He was named the starting point guard after three inconsequential years on the bench. And though he knew that Brett's vocal support as team captain had something to do with it, he also knew that his own skill had earned him his new status.

"Hey, you ready?" asked Brett as the boys took shots before their first home game.

"Yeah, I think so," said Billy. He glanced at the old wooden bleachers to his left and to his right. Above him hung cloth banners in his school colors of red and white. Each one represented a conference championship and some went back decades.

"Nervous?"

"A little bit."

"Well, just pretend we're playing at your house," said Brett.

"Thanks, man," said Billy, grabbing a loose ball that bounced his way.

As a loud buzzer sounded, indicating the start of the game, Coach Avery huddled the team together in front of their bench. "Okay, remember, West High has played a zone defense for as long as anyone can remember, so run the stack offense. Look for Hank inside and Brett on the three point line. Billy, if guys start to cheat too far to either side, don't be afraid to drive the lane and make them pay!"

A few players nodded. Brett slapped Billy on the shoulder. As Billy began to take off his sweats, Toby approached him. "Don't worry about screwing up, Dean," he muttered quietly in Billy's ear. "I'll be here to clean up your mess."

Brett turned toward Toby. "What did you say to him?"

"None of your business," replied Toby. "I was just giving the *temp* some advice."

"Yeah, well, you can do that from the bench," said Brett.

The two boys faced each other before Toby slowly sat down.

"Don't worry about him," said Brett to Billy. "Just play your game. We're in your driveway, remember?"

Billy smiled and nodded. He then took in a large breath of air and blew out slowly.

In the initial play of the game, Hank lost the jump ball to the opposing center. The boys quickly went to their man-to-man defense, calling out the numbers of five different jerseys.

"I got twenty-four!" said Brett.

"I got eight!" said Billy.

"I don't remember seeing you before," said Billy's man.

Billy remained silent. He marked his man, staying between him and the basket. Billy was surprised at how careless he was with the ball. It appeared that he was daring him to take a swipe. Billy hesitated. He knew if he were too eager, it could result in a foul. Or, he could overcommit, allowing his man to blow by him. Thoughts of his coach yelling and waving him off the court raced through his mind. He pictured Toby looking at him with a huge smirk on his face as he took his place in the game.

"Run the wheel, run the wheel!" called out the opposing point guard.

Suddenly, Billy made his move. He reached out with his long right arm and knocked the ball loose. It rolled over to Brett, who without hesitation threw it up court. Billy shot off like a rocket. Before anyone could react, he grabbed the ball off the bounce and raced toward the basket. As he passed the free throw line, he took two more steps and planted off his left foot to lay the ball in. With so much adrenaline running through his body, his leap took him much further than he expected. As he rose higher and higher, he actually hesitated in the air before slamming the ball hard through the rim with two hands. As the ball hit the floor, Billy held on to the rim a few seconds before swinging in the air. He finally let go and drifted back down to the hardwood.

Time stood still for a few seconds, but as Billy quickly regained his bearings, he was suddenly overwhelmed by the sound of the gymnasium exploding in cheers. Players were jumping off the bench as Billy came jogging back down the court with a huge grin on his tan face. Even he could not believe what he had just done. His teammates mobbed him, patting him on the back and slapping his head. Brett then shouted at them to get back on defense.

The second time down the court, the opposing point guard had a completely different look on his face. "Who are you?" he shouted as he dribbled the ball cautiously, keeping his body between Billy and the basketball. As the game went on and the team settled down, Billy knew. He was better than his opponent. Faster. Stronger.

When the team's power forward grabbed a rebound and passed it to Billy, he dribbled down the court with new confidence. Calling out the play, Billy could not help but see how much room he was receiving. After the ball went back and forth from one side of the court to the other, Billy then rose for a jump shot just beyond the free throw line. It swished softly through the net.

"Hey, save a few points for the rest of us," said Brett as they ran back on defense.

By the end of the third quarter, Billy and the other starters were called to the bench. They had run up the score and were winning by twenty points. Coach Avery replaced them with the second unit and even a few third unit players who rarely played. Billy led all scorers with twenty points. Brett was next with fifteen.

Once seated on the dark wooden bench, Billy felt a special pride upon receiving a water bottle and a towel. Throughout the fourth quarter, he watched with interest, cheering his teammates on until the final buzzer.

"Hey, Chet!" called out Billy, handing him a towel and a fresh water bottle.

"Thanks, Billy," he wheezed. Though Chet was apt at using his girth to his advantage in the key, he had trouble getting up and down the court. He took a big gulp and returned the bottle to Billy. Wiping the sweat from his face, he said, "Man, I'm not used to playing this much."

The opposing coach walked over to Coach Avery and congratulated him. "So, Tom, who's the new boy? He a transfer?"

Coach Avery shook his head from side to side. "Not at all, Frank. He's been with us for a while."

"Why haven't I ever seen him before, then?"

"He was here. Just sick, that's all," replied Coach Avery.

"Sick, huh? Well, if you don't want to tell me, that's fine. I just hope you're not breaking any league rules."

7

BILLY WAS NOT accustomed to his newfound popularity. Word of his opening dunk in the first game of the season spread quickly. Even a few cheerleaders, as well as other popular girls, were starting to notice him. In the past, they had never done more than acknowledge his presence, but after his first game, some of them went out of their way to greet him and congratulate him on the team's victory.

Besides the attention he received at school, Billy took special pride in hearing his name announced on the loud speaker at each game. As the starters rushed to the center of the court to shake hands with the opposing team's players, their names echoed throughout the oval shaped gymnasium.

The drought was over. Billy was making a name for himself as the season wore on. With each game, his confidence grew by leaps and bounds. He became more assertive and actually discovered a special joy in exploring his talent. Instead of questioning how people would react to his failure, he began to wonder just how good he could become.

As he sat on the wooden floor stretching before his next game, a voice interrupted his thoughts. "You might as well strap your saxophone on and join us!"

Billy turned quickly. Sitting only a few spaces above the bench the team occupied was Steven, the drum major of the school band. He was wearing a large red and white hat, which matched the colors of Billy's uniform. Billy smiled. He was accustomed to the running joke that he should sit next to his fellow band members during games. Pushing off the hardwood floor, he quickly got to his feet and walked over to Steven.

"Not this time," said Billy.

"I bet you can't get thirty."

"You're on," replied Billy. "But if I do, you have to go to the microphone and tell everyone that you're going to do a trumpet solo dedicated in my honor."

Steven laughed. "Let me guess. The Star Wars™ theme, right?"

Billy nodded, and then pointed at Steven with a gun formed with his thumb and index finger.

"I have a better idea," called out a soft voice.

Billy turned, and then quickly moved his head back in surprise. Standing next to him was a girl dressed in a white sweater and a red skirt. Her silvery flute dangled in her right hand. With dark brown hair, blue eyes, and a fresh white face that appeared to have been scrubbed clean, she could have easily been cast in an Ivory™ soap commercial.

"Lor...Lorraine?" stammered Billy.

"How 'bout if you get thirty points, I buy you a hamburger and fries."
Billy continued to stare.

"Okay, how 'bout twenty," she continued, smiling. Her polished white teeth only served to distract Billy further.

"Uh, sure, okay," said Billy. "I'll just have to talk to my parents and, uh, shower of course."

"Yes, showering is a good idea," said Lorraine.

"So, I'll meet you outside later?" asked Billy.

"Sure," she replied.

With his eyes fixed firmly on Lorraine, Billy almost stumbled to the gym floor when an arm suddenly slithered around his neck, choking him. "Billy! Get your butt over here!"

"Huh?"

"The game's about to start!"

Billy struggled to see Brett's scowling face. As he was being dragged away, he clutched at Brett's arm and pushed him off. "Wait! Hold up!" He quickly ran a few steps to get closer to Lorraine. "What if I can't score thirty? Or even twenty?"

Lorraine giggled. Her laughter was sweet and exuded confidence. She quickly covered her mouth. Then, rubbing Billy's bare shoulder, she said, "Oh, come on, Billy. You will. But even if you don't, I'll be waiting for you outside."

8

THERE WAS EXCITEMENT in the air. In every hallway of Bloomington High School students were busy painting banners. Billy could not go anywhere without hearing his name. The playoffs had begun.

In the first round against Central High School, both teams exchanged their best blows. The crowd was on its feet. Brett would make a three-point basket, but the other team would counter. Hank would score on the post, and then the opposing center would answer. The second quarter was more of the same.

While in the visiting locker room during halftime, Coach Avery pointed to Billy. "Everyone's good in the playoffs. I told you boys that there would be no easy games, especially on the road. We're down by two, but I do believe we have one strength they can't counter, and it's at the point. Billy, I want you to be a little more selfish during the second half. I want you to take your man off the dribble and take it all the way to the rim, or if they collapse, pass it off to the open man."

At the start of the third quarter, Billy began the team's high-low offense. Instead of a pass and screen, however, he drove to the basket. The opposing team was taken off guard as Billy laid the ball in for two points. The visiting side of the bleachers, full of Bloomington residents, cheered loudly.

"That's it, Billy!" shouted Coach Avery as he walked back and forth in front of the bench.

Billy glanced over his shoulder in the direction of the bleachers. He could see his parents. His father was nodding affirmatively. Further down sat Lorraine with a group of her friends. She was smiling. After a missed three point attempt by Central High, Brett grabbed the rebound and threw it to Billy. The quick pass jarred him, and he bobbled the ball.

"Take him!" shouted Brett.

Billy nodded. He sized up his man. Dribbling the ball back and forth between his right and left hand, he flew past his defender. Once again, he scored.

"They can't stop you!" said Brett.

After another miss, Hank threw an outlet pass to Billy. Instead of waiting for his teammates, he raced to the other end of the court. As he drove past two defenders on his way to the rim, he was hit hard as he drove into the lane. While still in the air, Billy twisted his body, keeping his eye on the basket. He then released the ball hard off the backboard. He was just able to see the ball fall through the net when he landed on the top of a shoe instead of the gym floor. His ankle wrenched violently, causing Billy to collapse onto the hardwood floor. His smile quickly faded as a sharp pain exploded through his leg. Billy clutched his ankle, gritting his teeth. As he writhed in agony, his teammates quickly surrounded him.

"Give him some air, everyone!" said Coach Avery. "Can you walk, Billy?"

"I can try," he gasped.

Billy slowly got up, moaning in pain. He gingerly placed his left foot on the floor. Coach Avery shook his head. "It's no use, son."

"Billy, put your arm around me," said Brett, helping him to the bench. Then, turning to a few members of the second unit, Brett ordered, "Scoot over, guys. He needs room."

"Hey, Coach, he going to be able to shoot his free throw?" asked one of the referees.

Coach Avery turned toward Billy, who was grimacing in pain. "I don't think so. I'm going to have to sub."

Toby enthusiastically tore off his practice sweats. "I'm ready to go, Coach."

Coach Avery inclined his head, scratched his chin, and nodded. "Okay, go check in."

Passing Billy with a smirk, he muttered, "Tough luck, Dean."

"Hey, don't worry, you're going to be okay," said Brett.

"Yeah," Billy replied flatly, extending his leg horizontally on the bench.

"Brett, we need you in there," interrupted Coach Avery. "I want you to take Billy's free throw."

"Hey, don't go anywhere," said Brett, smiling as he gently slapped Billy on the back of his head. "We'll win this one for you and then you'll help us get the next one."

As Brett ran onto the court, a few players helped Billy take off his shoe. A trainer then came over and put a large bag of ice around his ankle and lower shin. Several adults shouted encouragement to Billy from the stands. His own father worked his way down to the team bench. "Come on, son," he shouted. "I've seen a lot worse. You gotta walk it off!"

"Dad, I can't," said Billy.

"Rick, please, it looks bad," said Coach Avery.

Billy's father frowned. "Come on, Tom, you can't coddle the boy! You need him out there!"

"Rick, could you please sit down!" said Coach Avery. Then, turning to Billy, he continued, "Uh, I didn't mean *real* bad, Billy, but I don't want to take any chances. You're too valuable to the team. Just rest for now and keep that ice on your ankle. We'll be needing you for the county finals."

Billy managed a weak smile in return, but when he looked at his ankle, it had swelled to the size of a softball. He knew what no one else would say. He had played his last game of high school basketball.

9

BILLY HAD FRACTURED his ankle in two places. His leg was set in a cast that reached his lower knee. As he lay on the hospital bench in the small doctor's office, he continually shook his head.

"You're going to need these for about six weeks, Billy," said Doctor Warner, an elderly gentleman with thin gray hair. He handed Billy a pair of crutches. Then, turning toward Billy's mother, he instructed, "You need to make sure he keeps that leg elevated, Trisha, especially the first month."

"Got it," she replied.

Billy put the crutches under his armpits and took a few steps. After doing so, he nodded with a sense of satisfaction.

"Well, you're going to build up your arms," said his mother, smiling.

As they left the medical clinic, Billy used his crutches and his one good leg to make his way to the car. He attempted to open the front door.

"Um, Billy, I don't…"

"Oh, yeah," said Billy. He closed the door and hopped a few steps back. Opening the back door, he shoved his crutches down to the floor and then dragged himself backward on his rear end. He then reached to close the door, but found he could not do so.

"This is ridiculous!" shouted Billy. "Why me?"

"Oh, come on, now! It's not the end of the world," replied his mother. "I'll close the door for you."

10

THE PASSIVITY RETURNED. His newfound confidence began to **wane**. When Billy first returned to school, he received his fair amount of sympathy, but as the days turned to weeks, people paid him less attention. The girls that had finally noticed him slowly vanished. His new friends disappeared, preoccupied with their own activities. Gradually, Billy found himself alone.

"Excuse me, but do you take visitors on weekends?" asked his mother, opening the door to his room.

Billy lay in his bed, dressed in shorts and an athletic jersey, exposing his tan, practically hairless skin. "Very funny, Mom. Who is it?"

Brett suddenly jumped through the door. He threw both of his hands up, each one with a baseball mitt. "Tuh-duh!"

"Oh, it's you," said Billy with a long face.

"Is that any way to greet your best friend?"

"Sorry," muttered Billy. "It's just that I thought…"

"…I was Lorraine?"

"Yeah," said Billy, frowning.

"Aw, forget about her," said Brett, jumping onto Billy's bed.

"Hey! Watch it! You almost landed on my foot!" said Billy, scooting over the best he could by lifting both of his legs.

"It's in a cast," said Brett, rolling his eyes.

"So? It's still tender." Billy stroked his open knee. He then began to whisper. "Lorraine. She plays the flute. She has a sweet smile. She has a sweet voice. She's the perfect girl."

"I wouldn't say that," said Brett. He got up off the bed and settled into a chair next to Billy's old wooden desk.

"I would," said Billy. "Beautiful smile, soft skin, fluffy brown hair. She's almost like a younger version of my mom."

Brett crinkled his nose as he leaned back into his chair. "Your mom? That's weird, Billy."

Billy shrugged. "What? Don't you think my mom's pretty?"

Brett furrowed his brow. "You've been spending too much time alone, man." He threw one of the baseball mitts at Billy, hitting him on the side of his face. He then smiled widely. "Now, if you want to talk about your sister, I'm game."

Billy grinned as he placed the baseball mitt on his left hand. "You're too young for her, and besides, she's in Florida."

"Three years ain't that much," said Brett, arching his eyebrows. Then, turning more serious, he asked, "Hey, when are you going to get that thing off, anyway?"

"A few more weeks, why?"

"That's great! You can get back in the marching band!"

"No, Brett, it's not that easy. I get my cast off in a few weeks, but I still have to use my crutches and then go through physical therapy." Billy paused. He stared at Brett for a moment. "Since when did you care about the band?"

"Since I saw Toby carrying Lorraine's books," said Brett.

Billy's mouth dropped open. He shook his head slowly. He then rubbed the back of his head.

"There's always the school choir!" said Brett. "There's a lot of cute girls there. Do you sing?"

"Not helping," said Billy.

"Well, it's a nice day and I don't want you to waste it. Come on, let's play catch. You can throw the ball at me as hard as you want."

Billy smiled weakly. "Fine, it will be the highlight of my year. Help me down the stairs."

11

BILLY HAD MADE his father proud, but his mother was not so happy. As they sat around the large dining table, both of them made their viewpoints abundantly clear.

"So you take off for Indianapolis tomorrow morning?" asked Billy's father.

Billy nodded. He then began to shovel chicken and mashed potatoes into his mouth.

"Take a breath, Billy!" said his mother.

"I'll drop you off at the bus station," said Billy's father.

"I still can't believe you're not going to college!" said his mother.

"Come on, honey," said Billy's father. "College isn't for everyone."

"You're just saying that because you didn't go," she replied quickly.

Billy's father suspended his fork in the air. He clenched his thick perpendicular jaw. "There was no reason for me to go! I had already served my country and was accepted into the police academy."

"You were fortunate, Rick. When you served nobody put up a fight. Things are different now. Have you ever stopped to think about the risk? It's bad enough I have to worry about you all the time, and now I have to worry about my only son, too?"

Billy began to fidget in his chair. His eyes darted back and forth from his father to his mother. "Mom, everything is going to be fine! With my score on the ASVAB, I qualified for the military intelligence division. Even if I do see action, I'll probably be behind a computer somewhere. Anyway, I'm going to be able to travel the world, serve my country as a patriot, and still earn money to go to college."

"You sound like a commercial, Billy," said his mother. She crinkled her little nose. "Have you ever thought about how political these wars are? You had enough trouble with a broken ankle. How would you deal with losing an entire leg, or an arm…or your life? And for what, Billy? For people who resent us?"

"Honey, don't discourage him!" said Billy's father. "That's the problem with you liberals! You don't even have pride in your own country!" Then, turning to Billy, he smiled approvingly and said, "Don't worry, Billy. You're Irish—the fighting Irish! It's in your blood! To be honest with you, I was starting to wonder, but you proved it with that last basketball season of yours."

"Thanks, Dad," said Billy, releasing a slight smile.

"It's not a real man's sport like wrestling or football," his father added as he put a large piece of chicken in his mouth, "but at least you showed you got some heart."

Billy's smile instantly disappeared. He furrowed his brow and looked down at his food.

"We have pride," said his mother.

"Huh?" huffed his father.

"We liberals have pride," continued Billy's mother. "We just don't believe the United States should serve as the world police, especially in countries that don't even want us there!"

"Where did you learn that, Trisha? From some professor at Indiana University that calls me crying about a little sound he heard in the middle of the night?"

Billy's mother raised her hand to comb back the brown bangs that fell over her forehead and into her hazel eyes. "I probably did, Rick, and maybe you would have, too, if you had gone to college."

Billy watched his parents uncomfortably. "How did a conservative Republican marry a liberal Democrat, anyway?" asked Billy, shaking his head.

"I don't know," said his father. He wiped his slightly stubbled face and threw down his napkin. He then brusquely pushed his chair back and stood up. "I guess because your mother was so damn pretty. I'll see you in the morning!" Turning to face Billy's mother, he added, "I have to get up early to make sure my son becomes a man!"

Billy's father left the room. For a brief moment an awkward silence followed.

"I guess I'm too opinionated sometimes," said his mother.

"No, Mom, really?" replied Billy, arching his eyebrows.

"It's just that it makes me so mad to think about so many fine young men—and women—leaving to far off countries that don't even share our values. I mean, they don't even want us there!"

"Many of them do," said Billy. "And sometimes you have to fight. Sometimes it's necessary."

"Well, why do you have to be like your father? Why don't you go to IU like me?"

"Do we have to go through this all over again?" asked Billy. "Anyway, it's too late. I missed all the deadlines. I didn't even apply."

His mother frowned at him, then after a slight pause, said aloud, "So, you just turned eighteen. What's your political affiliation?"

Billy curled his upper lip. "Independent!" He then got up from his chair. Collecting his plate and stacking it on top of his father's, Billy disappeared into the kitchen. Returning briefly, he kissed his mother on the cheek. "Don't worry, Mom, I'll be fine. You'll send me cookies and I'll thank you each month. That's the way it works."

12

IT WAS EARLY in the morning. The air was crisp and cool. Even so, the sun was shining brightly in a blue sky filled with but a few white puffy clouds. After a strong handshake, Billy walked toward the large bus that was bound for Indianapolis. He walked up the steps, passed the driver, and noticed a few young men his age scattered throughout the seated passengers. He gathered they were there for the same reason.

Billy quickly found an empty seat and promptly placed his large duffel bag on the metal rack that stretched throughout the top of the bus. He stared out the tinted window at the imposing figure standing on the smooth pavement below. His father was getting older, nearing fifty, yet he stood six feet tall and possessed the broad shoulders, thick neck, and square jaw that immediately marked him as an officer of the law—even while dressed in blue jeans and a dark windbreaker. He showed no emotion. There were no tears. He merely turned around and walked toward the entrance of the station.

Watching his father disappear, Billy continued to stare at the passing buildings. The brown and red traditional structures made of brick were familiar to him. They, too, though, began to slowly disappear, replaced by rolling green fields and thick masses of shrubs and trees. Billy's thoughts drifted to his classmates—or former classmates. They all seemed headed in different directions. Brett had been given a minor league baseball contract by the Indianapolis Indians. Billy wondered if he would be in the city or off somewhere on a road trip. Perhaps he could see him.... Others were off to various universities, and some would stay in Bloomington for the rest of their lives.

After a little more than an hour, the bus pulled into the Indianapolis recruiting center. There, Billy met his personal recruiter in the lobby, a fit black man dressed in army camouflage and brown boots.

"Good morning, Sergeant Wilkes," said Billy.

"Hey, William, right on time."

Billy was led to a waiting room along with several other young men. There, he was instructed to strip for medical examinations. Though he felt uncomfortable, he followed orders as did the others standing to his right and to his left. Soon afterwards, he participated in exercises which assessed his strength, coordination, and speed. A few recruits struggled, but Billy passed each skill set with ease. Once finished, however, he was told to meet with an Army physician before giving his oath of service.

"X-rays show you fractured your ankle pretty badly," said the physician matter-of-factly, his head tilted downward toward a clipboard full of papers. His black hair was thinning rapidly, forming a large bald spot on the crown of his head. The front of his teeth had several gaps, and there was simply something in his small, narrow face that Billy found irksome. Unlike the rest of the commissioned military men at the center, he wore a white coat with a name tag. A stethoscope dangled across the back of his neck and shoulders.

"Yeah, it clicks a little, but I feel good. I'm running now," replied Billy.

"But did it click before?" asked the physician.

"Well, not exactly."

"I'm going to have to reject you. It hasn't healed all the way, and it may never be a hundred percent again. It might wear down in boot camp."

"But my family doctor approved me!" said Billy. "He said I should have a full recovery!"

The physician lowered his charts, made eye contact for the first time, and snarled at Billy. "We are the top medical physicians in the world! What some little country doctor tells you means nothing! Do you understand me?"

"Yes, sir," muttered Billy.

"Okay, you may leave now. Talk to your recruiter. We'll put you on a waiting list and see you in a year for reevaluation."

13

BILLY LAY ON the soft leather couch of his living room, his feet hanging over the puffy cushioned armrest. In his hands was a magazine. Though he recognized the sound of his mother's footsteps quickly approaching, he did nothing to acknowledge her, hoping secretly that she would pass by without saying a word. Instead, she stopped directly in front of him.

"What are you doing?"

"Oh, nothing," said Billy, not bothering to look up, "just reading some articles on Indiana's recruits for next year."

His mother smiled. "Are you studying their basketball program?"

"Yeah," said Billy wistfully. "Reading, dreaming, thinking about what might have been. Trying to come to grips with the fact that I failed at everything I ever tried."

Billy's mother laughed.

"It's not funny," said Billy, lowering his magazine.

"Sorry, but I couldn't help it. It's just that…"

"What?"

"Well, you sound so pathetic."

Billy glared at her. She was dressed casually in jeans and a yellow cotton shirt. On her hands were white gardening gloves. "Mom, don't you have somewhere to go?"

"No, I'm enjoying my vacation, and it looks like you are, too."

"What's that supposed to mean?"

"It means that every morning you come down here, watch television or read a magazine. The only time you get up is to raid the refrigerator. Remember, I tried to tell you that you should have applied to Indiana University. I might have even been able to help you."

"You know, now is definitely not the time for a lecture," said Billy, raising his magazine over his face.

"Well, Billy, I'm sorry, but you should have had a contingency plan. Even your school counselor told me that you ignored all of her advice!"

Billy turned the page quickly, making a whipping sound.

"You know, a plan B or even a plan C. I bet you would have gotten some really good grants or even scholarships," continued his mother. "If not my alma mater, you could have gone out of state like your sister. At the very least you should have applied to a community college like Ivy Tech. I've heard they've got a criminal justice program."

"Yeah, Mom, I'm sure you're right. Too bad I'm not as smart as you," said Billy, getting up from the couch.

"I'm just trying to help."

Billy passed his mother, patted the top of her thick brown hair, and made his way over to the closet. He fumbled through a few sporting items until he found his basketball, and then headed outside. Just before he opened the door, his father called out to him. "William, I need to talk to you."

Billy paused. "Can it wait? I need some fresh air."

His father passed through the living room and stopped directly in front of him. "Actually, it can't."

"What's so important?"

"Your future, that's what."

"Dad, my future was ruined, remember?" said Billy. "In fact, it was ruined twice."

"William, it's not that bad. Besides, your mother and I have been talking and, well, you can't just stay here doing nothing."

"That's right," interjected Billy's mother.

Billy frowned at her. Turning to his father, he asked, "Could we go outside and have this talk on the patio?"

"Sure."

The two walked over to the wooden patio just outside the door. Billy, basketball in hand, plopped himself down in a chained rocking bench that hung from the wooden rafters while his father sat in one of the green deck chairs. "Son, I'm sorry about the Army. I really am. I know you wanted to keep the family tradition, but you're eighteen now and we need to set some ground rules."

Billy winced. "Ground rules?"

"Yeah, 'cause if you plan on staying here, things have got to change."

"Dad!" said Billy. "I can't believe you're saying this to me! Now's not the time! I'm going through a lot!"

Billy's father rubbed the stubble on his square chin. "Oh, come on now, things aren't that bad."

"Not that bad?" Billy shook his head. "Hmmmm. Where do I start? Okay, first, I broke my ankle and it may never be the same. Second, I didn't get to finish my senior year of varsity basketball. Third, the Army rejected me. Forth, all of my friends have gone off to college and I'm stuck here." Billy paused for a moment, then added, "Oh yeah, and the first really pretty girl that ever paid attention to me went to the prom with the one kid I'd like to smack in the face!"

Billy's father took in a deep breath. "I'm sorry about all that, but if you want to stay in our house—"

"Your house?" exclaimed Billy. His eyes flashed. "What are you saying?"

"I'm saying that this house belongs to your mother and me and now you've become a visitor."

Billy put his feet down on the deck. He inclined his head. "A visitor? What the heck is that supposed to mean?"

"It means that you will always be our son, but you're not our little boy anymore to take care of."

Billy rubbed his temple. "Are you telling me all this because I didn't keep up the Dean tradition?"

"That has nothing to do with it, William."

"Well, haven't you always said 'God and country'?" asked Billy, looking at his father accusingly.

"Yes, I do say that and to your credit you tried. But it's time to move on, son. You can't keep feeling sorry for yourself."

"I don't remember you having this conversation with Jill."

"I didn't have to," replied Billy's father. He then raised his voice. "To be honest, she's a lot different than you! She insisted on Florida even when your mother and I were totally against it! You know your mom begged her to go to IU. We hardly see her now."

Billy began spinning his basketball in his hands. "So you're saying that you wish she would have stayed but you want to get rid of me?"

"Look, I'm just saying that Jill was a lot more independent, that's all. You're welcome to stay here—for now—tell you figure things out—but if you want to use the car, you're going to have to pay for the gas. If you need clothes, or if you want to go out with friends, you're going to have to pay for it; no more asking us for money. No more taking things for granted. And I don't see this lasting more than a year."

Billy threw his basketball up in the air and then clutched it hard with both hands. "Man! I'm surprised you're not charging me rent! How am I supposed to do all that?"

"Get a job, son! That's the American way!"

"Dad, did you know that some of my friends got cars for graduation? And a lot of their parents are paying for them to go to college, too. What did I get? Nothing! Honestly, I don't know why you're treating me like this! Even Brett got a brand new car!"

Billy's father cocked his head back. He brushed back the thick bristles of light brown hair that stood on top of his forehead like a brush. "Yes, he did, and his father told me that he got it himself with his signing bonus, so while he's trying to make it in the big leagues, you're here feeling sorry for yourself! Summer is almost over, son, and you're still here moping around without any direction."

"Dad, I told you, there's nothing I can do about that! This semester I have to wait—maybe even the entire year. Then you and mom can help me get into Indiana University."

Billy's father shook his head. "William, maybe we could do that for you, but I'll tell you right now, it wouldn't be right. When I was your age, my dad made it very clear that once I finished high school, it was time to move on. He gave me a week to pack my bags. I stayed with a friend for a while then went straight to boot camp. My parents didn't help me at all. I had to do everything on my own."

Billy looked up, opened his mouth, but then slowly closed it.

"Do your best and I promise you that your mother and I will help you every step of the way," continued his father, "but you have to grow up, son, become independent. It's part of becoming a man."

"Dad, please," pleaded Billy. "Grandpa just had the farm, but you and mom have good jobs! It's different. Why can't you see that?"

"Because it don't matter, William," replied his father. "The fact that I grew up poor ain't the point. What we're talking about here is your character, about being a man and knowing how to take care of yourself."

Billy began spinning his basketball on his middle finger. "So now you're saying I'm not a man?"

"If you expect others to do everything for you, then no, you're not! That's how a boy thinks, William, not a man. A man has to learn how to take care of himself, and once he's done that, he can start taking care of others. Right now you're not showing me that you know how to do that."

Billy paused. His hand fell limp, causing the spinning basketball upon his finger to come to a halt and fall to the floor. "Okay, I'll tell you what. Help me find a college—any college—even a cheap one. It doesn't have to be IU. Pay for everything, and once I'm done, I'll have a good job and I'll be able to pay you back! I promise!"

"William," his father replied in his deep baritone voice. "Are you listening to a word I'm saying? Look, this is the way it works. You work for a year, earn money, and meanwhile you look for a college on your own. It doesn't have to be IU, you know. You could find something cheaper."

"I don't know."

Placing his strong, calloused hand on Billy's shoulder, Rick Dean stood up, indicating that the conversation had come to an end. "That's a lot better deal than I ever got and it's a lot better deal than anyone else will give you. I guarantee it."

Billy rubbed his forehead, but said nothing.

"Son, if I haven't made myself clear, those are the conditions…"

"…to stay," interrupted Billy.

14

"Any luck?"

Billy turned to see his mother entering his room while holding several pairs of athletic white socks. He turned off the flat television screen on his desk. Besides, nothing interested him; he had been randomly changing channels for over an hour.

"Do you ever say 'good morning' anymore?" asked Billy.

His mother smiled. "Good morning. Any luck?"

She passed his desk and made her way to a large wooden dresser composed of four drawers, the top one almost reaching the one window in his room. There, she dumped the rolled up pairs of socks.

"No," huffed Billy in a tone that dispelled his exasperation.

"Maybe you could babysit. That's what your sister used to do. Of course, shorts and a tank top won't be acceptable."

"Mom, please!" said Billy. "I'm going jogging before it gets too hot."

Crinkling her nose, she asked, "You're going jogging in your room?"

Billy got up from his desk and glared at her as he headed for the door.

"When are you coming back?"

"I don't know! I need to think—figure things out before my parents kick me out of my own home."

His mother's face broke into a slight grin. "Okay, have fun... meditating."

"Yeah, yeah," muttered Billy as he left his bedroom and flew down the wooden stairs, his leaps making a loud thud on each landing. Making his way to the green grass in front of his house, he stopped to stretch his legs and hips. He then took measured steps down the familiar black, paved road. He looked at the houses he had seen all of his life. There were a few white fences in the front yards, but none that separated neighbors. Though slightly different, they shared many of the same characteristics. Green lawns full of both trimmed grass to walk on as well as fields of long unkempt stalks that grew as high as one's knees; flower bushes and trees; and open windows with no curtains.

Billy was aware that the freshness of the morning air would soon be gone, replaced by a hot, humid afternoon. In recognition of this, he began to trot through the beautiful landscape of his hometown. His ankle felt good, but the clicking sound had not gone away. As he passed street upon street, waving to acquaintances as well as strangers, he made his way toward Indiana University. Entering the campus, he slowed down and began to walk onto one of the white cement walkways. The clicking sound stopped.

Billy observed the many students moving into the dormitories. They were carrying large bags and suitcases. Some were accompanied by their parents. Others scuffled along in what seemed to be large packs of friends. His eyes turned dark with envy. With a deep breath, Billy began jogging once again. First, he passed the intramural center. As he did so, his thoughts turned back to the previous summer when Brett had talked him into playing there during an open gym session. He had held his own against some of the best high school players in the county as well as a few college players.

Lost in distant memories, Billy smiled unconsciously as he made his way to the arboretum. It was beautiful, surrounded by a waterfall, rock formations, and surrounding trees. Billy enjoyed the shade given by the large tulip trees. He sat down on a large rock. He was alone except for the sound of running water that was occasionally interrupted by the treble chirping of the birds found overhead. Or so he thought.

"Hello," flowed a soft voice toward Billy.

Only a few feet away sat a young lady. She had long dark hair that enclosed a round, alabaster face. Billy found her exceptionally attractive. "Oh, hey," he replied.

"You have been here long?" she asked.

"Uh, for a little while. Sometimes I come here to—you know—clear my head."

"Yes, this is a beautiful place," said the young lady. "But I meant to say…. How long have you been studying at the university?"

Billy wagged his head vigorously. "Oh, I'm not a student—I mean—I'm going to be—maybe next year. Are you a student here?"

"Yes," she replied, "I am a graduate student. I am earning my Master's degree in education. I will be a teacher. Maybe here or maybe in my country."

"Oh, where are you from?" asked Billy.

"I am from China. I graduated from Zhejiang University."

"Wow," said Billy. "You came here all the way from China!"

The young lady laughed. "Yes, I was able after five attempts."

"What do you mean?" asked Billy.

"At first, I was denied to come."

"You were denied? But why?"

"I am not sure," she replied. She then touched her forehead, removing a sliver of thick black hair that hung over her eyes. "I think, maybe, I did not have the highest marks, so, the government, they do not approve my Visa."

Billy furrowed his brow. He looked down at the water that flowed down a rocky path. "What are 'marks'?"

The young lady blinked a few times. "Marks. The number the professors give you after an assignment. Did you not understand? Did I not choose the right words?"

"Oh, no, your English is perfect!" said Billy. "You speak it better than I do and I'm American!"

The young lady laughed. "No, you are too kind."

Billy smiled. A brief silence followed. "My name is William. I've always gone by Billy, but I'm starting to like William more now."

"Hello, William, my name is Fan."

Billy extended his hand. Fan gently touched his fingers.

"You are sad?" she asked.

"Me?" said Billy, pointing his hands inward.

"Yes."

Billy slowly opened his mouth and stammered, "Well, maybe a little. How—how could you tell?"

"Because Americans speak very openly."

Billy looked at her questioningly. "But I didn't say anything."

"Yes, you did. With your mouth, and your eyes, and with these…. How do you say it?"

Fan reached out and touched Billy's face. He moved back slightly, but relaxed at the gentleness of her light caress.

"Oh, eyebrows."

"Yes, with your eyebrows," said Fan.

Billy smiled. "So what did my eyebrows tell you?"

"They told me that you are sad, that you are discouraged. They told me what your words do not."

Billy paused. Once again he looked at Fan. Her round, white face was soothing. "I don't even know where to begin," he said, gesturing with his hands. "I have to get a job. I want to come here, but right now, well, I can't. Truth is, I can't go anywhere. My dad won't even help me. It's just so complicated."

Fan smiled gently. "William, this is not complicated. This is normal. In my country, many people are poor. There are only a little people who are rich. It is not like here. In China, everyone struggle. Even the young people, like me, must study many years at the university, and when they work, they are paid two thousand Renminbi each month."

Billy's eyes narrowed. "Is that a lot?"

"No, William," said Fan. "It is only, maybe, three hundred dollars?"

Billy cocked his head back suddenly. "People who graduate from college only make three hundred dollars a month?" he exclaimed. "How do they even live off that?"

"It is different in China," said Fan. "Sometimes, we live in large dormitories. We share rooms. I never had a car in China. I always took the bus or I had to walk. Some people ride bicycles."

Billy shook his head in disbelief. "Gosh, you're such a nice girl, Fan, and pretty, too. I'm sorry your life was so hard in China; at least you're here, now."

Light laughter proceeded from Fan's mouth before she stifled it with her hand. "My life was not hard. It was a good life. The factory workers— or the farmers—they are the ones who have difficult lives."

"Well, it sure seems hard to me," said Billy. He looked away toward the splashing water of the small water fountain. "At least you knew what to do. You're going to be a teacher. I don't know what to do. It seems like every time I think I do, something goes wrong."

"Do not try to understand all at once. Just know what you will do today. The rest will follow."

"What do you mean?" asked Billy.

"We have a saying for this. 千里之行 始于足下."

Billy smiled upon hearing Fan speak Chinese. Unlike her English, she spoke quickly and fluidly, aptly producing a variety of phonemes and intonations.

"Wow," said Billy. "That was really cool. Could you do that again?"

Fan laughed. "You are so funny. Why don't you try?"

Billy shook his head. "No, I could never speak Chinese."

Fan widened her eyes and raised her brow. It was an endearing expression. "Listen." Slowly, she proceeded to sound out each word. "Qiān lǐ zhī xíng, shǐ yú zú xià."

Billy attempted the first few words with little success. Finally, his face broke into a wide smile. "Sorry, Fan, I guess I'm not so good at other languages."

"No, you did fine, William. Maybe, first, I explain in English. And then you try, yes?"

"Yes," said Billy.

"The journey of a thousand miles must begin beneath your feet."[5]

Billy nodded. "That was beautiful, Fan."

She slowly stood up from the horizontal rock slab which she had sat upon. "I am sorry, but I must go now. I hope you will come here again and we will practice more Chinese. And when you do, and I see your face, you will tell me that you are no longer sad."

Billy blushed slightly. "Gosh, thank you, but the truth is things aren't easy right now, and until they get better, I'll probably look the same."

Fan took a few steps, then turned and said, "William, who made you believe that your life is to be easy?"

Billy opened his mouth, but said nothing. He watched as Fan smiled, waved, and then disappeared along the cement path along the trees.

15

THE SUN WAS shining brightly, and the temperature had risen considerably. It was almost noon, and Billy was hungry. Leaving the beautiful campus behind, he headed downtown. He trotted past the many eateries, taking in their various aromas when he suddenly turned his attention to a yellow ladder perched against one of the walls. Standing on the top step was a short, plump figure with bushy unkempt dark hair.

Filled with curiosity, Billy inspected the site more closely. He was then able to see a man dressed casually, with brown khaki pants and a white shirt with rolled up sleeves. He was making rotating turns with his elbows. Finally, with screwdriver in hand, he seemed content with his work and began his descent. Billy stared at the old-fashioned, wooden sign that hung above a green door. It was painted in the shape of a flag with colors of green, white, and red. In stylish calligraphy were the words *Marcelo's Pizza Ristorante*.

"*Buon pomeriggio!*" said the man at a gawking Billy. "I'm Marcelo. We're not open yet, but you come back on Monday and I make you anything you want. Pizza? Calzone? How about a delicious hot sandwich?"

"Hi, I'm Billy—I mean, William—William Dean. I'm sure the food is delicious, sir, and I am a little hungry, but I was actually interested in a job. I saw you putting up the sign. This place is new, right?"

"Yeah, that's right. You looking for a job, you say?"

"Yes, sir."

"You got a license?" asked Marcelo.

"A license?" repeated Billy.

"Yeah, a license. You know, to drive. I gonna need a delivery driver."

"Oh, yes, sir," said Billy, the tension leaving his shoulders. "And I know B-town as well as anybody!"

"You got a license, you know the town, you got a job!" said Marcelo.

Billy smiled widely as the two shook hands.

"You want a tour?" asked Marcelo.

"Um, sure," said Billy.

Signaling for him to follow, Marcelo entered the building with Billy following closely behind.

"This is the dining room," said Marcelo, "and over there is the kitchen—the most important part, you know."

Billy nodded. He then raised his hand as if her were in a classroom. "Sir?"

"This wood, beautiful, no?" Marcelo stroked the top of one of the rectangular shaped tables. "Roasted and oiled to perfection!"

"Yes, they're nice," said Billy, "But I was wondering—"

"You like the colors?" interrupted Marcelo. "Green, white, and red. The colors of my country!"

"Yes," said Billy.

Pointing to his right, Marcelo continued, "Behind that counter is where we make the sandwiches."

"Sir?"

"And over there," said Marcelo, pointing frenetically, "over there is my baby! Come! Come with me!"

Billy was then led behind the green counter and through the red swinging French doors. He stopped suddenly at the sight of Marcelo caressing a large silver oven. It had two heavy metal doors, no more than a foot in height and several feet in width.

"Sir?"

"This is the cutting board. And over here—this machine here—is where we make the dough," continued Marcelo. "And that refrigerator is where we keep all the ingredients. Everything is fresh!" Billy nodded politely as Marcelo continued toward another room. Billy, however, remained. "Over here we have the wash room! Lots of pans. Lots of dishes."

Billy slowly made his way to Marcelo, his eyes nervously darting in all directions.

"What's the matter, William? You change your mind? *Non ti piace la pizza?*"

Billy shrugged his shoulders. Marcelo then let out a big, hearty laugh that filled the entire room.

"I asked you if you like pizza," said Marcelo. "You gonna learn a little Italian, *ti prometto*!"

"Oh, yeah, of course I like pizza! Actually, I love pizza!" said Billy. "I would eat it every day if I could!"

Marcelo laughed. It was a booming sound that seemed to proceed from deep within his diaphragm. "Then what's the matter with you? You're going to get your chance but you don't look so happy."

"Well, I'm sorry, sir, but I thought I was just going to deliver pizzas. Do you want me to do more than that?"

Once again, Marcelo let out a big gust of laughter. He then slapped Billy hard on the back. "William, I like you! You a funny guy! Okay, so you want to know what you gonna do? The answer is everything! I gonna teach you myself! But yeah, you start with the truck. Think you can do that?"

"Oh, sure!" said Billy. "Like I said, I know Bloomington really well! I grew up here and I know most of the other towns, too."

"*Fantastico!*" said Marcelo. "You are—you are—how you say it? *Tu sei la risposta alle mie preghiere!*"

16

BILLY HAD BECOME William, and William took great pride in wearing his white polo shirt that had stripes of green and red splashed horizontally across the chest. He was not so fond of the green apron strapped across his waist, but he did not complain openly about this. William enjoyed working for Marcelo. He also enjoyed working with one of the waitresses that Marcelo had recently hired. Her name was Maria. She had dark brown skin and thick black hair that curled upward at the nape of her neck. A petite girl, she stood five feet only with the aid of the thick black heels that supported her shoes.

William felt a deep attraction to her **vivacious** personality. He also loved her smile. Whenever she released it, she revealed her perfectly white teeth and her large dark eyes literally seemed to sparkle.

Watching Maria wipe the wooden tables in the dining room, William quickly left the kitchen and walked over to her. "*Puedo asistir tú?*" he asked, holding a large white cloth.

Maria laughed. "*Sí, me puedes ayudar,*" she replied.

"Oh," said William. He rubbed his temple for a moment. "*Puedo ayudar tú?*"

"*Sí, gracias!*" Maria smiled. "I'm impressed, William! You're getting better! But just say it like this: *Te puedo ayudar en algo?*"

"Thanks," said William, smiling. "I've been studying. I'm thinking about majoring in international studies, so I've been going to the library and reading about other cultures. I grabbed a used Spanish book, too. I figure it's easier than Chinese."

Maria furrowed her brow. "Huh?"

"Never mind," said William.

"Well, you're doing great, *Memo.*"

"*Memo?*"

"Yes, *Memo.* It's short for *Guillermo.* William is *Guillermo* in Spanish."

"Oh," said William. "I get it. *Memo's* easier."

"Yeah, I guess," said Maria. "But that's not why I called you *Memo.*"

"Then why?" asked William.

"Because in my culture, if you like someone, you call them by a nickname. It's a term of affection."

"Oh," said William, smiling shyly.

Maria, too, smiled widely, revealing her lovely teeth.

"William! William! What are you doing out there? We've got pizzas ready!" called out the booming voice of Marcelo.

Looking at Maria, William grinned and quickly made his way to the kitchen.

17

As THE MONTHS passed by, the warm Indiana summer turned into a beautiful multi-colored autumn, and then a cold, white winter. But amidst the fog, or rain, or even snow, William felt happy. His dreariness had slowly vanished. By working every shift available, he was earning enough money to attend college. Also, his father seemed genuinely proud of him. But more than this, William looked forward to seeing Maria. Each week he secretly cross referenced the employee schedule to see when the two would work together.

One afternoon, as he walked into the kitchen, he was surprised to see Maria peeking into the oven. "Hey, what are you doing?" he asked.

"What does it look like I'm doing?" Maria replied, turning her head slightly to make eye contact.

"But, you're not a cook, you're a waitress," said William. "Don't you belong behind the register?"

"Well, now I make pizzas and I'm a cook and I belong in the kitchen," said Maria.

"But how did this happen?"

William watched as Maria carefully held the large shovel like tool to take out a pizza that lay deep inside the top drawer of the oven. Using both hands, she placed both shovel and pizza on the white cutting board. She then closed the thick metal door, gripping the black rubber grip on the handle.

"Why are you so surprised, *Memo*? I just wanted to learn, that's all. It looked like fun, so I asked Marcelo and he said that it would be great to have another cook, so he started teaching me. A few days ago he told me I was ready."

"You really can do anything!" said William. "You're still in high school and you're already a waitress, and you speak Spanish perfectly, and now you're a cook, too!"

"You make it sound like such a huge achievement!" said Maria, grinning at him. "Anybody can cook. I do it all the time at home! And I speak Spanish because it's my first language. In fact, that's *all* we speak at my house."

"But your English is perfect, too!"

The expression on Maria's face was one of amusement. "You're so funny, *Memo*. Maybe I speak English pretty well now, but trust me, it wasn't always like that. When my family first came here, I was ten years old. I used to go to a special class every day. Most of the time I didn't know what was going on. I felt lost. But that only made me want to try harder. Then, when I started junior high, I felt more comfortable."

"Maria, I never knew," said William. "I thought you were born here. I didn't know you were from Mexico."

"I'm not," said Maria, contorting her face. "Why does everybody here think that only Mexicans speak Spanish?"

"Oh, I'm sorry."

"Don't be," she replied, smiling. "It's just that I get that a lot. I'm from Nicaragua."

"I guess I just assumed. I'm sorry."

"Quit apologizing! It's okay! *No te preocupes, Memo.*"

William looked at her, shrugging his shoulders.

"I thought you knew that," said Maria. "It means not to worry."

"Oh," replied William. Then, after a brief silence, he asked, "Maria, is there really that much of a difference?"

Maria did not answer right away, but instead took out a large pizza and slid it onto the white plastic cutting board. She then grabbed a huge knife and with both hands began cutting the pizza into halves, then two diagonal cuts turned it into sixths, and then finally into twelfths. From there, she used a giant spatula to scoop it up and place it onto a circular metal pan.

"William! William!"

William looked up to see Laura, an attractive waitress who attended Indiana University. She was rolling her blue eyes at him. "Are you going to stare at Maria or grab those tickets I put up, like, five minutes ago?" she asked, her voice filled with a noted tone of superiority.

"Oh, sorry, I'm on it," said William. He quickly grabbed one of the pink tickets that hung on a metal strip, read the order, and began making a medium sized thick crust pepperoni and sausage pizza. Laura then flipped her hand through her blonde bangs that dangled on her forehead, shook her head, and walked away.

"William, think about it!" said Maria. She set a pizza on the kitchen counter and rang a small metal bell. Then, she too, grabbed an additional ticket, searched for the proper crust size, and began spreading sauce over the dough. "How would you like it if everybody you met assumed you were from England just because you're white and speak English?"

"That doesn't make any sense. People from England have a totally different accent," said William, frowning. "Besides, it's not like they're the only ones who speak English."

"Exactly!" said Maria, her eyes flashing. "But what if nobody knew that?"

William looked at her and nodded as he placed pepperoni over the sprinkled mozzarella cheese on his pizza.

"We have our own culture, our own way of saying things," continued Maria. She deftly spread chunks of sausage and slices of mushrooms on her own pizza between her thumb, index finger and middle finger, emulating a vending machine. Bumping William with her hips, she announced, "Beat you again."

She then opened the top oven door and placed her pizza in the very front. Then, curling her upper lip, she rang the counter bell. A few moments later, Laura appeared.

"Are you going to stare at those IU guys all night or attend our customers?" asked Maria.

Laura blinked at her a few times. "Whatever," she replied as she grabbed the pizza.

William smiled as he moved past Maria to open the oven door and place his pizza next to the one she had just set down.

"Don't close it, William!" said Maria. "I think that delivery order in the back is ready."

She then grabbed the oven shovel and slid it under a pizza that lay in the very back. "I'll cut it up and you're off for another tip."

As William opened his mouth to answer her, Marcelo suddenly peered over the swinging kitchen doors. "Maria, you're doing a great job!" he said. "I think you must be half Italian!"

Maria smiled widely. Marcelo then waved his hand rigorously at William.

"Um, Marcelo," said William, "Maria's preparing a delivery. I was just waiting for her to finish."

"It's okay. You come with me to the front. We have a little chat first."

William glanced at Maria, but she had turned her back to him and was busy slicing a large combination pizza.

"Maria! If we take too long, you put that pizza in the holding oven, okay?"

"Yes, Marcelo," replied Maria.

As William made his way to the counter, Laura walked past him with a tray full of sandwiches. "Looks like someone's in trouble," she said with a slight grin.

Standing next to the soft drink dispenser, Marcelo began, "William, how long you been delivering pizzas?"

"Um, about six months."

"What you do besides deliver pizzas?" Marcelo asked.

"Hmmmm," William pondered, "I make them…and I wash dishes."

"*Mamma mia*!" said Marcelo in his thick Italian accent. "You telling me that's all you can do?"

William inclined his head.

"You a big boy," continued Marcelo. Then, grabbing William by the biceps, he added, "and strong. I see you with that basketball. How tall are you?"

"About six feet," said William, "six one."

"You gonna go to college, right?" Marcelo continued.

"Yes, Marcelo, that's why I'm here," said William. Then, as an afterthought, he added, "but I plan on working here part-time even after attending IU."

"So you're smart, too," said Marcelo.

"Pretty smart," said William.

"Then why you have top mind but only do *okay* work?" Marcelo asked, pointing his finger in William's face. "Why you have big strong body but you not work hard?"

William inclined his head once again. Then, suddenly, his body stiffened. "What do you mean, Marcelo? Aren't I doing a good job? I'm sorry if I'm not fast enough. It's just that you said I have to drive carefully. Please, don't fire me. I'll do better, I swear!"

"No, no, no, you not understand," Marcelo interrupted. "I like you too much to fire you. *Guardi*, William, *guardi*. You deliver pizzas. You do it good. But that's all you do. You a nice guy, you deliver a pizza, you talk a little to the people, you get yourself a soda, then maybe you look around and help make a few pizzas." Marcelo waved his hands back and forth, emulating a slow, rocking motion. "Anybody do that. But not anybody can cook the pizzas right or work the register or be nice with customers or count the money and not cheat me, you see? William, you a nice guy, but you gotta try more. You gotta do more. You gotta show a little more *desiderio*—a little more *passione*! I watch you and Maria and she works, like, twice as fast as you. She asks me lots of questions. She learn new stuff, but you…" Marcelo paused, folded his hands toward his chest, and then spread them out quickly in a single motion, crossing them in the air. "*Nulla! Niente!* Nothing!"

William remained silent.

"You think I know how to do all this stuff easy like?" asked Marcelo.

"I guess so. I mean, you are Italian…and the owner."

"No, you guessed wrong *il mio grande ragazzone!*" Marcelo laughed, which resulted in William exhaling deeply. "Lots of stuff I don't know. And when I first started in Italy before I came here, I knew even less! Believe it or not, not all Italians know how to cook! And me, a bachelor! So…what I do? I ask people! I ask for help. I mess up. I try again. I mess up. And I try again. Some people, they make fun of me, but I just keep trying and trying till I get it right! I still don't know much about…*come si dice*? Payroll, that's the word, so my friend, he helps me. He's an accountant. He always helps."

William nodded, looking down slightly on Marcelo to maintain eye contact.

"How 'bout I give you a key to this place and make you the night manager?" asked Marcelo.

William jerked his head up suddenly.

"You finish the last couple hours by yourself. You cook, you work the register, you make sandwiches, all that stuff, and I give you a raise!"

"Wow," William replied. "That would be great, but I don't know how I could do all that. Are you sure you shouldn't be talking to Maria?"

"William, *ragazzone!*" said Marcelo. "Maria's only seventeen; she's too young. She can't serve alcohol, and besides, her *zia* don't want her to work too late."

William gave Marcelo a puzzled look.

"Her *zia*—her aunt—she's like the one in charge of the family." Then, pointing one of his thick stubby fingers in William's face, Marcelo added, "You going to college so that you become a professional, right?"

"Well, yeah," William replied meekly.

"Well, now's your chance!" Marcelo stepped closer to him and put his hand on his shoulder. "So what's it gonna be, you gonna help me out or not? You want to be my night manager? Couple nights a week?"

"Of course I want to help you, Marcelo, but I'm afraid! It's just…"

"It's just what?"

"It's just that I don't want to let you down, that's all."

"*Non ti preoccupare*, William!"

"That means not to worry!" exclaimed William, his eyes widening.

"Hey, you getting it!" Marcelo replied, patting William on the back. "I told you that you learn Italian!"

"It's kind of like Spanish," said William.

"Yeah, that's right. Okay, listen, you don't worry about letting me down. You gonna mess up, but don't worry about it! Everybody, they mess up! I still mess up! Maria, she mess up too, but it's okay because she's good. She's really good. So you just do your best, huh?"

"If that's what you believe," said William.

"William, *credo in te*! I believe! Do you believe?"

William could not help but let out a small smile. "Yes, I believe."

"Okay, then it's settled. You my night manager."

"Marcelo," said William, "I want to learn as much as you will teach me."

Marcelo laughed. "Yes, yes, I teach you! You make me laugh, William. *Tu sei un bravo ragazzone!*"

William shrugged. "I guess I better deliver that pizza. I mean, you still want me to do that, right?"

"Yes, you still deliver pizzas until I train you and then we get someone else to do it."

As William turned to leave, Marcelo called out to him, "*Aspetta!* I'm not finished. *Torna qui!*!

William stopped. He grinned slightly. "What?

"Nothing, nothing, I just told you to come back. You gotta learn more Italian." Marcelo's face suddenly turned more serious. "Let me ask you something. You think I talk to everyone like this?"

"I don't know."

"William, I talk to you like this because I like you! But it's more than that, you know? You have a lot of, a lot of *potenziale! Potenziale*. You know this?"

William thought for a moment. Suddenly, it came to him. "Potential!" he exclaimed.

"Yeah. That. Potential," continued Marcelo. "I see you carrying that basketball with you. You a strong kid, you a smart kid, but most of all, you a good kid. I expect more from you, you understand? I'm not angry at you, William. I just want you to do better. *Alcune persone non vale la pena!* But William, you not like that. You worth it!"

18

THE NEXT FEW weeks William often stood next to Marcelo, watching him carefully. He observed how Marcelo maneuvered each pizza, from the back to the front, and then turned them a hundred and eighty degrees to the right.

"My baby doesn't heat all the same," said Marcelo, peering into the hot oven. "She's a lot hotter in the back, so you put the fresh ones there first and move the others to the front so you can keep a good eye on them."

"Why do you keep turning them?" asked William.

"Because she's also hotter on the walls," he replied.

William nodded while holding in laughter at the affection Marcelo had toward the large double door oven.

"Lots of details, William. The deep dishes, you gotta give them time because they so thick, and the black pans, they thick, too. You can't see them so well. The thin crust. They easy. Look at this extra-large combination."

William stared at the light buttery brown texture of the crust and the slight darkening of the cheese.

"Go ahead and take it out and cut it up for me," said Marcelo.

"Yes, sir," replied William, putting the flat metal shovel underneath the circular wired rack where the pizza lay. With a quick thrust, he inserted the shovel underneath and lifted it up. Then, holding the pizza with one hand, he closed the oven door with the other. The expression on Marcelo's face held a surprised look of satisfaction.

"That's very good, William. Not even Maria can do that."

"Really?" said William as he slid the pizza onto the cutting board.

"Yeah, the big ones are too heavy! Maria, she has to use two hands, put the pizza on the counter, and then come all the way back just to close the oven." Marcelo frowned. He wiggled his index finger. "That's not good. It's dangerous. Someone not looking and boom! He gets burned."

"You mean I can do something better than Maria?" asked William, smiling.

Marcelo laughed. "Okay, let's see you cut it."

William nodded. He closed his eyes for a split second, visualizing Marcelo slicing the pizza before him. Then, taking a deep breath, he placed his left hand on the far end of the outer edge of the large knife and his right hand on the handle. With great precision, William made his first cut down the middle. He then made two diagonal cuts. One last horizontal cut created the desired ten slices.

"Well done, William. I think you got it," said Marcelo. "Why don't you take a break…" Then, with a wink, he added, "I think Maria she be alone over there."

"Oh, thank you," William replied shyly. He then took off the green apron around his waist and poured himself a drink from the soda machine. With cup in hand, he walked to the staff room, a small area just behind the dish room. It barely accommodated a small square table. On the side was a small metal counter with a plastic utensil organizer and napkin dispenser.

"Hi, William!" Maria flashed a wide smile full of white teeth. "How's the training going? Ready to take over?"

"Hardly," said William.

"You'll do fine. And you know you have me."

"Thanks, but you leave before we close," replied William. "May I sit with you?"

"Of course!" Then, pointing to the pizza in front of her, she continued, "I made this deep dish Hawaiian, and I know I'll never finish it by myself."

Sitting across from Maria, William said, "This is actually my favorite pizza."

"Yeah, mine too."

"Canadian bacon and pineapple make a great combination," said William.

Maria nodded. After a brief moment of silence, William looked at her. He raised his soft drink to his mouth several times. Finally, he asked, "Maria, you're not mad at me, are you?"

Maria cocked her head back. "William, why would you say such a thing?"

"Well, you seemed a little upset when I made that comment."

"You mean when you said that I was from Mexico?"

"Yeah."

Maria laughed. She took another bite of her pizza, and followed this with a drink of water. "No, William. I wasn't mad at you. It's like I told you; I just get tired of hearing that all the time. And, well, it's not always easy being a *Nica*. I guess I'm a little defensive."

"What do you mean?" asked William. "What's a *Nica*?"

"It's just a shortened word for *Nicaraguence*, or Nicaraguan in English."

"But what's so bad about being from Nicaragua?"

Maria paused for a moment. She inclined her head. "Well, nothing.... It's just that a lot of people look down on us."

"Why?"

"Because we're poor, and dark, and I guess some people think we're not as good as them."

William shook his head. He noticed the moisture forming around the edges of Maria's eyes. "That doesn't make any sense," he said. "There's no shame in being poor, Maria. And who cares if your skin is dark? In my family, we always make fun of my sister because she's so white!" William raised his hands over his eyes and squinted. "I mean, when she wears shorts we have to put on our sun glasses!"

Maria laughed. "Thank you, William." After a brief pause, she asked, "Would you like to know about my country?"

"Of course!" said William. "I would like to know everything I can about you."

Maria smiled. "William, that's what I like about you. You're so sweet, and you're not conceited."

William furrowed his brow. "Why would I be conceited?"

Maria rolled her eyes and shook her head. "And innocent," she added. "Anyway, well, let's see, where do I start? Nicaragua is a little country in Central America. It's been torn apart by many wars—America's been involved in some of that."

"We have?"

"Yeah, a long time ago. They were trying to help people to fight against the government."

"Why were they—or we—doing that?"

"I think it had more to do with wanting our land, but later I think America was afraid we were going to become Communists."

"Oh, that explains it," said William.

Maria took a few more bites of her pizza. While she continued to chew, William asked her, "So, Maria, did your family come here to escape the fighting?"

After swallowing, she took a large drink. Then, to William's surprise, her eyes suddenly looked **forlorn**. "Not exactly," she replied. Her tone then became softer. "The fighting stopped a while ago, William, but it had its effect. Like I said, Nicaragua is a very poor country. Most people are lucky just to find work. My family was poor, too, but we were making it. Then my father—he was killed—and my mother was left to take care of me and my two younger sisters. No one would take us in."

William furrowed his brow. His eyes reflected his compassion. "Maria, I'm so sorry. We don't have to talk about this anymore."

"No, it's okay. It actually feels good to talk about it with someone—with a friend." Maria then released a halfhearted smile. "My father was a guard at a department store in Managua, and it was robbed. They had guns. My father had a stick. He never had a chance."

"That's so wrong, Maria," said William. "I—I don't know what to say. My father's a police officer and my mom, well; she worries about him a lot. He's had a few close calls, and once one of his partners got shot and went to the hospital. It could have been my dad."

"But it wasn't," said Maria.

William shook his head slowly. The two proceeded to eat in silence. Slowly, he attempted to make eye contact. "So that's why you came here?"

"Yeah, after we lived in Costa Rica for a year," Maria replied.

William furrowed his brow and bit his lower lip.

"You've never heard of Costa Rica either, have you?" asked Maria.

"Sorry. Is it by Puerto Rico?"

Maria released a small chuckle. "You're incredible, William! Puerto Rico is in the Caribbean. I already told you that Nicaragua is in Central America. It's a little strip of countries between Mexico and South America."

William nodded affirmatively. Maria smiled at his serious expression. "Anyway, my country shares a border with Honduras and Costa Rica. Honduras is just as poor as Nicaragua, and probably more violent, so most

Nicas cross the border and head for Costa Rica. The trouble is, though, that most of the *Ticos* don't want us there."

"What does *Tico* mean?" asked William.

"Oh, sorry," said Maria, "*Ticos* are *costaricenses*. Costa Ricans in English."

"They were mean to you?"

"Kind of," replied Maria. "I mean, not all of them, but enough. In my school there were only a few other kids like me from Nicaragua, so most of the *Ticos* called us names. They said we were stupid and ugly and talked funny and that we were ruining their country."

"Wow," said William. "That's terrible!"

"I hated those kids when I was a little girl, but now I actually understand a little more why they were so mean to us."

"I'm lost," said William. "What do you mean?"

"Well, a few months ago, I went to Terre Haute to attend Girls State. I met this girl from Costa Rica," began Maria. "Her name was Hanni."

William swallowed, then quickly blurted, "You were chosen for Girls State?"

"Stop doing that!" said Maria. She reached over and playfully slapped William's hand.

"Sorry, it's just that you never cease to amaze me," he replied.

"As I was saying," said Maria, shaking her head slightly, "I met this girl and had to compete against her. I still had some resentment toward Costa Ricans, and to make it worse, she kept saying things that got me angrier and angrier..." Her voice faded. Maria seemed lost in thought. Finally, she grumbled, "But I have to admit that she made some good points."

William furrowed his brow. "I don't get it."

"I'm not explaining this very well, am I?" asked Maria.

"Not really."

"All right, let me start over. I was chosen to be the lead defense lawyer of my team in the mock trial. It's a big event at Girls State—the culminating activity of the conference. Both teams were given a case study about a man who was being charged with illegally entering the United States as well as the falsification of papers."

A quizzical look appeared on William's face.

"You know, a fake driver's license, social security…" began Maria as she vividly recalled the event to William.

The room was large, laden with brown wooden walls. Front and center, above the rest on a vanilla carpeted platform, sat a female judge. Her chestnut brown hair was pulled back into a sophisticated bun. She wore a black robe. There was a serious, graceful aspect to her. In the middle of the room were two large rectangular tables, each assembled with three young ladies and an array of scattered documents, pens, and pencils.

Maria was dressed formally in a business suit, complete with a gray vest, a white collared blouse, a gray skirt, black stockings, and black leather shoes with high heels. Across from her sat the prosecution team. One of them, a tall slender young lady with a white complexion and auburn hair, whispered instructions to the others.

The jury members, composed completely of teenaged girls, were seated to the side of the courtroom. At the very back sat a collection of faculty and students. On the witness stand was an attractive girl with light brown skin, large eyes, and long black hair that fell just below her shoulders. She wore a white collared shirt with an oversized red tie. Giving her a comical element was the obviously fake black mustache she wore on her upper lip.

Hanni asked the witness several questions. Then, Maria arose and did the same. Afterwards, both girls were asked by the judge to make their closing arguments, with the lead prosecutor addressing the jury first.

"Ladies and gent—well, ladies of the jury." Laughter was heard from the jury as well as the many other girls throughout the audience of the courtroom. "You have heard the testimony of many witnesses regarding the state of Indiana versus said Ignacio Cortéz. In sum, we know the following to be true. He entered the United States illegally. He brought his wife and his first two children here—illegally. He falsified his records. Yes, he says that this was done in order to work and support his family, but are we to merely take him at his word? After all, he has already established himself as someone who perpetually deceives others—including the U.S. authorities. Identity theft is quickly becoming one of the most dangerous issues we face today."

The young lady paused for a moment. She brushed the sides of her long auburn hair that fell softly over her ears. "Before I conclude, I would like to tell you my personal experience with illegal immigration, lest there are some that think the act of illegally crossing a border is a slight matter. My name is Hanni Mora Sanabria and I myself am an immigrant—a legal immigrant. My country of origin is not the United States, but Costa Rica. The name of my country is translated *rich coast*. Many people referred to Costa Rica as the jewel of Central America. Others called it a paradise. Note how I use the past tense."

Maria's eyes widened. Her brow furrowed deeply. Her hips shuffled on the wooden chair in which she sat and her elbows, propped firmly on the table, slid a few inches. The girls next to her sat in stony silence, seemingly unaffected and somewhat disinterested.

"As a child, I fondly remember traveling to Heredia to visit my grandfather. He would speak of a Costa Rica that I never knew. It was a time when women visited their neighbors at all hours of the night. It was a time when children played in the streets. It was a time when people left their doors open when they attended Mass. Now, women rarely go out alone even during the day. Now, those same streets are empty. And the homes? Now, they are guarded by huge metal gates, armed guards, and the doors and windows are covered with iron bars.

"Costa Rica has always prided itself in being a peaceful nation. A nation that builds universities instead of armies. A nation that invests in parks, not weapons. Unfortunately, our neighbor to the north does not share our culture." Pausing, Hanni glanced at Maria. "Though we share a common language, the Nicaraguan and the Costarican are two very distinct people. Whereas the Costarican seeks peace, the Nicaraguan seeks violence. Whereas the Costarican takes pride in being educated, the Nicaraguan takes pride in destruction."

A few of the girls in the jury box exchanged surprised glances. Maria twisted her lips and began to tap her pen on her notebook.

"I respect the United States and I respect the laws established here, yet I fear I am witnessing the decline of a great nation. The Nicaraguans came to Costa Rica uninvited; and in allowing them to come, we did not save their country, we simply lost our own." Maria grimaced. A few of the girls in the jury nodded, a glint of sadness in their eyes. "And lastly," concluded Hanni, approaching the jury box so closely that she was able to lean against the wooden rail, "to those who may feel that my words are harsh, I leave you with the following quote attributed to former President Ronald Reagan: 'A nation that cannot control its borders is not a nation.' "[6]

Maria sat at her table brooding. The judge called out to her. She called her name again and again. "Maria? Maria?" The voice was different, deeper, younger…

"Oh, sorry William," said Maria, shaking her head.

"Your eyes went blank for a minute," said William.

"Yes, sorry." Maria took a long drink of her water. "I guess the memory still bothers me. Even after the trial, she started telling everyone that all the *Nicas* are *chapulines*."

William crinkled his forehead. "Huh?"

"*Chapulines*—grasshoppers."

William smiled broadly. "What are you talking about?"

Maria laughed. "Oh, sorry, William, that's just the slang they use for the gangs. Mostly, they're boys who can't find work, so they jump out at people and steal their stuff, but usually they're not too violent. I mean, they may hit you or something, but most of them don't carry knives or guns."

William nodded his head slowly. He shifted his eyes away from Maria.

"Go ahead," said Maria.

"Go ahead and what?" asked William.

"Go ahead and say it."

William furrowed his brow. He grabbed one of the few remaining slices of pizza.

"You're wondering if she was right," pressed Maria. "You're wondering if we ruined her country."

"I—I don't know what to think, Maria," stammered William between bites of his pizza.

"Well, maybe some of the things Hanni said were true." Maria took a deep breath. "But still, William, you have to understand that most people in Nicaragua are dirt poor. You have no idea what it's like! Costa Rica was my family's only chance. It took everything we had for my mom to get us there. We lived in a little room—all of us—my mom, me, and my little sisters. I wore the same clothes to school every day. My mom worked as a housekeeper for three different families, William. Three!" Maria held up three of her fingers. "She washed other people's clothes, cooked for them, scrubbed their floors. We barely saw her." Maria inclined her head.

"Sometimes, things were so bad that I had to ask neighbors to give my sisters and me something to eat."

William pressed his lips together. He then moved his tongue across the front of his teeth.

"We didn't commit any crimes, William!" said Maria. "We didn't try to hurt anyone! My mother did everything for us until my aunt was able to come and bring us here." Maria stopped. She seemed to be waiting for a response, but William did not offer any.

"Is it so wrong for a rich country to help a poor one?" asked Maria.

"I don't think so," William replied meekly.

"I know it's wrong to break laws," continued Maria, "but what was my mother supposed to do? Let her children die?"

"Of course not!" William reached over and gently rubbed the top of Maria's hand. "I think—I think we just need to find a better way of letting the good people in and keeping the bad people out."

"William," said Maria, her face breaking into a wide grin, "you should be President!"

Before William could respond, Marcelo appeared.

"I make him assistant manager and now he's *il Presidente*!"

Laughing, both Maria and William got up from the table.

"Sorry, Marcelo, I guess we lost track of time," said William apologetically.

"It's okay, it's okay, that's what happens *con amore*, but I need you both now. The dinner crowd's coming."

William and Maria both raised their eyebrows, smiling mischievously as they returned to the kitchen. Before returning to the register, however, Maria lingered for a moment.

"William, most immigrants are good people."

Turning to face her, William cocked his head back in surprise. "Maria, you don't have to say that. All of us were immigrants at one time or another."

"I know; it's just that some of the things that I said to you were pretty negative. I just don't want you to get the wrong idea about Nicaraguans." She quickly moved her head in both directions. Grabbing William by the arm, Maria said in a commanding tone, "Come!"

She led him to the small hallway next to the restrooms. William lowered his eyebrows at Maria, staring at her as if she had lost her mind. Inwardly, however, he took some pleasure from her aggressive act.

"Most *Nicas* who cross the border are just trying to survive, William. They go up in the mountains and pick the coffee berries by hand, and in the city they work in construction with cement and stone and little chisels. Probably half of Costa Rica was built by *Nicas!*"

William looked at her, a bit taken back by the intensity in her voice.

"Do you know what I remember most about Costa Rica?" asked Maria.

William shook his head from side to side.

"I was walking home from school when I see this old *Nica* cutting the grass of a really nice house. It was in *Tres Rios*. He was bent down, waving his machete—"

"A machete?" interrupted William, his eyes suddenly widening.

"That's how they cut the grass."

William arched his brow. "They cut grass with machetes?"

"Yes!" said Maria, hitting him on the shoulder. "Now quit interrupting!"

"Sorry," said William, smiling slightly.

"Anyway," said Maria, "this rich Costa Rican man—he had a suit on. He comes out and hands the old man some money. You know what he did with it, William?"

"I have no idea."

Maria raised her hand in the air and began to demonstrate. "This little old man held the money in his withered hand, made the sign of the cross in the air, and then kissed the money. And it was only five hundred *colones*."

"I'm betting that wasn't a lot," said William.

"It's not. It's a dollar or two."

Looking down on Maria, William gently put both hands on her shoulders and looked her squarely in the eyes. "Maria, you don't have to say anymore. *No te preocupes*—I believe you—and all the Nicaraguans I've ever met are really wonderful and beautiful people."

Arching her eyebrows, Maria asked, "You've met people from Nicaragua?"

"Well, actually, only one."

19

WILLIAM SLOWLY BECAME comfortable closing the restaurant as the night manager. Still, he knew that there would be nights when he would be challenged. On one such night, with only a few staff members remaining, he observed Laura as she joined two young men at their corner table. She put three slices of cheesecake down and helped herself to one of them. William waited a few minutes, trying to decipher if she was merely being friendly or blatantly disregarding her responsibilities. Finally, he decided he had seen enough. William approached the table. He cleared his throat loudly. The sounds of chatter mixed with laughter slowly came to a halt.

"Yes?" asked Laura, a reflection of mockery in her eyes.

"Laura, you're in the middle of your shift," said William. "I had to wait on a customer while you were sitting here."

"So you're good enough to be night manager but you can't even help one customer?" she asked. The two young men sitting next to her broke into laughter.

"Hey, man, aren't you the delivery boy?" asked one of them. He then wrapped his arm around Laura's waist.

William looked at him, observing his Indiana University sweatshirt. He had a red cap that covered his shortly cut blonde hair. William then looked at the other young man who was sitting across the table. He was chubby. His white sleeves from his thermal shirt extended past his plaid, collared shirt. William did not care for the smirk on his face. "Laura, did you even pay for that?"

"You're taking yourself too seriously," she said as she tossed her wavy blonde hair. "I mean, please, you're younger than I am."

"Let me make this clear to you," said William. "While you are working, you're expected to do just that. Now, you need to get back behind that register right now. You also need to write out a ticket and pay for these cheesecakes. If not, I'm going to report this to Marcelo."

"Look, man, you can't talk to my girl like that," said the young man sitting next to Laura.

"Ashton, it's okay, he doesn't mean it," said Laura, tugging at his shoulder. "He's just mad because his girlfriend isn't working tonight. Really, William, what do you even see in her?"

William paused for a moment. He felt his cheeks redden slightly. He scratched the side of his short brown hair. "Laura, I meant every word. And Ashton—that's your name?"

"Yeah."

The other young man raised his chin defiantly. "And I'm Brice!" he said.

William shook his head slightly. "Well, guys, you do understand the difference between a date and a job, right? Laura gets paid to work here, and I get paid to watch over the restaurant when Marcelo's not here. He's worked too hard and put too much trust in me to let him down."

"Who is this guy?" asked Ashton, gesturing to Brice. Then, turning to William, he said, "Come on, man! Relax! There's hardly anybody here!"

"Why don't you go back to the kitchen?" said Laura. "You're embarrassing yourself."

William moved his head up and down in small movements. "Okay, I asked you nicely. Now, I'm going to write an incident report."

William turned and began to walk away.

"I'll pay for your stupid cheesecakes!" said Ashton.

William stopped, turned to face them, and said, "Fine, but she needs to return to the counter until her shift is over."

Laura nodded to the two young men and promptly stood up. As she passed William, Brice muttered, "What a jerk."

"Yeah, I didn't know delivery boys could boss everyone around. This place is going down fast," said Ashton.

William considered ignoring their remarks, but something inside him would not let him do so. "Excuse me?" he asked.

"What?" asked Ashton.

"What did you just say?" asked William.

"I was saying how thirsty I am." He picked up his glass mug and waved it back and forth in the air. "Now why don't you go get us another beer."

"No, I don't think so," replied William. "You won't have time."

"You don't close for another hour!" said Ashton.

"I know, but you're leaving," replied William.

"Huh?"

"I think you guys heard me," said William. "Please pay your bill and leave."

"You're kicking us out?" shouted Brice.

William inhaled deeply through his nostrils as both Ashton and Brice stood up and approached him. Each of them stood a few inches shorter than William.

"Yes, we have the right to refuse service to anyone," said William in the most professional tone he could muster. "Your attitude isn't what we want here. You can pay Laura at the register and say goodbye. And if I have another incident with you guys, you won't be allowed back."

"You can't make us leave," said Brice.

"Oh, yes he can!" called out a voice. Slowly, an elderly woman emerged from several tables away. "I've listened to you two insult this young man and treat him disrespectfully. I know his father, Rick Dean, who just happens to work for the Bloomington Police Department. Now, if he tells you to leave, then you better get!"

William observed the old woman with curiosity. She was small, with puffy gray hair and a heavily wrinkled face. He then turned his attention to Ashton. He appeared to be assessing the situation. Pressing his lips together firmly, Ashton swallowed and then nodded to Brice. He then placed a few bills on his table, walked over to Laura, and promptly exited the restaurant with his friend at his side.

"Thank you, ma'am," said William. "That was so nice of you."

"That's okay, Billy. Like I said, I know your father," she replied. "Known him for a long time. I know your mother, too."

"Did my dad help you?"

"Yes, he did," she replied. Then, motioning to an older man wearing blue overalls, she walked off toward the front counter.

William quickly followed her. "Ma'am, if you don't mind me asking, when did my father save you?"

"Save me?" repeated the woman, laughing. She shook her head. "Nothing that dramatic, son. Your dad used to cut my grass when he was a boy."

Billy furrowed his brow in silence. The woman turned to her husband and said, "Okay, Herb, pay the bill!"

"Yep," replied the man in a monotone voice.

William quickly grabbed the small slip of paper. "This one's on the house."

"So they're eating for free?" asked Laura, her lips curled aggressively.

"No, Laura," said Billy, shaking his head, "I'm paying."

"Thank you, son," said the man. "I see the apple doesn't fall far from the tree."

The elderly couple walked toward the front door with their arms linked. William raced past them and opened it for them. As he did so, the old woman smiled and extended her thumb high in the air.

20

As the months rolled on, William established himself as a leader. He found that he was a quick learner, and when he did run into an obstacle, he simply asked others to assist him.

"Hey, where's Marcelo?" asked William to a recently hired pizza delivery boy who had just entered the kitchen.

"Doing his thing."

William smiled at the newest member of Marcelo's crew. He was a small and possessed a boyish face that made him appear even younger than his sixteen years.

"Things are kind of slow right now. Why don't you grab a drink and then go in the back and wash trays."

The boy nodded. "You got it, William."

Exiting the kitchen, William spotted Marcelo speaking gregariously with a customer at the front counter. He then saw Maria wiping tables in the far corner of the dining room. He quickly grabbed a wet cloth and joined her. The two then began to form circular strokes in silence until William began making clicking sounds with his tongue.

Smiling, Maria said, "Yes?"

"Maria, I was thinking…" began William. "We've worked together for almost a year, now."

"Uh-huh," she replied as she continued to wipe the large wooden table.

"And we've had some really good talks," continued William.

"Yes, we have."

"Well, maybe we could do something together when we're, well, not working."

"William…*Memo*," began Maria slowly, "I would love to—"

"Great!" interrupted William, releasing a wide smile. "How about a movie?"

"—but I can't."

William inclined his head. A large frown quickly formed upon his face. Maria seemed to notice this. She placed her hand gently under his chin and lifted his head up until their eyes met. "I didn't say I didn't want to go out with you. I said I *can't*."

William grimaced. "I don't understand."

Maria inhaled and exhaled deeply. She moved to another table. "It's hard to explain. It's just us—all girls. My aunt married an American, but he passed away. He was a lot older than her. She never had any kids of her own, so we're the only family she has."

William released a weak smile. "I respect your family, Maria, but why won't they let you see a movie with me? Or get some ice cream? I mean, we're here together all the time."

"I know. But it's different. Marcelo's here, and we're in public."

"A movie theatre is a public place. So is an ice cream parlor."

"William," said Maria very softly. So softly, in fact, that William could not recall ever hearing her voice sound so tenderly feminine. "Trust me, I would love to do that with you—and only you. But I'm the oldest, and they're afraid something will happen to me."

William furrowed his brow. "I would never let anything happen to you."

Maria smiled. "I know."

William stood across from Maria and continued to assist her but without the previous vigor he had demonstrated.

"I'm sorry," said Maria, "but I am planning on going to IU in the Fall, and I know we'll be able to see each other there. You're going, right?"

William nodded. He and Maria then proceeded in unison to stoop down in order to wipe the wooden benches on both sides of the table.

"I've already been accepted," said William. "I'm even thinking of trying out for the basketball team as a walk on."

"That's wonderful!" said Maria.

"Yeah, wonderful," repeated William in a tone void of all excitement.

"Slowly, things will change," said Maria. "You'll see."

Maria moved to a nearby table and began to wipe. William did not follow her. He lingered a bit, and then said quietly, "Maybe we'll have some of the same classes. It would be fun to study with you."

"I would like that too," she replied.

After an awkward pause, William added, "I guess I better get back to the kitchen."

Maria smiled and nodded. Suddenly, she called out, "Don't give up, William. I don't want you to…" Her voice trailed off as she glanced in the opposite direction.

William stopped.

"…ask some other girl to study…or get an ice cream."

"No," said William, shaking his head. "That would never happen." Then, frowning, he added, "I just wish we didn't have to wait so long."

"Maybe we don't," said Maria. Her dark eyes flashed. "If you really want to be close to me and improve your Spanish, why don't you come to my house and have lunch with my family?"

"I could do that?" stammered William. "Your mom—or your aunt— wouldn't care?"

"Yes, you could," said Maria. "It might be a little awkward at first, especially with my mother. She doesn't speak much English. But I'm worth fighting for, right?"

"Of course you are!" William shouted loudly.

"Shhhh!" hissed Maria as she raised her index finger to her lips. "But we won't have pizza." She then shot William a gesture of mock seriousness. "Or tacos!"

Laughing, William asked, "So what is Nicaraguan food like?"

"It's great! How does *carne asada, gallopinto, maduros* and *ensalada* sound?" asked Maria.

"I don't know. I don't even know what that is, but I look forward to eating it with you."

"And my family," Maria quickly added.

"Yes, and your family," said William. "And then it will be your turn to have dinner with my family."

"It's a deal," said Maria, holding out her hand.

William grasped it and did not let go. As the two locked eyes, Marcelo passed by. He shook his head and laughed. "*Che figata!*" He then sang heartily, "When the moon hits your eye like a big pizza pie, that's *amore!*"

MULTICULTURAL DILEMMA

1

Born in Buenos Aires to an affluent family rich in history and culture, Miranda Frondizi felt **privileged** from the start. She was the firstborn, a *Porteña*, and conspicuously beautiful. Even as a child, she was capable of causing a small commotion. Complete strangers would stop in the middle of a pebble lain street and stare at the symmetrical perfection of her tan face. Miranda did not shy away from such attention. Instead, she would sing and dance for them. Her admirers, young and old, would inevitably applaud and laud her with superlatives. Some of the men tipped their hats to her and offered her candy. Women dressed in the finest linen of Argentina would stoop down and kiss her on the cheek.

"*Qué hermosa!*"

"*Qué linda!*"

"*Dios mío! Ella es una muñeca!*"

Miranda smiled, hypnotizing each and every one with her bright green eyes and the soft blonde hair that fell across her forehead and around her ears. Upon a brief recognition of the small crowds that developed, her parents would whisk her away.

After Miranda came Raúl, Eva, Amanda and little Arturo. There was a pleasant aspect to them. Yet, somehow they understood that their oldest sister was different, as if destiny had granted her an inexplicably higher status.

Miranda's father was a banker. A senator, too. Her mother was a former beauty queen. By most accounts, they had led a charmed life and were well-known amongst the highest social circles of Buenos Aires. Neither had known the pain of uncertainty until an economic collapse occurred. It spared no one.

As the upper class felt the hard waves of inflation and the devaluation of the Argentine *peso*, many began to relocate. For the Frondizi family, this meant living in America. Miranda was nineteen at the time and enjoying her first year at the university. Naturally, she was none too pleased with the announcement.

"*Pero papá*, you know we can't leave! My life is here! I must stay at the *Universidad de Buenos Aires*!" exclaimed Miranda. "Must we suffer because of your failure?"

José Raúl Frondizi was a proud man, and one not accustomed to being addressed in such a manner. Upon hearing Miranda, his face contorted, forming an expression that displayed both frustration and anger. His next movement was to nervously run his fingers through his thinning brown hair. From there, he transitioned to a slight caress of his light mustache by simultaneously moving his thumb and forefinger.

Miranda's mother, the lovely Mireya Frondizi, did not speak much English, but she understood more than she let on. Standing next to both husband and daughter, she appeared anxious to join the conversation.

Miranda spoke four languages. Spanish, Italian, French, and English. She took full social advantage of this. When she did not want her mother to actively participate in a conversation with her father, she chose English; and when she did not want her father to interfere, she spoke French with her mother.

"Miranda, how dare you speak to me in such a manner!" said her father. His hazel eyes began to glow, as if they were burning. "Is there no limit to your impertinence?"

"Oh, *mil disculpas, papá*," said Miranda with a smile that not only gushed with confidence but seemed to mock her father as well.

At first, he stared at her, but then, like most men, he wilted. There was no way around it. Miranda was a stunning beauty and quite aware of the power she held over people. Tall and possessing an alluring figure, her skin remained a perpetual bronze color. Her symmetrical face was complemented by perfectly shaped white teeth and green eyes that were accentuated by thin dark brows that were curved slightly at the ends. Feathery blonde hair fell in waves along her cheeks and marked the wide jawlines that flowed harmoniously from below her ears to her chin.

"Forgive my blunt speech, *papá*. I am not a politician and thus I have no use for half-truths," continued Miranda without the slightest fear of repercussions. "Yes, I very much prefer to speak clearly without any pretexts whatsoever. Does that offend you?"

"*Qué estás diciendo, Miranda? Decime en español!*" interjected Miranda's mother in her thick Argentine accent. Though well into her forties, it was conspicuously evident that Miranda owed much of her beauty to her mother. The slight lines beneath her eyes, as well as along the edges, did little to distract from the healthy glow of her face and the thick blonde hair that just reached her shoulders.

"*Un momento, mamá,*" replied Miranda. Then, turning once quickly toward her father, she continued, "Well, I am waiting…"

"Darling, we have done our best to give you everything you have ever wanted. Your mother and I have provided you with the finest schools, clubs, music lessons—"

"Still waiting!" interrupted Miranda.

Her father's mouth fell open. He looked more like a beggar than a government official of high rank. "*El Congreso no es muy popular, corazón.* As a senator, I am up for reelection and the people are crying out in the streets 'out with them all!'"

"But you are the vice-president of *el Banco Nacional!*"

"*Paloma*, our investments are practically worthless. Many of our loans are unpaid. The bank will be dissolved. It is just a matter of time, I'm afraid."

Miranda crinkled her nose and forehead.

"If we act quickly," continued her father, "we can sell our home and still receive something in return, even though it will be very little. But all is not lost. I have some contacts in Los Angeles that have offered me a position at the main branch of their finance department. We may not live quite as well, but it will allow us some sustenance until our economy becomes stable once again."

"*Ya se lo dijiste, José? Ya le explicaste que nos vamos a quedar en Los Angeles?*" asked la señora Frondizi.

"*Sí, mi amor,*" replied el señor Frondizi.

After a brief silence, Miranda replied somewhat coldly, "Well, *papá*, I am sorry for your misfortune, but I will not accompany you. I shall continue with my studies and remain here. I know *tío Alfonso* will agree."

"Honey, *paloma*, you cannot," said her father. "We must stay together."

"No, *papá*, I am staying."

Miranda's father swallowed deeply. "You are not."

Miranda glared at her father, and then at her mother. Seeing that they would not recant, she shut her eyes and stomped the floor. *"Esta es una gran injusticia!"* she screamed. *"Oigan! No los voy a perdonar! Nunca!"*

Miranda quickly walked to her room and closed the door. On the other side, her father spoke to her about the virtues of living in America, trying in vain to **appease** her.

2

THE FRONDIZI FAMILY settled into one of the nicer suburbs of Los Angeles, a place called Glendora. The community boasted a balance of modern and antique buildings. The Historic Village, with its smaller businesses and friendly store owners, reminded Miranda to some extent of her favorite boutiques in Buenos Aires. But, overall, she found very little that would make her forget her depressed state of mind. As each day passed, she spent more time in her bedroom, pining away for her former life.

"Vení, Miranda," called out her mother. *"Tu papá nos va a llevar a un restaurante cerca de la playa."*

Miranda's eyes flashed. *"La playa? En serio? Hasta que por fin puedo ver algo de belleza!"*

"Sí, mi amor, ponete shorts. Todos andamos en sandalias y gafas de sol."

Miranda quickly changed and then followed her mother outside the house. There, in the driveway, she saw the rest of her family seated in their blue mini-van. She entered and sat next to her brother, Raúl, in the second row of chairs.

"Listos?" asked el señor Frondizi.

Miranda, as well as her brothers and sisters, nodded. El señor Frondizi then slid the large door shut. Along the way, Miranda did not say much, preferring to listen to music. When they finally arrived, however, she removed her earphones and joyfully looked out the window.

"*Papá*, this is a delightful place! What is it called?"

"Newport Beach, *paloma*."

Miranda stepped out of the mini-van, stretched her shoulders, and smiled widely. "Why in heavens didn't we come here?"

"We are here," said Raúl.

"I meant to live, silly," said Miranda.

"Come! Come! *Todos! Vámonos al restaurante! Unos colegas míos me dijeron que tienen un ceviche excelente!*" said her father.

They walked across a small bridge. Miranda inhaled deeply. "*Qué aire más fresco!*" she exclaimed.

"*Sí!*" said Eva. "*Cómo se llama esta parte del océano, papá?*"

"*Um, se llama…*"

"It's called a harbor," said Miranda.

"Those are cool boats," said Raúl.

"They're referred to as yachts," said Miranda.

Raúl smirked. "Same thing," he muttered.

"Not really, any common fisherman may own a boat," said Miranda. "These beautiful vessels belong to someone of importance."

"The climate *es perfecto!*" said Amanda.

The family of seven, led by their father, entered the restaurant and proceeded to an outside patio area. They were fortunate to find one large table available. People of various ages were busy in conversation, displaying such mannerisms as to give them an air of the upper class.

"Don't tell me," began a young waiter. "You're involved in one of the soaps."

Miranda, seated casually, lowered her large sunglasses. She peered up at the handsome figure before her. He had blonde hair, brown eyes and a golden tan that could be seen beyond his rolled up sleeves. "Wow! Look at those green eyes!" he proclaimed. "Now I know I've seen you before!"

"I beg your pardon," replied Miranda.

"You're in one of the soaps, aren't you? Let me guess. General Hospital™?"

"No," said Miranda quizzically. "I'm not in any hospital. Why would you assume such a thing?"

"No, no, no," said the young man as he served water to each member of the Frondizi family. His hands shook gently as he let out a gust of laughter. "I'm talking about the soap opera! You're an actress, right?"

Miranda, placated by the young man's explanation, smiled at him. "Oh, no, not really, although I have done some modeling. We have just moved here from Argentina, but perhaps you shall see me on television soon here."

"I'm sure I will," he said. "I've had a few parts myself. I played Conner, the lifeguard, on Guiding Light™. If you're interested, give me your number and I'll see what I can do about an audition."

Miranda quickly took out her cell phone.

"No, that will not be necessary," interrupted her father. "I believe we are ready to order."

"Oh, yes, sir. How may I help you?"

"*Miranda va a ser actriz?*" asked Eva.

"*Cómo?*" replied her mother, furrowing her brow.

"Nobody is going to be an actress!" bellowed el señor Frondizi. "Now, please, I suggest we order and if this young man is able to refrain from socializing, perhaps he can bring us our food."

The waiter nodded. Then, with a serious expression, he pulled out a pencil and pad of paper. He quickly recorded the petitions for food and beverages. "You're going to love our fish and chips and ceviche, sir."

"Yes, if it ever comes, I'm sure that will be true," replied el señor Frondizi.

Turning toward Miranda, the waiter added, "I know a lot of agents that would be interested in a beautiful girl like you. Maybe I could introduce you to a few of them. Since you're new here, I could show you around, too."

"Thank you," said Miranda.

Once the waiter had left, el señor Frondizi began to fidget, continuously moving his napkin through his thumb and forefinger.

La señora Frondizi turned to him and asked, "*Qué te pasa? Estás enojado con el mesero?*"

Miranda smiled and quickly asserted, "It's innocent flirting, *papá*! Please don't be so cross!"

"*No es eso,*" replied her father.

Miranda reached into her purse. She brushed aside her wavy blonde hair and inserted a pair of small pink earphones. "Fine, if you choose not to share your true feelings, then I shall enjoy this beautiful place while being serenaded in Italian by Bocelli."

"Wait, Miranda, there's something I need to tell you."

Miranda moved her head back and forth slowly.

"*No te puede oír*," said la señora Frondizi.

"Miranda!" shouted her father.

Miranda jerked suddenly. She glared at her father and then quickly removed her ear phones. "*Che cosa hai detto?*"

"*Perdón? Vos sabés que no entiendo italiano.*"

"Oh, sorry, *papá*," said Miranda. "But what in heaven's name has possessed you to shout at me so?"

"*Miranda, prestáme atención. Tengo que decirte algo*," said her father.

"*Algo bueno o algo malo?*"

"*Algo malo.*"

"What could be worse than what you have already done?" asked Miranda, effortlessly flowing from Italian to Spanish to English.

"Well, you see, our paperwork is taking much longer than expected. I think it's our embassy—or maybe it's the Americans—perhaps it is just…"

"Father, please!" interrupted Miranda. "I cannot understand your gibberish!"

"What I'm trying to say is that we are still waiting on official documentation. I'm afraid you won't be able to attend one of the universities until we finish this process."

"What?" shrieked Miranda. "*Papá*, how long must I wait?"

Her father paused. At that moment the waiter appeared with two loaves of bread and several bowls of soup.

"An entire semester?" continued Miranda.

"Possibly more."

"*Increíble!*" said Miranda. "*Cómo me has hecho sufrir, papá!*"

"Everything okay?" asked the waiter. "I'll have the main courses ready in about five minutes."

"Yes, thank you," said Miranda's father flatly.

The waiter nodded. He then put an extra napkin next to Miranda's plate. On the top were ten digits scribbled in blue ink. He left the sunny patio area, disappearing into the entrance of the restaurant.

After a period of awkward silence, el señor Frondizi said, "You could attend the community college. I hear it is quite nice, and it is very close by."

"You would have me attend classes with people so uneducated and uncultured?" asked Miranda with a look of disgust.

"Miranda, it is better than staying at the house for an entire year... or more."

"Or more?" repeated Miranda. "Oh, father, you are making my life an utter nightmare!"

3

AGAINST HER WISHES, Miranda enrolled in Glendora Community College. To console herself, she announced to her family that it was a temporal arrangement until she could convince the Argentine Embassy to expedite her family's paperwork. In the unlikely event that this would not occur, Miranda vowed she would return to Argentina alone. Her father shook his head. Her mother said nothing.

"Why do you want to leave so badly?" asked Raúl. "I like it here."

"Because this isn't our home, Raúl!" replied Miranda. "And unlike you, I'm not obsessed with movies from Hollywood!"

"They're not all from Hollywood. There's Warner Brothers™. There's MGM™. There's Paramount™. There's—"

"*Papá!*" interrupted Miranda. "I told you he should have gone to *la Academia Británica!* Sending him to that American school has brainwashed him!"

"Now, now, Miranda, *calmate, por favor!*" said her father.

"Well, now we are all Americans!" said Eva, standing up with a large smile.

"Oh! *Por Dios!*" said Miranda. "Am I the only sane person left in this family? *Mamá, sos gringa ahora, tambien?*"

Her mother laughed. "*Por qué me decís esto, Miranda?*"

Miranda put both of her hands over her head and massaged her temples. *"No te preocupés, mamá. Me llevás a la universidad? Tengo que hablar con los orientadores."*

Raúl smirked. "University?" he scoffed. "Don't you mean *community college?*"

Miranda glared at him before ordering her mother to hurry. Leaving the house quickly, they entered a cream colored Mercedes Benz and drove a few miles to the college campus. Once there, Miranda instructed her mother to wait in the lobby while she spoke with a counselor.

"Well, from what you've told me, probably the best thing to do is to enroll you in some of our courses in American history and literature," said the middle-aged woman from the other side of the desk. She stroked her short dark hair and perused the school course catalog. Without bothering to make eye contact, she continued, "Your assessment scores are very high, so that's all I can really suggest at this point."

"That would be nice," said Miranda. "I mean to say it will at least occupy my time. I will not be here long, you know. I may not even finish this term before I transfer to a university where I belong."

The woman nodded. "Yes, of course."

"Perhaps I could take a few classes in French and Italian?" asked Miranda.

"We don't offer Italian, but we do have courses in French. If you would like, you could go to the foreign language building and see if any of the French teachers are around. There are only two instructors."

Miranda curled her lips somewhat condescendingly. "Could you orient me as to the classroom?"

The counselor furrowed her brow. "Excuse me?"

A young man approached. "I believe she is asking for directions," he said.

"Oh, Ben," said the counselor. "Would you mind?"

"Not at all."

Miranda hesitated. She took a long look at him. To her surprise, she found him quite handsome. He had fair colored skin, and light blue eyes that were somewhat hidden by the black rims and the thick lenses of his glasses. His thick black hair was neatly trimmed and combed to the side with gel, displaying his square forehead. He was slight of stature when compared to the typical American, and conservatively dressed with dark slacks, black shoes and a white collared shirt. He reminded her of the boys in Argentina.

Ben motioned with a sweep of his hand that Miranda proceed out the door. "After you."

Miranda nodded. She then got up and walked past her mother, saying quickly, "*Ya vengo, mamá. Esperame aquí.*"

Walking past several buildings on a wide cement path, Miranda waited impatiently for Ben to speak. She looked at him, but he seemed fully concentrated on the buildings. Finally, he said, "The campus seems large, but I'm sure that's true of any college."

Miranda frowned. "Actually, I find the campus quite small, especially when compared to the University of Buenos Aires."

Ben's eyebrows arched. "Buenos Aires? You're from Argentina?"

Miranda stopped and smiled. She looked directly into Ben's eyes. "Why, of course, what did you think?"

Ben hesitated for a moment. "I thought that you were British."

"No, silly," said Miranda. "I am Argentine."

Ben inclined his head. "Well, we're almost there."

"Yes, we are," said Miranda.

Ben turned his head in both directions. The two stood closely. In front of them was a gray, rather drab cement building of two floors. Ben pointed and continued to walk. Miranda crinkled her nose and then slowly followed him. After a dozen steps, Ben stopped. "I hope your stay will be a pleasant one."

Miranda's eyes widened. "What did you say?"

"I said that I hope you will enjoy your stay here."

Miranda smiled. "Well, I am starting to believe that I shall."

Ben smiled. It was a bashful smile that seemed to ask permission to do so. "Well, I guess I better let you go so you can inquire about the French classes."

He slowly began to walk away when Miranda suddenly blurted, "Excuse me!"

Ben turned. "Yes?"

Miranda approached him and extended her cheek. "Did you know that in my culture friends dismiss themselves with a kiss on the cheek?"

Ben blushed as he released a nervous smile. Slowly, a bit hesitantly, he kissed Miranda. He then lingered a moment before quickly walking away.

Miranda watched him as he strode across the wide cement path. She sighed, brushed back her wavy blonde tresses, and proceeded to locate the French department. Entering the building, she walked down a long, narrow hallway. After passing many rooms, she saw an office with a class schedule posted on a transparent rectangular glass section of the door. It was written in French.

"Hello, hello, hello," said a young man with long brown hair. He wore a loose white T-shirt that fell untucked over his faded blue jeans which sported a few holes near the knee.

"Hello," said Miranda, smiling at him.

He continued to face her as he walked forward, which resulted in a large thud as he crashed against a water fountain that slightly protruded from the wall. Miranda could not help but laugh.

"Uh, water fountain," he shouted, pointing to the dark metal structure. After an awkward grin, he added, "But you were worth it!" He then disappeared down the hall.

Knocking on the office door, Miranda heard a voice beckoning her to enter. Turning the knob, she saw a woman writing basic French greetings on a small white board display. Miranda frowned slightly at the sight of her. She was wearing dress slacks with a light blue blouse. Her dark hair was very thick, woven into a bun, and she wore cat like glasses with dark rims that blended nicely with her tan skin.

"Excuse-moi, êtes vous le professeur de français?" asked Miranda.

"Yes, wow!" replied the instructor. "You speak French so well! I am Madame Thompson."

"Enchante! Je suis Miranda! Oui, je parle français depuis que j'étais un enfant. Et chaque été, ma famille visitais Paris et Venice," said Miranda.

Madame Thompson smiled, then replied, *"Impressionnant! S'il vous plaît, asseyez-vous."*

Miranda closed the door behind her and sat down on an old, slightly padded chair. She crossed her legs, pausing to allow Madame Thompson to continue, but she did not. Miranda then inquired as to how she had learned the French language. *"Excusez-moi, professeur, où avez-vous appris le français? Si je peux vous demander?"*

Madame Thompson furrowed her brow. Then, she replied, "*j'ai étudié à la université…et j'ai passé…un été en Beligique.*"

Miranda frowned deeply. Her initial excitement vanished, replaced by disappointment and even pity. "I'm sorry, Madame, but I cannot even consider you a **fluent** speaker. How can you teach French when your accent is dreadful and you must pause to utter even the most basic sentences?"

Madame Thompson's mouth dropped open. She then crossed both of her arms in front of her slight bosom. "Most people compliment me whenever I visit Europe," she said dryly.

"Yes, I am sure they do. They say, however, that when people *stop* complimenting you is when you have truly reached a satisfactory level."

The face of Madame Thompson reddened slightly. "Well, I never claimed to be an expert."

"Then may you explain to me how someone who is not an expert teaches literary analaysis of such classics as *Le Compte de Monte Cristo ou Cyrano de Bergerac?*"

"We don't teach those works!" said Madame Thompson. "That is very advanced! I myself would have trouble with such works. We teach basic French—conversational French. I'm sorry if you misunderstood."

Miranda paused at this admission, but ultimately remained unmoved by Madame Thompson's sincerity. "Please do not apologize. I suppose you are not to be blamed for being an unqualified instructor residing at a school with such low standards. As Cicero would say, 'To each his own.'[7] In my case, however, that would never do. I had two French teachers who impacted me greatly in Argentina. Both were from France, educated in France, and with Degrees in the French language. They inspired my parents to make frequent visits to Paris to understand the culture and the language from its purest source. I have spoken French since elementary school."

Madame Thompson furrowed her brow. "So you're from Argentina?"

"Yes, I am," said Miranda, lifting her chin proudly.

"But your accent…it almost sounds British."

"Yes, I attended a British school in Buenos Aires," replied Miranda, tossing her blonde hair back slightly. "Every student was required to take classes in English and Spanish. Later, we were exposed to Italian and French. Of course, not all students chose to take these courses, and even less pursued them with any type of passion; but my parents insisted. I do love Italian, and it is part of my heritage, but I must say that my mother and I believe French to be the sweetest of all languages. *Le français* is an incredible language! *J'adore la langue francais! C'est la plus belle langue du monde!*"

Madame Thompson paused again. She appeared to be studying Miranda. "Well, uh, maybe you would like to visit one of our classes. You could be a guest speaker and share your experiences in Paris."

Miranda displayed her bright dazzling smile. "Yes, that is a wonderful idea! I will be happy to oblige, but at the same time, it could be a bit demoralizing for your students."

"I don't follow you."

"Don't you?" said Miranda, her face revealing a **condescending** frown. "Well, silly, once they see how beautifully I speak, they will be terribly embarrassed by their actual level. I would not want to dishearten them now, would I?"

Madame Thompson bit her lip. She then lowered her head. After a brief silence, she walked past Miranda and opened her office door. "I'm sorry. I just remembered I have an appointment soon and I—I really need to finalize a few things I'm working on. *Salut.*"

"Au revoir! Passez une bonne journée!" said Miranda, smiling and waving as she walked away, **oblivious** to the fact she had offended the woman.

4

It did not take long for the male students to notice Miranda. Although there were many attractive young ladies on campus, Miranda was still very conspicuous. Not only was she amazingly beautiful, but she had a certain exotic aspect to her that captivated each young man who laid eyes upon her. As she left one of her classes just before noon, she was practically mobbed by four popular football players.

"Hey, hold up!"

Miranda continued to walk down the wide cement path.

"Hey! Hey! Wait up! Are you gonna eat lunch?"

Finally, Miranda slowed down and peered over her shoulder.

"You're new here, aren't you?"

Miranda looked up to see a chiseled brown face. He stood a solid six feet and had shaved black hair and thick dark eyebrows. His muscular body was easily seen through his tight blue jeans and white T-shirt. Miranda smiled at him and replied, "Yes, I am from Buenos Aires."

"Cool. I'm Carlos. Maybe you've heard of me. All league running back?"

Miranda responded with a quizzical expression.

Carlos, undeterred, smiled and continued. "These here are my boys."

Miranda quickly observed three well-built young men, two being black and the other white. "Dillan, Darnell, and this guy over here is Harrison Jones, but that's kind of boring, so we call him Jonesy."

Dillan and Darnell laughed. Jonesy ran his hand through his short blonde hair and released a wide smile. Darnell, who was wearing a white tank top, gripped Jonesy's shoulder with his muscular arm and shook him playfully.

"Pleased to meet you all," said Miranda. Then, looking directly at Carlos, she added, "So, you run?"

Carlos nodded. "Yeah, for the football team. Do you like football?"

Miranda smiled weakly. "American football? No, not really. I much prefer real *fútbol*."

"Oh, yeah, soccer," said Carlos. "Yeah, it's cool, too, I guess. Buenos Aires. Is that in southern Cal?"

Miranda puckered her lips slightly. "I beg your pardon?"

"I've heard of Buena Park but not Buenos Aires. Is it around here?" But before Miranda could reply, Carlos continued, "You seem different. And you say words in Spanish really good. Are you from Mexico?"

Miranda stopped. She shook her head and rolled her eyes. "Please tell me you are not serious."

Carlos bit his lip. He turned to his friends once again. None of them said a word. Darnell offered Carlos nothing more than a shrug of his muscular shoulders. Jonesy merely arched his eyebrows. Continuing, Carlos stuttered, "Uh, yeah, I was just saying I noticed your accent. It's different. You speak so clearly. So I was right? You're from Mexico? What part?"

Miranda's green eyes suddenly flared. *"Escuchame bien, yo no soy ninguna ignorante mexicana! Ese comentario fue un insulto! Soy argentina y aún más, soy Porteña!"*

As Miranda walked off, the boys remained standing. Carlos, in particular, was as rigid as a statue.

"Hey, man, what did she say to you?" asked Dillan.

"It sure didn't sound good," said Darnell.

"Maybe I ought to give it a try," said Jonesy.

"Hey, back off, I got this!" growled Carlos.

"So what did she say?" asked Darnell.

"I didn't get it all!" replied Carlos. "She spoke too fast! But see! I was right! She's like one of those fine babes you see on the Mexican channels!" He quickly ran up to Miranda as she approached the cafeteria. His friends followed in pursuit. "I'm sorry," began Carlos, "I don't get you. *Qué quiere decir 'Porteña'? Es como 'Sureña'? Estás en una clika?* That's hard to believe 'cause you're way too pretty to be gang banging."

"What is wrong with you?" asked Miranda, **gesticulating** her exasperation by shaking her head and crinkling her nose and forehead. "I cannot understand your English or your Spanish!"

With that, Miranda quickened her pace and walked away, leaving Carlos and his group of friends standing together, speechless. Finally, Darnell spoke up. "Yo, homeboy, I think you just got played!"

"Yeah, that's the first time I've seen you shut down, bro," said Dillan.

The entourage of athletic boys that followed Carlos then began slapping each other's hands and laughing. Carlos frowned. "You know what? I think I'm either completely fascinated by that chick or totally repulsed by her. Come on, let's get some grub. Who's driving?"

5

As MIRANDA SEARCHED for a place to sit, she noticed students eating both inside the cafeteria as well as outside on cement benches. Observing them, she was struck by a certain **eclectic** nature found within their entirety; they seemed to come in all sizes, shapes, colors, and generations. Some students appeared to be the age of the professors whereas others were clearly teenagers who were just beginning to leave the era of adolescence. Their style of clothing, too, demonstrated a marked contrast; a few were dressed quite formally but most displayed a casual variety of jeans or shorts, cotton shirts, sandals or tennis shoes.

Miranda herself was quite conspicuous, readily visible with her snug white pants that reached her ankles, her bright yellow blouse that displayed a hint of cleavage, and her black shoes that made a loud clicking sound each time the two inch heels touched the floor. She hesitated, surveying her possibilities, quite aware of the many eyes upon her.

"Hey, you, come on over," called out a petite brunette. "I'll save you from the wolves."

Miranda looked at the girl, somewhat confused.

"I'm Tawny. I'm in your American Lit class. You want to hang out with me and my friends?"

"Are you inviting me to sit with you?" asked Miranda.

"Yeah, sit or stand, whatever. Follow me and you can kick it with us."

Tawny then motioned for Miranda to follow her. As the two girls carried their card stock paper lunch boxes outside to a grassy area underneath a tree, a boy passing by proclaimed, "Man! You're hot!"

"Oh no, just a little," replied Miranda. "The truth is that you have wonderful weather here in southern California."

The boy furrowed his brow. "Huh?"

"I said you have beautiful weather here," repeated Miranda.

"Um, yeah, whatever. Hey, you need any help? I could carry your food. What's your name?"

"Her name's none of your business!" interjected Tawny. "Now, I suggest you get lost unless you want your picture on the front page of the school paper with the headline: *Stop Harassment by Clueless Losers.*"

"*Sorrrrry,*" said the boy, shaking his head. As the girls walked away, he called out, "Nobody reads that thing anyway!"

Tawny dismissed him with a wave of her hand. Leading Miranda, she stopped in front of a group of students sitting beneath the shade of a large tree. "This is Reggie; Steve, with the guitar; and that's Luis."

Each of the boys smiled and waved at Miranda.

"Over there are Bryanna, Meling, and Sharon," continued Tawny.

They also smiled and waved.

Miranda sat down on the soft green grass and put her food on her lap, following the example of the others. She took a small bite of her sandwich. "Hello, pleased to meet you all. My name is Miranda Silvini Frondizi." She then looked downward, concerned that the grass might stain her white pants.

"Wow! That's quite a mouthful!" said Tawny. "I think we'll just stick with *Miranda*. So where are you from?"

"Buenos Aires," said Miranda, pronouncing her city of origin proudly with her Argentine accent.

Steve, a thin boy with long brown hair and tan skin, instantly began to strum his guitar and sing, "Don't cry for me Argentina…"

Miranda smiled. "Yes, yes! Finally, someone understands! It is simply dreadful that everyone thinks that I am from Mexico!"

Luis, a chubby young man with dark brown skin and long black hair that slovenly fell over his forehead, cocked his head back. "Well, it's not like they're accusing you of committing a crime."

"Oh, yes, I know, but there is such a huge difference, especially with the Mexicans that live here," Miranda replied.

Suddenly, Steve stopped singing and strumming his guitar. The flow of several conversations that were taking place within the group abruptly came to a stop.

"Well, hold on there, Miranda," said Tawny. "What exactly are you trying to say?"

Miranda smiled and proudly continued, "I'm only stating the obvious! We Argentines are the pride of South America! We are creoles that have descended directly from Europe, primarily Spain and Italy. I have absolutely no Indian blood. There are very few *Mestizos*, and even less mulattos, in Argentina…. At least not in proper society."

Reggie, sporting baggy jeans that sagged low on his hips and a gold basketball jersey that contrasted with his black skin, turned to face Miranda. "I don't get you."

"I believe I have been quite clear," replied Miranda. "My English is impeccable. In fact, I am shocked at how badly you Americans speak the English language. Why do you always say 'get' to everyone? What is that supposed to mean, anyway?"

"Okay," Reggie said slowly, anunciating each word with great exaggeraton. "I do not un-der-stand what you mean by say-ing that you have no In-di-an blood."

"Oh," said Miranda, smiling. "Well, one normally infers such a thing in public, but if I must say it to educate you all, then I guess I shall. I'm simply amazed at how ignorant Americans truly are! We creoles have superior genes. We are white *hispanoamericanos* of European ancestry. We have very little in common with the typical Mexican who has migrated here in search of manual labor."

Reggie's eyes widened as he turned back toward the others. A few people stopped chewing their food. Finally, Tawny broke the silence. "Miranda, I don't get—I mean—are you saying that you are better than Mexicans because you're whiter?"

"Of course!" exclaimed Miranda. "I mean, certainly there are exceptions. One must only look at the popular *telenovelas* to see that some Mexicans have European features and surnames, but sadly most are not so fortunate! Surely you must understand?"

Tawny shrugged her shoulders.

"Why, just look at you!" continued Miranda, pointing to Tawny. "You have pretty brown hair—although it is much too short—and you have blue eyes and a cute little nose I might add. If you were Indian, or sorry…" She paused to look at Reggie, who was African American, and added, "*Moreno*, then you would not have such nice features. I mean, you might still be attractive if you were fortunate, but of course you would be very limited indeed. Well, and those are just the physical aspects. We haven't even begun to discuss such things as the typical lack of education, culture, and manners one finds with these people."

"Miranda, what the hell is your problem?" shouted Tawny. "Are you some kind of damned racist?"

Miranda furrowed her brow, startled by Tawny's reaction. Seeking to maintain her composure, she adopted a much more conciliatory tone. "Oh no, I talk to everyone. I pride myself on being charitable to the less fortunate."

"*Mírame!*" said Luis, standing up and walking over to Miranda. "*Soy mexicano* and I have brown skin."

"You're Mexican? I thought you were American," Miranda replied.

"Well, yeah, I'm American, but my race is Mexican."

"Your race?" Miranda repeated, puzzled by the statement. "Being Mexican is not a race but a nationality. That would be like saying *Brazilian* or *Canadian* is your race. You are a *mestizo*."

"I don't even know what the hell that is!" said Luis. "All I know is that people look at me and see *Mexican*, all right?"

"Were you born in Mexico?" asked Miranda.

"No, but my parents were."

"Then perhaps your parents are Mexican, but you are obviously American."

Luis shook his head. "Look, whatever, my family's Mexican. My dad barely speaks English. He's dark. And you know what? The reason he's so dark is because he's worked in the sun all his life for rich little *fresas* like you! In fact, my dad works his ass off so that me and all my brothers and sisters can have a better life! So are you saying that you're better than him? Are you saying that you're better than me?"

"Please do not be angry," Miranda said calmly, looking up at Luis. "I am quite sure your father is a fine man."

Luis breathed heavily. His jaw began to tighten. Steve then stood up and with his guitar attached by a shoulder strap, walked over and patted him on the shoulder. "Take it easy, bro."

"You don't have to feel sorry for us," said Meling, a young lady with long black hair and a nicely shaped square face that showed a few sprinkles of freckles. "My grandparents are from Taiwan, so just out of curiosity, are *yellow* people inferior, too? You know, Asians?"

Miranda took a quick panoramic view of the students around her. Their faces were serious and somewhat threatening. "Um, it was nice meeting you all," she began, standing with her lunch box in one hand. "I must be going now. Have a nice day."

As Miranda proceeded to walk away, Reggie called out, "Watch out for all them black folk!"

The group broke into laughter. As they did so, Reggie shook his head vigorously. "Man, that girl's a trip!"

"Yeah," said Tawny, "a serious head case. Who the hell does she think she is?"

"It's cool," Luis replied. "You and Steve can hang out with her 'cause you're white. We'll understand."

Tawny punched Luis hard on the shoulder. He flinched before his face broke into a large grin. Then, in a tone dripping of sarcasm, he added, "Sharon, you better stay clear, and you too, Bryanna. Meling, I think you're like in the middle or something so I guess you can go either way."

A few in the group laughed.

"Yeah, what's up with *yellow?*" asked Reggie. "Aren't you white—or tan—or something?"

Meling crinkled her nose and shrugged. Bryanna, an attractive girl who had a joyful, even innocent air about her, released a large smile as her eyes widened. The black hair that covered her honey colored skin and flowed to her shoulders in evenly cut waves danced from side to side as she shook her head. "Wow! I've never met anyone like her before! I guess I never thought about those things! But just so everyone knows, I'm not really Mexican. I've never even been to Mexico and nobody in my family speaks Spanish. I mean, maybe my great-grandparents or something like that but not me. I'm American, right?"

"Of course you're American!" said Tawny. "We all are!"

Luis curled his lips and shook his head.

"I don't know," Sharon replied. She adjusted her glasses. "I think she's just ignorant. I don't think she's actually all that bad. I don't see her saying anything with hatred."

"Are you crazy?" Tawny asked. "She's a racist prick!"

"But she's hot!" said Steve as he strummed his guitar and then sang, "Don't cry for me Argentina! The truth is I neeeeever left you…"

He did not get past the first few lines of the song before being pelted with food.

6

MIRANDA WAS RELIEVED that her first week of classes was coming to an end. The last few days had been stressful. She was finding it difficult to relate to Americans. Most of the female students avoided her, the male students frightened her with their forward behavior, and the teachers did not seem to appreciate her comments during class discussions.

While studying in the library, Miranda had seen Tawny and a few other girls, all with cameras attached to lanyards of different colors dangling from their necks. Miranda smiled and waved at her, but instead of reciprocating, Tawny rolled her eyes and then whispered something to the other girls. They immediately frowned and walked away.

As the evening approached, a pretty sunset emerged, creating a beautiful sky of a dark blue and gray hue. In the background were the beautiful San Gabriel Mountains. Miranda admired this setting for a brief moment, stretched her arms and legs, and then left the school's main buildings. She continued until she crossed the parking lot toward the main boulevard, where she knew her mother would be waiting for her.

An hour passed; Miranda looked at her watch impatiently. The sun had faded, replaced by darkness, and the cool night air had descended upon her. She looked at her phone; there were no text messages. As Miranda peered down the street, she was so upset that she failed to recognize three approaching boys.

"Yeah, that's gotta be her!" proclaimed one.

"Hey, what's your name?" asked another. He stood so closely that he actually nudged Miranda's arm with his chest.

Her feminine nature quickly told her that this was not mere flirtation but a truly dangerous situation. Still, Miranda did not panic. She was almost as tall as all three boys and could see a few students passing by in the distance. "Excuse me, but could you please give me some space? You're much too close. Please—please step aside."

"Yeah, back off!" said a third boy who was larger than the others. He had a certain roughness to him. Below his light brown mustache were sharp, jagged teeth covered with yellow streaks. His breath reeked of cigarette smoke. "Anyone dressed like you wants attention. So I hear you like white guys," he continued while stroking Miranda's hair and the back of her neck.

"You know, my mother will be here at any moment," said Miranda, "and there are people everywhere watching us. I am asking you for the very last time to leave, or you are going to find yourself in a very unfavorable situation."

"Yeah, watch out, Tony!" said a boy whose face was covered with acne. "Anyway, I'm the one who spotted her!"

"Shut up!" snarled Tony before quickly returning his attention to Miranda. "I'm not even sure what you said, babe, but if you're talking about trouble, well, I get into trouble all the time. In fact, I just got done with a two year bit..." Tony's voice trailed off. Then, with a deep snort, he said, "But looking at you, I think it'd be worth pissing off my probation officer." He then pulled Miranda toward him, pressing her firm bosom against his chest.

"Stop!" Miranda cried.

But to her surprise, nobody interfered. One girl in the distance lingered for a moment, but left when the boys shouted obscenities at her. Tony slowly began to caress Miranda's upper arms despite her shouts to the contrary. He then clutched the nape of her neck and forced her face forward. As he opened his mouth to kiss her, a voice called out, "Hey! What's going on over there?"

Tony stopped suddenly. "None of your damn business!" he shouted. "Now get the hell out of here!"

"Are you okay?"

"No!" Miranda cried. "Please! Help me!"

"Gentlemen, you have two choices," called out the same voice from within the darkness. Somehow, it seemed familiar to Miranda. She strained to follow the sound of the gentle, yet firm tone, but could see no one through the blockade formed by the three boys. "Leave her alone and walk away, or continue and I'll report you to the school authorities *vis a vis* the police. Do you know how serious a charge sexual assault is? You will all be arrested immediately."

The three boys exchanged glances. Tony then threw Miranda toward his two friends and walked a few steps away. Scowling at the intruder, he hissed, "Little boy, I ain't playing around. Unless you want to get seriously hurt, you better back off."

"I'm not going anywhere," replied the voice.

Tony spit on the ground. "I swear I'll kick your teeth in!" he shouted.

A white, slender arm reached through the boys toward Miranda. "Come with me."

Miranda was just able to see the image of a young man. He possessed a soft pale face, black hair, and glasses with dark rims. She attempted to grasp his hand, but just as their fingers touched, he suddenly gasped and fell to the ground. A loud thud filled the air, and then another and another, until replaced by the sound of glass and plastic cracking against the pavement. She screamed instantly.

Tony grabbed Miranda firmly by the arm. "Hey, take it easy!"

"Who is this little school boy?" asked the young man whose face was covered with acne.

"I don't know, but get rid of him!" said Tony.

At that moment a cream colored Mercedes Benz pulled up to the sidewalk with headlights flashing brightly on Miranda and the surrounding boys. As they squinted and covered their eyes, an elegant woman emerged from the car and shouted, *"Qué está pasando aquí?"*

"Mamá! Mamá!" cried Miranda between tears as she rushed to her mother.

Her mother embraced her and whispered, *"Ya, ya, qué pasó mi amor?"*

Tony began to fidget. He then motioned to his friends. "Come on, there's too many people!" he shouted.

The two nodded. The three of them quickly passed Miranda and her mother. As they did so, Tony whispered, "Hey, babe, don't worry, I'll be back." He and the other two boys then ran into the parking lot and disappeared into the darkness.

A small crowd quickly formed. "Ben? Is that you?" asked one young lady with curly brown hair.

"Yeah."

"Hey, man, you okay?" asked a young man casually dressed in jeans and a T-shirt. "Here, let me help you up."

Ben winced as he was helped to his feet.

"Here's your glasses," said a young lady with long dark hair.

"Thank you," said Ben, holding the black rims. They were bent beyond repair.

Releasing her mother, Miranda shouted, "You!"

Ben picked up his backpack. He then inserted his twisted glasses into his shirt pocket. "Hello."

"Estás bien?" asked Miranda's mother.

Ben furrowed his brow.

"Mamá, él es gringo, por supuesto que no habla español! No sea tonta!" said Miranda. Then, turning to Ben, she continued in a much more agreeable tone, "You poor thing! Are you okay?"

"Yes, thank you."

Miranda smiled. "I believe we have met before."

"Yes, I believe we have," replied Ben.

"May we offer you a ride home?"

"Thank you, but I can take the bus."

Miranda caressed Ben's arm. "Please," she said, "I do not know what might have happened if you had not intervened, and I seriously doubt that a bus can take you directly to your door."

"Well, you're right about that," said Ben. "You're sure it's no trouble?"

"Not in the least, now come!" beckoned Miranda, motioning toward the car.

Miranda opened one of the doors located on the side of the car as a crowd of onlookers developed on the curb. "We will take you home, but you are sure you do not need any medical assistance? Perhaps we should take you to see a doctor."

Ben slowly sat down in the leather seats in the back of the car. "No, no, I'm fine, really."

"We are new to your city," said Miranda. "Actually, we are new to your country. But if you explain to me where you live then I will tell my mother."

"Sure, we just need to go a little way into Glendora."

After translating directions to her mother, Miranda recounted the day's events in vivid detail. This was followed by a diatribe of how her mother had put her life in danger. As her voice became more and more animated, Ben gently rubbed his ribs.

"Well, I am so sorry for what happened to you," said Miranda, turning in order to make eye contact with Ben. "You were very brave to deal with those ruffians. Of course, it was entirely my mother's fault. She still does not know her way around and has always been quite the brute when it comes to directions! I hope we do not find ourselves lost while searching for your home!"

Miranda then proceeded to laugh. Ben turned his head toward the window.

"It is so hard to find good help these days!" Miranda continued, pointing to her mother.

"Excuse me," said Ben, "but do you find it appropriate to make rude comments to your mother? She, too, helped you. And now she is helping me."

"Oh, it is okay. She understands very little English," Miranda replied flippantly.

"Oh, I see." Ben paused for a moment. Then, slowly, he added, "Does that change anything?"

Miranda gave him a puzzled look. "I do not understand."

"Whether the person hears you or not, understands you or not…isn't it the intention of your heart that matters?"

Miranda stared at him. "I—I guess I never thought about it that way."

"The feelings of others?" asked Ben. Miranda opened her mouth as if to say something in her defense, but instead she stopped and smiled.

Ben pressed his lips together. For a moment, they continued in silence. Finally, Ben pointed and said, "Please tell your mom to make a right on the next street and stop at the house with the black car parked in front."

The car came to a halt in front of a house of yellow wooden side panels and white window shutters. Ben then quietly gathered his backpack and walked over to Miranda's mother. She lowered her window.

"*Muchas gracias,*" said Ben in a rather thick American accent.

La señora Frondizi smiled. "*Con mucho gusto y más bien, gracias a vos.*"

Ben nodded, smiled, and waved goodbye. Miranda watched him intently as he made his way to the door.

7

MIRANDA AND HER father sat in front of a large wooden desk.

"What kind of college is this, Mr. Howard?" shouted el señor Frondizi. "I still can't believe what happened to my daughter!"

"*Papá*, please! Control your temper!" said Miranda.

Mr. Howard was a large gentleman with patches of blonde hair that strained to reach the top of his forehead despite obviously being combed in that direction. He sat calmly at his desk while Miranda's father continued his tirade. Finally, he said, "Mr. Frondizi, I can assure you that we have security on campus at all times. There are, however, certain areas that have less vigilance. I am as shocked as you are that these young men would be so brazen as to do this in public. Technically, from what you both have told me, Miranda was standing on the edge of the parking lot, so all kinds of people walk by there. It wasn't as if this happened in the center of our campus. At this point we're still not sure if they are even students of ours."

"I do not believe so, sir," said Miranda, "but being new here, I cannot be certain. I know they called one of the boys 'Tony.' He was actually the one who…"

Miranda inclined her head. Her father leaned out of his chair and put his arm around her.

Mr. Howard wrote down the name. "I know this is hard, Miranda, but is there anything else you can tell me?"

Miranda thought for a moment. She had no desire to recollect the ugly incident that occurred the week before. "Well, it was dark, you know. I do remember one of the boys showing the others his cell phone," she began, looking down in embarrassment. "I think it was a picture of me."

"How do you think they obtained that picture?" asked Mr. Howard.

"I do not know," said Miranda. "Some boys have taken pictures of me as I have walked to my classes."

"*Escuela de mierda!*" said Miranda's father. "You allow this?"

Mr. Howard paused. "Mr. Frondizi, kids taking pictures of each other is nothing out of the ordinary. If Miranda feels it is a form of harassment then she needs to report this to us."

"So my daughter is responsible for everything?" Miranda's father raised his index finger. "Tell me, Mr. Howard; are you not the Dean of Students? What is it that you do, exactly? I'm beginning to feel I will need to hire a lawyer!"

Mr. Howard took a deep breath. "Sir, I will talk personally to our school president and our campus officers about this incident. We want your daughter—and all of our students—to feel safe while on campus."

"You are pressing criminal charges against them, aren't you?"

"I would like to get more information, but yes, we will report this incident to the Glendora Police Department right away."

"My daughter has told you all that she knows, but there was a young man, a student here, who helped her."

"Then we need to speak to him," said Mr. Howard.

"I know where he studies in the library," said Miranda, her downcast face suddenly expressing a hint of joy. "I'll talk to him and bring him to you!"

"That would be great," said Mr. Howard. "In the meantime, I want to say to both of you that we have great students here, overall, but we are not a private school and some of our surrounding neighborhoods are a little rough. I would suggest that Miranda walk with other students if she is going to take evening classes and wait for her mother in one of the parking lots. I wish it were not so, but as a father of two daughters myself, we have to realize that we live in a dangerous world. Miranda is a very pretty young lady and naturally draws attention. There's safety in numbers. Do you understand what I'm saying?"

Miranda nodded.

"We are still learning your culture," said el señor Frondizi, combing back his thinning brown hair. "But it is no different than where we are from. But having said that, I want to make it clear that I will hold this school responsible if anything happens to my daughter!"

With lips pressed firmly together, Mr. Howard nodded. "Yes, of course."

With that, the two men shook hands.

As Miranda and her father turned to leave the office, Mr. Howard asked, "May I have a word with you in private, Mr. Frondizi?"

"You want to speak to me alone?"

"Yes, it will only be a moment."

"Danos un momento, mi amor," Miranda's father said to her.

As soon as Miranda closed the door behind her, Mr. Howard began, "I need to be very direct with you, Mr. Frondizi, and although what I am about to say might sound offensive, I want you to know that it is not my intention."

El señor Frondizi furrowed his brow. "Yes?"

"Miranda is a very beautiful girl. We have many attractive young women on our campus and this is not the first time that I have had this conversation. Usually, I prefer to speak directly to the student, but since you're here, and Miranda is new to the states, I think it may be better if you speak with her about a certain level of modesty in the way she chooses to dress."

El señor Frondizi leaned forward in his chair. "My daughter takes pride in her appearance, sir, and we have raised her to be successful. Her mother has personally assisted her to choose the most fashionable clothing that can be found around the world. Should Miranda attempt to hide her beauty because a few hooligans with no honor chose to harass her? I think you are condemning the wrong person, Mr. Howard."

"There is a difference between being attractive and provocative, Mr. Frondizi."

"Yes, well, I would never presume to tell you how to raise your family," replied el señor Frondizi. Then, pointing his finger once again at Mr. Howard, he added, "And I suggest you not tell me how to raise mine."

An awkward silence ensued as both men faced each other. Finally, Mr. Howard spoke. "I sincerely wish that you do not misconstrue anything I've said to you. I want to be very clear. I will do everything possible to find the boys who harassed your daughter—"

"—assaulted," interrupted el señor Frondizi.

Mr. Howard paused for a moment. He scratched the bridge of his nose. "Yes, and I promise you that the full force of the law will be utilized to bring about justice."

"I sincerely hope so," replied el señor Frondizi, standing up in his chair. He then proceeded to leave the office. Outside in the main building, Miranda sat waiting for him.

"May I inquire as to what that was about?" she asked.

"Oh," replied her father, "Mr. Howard simply said you need to be careful, *mi amor*."

"*Por supuesto, papá*."

"And find that boy and tell him to report everything he saw," her father continued. "Maybe he can walk you to meet your mother when you have your evening class."

"*Sí, tenés razón*," said Miranda with a twinkle in her eye.

305

"Perhaps you could invite him to dinner," added her father. "I would like to thank him personally."

"*Sí, papá.*"

8

BEN AND MIRANDA found a table alone located at the far edge of the cafeteria. The large room was filled with the noise of chatter and the clanging of utensils caused by the many students that surrounded them.

"I recognized one of them," said Ben. "I think he goes here. But the others? I've never seen them before."

"American boys are such animals!" exclaimed Miranda. "So vulgar. So uneducated. So unlike the boys in Argentina."

"All American boys?" asked Ben.

Miranda smiled. "Of course not. I am happy to observe that there are some exceptions."

The two took a few bites of their meal. Miranda enjoyed her ham sandwich while Ben picked at his salad which was sprinkled with strips of broiled chicken.

"I must say," began Miranda, "that I am impressed with the school cafeteria. The food here is delicious. Would you like a bite of my sandwich?"

Ben hesitated. "No, thank you."

"Please, Ben," insisted Miranda. "I don't think I can eat it all. Why don't you take the other half?"

"No, really, why don't you save it instead?"

"Oh, well, if you insist." Miranda wrapped her sandwich with napkins and neatly stored it in her purse. "I will be leaving for home, soon, so I think it will be okay to offer it to one of my siblings. My brother, Raúl, loves American sandwiches. Actually, he loves everything American."

Ben nodded.

"May I ask you a personal question?" asked Miranda.

"Of course," Ben replied.

"I know I am not American," said Miranda, "And, unlike my brother, I have never attended an American school until now. Perhaps, I do not fit in so well?" Her green eyes reflected a certain pensiveness, even melancholy.

"No one seems to understand me," continued Miranda. "It's as if I don't belong here."

Ben inclined his head. He held this position for a brief moment before answering. Putting his hands together as if praying, he began, "Miranda, I can only tell you what I know based on a few comments I've heard from others, and, well, our conversation in the car. I don't know how valid my opinion will be."

"Go on," said Miranda.

"Well, some people have said outrageous things about you, but you know how that goes. What I can tell you is that Tawny, the editor of the school paper and not someone you want on your bad side, by the way, claims you made some very derogatory statements about her friends. According to her, your remarks were even racist. And to make it worse, she said that everyone was trying to be nice to you."

Miranda frowned. "I do not see why she is so upset," she began rather smugly. "I would never be intentionally cruel to her friends even though they may be less fortunate."

"But that sounds really condescending," interrupted Ben.

"You must understand. I was forced into such a position. And it is not in my nature to lie."

"So it's true? You do think you are superior to others?"

"Well, not just me," said Miranda. "I merely stated that people like us have certain advantages."

"People like us?"

"Yes," said Miranda. "People like us, people of European descent, people of a certain status. Isn't it true that we have always been the leaders of society?"

Ben frowned. "I doubt if that's true in China or Japan or the Middle East or Africa—"

"I was not referring to those places," interrupted Miranda. "I was simply communicating that I am a white European Creole and do not have any Indian blood. My heritage is from Europe, as is yours. We are of the highest social order. Why, one only has to look at the top schools, or the government, or a *telenovela*, to see this."

"A what?" asked Ben, furrowing his brow.

"*Una telenovela,*" repeated Miranda, "a show, Ben. People on television throughout Latin America are of white European descent. You are not going to see a dark little Indian woman with protruding cheek bones playing the love interest in a *novela,* now, will you? Or some short, plump Indian man reporting the news?"

Ben shook his head. His eyes moved downward.

"Why are you so concerned?" asked Miranda. "You have white skin and I love your blue eyes. It is such a nice contrast with your black hair. You look like Superman™!"

"Well, thank you," replied Ben. "But even without my glasses I think I'm more Clark Kent™ than Superman™. Instead of being the captain of the football team, I'm the president of the chess club."

"Oh, I love chess!" gushed Miranda. Her eyes suddenly lit up. "My father belonged to the chess club in Buenos Aires! Oh, that reminds me, he wants you to come visit us for dinner! Perhaps this Friday?"

Ben paused. He appeared lost in thought. Then, slowly, he raised his hand in protest. "Miranda, wait, we're not finished. Your comments… they concern me. Not only do I believe they're wrong, but I'm personally offended by them."

Miranda gave Ben a puzzled expression. "I don't understand."

"I suppose it has to do with my race," said Ben in a tone barely above a whisper.

"Your race?" asked Miranda. "Why are Americans so confused about this?"

"I'm not confused."

"Yes, you are! Being American is not a race!" said Miranda.

"Perhaps you're right, but in my case it's—it's different.

"And why is that?"

"Because I'm Jewish."

Miranda pursed her lips and smiled. "Oh, I had no idea," she replied calmly, "but that is nothing to be ashamed of. The Jewish people have a very rich tradition!"

"Yes, we do," said Ben, "but you do know that my people have had to fight hatred and bigotry throughout all of our existence. Do you have any idea what it's like to be Jewish?"

Miranda paused, wrinkled her forehead, and then shook her head and replied, "No, I suppose not."

"Do you have any idea what it's like to be anyone besides yourself?"

"What do you mean?"

"Close your eyes and I'll show you."

"Close my eyes? Whatever for?"

"Trust me," said Ben "and I'll show you."

Miranda looked nervously around the cafeteria. A few young men made eye contact with her as she surveyed the large room, but each table of students seemed preoccupied with their own conversations. She fixed her gaze upon Ben. "How will you show me anything with my eyes closed?"

Ben arched his brow.

"You are not going to try to kiss me, are you?" asked Miranda, smiling flirtatiously.

Ben did not respond, which prompted Miranda to finally consent and close her eyes. He then began, "I want you to imagine the following: You live in Somalia. You are hungry. In fact, you have not eaten for two days. Your family is starving. You live in a place that has been devastated by drought. Each day your main purpose is to survive."

Miranda's smile quickly faded. She opened her eyes. "I do not like this game."

"We're not finished yet," Ben said curtly. "Now close your eyes and focus."

Miranda puckered her lips and pouted, but Ben would not be moved. "You and everyone around you are refugees," he continued, "and nobody has time to be nice to you. There are no special commodities. No television, no cell phones, no hairdryers, no makeup, no designer jeans—not even soap or toothpaste. You live in a small tent made of anything you can find that others have discarded."

"This is dreadful," Miranda said with her eyes still closed. "May I— may I ask how I look?"

"Certainly. You have short, thick, tightly curled black hair. You have dark skin. Your eyes are brown. Your face is a mess, you are dirty, and you smell. You are very skinny. In fact, you are so malnourished that your rib bones protrude from within your skin."

Miranda opened her eyes once again and said, "Ben! I do not understand! Must we really do this?"

"Yes, we still have a ways to go."

Miranda looked at him doubtfully, but then dutifully closed her eyes.

"Let's try again. Now I want you to imagine you have white skin," Ben continued. "You also have blonde hair."

Miranda smiled.

"You were born in Europe—Eastern Europe—in the mountains. You are part of a forgotten people, a dying village. Each day men leave in search of work. They travel to France, or Germany, or Italy. Your father is among them. Years pass until you can no longer recall how he looks, or the sound of his voice, or the texture of his lips upon your cheek."

Miranda began to squirm and wince, but remained engaged with her eyes fully closed.

"Your mother does her best to nourish you and your brothers and sisters, but all she can offer is an occasional piece of bread and some goat milk. You are illiterate. You have tattered clothing. Your mother worries that none of you will survive the winter."

"That's enough, Ben!" interrupted Miranda, opening her eyes as she leaped to her feet. Several people nearby turned their faces toward her. "Why in the world would you have me imagine such horrible things? I refuse to participate any further!"

"Miranda, wait!" said Ben, standing up as well. "I told you these things because they are real."

Miranda looked at him, still upset.

"Please, sit down," said Ben in a tone which clearly sought to appease Miranda. "Besides, people are staring."

"I do not care."

"Please," said Ben softly. "Let me explain."

"Very well," said Miranda, settling back into her chair. "But I still do not understand. I thought you were a nice boy. Now I am not so sure."

"I just want you to see that the world is so much bigger than you and me. Don't you understand? We are just two little lives—a blink of the eye—and we share this world with people of different colors and races and cultures. Some are born with light skin and some are born with dark skin.

Some are born into poverty and some are born into wealth. They didn't ask to be born a certain way or in a certain place.... They were just born."

Miranda stared at Ben. For perhaps the first time in her life, she did not feel the need to interrupt due to an innate belief of superiority.

"Did you know that scientists have concluded that you can take any two people from any race or nationality—two totally different people, mind you—and the basic genetic differences among them would be calculated at about two tenths of a percent?"

Miranda waved her head from side to side, and then brushed a strand of blonde hair from her forehead.

"And are you aware of those minute differences?" asked Ben.

"No, I must confess that I am not," huffed Miranda.

"Basically, we're talking about skin color and the shape of the eyes because all people have a variety of hair color and eye color, or height or shape. Maybe someone has lips that are fuller or a nose that is broader, but that also can happen within the same race as well."

"Ben, how do you know these things?" snapped Miranda, still somewhat irritated.

"I did a research paper in my anthropology course last year. But, more than that, my interest has always been personal..." Ben's face suddenly turned sullen, revealing the pain of **vicarious** memories. "The Nazi scientists believed that the Aryan race was superior, that they were different, but their extensive studies proved quite the opposite. They discovered that human beings are remarkably alike."

A silence ensued as Ben stopped talking.

Miranda reached out and gently touched his shoulder. "Ben," she said softly, "what is it? What troubles you so?"

"The stories..." His voice trailed off. "The stories of my grandfather. He escaped Nazi Germany as a child."

"I am so sorry," said Miranda, softening her tone. "I can only..."

"Imagine?"

"Yes," replied Miranda. She curved her lips slightly, forming a very light smile that indicated that she had conceded.

Ben nodded. "Have you ever heard of the term 'melanin'?"

"No, I have not."

"It's a dark pigment that's produced in special cells in our skin. It determines our skin color. If we produce a little melanin, then we are basically classified as white. If our skin produces a strong amount of melanin, we are classified as black. And in between, of course, are all shades of brown. There are no other significant skin pigments. And want to know something else?"

Miranda raised her brow, silently prodding Ben to continue.

"The amount of melanin that we have is more of a genetic potential!" said Ben, his voice becoming more animated. "This means that our color can change due to sunlight. My skin, for example, is white, even pale I'm afraid to say, whereas you have a beautiful golden tan." He rubbed his arm, and then did the same to Miranda. "You have more melanin than I do and probably spend more time under the sun than I do. Now, over generations, or intermarriages, this amount of melanin can change and often does. Virtually, skin color within a family can change within two to three generations. The same goes for other features, such as hair or lips."

"Is this a clever way of proposing to me?" asked Miranda coquettishly.

Ben released a rather timid smile, and then replied, "Well, actually, what I'm saying, Miranda, is that if you marry a black man, and you both have a son that marries a black woman, then chances are your grandchildren will look no different than any other black person."

Miranda inclined her head.

"Don't you see? Every human being—dark, light, fat, skinny, tall, short, rich, poor—is basically the same. Where we are different is in here..." Ben paused to rub his temple. "And in here." He then touched his chest.

Exhaling, Miranda replied, "Yes, Ben, I see your point. Maybe we are not so different after all. Maybe I have been wrong. Still, you do at least agree that some people, some cultures, are better than others, don't you? I'm not trying to be cruel. I'm just stating a fact, aren't I? I mean, some toothless Indian woman living in the jungle cannot be compared to a Venezuelan beauty queen who has been raised in high society."

"Miranda," said Ben, his voice becoming raspy, "who defines those terms? I think that everyone has a different definition of beauty. What is beautiful in one culture may not be so in another. It's all very subjective."

Miranda leaned forward and whispered quietly, "Ben, do you believe that I am beautiful?" She stared at him with eyes that refused to blink. The green hue seemed mesmerizing. Her soft blonde hair fell lightly around the harmonious bone structure of her face, her flawless skin, finally resting on her shoulders and upper back.

Ben remained with his mouth open for several seconds before answering. "You are incredibly beautiful, Miranda...on the outside."

Miranda arched her eyebrows. "Why do you—why do you word it so?"

"Because on the inside, there are still some ugly parts."

"How can one measure beauty if it is on the inside, Ben? You cannot see the inside."

"Yes, you can. If you look deeply enough."

9

"WEAR YOUR BLACK shirt with these slacks," said Ben's mother, a plump woman with dark hair. Her square forehead led to a wide face, and her dress, composed of a simple striped pattern with long white sleeves, placed her in a different generation altogether.

"Make sure to wear a tie!" called out his father from the living room. "And be careful with the car!"

"I can't believe you two," said Ben to his mother who continued to hover over him. "I'm almost twenty years old! I think I know how to dress myself." Then, raising his voice, he shouted to his father, "And I promise I won't do anything to your precious Oldsmobile!"

"You are our youngest son, Benjamin, and you will always be my baby boy," replied his mother, "and you know your father's car is a classic."

"Mother, it's not a classic; it's just old. Now let me shower and get ready," said Ben, gently leading his mother out his bedroom door. "I don't want to be late. My friend said dinner will be served at seven o'clock."

"What did he say?" shouted his father.

"He said that he has to meet his girlfriend by seven!" said his mother in reply.

"Mother! She's not my girlfriend. She's just a friend."

"You seem to be spending a lot of time with her," said his mother, her palms demonstrably open. "Are you sure she knows she's not your girlfriend?"

"When are we going to meet this girl?" shouted Ben's father once again. "And what are her beliefs?"

Ben brushed by his mother and walked over to his father who was seated comfortably on the family sofa in the living room. He was a slight man, with black hair that grew only on the sides and the back of his head, leaving the rest of his scalp completely bare. His polyester pants and collared shirt somehow made him seem older than he was. Lying next to him was a metal walker with four black plastic rubber ends.

"Father, she's not Jewish if that's what you're getting at."

"She's not Jewish!" bellowed Ben's father. "Is she open to our faith?"

"Benjamin, you need to very careful," said his mother. "We've told you many times that you cannot simply give your heart away."

"For the last time, we are just friends. She..." Ben inclined his head and sighed. "She could never be interested in me."

"And why is that?" asked his mother, walking closer to him.

"Because she's so different than any other girl I've ever met. She is so beautiful that she doesn't even seem real, and she's traveled the world and speaks several languages."

"Well, you speak three!" replied his father.

"I speak English," said Ben, frowning.

"No, you speak English, German and Hebrew!" said his father before turning his attention to his wife. "Sweetheart, could you get me some hot tea and adjust my pillow?"

"Yes, dear," replied Ben's mother, hurrying to the kitchen.

"I speak some Hebrew and a few German phrases that I learned from Grandfather," replied Ben. "That's not the same. And mother, you need to stop spoiling him or he's never going to walk."

Returning from the kitchen, Ben's mother placed a cup of hot tea in front of her husband and adjusted his pillow. As she lifted his back, he moaned lightly. Upon hearing this, Ben rolled his eyes.

"Benjamin," began his mother, "you are very intelligent and very handsome. And any girl would be very fortunate to call you her own. We are so proud of you for what you did. We know it was a sacrifice."

Ben kissed his mother on the cheek, "I told you not to talk about that. It's over. It's done."

"Okay, okay, go ahead and get cleaned up. We'll leave you alone. I promise."

"Thank you," said Ben.

"Don't forget your new glasses!" shouted Ben's father.

10

STANDING ON A light brown wooden patio, Ben waited nervously. To his left, located on the white side panel of the house, was a small sign. It was painted with light blue stripes at the top and the bottom and a shining sun was in the center with the word *bienvenidos* splashed across in large black letters. After what seemed like an eternity, Miranda opened the door and smiled. "How do I look?" She then placed her right hand on her hip and her left hand on the back of her head. The pose fully displayed her tight gray skirt that accentuated her shapely tan legs. If that were not enough of a distraction, her white sleeveless blouse blended perfectly with her blonde hair and accentuated her hourglass figure.

"Um, fine," said Ben between small gulps of air. His response was almost comical, a somewhat tormented attempt to not make direct eye contact. He pressed against the black bridge of his glasses. He moved his head in all directions. He adjusted the white tie that contrasted with his solid black shirt.

"Only fine?" asked Miranda, widening her eyes playfully.

Ben smiled. "No, actually, much better than fine."

"That's more like it. Please come in," said Miranda. She leaned forward, brushing her smooth cheek next to Ben's lips. They exchanged kisses. Ben paused for a moment. A wide smile broke upon his face. It did not last long, however, as Miranda's mother approached him and greeted him in the same fashion.

"So, this is our hero," said Miranda's father, extending his hand.

Ben shook it firmly, then replied, "*Mucho gusto, señor. Soy Ben Kurtz.*"

"*Mirá!*" said el señor Frondizi, turning toward Miranda before facing Ben once again. "*Usted habla español? Me llamo don José Raúl Silvini Frondizi.*"

Ben's eyes widened. He opened his mouth, and then slowly replied, "Actually, sir, I speak very little. I've only taken one course."

"Yes, no problem," said el señor Frondizi. "Miranda's mother speaks little English. Besides Spanish, French is her preferred language. I, on the other hand, studied international business and felt that I must learn English." He motioned for Ben to follow him. "Here, come with us and sit down at the dinner table and meet Miranda's younger brothers and sisters; they all speak English except for the little one, Arturo, who is still learning."

"Thank you, sir," said Ben. He turned to Miranda's mother and handed her a small box wrapped in red decorative paper. "Oh, and this is for you. It's a housewarming gift. My parents insisted."

"Es un regalo de sus papás," said Miranda.

La señora Frondizi smiled warmly. *"Muchas gracias! Mandales saludos y deciles que muchas gracias de nuestra parte."*

Ben smiled awkwardly.

"My mother said to greet them for us and to thank them," said Miranda. "She speaks to you in the familiar style. That means she likes you!"

Ben smiled and gave a sincere *"gracias"* to Miranda's mother.

On the deeply stained rustic brown walls of the dining room were several paintings that reflected various locations in Europe. The Eiffel Tower, the Louvre, the Basilica of Saint Peter, the Grand Canal of Venice. Ben sat down next to Miranda at a very large, dark wooden table. There, he was introduced to the rest of the Frondizi family.

"Miranda informed us earlier that your parents were unable to come," said el señor Frondizi.

"Yes, sir," replied Ben. "My father had an accident over a year ago. He broke his hip and shattered his knees. It was pretty bad. He was in the hospital for quite a while, and since then has been confined to a wheelchair."

"Ben, you never told me," interrupted Miranda. "I am so sorry."

"Yes, I usually don't talk about it, but I didn't want your parents to think that my family did not appreciate their offer. My father's doing much better, now. He uses a walker—or at least he's supposed to."

"That is a tragedy," said el señor Frondizi.

"Qué es una tragedia?" asked la señora Frondizi.

"*No sé, mamá,*" said Miranda. "Ben, do you mind if I inquire how this accident occurred?"

"Miranda, I do not think that to be an appropriate question," said her father.

"Ben and I are very close, *papá*," replied Miranda. "He is not offended by personal questions."

Ben shrugged. "Well, supposedly he was hit by a drunk driver."

"That is dreadful!" said Miranda.

"Was justice served?" asked her father.

"I'm afraid not, sir," replied Ben. "From what we were told, the police had a few leads but nothing ever came of it. They officially ended the investigation after a few months."

After an awkward pause, Miranda's father shook his head and said, "Terrible! That is just terrible! This world is full of injustice! I fear the same results in our situation as well."

Ben nodded. "Yes, I spoke to Mr. Howard."

There was a brief moment of silence. Miranda's father then clasped his hands together, making a clapping sound. He smiled. "Well, let's try to think about more pleasant things for the moment." He motioned toward the food that was set before them. "Let's eat and drink and be thankful for friends and family."

"Ben, have you had Argentine food before?" asked Miranda.

"No, I have never actually tasted authentic Argentine food."

"I told you we should have ordered a pizza," said Raúl.

"Ben is very cultural unlike some people," snapped Miranda.

"I'm just saying he may not like it," continued Raúl.

"I'm sure it will be delicious," said Ben.

"We usually make lunch our main meal, but we know that you Americans think differently, so Mireya has prepared a delicious dinner in your honor," said el señor Frondizi, smiling.

Ben inclined his head. "Sir, that wasn't necessary. I just did what anyone would have done."

"I disagree. You did what no one else did."

Miranda smiled at Ben.

"*Yo quiero guiso de patatas!*" said Miranda's youngest sister, Amanda.

"*Un momento, hijita,*" replied el señor Frondizi. "*Primero, nuestro invitado.*" Turning to Ben, he continued, "Please try our potato soup. You will find it delicious. After that, we have filet mignon with grilled onions."

"And after that," added Miranda, "*los postres!*"

Ben raised a spoonful of soup to his lips. "Wow," he said, "it's incredible."

As the appetizer transitioned into the main course, and the main course to the dessert, Miranda looked at Ben with great anticipation. Handing him two small plates, she said, "Here, Ben, you must try our cherished *postres.*"

"Both?" asked Ben.

"Yes, this one is *dulce de leche* and the other we call *alfajor de maizena,*" said Miranda.

"Cheesecake and a cookie," said Raúl.

"Not exactly," said Miranda.

"They both look delicious, but I don't know if I can," said Ben, gently rubbing his stomach.

"Ben, please, you must. If you do not finish, it is okay."

"I'll eat whatever you can't," said Raúl with a large smile.

Ben nodded. He then took his spoon and took a bite of each dessert. After doing so, his eyes widened. "Wow!"

Laughter broke out from both sides of the table.

"I knew that you would be pleased," said Miranda.

"Yes, very much so!" said Ben. "Your mother is amazing!"

"*El dice que vos sos increíble!*" said el señor Frondizi to la señora Frondizi.

La señora Frondizi smiled at Ben. "Thank you."

"*De nada,*" replied Ben.

"You should try the desserts in *las pastelerías de Buenos Aires!*" said Miranda, her eyes lighting up. "There, they actually melt in your mouth! My mother does her best, but of course it is not the same."

Ben frowned. "Well, I think your mother does just fine."

"Excuse me, but may I steal our guest away?" asked el señor Frondizi. "Ben, I want to show you something."

Ben turned to Miranda.

"It's okay. Go!" she said, smiling. "I will join you after helping my mother."

"Are you sure?" asked Ben. "I could help clear the table."

"No, no, come with me," said el señor Frondizi, leading Ben to a nearby den. "I hear you play the royal game." He then gestured toward an exquisite, antique chair. Ben sat down. Between the two lay a complete set of beautiful wooden chess pieces, placed upon light and dark squares that were carved into a coffee table. Along the side of the table was a classic wooden chess clock. El señor Frondizi grabbed two pawns and proceeded to put them behind his back. Ben gestured toward his left hand, which upon opening, revealed a black pawn.

"I suggest we set the clock to thirty minutes," said el señor Frondizi. "I would prefer more time, but I don't want to keep you captive here too long."

"Thirty minutes is fine, sir."

"Of course, the game may finish much earlier," added el señor Frondizi with an air of confidence.

Ben pressed the button of his clock, activating the mechanism. El señor Frondizi opened by advancing his king's pawn two squares and promptly pressed his button down. Ben answered by pushing his queen's bishop's pawn one square. El señor Frondizi frowned and then pushed his queen's pawn two spaces. Ben did the same.

"The Caro-Kann defense," stated el señor Frondizi, nodding slowly.

Ben nodded and replied, "Yes, it was my favorite player's defense."

"And who is that?" asked Miranda as she entered the room.

"J.R. Capablanca. He was from Cuba. He was also a diplomat," replied Ben. "Many people think he was the greatest player of all time or at least the most gifted."

"You have studied Capablanca?" asked el señor Frondizi. "I thought a young American would study Bobby Fischer or Gary Kasparov or perhaps the great Indian grandmaster, Viswanathan Anand."

"I do," replied Ben, "but I think it's important to study the games of the great players of the past. I enjoy the history of the game and seeing how chess theory has developed over the years. It's fascinating to see how each champion has his own unique style."

El señor Frondizi nodded before turning his attention to the board. As he made his next move, and Ben countered, the opening slowly transitioned into the middle game. Both players exchanged minor pieces, struggling to gain the upper hand. Then, after several minutes of silence, Ben placed a knight beside his other knight so that they stood proudly together like a sturdy wall. He pressed his clock and released a gust of pent up energy.

El señor Frondizi sat back in his chair and lit a black wooden pipe. His eyes darted horizontally and vertically. "I'm afraid you have left your king unprotected."

Ben did not reply, but continued to develop his pieces on the queenside. After a series of preparatory maneuvering, el señor Frondizi moved his queen in for the attack, placing the piece onto the board with force. He pressed the button of his clock, sat back in his chair, crossed his legs, and exhaled smoke triumphantly into the air.

"My father has won several tournaments in Argentina," said Miranda, leaning on the side of Ben's chair. "Nobody in the *Congreso Nacional* could beat him."

El señor Frondizi smiled. Ben, with a look of calm, nodded politely as he finally castled on the queenside. El señor Frondizi instantly furrowed his brow. "Hmmmmm. That was somewhat unexpected."

"Ben, why are you placing your pieces on the opposite side of my father's pieces?" asked Miranda.

"Um, well, we're both simply seeking control of different parts of the board," Ben replied.

"My father is an incredible chess player. You should feel very proud of yourself, Ben. I don't think I have seen him think this much before. Isn't that right, *papá*?"

Her father did not answer, but instead crinkled his forehead and curled his lips. His eyes darted toward the clock. Ben had ten minutes whereas el señor Frondizi had a mere two minutes remaining.

"Isn't that right, *papá*?" repeated Miranda.

"Well, yes, *paloma*, but it is not proper etiquette to speak when two people are involved in a match." He then stroked his thinning hair several times.

"If I am not mistaken, you won a tournament held in the Senate in Buenos Aires shortly before we left for the United States," Miranda continued.

Ben smiled politely as Miranda's father let out a few heavy puffs from his pipe.

"I do enjoy the game, but sadly I have never passed the level of a beginner," said Miranda.

Her father scowled at her. Ben then pushed his pawns on the kingside forward, sacrificing them in order to open up both files for his rooks.

"Oh, it looks as if you have lost your pawns, Ben," said Miranda in a tone full of compassion that displayed her sincere concern.

Ben smiled at her naïve form of innocence but never turned from the chess board.

"Perhaps you could teach me some day," said Miranda, placing her hand on Ben's shoulder. "My father is much too impatient. But I really think I could become a strong player if someone would take the time to truly explain to me the proper strategies."

"*Miranda, vas a seguir hablando durante todo el juego?*" snapped her father.

"*Papá*, why are you so cross?" asked Miranda. She frowned briefly, and then looked at Ben. His hand was hovering over his dark squared bishop that he had just moved. Just as he was about to lay down the piece, their eyes met. Miranda quickly changed facial expressions. Her frown transformed into a soft, feminine smile. Ben seemed to lose his concentration momentarily, practically dropping his piece on the board.

"Oh, excuse me," said Ben.

"Miranda, perhaps you should leave until we are finished. I believe you are upsetting our guest...or at least distracting him."

"Father, do not be absurd!" replied Miranda, squinting her eyes. Then, she added, "Ben, you must be playing very well since my father has become so surly!" Miranda broke into laughter. "I certainly am fortunate that I never inherited his insecure character!"

El señor Frondizi fidgeted in his chair. He began puffing on his pipe much more quickly.

"On the contrary," said Ben. "I think you should be grateful for the many things that you have inherited from your father."

Miranda furrowed her brow. She puckered her lips in a sympathetic expression. Then, she smiled at Ben. Her eyes had a surreal quality to them. The **dichotomic** nature of Miranda was on full display. She was just as able to astonish with her arrogance and narcissism as she was to enchant with her beauty and tenderness.

El señor Frondizi rubbed his forehead. His position was lost. On his clock, he had less than a minute remaining before his flag would rise and fall. A resignation would have been the dignified thing to do, but instead he continued, a gesture that seemed to indicate that he preferred to go down fighting than to lose gracefully. In a desperate attempt that would merely slow down the inevitable checkmate, he sacrificed the most powerful piece on the board, his queen. Ben immediately reached for his bishop, then, in a sudden change of movement, instead touched the button on his clock. As he pressed it to the halfway mark, balancing both sides, the mechanism came to a stop.

"It looks to be a draw," said Ben, stretching out his hand. "I don't see any reason to continue."

El señor Frondizi nodded as he quickly grasped Ben's hand. A tinge of happiness could be seen in his eyes. "You are very skilled, Ben, and I hope we can play again very soon."

"I would enjoy that very much, sir."

El señor Frondizi began to restore the pieces on the board, to which Ben did the same. "Ben, you seem to be such an intelligent boy, and Miranda tells me you live in a very nice neighborhood. If you don't mind me asking, why are you attending a community college?"

"Well, actually, I was accepted to a few universities, but my father's accident occurred at the end of my senior year in high school, so I stayed to help my parents."

"I see. That was very noble of you."

"Ben, do you have brothers and sisters?" asked Miranda.

"Yes, I have an older sister, who is married, and a brother who is working on his doctorate degree at Stanford," said Ben.

"That is impressive," said el señor Frondizi. "What is his field of study? Medicine?"

"No sir," Ben replied, "mathematics."

El señor Frondizi laid down his pipe and slowly got up from his seat. "Well, it is getting late. I think I will check on my other children. Miranda, will you be so kind as to walk our guest to his car?"

"Certainly, *papá*," replied Miranda.

"*Fue un placer conocerlo,*" said el señor Frondizi as he left the room. "*Buenas noches.*"

"Oh, yes," replied Ben. "*Buenas noches.*"

Miranda led Ben toward the front door of the house. The two then walked outside together. It was dark and cold. As they reached an old light blue sedan, Miranda put her arms in front of her bosom. Ben opened the front door, and then awkwardly turned to face Miranda. After a short pause, he said, "Well, thank you for dinner. You have a wonderful family."

"Yes, I suppose," replied Miranda.

Ben furrowed his brow. "You suppose?" he repeated.

"Well, if it were not for my father's failure, I would still be in my beloved country," said Miranda. "It has been very difficult for me here, Ben. You are my only friend. I am not happy in the least. I miss my university; I miss my friends; I miss Buenos Aires."

Ben nodded.

"I miss the people," continued Miranda. "I miss knowing where I am going. I miss the little things, like walking along *la avenida de Mayo y* la *plaza Italia*. I miss the taxis and shopping in the Palermo." Miranda's green eyes practically began to glow in the night. "Did I ever tell you that once, while looking for shoes, I was offered a position as a model at one of the boutiques?"

Ben shook his head.

"It was the *Desiderata*," continued Miranda. "Why, that very moment they paid me. All I had to do was return the following day and wear a number of outfits!"

Ben was silent. He seemed to be studying the brief smile that had erupted onto Miranda's face, only to be replaced by the sadness in her eyes. "May I hold you," he asked, "to keep you warm?"

"Yes, please do."

Embracing her, Ben said, "I know this must be a difficult transition for you. I can only imagine the differences in culture."

"Well, you have made it more bearable," replied Miranda, gently putting her head next to his, causing their cheeks to touch.

Ben lightly caressed her upper back, making light contact with the soft texture of her skin and hair. Moving slightly closer, their noses brushed. "Try to be grateful, though, for all that you do have."

"And what is that?" asked Miranda, pushing away slightly in order to make direct eye contact. "Everything was taken away from me when we came here!"

"No, Miranda, on the contrary, the truth is that you have so much. You have yourself, and that can never be taken away from you." Caressing her dark curved eyebrows gently with his thumbs, Ben continued, "I actually think you are the most fascinating girl that I have ever met, and it seems to me that your parents have done their very best to provide for you."

"Bringing me here to attend a little unknown college is the best they could do for me?" asked Miranda. "I'm sorry, Ben, but I deserve so much more."

"According to whom?"

"Why, according to me of course!"

"But Miranda, what do you have that was not given to you?" asked Ben. Miranda crinkled her nose.

"Think about your life. Think about how fortunate you are!" said Ben. "Maybe it's time to stop complaining about what you don't have and focus on all that you do! I mean, come on, Miranda, be sensible."

"I am being sensible! I am always sensible!" replied Miranda.

"Then you should be aware that you inherited your looks and your intelligence from your parents! Your mother is beautiful. It's obvious she has some sort of aristocratic background. She's very elegant. And your father is a very successful, educated man. Your own home literally breathes education and culture! How many people can boast of such an upbringing?"

Miranda flashed her dazzling smile of perfectly shaped white teeth, easily seen in the dark of the night. "I must say, Ben, that you make my life appear as though it inspires envy."

"Miranda," Ben began slowly, "You inspire envy. You are the most beautiful and the most interesting girl I've ever met! If only..."

"If only?" asked Miranda, gazing directly into Ben's eyes. "Don't be afraid. I know what you are about to say."

"If only you were a little more humble," Ben continued. "A little more grateful. A little more sensitive to the feelings of others. You could be such a powerful person!"

Miranda crinkled her forehead and puckered her lips.

"Miranda," Ben continued, "if someone who is so beautiful, so talented, so knowledgeable. If someone like that—if someone like you—showed kindness to others it would make such a huge impact!"

Miranda looked away, clearly disappointed with the direction of the conversation. Finally, she said, "But, why me, Ben?"

"Because you have so much to give!" Ben blurted out loudly, his voice echoing in the quietness of the night. "Most people judge others by how they look or by how much money they have or even the clothes they wear! It may not be fair, but it's reality. Don't you understand? If someone like you led the way and showed people that those things aren't so important, then others would see your example and follow. I just know it!"

Miranda became very quiet. After a long pause, she replied, "I must confess that I do not even know how to do such things."

"It's so easy," said Ben, practically sighing. "All you have to do is smile at some poor lonely boy, or greet him with a simple *hello*. Or if you see girls who are not so attractive and you talk to them and befriend them—trust me—you could change their lives."

Miranda stared at Ben, but said nothing.

"Sometimes, I wish I were completely blind," said Ben, "to the point that these glasses would be useless."

"Ben, why would you say such a thing?"

"Because then I could only see real beauty; the beauty from within," replied Ben. "I wouldn't be affected by anything else."

"Are you telling me that you do not appreciate physical beauty?" asked Miranda. "The beauty of a sky full of stars? The beauty of the mountains that surround us? The beauty of a lovely woman?"

"Yes, I do. But I would rather see the beauty of love."

"Okay, then," said Miranda. She then placed her hands around his glasses and gently removed them.

"What are you doing?" asked Ben.

Without hesitation, Miranda touched Ben's cheeks, then the back of his neck, and then kissed him softly on the lips. "I am showing you the beauty of love."

11

THE SUN SHONE brightly, yet the reputation of beautiful Southern California weather in autumn remained intact. A cool breeze followed Ben as he walked past one of the many college cement walkways and onto a grassy field. With a brown paper box in one hand and bottled water in the other, he paused by a large tree. In front of him, sprawled in all directions sat Tawny and her usual group of friends.

"Hey, Ben, what's up?" asked Tawny.

"Oh, nothing, I just thought I'd eat lunch with you guys today."

"Really?" replied Tawny. She arched her eyebrows. "And why is that? I haven't seen you since we did that article on you last year."

"What article?" asked Sharon.

"Ben's our resident genius," said Tawny. "He gave up—"

"Okay, you're right," interrupted Ben, "I did come here with ulterior motives. Look, Tawny, I came here to talk to you about Miranda. I know she got off to a bad start with you—"

"Not just with me!" interrupted Tawny between bites of her homemade veggie sandwich. She pointed at the others who were circled around her. "Try everyone."

"Well," continued Ben, "I've been talking with her and I've gotten to know her pretty well and—"

"So I've heard," interrupted Tawny once again.

"And I think she just needs exposure to different kinds of people to better understand—"

"You got that right!" interrupted Luis.

"Look, guys," said Ben, adjusting his glasses. "Miranda definitely has some pride issues and some cultural bias but I really think—"

"Dude, why are you defending her?" interrupted Reggie.

"Yeah, Ben," added Tawny, "I'm really disappointed in you. I mean, I've always respected you. Everyone knows you're going places. But come on, give me a break! If Miranda were ugly, you wouldn't even be here talking to us! I'm not trying to hurt your feelings, but the whole thing is kind of sad!"

"Sad? What's sad?" asked Ben.

"You coming over here to represent her!" replied Tawny. "Yeah, it's pretty obvious. Don't look so surprised. I can see the headline now: Foreign Babe and Local Geek Hook Up!" Tawny motioned with her hands in the air as the rest of the group broke into laughter. "Everyone's seen you following her around like a little puppy dog. Just admit it! You've got a huge crush on her, but deep down you know she's nothing more than a racist, conceited, pretty little rich girl!"

"So it's wrong to be pretty and rich?" asked Ben.

"Oh, get off it, Ben!" continued Tawny, scowling as she pointed her sandwich at him. "You know what I mean. Get real! She wears her little designer clothes and high heels that go *clickety-clack clickety-clack* everywhere she goes! It's like, 'Hey everyone, look at me! Look at me and my beautiful blonde hair!' " Tawny made a mocking gesture, using the back of her hand in an attempt to move her short brown hair.

"You forgot to mention her body!" added Steve while he fiddled with his guitar.

Tawny crinkled her nose. "See what I mean? She gives us real girls a bad name! Guys only like her for her looks and ignore her stupidity and pompous attitude!"

"You know, Tawny, there are many forms of prejudice," said Ben.

"You can defend her all you want," Tawny retorted quickly, "but I'm sorry to say that you're just a tool! She's using you to help her pass her classes!"

Some of the others in the group nodded and smiled affirmatively.

"Actually, she's a very independent and intelligent girl," replied Ben. "She doesn't need my help."

"Look, man," said Luis, "if you know her so well, then what are you arguing for? If you want to be friends with her, go ahead! But don't come here trying to tell us what to do. We were cool with her, you know, and she said straight out that she was a racist! She didn't even try to hide it, man!" Luis turned from Ben and raised his hands toward the rest of the group. "Didn't she say to all of us that white people are superior? Come on, man, that's the problem with white people. They think they're better than us."

Reggie nodded. Steve inclined his head. Others in the group remained still.

"Like I said, prejudice can take many shapes," replied Ben. "Luis, you just made a very racist statement. Tawny, you don't have anything to say about that?"

"Hey, just 'cause I'm white doesn't mean I don't recognize that a lot of white people are prejudiced, especially in the past," replied Tawny. Then, after gulping down half of her soda, she added, "That's why I do my part to make up for all of that."

"Yes, the past does teach us a lot about prejudice," said Ben. "It teaches us that white people have treated others shamefully. There's no justification for that. But really, when you think about it— everybody—every dominant race—has shown prejudice in some way or another. It's an evil within human beings that must be overcome."

Reggie and Luis exchanged glances.

"Are you going to deny this?" asked Ben.

"Well, who's constantly talking about deporting people? White people aren't even grateful that Mexicans do all of the hard work around here," Luis shouted. "And remember what they did to black people, too. You know, slavery and segregation and all!"

"Ain't nobody ever told whites where they have to live!" added Reggie.

"Yes, there is some truth to that," said Ben.

"Some truth?" repeated Reggie.

"Yes, some truth," said Ben, "and I mean some truth because yes, many white people have done horrible things to minorities in this country; and there is no excuse for that, but you used an overgeneralization, and when you do that, you're creating a stereotype, and that leads to racism, or prejudice."

"So now you're calling *us* racists?" asked Luis in an angry tone.

"If you believe that an entire race acts a certain way based on the actions of a select group of individuals, within a select period of time, then yes, I would call you a racist. You guys mentioned history, and you're right; history is embarrassing for all of us. It's shameful what our ancestors have done and what people continue to do. But you guys are wrong if you believe that history concludes that a single group of people have always been the worst. History teaches us that every nation in power has traditionally abused others, and there are no exceptions. Everyone, and I mean everyone, has done it. Whites, blacks, Asians, Hispanics,

Arabs—even Indian tribes have preyed on smaller, weaker ones. That's why Jorge Santayana stated that we have to learn from it."

"Santayana?" repeated Luis, "He sounds Mexican."

"He was Spanish," said Ben, "from Spain. But he lived much of his life here before traveling throughout Europe. I doubt that he would claim any one country as his own. He was very international."

"Well, what's your point?" asked Reggie.

"Jorge Santayana said that 'those who cannot remember the past are condemned to repeat it,' " stated Ben.[8]

"We don't need a boring lecture, man!" said Reggie. Then, he turned around to face the rest of the group. With a mischievous smile, he added, "We can go to class for that!"

A few of the others laughed.

"Fine, you don't have to listen to me," replied Ben, "but just tell me if you agree or not. That goes for all of you."

Tawny took another bite of her sandwich and then furrowed her brow. "Agree with what?" she asked while continuing to chew.

"Agree that there are white people who mistreat other white people and black people who wrong other black people," said Ben. "And are you going to tell me, Luis, that Mexicans never hurt other Mexicans? Or Hispanics have never harmed other Hispanics? Have Asians never fought against other Asians? Have Arabs never attacked other Arabs? Prejudice is a horrible act and it's not always about race or color. It can be based on religion, socio-economic class, even gender! I mean, who has suffered more than women?"

"That's right!" said Sharon as she shot a menacing look at both Luis and Reggie.

Luis bit his lip and inclined his head for a moment. Then, taking a deep breath, he redirected his attention to Ben. "Look, man, everything you're saying…. It don't mean nothing! You might be smart, but I've lived it! And I'm not going to listen to a rich little white boy talk to me about prejudice! Just get rid of all the racist laws and then we'll have something to discuss, all right?"

"It takes time, Luis!" Ben replied. "Although history exposes the abuse of prejudice, it also points to the progress we've made. We all owe thanks to people like Lincoln, Gandhi, and Martin Luther King Jr. just to name a few.

"What about César Chávez?"

"Yes, César Chávez!" replied Ben. "We all have to recognize that everyone is equal—"

"Equal?" shouted Luis, "You think everyone is equal? Maybe in your neighborhood, but where I live Mexicans come just to find work and they can't even get a driver's license! My uncle—"

"Look," interrupted Ben, "I can see this is very personal for you. Remember though, every country has immigration laws. Most countries treat immigrants much worse than the United States. We're actually one of the most hospitable countries in the world. I know how you feel, though—"

"What?" exclaimed Luis. He took a few steps toward Ben. With a deeply furrowed brow, he shouted, "What are you talking about? How would you know how I feel? Have you ever worked in the fields? Have you ever worked in a packing shed? Have you ever translated for your parents while people give you a look that makes you feel like trash?"

"Hey guys, maybe we ought to drop this," said Tawny.

"You're right," said Ben. "I shouldn't have said that I know how you feel because I don't—nobody does. I guess I meant that I understand how personal prejudice can be. Some of you know that I'm Jewish. My family knows about racism. People think of Jews and only think of the Nazis, but Jews have struggled as immigrants in countries all over the world because of our beliefs. Many people hate Jews, and so it's not always easy."

Luis inclined his head. Reggie licked his lips. For a brief moment, nobody said a word.

"You're Jewish?" asked Meling, breaking the silence.

"Yes," replied Ben. "My grandfather was actually in a German concentration camp as a little boy."

"That's deep, man," said Reggie. "But let's be real. That was him, not you. You didn't live back then, so it's not the same."

"Yes, and the same could be said of you," retorted Ben.

Reggie bit his lower lip. He nodded slightly. "Okay, okay, I feel you. So let's talk about your grandfather. You telling me he didn't hate German people? You saying he didn't wish he could have killed one of those dudes?"

Ben adjusted his glasses. "I'm sure he struggled with that, but he was German too, you know. Just because he was Jewish doesn't mean that he didn't consider himself German. He was born in Germany. It was his home. And anyway, not all Germans belonged to the Nazi party. Some even gave their lives to help Jews."

"Maybe so," replied Reggie, "but most didn't do a damn thing just like most whites didn't do a damn thing when blacks were suffering." He nodded toward Sharon. "That's why people got to help their own."

Ben inclined his head. After taking a deep breath, he whispered, "Yes, you make a good point."

Silence ensued. Finally, Sharon walked up to Ben. "Your grandfather. Did he forgive them?"

"I don't know," he replied, "but I do know that he has a saying for this. *'Wir dürfen nicht alle für die sünden der wenigen verurteilen.'* It means that we must not condemn all for the sins of the few."

Luis furrowed his eyebrows. He seemed to be studying Ben. A few people turned to Tawny, who had been uncharacteristically quiet.

"I don't deny that racism exists," said Ben softly, "and I don't deny tension exists between certain races, but if we're ever going to overcome that, then we have to see people for who they are. When it comes down to it, everyone has experienced some form of prejudice or discrimination. Being left out—abused—for whatever reason. And if we're going to break that pattern then we have to do what Martin Luther King said and not judge people 'by the color of their skin but by the content of their character'.[9] Otherwise, we just keep hurting each other."

"That makes sense to me," said Sharon. "I think Ben's right. I'm black, and I'm proud of who I am, but I'd be proud of myself if I were white, too. Or any other color. It's what's on the inside that counts."

Ben smiled. A few of the others nodded and voiced their support.

"Yeah, yeah," interjected Reggie as he wrapped his arms around Ben and Sharon. " 'We are the world, we are the children.'[10] That's all great, but everyone's forgetting how this whole thing got started! It was your friend, dude! We were just being cool with her, and she basically put us on blast—or at least most of us. She's the one you should be talking to!"

Ben took a deep breath. "You're right, and I have been talking to her, Reggie. I can tell you that Miranda's not hateful, she's just been isolated most of her life. And that's a big difference. You asked about forgiveness? Well, I'm here asking all of you to forgive her."

"Hey, I'm a musician," said Steve, moving his long sandy brown hair out of his face. "We're cool with everyone! I never had anything against her in the first place. I'm not even a part of this."

"Are you a part of anything?" asked Ben, frowning slightly.

"Huh?" huffed Steve.

"I'm saying it doesn't take a lot of courage to simply stay neutral," said Ben, "but it does take courage to speak the truth. Tawny, I know you're not afraid to stand up for what's right. I remember a column where you quoted Edmund Burke."

Steve shrugged his shoulders. Reggie frowned. Luis furrowed his brow.

"Okay, Ben," said Tawny, "bring her here tomorrow and we'll give her a second chance. But I want to hear it from her, not you."

Ben let out a shy smile. "Thank you. You won't regret it."

"I hope not!" Tawny said before releasing a smile.

Ben nodded and turned to leave. As he did so, Tawny shouted one final admonition, "For your sake, this better work!"

"I heard that!" added Reggie. Then, shaking his head, he added, "Man, that dude's exhausting! I eat lunch to relax, not to get into some big old deep discussion! I just might have to cut my next class!"

12

WHILE MIRANDA SAT comfortably at the kitchen table, Ben's mother admonished her, "Have some more chocolate torte, honey."

"Thank you, Mrs. Kurtz, it truly is delicious," replied Miranda, "but I don't think I could fit another bite."

"Look at her, Benjamin," she continued. "Isn't she a doll? Come on, take another piece. One more bite isn't going to hurt a girl as pretty as you are."

"Okay, but just a small slice, please," said Miranda.

As Ben and Miranda ate their dessert, Ben's father walked slowly into the living room. Each step was preceded by his walker. A grimace could be seen on his face.

"Wow! Look at you!" proclaimed Ben.

"Did you think I was going to let you two have our guest all to yourselves? Miranda, let me tell you about these pictures."

"Father, I don't think she's interested," said Ben.

"Then you do not know me very well," replied Miranda. "I would love to know more, Mr. Kurtz."

"See, Benjamin, this young lady appreciates history."

Ben shook his head as he released a slight grin.

Pointing to the several framed pictures that hung from the white wall of the large kitchen, Ben's father continued, "This picture goes back to 1938. It was taken in Berlin, Germany. This boy you see here with the cap on his head was my father—Benjamin's grandfather."

"Yes, Ben has mentioned him to me!" exclaimed Miranda, standing up from her chair to get a closer look of the photograph hanging on the wall.

Ben's father paused and swallowed. "Out of the seven people you see there, only he and his brother survived."

Miranda studied the picture. Her face took on a somber expression. "Excuse me, but if it is not too forward, may I ask a personal question?"

"Certainly."

"Is your father still alive?"

"Yes, he is, but he's very old. He's in a nursing home in Pasadena."

"Ben, I would so much like to meet him!" said Miranda, smiling.

"Then we shall," said Ben.

"My father is a great man," continued Ben's father. "He kept his younger brother alive during Nazi Germany and survived two different concentration camps. With the help of a few relatives, he and his brother later established our family business. They were clockmakers and watchmakers. The Kurtz have known this skill for generations! Nowadays, these are two different trades, but we can do both!"

"That is fascinating, Mr. Kurtz," said Miranda. "So Ben has this skill?"

Rocking his head back and forth, Ben's father replied, "Well, yes, he knows a little. They all do, but it's Ben's sister and her husband that work at the store. Someday, they'll run the business."

"You have no interest in this?" asked Miranda to Ben.

"No, I have other plans," replied Ben.

"Benjamin and his brother are too intelligent to bother with us!"

"Father!" said Ben. "Don't say it like that."

"How so?" asked Miranda.

"His brother, Joseph, is studying at Stanford University. He's going to work for NASA."

"Yes, I have been told. You must be so proud!" gushed Miranda. "That is an extraordinary achievement."

"Yes," interrupted Ben's mother, "but this one here is the one we're most proud of!"

"I think Miranda has heard enough," said Ben, lightly touching her on the shoulder.

"What, we can't say we're proud of you?" asked Ben's mother. Then, turning to Miranda, she added, "Here, have another slice."

Miranda reluctantly accepted another piece of chocolate torte.

"This is Joseph right here!" said Ben's father, pointing to another portrait. "And this young lady in the wedding gown is his sister, Rachel. That's Asher, her husband."

"Well, I think Miranda has seen enough of our family history," interrupted Ben. "I want to show her the backyard—alone."

"That would be nice," replied Miranda, "but I still don't understand why you have no interest in taking over your father's business. I mean, it must be quite lucrative."

"Because he wants to be a lawyer!" said Ben's father.

"Really? Oh, that is wonderful, Ben!" said Miranda. "But you will have to study very hard to get into law school! It's not so easy, I'm afraid."

"This one? Study?" said Ben's mother. "Honey, that's all he does!"

Tapping his forehead, Ben's father added, "And he remembers everything! Getting into a law school is the least of his worries!"

"It's more like which one!" said Ben's mother.

"I don't understand," said Miranda, looking at both of Ben's parents.

"Young lady, all of my children are very intelligent, but Benjamin's the smartest of the bunch!" said Ben's mother. "Not only was he accepted into Stanford like his brother, but schools like Harvard and Yale wanted him, too! Benjamin, go get the article from your room!"

"Mother, no," said Ben. "She probably wouldn't understand. Her school system is completely different than ours."

"It doesn't matter!" said Ben's father. "Show her the article."

"I'd rather show her our garden," said Ben. "You'll love it, Miranda. It's very, um, peaceful."

Ben took a few steps forward. He motioned for Miranda to follow. Before she could move, however, Ben's mother suddenly returned with a small wooden frame. Inside was a newspaper article that had a picture of Ben at the very top just below the headline.

"This is how smart Benjamin is!"

Miranda eagerly took the small frame into her hands. As her eyes darted from left to right, her smile widened. "The top student in California," read Miranda. Then, reading further into the article, she exclaimed, "Ben, it says here that you were going to attend Harvard on a full scholarship!"

Blushing slightly, Ben nodded his head affirmatively. Then, he grabbed Miranda gently by the elbow and led her away from his parents. "Okay, okay, that's enough. Show's over, folks. Come on, Miranda, let's go before we overdose on my mother's torte."

Following Ben, Miranda refused to let go of the small frame in her hands. She passed through a dim room and then outside to the sunlit beauty of a garden divided by a variety of small cement gullies that sprung from a cobblestone waterfall. On one side of the garden were vegetables and on the other, roses. Ben sat down on a white wooden lawn bench. Still reading the framed article, Miranda slowly positioned herself next to him.

"I love this place," said Ben. "I always come here to think—to pray—to clear my mind—to listen to the birds.

"Ben," said Miranda, still staring at the framed article.

"Yes?"

"It says here that you achieved a perfect score on the scholastic aptitude test," said Miranda, pointing at the article. "It also says that you were the only one in the nation to have done so."

"I think I missed a few multiple choice questions, but on the curve they give I guess—they were generous—I probably got lucky."

"This test," continued Miranda, looking at Ben, "is necessary to attend your universities, correct?"

"Yes," replied Ben.

Looking back at the article, Miranda then blurted, "According to this man Doctor Levenson, the average mark for a student attending Harvard is twenty two hundred! And you scored twenty four hundred! Ben, that is amazing!"

Ben pressed his lips together and turned his face toward the garden.

"So now I understand the mystery behind Ben Kurtz," said Miranda, trying to establish eye contact. "You did not go. You stayed for your family. That is why you are at a community college and not a prestigious university."

"It's not a big deal."

"You never cease to amaze me!" said Miranda, turning to face him more closely. "It certainly is a "big deal" as you put it! Please, Ben, I know it must bother you! You do not have to pretend with me. It must be so hard for you to be forced to associate with people who are not at your level."

"I wouldn't say it like that."

"Then how would you say it?" asked Miranda, playfully touching the middle of his black rimmed glasses with her index finger.

Adjusting his glasses, Ben replied, "I've learned a lot at GCC. There are some challenging courses there. And the professors are very personal. I've even had lunch with some of them, which is something I doubt I could do at Harvard. Anyway, my father needed me. It wasn't a hard decision."

"Even so, you simply cannot compare Glendora Community College with Harvard University," said Miranda.

"Yes," said Ben, "but it does have some things that you can't find in the prestigious universities, you know."

Miranda arched her eyebrows sharply. "Name one!"

Ben inclined his head, then whispered, "Well, you, for instance."

Smiling, Miranda bent over and kissed Ben on the cheek. After a short pause, Ben kissed her on the cheek as well. He then pivoted his face until their lips touched. Soon, they embraced and began kissing each other more vigorously. Suddenly, Ben withdrew. Miranda kissed him once more as he touched her shoulders and inclined his head.

"What?" asked Miranda. "What is the matter?"

"We better stop."

"Why?" asked Miranda. "Everything is perfect. The sun is just fading. The air is cool. Your garden is absolutely lovely, and we are here—alone."

"If only that were true," said Ben. "Trust me, Miranda, you don't know my mother. I wouldn't be surprised if she's watching us right now through a window. She'll probably come out any minute to offer us some iced tea."

"I seriously doubt that," said Miranda, pressing her face against his.

Ben began to caress the side of her head, running his fingers through the soft strands of blond hair that fell to her shoulders. "Well, we shouldn't get too distracted," whispered Ben, "because tomorrow is a big day for us."

"And why is that?" asked Miranda. She put one foot down and pushed off the cement, causing the lawn bench to rock up and down. Ben smiled, seemingly amused by this free, childlike act. "What a beautiful blue sky!" continued Miranda. She then looked up at the spherical blue expanse, interrupted only by a few streaks of clouds. She wrapped her arm around Ben's, holding on to him snugly as the bench swung up and down.

"Tomorrow is the day we reconcile you with Tawny and her friends," said Ben.

"Yes, that would be nice," replied Miranda absentmindedly.

"I think it's very important to show her who you really are."

"Uh-huh."

"It's sad," said Ben, "but I think there is an element of jealousy that pretty girls must always combat. I mean, just look at you. You're so—so—perfect. It's unfair, really. Yet, it's not your fault. I mean, you can't be blamed. It's a good thing, but I imagine some girls treat you badly because of your beauty. That is a form of prejudice as well."

"Ben, what are you expounding on now? Wouldn't you rather do something else?" asked Miranda, looking directly into his eyes.

Ben swallowed hard, which caused Miranda to smile. She was pleased by his nervous reaction to her **innuendo**.

"Miranda, believe me, there is nothing more that I would rather do right now," said Ben, "but we need to talk about this and make sure you say the right things."

"The right things?" asked Miranda, crinkling her nose.

"Yes, tomorrow, at lunch. We're going to meet with Tawny and you will apologize."

"What?" gasped Miranda, sitting up abruptly. She quickly dug both shoes sharply onto the ground, her heels screeching against the cement and causing the bench to come to an abrupt halt. Facing Ben, she screamed, "Apologize? What in God's name are you talking about?"

"Miranda, what's wrong?"

"I said what in God's name are you talking about?" repeated Miranda, her tone tinged with anger.

"First, could you please not use God's name in vain," said Ben, "and second, we both agreed that you spoke badly to Tawny. Actually, you were rude to all of her friends. Now is your chance to redeem yourself! They're waiting for you!"

"They are waiting for me?" repeated Miranda, becoming more upset by the moment. "And why would they be doing that?"

Ben paused for a moment. "Well, because I spoke to them."

Miranda pressed her lips tightly together. She folded her arms in front of her. "And what did you say?"

"I—I told them that you fully understand that you were wrong to say the things that you did," stammered Ben.

"*Por Dios,* Ben! *Estás loco?*" Miranda stood up and took several steps away from the bench. Pacing back and forth, she said, "*No puede ser! Cómo se ocurre?*" Then, stopping directly in front of Ben, she looked down at him with fire in her green eyes. "Have you completely lost your mind? I do not recall ever giving you permission to speak on my behalf!"

"Miranda, I did it for you!" replied Ben. He quickly stood up and reached for her shoulder.

"Don't touch me!" said Miranda. "How dare you, Ben? I thought you respected me! I thought you were my friend!"

"I am your friend, Miranda! I care deeply for you."

"Really? And yet you think I should apologize and humiliate myself so that some insignificant people may approve of me?"

"No, I think you should apologize to them because it is the right thing to do!"

"Well, I hate to disappoint you," said Miranda, "but if things go as planned I will not even be at this school once this semester is completed, and what a few ignorant Americans think of me is of little consequence. Why, I do not even know if I shall remain here in this country!"

"Miranda, please," Ben pleaded. "You're taking this all wrong."

"I think we are finished here and I wish to leave," said Miranda without a hint of tenderness in her voice.

Ben removed his glasses. He rubbed his eyes. "Please, don't..."

"I am sorry, Ben, but I must insist!"

"Okay, I'll drive you home."

"No, that won't be necessary," said Miranda. "It is a lovely day. I think I will walk a bit, and I can call on my mother to fetch me."

As Miranda began to walk away, Ben quickly caught up to her. Standing directly in front of her, he attempted to block her path. "Then let me walk with you until your mother arrives."

"Goodbye, Ben," said Miranda in a businesslike tone. "I can see my way out. I want to—*despedirme*—with your parents." She walked around Ben and then toward the patio door of his home. Ben remained standing. Upon entering, Miranda lingered a moment, turned and added, "If anyone should apologize, it should be you for attempting to humiliate me so." With a condescending frown, she was gone.

13

PASSING THE CAFETERIA, Ben mumbled his prepared speech quietly to himself. He turned the corner of the large building when suddenly he struck a large object.

"Watch it, runt!"

Ben stumbled back, almost falling to the ground. He slowly adjusted his glasses. In front of him stood a large young man with spiky brown hair, chubby red cheeks, and a thick nose which possessed a huge crease at the top. In one of his hands was a can of Root Beer, in the other, a brown paper box. On his shirt were smudges of red catsup and soda.

"Great! You made me drop my food!" he bellowed, scowling at Ben. "And my shirt's wet!"

"I'm sorry," said Ben. He inclined his head. On the ground were the remains of a large hamburger and scattered French Fries. "I didn't see you."

"How could you not see me? Are you dense or what?"

"I'll pay for your sandwich," said Ben as he pulled a black wallet from the back of his gray slacks.

The large young man snatched the wallet from Ben's hand. "You bet you will!" he snapped. "This twenty ought to do it. So what else do you got in here?"

"Look, I'm sorry about what happened, but it was an accident," said Ben. "Now, please, give me back my wallet."

Instead of granting Ben's request, he laid his beefy hand on Ben's shoulder and began to shake him. "Forget it! You ruined my shirt, too!"

"Hey, Hansen, what do you think you're doing to my friend over there?" called out a deep voice.

Upon hearing his name, Hansen's small eyes squinted beneath the thick layers of his cheeks. "Carlos?" he stuttered.

"Let him go."

Ben's eyes shifted somewhat nervously toward Carlos and his ever present entourage.

Hansen then crinkled his brow, making his wide nose resemble the snout of a large pig. "Hey, Darnell. Dillan. Jonesy."

"Let him go, bro," said Darnell.

Hansen hesitated. "You know this guy?" he asked.

Carlos stepped closer toward Hansen until the two stood inches apart. "Yeah, I already told you that he's a friend of mine. Didn't you hear?"

Hansen slowly released his grip on Ben's shoulder. "This guy owes me money," he snorted.

Carlos smirked. "For what?"

"He ruined a perfectly good double cheeseburger and fries!"

Carlos and his friends broke into laughter.

"Hansen," said Darnell, "that's the last thing your fat ass needs!" He pressed his lips together and shook his head. "Now, get on out of here. And return the wallet."

Hansen frowned. He slowly handed Ben his wallet.

"Thank you," said Ben.

Carlos then grabbed Hansen by the nape of the neck and squeezed it as he pushed him away. "We're doing you a favor, man. You know Coach says you're too slow off the line."

Ben straightened his white collared shirt. He then smiled awkwardly at the group of football players assembled before him. "Hey, thanks, Carlos," he stuttered. "I did bump into him and make him drop his food, though."

"Don't even sweat it, man," said Carlos, putting his arm around Ben's neck so that it remained in a loose fitting headlock. Then, turning to his friends, he said, "Listen up! If you ever need help with your work, this guy is the man! He can tutor you in anything!"

"Cool," said Jonesy, offering his fist to Ben.

Ben grinned and then met the boy's fist with his own.

"Yeah, don't worry about Hansen," continued Carlos. "He's mostly dead weight, and not the brightest guy in the world. You know what I mean? Anyway, so Kurtz, what's up with you and that new chick, Miranda?"

"I—I don't know. We've been getting to know each other, but she's kind of...complicated."

"Yeah," said Carlos, "I agree. She's really fine, though, and from what I've heard, she's all yours."

Ben inclined his head. "I don't know, Carlos. I wouldn't say that."

Withdrawing his arm from around Ben's shoulders, Carlos nodded to his friends. "Okay, Kurtz, we're out of here. Take care of yourself, man."

"Thanks," replied Ben. Then, as the group walked away, he shouted, "Hey! When are you going to come to the chess club?"

Carlos turned and smiled. "One of these days, Kurtz! We need to play again! None of these fools are a challenge!"

"One of these days," Ben repeated quietly. He then shouted, "That's what you always say!"

Carlos waved as he and his friends disappeared down one of the many cement walking paths found throughout the campus. Ben then took a deep breath. He made his way toward a grassy area that surrounded a large tree. There, a range of sounds could be heard that ranged from the chomping of food, to laughing, to shouting, and then to the pleasant sound of a guitar.

"Hey, Ben," said Tawny quite casually.

"Hi, Ben," added Sharon.

Luis stood up and stretched forth his hand. "Hey, Ben, how you doing, man?"

Ben shook his hand somewhat awkwardly. "Oh, uh, I'm fine. How are you, Luis?"

"I'm good," he replied.

Reggie then waved at Ben. "What's up, professor?"

Ben nodded and replied, "Hi, Reggie."

Steve paused to raise both thumbs toward Ben before strumming his guitar once again.

After a brief silence, Tawny said, "Well?"

"I'm sorry," Ben stammered, "but Miranda isn't coming."

There was a collective moan heard from within the circle of students.

"I knew it!" said Tawny. "Now do you believe me?"

Standing rigidly, Ben turned toward the trees and the many flowered plants that lay in the distance. "Sometimes," he said, "it takes time for people to grow."

"Why don't you join us?" asked Sharon. "It's not your fault."

"Thanks, I wish I could," Ben replied, "but I have a chess club meeting."

Reggie laughed. "Man, are you for real?"

"What's wrong with chess?" asked Sharon. "My dad played in the Army and still plays with his friends!"

"Okay, okay," said Reggie, shaking his head. "I guess it sounds all right when you say it like that."

"I'm really sorry, everyone," said Ben, "and maybe tomorrow I'll bring my lunch and eat with you all."

Suddenly, the group became quiet. Tawny's eyes widened. Reggie's smile quickly faded.

"What?" asked Ben.

No one said a word in response.

"I apologize for being late," said Miranda. She was carrying a lunch box and a small bottle of juice.

Ben, whipping around quickly, exclaimed, "Miranda, you're here!"

"Of course," replied Miranda. "Where is your lunch, Ben? Do you not understand that it is rude to socialize without eating?"

"I...I..." stammered Ben.

"I guess she made it after all," said Tawny, arching her eyebrows.

Taking a panoramic view of the diverse group of students, Miranda inhaled and began, "Hello again. I suppose you all know why I am here."

Miranda could see a few faces that appeared happy to see her whereas others had a look of skepticism. Undaunted, she continued, "I really am sorry for the way I behaved upon meeting all of you. I do not always communicate my true feelings properly—*y—bueno*—during my upbringing, you see, my family and my culture..."

Ben began to shake his head. His brow was deeply furrowed.

Miranda looked at him and then at the rest of the group. "Well, actually, it is true that I come from a different culture—but that is not to blame—and neither is my family. While each member of my family is somewhat privileged, I must confess that I am the worst. My brothers and sisters are actually quite sweet. I struggle with my temper and my arrogance and my pride, but I want to overcome these defects. I really do."

Miranda glanced at Ben, who nodded encouragingly. Tawny and her friends expressed little emotion.

"I know now that I was wrong and for that I am truly sorry," continued Miranda. "I would be so grateful if you all could find it in your heart to forgive me for any and all offensive remarks that I have made. Nobody is any better than anybody else." Miranda paused for a moment before adding, "And I only wish to be your friend."

All eyes seemed to turn toward Tawny, who slowly got up, walked toward Miranda, and stood directly in front of her. She was the smaller of the two girls, but possessed a certain demeanor that was quite intimidating. Ben bit his lip nervously. Everyone waited. Finally, Tawny smiled and wrapped her arms around Miranda. "Apology accepted," she said.

Relieved, Miranda exhaled profoundly and said, "Thank you! Thank you so much!"

"Come here!" said Reggie, smiling. He, too, gave Miranda a tight embrace.

"*De acuerdo,*" said Luis, offering his hand. "I mean, we *Latinos* have to stick together, right?" Luis shot a mischievous grin at Ben. "Hey, just kidding, man."

"Don't even go there or we're in for another lecture!" said Reggie, rubbing his temples with both hands.

One by one, each remaining member of the group embraced Miranda.

"I'm going to make it my personal challenge to Americanize you," said Tawny to Miranda. She then turned to Ben and added, "Hey, Ben, why don't you grab something to eat and hang out? I don't think the nerds in the chess club will miss you that much!"

Miranda's eyes suddenly widened. "Oh no!" she exclaimed. "The chess club. Ben, we will miss the meeting!"

Tawny moaned. "Please tell me you're not serious!"

"Why, of course!" replied Miranda. "Ben is the president and a truly splendid player! Would you mind if I eat lunch with all of you tomorrow?"

Tawny rolled her eyes. "You're gonna bounce?"

Miranda furrowed her brow.

"You're leaving?" said Tawny.

Miranda glanced at Ben. She then looked at Tawny, pleading silently through her deep green eyes.

"Yeah, yeah, go ahead and hang out with the nerds! We'll see you later!" snarled Tawny, shaking her head.

"Hey, hey, hey!" said Steve. He began strumming his guitar. "None of that nerd talkity talkity talk talk talk! Chess is *coooooolllll*." He then moved his fingers quickly up and down the frets, completing a complicated range of notes that ended with a dramatically loud crescendo. When he stopped, Miranda smiled curiously. Tawny's mouth popped open. Reggie cocked his head back.

"Ooo-kay," said Tawny, elongating the word as she frowned at Steve.

"What?" asked Steve. "Edmund Burke. I'm standing up! Right, Ben?"

"That's right," replied Ben, smiling widely.

"Who the hell is Edmund Burke, anyway?" asked Reggie.

Tawny extended her arms up into the air. "Doesn't anyone here read my column?" she shouted.

"The only thing necessary for the triumph of evil is for good men to do nothing," said Ben.[10] He then gently caressed Miranda's shoulder.

Miranda smiled. "Goodbye, everyone, and I do look forward to eating lunch with you tomorrow."

As they headed back toward the main buildings, Tawny lamented, "We have really got to work on that girl. I mean, come on, picking the chess club over us?"

"Yeah, that's messed up," said Meling in a lighthearted tone.

A few of the others nodded.

"Is it just me," said Bryanna aloud, touching her lower lip with her index finger, "or is Ben really hot?"

She was instantly pelted with food.

14

THE SMALL ROOM was full of students seated across from each other in rectangular tables which were covered with unfolded cloth chess boards. When Ben entered, nobody seemed to notice, but when Miranda followed him soon thereafter, it was as if time stood still. Suddenly, students stopped moving pieces, mouths dropped open, and the only sound that could be heard was the rhythmic ticking of the old fashioned chess clocks.

"Hey guys, I brought a new member!" announced Ben. "Anybody want to play Miranda?"

Instantly, several young men jumped out of their seats, forming somewhat of a mob as they jockeyed for position next to Miranda. With only a few female members in the club, Miranda was all the more conspicuous.

"Easy, boys, easy!" shouted Ben, trying in vain to control the crowd.

"If you do not mind," said Miranda, "I would prefer playing with the girls for now."

A collective sigh was heard throughout the room as several young men returned to their original places and resumed their games. Miranda then approached one particular girl who was sitting alone with a book in her hands.

"Hello, I am Miranda Frondizi."

"Uh, hi, I'm Molly."

"Pleased to meet you," said Miranda, extending her hand. "Would you like to play?"

Molly offered a limp handshake and replied, "Sure, uh, I usually just study from this book until someone plays with me."

"You are studying chess?"

"Yeah," said Molly, displaying the book to Miranda.

"Well, then you must be very good," said Miranda, smiling. "I hope you will extend to me at least a smidgeon of compassion."

Molly smiled. "Sure, no worries."

The two girls created a stark contrast. Molly had thick frizzy brown hair and dull eyes that melted unnoticed into a white, slightly reddish face that was riddled with freckles. She was overweight and slovenly dressed, wearing loose blue jeans and a large green shirt that hung over her pants.

Her old tennis shoes were faded with wear. Miranda, on the other hand, had perfectly fitted Gucci™ jeans that hugged her body. There were a few torn areas and holes that gave her that perfect "worn in" look. Her white ruffle blouse covered only one of her perfectly tan shoulders. The image of Miranda playing chess conjured up images of a photo shoot for a supermodel.

As playing resumed, all eyes were on Miranda. A few pieces dropped to the floor as a result of this distraction. One boy bent over and began touching the floor blindly, searching in vain for the fallen piece. He continued stretching until he fell over onto the floor. Several of the other boys pointed and laughed. Miranda looked at him and smiled.

Despite an admirable struggle, Miranda eventually lost her first game. "You play very well," she said to Molly.

"Thanks, so do you, especially for your first day in the club."

"I'm next!" said one boy as he nudged Molly on the shoulder.

"No, I'm playing her!" said another, shoving the boy in front of him.

Ben quickly approached the table to establish order. "Guys, look, we'll go by—uh—last names. And that's after Miranda plays Lorna."

"That's okay," replied Lorna, the lone remaining female in the room. She snarled slightly and added, "I'd rather play someone else."

"Then it's settled!" said one of the boys.

Once again, the shoving began.

"Wait! Wait! Wait!" said Ben. "Alphabetical order, remember?"

"You gotta be kidding!" said a boy with red hair and freckles. "How does that make any sense?"

Ben arched his brow. "Do you have a better idea?"

As each boy anxiously waited his turn, Miranda graciously played with each one. Ben, for his part, played with Lorna and then several others. As the meeting officially ended, a line of boys formed to shake Miranda's hand and welcome her to the club. Each of them made her promise that she would return.

Ben patiently put away the remaining cloth boards, chess clocks, and pieces into several cabinets reserved for the club. Miranda, for her part, waited until the two were alone.

"I think you've achieved celebrity status," said Ben, smiling, "and in less than an hour at that. I have a feeling our membership is going to increase if you continue to come."

"Oh, Ben, I had so much fun!" exclaimed Miranda. "I must say that I am even better than I suspected! It is true that my father is a strong player, but I never knew that my level was so high! I started off a little slow, but did you know that after my first loss I won every game?"

"Yes, I noticed. That was quite a winning streak," said Ben in a playfully sarcastic tone.

As he placed the last of the chess boards into a drawer, Miranda approached him. "Ben, I owe you an apology, too. I said cruel words to you—words that never should have been spoken."

Breaking eye contact, Ben turned away from her.

"Is something wrong? Do you not accept my apology?" asked Miranda.

"No, no…it's not that," said Ben.

"Then what?" asked Miranda, walking up to him so closely that her body rubbed against him. Looking deep into his eyes, Miranda furrowed her brow. "Ben, what is it? You look as if you are in pain. Are you cross with me, Benjamin Kurtz?"

"No, I—I just get irritated at how much power you have," Ben stammered. He then frowned at Miranda. "It's so unfair. It makes me feel so weak."

"Weak?" repeated Miranda, touching his nose with her own.

"Yes," replied Ben in soft tone little more than a whisper.

"Too weak to stop this?" asked Miranda softly. She then removed his glasses, revealing his light blue eyes, and kissed him firmly on the lips.

Ben smiled. He gently put his arms around Miranda. "I'm so proud of you," he said. "I was afraid you weren't going to come or that I might not see you again."

"I must confess that I was very upset at first," said Miranda, flashing her lovely green eyes. "I wanted to stay away from you, for a while, to make you suffer."

Ben remained silent.

"Well, did you?" asked Miranda. "Did you suffer?"

"Yes, very much so."

"Well, I found myself suffering also. But, I had to—I had to see you."

"So that's why you came?"

"Yes. I could never disappoint you, Ben."

"It took a lot of courage to do what you did," Ben replied, tightening his arms around her lower back. "You're a leader, Miranda. I knew you were. I knew you could lead others."

As she held on to Ben, with her head next to his, Miranda closed her eyes. "I hope so, Ben. I am still not sure how."

Ben caressed her dark eyebrows. Softly, he whispered in her ear, "By example, Miranda, by example."

Novel 8

TO BE A CHAMPION

1

BONG-CHUL AND IK-JONG were second generation. Their parents, Jae-Pil Kim and Song Park, had come to America from Seoul, South Korea. A beautiful and mysterious city, Seoul boasted over ten million people and six hundred years of history. Located on the Han River in the center of the Korean Peninsula, Koreans from generation to generation took great pride in its palaces and pagodas, markets and museums, shrines and skyscrapers. All of that paled, however, in comparison to their most treasured martial art: Tae Kwon Do.

Jae-Pil had learned Tae Kwon Do from his father shortly after he had taken his first few steps, and his father had learned from his father. Thus, it was a way of life, a family tradition. Each son carried the family burden to earn his black belt in Tae Kwon Do. But even that was not enough. They were expected to become champions.

Jae-Pil was a champion. He had proven himself by winning several tournaments as a young man. He had also proven himself as an officer in the military. He had even been bestowed with the title of *Hwarang*, a name given to only a select group of Korean men who had proven themselves in combat.

Hwarang, the way of flowering manhood. These men were the most esteemed of all Korea. They studied *taek-gyeon*, Confucianism, Buddhism, history, ethics, social skills, and military tactics. Their guiding principles were based on Won Gwang's five codes of human conduct: loyalty, filial duty, trustworthiness, valor and justice. The *Hwarang* were not like other men; they were men of steel, forged with fire and pounding until all weakness had left their bodies.

2

A WOMAN AS beautiful as her name, Song Park made an odd pairing with her husband. Jae-Pil Kim was hard and often distant; Song Park was happy and sweet. He had a very square, even harsh looking face, while hers was round and gentle. His skin was rough, marred with scars and scratches; hers was soft as cream. He was deeply rooted in tradition, tracing his heritage back to a time when there existed only one Korea. She knew Korea more through stories. Jae-Pil had come to America as a young man, his identity already established. Song had come while still a small child, her identity still forming.

When Song fell in love with the young Tae Kwon Do instructor, she tried to convince him to adopt the name of Phillip, but Jae-Pil sternly refused. He was completely **intolerant** of ideas that did not find their base in the *Hwarang* tradition. Even so, Song insisted on referring to their first born son, Bong-Chul, as Paul, and the second born, Ik-Jong, as John.

Paul was born two full years ahead of John. He was the pride of the Kim family. Handsome and strong, Paul was favored by Jae-Pil over the less attractive and weaker John. As the eldest son, he was the heir and according to Jae-Pil, the most worthy to continue the *Hwarang* code of the warrior. And though Song sought to comfort John, she could not overcome her husband's blatant disregard for him.

3

WHILE PAUL SPENT every possible moment at the *dojang* with his father, John preferred to help out at his uncle's restaurant, a popular Korean Barbecue. One particular day, John practically ran to the back row of the buffet where his uncle was supervising several servers as they filled the metal bins with prepared Korean dishes. John stood patiently until his uncle turned to face him.

"I hear you have something special to show me!" said his uncle, known by his Korean title of *Samchon*.

"Yes!" John replied, looking at the older man with excitement. He had a special love for him. Samchon, the eldest brother of his mother, had always encouraged John and treated him with much affection. Looking at the slender man who was no taller than himself, John proudly proclaimed, "Samchon, I finally have an official work permit!"

"You mean now I really have to pay you?" asked Samchon with a gleam in his eye. "No more extra dishes of *kimchi* and *bulgogi* and loose change from tips?"

John laughed at his uncle's remark. "Samchon, I'm fifteen now! Besides, who's going to run this place when you retire?"

Samchon laughed loudly. "Look at this!" he said, gesturing to Song and a few others. "His first official day and he's already taking over! You going to rename the place 'John's Korean Buffet' too?"

"When you take over will you give me a raise?" asked Song, releasing a tender smile of beautiful white teeth.

"Me, too?" added another waitress.

"Of course, and I won't make you work as hard as Samchon!" said John.

"He's got my vote," said Song, smiling at her older brother.

"I'm ready, Samchon," John pleaded, redirecting his focus toward his uncle. "So what do you say? Assistant manager?"

Samchon gripped his chin and began rubbing the few careless gray hairs with his thumb. "Hmmmm--assistant manager, eh? You really think you can run this place?"

"Yes!" John replied.

"You ready to learn everything there is to know?"

"Yes!" John replied eagerly.

"You ready to work hard like me?"

"Yes! Yes!" John replied emphatically.

Turning briefly toward John's mother, Samchon continued, "Okay, okay, the boy shows promise."

Song smiled as she walked toward the register which was located in the corner of the restaurant. She took a paper slip from a Korean man who was holding onto a credit card.

"Tell you what I'm going to do," continued Samchon.

John looked at him expectedly.

"Because you my favorite nephew, I going to give you the best position in my restaurant. This position is only one where you have to work with everyone—and I mean everyone! You can't be too shy!"

"No, Samchon," replied John very seriously.

"You have to be fast on your feet!"

"Yes, Samchon!"

"You have to have quick hands!"

"Of course, Samchon!" replied John, releasing an impatient smile.

Then, making hand motions that resembled karate chops that cut through the air, his uncle finished, "You going to need that Tae Kwon Do!"

John put his head down. The mere mention of the Korean art was enough for him to feel paralyzed with fear. As he stared at his uncle, his thoughts raced backward to a different time and a different place.

"Jwa-woo-hyang-woo!" said Jae-Pil.

Standing in the middle of a wooden floor, two small boys faced each other. Paul, the larger of the two, reached down and caressed the blue belt strapped tightly around his white *do-bok*. John did no such thing, for unlike Paul, he wore his white belt with a certain amount of shame

"Sijak!" ordered their father.

The boys instantly assumed their fighting stance. After a feeling out period, Paul struck, kicking John firmly in the stomach with a side kick. Upon impact, John flew back, landing on his rear end. Paul released a sly smile. He then walked over and offered his hand to John.

"Mumcho!" said the boys' father with a look of disapproval. He wagged his index finger at Paul.

Seeing the anger expressed in his father's face, John slowly rose to his feet as Paul backed away. Wobbling, John raised his fists and approached Paul. Both boys threw a few kicks and punches, neither connecting with any force. Then, John rushed Paul. He recklessly threw a triple punch, the last of which connected firmly on Paul's chin.

Rubbing his face, Paul remarked, "That's going to cost you, *neo.*"

Then, bellowing a *gihap* that echoed throughout the room, Paul jumped in the air, spun, and kicked John squarely on the jaw. John immediately crumpled to the ground, faintly recognizing his brother standing over him. Lying on the wooden floor, everything became a blur. John felt dizzy and disoriented. Struggling to prop himself on his elbow, he saw his brother bowing to his father, whose lips were pressed firmly, but slightly curved, allowing as much as a smile as his **austere** mind would allow. "*Haecho,*" said his father to Paul.

At the sound of the snapping of fingers, John awoke from his mental stupor and regained his focus. He suddenly was aware of his uncle standing before him.

"Hey, where'd you go?" asked Samchon, waving his hands directly in front of John's face.

"Oh, sorry Samchon," stuttered John. "Thank you so much."

"'Thank you?'" asked his uncle, raising his eyebrows in confusion. "Thank you for what?"

"For making me the new assistant manager!" replied John, his smile returning to his face.

Samchon raised his hands in the air. "Whoa, whoa, whoa. When did I say that?"

"But you said…" John protested before recalling his lapse into the past.

"No, no, no! I said it was best position in the restaurant. Not even your mother have so much responsibility, but I never say anything about being manager."

While John stared at his uncle with a confused look on his face, a large white towel was placed on his shoulder.

"Congratulations! You my new bus boy!"

A burst of laughter was heard throughout the restaurant, fostered all the more by John's long face.

"Oh, come on, John, it will be fun!" said his mother, giving him a tight hug while she ruffled his black spiky hair with her hand. "You will be the best dishwasher in all of Los Angeles!"

"See?" began Samchon as he smiled at John. "How can I go wrong? I now have prettiest waitress and best bus boy!"

4

THE LAST FEW weeks of a blissful summer had come to an abrupt end. As John wiped down a table at the Korean Barbecue, he constantly kept one eye on the clock. His mother, he noticed, did the same; though for entirely different reasons. Unlike John, she was actually excited. Father and number one son had been in South Korea for specialized training at the *Kukkiwon*, considered the paradise of Tae Kwon Do. The instruction was widely regarded to be the very purest form available, and many of the greatest instructors from around the world gathered to share technique and theory each year. For John, it was simply two weeks where he could breathe without fear of judgment.

"Hey, look everybody! Bruce Lee is back!" said Samchon with a wide grin.

John instantly felt his heartbeat. As his pulse began to race, he pretended not to notice his father and brother enter the restaurant. His mother raced to meet them, kissing them both on the cheek. Paul released a wide smile, showing off the beautiful white teeth he had inherited from his mother. To John's chagrin, it seemed that whereas Paul had received the best features of their parents, he had received none at all. People often commented on Paul's muscular physique, his square jaw, and his bright, shapely brown eyes. In contrast, the only comment John ever heard was that his long face and slender body resembled that of his uncle.

Paul embraced his mother and tenderly kissed her on the forehead. Jae-Pil, however, appeared mildly irritated by the public display of affection. Instead of kissing his wife, he turned to Samchon and bowed.

"Hyeong-nim," stated Jae-Pil, *"Annyeong hasyeoss-eoyo. Jal jinaesyeoss-eoyo"*

Samchon shrugged off Jae-Pil's formal behavior and continued, "Yes, yes, I'm fine, and good evening to you, too." Then, turning to Paul, he asked, "So, you guys here to tell us about the trip or just to mooch some food?"

"Hopefully a little of both!" replied Paul, grabbing a plate and walking through the buffet, using the large black tongs to choose his favorite meats, *kimchi*, and Korean vegetables.

Jae-Pil sat down **stoically** as Song brought his food to him. As she did so, a few men passed, bowed, and greeted him. Some referred to him as *Hyeong-nim*. Others called him *Chung sa nim*. Jae-Pil nodded quickly in response.

"So, tell us about your trip!" implored Song.

Jae-Pil sat very stiffly, used his chopsticks to take a few bites of white rice and *bulgogi*, then replied **tacitly**, "Good training."

"Wow!" said Song. "That is so exciting, honey! I can't believe you had so much fun without me!"

Everyone laughed except for Jae-Pil, who continued to eat in silence.

"It was awesome, mom!" Paul exclaimed. "I even got to go out to the best clubs in Seoul!"

"Really? Your father took you to the night clubs?"

"Well, he didn't go, but I went with some of the guys I met there. They were really cool, especially this one guy named Min. He was incredible! His *yeop-chagi* was out of this world!"

"You mean someone is actually better than you?" asked John.

"Hey *Dong-saeng*, is that a dress you're wearing?" Paul replied, frowning. John scowled at his brother. "No!"

"Actually, it's an apron!" said Samchon. "He our newest bus boy and dishwasher!"

"Whoa!" Paul exclaimed, "Congrats, little bro! You finally found something you don't totally suck at!"

"Very funny," replied John, "but you never answered my question. So you met a lot of guys over there who are better than you?"

"What are you talking about?" asked Paul. "I'm going to the Olympics soon, *Dong-saeng*."

"Well, hopefully you won't go against your buddy with the great side kicks," John retorted.

"Not a problem," said Paul. He wiped his face with his napkin as he stood up from his booth. Then, raising his right knee, he slowly lifted his entire leg with perfect form, bending low at the hip, so that his foot lay arched in knife position only inches from John's face. "Min taught me everything he knew."

John glared at his older brother as several customers applauded. A few boys pointed, chattering with great excitement in their voices.

"Man, if looks could kill!" said Paul, laughing as he lowered his foot smoothly to the floor. "Dude, don't dish it out if you can't take it! Get it, dish?"

"Hey, now," Samchon interrupted, "remember, you make fun of my employees you making fun of me."

Paul smiled confidently and patted his uncle on the shoulder. He then turned to John and added, "Don't take it to heart, Johnny boy. I'm just messing with you."

John, frowned deeply. "I better get back to work."

"Okay, okay!" replied Samchon. He then led John into the kitchen and shouted in Korean to the men in the dish room, "Everyone here knows my nephew! He in charge back here! Everyone needs to respect him. If you disrespect him, you disrespect me, got it? Okay okay. Let's go!"

John looked at his uncle, slightly stunned. "Samchon?"

"Yeah, you heard me, you in charge of this kitchen! Being a bus boy is training for manager!"

John smiled, then replied, "But these men are older than me."

"Yes, but none of them are my favorite nephew."

John paused, then whispered, "*Jeongmal gamsa-habnida,* Samchon."

"You're welcome, you're welcome. Now make sure these guys do a good job!"

As John lowered a large plastic bin on the metal sink counter, Samchon stood at the entrance with his arms crossed. John observed the serious expression on his uncle's face as he proceeded to load an array of dishes into a thick green plastic tray. John then grabbed a black hose with a large metal head, sprayed the entire tray, and shoved it into a large square metal washer. Samchon nodded, smiled, and then returned to the table where the Kim family remained seated.

"I got room for one more if you're interested," he said to Paul.

Paul inclined his head, avoiding eye contact. Finally, he replied, "Uh, thanks Samchon, but I don't think so."

"What? You too good to be a dishwasher? You know Bruce Lee was a dishwasher?"

Jae-Pil finally broke his silence, shouting, "Yes, Bong-Chul too good to be dishwasher! And stop this nonsense about Bruce Lee! He not Korean and he not have nothing to do with Tae Kwon Do!"

"Excuse me!" replied Samchon. He then walked away.

Song lowered her eyes. "You're tired, dear, from your flight," she said, stroking the broad shoulders of Jae-Pil. "Why don't you and Paul go home and rest?"

"Yes, you are right."

Jae-Pil then quietly walked up to Samchon, bowed, and apologized.

5

IT ONLY TOOK a few weeks into the new school year for the first newsworthy event to occur. An epic fight had taken place that students could not stop talking about. Normally, John would not have paid much attention to such events, but this particular case held a special interest for him. The boy who had been beaten up was none other than Joe Bok, a red belt who trained at the *dojang*. He was known as a fighter, even a bully, so the sight of him lying unconscious on the ground had the entire school buzzing. Rumors began to fly instantly. John listened to a dozen different versions of the fight, but the one fact that nobody seemed to know was the identity of the other student.

"Listen, I don't know his name, but I did find out he's new to our school," said Narayan Rajiv, John's closest friend. Dark skinned with straight black hair that fell over his forehead, his thin legs matched John stride for stride as the two boys continued to walk across the campus. Dressed in baggy jeans and collared shirts and with small backpacks slung across their shoulders, they formed a sort of mirror image. "From what I gather," continued Narayan, "he's just a little Mexican boy. Well, I mean, he's our size."

"That's impossible," John interrupted, "The only one who can beat Joe Bok is my own brother! Nobody messes with him!"

"Well, it did happen," said Narayan.

"You've seen him?" asked John.

"Yes, he was suspended for a few days, but I hear he's back now."

"Have you talked to him?"

"Are you off your trolley?" said Narayan, lowering his eyebrows. "Why would I want to know the person who bullied the person who bullies me?"

"What?" replied John, shaking his head. "Anyway, it just doesn't make sense. I mean...how, Raj?"

"I don't know, but I still remember Joe constantly bumping into me last year. Once, it was raining, and my books fell into the mud! So, it's not like I'm terribly disappointed that it happened."

"Yeah, but Joe hasn't done that this year, has he?" asked John.

"No, now that you mention it, I've rarely seen him." Narayan scratched his forhead. "Maybe he's searching for a fresh supply of freshmen to torment." Then, smiling, he added, "John, don't pretend that you're not happy about this."

Grinning, John confessed, "Okay, maybe a little. Joe's definitely…"

"A Neanderthal? A dimwit? A complete arse?" said Narayan.

Laughing, John replied, "Yeah, all of the above. Except for maybe the 'arse' part."

"Well, that's how we say it."

"But that's not what I was thinking."

Narayan arched his eyebrows. "You're wondering how he did it."

Nodding his head, John replied, "Raj, Joe's strong and tough. He can break boards. I've seen him rough up people twice his size. And he never backs down. I don't get it."

"Maybe the other fellow knows karate, too."

Looking at him condescendingly, John replied rather **pedantically**, "We don't train in karate! That's Japanese! My father teaches Tae Kwon Do. It's Korean!"

"Oh, I thought it was all the same," said Narayan.

"Why would you think that?" asked John. "You don't know the difference between the martial arts?"

"I'm Indian, John. If we get mad at somebody, we just set their entire village on fire."

John broke into laughter. "Man, shut up, I know you grew up in England."

"I know, I know, but my Indian heritage is still in there," he said, pointing to his heart. "Besides, I don't know why you're so upset. I thought you stopped training with your father."

John shot his friend an irritated look, and then muttered quietly, "Never mind."

The two boys then exchanged farewells as they headed for different classes.

6

THE NEXT SEVERAL days at school became a personal investigation for John, and though he had direct access to Joe Bok, that was not a source he wished to tap. When he pressed other students for details, their answers did little to satisfy him. John was actually beginning to consider the possibility that the mystery student did not exist.

"John, I found him!" shouted a fast approaching Narayan.

"Yeah?"

Panting heavily, Narayan continued, "Yes, and he's standing just outside the cafeteria."

John looked at his friend, slightly puzzled, and then replied, "Are you sure?"

"Yes, I'm sure! No more clangers, I promise!"

"Come on," said John, "let's go!"

The two boys quickly descended a long flight of stairs, dodging several students as they ran through an outside hallway that led to their final destination.

"Right over there, standing by the door," said Narayan, pointing at a boy casually dressed in loose fitting slacks and a white cotton shirt.

"Time to put this to rest once and for all," said John, walking toward the entrance of the cafeteria.

"No!" said Narayan, grabbing him by the arm.

"Man, what's wrong with you?" asked John.

"What's wrong with *me?*" repeated Narayan, his eyes flashing. "Have you forgotten that Joe's your brother's best friend? You are guilty by association, John."

"Then you go talk to him," said John.

"No, no, no," replied Narayan, wagging his head. "Sorry, out of the question."

"He looks harmless," said John absentmindedly, "and you were right; he's kind of a little guy!"

"Well, looks can be deceiving," said Narayan. "Besides, I spent a lot of my wits trying to find him, so we have to approach this entire situation quite delicately. Please, John, don't botch it up!"

"Raj, you're so..." began John, searching for the precise word.

"Brilliant? Dramatic? Diplomatic?"

"I was just going to say *strange*," replied John.

John walked toward the boy. He was of the same height, standing well under six feet. He was also slenderly built, but lithe, not willowy, like John; and definitely not thinly boned, like Narayan.

"Hey, what's up?" John announced.

"Hello," replied the boy, turning to face John.

He was nothing like what John had envisioned. His tone was cordial, and with his thick brown hair, olive colored skin, and brown eyes; he was actually quite handsome.

"I'm John Kim, and this is my friend, Raj," John continued, offering his hand.

The boy responded with a firm handshake. He then gave John a quizzical look. "Your friend?"

John turned to see Narayan leaning against one of the large circular cement posts that supported the sundeck of the cafeteria. John frowned and angrily motioned with his hand. With a nervous smile, Narayan quickly approached, his long thin legs taking such great strides that the image made John think of a large bird such as a crane or flamingo.

"Pleased to meet you," said Narayan as he nodded his head and smiled. "Thank you."

"What's your name?" asked John.

"My name is Robson Da Silva."

"Cool," replied John. "Hey, um, if you don't mind me asking, how long have you been here? I mean, I've never seen you before. You're new, right?"

"Yes, I have visited Los Angeles before, and other places in the United States, but now I am here to stay," said Robson. He spoke slowly, as if measuring each word so as not to make a mistake. "This is my first time to attend school here."

"You speak English very well," said Narayan. "I myself speak three other languages, and I'm learning yours." Clearing his throat, he continued, *"Estoy aprendiendo a hablar español...porque...las muchachas de México... son muy guapas!"*

Robson smiled. "Yes, I agree, but I am not from Mexico. *Eu sou de São Paulo, Brasil. Entendo espanhol mas falo Português.*"

"Did you say you're from Brazil?" asked Narayan.

"Yes," replied Robson.

In unison, John and Narayan nodded, saying, "Oooohhhhh."

Robson smiled once again, then turned his head from side to side. He seemed to be searching for someone. "I was about to eat lunch. Please excuse me."

John glanced at Narayan as Robson began to slowly walk away from them. "Hey! Wait up!" He called out. "You're the one who beat up Joe Bok, right?"

Robson stopped suddenly. His upper body seemed to tense up. "Look, I really do not want any trouble."

"No, you misunderstand," said Narayan. He smiled widely, displaying his very white teeth that contrasted nicely with his dark skin. "We very much approve of what you did! We're just curious to know *how* you did it."

Robson inclined his head. Slowly, he replied, "I did not want to fight him. I was simply eating lunch with my cousins. He approached us and became quite vulgar with Gabriela. I asked him to leave her alone. I only intended to talk to him, but then he threatened me. I stood up, and that is when he tried to punch me, so I was forced to resist him."

Narayan furrowed his brow. John began to study Robson with a mixture of curiosity and fascination.

"*Oi*," interrupted a slow, seductive voice, marked by a similar Brazilian accent.

The three boys turned to see two young ladies, both quite attractive. One possessed dark eyes and long black hair. She wore tight shorts, revealing thick, shapely legs. The other girl was actually stunning, displaying darker skin and light brown, almost blonde hair. Her eyes were incredibly blue, all the more so due to the contrast with her skin tone. The mere sight of her caused John and Narayan to stop suddenly, as if struck by a temporary form of apoplexy.

"*Oi*, Kayla!" said Robson, kissing the dark haired girl on the cheek. He then kissed the golden haired girl. "*Oi*, Gabriela!"

"*Tudo bem?*" asked Kayla, scowling slightly at John and Narayan.

"*Sim, prima. Vou te apresentar uns amigos,*" said Robson. "This is John and this is Raj."

"Hello," said Gabriela, extending her hand first. Both boys eagerly responded. Gabriela laughed before choosing to take the hand of Narayan first and then John's.

"I'm Kayla," greeted the other girl. She squeezed each of the boys' hands very firmly, so much so that her grip caused Narayan to wince. Then, holding up a large brown bag, she asked Robson, "*Voce está com fome?*"

"*Sim,*" replied Robson. He then turned to John and said, "We have to go. It was nice to meet you."

Gabriela smiled at both boys through her thick pink colored lips and said sweetly, "*Tchau.*"

"Goodbye," replied Narayan, waving to her.

John watched as the three Brazilians disappeared toward one of the outside circular stone lunch tables. "Raj," he said, looking at his friend who seemed lost in a trance. "You can put your hand down now."

7

It was no use. Try as he might, John could not concentrate on his homework. As he sat at his desk in his bedroom, his eyes would glaze over each time he began to work on one of his geometry problems. His mind wandered toward Robson. There was something about him that provoked admiration, and yet, in a way, John harbored resentment toward him. He was not quite sure why. Robson had been polite enough to him when they had met. He definitely was not conceited like his brother, and he was not intimidating like Joe, so what was it about him that bothered John so much?

After pondering his many thoughts, John reluctantly came to the conclusion that part of it had to do with his own low self-esteem. He was envious of Robson just as he was envious of his brother. Like Paul, Robson was handsome. He had nice features and was constantly surrounded by two incredibly beautiful girls. As John struggled to overcome his resentment, his thoughts were interrupted by the heavy thud of his bedroom door, which was flung open so harshly that it richoceted off the wall. Paul and Joe Bok then entered the room.

"Hey, man," began Joe, "I heard you were talking to that Mexican kid who fights dirty! What's up with that?"

John did not bother to make eye contact. "The door was closed for a reason," he mumbled rather monotonically.

Paul then yanked John's textbook off of his desk. "This is my house, too, little bro."

"What do you guys want?" asked John as he reached for his book.

"I already told you, dumbass!" said Joe. He furrowed his brow and stuck his chin out. His lips were pressed tightly together. John stared back at the angry face, tired of Joe's constant **belligerence**. Even his appearance was audaciously hostile. With his spiked, blonde hair and the green dragon tattoo on his bicep, it was impossible for Joe to go unnoticed.

"Look, he isn't Mexican, and who said he fights dirty?" asked John.

"Well, he ain't Korean, that's for damn sure!" Joe snapped, practically spitting the words at John. "And unless you're deaf, I just told you that he fights dirty! That little punk grabbed me from behind just when this new chick was coming on to me!"

"That's not what I heard," muttered John.

"Is that right?" asked Joe in a menacing tone that seemed to dare John to continue.

"Yeah, that's right. I heard that you were harassing that girl and so Rob..." John paused suddenly, catching himself. He then continued, "...so he threw you down and elbowed you in the face and knocked you out!"

Joe slapped John hard on the head. "You calling me a liar?" he asked.

"Ouch!" whimpered John as he cowered back.

"Hold on, Joe," said Paul, motioning with his hand. "*Dong-saeng*, why do you always have to rebel?" Paul paused for a moment as John rubbed the top of his head. "Look, just stay away from that kid 'cause I'm going to have to rough him up. You know, make an example out of him. We can't let him disrespect us."

"Us?" asked John. "Look, he didn't do anything to you, Paul. You know how Joe is."

"Your little brother has a big mouth!" said Joe, his scowl still prominently on his face. "And you should refer to me as *Hyeong*!"

"I don't even call Paul that!" said John.

"All right, all right, both of you. Just take it easy!" said Paul. He then took a step closer to John and asked, "Is there something you're not telling us, little bro?"

John stared at Paul for a moment, started to open his mouth, and then closed it as he turned back toward his desk.

"He asked you a question!" said Joe, grabbing the back of John's desk chair and swinging it around so that John was forced to face them.

"You have a serious problem, Johnny boy," said Paul. "You know nothing of *chung seong*. You don't even know the difference between family and a bunch of foreigners."

"That's because he stopped training!" said Joe.

"Yeah, come to think of it, I can't even remember the last time I saw John at the *dojang*," Paul continued. "Maybe he needs a private lesson."

Paul raised his thumb. Joe smiled, then instantly grabbed John and lifted him out of his chair and up to his feet.

"Stop it! What are you guys doing?" John shouted, struggling in vain. "*Naebeolyeo dwo*!"

"*Mian-hada, Dong-saeng,* but this is for your own good," said Paul, grinning widely.

"Ready to train, John?" mocked Joe as he held both of John's arms tightly behind his back.

"Get over here!" said Paul, grabbing John by the back of the neck with his left hand as he cocked his right hand in a tight fist. "This is your lucky day, *Dong-saeng. Museowo*? Don't be. This is exactly what you need. A lesson about *jon gyeong!* About *chung seong*!"

"Yeah! Respect and loyalty!" echoed Joe, nodding approvingly as Paul prepared to attack.

John did not say a word, but instead closed his eyes and lowered his head.

"Look at him! How pathetic!" said Joe, laughing as soon as the words left his mouth. "It's not enough that he's an embarrassment to his *gajok* and the entire *cheyug-gwan*, but he won't even face his discipline with pride!"

"Sorry, Johnny boy, but Joe's right. You need to see this!" said Paul, digging his thumbs into John's eyebrows so as to raise his eyelids. "I mean, come on! People pay to see the great Paul Kim perform a *sibeom*! Here it is! A *baro jjireugi* to the face..."

"We're going to force you to respect your heritage!" Joe said. "Even if it means pounding the weakness out of you!"

"Set," said Paul with his fist cocked. "*Dul*," he continued, his eyes fixed on John's nose. "*Hana!*"

With a shrill *kihap*, Paul feigned a punch at John's face, stopping his fist only inches from John's nose. Relieved, John began to relax and breathe normally. Paul, however, quick bent his knees and changed levels to throw a straight punch directly at John's midsection. At the point of impact, John let out a gasp and slumped to the ground, holding his stomach.

"Lesson number one," said Paul, sounding quite professorial, "always exhale and tighten your abs before a punch. If you would come to the *dojang*, you would know that."

"It's all about the abs, John," said Joe, raising his shirt to display his firm abdominal muscles.

"That's right," said Paul. His face broke into a wide smile as he, too, lifted his shirt and revealed a flat stomach composed of tight squared muscles that outshone Joe's own. Then, wagging his head condescendingly at John, he said, "Come on, Joe. We don't want to be late for class tonight."

"*Tto boja, Dong-saeng!*" said Joe between laughter.

Remaining on the floor, John watched helplessly as the two boys left his room. He was in pain, yet inwardly he knew that Paul had not seriously tried to hurt him. John had seen his brother break thick wooden boards in demonstrations and was fully aware of what he was capable of doing.

8

AFTER ATTEMPTING TO brush his thick black hair to the side, John lingered for a moment in front of the mirror. With each stroke, his short spiky hair resisted any control and continued to stand up. He straightened his blue collared shirt over his khaki pants and began to turn away, but then suddenly stopped. Stroking his chin, he observed his long downward jawline. It was not square like his father's. He then made a face, exposing his teeth. They were large, too large for his mouth, and unlike the perfectly shaped teeth of his mother, John had a slight overbite.

He looked at his nose, which was a bit long. He then moved his face from side to side, observing various angles. John frowned. He had had enough of his reflection. He did not possess the rugged strength of his father, nor had he inherited any of the soft, beautiful features of his mother. All of that had gone to Paul. It was not fair. John would never know what it was like to be handsome. He would never experience the sensation of knowing people were purposely looking at him. He tried to convince himself that it did not matter, but somehow he was unable to do so.

Looking at his watch, he decided that if he rode his bicycle quickly, he would arrive in time to drink a soda and help himself to one of the desserts before starting his shift. Making his way out of the bathroom and toward the living room, he was surprised to see the familiar figure of his father heading his way. Short black hair that shadowed a tan square face, the gray dress shirt that hung loosely over dark slacks, and the polished black shoes. This was the image John had of his father for as long as he could remember.

The narrow hallway made it impossible for John to avoid him. As the two stood face to face, his father asked, "Ik-Jong, you leave? Bong-Chul say you train tonight."

Bowing respectfully, John stuttered fearfully, "*Abeoji*, I am so sorry for the misunderstanding. I never told such a thing to Paul. I—I have to work with Samchon and *Um-ma*. I must leave now."

Jae-Pil remained in front of John with steely, unflinching eyes. Though not a particularly large man, he was the most intimidating figure John had ever known. "*Moreugess-seubnida...* Bong-Chul say you prepare apology. You resume training and regain honor."

John, squinting his eyes, slowly shook his head from side to side, "*Anio—joesong-habnida*—I never said such things."

"So you care more to clean dirty dishes of strangers than your heritage?" asked Jae-Pil, his voice rising with each word.

"*Abeoji*, Samchon needs me to arrive on time. *Anyeonghi gyeseyo.* I must go."

John bowed once again and attempted to pass, but his father would not allow him to do so. John then looked at him and began to shake in fear. Suddenly, his father reached up and pinched his cheek, pulling the skin with a fierce vice of finger and thumb. His father then yanked him closer, causing the two to bump foreheads. John, horrified by his father's actions, began to sweat profusely.

"It better if you born a girl." Jae-Pil uttered the words slowly, each one dripping with contempt. *"Haesan!"*

John dare not say a single word. Instead, to further his humiliation, his pent up emotions resulted in tears forming and slowly descending down his face. He hoped his father would not notice, but he did. Jae-Pil shook his head slowly. The left side of his lip curled upward. Finally, he walked past John, brushing his shoulder as he disappeared into his bedroom at the end of the hall.

9

THERE WAS NO smile on John's face. He passed customers without saying a word. Even when they greeted him, he merely nodded. As he wiped tables and collected an assortment of plates, glasses, silverware and used chopsticks, his mother approached him. "What's wrong, honey?" she asked.

"Nothing!" replied John.

"Please, tell me."

John stopped. The large white dishcloth in his hand limped downward, allowing drips of water to fall onto the table. He gazed at his mother, admiring her pretty round face and creamy white skin. Her thick black hair seemed to always flow perfectly around her shoulders. Even in her uniform, a black blouse attached to a white skirt, she was stunning. It was not fair.

"Mom, it's just that..." His voice trailed off. Suddenly, his entire countenace changed. He glared at her. "Oh, never mind, it's not like you're going to do anything. You never do."

Song arched her eyebrows. "John?"

Throwing the damp white cloth in his hand onto the table, John shouted, "Forget it!" He then grabbed his cleaning cart and pushed it with great force, causing the glasses inside the plastic tubs to crash against the many utensils. A clanging sound was heard as John hurried off to the dish room.

With eyes that expressed her sadness, Song walked over to Samchon. After exchanging a few words, he nodded and left her. Pointing to John, he said, "We need to talk."

"But Samchon, there's a lot of dirty dishes," said John.

"Family comes first," he replied. "Now take off your apron and come with me."

John nodded and followed his uncle to his office, which was located out of sight, far into the very back of the restaurant. Samchon was an unpretentious man. His wooden desk was very old and was covered with papers. Nobody dared clean up the mess; however, as Samchon claimed that he knew where every single artifact lay. As John took a seat on the opposite side of the desk, Samchon asked him, *"Joka, museun il issni?"*

"I'm fine," muttered John.

"I don't believe you."

John quickly looked downward. After a moment of silence, his uncle tried once more to reach him. "John, come on, it's me, Samchon! You know you can talk to me about anything."

John continued staring at the floor, observing the cheap tile and its design of intersecting squares. As he focused more deeply, the images slowly blurred and began to move, changing shape. He was lost in his own world. He was safe. Safe! Safe from his father and safe from his brother and safe from anyone else who might hurt him!

After enduring John's silence, Samchon finally interjected, "Well, I'm here if you need me. Anything at all. You just let me know. Okay?"

John felt his eyes welling up in response to the gentle tone of his uncle's voice. He struggled to repress his emotions. According to his father, tears were a sign of weakness and the man who shed tears dishonored not only himself, but his father as well.

10

STUDENTS WALKED ACROSS the green grass underneath the bright sunlight. John strained to find Robson among the many boys and girls that passed him in all directions. Finally, in a somewhat isolated spot, he found him sitting between the same two pretty girls at one of the circular, white stone tables on campus. As John approached, he heard the sound of a foreign language mixed with the delight of laughter. It was an appealing sight: three attractive young people laughing and playfully caressing each other. When John finally reached their table, he saw Kayla with her arms around Robson's neck, seemingly strangling him from behind while Gabriela had her hands placed against his eyes, covering them completely.

Robson giggled as he clutched one of Gabriela's wrists with both hands and then slowly bent it. She cried out in mock pain, *"Ai! Monstrinho!"*

"Imagina!" shouted Robson between giggles. He then made eye contact with John. "Hey! Save me, my friend! I've been caught by a *jacaré!*"

"Do not listen to him," said Gabriela. John stared at her. She was truly a beautiful specimen. He had never seen a girl with such a combination of caramel colored brown skin and bright blue eyes. "He deserves it," continued Gabriela in the same seductive voice that had been recorded in John's mind from the moment he had first laid eyes upon her.

"I had some salad stuck on my tooth and he said I looked like a *jacaré!*" shouted Kayla.

John smiled awkwardly. "I don't know what that is."

Laughing, Robson said, "These two are *jacarés!*"

"What did you say?" asked Kayla, tightening her arms around Robson's neck.

"Okay, okay," said Robson, gently tapping Kayla's shoulders. She smiled and released him.

"A *jacaré* is like a crocodile. We have many in Brazil," said Kayla.

"Oh," said John, smiling uneasily.

"Do you want to sit down?" asked Gabriela.

John blinked twice, surprised that the blonde, tanned beauty before him would address him so casually.

"What was your name again, my friend?" asked Robson.

"John—John Kim."

"Yes, John. Come sit with us if you dare," said Robson in a playful tone. "But watch out because this one…" He paused to point at Gabriela. "…will break your heart. And this one over here…" Once more he paused to point at Kayla. "…will break your arm!"

Both girls slapped Robson on each side of his shoulders, which only served to make him laugh more loudly. Gabriela then moved slightly, motioning to John to join them at the table. He did so, but remained quiet, somewhat intimidated by the closeness displayed by the three.

"My friend," continued Robson, "Gabriela makes all the boys fall in love with her. Then, she tells them she only wants to be their friend. So, she is really the *jacaré*." Robson then made the shape of a large mouth with his forearms touching at the elbows. "She just waits, looking at them with those blue eyes of hers, luring them closer…closer…and then…snap!" Robson then slapped his hands together for emphasis. "Kayla, on the other hand, is a purple belt in Jiu Jitsu. She is more like an anaconda. She doesn't pretend. She goes straight for the kill!"

John felt captivated by Robson's personality. He was confident, even effervescent. This helped John overcome his own self-doubt, allowing him to slide between Robson and Gabriela on the circular stone bench.

"Jiu Jitsu. So that's how you did it," said John as he looked straight at Robson.

"Did what?" asked Robson.

"Oh, nothing," replied John. Then, motioning to the girls, he asked, "Do you all train in Jiu Jitsu?"

"I do not," replied Gabriela.

"I have trained for…" said Kayla, pausing to count on her fingers, "five years. I started when I was twelve."

"And you?" John asked Robson.

"*Desde que ele era um menino!*" said Kayla. She then reached out and playfully began to ruffle Robson's dark brown hair.

"Yes, it's true," said Robson with a large grin across his face. "I grew up fighting. But my uncle is the one who saved me."

John looked at him quizzically.

"Robson is very, very good," added Gabriela, smiling proudly. "He is a great fighter. Everyone in Brazil knows him. They understand that he is special."

"Everyone except Uncle Mario!" interrupted Kayla.

"What do you mean?" asked John.

"He won't give him his black belt until he turns eighteen," replied Kayla. "Robson is already an instructor."

John listened, then suddenly soured upon reflecting on what he had been told. "Your uncle," he began. "He's holding you back? He doesn't respect you?"

Robson cocked his head back quickly, then shook his index finger at John. "No, no, my friend, never say that. My uncle has done everything for me. He showed me the importance of family and he taught me a new way."

"A new way to fight?" asked John.

"A new way to live," replied Robson.

"But, shouldn't you be a black belt? If you're a great fighter, you've earned it."

"I earn it when my uncle says that I have earned it," replied Robson.

"Maybe you should teach people on your own? I'd be willing to pay you. I bet some of my friends, like Raj, would too!"

"John," replied Robson calmly, "my uncle is Mario Da Silva. He is a great man. If he says I need to wait, then I will wait. He knows what is best for me. I would never betray him like that. If I train, it is in his school. If I wear a belt, it is the belt he gives me."

John inclined his head.

"It's okay," said Robson, patting John on the back. "You have heard of my uncle?"

Shaking his head, John replied, "No, I haven't."

"You have heard of Brazilian Jiu Jitsu?" asked Kayla.

"Yeah, I know about it."

"Have you ever trained?" she asked.

"Well, not in Jiu Jitsu, but in Tae Kwon Do. My father's actually a former champion and my brother's won lots of tournaments." After a slight hesitation, John reluctantly added, "He's training for the Olympics."

Robson frowned and nodded respectfully, as did Kayla.

"Who is your brother?" asked Gabriela.

"Paul Kim," said John.

"*É mesmo?*" blurted Gabriela, her eyes flashing.

"*Você o conhece?*" asked Kayla.

"Yes, he is so cute," replied Gabriela.

John became irritated at her response until Robson also entered the discussion. To John's delight, he had a serious look on his face. "I also know your brother. He challenged me in front of the entire school, but I told him that I was forbidden to fight again. He then accused me of being afraid, so I told him that he is welcome to come to our school and I will fight him there."

"Cool!" blurted John. "I would love to see you kick his ass!"

Robson arched his brow. "You wish that I defeat your own brother?"

"Of course!" replied John without the slightest hesitation.

"But why?" asked Kayla.

"Because he thinks he's better than everyone!"

"John, even if that is true, we should never fight to…" pausing, Robson turned to Kayla and Gabriela before continuing. "*Como podes dizer a palavra…humilhar?*"

"Humiliate," replied Gabriela.

"My friend, we should only fight for honor. We should never try to humiliate our opponent."

John looked at Robson, and then looked down. After a moment of silence, he asked, "Robson, can anyone train at your school?"

"Yes! Jiu Jitsu is for all people!"

John smiled upon hearing Robson say "Jiu Jitsu." Instead of a hard "J," he pronounced it with a type of "zsh" combination that gave the word a vibrating, humming sound.

"Well, like I said, I've trained in Tae Kwon Do for many years," said John, hoping to impress Robson.

Instead, he **nonchalantly** replied, "That is nice. Now, do you want to learn Jiu Jitsu?"

"Yes," said John softly. "But it doesn't matter that I'm not Brazilian?"

Robson laughed, then replied, "No, of course not. We only have a few Brazilians in our school. Most of them are American."

"Oh," said John, his eyes suddenly perking up.

"You thought only we could learn Jiu Jitsu?" asked Kayla.

"Well, no, it's just that my father only allows Koreans in our school. He says that we shouldn't share our heritage with *oegug-in*."

A dubious look fell upon the faces of Robson and the girls.

"What is that?" asked Robson.

"That's the name Koreans give to foreigners."

Nodding, Robson replied, "Yes, I understand. Some Brazilians are like that, too, but my uncle believes that Jiu Jitsu belongs to everyone. He says that we are all a family in Jiu Jitsu, and besides, Brazil is like America. We have many different people there."

"Just so you know, I'm not like that." Suddenly, John's eyes narrowed. His jaw tightened as he said, "It's my father! He's too damn traditional!"

"You have so much anger," said Gabriela. She reached out and gently rubbed John's neck. "You need to smile more."

John looked at her for a moment, and then promptly lost himself not only in her comment, but in the **succulent** tone of her voice and the blue eyes that projected so deeply from her golden brown face.

"John...John..."

But there was no answer.

"*Eu acho que ela hipnotizou ele*," said Kayla to Robson, who smiled and nodded. She then reached past Gabriela and thumped John on the side of his head.

John grimaced. A guttural "huh?" followed. Then, realizing what had happened, he instantly felt embarrassed.

"Don't worry," said Robson between laughter. "She does that to everyone. I'm only...*impérvio*?" he paused, turning to his cousins, who both shrugged. "Uh, I don't know this word in English, but I have, like, a special power against her because she is my cousin. Anyway..." Robson stopped, turned, and reached into his backpack. "Here is my uncle's card. It has the address of our school and a class schedule on the back. Come and you will be my guest."

11

JOHN MADE HIS mother promise him that she would not tell his father anything about his visit to the Da Silva Jiu Jitsu Academy. He had always been told that it was betrayal to consider other martial arts. At first, she refused, but as he pleaded for her **collusion** day after day, she finally gave in to his request.

"Okay, mom, see you around nine," said John as he got out of the car.

His mother responded with nothing more than a nervous smile and a quick nod. Waving goodbye, John took a few steps toward the entrance and slowly turned the doorknob. He could feel his heart pounding. He had not trained in martial arts for well over a year, and his most recent memories were not pleasant. Quite the contrary, they were filled with the countless times he had striven in vain to win his father's attention. When Jae-Pil did randomly pass by, he only stopped long enough to frown disapprovingly at John's technique before quickly moving on to help Paul or another of his promising students.

"You came!"

It was Kayla. She was seated behind the front desk, dressed in a thick, black kimono that blended magnificently with her dark eyes and long black hair. John observed her, not sure if she was smiling or smirking at him. Having only looked at her next to the golden skinned Gabriela, he had failed to see that she was quite the beauty herself. She was larger than Gabriela, and much more strongly built. Her roundish yet firm white face contrasted nicely with her darker features, and further adding to this contrast was a sprinkle of freckles on each cheek.

"Hi," he replied somewhat timidly. "Do you work here?"

"*Professor* Mario is my uncle, too," said Kayla. "I train here, but Robson and I help out as well. We also have Mauricio Reis. He is a very good blackbelt and our main assistant instructor."

John nodded politely.

"You can go back there. Robson is probably warming up."

"Thank you, Kayla."

"Yes," she said before turning her attention to a magazine.

Tentatively, John left Kayla and walked down a narrow hallway that almost immediately opened up into a very large room, much larger than he had expected. It was divided into two large mat areas, one white and one blue. Between the two training areas was a fairly large carpeted section laced with simple white plastic chairs. Several people remained there, casually seated and dressed in kimonos similar to Kayla's. Others were dressed in normal clothing and appeared to be spectators.

On the white mat to his left were people participating in Brazilian Jiu Jitsu. Each one possessed a kimono with a different colored belt tied at the waist. As John observed them grapple, he heard the snap of rapid combination punches as well as the thud of heavy swinging kicks. He turned to the right where men wearing board shorts and rash guard T-shirts of various colors were training on the thinner blue mat. Their hands sported small black gloves that contained separate thumb and finger outlets for dexterity. Some of them were training with heavy bags while others trained with kicking shields or hitting pads held by an instructor.

John's eyes darted between the two sites. He then spotted two locker rooms at the very end of the building. Entering, he removed his shoes and changed into his Tae Kwon Do gi and slowly walked toward the white mat in search of Robson. There, John found him dressed in a dark brown kimono standing with bended knees on the white mat.

Robson was holding the pant legs of a much larger man. He, in turn, was gripping Robson's sleeves around the wrist. They battled back and forth until Robson was able to use his knee and shin to pressure one of his opponent's legs down to the mat. He then hopped over to the other side and sprawled over the man. John watched, fascinated by the movements. Suddenly, Robson propped himself up and put his knee on the man's chest. He tried in vain to push Robson off, and just when he was able to do so, Robson quickly turned to the other side. In one quick movement Robson grabbed the man's forearm, threw his legs over the man's face and chest, and then fell to his bottom with his back slightly arched. Robson then stretched the man's arm, locking it at the elbow. It appeared as though Robson would break it, but instead he merely held the position. The larger man struggled for a moment, but then ultimately tapped Robson on the top of his leg. The grip was promptly released and to John's surprise, the two competitors shook hands and smiled afterward.

As John contemplated this act of camaraderie, he turned his attention to the other area of the academy. The sound of kicks and punches were more familiar to him. Except for the fact that it had a thinly padded blue mat instead of a hardwood floor, it could have been mistaken for any Tae Kwon Do school. Several men were sparring, throwing combinations of strikes and kicks. John decided to approach Robson when suddenly one of the men training lunged at his sparring partner, wrapped his arms around the insets of his legs, and wrestled him down to the mat. The fallen opponent did not panic. Instead, he wrapped his legs around the other man and quickly tied up both of his arms so that he could not be punched. John remained still, mesmerized by the action.

"Excuse me, bro," said a young man with light brown hair who appeared to be in his twenties. He walked past John, took off his sandals, and walked on to the white mat where he greeted another student and began to stretch.

"Hey!" called out a voice with a distinct accent that John instantly recognized. "Over here!"

John slowly walked toward Robson, who promptly reached out and began to run his fingers through John's gi. "What is this?" he asked with a bemused smile.

"It's my kimono," replied John matter-of-factly. He then showed Robson the emblem on the back, which revealed the Kim name and a large design of a Tae Kwon Do fighter flying through the air with a high sidekick.

"That's nice," said Robson, "but it won't last long here. If you continue to train, you will have to buy a BJJ gi. Feel this."

John touched the coarse material of Robson's collar. "Wow! It's really thick!" he exclaimed.

Robson inclined his head toward John and pointed. "So you are a yellow belt?"

Pressing his lips together, John hesitated as he looked at the old, faded brown belt wrapped around Robson's waist.

"I should be green—that's what a lot of people told me—but my father…"

"No, it's not that," interrupted Robson. "How do I say it? Jiu Jitsu is a different art, John. If you decide to train with us, you will have to start over. Belts do not come easy in Jiu Jitsu. It takes a lot of hard work. Since you are just beginning, you will have to wear one of those."

Robson pointed to a man wearing a white belt. He was struggling helplessly underneath another man wearing a purple belt.

Exhaling loudly, John exclaimed, "I really don't want to wear a white belt." He then gripped his own belt. "It's bad enough that I still have this."

Robson arched his eyebrows. "John, do not feel bad. We all start at white belt. Besides, there are some white belts who are very good. In the end, it is our technique that counts, not the color of the belt we wrap around our gi."

John was not convinced.

"Well, just keep it on then," continued Robson. "Come on. I want to introduce you to my uncle."

John was led to a man who appeared to be in his late thirties. He was of good size, taller and heavier than both boys, and sat on the mat comfortably in a similarly thick course white gi. Around his waist was a faded black belt.

"*Tio*, this is my new friend, John," began Robson. Then, turning to John, he continued, "John, this is Mario Da Silva, my uncle and lead instructor."

John bowed to the man three times without making eye contact. When he finally did so, he paused for a split second. Mario had a very handsome face when seen from his right side, but the left side revealed the remains of deep scar tissue. His ear was almost non-existent, revealing little more than a small hole, and his eye looked slightly deformed due to the thinner, stretched skin that surrounded it. Even the short black hair on the left side of his face came in patches, dominated by wrinkled, reddish, knotted skin grafts.

"I like your friend," said Mario to Robson. His voice was deep, but possessed a calm, almost gentle resonance. Then, turning to John, Mario added, "Please, though, a simple handshake will do."

John hesitated. He swallowed deeply.

"It's okay," said Mario, extending his hand further.

"I'm sorry, sir," stuttered John, "but…"

"Yes?"

"Is it not a dishonor for you to shake my hand?"

Mario turned to Robson and shrugged his shoulders. He then said to John, "It is never a dishonor to shake hands with a future student, and Robson has told me that you have befriended him at school, so how could this be a dishonor?"

John stared at the black belt around Mario's waist, and then slowly touched his offered hand. Fear overwhelmed him, a combination of Mario's appearance as well as his stature as a great fighter. John expected Mario to squeeze his hand tightly, a proud demonstration of what was sure to be a powerful grip, but instead he did no such thing. His hand gently and softly wrapped around John's own and then with a calm smile on his face, he released it.

"We're glad to have you," said Mario. "Robson will help you. Now, go and have some fun."

377

John, slightly dazed, did not move.

Robson smiled slightly and grabbed him by the arm. "Come."

John walked over to a far corner of the large white mat. There, he began to observe the action around him much more closely. Some people were standing up, others were on their knees, and some were even seated yet apparently in total control of their opponents.

"Sit down," said Robson. "You need to stretch."

"This is so strange to me," whispered John as he moved his head in circular movements.

"What is so strange?" Robson asked. He then touched the tips of his toes and began to rock back and forth on his back.

"Everything," John replied. He then swiveled his torso from side to side. "People laughing and talking—nobody bowing to Master Da Silva—and the movements."

"John," said Robson, touching the top of his head with his heel. "We respect everyone. We are all family, from white belt to black belt. And yes, we like to talk and have fun."

At that moment Mario walked to the center of the mat. Students quickly stopped what they were doing and formed a circle around him. Mario then lowered himself to the mat and demonstrated the technique. "When practicing the snake drill, make sure you lift off your foot and raise your hips. Then, while on your side, push off with as little friction as possible, moving out and back like this." He then stood up and walked to the outer padded wall. "Okay, let's form our lines."

"Follow me," said Robson. He then walked to the back of one of the four lines that were quickly forming.

"Aren't you going first?" asked a young man. He was wearing a blue belt around his waist.

"No, I want to go in the back so I can help my friend. It is his first day," replied Robson. "Go ahead. You lead. We'll go last."

"Okay," replied the young man as he lay down on his side.

John watched the first of the students begin as Robson commented on their movements.

"This first guy is pretty good. Yeah...smooth." Then, shaking his head disapprovingly, he continued, "No, he needs to get his bum off the ground." A mischievous smile formed across Robson face. "Now, *that* is nice form." John followed Robson's eyes to another line. There, Kayla was moving quickly across the mat in strong, tight movements. "Okay, it is our turn. Watch me and do your best to do what I do." Robson then reached out and touched John on the shoulder. "Don't feel bad if it's hard. Just go slow and take your time."

John nodded. He watched Robson intently as he knelt down on his right side and proceeded to glide along the mat, doing so as effortlessly as Mario had done during his demonstration. With a deep breath, John lay down and assumed the position on the mat. As he attempted to move, however, he found his body simply did not cooperate. Aware that he was falling behind, he broke into a nervous sweat. He looked forward and noticed that Robson had not only reached the end of the mat, but was standing in place with the rest of the students.

One of the lines had moved more slowly than his own. John looked over to see one remaining student who also was struggling. He had a large belly and unkempt sweaty red hair. He stopped often to catch his breath. Even he, however, was beginning to pass John. Struggling mightily, John tried a few more times to move, but it was futile. He seemed to have no control over the direction of his movements. He slowly became aware of the eyes staring at him as he had only progressed a few feet beyond his original starting point. John perspired more profusely. He could hear the murmuring from the other side of the mat.

"What school is that guy from?"

"I don't know, but whatever a yellow belt is, he definitely doesn't deserve it if he can't even do a simple drill."

To John's dismay, none other than Mario Da Silva walked toward him. He knelt down on the mat next to him. Before he could say a word, John blurted out, "I'm so sorry, master!"

A large smile broke onto Mario's face, followed by laughter. Then, several others who had heard John's loud apology began to laugh as well. John, noting this, slowly stood up and began to walk away. Mario turned the palms of his hands upward and shook his head. He then motioned to Robson.

"John! John! What are you doing?" shouted Robson as he ran after John.

Unable to make eye contact, John bowed his head low. "I am so sorry, Master Da Silva. I am sorry, Robson. I have shamed you both."

Once more, Mario began to smile. The other students stood there, a mixture of perplexity and amusement on their faces. Mario then grabbed John by the shoulder and pulled him toward him. "John, I was only going to help you."

"Like this, John," said Robson as he knelt down on the mat and fluidly turned to his side. From there, his body moved sideways and forward.

John nodded and slowly lay down. Mario then placed John's left foot on the mat and then grabbed his right hip and lifted it a few inches off the mat. "Now, push off."

John did so as Mario assisted him. Robson sat close by with a joyful grin on his face.

"That's it!" said Mario. "Now, switch to your other side and do the same thing. Put your right foot on the mat and push off, moving your bum and hips back."

Once more, Mario assisted John as he continued the movement. As John slowly began to move forward on his own, Mario began to clap. "It's his first day! Let's encourage him!"

The other students, smiling, followed his example. They cheered John to the edge of the mat that suddenly did not seem so long nor wide.

12

EYEING THE GREEN bill that lay folded on top of the napkin dispenser, John waited patiently as he cleared the many plates and cups from the table, dumping them into a large dark bin that lay on the top of his cleaning cart. Next, he pulled out a wet cloth and began wiping vigorously, removing bits of white rice, *bulgogi, bibimbap*, and *eomug bokkeum*. Finally, he pulled out a thick brush with which he began to scrub the charcoaled meats that had stuck to the grill located in the center of the table. Satisfied with his work, he eagerly grabbed the tip. Fifty dollars! John straightened it out. His eyes widened. He licked his lips vigorously. He had never received such an incredible sum of money. He looked admiringly at the front, observing the details of Ulysses S. Grant with his beard and bow tie. Then, he turned the bill around in his thumbs and index fingers, but as he stared at the Capitol building, John sensed something was wrong. It seemed oddly faded and the dimensions were out of place.

Staring at the bill, John said aloud, "What the...?"

His thoughts were then interrupted by laughter.

"Man, this is classic!" said Joe Bok as he held his phone high in the air. "I got the whole thing right here. I'm posting this right now!"

"Think of a good title!" said Paul.

"How about 'John gets punked...again!' " said Joe.

Paul burst into laughter as he held both thumbs up. John, seething with anger, pushed his cart to their table. He stared at both Joe and Paul, and then at the attractive Korean girls sitting next to them. "You think that's funny?" he shouted.

A few customers who were sitting in adjacent booths suddenly stopped talking.

"Yeah," replied Joe, a prominent smirk on his face. "I do." He then grabbed the girl who sat beside him around the waist and pulled her toward him until their shoulders touched. Placing his hand around the nape of her neck, Joe planted a firm kiss on her lips. He then waved his phone in John's face. A clip of the video was displayed on the screen. "And so are all of my friends once they see this!"

Both girls burst into laughter.

"And don't forget the entire school!" said Paul. Then, frowning, he continued, "The only bad part is that nobody even knows John. It's kind of hard to humiliate him."

"No worries," said Joe, pointing to the video on his phone. "Everyone's gonna know him soon enough!"

John glared at them.

"Look at him!" said Paul. He laughed loudly as he pointed his index finger in John's face. "If only he could harness that *ki.*"

"You mean horse power!" said Joe.

"Don't call me that!" said John, squinting his eyes in anger.

"I don't get it," said the girl next to Joe.

"It's his nickname because he has such a long face," said Paul. "We call him horse. John's got that long jaw and those buck teeth."

"What?" replied the other girl, crinkling her nose. "No, that's not true. Don't say that."

Joe whinnied as he pointed at John. A few people in the restaurant began to stir as a result of the commotion. A waitress walked by, frowned, but did nothing.

"Hey, let me get some more pics for my post!" said Joe. Stretching upward, he lifted his phone up to John's face. "Horse, say something in your language!"

John glared at Joe, and then noticed his brother and the two girls. They were laughing at him. As the anger rose in his body, Joe put his phone down and grabbed two chopsticks. With his right hand he held them in the front of his mouth. With his left hand he stuffed his face with rice and attempted to chew by moving his lower jaw from side to side.

"Is that a horse or a cow?" asked Paul amidst laughter.

Grabbing a glass of water from his cleaning bin, John hurled it at Joe. He then grabbed another and dosed his brother as well. The girls jumped and shrieked as chunks of ice and water splashed over them and dampened their faces and long black hair. Wiping his face with a napkin, Paul cursed through gritted teeth.

"Get him!" said Joe, rising up as he brusquely pushed the girl next to him out of the way. Paul then gently nudged the girl next to him and stood to his feet. With a furious scowl on his face, Joe grabbed the front of John's neck and began to squeeze. Instinctively, John placed both of his hands on Joe's wrist and ripped Joe's hand away. Joe froze. His eyes widened. John then seized the moment and pushed Joe backward, causing him to stumble and fall onto the lap of the girl who had been sitting next to him.

"I'm taking you outside, *Dong-saeng*!" screamed Paul, grabbing John by the bicep.

As Paul attempted to pull John away, John pummeled his hand underneath Paul's arm. With a tight underhook, John controlled the right side of Paul's body. Paul squinted, hesitated, and began to struggle. John then cranked Paul's shoulder, painfully forcing Paul to bend down to relieve some of the pressure. John slowly took a few steps over to the table and began to smash his brother's nose into a plate of spicy *kimchi*. As he did so, Joe Bok hit him on the side of the face with a hammer fist. The blow stunned John, causing him to release his hold and fall to the floor.

"Enough! What are you boys doing?"

The three boys suddenly stopped. In front of them stood a glowering Samchon.

"I'm going to break you, John!" said Paul as red blotches of *kimchi* dripped from his face.

"Paul, I said enough!" said Samchon, raising his hand high into the air.

Paul took several quick short breaths. His nostrils flared. One of the girls quickly handed him a napkin. Snatching it out of her hand, Paul wiped his face for the second time. "Out of respect for Samchon, I'm leaving. But this isn't over."

"Damn right it ain't!" said Joe, grabbing his date by the arm as he led her away. He then kicked John as he stepped over him.

With a deeply disapproving frown, Samchon muttered, "Get up!"

John attempted to make eye contact, but his uncle more seemed preoccupied with the mess the boys had made than anything else. A mixture of water, ice, and food covered the table as well as the booths on each side and the floor below. Several customers were pointing and whispering.

"Ladies and gentlemen, just a little family squabble," announced Samchon, waving his hands in the air. "You know how it is. Respect has been restored. Please go back to eating. I promise this will not happen again."

A few people nodded and resumed eating.

"Clean this up right away and then come to my office!" said Samchon in a very unfamiliar tone.

"Yes, *sajang-nim*," replied John, slumping his shoulders in regret.

"*Sajang-nim?*" repeated his uncle. "No, John, I am *Samchon*...always *Samchon.*"

He turned to give some instructions to a few waitresses before leaving toward his office. John watched in silence. A waitress quickly approached him and handed him a mop. Setting up two bright orange cones, John audibly sighed and began cleaning the floor. He noticed a pair of brown dress shoes. He looked up to see an older man with a very large, wide face. "Sorry," said John. "I'll be done in just a minute."

The man frowned and proceeded to the other side of the restaurant in an effort to pass. John pulled out several white towels and scrubbed the table and the padded booths. He bent over and grabbed several chunks of ice. Finally, seeing that the table was suitable for customers, John collected his cleaning supplies and headed back to the dish room. He dumped the dirty water and shouted angrily to the men working there, "We always dump dirty water in the sink! We never just put it back in the closet!"

John was met with blank faces. One of the men rolled his eyes and shook his head. John then proceeded to his uncle's office, where, to his surprise, he found the door closed. After a slight hesitation, he rapped the door a few times with his knuckles.

"Come in!" shouted his uncle.

Opening the door slowly, John sat down on one of the two wooden chairs in front of his uncle's desk. They were old and simple chairs with absolutely no padding.

"John, I am not happy with you."

"I know, Samchon. I'm sorry. It's just that they started calling me names—"

"You don't have to explain," interrupted his uncle. "You think I don't know what's going on?"

John lowered his eyebrows and cocked his head back.

"You are training again," continued Samchon.

"How—how did you know?" John stammered.

Samchon shook his head. He then got up from his chair and walked around his desk. He stopped when he stood directly in front of John. "First, I know because I hear you telling lies about these," he continued, touching John's cheek where a shaded rough patch had formed. Then, he grabbed John's wrist and stretched out his arm, revealing a large, slightly purple bruise. "These marks are not from burning yourself in the dish room or bumping into the crates."

John put his head down and stared at the floor.

"You cannot lose control of your emotions," continued Samchon. "This is my restaurant. When you do childish things like that, you don't just shame yourself, you shame me, too. And if your mother working tonight, you shame her as well."

John nodded. "I'm sorry. You are right. I have shamed you." He hesitated a moment before adding, "I will resign immediately. You don't even have to pay me this month."

John got up and began to untie his apron. Wagging his head, Samchon put his hand on John's shoulder and pushed him down gently. "Sit down," he instructed. "You are not dismissed, but you must be more careful. If your brother—or anyone else gives you trouble—you come tell me, okay?"

With a slight bow, John replied, *"Gamsa-habnida."*

"It's okay. I understand. I am sure your father is very proud of you."

"Wait…. What?" asked a bewildered John.

"You've let your brother bully you for too long and his funny looking friend, too. But you must keep your sparring at your father's school, and not let what happens there carry on to my restaurant!"

"But Samchon, I'm not training with…" John paused. Swallowing deeply, he changed course. "Yes, I'm sorry, once again, you are right. *Joesong-habnida.* I promise I won't embarrass you again. May I leave now?"

"Did you clean up that mess?" asked his uncle.

"Yes, Samchon."

Samchon combed back his thinning gray hair with his long, bony fingers. He then went back to his desk, where he sat down and rested his cheek on his fist. He let out a deep breath. John promptly stood up, smiled, and walked out the door.

13

JOHN SAT NEXT to Robson on the large white mat. As Mario gave instructions, a man in a blue kimono tiptoed onto the mat and quickly knelt down.

"Okay, good to see everyone again. Good to see you, Thomas," said Mario.

The man nodded and waved. He had a purple belt around his waist.

Robson whispered to John, "Thomas is a lawyer. He's also one of my uncle's first students here in the United States. He doesn't train so much anymore, so his endurance is poor, but he still has very good technique."

John raised his eyebrows as he observed the man. He had blonde hair and sported a clean-shaven face.

"Why is your uncle so happy to see him if he isn't dedicated to his training?" asked John.

"Because he has been with my uncle since the beginning. He's very busy. Besides, he is a very nice man."

"Oh," said John, somewhat surprised by Robson's simple answer.

"Ssshhhhh!" hissed Kayla with a threatening scowl.

John closed his mouth while Robson appeared as though he were going to break into laughter at any moment. Kayla then raised her middle finger and index finger toward her eyes before pointing both fingers menacingly toward Robson. He puckered his lips in response and made kissing motions toward her. She then smiled widely. Her eyes, too, began to sparkle.

"All right, let's start with some basics from the closed guard," continued Mario, standing in the middle of the large white mat. "I want to see arm bars, triangles, and then a basic sweep that lands in a mount. Make sure no white belts are together." Mario pointed to four white belts and divided them up between others. Gesturing toward John and Robson, he asked, "You two are going to stay together?"

"*Sim, Tio*," replied Robson.

Robson and John found a space on the mat that gave them some room to maneuver. John then pulled Robson into his closed guard by wrapping his legs around him. Robson put both of his hands on John's chest, to which John reacted by grabbing Robson's right wrist with his left hand, using his four fingers to grip the gi sleeve. John then reached for Robson's right elbow with his own right hand, pulling it toward him. Robson remained calm, allowing John to make each move. Smoothly, John put his left foot on Robson's right hip, lifted his right leg further up Robson's back, and then moved his hips and swung his left leg around Robson's head. Robson nodded encouragingly and tapped John lightly on the shoulder. "Yes, John, you got it, man! Maybe you can turn my wrist a little more, but really, you got it down."

John smiled and then locked in the arm bar.

"Whoa, man, easy there *Assassino*. I tapped!"

"Sorry," John replied. "I was just trying to make sure I really had it."

"No problem," said Robson, rubbing his elbow. "You know what? I think you are a natural. You did not even have to push my head back. You just whipped your leg around me—very fast."

"Well, I'm pretty flexible from Tae Kwon Do," said John. Then, his face fell. "If only I weren't so skinny. I'll never be strong like my brother."

"You are strong!" Robson exclaimed. "Anyway, you don't want to be too strong."

"What do you mean?"

"I mean that some guys are too muscular—too big. A fighter needs to be flexible and have good cardio."

Nodding happily, John practiced the other drills until Mario walked once more to the center of the mat. "Okay, time for sparring."

John started out on his knees whereas Robson remained in a sitting position with one foot on the mat and the other knee bent in a perpendicular fashion. As much as John tried, he could not get past Robson's defenses. He attempted to control Robson's sleeves, but Robson always ended up rotating his hands, breaking John's grip and establishing one of his own. John then began to stand, but Robson grabbed his lapel collar on one side and his wrist on the other. Robson then climbed up John's body through his hips and shoulders. Before John could react, Robson's had pulled him down and had placed his legs around him in a figure four.

Smiling, Robson announced, "Triangle choke, my friend."

John would not concede; he continued to fight. Using his free arm, he pushed Robson's right knee, but it was in vain. Robson began to pull down on John's head slowly. Soon, John could feel himself becoming lightheaded. He then tapped Robson on the thigh several times. Robson released John and then displayed his agility by disconnecting his legs and bringing them over his head and somersaulting backward in one fluid motion. He reached out his hand, which John grudgingly shook.

Laughing, Robson said, "Don't get discouraged, *Assassino*! You're doing great."

"Then why do you always submit me, like, ten times in five minutes?" asked John.

"No, not so much. You must remember I have been doing this since I was a child, and my teachers were all the very best. Growing up in Brazil, I had the best instruction possible. Jiu Jitsu is like Portuguese to me. It is my mother tongue. But I can tell you that you are learning very fast."

"Thank you, Robson," replied John. Then, with a bit more of confidence, he added, "I've been submitting most of the white belts my size and I've even beat a few blue belts."

Smiling, Robson patted him on the shoulder. "See? There you go. Don't compare yourself to me. That's like me comparing myself to my Uncle Mario."

"Have you ever beaten him?" asked John.

Robson's eyes widened as he shook his head vigorously. "No, never! He is much too difficult. Not only is he bigger than me, but he sees things much faster than I do. Even though he's retired now, a lot of people say he could still win the *mundial* if he chose to compete."

"What's that?"

"The *mundial de Jiu Jitsu* is the world championship."

"Wow," said John. "So why doesn't he compete? Was it…because of his injury?"

With a very serious look on his face, Robson replied, "No, he stopped because…" Robson paused. He turned his face for a moment. Slowly, he continued, "My uncle got married, and he said he found something greater than gold medals."

As John opened his mouth to ask another question, Robson quickly changed the subject. "All right, now I want to help you a little with your posture. You are allowing me to get you too—how do you say it? You are bending too much. You are using your back instead of your legs."

"I can't help it," replied John. "You're stronger than me."

Robson waved his index finger in John's face. "No, no, no, John. You must stop thinking like that. Maybe I am stronger than you, but that is not the reason I keep pulling you down. It's because you have your legs too far back. You must keep your back straight."

"But how do I do that if you're pulling down on me with all your weight? Your legs are stronger than my arms."

"Yes, you are right. Now you are thinking in the language of Jiu Jitsu. So, the answer is simple. You bend your legs to keep your posture. Here, like this. Let's switch positions."

Robson stood up as John sat down. "Grab my collar with your right hand and here, take my sleeve with your left hand." John did as Robson instructed. "Now, put your right foot on my hip and your left foot against my knee—or my other hip—whatever you want to do. Just play around a little."

John did so, pulling with all his might. Robson then placed his left leg back and his right leg forward. Tucking in his right elbow, he prevented John from pulling his arm forward. Methodically and patiently, Robson worked to secure the pant leg of John's right leg with his left hand. He then pinned it down to the mat and crossed over with his right knee. Grabbing underneath John's left shoulder with his right hand, Robson slowly transferred more and more of his weight onto John's torso until he passed to John's side. John scrambled to his right hip, but it was too late. Robson had gained control of his legs by gripping his gi pants, and with his arm around John's head, he had established a dominant sidemount position.

"Like that," said Robson, releasing John.

John slowly sat up, breathing heavily. "How come you're never out of breath?"

"I do not get tired very easily," replied Robson. "I know how to take small breaths and I do not exert myself unless it is very necessary. You are still learning that."

"Hey, you want to hit the heavy bags?" asked John.

"Yes, let's do it."

As the two boys stepped off the mat and onto the carpet, John paused, staring at the continued action. His eyes moved towards Kayla. She had a young man trapped in a collar choke from her full guard. Shaking his head, John said aloud, "Man, Kayla's really good."

Nodding, Robson said, "Yes, she is wonderful."

John furrowed his brow, surprised by Robson's choice of words and the soft, almost subconscious manner in which he had said them. He could not decipher the exact meaning, but decided against pursuing the matter.

"Let's see some of those kicks of yours, but remember, throw in some Muay Thai."

John nodded as both boys walked onto the blue mat. Approaching the large black bags, they took a low stance with bent knees. Robson then lifted his right knee, swiveled his hips by rotating on the top of his left foot, and swung his right leg with such force that when his shin made contact, a large thud resounded within the academy. Several people turned in response. John repeated the movement, hitting the bag but with less force.

"John, you are still trying to kick the bag with your feet," said Robson. "Do not do this. You could break your bones in a real fight. Use your shin. And look, don't stop; it's one fluid motion."

Once again, Robson raised his right knee high in the air and then fluidly swirled toward the bag, swinging his leg like a sledgehammer. Time and time again, they pounded the bag relentlessly with both their right and his left shins. John then danced around in agile fashion, mixing an array of front kicks, back kicks, side kicks, and spinning kicks until he was drenched in sweat.

A few men walked by and nodded approvingly. "That kid's got skills," said one of them.

Smiling, Robson shouted above the noise, "Now *this* is your mother tongue!"

John nodded as he continued to kick the large bag, knocking it to the left and to the right, then back and forth. Slowly, it began to blur as his thoughts reverted to the past...

"John, I'm sorry," said Mr. Lee. He had short black hair like John's father, but instead of the rough, blocky face, Mr. Lee had soft eyes and a kind oval shaped face. "I spoke to your father and he actually became upset with me. He said that it was very disrespectful of me to bring up such a topic."

"But why?" asked John.

"According to your father, promotions are completely the judgment of the head instructor of the *dojang*. In fact, he said that if I bring it up again, I will be forced to leave the school."

John looked down to the floor. "*Sabeom-nim,*" replied John. "I understand."

"You are much too good to be a yellow belt," said Mr. Lee. "Your brother isn't *that* much better than you and your father has already awarded him his black belt. I was twenty-eight years old when I got mine and your brother is what, sixteen? The only words *Chung sa nim* said was 'John has the *Tae* and the *Kwon* but he does not have the *Do*. Unless he changes from within, he will have to go to another *dojang* in order to advance.' "

Mr. Lee paused. He put his hand on John's shoulder. "For what it's worth, I don't agree."

John fell silent.

"I tried, John. There's nothing else I can do," added Mr. Lee before walking away.

Suddenly, John became aware of his surroundings. He was in Mario Da Silva's academy and Robson was standing next to him, his eyes wide with admiration. John was sweating. He was breathing heavily. His heart was pounding.

"*Nossa*! You kicked the hell out of that bag!" exclaimed Robson.

John nodded, but said nothing. His rage had come and gone. He felt tired.

14

THE FOUR KOREAN boys huddled together.

"Look at him!" said Paul. "Talking and laughing with those *oegug-in*!"

"You have to admit that Gabriela's pretty hot!" said Richard, who had short black hair and glasses.

"You got that right. I could see how she distracted Joe," said Jun, a boy with a large face covered by thick bushy dark hair that seemed to have a mind of its own.

"Shut up, Jun!" barked Joe.

"It's okay, Joe," said Paul. "Jun and Richard are right. She is hot. If it weren't for my father, I would've had her by now."

Jun nodded and then exchanged a fist bump with Paul.

"Let's do something!" growled Joe. "Come on, man! We owe those guys!"

"No can do, bro," replied Paul. "I already challenged that kid. He won't fight me."

"I thought he said he'd fight you at his *dojang*," said Richard.

"Dude, like I'm going to go fight him in front of his entire school!" said Paul. "Once I kick his ass I'd have like twenty Mexicans—or Brazilians— or whatever the hell he is—after me."

"What about John?" asked Jun. "You and Joe still haven't gotten him back."

"His mommy's protecting him!" interrupted Joe.

Jun crinkled his forehead. "Huh?"

Nodding, Paul said, "Yeah, that little weasel! He must have talked to my uncle because he told my mom that we were causing trouble. She said she may never speak to me again."

Joe released a large smirk. "Yeah, but it's not your fault if he has a little accident."

The others burst into laughter.

"Go challenge him," said Richard, pointing directly toward Robson.

"I already did, man!" replied Paul.

"Yeah, but that was a long time ago," said Jun. "Maybe he was afraid to get into trouble after he beat..." He paused. "I mean, after he and Joe got into it."

"I don't know," said Paul. "I got too many things happening right now to waste my time on this little punk."

"Your mom can't do nothing to me," snarled Joe, "and I don't give a damn if I get suspended!"

Joe then marched off with the other three boys closely behind. Without even the slightest hesitation, he walked straight up to the circular bench table. "Hey! Indie! Where's the money you owe me?"

Suddenly, the laughter and chatter stopped.

Looking up at Joe's familiar scowl, John replied, "Just ignore him, Raj."

"Like hell he will!" said Joe. "This fool owes me money!"

"And why do I owe you money this time?" asked Narayan.

"For not kicking your ass all year!" said Joe.

Laughter could be heard from Paul as well as the other two Korean boys.

"Don't give him anything," said Robson.

"Yeah," added Kayla.

Joe turned to face Robson. "Stay out of this!" he barked. "Or do you want to go at it again? This time I'm ready!"

Robson's jaw tightened. His brown eyes suddenly narrowed.

"Follow John's advice," interrupted Kayla. *"Simplesmente ignorá-lo."*

Standing up, Gabriela walked over to Paul. She flashed her deep blue eyes directly at him. "Paul, I thought you were a nice boy," she said in a sweet, pleading tone.

Hesitating, Paul smiled weakly at her. Her full image—the thick pouting lips, the white blouse that showed a tad of cleavage, the tan shapely legs—were on full display. "Come on, Joe. Leave him alone."

Joe remained as rigid as stone.

Paul moved his head from one side to another, motioning to Joe.

After a brief pause, Joe shouted, "All right, all right! I'm sure I'll see this little punk again."

He then pushed Narayan hard in the face. Robson quickly rose from the bench.

"*Acalma-te*," hissed Kayla.

As Joe approached Paul and the other two boys, Robson walked up behind him and pushed the back of his head.

"What the—?" said Joe, turning around quickly.

"Now you both are even," said Robson.

Balling his hands into a fist, Joe approached Robson and began to curse at him. Robson took a few steps back, creating distance between himself and the stockier Joe Bok.

"Well?" shouted Joe. "Do something! Do something!"

Robson remained with his lips pressed together. His nostrils moved slowly as he took in short gusts of air. His eyes remained locked on Joe, but he said nothing.

Paul walked forward until he stood beside Joe. "What's wrong?"

"I promised my uncle I would not fight again at this school, but if you—"

"Shut the hell up!" interrupted Paul. "I know what you're gonna say. If we want to fight you we can go to your school. Man, that's bullshit! Who do you think you are, anyway? We're seniors! We rule this school! You can't just come in here and start calling the shots! If we say right here and right now then you either fight or get your ass kicked!"

"Either way he's getting his ass kicked!" added Joe.

His tone calm and steady, Robson replied, "I am not trying to fight anyone. I attend this school just as you do. You do not have more rights here than we."

"Us," said Kayla, who had approached Robson with John and Narayan at her side

"Actually, I believe *we* is correct in this case," said Narayan. "It is not used often, but then again you cannot trust Americans with correct grammar."

Joe and Paul frowned and then exchanged quizzical glances.

"Besides," continued Robson, "I was not the one who harassed Gabriela. That was this one here." He then pointed at Joe. "I was not the one to make a challenge. That was you. And I am not the one right now... *Como você diz provocar?*"

"I don't know," replied Gabriela.

"Provoke!" said Kayla.

Joe raised his hands demonstrably. "What the hell is this? A damn English lesson or what? Just shut up already and fight me!"

Robson raised his hands. "Wait."

Joe disdainfully blew out a puff of air as Robson walked toward John and put his arm around him.

"Come." The two slowly walked away from the rest of the group. "Look," continued Robson, "I cannot fight him here, but you can."

John's eyes flashed. "What?" he exclaimed. "You want me to fight Joe Bok?"

"Yes, now it is for honor; the honor of your friend. Fight to defend him."

"Robson, I can't! He's too big! He's too strong! He'll destroy me!"

"No, he will not. You are a good fighter. You will beat him with superior technique."

John inclined his head and whispered, "I can't fight him. He's worse than Paul. I remember our *gyeorugi* at my father's *dojang*. I hated going up against him. He—he would hurt me—on purpose!"

"That was then. This is now." Then, nodding subtly toward Joe, Robson added, "And if he does outstrike you, move around and wait for your chance. That is when you take his back. Or, if he rushes you like he did me, it will be easy. All you have to do is put him in a guillotine."

As John listened to Robson, Joe suddenly appeared. Putting his hands around the napes of their necks, he squeezed each boy with a viselike grip. "I'm tired of waiting! Why don't we just make this simple! Paul and I will kick both of your asses and then after we're done, I'm coming after you!" Joe scowled as he pointed toward Narayan.

While Joe continued his threats, Robson bent his knees, lowering his stance. He then swiveled his neck and encircled Joe's wrist with both hands. With one quick lunge, Robson removed Joe's hand from his neck. He then extended Joe's arm and in one single motion twisted Joe's arm behind his back. Robson held on tightly to the fleshy part of Joe's palm with his fingers and applied pressure to the bony part of Joe's hand with his thumbs, creating a painful wristlock. Joe cried out instantly as Robson applied more pressure.

"Let go of me you little—" shrieked Joe.

Before he could finish, Paul flew toward Robson with a precisely placed *Ttwieo-chagi*. Robson was just able to release his grip on Joe and raise his forearm before Paul's foot made contact. The impact resonated with a loud thud and caused Robson to fall down to the ground. Paul instantly attacked again with a downward axe kick, but he was met with nothing but air as Robson rolled on the grass before deftly springing back to his feet.

"Yeah, Paul!" said Joe. "Kill that little bastard!"

John desperately wanted to help Robson, but he was unable to do so. His body simply would not move. He first looked at his brother. Paul had bent his knees. His left foot was perfectly placed forward to give him the balance to launch an attack from any angle. His *gyeorugi seogi* was impressive. John then looked at Robson. He was practically unrecognizable. His jaw was clinched. His back was slightly hunched like a cat ready to pounce. His fists were held in front of his face. But there was something more. Something that John had never seen before. Something in Robson's eyes. They were filled with rage.

"Robson, no!" shouted Kayla. She ran to him and threw her body on top of him. Robson, seemingly stunned by her action, wrapped his arms around her as the two fell to the grass below.

"Come on, get up!" screamed Paul. "You can't hide behind a girl!"

Robson began to push Kayla, but she reached around his head with her right hand and with her left arm she underhooked his shoulder, holding him tightly.

"*Pare*, Kayla!" growled Robson, bearing his teeth. "*Não te quero machucar!*"

"I'm not going to let you do this!" said Kayla. "And I don't care if you hurt me!"

Robson slithered to his side as he put his forearm into Kayla's throat. He then began to push her back. She attempted to resist him, but Robson then used his other free hand to grip the back of her head, causing her to gag. Kayla's dark brown eyes widened, expressing her fear. Then, unexpectedly, she pulled Robson's face toward her own. As they faced each other, she kissed him deeply on the lips. John watched in amazement. Slowly, Robson's face was transformed. The rage had lifted. His calm demeanor returned.

"This is getting weird!" said Jun. "Come on, let's go!"

"I told you he always has a girl saving him," said Joe, shaking his head. "Now do you all believe me?"

Paul spit only inches away from where Robson and Kayla lay on the ground. "Told you he was nothing."

Robson moved a bit, but Kayla put her hand on his forehead. Caressing him gently, she said, "*Não escuta eles.*"

As the boys walked away, John slowly approached Gabriela. "What just happened?"

"Kayla saved your brother," whispered Gabriela.

John shook his head. "But...Kayla...she..."

"Yes," replied Gabriela, smiling slightly. "She is in love."

"But they're cousins!" exclaimed John.

"Come. We must go," said Gabriela.

John followed Gabriela. Then, with mouth agape, he turned to Narayan. But Narayan did not offer any answers. Instead, he returned John's gesture with a blank look of his own.

15

THE PHOTOGRAPH SHOWED a jubilant young man standing on top of a platform, a gold medal placed around his neck. It was one of many that adorned the walls of the main entrance of the Da Silva Jiu Jitsu Academy.

"*O campeonato do São Paulo, Brazil,*" said a beaming Kayla, standing next to John. "Robson is the youngest brown belt to win."

John looked at her, startled by her sudden presence. "I didn't even notice you. How long have you been here?"

"I was filing some papers in the back," said Kayla. "I saw you come in. You're early."

"Yeah," replied John. "Robson told me to meet him. He's going to help me before the tournament." Then, after a slight hesitation, he asked, "Is he here with you?"

"You mean in the back room? Alone with me?"

John, somewhat embarrassed, paused before attempting to answer her. "No, I—he said he would meet me here at six thirty—before the tournament—to help me."

"Robson is Brazilian, John," replied Kayla. "If he is here by seven, for him, that will be early."

John nodded before turning his attention back to the many framed pictures. Pointing to a beautiful woman dressed in nothing more than a white bikini and black high heeled shoes, he blurted, "Who is that?"

"Why do you ask?" replied Kayla. She arched her eyebrows and released a half smile with closed lips. It was a knowing smile. Kayla seemed to have an innate talent for making others feel uncomfortable. It was as if she disdained any speech that could even be accused of being disingenuous.

"She looks like a model," said John.

"She *is* a model and a movie star. Her name is Adriana Oliveira. At least it was before she married Uncle Mario. Now it is Adriana Da Silva."

"That's Master Da Silva's wife?" asked John, his eyes widening.

"Yes, she is very famous in Brazil. Everywhere, really. She is in many magazines, and even television."

"She lives here?"

"Yes, of course, with Uncle Mario, but she spends much of her time traveling."

John continued to gaze at the dark beauty in the photograph. Her black hair was cut very trim, accentuating an angular face and stunning cheek bones. Her pronounced jaw line led to a muscular neck, firm breasts, a curvaceous torso, and long, shapely legs; all given full exposure by the white bikini she was wearing in the picture.

"Here she is with Uncle Mario," said Kayla, pointing to another framed picture. There, in the snapshot, was a triumphant Mario Da Silva being kissed by the mysterious beauty.

"Wow," said John, a bit incredulous.

"Of all the pictures, this one is my favorite," said Kayla, taking a few steps toward the main entrance that led to the large training room.

"Is that Master Da Silva?" asked John.

"Yes," said Kayla.

Mario Da Silva was standing on a platform, smiling and shaking the hand of another man who was standing just above him. He was dressed in a white kimono that was loosely wrapped around his muscular chest. Just below him was a third fellow who was pointing not at the man who stood at the peak of the podium, but rather at Mario.

"Master Da Silva came in second? Who's the guy above him?" John took a step closer. "That guy even looks a little like him except that he doesn't..."

"That's Rodrigo," interrupted Kayla. "He is also my uncle. And he is famous, too."

"I guess so," said John, still observing the photograph. "If he could beat Master Da Silva then he must be really good!"

"No, he is not. He is not famous for his Jiu Jitsu. He is an actor. Uncle Mario is much better."

John stared at Kayla.

"They were to meet in the finals, but Uncle Mario forfeited the match." she continued. "That is not the way it is supposed to be. He is older and had won many more medals...but that is why I love him so much."

John nodded. He looked at the serious expression on Kayla's face, and then back at the framed photograph. Rodrigo could have been Mario's twin. Though he appeared to be a bit younger, he had the same short black hair and square jaw. But Rodrigo's face was complete. He possessed both ears and his eyes were symmetrical, his cheeks smooth.

"Kayla, what happened to Master Da Silva?"

"What do you mean?"

"You know..." stuttered John. "How did his face get like that?"

Kayla squinted. She stepped closer toward John. Her eyes pierced his own. "Never ask that question," she said in a dry, cold tone.

John took a step back. He did not know how to react. Fortunately, Robson entered the office along with two other students of the academy. "John, hello, how are you?" greeted Robson, smiling in his usual courteous manner. Then, turning to Kayla, he added, "*Há algo errado?*"

"No," replied Kayla.

"Hey, John. Hey Kayla," said one of the young men as he walked past them with a gym gag in his hand.

"Hello," said a second young man, a bit older than the others, as he, too, passed by.

Only Robson stayed in the office area. John looked at him, and then looked at Kayla once more, her words still ringing in his ears.

"Nervous?" asked Robson.

"A little. Why?" replied John.

"I don't know. You just seem a little quiet." Then, turning to Kayla, he said, "*Você não disse nada a ele, certo?*"

"*Nós não estávamos falando sobre isso,*" replied Kayla.

"Good, I thought she might have given away the surprise," said Robson, patting John on the shoulder.

"What surprise?" asked John.

"I'll tell you later, *Assassino*. You do not need any more pressure."

Kayla curled her lips upon hearing Robson's nickname for John.

"What's up?" greeted another student. "Have the other schools shown up?"

"Hello, Ted," replied Robson. "They will be here soon. Uncle Mario told me to get everyone ready first. It's his anniversary, so he will be a little late."

"Cool, I just wanted to talk to him about a few things before the tournament starts."

"If he is not here, Mauricio or I will help you," said Robson.

"Okay," replied Ted. "This is my first tournament, so I'm a little nervous." Then, turning to John, he asked. "Is this your first tournament, too?"

"Yeah," replied John before quickly adding, "Well, my first one in Jiu Jitsu."

"Yeah, I heard you were into Karate or something like that," said Ted. Then, touching Robson on the shoulder, he added, "Well, I'm sure you're going to kick ass 'cause you got this guy helping you."

"Thanks, man," replied John, "but we'll see. I'm nervous, too. What weight class are you, Ted?"

Exhaling in an exaggerated manner, Ted grabbed a roll of fat from his belly and replied, "Man, I should be in the middleweight division, but thanks to all of this, I'm going to have to compete against the heavyweights. I'm about two hundred—two ten—maybe two twenty—somewhere around there."

Robson laughed. "Then you will just have to be smarter than the rest. And you also have to stop eating those donuts."

"I can't help it!" replied Ted, grinning widely. "I work the night shift at the store and that's when they deliver them!" He then began to sniff the air. "Fresh, golden brown, chocolate, cream filled.... What's a guy to do?"

John and Robson broke into laughter while Kayla remained with the same serious expression. "You will be a better fighter and more handsome if you are not so fat," she replied.

"Isso não era muito agradável," said Robson, shaking his head at her.

"I'm just trying to help him," said Kayla.

After an awkward silence, Ted smiled and said, "Oh, it's okay. Well, I'm gonna put my gi on and warm up."

"Yes, we will do the same," said Robson. "Come on, John."

16

THE MAIN TRAINING room was quickly filling to full capacity. On the white mat several competitors were warming up. Robson, dressed in a chocolate colored kimono, worked diligently with John, who wore a basic white gi. Others, too, were making final preparations. On the carpeted area people moved about, greeted old friends, and searched for one of the few remaining seats; and the thin blue mat used for mixed martial arts was occupied with display tables.

Suddenly, all eyes turned to the couple who had just emerged through the hallway, Mario and Adriana Da Silva. Mario was dressed casually in black jeans and a yellow and green cotton shirt that had an emblem which read *Campeonato Brasileiro*. Holding his hand was a tall woman dressed in light blue jeans, perfectly fitted to accentuate her hourglass figure.

Her black cotton blouse was sleeveless, showing off her firm arms and shoulders.

"John, pay attention!" said Robson.

"I was just seeing what everyone was looking at," replied John. "Man, I never knew Brazilian women were so pretty!"

"Every woman has her own beauty," said Robson, "but right now you need to be thinking about your matches. Look, you have a nice open guard, so don't be afraid to use it."

"Then why do you always pass it?"

"Because I am a brown belt," replied Robson with a tinge of pride in his voice. "But this is a white belt tournament, so you don't have to worry too much. You might have some wrestlers, though, and they are always difficult. A lot of them are at blue or purple belt level in many ways, especially in their top game, so you have to be ready. Also, you must understand that what white belts lack in technique they make up in pure power, so survive the first minute and you will be fine."

"Okay, so what do I have to do if a guy gets a good grip on my pant leg?"

"First, you must sit up and reach for my wrist. Remember, your legs are stronger than anyone's arms. Try to break my grip, but if you cannot break my grip after grabbing me, place your foot here, on my bicep and go into your spider guard."

John crunched his stomach and bended his knees so that he could grab Robson's right gi sleeve at the wrist. He then placed the ball of his foot on Robson's bicep by turning his foot in a circular motion around Robson's fist. "Like this?"

"Yes," said Robson, "and now, whatever you do, do not let me straighten out your leg and do not go flat on your back. You do that and you're dead."

John looked at the serious expression on Robson's face. "What if I do all of this, Robson, and he backs away and then tries to run around me to get side control? That's happened to me before, especially with the tall guys."

"You have to keep the right distance. Don't let him have that space. You can't just let him do whatever he wants. If he backs up, you pull him back. Be agressive!"

"What if he's too strong?" asked John.

"Then you follow him. Hook him, or go for a sitting guard and grab one of his legs. Or, if you have to, back up and stand up with him. You know a few throws. You'll be fine. And if he is a wrestler—"

"Jump into guard," finished John.

"Yes, *Assassino*. Okay, there are only eight guys in your weight class. Win your first match and you're in the semi-finals! Easy, right?"

"But what if I lose?" asked John.

Robson held out his hand to pick John up off the mat. "Then, *Assassino*, you will do better the next tournament. That is all winning and losing means—nothing more. But no matter what happens, you are ready."

John lowered his brow. "I'm ready?"

"Yes, you are ready. And I am not the only one who thinks so."

Their conversation was cut short by a voice, marked by the familiar Brazilian accent, reverberating throughout the room. "All right, everyone, if I can have your attention, please." Various people within the crowd slowly quieted down and looked at the man standing at a podium in front of a silver microphone. He was wearing a dark kimono with a faded black belt around his waist. His head was shaven, making him completely bald, but his face showed him to be a young man in his late twenties.

"We're done!" said Robson. "Remember, the first minute is key!"

"I need everyone off the mat! We are going to divide it in half with black tape so that two matches may proceed simultaneously. Fighters, please look at your sections. Spectators, please take your seats or if you wish to stand, we ask that you remain in the very back. There, you will also see Jiu Jitsu and MMA merchandise on sale for a discounted price to all competitors."

A host of activity occurred as a result of the announcement.

"Since this is an invitatonal white belt tournament, we have limited the brackets to four weight classes: light, medium, heavy, and super heavy. Each match will be for five minutes, but if the referee determines that a competitor is stalling, he will stand both fighters up and an extra minute will be assessed. There are no age brackets. Tonight, we are all competing as adults."

Robson and John, as well as several others, walked off the large white mat and onto the carpeted area.

"Over here, *Assassino*," said Robson, motioning with his hand. "You will wait here with the rest until they call your name."

John nodded and joined several other competitors who remained in a corner next to the white mat. As he did so, he began to size up his competition. Except for one boy, they all looked older than him. One man even had gray hair mixed in with the fading black. Each one stood relatively still. Some mildly hopped from one foot to another. The only one who was not standing was a young black man who was dressed in a bright red gi. He was short and stocky. Sitting down on the floor with his eyes closed, he seemed to be in his own world as his head swayed rhythmically to the music barely audible through his earphones.

"I've never seen a red gi before," said John.

"Don't worry about him," said Robson. "Jiu Jitsu is not about image; Jiu Jitsu is about technique."

"Okay," said John, nodding as he took a deep breath.

"*Assassino*, I must sit down. Just relax and trust your instinct. Don't be afraid to do what you believe is right. When it is your turn, I will shout from the front row."

"Thanks."

Robson then walked away. He slipped on some plastic sandals, removed his gi top, and with nothing more than his gi pants and T-shirt sat beside Mario Da Silva. As he did so, several people patted him on the back and shook his hand. Some even posed for pictures with him.

"Ladies and gentlemen," boomed the voice from the microphone once again, "I am Mauricio Reis, assistant instructor here at the Da Silva Academy. Before I continue, I would like to introduce head instructor and five time absolute Jiu Jitsu world champion, *Senhor Mario Da Silva*."

Mario and his wife stood up, waving to the many people seated and standing.

"And I'm sure you noticed the beautiful woman at his side. She is Adriana Oliveira!" continued Mauricio to more applause.

"*Senhora Da Silva, por favor!*" she shouted.

"Yes," said Mauricio into the microphone, "she is Mrs. Da Silva. Now, we will begin our white belt tournament with the light weight division. Will the following fighters please come to the scale, weigh in, and proceed to the mat you are assigned. Hector Ramos, Blake Jones, Frank Garrison, and John Kim. Just a reminder to the fighters. Listen to the referees and follow their instruction at all times. Also, we remind all fighters that no leg locks of any kind will be allowed."

John stole a quick glance at Robson. He noticed Kayla sitting next to him, and next to Mario's wife was the golden toned Gabriela. The three ladies seemed to create a mild distraction for the majority of the male audience. After weighing in at one hundred and forty-five pounds, John was told to go to mat number two. He did so and met his opponent, a young man who appeared to be in his twenties. He, too, had a white gi that blended easily with his short blonde hair and reddish face. The two of them met at the center of the squared off area, shook hands, and backed away slightly.

At the hand signal of the referee, John kept low, keeping his legs bent and his hands staggered in front of him, a stance not so different than the one he had adopted while training in Tae Kwon Do. After circling each other, John reached for his opponent's collar, grabbed it, and then reached under his opponent's knee. He instantly followed with a push and a pull, sending his opponent to the mat.

The referee flashed two fingers high in the air.

"That's great, *Assassino!*" shouted Robson. He then turned to Kayla and announced proudly, "I taught him that!"

"John is learning quickly, but I don't think he is ready for that name," said Kayla.

"*E claro que ele é!*" replied Robson.

John attempted to get around his opponent, but instead was pulled into a closed guard. At first, John struggled, accomplishing little, but then he remembered to remain calm. He quickly resisted his adrenaline burst and began to take in quick, short breaths through partially closed lips. Establishing his posture, John first fought for sleeve control so that he could stand up. After several attempts, however, he was unable to do so. His opponent pulled at John's lapel with all of his might, forcing him down to his knees.

John switched strategy. He lifted his right leg, putting it out to his side in a perpendicular stance. Next, he lowered his grip and pushed off his opponent's chest with one hand and his lower abdomen with the other.

After some resistance, John's opponent began to breathe heavily and loosen his grip.

"Go for the sweep, Frank!" shouted someone in the audience.

Immediately John's opponent reached under his leg. John, anticipating this move, exploded upward and ripped himself out of his opponent's closed guard. While standing over him, he hopped over his opponent's legs and landed in a north-south position.

"That was a guard pass!" shouted Robson as he stood up and looked at the referee.

Wagging his head, the referee refused to grant John any points. John waited patiently in his dominant position as his opponent struggled to free himself. John remained patient and finally his opponent stopped, resting in his inferior position. John then made his move, working for one of his opponent's arms. John tugged at each one, but his opponent held his elbows in very tight to his body. John continued to put his weight on him, thinking of what he might possibly do. Finally, after several seconds of inaction, John shuffled to his opponent's side. Slowly, he worked his hand into his opponent's lapel. As John tightened his grip for a choke, his opponent rolled to his back and fought to get to his knees. John clung on to him, climbing on top of him and securing his position by sinking his legs into a grapevine. The referee held up four points for the backmount position. Then, he began waving his arms.

John looked around, somewhat disoriented, but then rose to his feet.

"Shake hands," ordered the referee.

After doing so, John's right arm was raised.

"Thank you," said John to the referee, bowing. "Thank you," he repeated to his opponent, bowing to him as well.

As he walked back to his area, Robson stood up and waved his fist in the air. John returned the gesture.

"Hey, nice match," said the eldest competitor. "You move well."

"Thank you, sir," replied John.

"Well, hopefully I'll win and see you next round," he said as he walked away.

John nodded. He lifted his hands to the back of his head and took in deep breaths. Passing him was the young man in the red gi. A minute later, he returned. Without any display of emotion, he promptly resumed his position on the floor and reinserted his ear phones. Though covered by his gi, John could see that he possessed a very thick and muscular build.

Five minutes later, the older man with salt and pepper hair returned, triumphant. The semi-finals had begun.

"Had to teach that youngster that us old guys can still compete."

"Yes, sir," replied John.

The older gentleman extended his hand. "My name's Sean by the way. Looks like he's about to announce the pairings. If we go up against each other, good luck."

John grasped his hand and quickly replied, "Thank you."

Walking up to the microphone, Mauricio announced, "Ladies and gentlemen, after a two minute rest, round two will begin. On mat one, Sean Donovan and Luther Wright. On mat two, César Sanchez and John Kim."

John grabbed a bottle of water and took a few drinks. He looked at the remaining competitors. Sean, the elder statesman, was sitting down and rubbing his neck with a towel. Luther Wright sat comfortably on the floor listening to his music just as he had done during previous rounds. And John's next opponent, César Sanchez, was pacing nervously, hopping from one foot to the other. After a brief resting period, all four took the mats to the applause of the audience.

"You can do this, *Assassino!*" shouted Robson.

John stood eye to eye with his opponent. They shared the same build. The main difference was in their faces. César Sanchez did not have the face of a boy, but of a man. He had a dark goatee and rough skin slightly scarred by acne. His ears were swollen, taking on an image of cauliflower. There was no doubt; he was a wrestler.

The two shook hands and waited for the referee. As soon as he lowered his hand, John began to look for a lapel grip. As he reached out his right arm, however, César shot in on him. John immediately sprawled, pushing César's head down as he did so, but it was too late. César secured both of John's legs and had lifted one of them off the mat, forcing John down to his left hip. John quickly wrapped his legs around César's waist and entrapped him in his closed guard. The audience cheered as the referee held up two fingers.

"That's okay, John, be patient!" shouted Robson.

John inhaled deeply and once again reached for his opponent's collar. As he did so, César reacted quickly, powerfully springing to his feet with John's legs still wrapped around him. John beat him to the next move, though. As César reached for John's lapel in an attempt to lift him off the ground, John grabbed his ankles and pulled with all his might, sending César hard to the ground. For a split second, John hesitated, surprised that his tactic had actually worked, but then he heard Robson's voice. "Mount him! Mount him!"

"*Tranquilo!*" said Kayla, tugging at Robson to sit down. "*Voce não pode treiná-lo!*"

Robson slapped her hand away, to which she frowned and shouted, "*Senta-se!*"

As Robson sat down, the audience burst into applause. On mat one, the referee was holding a red sleeve high into the air.

"One more, Luther!" a man called out.

A young lady then stood up. "Way to do it, baby!" she shouted.

John was too late. César was able to scramble and finally stand up. The match began anew. Not wishing to be taken down again, John decided to attack first. He bent low and shot in. As he put both arms around his César's right calf and ankle, he felt his head being pushed down. César then reached for John's lapel near his neck. John fell backward to avoid being controlled. Once fully stable, he assumed a sitting guard position. César then attempted to move around John, but John scooted on his rear from side to side, squaring up each time. Finally, César moved in to engage, lunging toward John in an attempt to control his upper body. John quickly raised his legs, placing them on his César's hips. To his surprise, instead of pulling back, César lunged forward. John then lifted him up in the air and continued until he did a backward somersault, landing perfectly on top of him.

Robson laughed, Kayla released a slight smile, and Mario nodded in approval. The crowd began cheering loudly.

John, seated over his opponent in a mounted position, grabbed at César's collar, seeking a choke. César thrashed about violently, trying to knock John off of him.

"One minute left, Cesar!" shouted a man from the audience. "You have to escape!"

Seeking to hold his position, John spread out his arms to maintain his balance. After another burst, César pushed on John's hips and dug his knee inside. John immediately pushed the intruding knee downward, but doing so caused him to lose his balance. His opponent was able to reverse the position with John holding him snugly in his closed guard. The referee awarded César two points. John put his feet on his opponent's hips. He worked for a sweep, but his strength was waning. A flash of panic struck him. He was not sure if he would be able to hold out much longer. Then, the referee stood threw his hands down. Tired and relieved, John looked up as the referee helped him to his feet and raised his arm in triumph. He had won by a score of six to four.

As John stumbled back to the waiting area, Robson left his seat. Mauricio motioned for him to sit down, but Robson continued toward John. Mauricio shook his head slightly as he made his way to the microphone. "We want to remind all members of the audience, including instructors, that no coaching will be allowed. Only participants in the tournament may be out of their seats and in the waiting areas. Everyone else must remain seated or in the back, away from the mats. We thank you for your cooperation."

"John! John! Are you okay?"

John lay on the floor with his arms outstretched. "Robson, I'm done. I can't fight anymore."

"You're in the finals! You cannot give up now!"

"Okay," muttered John without the slightest attempt to make eye contact.

"*Chega*, Robson!" called out a strong feminine voice.

Robson turned around quickly. Kayla was standing next to her chair, waving at him furiously.

"John! I have to go! You can do it, *Assassino!*"

As Robson returned to his chair, Mauricio intercepted him, asking, "*Será que ele vai continuar?*"

"*Sim, ele está pronto!*"

"*Okay, então vamos terminar isso!*"

Walking up to the microphone, Mauricio announced, "We are now going to conclude the lightweight matches. Will Luther Wright and John

Kim come to mat one. Let's show our appreciation to the fighters who have reached the finals!"

The audience burst into applause while several people stood up and shouted encouragement.

"As the lightweight finalists approach the mat, we would like the eight middleweight fighters to come to the waiting area and weigh in."

John lifted his weary body toward the large white mat. Luther Wright, his opponent, was already there. John glanced at him. He was puckering his lips with his chin held high, giving him an air of confidence. The referee called both fighters to the center where they shook hands. John looked at the timer, which was set for five minutes as it had been for his previous matches. For some reason, five minutes suddenly felt like an eternity. The scorer's table showed two large zeros. John and his opponent each took a few steps back. The referee then extended his arm between them and quickly brought it down.

"Go Luther!" a voice cried out.

John turned quickly to see a young attractive woman. She had dark skin, long black hair, and full red lips. Thoughts of envy began to flood John's mind as he supposed that his muscular, talented opponent had everything that he lacked, and he soon forgot his weariness. Instead, he extended his arms, palms down, with his elbows close to his body in a staggered stance. Luther also extended his hands, but with his four fingers together, forming a "C" shape with his thumbs. Then, very quickly, he exploded toward John, grabbed him around the head and shoulder, and hip tossed John into the air, slamming him down hard on the mat. While John fought to recover from the impact, Luther quickly cradled his body in a side control position. The audience burst into applause while several people whistled and shouted their approval. John glanced over to the score board to see the man at the table flip one side from zero to two to five.

Striving to clear his head, John began to assess his options. He was trapped in sidemount position. His opponent had one arm under the back of his head and one hand on his pant leg, stopping John from moving. Then, before John could even decide on his next move, a knee was suddenly thrust onto his chest. Luther then pulled on John's collar as he shoved his knee deeper into John's torso. With depleted strength, John used both hands to push away at his opponent's knee. It did not budge. Unable to breathe, John tapped his opponent's thigh three times. Suddenly, the weight that was crushing him ceased. A hand suddenly reached out to John. He grasped it and was quickly lifted to his feet.

"You did good, bro," said Luther. "We'll do this again when you're fresh."

"Thanks," said John, a little surprised by the unexpected gesture of sportsmanship.

The referee then came over and lifted the right arm of John's opponent.

17

JOHN, FULLY CLOTHED and with his gym bag strapped across his shoulder, watched the super heavyweight finals from a distance. It was nine o'clock. He glanced at the merchandise on the tables. One particular item caught his eye; it was a film about the life of two brothers, Mario and Rodrigo Da Silva. It had several captions in Portuguese as well as advertised subtitles in English and Japanese.

"The big guys are boring."

"Huh?" replied John. He looked up to see Robson.

"I said the big guys are boring. Not a lot of movement."

John nodded. "Robson, sorry I didn't do much in that last match. I was just really tired, and that guy was so fast and strong. He was just too good."

"No, no, no, *Assassino*, never apologize for doing your best. You were great. Uncle Mario was very impressed."

"Really?"

"Yes, even Kayla said you did well."

John let out a weak smile.

"While you were changing, I found out that the guy who beat you trains in Judo. In fact, they said he was very good."

"I believe it," said John as he looked at his watch.

"What's wrong?"

"I need to call my mother and have her pick me up. It's getting late, and I don't want anyone to worry."

"You should have invited your parents to come." Then, after a brief pause, Robson raised his eyebrows and added, "Maybe you did not want them to come?"

John inclined his head. "My dad would never approve of me learning a different martial art. My mom doesn't really want to get involved and my brother…"

Robson smiled. "I understand. You do not have to say more, but you cannot leave now."

"I have to," replied John. "If I come home late, my father will get suspicious and will start asking my mom questions. As far as he knows, I'm working at my uncle's restaurant."

As Robson was about to speak, the boys' conversation was interrupted by the sound of applause.

"Who do you think won?" asked John.

"Who cares?" replied Robson. "They're not from our school. Only you and Lenny made it to the finals."

"Yeah," said John. "Except that Lenny actually won."

"Lenny has been a white belt for more than two years. You have been one for less than a year. That is a big difference."

Strangely, the noise quickly subsided. Mario Da Silva had approached the podium. Speaking into the microphone, he announced. "I would like to thank everyone for coming tonight, especially the competitors. And, in their honor, we are going to do something very special. Medals will be granted to all except for the finalists. They will receive something far more precious—a promotion." Several members of the audience exchanged surprised glances. "I would now like the finalists from all four weight divisions to come forward to accept their new ranking."

The audience applauded enthusiastically. Several people shouted and whistled as well. Mario nodded and he, too, began to applaud.

"That is why you cannot go!" shouted Robson.

"What do I do?" asked John.

"Tell your mother that we will take you home."

John hesitated. He looked at Robson and then at the several men walking toward the front of the seated audience.

"Go! There is no time!" said Robson. "You are a blue belt now!"

18

THE NEXT TRAINING session at the Da Silva Academy was bittersweet for John. Though he proudly displayed the stiff bright blue belt wrapped around his white kimono, he also suffered some stifling defeats from a number of purple belts who fought with renewed aggression. As the class ended, members slowly made their way out the door. John, his kimono drenched in sweat, lingered along with Robson and Kayla.

"*Tio*, John wants to thank you personally for his belt," stated Robson.

"You don't have to thank me," stated Mario. "You earned it. I never promote white belts before one year of training, but you are an exception. Robson even says you are even starting to make *him* work!"

"He is just being nice, Master Da Silva," replied John.

"It is true. You deserve to be a blue belt. You fought hard," said Kayla.

"Thank you, Kayla," said John.

"John, I can tell you now," said Mario. "The decision was made before the tournament. I was prepared to give you your blue belt no matter how you performed."

John's eyes widened. "But how? What if I lost my first match?"

"Then you would have received your blue belt here tonight."

John paused. He inclined his head. "Sir, am I too skinny and weak for Jiu Jitsu?"

Furrowing his brow, Mario exclaimed, "Why would you ask such a question?"

"Because..." John's voice trailed off. A knot formed in his throat, and a flood of dreaded emotion rushed upon him. He fought hard to resist, but even so, he could feel moisture forming in the corners of each eye. "Because I trained for years in Tae Kwon Do and after earning my yellow belt, I expected to get my green belt. But it never happened. My teacher—my own father—told me that I would never be strong enough to advance... to be a champion."

Mario placed both of his hands on John's shoulders. "You do not need a big body to be a champion, John. You need a big heart."

"I want to be a champion," John whispered, "but I'm afraid."

"It's okay to be afraid," replied Mario. "It is natural to be afraid, to have fear. What matters is what you do with it, and you have already proven that you can overcome your fear."

Raising his head to look Mario directly in the eyes, John asked, "You mean because I came in second place?"

"No, winning does not make you a champion, John; how you compete makes you a champion."

A small tear seeped down John's upper cheek. "So you won't be ashamed of me if I fail?"

Mario sat down casually on the white mat. John, Robson, and Kayla followed his example.

"From my training, I have learned two important lessons. One, it is okay to fail. Everyone fails. It is part of the journey. And two, nobody becomes a champion alone. We all need a little help. Sometimes, we need more than help." Mario suddenly turned to Robson. "There are times when help is not enough—times when we need to be rescued. Isn't that right, Robson?"

"*Sim*," said Robson curtly.

"Kayla?" continued Mario.

"*Com certeza, tio*," she replied, nodding vigorously.

"John," said Mario, "do you know who made me a champion?"

John shrugged his shoulders. "Some teacher in Brazil?"

"No, it was my wife, Adriana."

John's eyes widened. "But how could *she* make you a champion?"

"By showing me that a beautiful woman could love me."

Silence ensued. For a long moment, nobody said a word. Kayla, who was sitting back in a relaxed state, her arms behind her to prop her up, sat up more rigidly and put her hands in her lap. She rotated her feet that peeked out of her gi pants and then wiggled her toes. Robson remained as in a sitting guard, his torso leaning forward against his bent knees.

"I was beginning to make a name for myself," Mario continued unprompted. "I was twenty years old and had just won my first big tournament in Brazil. It was in Rio, near Copacabana, a beautiful place. People were starting to notice me—other fighters, the magazines, the girls—and then just a little later, when I returned home, this happened."

413

Pausing, he turned to show the left side of his face, touching the reddish, stitched layers of skin that had been stretched to cover raw flesh. Kayla turned away.

"There was a fire in our building," continued Mario. "Both my brother and I were asleep in our room. I woke up first, and told him to get our little sister and leave immediately. I then called to my parents. I could hear them choking. I carried my mother outside, and then went back for my father, but the fire and smoke were too much—I stumbled. And then crawled toward the front door."

Mario paused. He inclined his head and rubbed his temple.

"I woke up in the hospital. The surgeons had completed several skin grafts because I had fourth degree burns. When I was finally released and they removed the bandages. I was given a mirror. My first thought was that it would have been better if I had died."

Kayla's mouth dropped open. "*Tio! Não diga isso! Você é um herói!*"

Mario raised his hand. "It's okay, Kayla. That is how I felt. I was young. I was on top of the world, and then suddenly everything came crashing down on me. People looked at me differently. The girls that used to chase me turned away in shame. The only thing left was Jiu-Jitsu. Once the skin on my face became rough and hardened, I was able to train again."

John stared at Mario, and then looked at the others. Robson remained serious, but his expression showed nothing of surprise. Kayla covered her eyes by rubbing her dark eyebrows with her left hand, as if the words were too much for her to bear.

"Even though both my left eye and ear were disfigured," said Mario, "I found that I could do everything that I had always done before. My teacher and the other members at my school welcomed me back and encouraged me. And, with fewer things to distract me, I poured myself into my training. I began winning again. In fact, I was consumed with winning. It was my only reason to wake up in the morning."

John suddenly blurted out, "But Master Da Silva, that is good, right? That is how you won a world title! A lot of people say you're the greatest champion ever!"

Shaking his head, Mario replied, "No, John, I wasn't a champion. I won medals, but I wasn't a champion. I was angry inside. Angry at the fire that took my father's life. Angry at the fire that did this to me...even angry at my little brother who was still handsome. So handsome that he stopped training to become an actor in my country." Mario paused. "Have you ever had so much anger that no matter what you did you still could not release it?"

John's eyes moved downward.

"I used that anger when I fought," continued Mario. "I hated my opponents." He then took a deep breath and continued quietly. "No matter what I did, nothing changed until the world championship of…in the absolute division…"

And then, for the first time, the untold story was revealed.

O Campeonato de Jiu Jitsu Brasileiro took place within the *Tijuca Tênis Clube* gymnasium in Rio de Janeiro, Brazil. There were over a thousand competitors, many of them from other lands. After eight brutal matches, each one harder than the other, Mario had once again emerged victorious. There was blood on his white kimono. Fingers on both of his hands were taped. His left shoulder was throbbing. Basking in the applause of ten thousand spectators, competitors, and trainers, he stood in the middle of a huge durable green foam mat that lay in the middle of a large arena.

At the conclusion of his final match, his teammates jumped over the rails of the stands and rushed onto the mat. They surrounded him and hoisted him onto their shoulders. The audience roared in approval. Suddenly, the crowd became even more boisterous. Young men from both sides of the stadium began to holler and whistle. Mario thought they were cheering for him, and so he raised both arms in triumph. But then he saw his younger brother, Rodrigo Da Silva, walking onto the huge mat. Next to him was a gorgeous woman scantily clad in a white bikini.

She was the most beautiful woman he had ever laid eyes upon. She walked up to him and put a gold medal around his neck. She then did something that gave him fear, more fear than all of his previous competitors combined, more fear than the threat of losing a championship in front of thousands of people. She puckered her luscious thick red lips and leaned forward to kiss him. He quickly turned, hiding the hideous scars and the missing hair of the left side of his face. But she raised both of her delicate hands; hands composed of long nimble fingers, beautiful tan skin, and perfectuly manicured pinkish fingernails; and with them she grabbed Mario's face and gently turned his head. She kissed his swollen eye. She kissed the burned reddish tissue of his cheek. She kissed the small hole where his ear had once been and she caressed the bald patches found upon that side of his head.

The wild cheering, the whistles, the chants.... They had all stopped. And Mario Da Silva, a man who had just conquered the most grueling tournament in the world, froze. He had thought that the fire had permanently damaged his tear ducts, but he was wrong. He rubbed his eyes. He then tried to say something, but no words came. He stared at her. She stared back. Then, she smiled, and escorted by Rodrgio, she slowly walked away.

At the conclusion of the story, John's mouth dropped open. Kayla inclined her head once again, and Robson, curiously, remained listening with no real change of expression.

"That night something in me broke," said Mario. "I cried. I didn't want to be angry anymore. I didn't want to hate. I wanted to feel love again, and Adriana taught me in that moment that I could. I decided to devote my life to a higher cause, to something greater than myself. Little did I know that years later Adriana would join me in my quest."

19

THE FAMILIAR SMOKE and aroma of grilled sirloin, chicken, and pork mixed with sesame oil, pepper and onion filled the Korean barbecue restaurant. As John deftly used his chopsticks to plop food into his mouth, Robson poked in vain at the mixture of rice, beef, and vegetables assorted on his plate. Finally, with a slight smile of achievement, he awkwardly brought some food toward his mouth; but just as it touched his lips, he lost control and it fell downward onto his plate and splattered onto the table. He shook his head before putting his chopsticks down on the table. With frustration pouring out of his voice, he announced, "*Não, não posso faze-lo.*"

"Huh?" blurted John as he continued to chew.

"I don't think I can do this."

John laughed heartily. "Don't give up, Robson! Look, like this." He then demonstrated by deftly grabbing a clump of sticky white rice and grilled chicken with his chopsticks. Afterwards, he clicked his chopsticks together several times. "You only move this one. The other one stays in the same place between your thumb and your finger."

Robson attempted to imitate John's movements only to fail once more. John could not help but smile. "It's okay, Robson. We have forks. You just have to ask."

"Yes, please get me one before I starve!"

John quickly got up from the counter. He returned with a fork in his hand and his uncle beside him.

"Hello, young man!" said Samchon, his voice ringing with his usual warm enthusiasm. "So you like Korean food? It looks like John only gave you beef and chicken and a little bit of rice! What about *haemul jeongol* or *Man-Du* or some *Gal Bi*?"

"Samchon, I don't think he'll like all that stuff," said John, sitting down as he passed Robson a fork.

"*Obrigado*," said Robson.

"At least give him some *kimchi*!" said Samchon.

"This is his first time here," replied John. "And besides, Brazilians love barbecued steak and chicken."

"Oh, you're from Brazil?" asked Samchon, raising his eyebrows. "I visited a long time ago. Beautiful beaches there..." He stopped for a moment as a wide grin developed on his face. "And the even more beautiful—the women!"

John looked at his uncle with a furrowed brow and a deep frown.

"I wasn't always an old man, you know!" replied Samchon with a twinkle in his eye.

"Yes, you are right," said Robson. "The beaches and the women are very beautiful!"

"Okay, I'll let you two eat," said Samchon. Then, turning to Robson, he added, "Next time you come, though, I want you to try some real Korean food!"

"Yes, I will," said Robson. He then grabbed several pieces of grilled steak with his fork. Lifting them to his mouth, he chewed enthusiastically. "This is very good! It tastes like *picanha*!"

"We call it *bulgogi*," replied John, continuing to eat with his chopsticks. "We like mixing it with rice and *kimchi* and *gochujang*, like this." John paused as he placed a red paste over a large lettuce leaf, then threw in pieces

417

of meat and slices of *kimch*i. Finally, he topped it all off with clumps of white rice. Rolling up the lettuce leaf, he picked it up with his hands and began to eat.

Robson nodded. "Now that I think I could do."

At that moment, a man passed by and greeted John. They exchanged a few words, and then John bowed to him as the man walked away.

"Who was that?" asked Robson.

"He's a regular customer," replied John. "He's very nice and always gives me a good tip after I clean his table."

"Yeah, he seemed like he was very friendly with you. What's his name?"

John shrugged before taking another bite. "I have no idea."

"I thought you said you knew him."

"I do, but he's older than me," replied John before finally taking another bite.

Robson furrowed his brow.

"I call him *Hyeong-nim*," explained John. "It means—like—honored older brother or uncle. I can't call him by his name. That would be disrespectful."

"I don't understand," said Robson as he continued to plop pieces of grilled chicken and steak into his mouth, obviously much happier with his fork than the previously used chopsticks which lay by his plate.

"In my culture," said John, "especially traditional Korean culture, manners are very important." He watched Robson voraciously chew on his food. "Like not eating with your mouth open."

Robson stopped for a moment, smiled, and then strained to swallow all of the food in his mouth. "Oh, sorry, it's just that it is so good."

"It's okay, man. Anyway, our culture is very strict. Like, when you first meet someone, you don't say, 'What is your name?' You ask, 'How old are you?'"

Shaking his head, Robson replied, "Really? You have to know their age?"

"Yeah!" replied John. "It's important!"

"But why?"

"Because that's how you know how to talk to them."

Robson let out a quick huff. "That's funny."

"Yeah, it's a Korean thing," said John. Then, looking at Robson, he asked, "You want me to put more meat on the grill?"

"Is it okay?" asked Robson.

"Yeah, this is an all you can eat restaurant, and besides, my uncle's not charging us," said John.

"Okay, then, my friend, yes, put some more steak and chicken on there. And throw on some onions and garlic, too."

"No problem," said John.

He then walked over to the buffet and piled raw beef onto one plate and raw chicken onto another. Balancing a third plate on his forearm, he loaded it with vegetables. The two boys eagerly grabbed their metal tongs and began to lay the meat on the grill, smiling at the hissing sound and the smoking aroma.

"Robson, that was pretty incredible what happened after class last week," said John quietly.

"You mean what my uncle told us?"

"Yeah, his story..." John stopped to observe Robson, who seemed more interested in the smoke rising from the grill placed in the middle of the table than their conversation. Finally, somewhat upset by his indifferent reaction, John asked, "Robson, are your parents in Brazil? I mean, how exactly did you end up living here with Master Da Silva?"

Robson did not answer, but continued to appear lost in thought. Noticing his hesitation, John paused for a moment, but then decided to go further. "And how is Kayla related to you? Is she from your father's side or your mother's?"

After a long pause, Robson whispered, "She is not from any side. She's just—she's my best friend."

Startled by his answer, John asked, "But I thought Kayla and Gabriela were your cousins?"

Robson remained silent.

"Because Master Da Silva is your uncle, and he's also their uncle, so that makes you cousins, right?"

"It is true that Mario is their uncle," said Robson.

Shaking his head, John continued, "Then why did you say—"

Before John could finish, Robson slammed his fist on the table. "He is not my uncle! Nobody is!"

John stopped chewing. "What?"

"*Maldição!*" blurted Robson as he waved smoke from the grill. He then grabbed some grilled sirloin and hastily shoved it into his mouth. Masticating the meat with renewed vigor, Robson continued, "Look, only a few people know this, and Kayla is one of them, but I—I was a *criança de rua!*"

Furrowing his brow, John remarked, "Huh?"

"A street kid, John!" shouted Robson. He paused and then bowed his head. In little more than a whisper, he continued, "A kid with no family. A kid with no home."

John stared at Robson. He opened his mouth to speak, but instead swallowed and pressed his lips together.

"Do you understand?" asked Robson.

John shook his head slowly.

Taking a deep breath, Robson began to reveal a murky past, a past full of gaps and shadows, a past full of dangers and darkness. It was an evening like any other within the *favela* of *Paraisópolis*. A cacophony of sounds and shapes, a myriad of connecting walls, the shifting engines of trucks and motorcycles, the shouts of men and women both young and old, barefoot children playing *futebol*, and the music of *baile funk*. And deep inside the *complexo*, somewhere within the maze of shanties composed of multicolored fragil wood and tin metal, a young woman stood staring at her child. He was sitting patiently on a little wooden bed, dressed in the only pants he owned accompanied by his one white collared shirt. His brown hair was combed neatly to the side. She released a deep sigh. Her eyes darted to and fro, acknowledging the filth and grime of the cramped room. A wooden bed, an old nightstand, a broken lamp, a pile of clothes on the floor. She grabbed a brush and plowed it through her long, tangled hair. She applied red lipstick that contrasted with her brown face. Finally, she raised the little boy into her arms and carried him out of the vacant room and into the vibrating streets.

She walked past young men squatting near the walls. Some of them held cigarettes in their hands; others held guns. A few of them nodded in her direction. She walked past several women scantily dressed on a street corner. They smiled and greeted her. One young lady—little more than a girl—reached out and affectionately caressed the boy's cheeks and hair.

His mother then put him down, and together, hand in hand, they moved onward.

After several blocks, they stopped. Several buses passed, off toward other destinations; but finally, their bus, the bus headed for the *avenida Faria* arrived. The young woman raised him once more into her arms, and the two entered together. In the very back, they settled onto a white plastic bench. The little boy could not remain still. He stood up to gaze through the window as the bus passed through many lights, and under an overpass, until slowly the roads became wider, longer, and even the cars seemed to change.

They disembarked onto hitherto unknown streets full of bright lights and huge structures that reached upward and disappeared into the skyline. Walking down the bristling white sidewalk, the two made their way to the Iguatemi São Paulo shopping malls. As they did so, the child often looked at the woman, jumped up and down, and pointed with great enthusiasm. She smiled at him, but then her face fell. Her eyes forlorn, she turned away.

Passing several quaint stores, they stopped in front of a large window that was lit with several cone shaped bulbs of light. It was a pastry shop. The child's eyes widened as he pointed to a chocolate *Brigadeiro*. The young woman kneeled and kissed him on the cheek before warmly embracing him. She then placed a bill of purple and white hue in his tiny hand. It was five *reais*. Pointing to the *Brigadeiro* with coconut strips, she gently nudged him forward.

He timidly entered the store. An elderly gentleman wearing a white chef hat smiled at him. Moving his head in all directions, he observed the many chocolate delicacies, the small cakes, the candied apples. He slowly made his way to the counter, tapped on the glass cover, and held up two fingers. The elderly man then handed him two chocolate pastries wrapped in white ruffled paper, one *real,* and a few *centavos*. He could not wait. He bit into one of the chocolates. He had never tasted anything so delicious. He took another bite. And then another. The chocolate quickly vanished.

The chef smiled at the little boy as he wagged his finger. *"Não mais. Guarde um pouco para mais tarde."*

The child nodded. He then dodged the large adults around him, his tiny legs carrying him toward the exit. *"Mamãe!"* He held the untouched chocolate in his little hand as high as he could. But there was no answer. She was gone.

He waited. And waited. Finally, he began to walk down the large white sidewalk. The night air felt cold on his ears. Tall men in dark suits and tall women in bright colorful dresses passed him by. He asked them if they knew his mother. They shook their heads and continued walking. Tears rolled down his cheeks as he walked several more blocks. Too weary to go further, he stopped. Climbing up onto a stone bench he curled into a ball in an attempt to keep warm. Once there, he cried himself to sleep.

In the middle of the night, the child awoke to a hard object knocking against his shoulder. A huge man with a tan bald head stood in front of him with a thick wooden truncheon in his hand.

"*Qual é o seu nome, menino?*"

"Robson."

"*Onde estão seus pais?*"

When Robson did not answer, the man scowled at him as he reached downward and yanked him off the bench and onto the cement below. A shriek burst into the night. Robson touched his forehead. His tiny fingers were covered with blood. His arm throbbed. It felt as if it had been pulled apart from his body. The man pulled him toward a black van with tinted windows. Robson shouted for his mother, but this only seemed to irritate the man further. He cursed at Robson as he grabbed his neck with one hand and opened the back door of the van with the other. Then, just as Robson was being hoisted upward, a group of boys surrounded them.

"*Polícia!*"

"*Alemao!*"

A host of rocks were thrown at the man. As he covered his face, the boys kicked him and beat him with sticks. A tall slender boy then grabbed Robson by the wrist and began to run, dragging Robson along with him. They ran and ran until they entered the *favela*. A blur of small shanties and walls full of *pichação* of various artistic shapes and colors—orange, green, red, and blue—raced by, scarcely seen through the narrow dimly lit streets. Robson experienced a vague sense of familiarity. He instinctively looked for his mother. But Paraisópolis had many *complexos*, and somehow he knew that she was far, far away.

Finally, in an abandoned alley, beneath a bright full moon that shone in the darkness of the night, the boys plopped down onto the hard cement. Robson panted, gasping for breath. His small legs ached. His eyes slowly moved toward the boy who had saved him. He had dark skin and a black, thick afro on top of his circular face. His name was Patricio and he promised Robson that he would protect him.

Living in the streets each day was an adventure. The boys would throw rocks at people, laugh, and then run away. They also stole food from ladies at the grocery stores, and if they could, they would snatch their purses as well. When they were bored, they dosed rags with paint and sniffed them. Then there were the days they met other groups of boys who had formed their own *gangue*, so they fought, willing to do anything to protect their little *zona* of the *favela*.

One day Patricio brought two girls to the boys. Like wolves, they quickly formed a circle around them. They reached out and touched their hair and stroked their arms. Patricio then began to remove the old tattered clothing that covered their malnourished bodies. One of the girls began to cry. Robson shook his head. He grabbed Patricio's arm and told him to stop, but he was quickly shoved to the ground.

That was when he ran. He ran so far that he no longer recognized the shanty houses that filled the streets. With nowhere else to go, Robson found a cement block by one of the little corner markets. There, he slept. Each time he heard a noise—a footstep, a shout in the night, the sound of a car—he quickly jerked and opened his eyes. He felt fear. Paraisópolis was not a safe place for a lone little boy. The next day a few older men approached him. They asked him to be their *avion*. They offered food and a bed indoors, and all Robson would have to do was deliver packages. He was hungry and cold, so he agreed. And so his life continued for days and months and years.

Each morning, Robson would venture far into the *favela*. He was searching. Searching for something. For someone. He passed the many shanties that were stacked one upon the other as they ascended up a cliff where they seemed to hang by a thread. He then crossed a dirt path full of construction, carefully avoiding the slush of the mud caused by the rain. Several men were painting over the colorful graffiti of the walls while a group of boys stood gaping at them. Robson, curious, stopped. *"Oi! e aí?"*

A boy dressed only in shorts replied, "*Tudo certo.*" He then told Robson that a man was inviting children from the *favela* to the city where he would teach them how to defend themselves. He said the man also fed them and handed them clothes. But he had never gone himself. He was afraid. He claimed that some of the boys disappeared after entering his *minibus*. And besides, the man looked scary. The boy referred to him as the *bicho-papão*. Robson shook his head. He folded his arms in front of his chest and declared that he wanted to meet this man.

"Master Da Silva." It was the voice of John Kim, bringing the past to the present, and the dream world to an end.

"Yes," said Robson. "When he saw me sitting there alone in the street, he asked me if I had a home. I told him I did not. And that's..." Robson's voice slowly trailed off. He wiped the moisture from his eyes. "That's when he said, 'Well, you do now.' He then announced that he was Mario Thiago Da Silva and that he had come to the *favela* to make champions out of little boys like me. I entered the *minibus* and left with him to Sao Paulo."

John shook his head in disbelief. "How—how old were you, Robson?"

Shrugging his shoulders, Robson replied, "I can't even tell you. Uncle Mario decided I was eight years old, so that is what I was, and that is why I am sixteen now."

"So he adopted you?"

"I trained with him every day, and I did whatever he asked. I was the most dedicated of all. He never said anything. He just took me in."

John became quiet. He grabbed his chopsticks and played with the white rice that had been left untouched on his plate. Finally, he asked, "Robson, what ever happened to your mother?"

Robson's jaw began to visibly tighten. "I used to look for her. I wanted to know why she left me. But I..." He paused and then inhaled deeply. "I didn't know her name." Then, raising his chin proudly, he continued, "My life is now, John. Mario Da Silva—and Jiu Jitsu—have taught me a new way."

20

THE SIMPLE SMALL corner building possessed two floors. Near the front entrance one could hear periodic shouting and the sound of intense colliding forces. John was well aware of the training being conducted at his father's school, for Paul was being prepared for the Olympic trials. As he reached for the front door, he glanced at Robson, and then hesitated.

"What's wrong?" asked Robson.

"This door," replied John, staring at it.

"It's just a door, John."

"It's more than that."

Smiling, Robson patted John on the back and replied, "Come, let's go in."

John led the way through a small hallway to a large wooden floor. On the opposite side was a long mirror that ran across the wall, instantly showing their reflection. In contrast to the casual blue jeans and untucked plaid collared shirts worn by John and Robson, Jae-Pil and Mr. Lee stood attentively while adorned in the traditional Korean *do-bok*, and the black belts wrapped around their waists only added to their solemnity. Paul, stripped down to his dark gi pants, thrusted powerful kicks and punches through the air under their watchful eyes. As he did so, drops of sweat poured down his face and onto his muscular chest and firm abdominal muscles.

John took off his shoes and socks, and then walked onto the wooden floor to approach the three men. Upon doing so, he bowed several times.

While Mr. Lee nodded politely to John, Jae-Pil continued his instructions to Paul. "*Cha lyeos, Junbi, jwa-woo-hyang-woo, kyeorugi, hana, dool, ses!*"

John waited patiently as his father refused to make eye contact. Finally, addressing him not as his father, but instead as the head instructor, John requested permission to speak. "*Gal lyeo! Chung sa nim! Joesong-habnida!*"

Paul stopped moving. He scowled at John. He then turned in the direction of Robson. His eyes narrowed, reflecting his disgust. The eyes of Jae-Pil also held a certain meaning. His eyes reflected his contempt for John. His eyes reflected superiority. His eyes reflected supreme disappointment.

"What the hell do you think you're doing?" asked Paul.

"I'm here to speak with *Chung sa nim*! This doesn't concern you!" John replied.

"Are you crazy?" asked Paul, shaking his head at John. "Have you lost all of your honor and respect? You think you can just walk in here and interrupt my training?" Then, pointing in Robson's direction, he added, "And what's he doing here? You actually brought a foreigner to the *dojang*?"

Ignoring Paul's comments, John continued, *"Chung sa nim*, and Mr. Lee whom I deeply respect, I have come to tell you both that although I am thankful for my training in our great art of Tae Kwon Do, I have decided to further my knowledge with Brazilian Jiu Jitsu and—"

Before John could finish, his father interrupted him. "Brazil? What is this?"

"Father, it is a different fighting style. My friend Robson is actually an instructor."

"Abeoji, that's the boy that I hurt," interrupted Paul. "He refused to fight me. He also refused to fight Joe Bok face to face, but instead hit him from behind like a coward."

"That's a lie!" said John.

"What did you say?" said Paul, his eyes narrowing.

"Maybe we should allow *Chung sa nim* to speak with John in his private office," said Mr. Lee.

"Be quiet, Mr. Lee!" shouted Jae-Pil. "My son dishonor me. He dishonor my number one son." Then, pointing his finger at Mr. Lee, he continued, "And he dishonor you!"

Mr. Lee lowered his head as he inhaled and exhaled deeply.

Directing his attention back to John, Jae-Pil continued, "Ik-Jong, is it not enough you never have fighting spirit of the Hwarang?" His breaths became heavy. His chest began to heave. "But now you deny your heritage?"

"I am not denying my heritage, father," John replied. "I am proud of being Korean and I am proud of Tae Kwon Do, but I have made my own choice now and I ask that you respect my choice. My choice, father."

Jae-Pil slapped John violently in the face, causing a loud echo to reverberate throughout the room. Robson, standing just outside the edge of the wooden floor, raised his brow. His mouth opened slowly. He lifted his foot and ripped off his shoe and sock.

"Silence!" shouted Jae-Pil. "You dishonor me! You were disappointment before, but now—now—you disgrace!"

John rubbed his cheek gently. Moisture gathered in the corners of his eyes. Quietly, he replied, "No father, I am not a disgrace."

"You are weak!"

"*Joesong-habnida,* father, but you are wrong. I am not weak."

"Then prove it!" screamed Jae-Pil. He stood mere inches away from John. "Strike me! Strike me!"

Robson walked barefoot onto the floor. "John, you did what you came for. Let's go."

"You stay out of this *oegug-in!*" said Paul. "You don't belong here! This is between family!" Then, addressing Jae-Pil, he continued, "Father, I ask your permission to make an example of this boy. And after I do that, I would like to do the same to John as well. He cannot be allowed to dishonor our family in this way!"

John shook his head. "Bye, father. Bye, Paul."

He nodded to Robson. They slowly began to walk away. As they did so, Paul's eyes darted toward his father, who nodded in response.

"Sorry little bro, but it's not that simple!"

Paul followed behind Robson. He cocked his fist back, but before he could release the intended blow, John lunged toward him, tackling him to the wooden floor. Once down, both boys pushed at each other until they struggled to their feet.

"John! It's okay! This is my fight!" said Robson, placing himself between them.

"Come on! Let's do this!" said Paul as he thrusted his fists in front of his body. "I'll fight both of you!"

Robson put his hands up in a boxing position. "You only have to fight me."

"Stop!" shouted Mr. Lee. "This is not what we represent! Paul, that's enough!"

"You not command my son!" said Jae-Pil. "You are too American, Mr. Lee! Do you not understand dishonor Ik-Jong bring upon me? Bring upon entire *cheyug-gwan?*"

"John has never done anything to dishonor any of us, *Chung sa nim,*" replied Mr. Lee.

Jae-Pil frowned deeply. His eyes burned. "You know nothing. Now step aside."

Mr. Lee furrowed his brow. His forehead became wrinkled. Shaking his head, he replied, "I should have done this a long time ago. Mr. Kim, you are a great martial artist and a great instructor, but it is you who does not understand the *Do* of our art. Your false pride and false concepts of honor are only going to ruin you and anyone foolish enough to follow you."

"You finished, Mr. Lee!" shouted Jae-Pil. "Never step one foot in *dojang* again or you regret! Entire Korean community against you! They listen to me!"

Mr. Lee faced John. He bowed to him. *"Jal issgeola."* Then, without another word, he quietly walked off the wooden floor and exited through the hallway.

"You see!" Jae-Pil said at John. "You see how disgrace spreads like— like disease? You know nothing of *chung seong* and *gajok.*"

"Father, I have only tried to honor you all of my life!" John pleaded. "But I was never good enough for you! The more I tried the more you humiliated me!"

"You forbidden to speak!" spewed Jae-Pil, his saliva flying from his mouth. "My father, he train me in the Hwarang spirit! I fulfill my destiny! I fight in military! Bring honor to my family!" He turned to Paul. "My duty as father pass code of honor to my sons, but only one worthy!" He then struck John on the forehead with his thumb several times. "I try to burn weakness from you! Beat the frailty of your nature into strength! But you fail me! And now your failure is my failure." He turned away, withdrew his hand from John's face, and took a few steps back. "Now one destiny only for you. Live as son of your mother in disgrace."

John stood speechless, staring at the back of his father's **silhouette**. Robson, shaking his head, grabbed John by the shoulder and began turning him back toward the edge of the wooden floor. In a whisper, he said softly, "Come on, *Assassino*, let's go. Come back with me—your real family."

"Abeoji!" screamed Paul. His voice bled with emotion. "He can't just leave! Please, father, give me permission to teach him one final lesson so that he will remember this day forever!"

Jae-Pil shook his head. "No."

"But I could kill him for what he has done today!" replied Paul.

Jae-Pil remained silent as Paul approached Robson. "Fight me!"

Robson squinted. Slowly, he replied, "I will fight you. But let me tell you, it will not be like when I fought your friend. This time I will not stop. I will hurt you."

Paul stepped back. His eyes moved up and down. Then, he inhaled deeply and raised his fists.

"Wait a minute!" John interrupted. "Robson, no! It's okay. I'm not afraid anymore."

"John, are you sure?"

"Yes, I'm sure."

Robson smiled slightly with closed lips, then replied, "Okay, but remember, I am right here."

"You should never have come here, *Dong-saeng*!" said Paul. Then, pointing at Robson, he continued, "And don't think I'm through with you, either!"

"Shut up, Paul!" said John. "Come on, let's do this! And when we're done, it's finished, okay?" He raised his fists.

Paul smirked disdainfully. "Okay, little brother." He walked in a circle around John. "Just remember, no holding back. This won't be a point match. We're going back to tradition."

Paul settled into his *mo seogi* fighting stance, moving his hands up and down as he approached John confidently. Then, without warning, he attacked with a *dollyeo-chagi* reverse round kick, which John was just able to avoid by quickly shuffling back so that Paul's heel narrowly missed making contact with his face.

Looking determined, John took a deep breath. He held his hands like a boxer, with his left fist out slightly and his right fist cocked closer to his shoulder. He then threw a left jab which brushed against Paul's nose.

"What is that crap?" asked Paul. "You think you're going to hurt me with that?"

Maintaining his focus, John kept his hands up, protecting his face. He pivoted to Paul's right, throwing several jabs at him. After slight contact was made, Paul charged John with a thrusting kick followed by a wheel kick and a punching combination. John quickly stepped back to avoid the kicks, but the last few punches landed hard against John's forearms and shoulder. The final blow stung the most breaking through John's defenses and grazing the top of his forehead.

Aware of the damage, Paul smiled and then began to sway back and forth in a type of graceful motion. He then let out a loud *kihap* and threw a flurry of punches and front kicks. Though beautiful to behold, they made little impression.

"You are okay, John!" said Robson. "Trust yourself! Trust your training! He can't hurt you if he doesn't hit you!"

Paul released a disdainful smirk. "Whatever," he muttered.

Once again, the two brothers squared up. Paul, being the aggressor, lunged forward with a *baro jireugi*. John stepped aside, avoiding the blow, and answered with a Muay Thai leg kick to Paul's left thigh, causing him to lose his balance temporarily. Crinkling his forehead, Paul's eyes flashed with anger. But John did not hesitate; instead, he whipped a second Muay Thai kick to the same exact spot. Paul's leg buckled. He almost fell to the floor. Squinting in pain, he looked confused, and John's confidence began to grow.

"*Pode crer*!" shouted Robson.

Jae-Pil stood in silence at the other side of the floor, his arms crossed, his expression without emotion.

Paul raised his fists, but his posture seemed more erect, more cautious. Both boys began to circle each other until John stepped in, throwing a four punch combination. Paul blocked the first two attempts, but as he ducked to avoid the final blows, John's left cross grazed him and his upper cut landed square in Paul's stomach. And though Paul's abdominal muscles felt as hard as a heavy bag, John could not help but smile.

Paul, visibly hurt, refused to back down. He quickly threw a front kick, catching part of John's hip and spinning him around. Furrowing his brow in anger, Paul quickly followed up with a downward hammer punch that landed on the side of John's head. Somewhat dazed, John fell to his knees. Paul quickly rushed in for the kill. He cocked back his leg to deliver a final blow. Before he was able to do so, however, John reached for his front leg, wrapped both arms around it, and quickly stood up. He then adjusted his grip, cupping Paul's heel and calf between his thumbs and fingers. John lifted Paul's leg high in the air. He waited for Paul to drop, but instead Paul extended his leg and hopped toward John in order to strike him. He threw several punches, hitting John in the ribs with his knuckles pointed outward. The blows stung and caused John to release Paul's leg.

"It's okay, John! He's very flexible! Keep fighting!" shouted Robson.

"Damn right I am!" shouted Paul in response.

John took several deep breaths. He could feel the weariness of his muscles. Paul, too, inhaled deeply, sweat dripping off his bare torso.

"*Il -gyeog-pil-sal!*"

Paul turned to his father with a furrowed brow as he continued to take in huge gulps of air.

Once again, the voice of Jae-Pil called out, "*Il-gyeog-pil-sal!*"

Paul then released a *kihap* full of rage. He charged John with a fury of punches and kicks. Several broke through the weary barrier of John's raised hands. Paul continued to swing wildly, cornering John. He then reached for John's throat. Clutching it, he pinned John's head to the wall. A singe of panic flared through John's body.

"Two on one, John, two on one!" shouted Robson.

With protruding eyes that revealed his fear, John strove to regain his composure. As he felt Paul crushing his windpipe, he grabbed Paul's wrist with both hands. In one movement, he lowered his stance and extended his arms, peeling Paul's hand off of his neck. Then, seeing he was in perfect position, John wrapped both of Paul's legs and took him down to the floor.

Once down, Paul threw a punch that brushed the top of John's forehead. It did nothing to stop John from fully mounting Paul, however. Then, from his dominant position, John punched Paul directly in the face several times with both fists, stunning his brother. Paul attempted a few counter punches, but from the bottom position he was unable to generate much power. Finally, in a vain attempt to escape his predicament, Paul twisted and turned recklessly like a fish out of water. But John would not let go. Instead, he hung on to Paul, wrapping his body around his backside like an anaconda. As Paul lay on top of him, John created a figure four with his legs in a vise like hold, causing Paul to gasp for air.

"Yes, John, yes!" Robson shouted. "*É isso aí!*"

Placing his arms around Paul's neck, John hugged his face against Paul's own. He then whispered, "You're done, Paul. Tell me you're done and we'll stop right now."

"You will *never* beat me you little..." Paul began to growl.

John tightened his arms. Paul gagged on his words, and then awkwardly attempted to reach back as far as he could in order to strike John. When that became useless, he blindly clawed at John's face.

"*Sim! Sim! Mata Leon! Obrigado e boa noite!*" shouted Robson, raising both arms in the air. "Choke him out, John!"

And then there was silence. Slowly, Paul's body went limp, showing no sign of struggle. John pushed him off of him. Paul's limp body rolled to the floor.

"You did it, *Assassino*, you did it!" said Robson, running over to John.

Looking through weary eyes, John nodded and slowly sat up. Jae-Pil approached quickly. He inclined his head toward Paul and turned him over. He then gently held Paul's head in his hands and rubbed his temples.

"What—what happened?" asked Paul, groggily.

"Nothing. Just rest," replied Jae-Pil.

Robson extended his hand and lifted John off the floor. "Come on."

The two began to walk off when they heard a voice call out. "Stop!"

John hesitated. Robson then grabbed him by the shoulder, nudging him to continue. As John turned back, he observed his father briskly approaching them.

"*Adeul!*" announced Jae-Pil, extending both of his fists.

Robson raised his arms.

"No," said John, stepping in front of Robson.

Jae-Pil smiled. "*Adeul*, you now show me spirit of *Hwarang*! You remove my shame! I will restore your honor! You now the son of Jae-Pil Kim!"

Then, to John's utter amazement, his father bowed to him three times. John looked at him in silence. Then, slowly, he uttered, "I am John Kim. That is my honor."

With a slight nod of the head, Robson led the way as the two walked out the door.

EYES WIDE OPEN

1

AT SEVENTEEN, BETANIA Solíz never expected that she would have to transfer to a new high school, but it was a necessity that could not be avoided. Whispers surrounder her since new students were a rarity in Cedar Falls, and the somewhat exotic persona that Betania emanated only added to the **speculation**. She possessed light creamy skin and a firm jawline which supported her plump lips, her small nose, and her dark alluring eyes. And flowing from her harmonious face were long intertwined strands of golden brown hair that were naturally thick and wavy. Her mannerisms, too, were marked by a certain ambience of culture not often found in the simple farm life of Iowa, for she was dainty and feminine, her voice soft and sweet.

Some claimed that Betania was from a prominent family in Spain. Others swore that she was a young actress from Mexico, even stating that they had seen her on television. Betania never tried to clarify their **conjecture** because she had not come to Cedar Falls to talk about her past, but to escape it.

2

RICH IN BOTH history and culture, Veracruz has often been referred to as the cultural jewel of Mexico. Legend stated that the original name of Veracruz was *La Villa Rica de la Vera Cruz*, a name supposedly given by none other than Hernán Cortés, the great Spanish explorer and *conquistador*. Stretching along the rich coast of the Gulf of Mexico, the city proudly displayed its Baroque architecture that resulted in stunning

433

cathedrals, palaces, and lighthouses. More than that, however, Veracruz was marked by its inimitable cuisine. From every part of the world, people would come to eat the delicious food, enjoy the cool ocean air, and to drink the famous *Kahlúa*.

Betania knew her personal connection to the mythical city quite well. It began with her grandfather, the first true *jarocho* and a man she only knew as Don Teófilo. In a market place called *La Pescadería*, he cleaned tables and washed dishes in one of the many restaurants. Forever at his side was a small boy, Eduardo, but no one knew him by that name. That would come later. In his childhood, he was known to all simply as Lalo.

Father and son worked diligently together, but made very little earnings. Occasionally, someone would have compassion on little Lalo and give him a *propina*.

"*Oye, chico, por qué no estás en la escuela?*" asked a gentleman with a nice suit and tie.

Lalo cleared the table and replied, "*No puedo, señor. Tengo que ayudarle a mi papá aquí.*"

The man frowned. He shook his head slowly. "*Dale a tu papá esto y dile que tú debes dedicarte a algo diferente.*" The man then handed Lalo one hundred pesos.

Clutching the money tightly, Lalo ran to Don Teófilo. "*Papá, papá, mire!*" Lalo held up a reddish bill. "*Un señor rico me lo dio y me dijo que es suyo!*"

"*Es una fortuna!*" said Don Teófilo. He wiped the last of the round white dishes, and then put them into a neat stack and stammered, "*Pero, por qué? No entiendo.*"

"*No lo sé. Creo que él quiere que yo estudie en la escuela.*"

Inclining his head, Don Teófilo replied, "*Dámelo, hijo.*" Lalo obeyed, handing his father the money. "*Si quieres salvarte de lavar platos toda la vida, allí está tu escuela.*" Don Teófilo then pointed to the kitchen. There, cooks were busy frying, cutting, and splashing ingredients into various pans and pots. Lalo became fascinated with the artistic creations of the best chefs of Veracruz. Year after year, he snuck out of the dish room to assist them, learning their secrets, and waiting for his turn. In time, the cooks took him in and began training him as one of their own. Lalo never knew that his father had given them one hundred *pesos* to do so, but Eduardo Solíz did.

Betania's father slowly gained a reputation as one of the finest chefs in all of Veracruz. As head *cocinero* of a restaurant called *La Garlopa*, his signature recipes included *huachinango a la veracruzana*, a dish composed of red snapper drenched in a spicy red sauce filled with green olives; *chile habanero*, which was made of tomatoes and burning hot Cuban chili peppers; *pollo encacahuatado*, a local favorite made of thick chicken breast covered in a peanut sauce; and of course, *arroz a la tumbada*, a rice dish baked with a variety of seafood. Eduardo's personal favorite was *caldo de mariscos*, a seafood soup **reputed** to cure hangovers caused from drinking too much alcohol.

3

BETANIA'S MOTHER, ERNESTINA Solíz, was a plump, simple woman with a sweet demeanor. She had brown skin, thick black hair that just reached her shoulders, and dark eyes that communicated more than her words. She was born and raised in La Antigua. With pride in her voice, she often told the story of how nobody in her family had ever been born in a hospital. Each of her brothers and sisters had entered the world in the same home. And that home, Betania's home, her mother's home, and her mother's mother's home, despite the sentiment, was actually quite simple— impoverished by most accounts—though Betania was unaware of this. There was no air conditioning. There was no heating unit. There was not even indoor plumbing. When members of her family, or *huéspedes*, had to use the bathroom, they walked outside to a small outhouse. Inside, placed in the corner, was a large plastic barrel of water with a plastic cup floating at the surface. Since the toilet did not flush, they had to gather the water and slam it violently into the hole located at the very bottom. This was the only way for everything to move down into the septic tank.

Bathing was not an easy task, either. In a small room with a cement floor and a drain in the center, Betania would wait for her mother to bring a pot of warm water from the stove to pour over her. During the summer it was not so bad, but in the winter she would shiver as her mother quickly wrapped a towel around her.

Despite these hardships, life in La Antigua seemed wonderful to Betania. Her childhood was filled with nothing but happy memories. Memories of the succulent aromas of her father's cooking. Memories of her mother sewing a new dress. Memories of her older sister playfully chasing her throughout the house. And perhaps the fondest memories of all arose from the times she would sit next to her *abuela*, who sat comfortably on her rocking chair, telling stories of the historic buildings scattered throughout La Antigua.

4

OF ALL THE people in Betania's life, there was only one that she truly idolized, and that person was her older sister, Pamela. An eternal optimist, an extrovert, and always ready to take a challenge head on, Pamela stood in stark contrast to the **introspective**, even timid, Betania. As the two girls entered adolescence, their differences became more acute, prompting the inevitable surprise when others learned that they were sisters. Whereas Pamela possessed dark skin, short black hair, and a stocky square frame, Betania's skin color was light, her long hair a golden brown, and her body petite yet shapely.

The **disparity** between Betania and her sister even extended to the classroom. Pamela was not happy to attend a school so far away. The public school in La Antigua was much better, she reasoned. She would be able to sleep more, and besides, all of her friends from the *barrio* were there. Betania disagreed. She looked forward to the long bus ride and considered herself fortunate to attend the prestigious *Colegio de las Américas de Veracruz*. Her favorite subject was science, and anatomy, in particular, simply fascinated her.

But Veracruz was changing. Some parts of the grand city were no longer safe. Betania had heard the stories. A public figure shot and killed, a child who had disappeared, a lifeless body found in the middle of the night. At only thirteen years of age, Betania would find that the violence in Mexico was not made of mere stories. It was real.

One day, against her better judgment, Betania allowed herself to be coaxed into skipping school. Pamela had promised Betania that she would take her shopping at the famous *Punto Plaza*. Betania did not know how her sister was able to pay for such things, but she never questioned her. After buying several cannisters of expensive perfume, the two made their way through the crowded streets of the *Centro Comercial*. It was then that they noticed a conspicuous yellow cab of a certain *taxista* had begun to follow them. This continued until a wide face leaned out of the front window. The loose fat of the man's neck jiggled as he smiled. He then rubbed the sweat of his forehead onto his thick black mustache. Calling out to the girls, he offered them a ride to any destination they desired. Betania looked at Pamela, who furrowed her brow and shook her head slowly from side to side.

The girls continued walking in silence, but the man would not be deterred. He continued to shout. He offered them jewelry, saying that all pretty girls deserved such beautiful ornaments. At that point Pamela began screaming obscenities at him. The man's pleasant smile vanished. He brought his car to an abrupt stop, waddled his way out, and then grabbed Betania by the arm. Her squeals caused a few onlookers to gasp, but they did nothing. Pamela, however, did not hesitate. She immediately wrapped both her arms around Betania and would not let go. Still, it was not enough. The man was overpowering her. He retreated toward his car, dragging Betania with him. That was when Pamela let go. Betania's eyes flashed a look of horror. But Pamela had not given up, she was merely changing strategies. Slipping off both of her shoes, she clutched each one and began to strike the man in the face with their sharp heals. Crying out in pain, he finally released Betania and hurriedly sped away in his car.

The two sisters walked miles until they made their way to their father's restaurant. When they entered *La Garlopa*, they were completely out of breath.

"*Papi, Papi, un hombre casi nos secuestró!*" screamed Betania.

El señor Solíz, dressed in a white uniform, quickly left the kitchen. "*Qué?*"

"*Es cierto, papá,*" said Pamela. "*Caminamos por la Poza Rica y un taxista nos dijo que guapas somos y nos ofreció cosas. Cuando le dijimos que se fuera, trató de agarrarle a Beti!*"

437

Betania's father raised her hand to his face. *"Oh, Dios mío!"* he shouted.

"Me agarró del brazo," said Betania between deep, agitated breaths, *"pero Pamela le pegó con los zapatos!"*

"Sí, le pegué con el tacón!" said Pamela, taking off her shoe and waving it as if it were a trophy.

5

BETANIA WAS SURPRISED to see her uncle sitting inside her living room speaking with her father. Even more surprising, he had come alone.

"Dónde está tía? Dónde están mis primos?" asked Betania.

Her uncle's eyes shifted toward Betania's father, who cleared his voice and called out, *"Qué vengan todos, por favor."* Gathering the family together, he announced that they were going to live with tío Rodolfo in Texas. Betania was perplexed. Turning to her mother, she noticed something in her face that displayed a tint of sadness. Pamela, to Betania's surprise, released a wide smile.

"Papi, entonces, abuela también?" asked Betania.

"Pues, no, hija. La patrona es muy grande. Se queda aquí en México. Va a vivir con tu tío Martín en Yucatán. Ya se fue con la familia de él."

Betania frowned. Tears began to form in her eyes. *"Entonces, no puedo despedirme de ella?"*

Her father inclined his head. In a very serious tone, he replied, *"Lo siento, hija."*

"Cuándo nos vamos, papá?" asked Pamela.

"Ahora mismo. Tu mamá ya empacó tus cosas."

"Qué buena honda! Vamos a vivir en los Estados Unidos!" said Pamela, her face beaming.

Betania's eyes darted toward an empty rocking chair. She then ran to her room. The wooden bed she shared with her sister was bare, stripped of all sheets. Even so, Betania plopped herself down on the old mattress and stared at the white barren walls. She heard her father's voice prompting her to join her family outside. They were putting the last of their belongings inside their uncle Rodolfo's large red truck. Begrudgingly, Betania joined them, squishing her slender body between her mother and her sister in the back of the double cab. She cried the entire trip.

6

BROWNSVILLE, WITH ITS evergreen plants and palm trees, seemed inviting to the Solíz family. Though different from La Antigua, it possessed many of the same qualities. The girls were happy to see their cousins, but the little two bedroom house made everyone feel cramped. Betania's parents slept on the couch, which folded into a bed, leaving only the floor for Betania and her sister.

The first few days did not feel like a foreign country. From stores to restaurants, Betania was able to speak Spanish with others and enjoy life as it was in Mexico. Her father quickly found work at a local restaurant, and though he criticized the limited menu, he seemed very happy. *"No se preocupen,"* he said to the entire family. *"Bien pronto mi hermano se irá y esta casa será nuestra. Y te digo una cosa, un día voy a tener mi propio restaurante y enseñarles a esta gente lo que es un plato de mariscos de verdad!"*

7

IT WAS NOT until Betania attended her first day of school that culture shock finally set in. Due to her limited English, she was placed in a special program. There, she found herself with other junior high students who had recently arrived to the United States. Most of them were from Mexico, but a few had come from Guatemala and El Salvador. Although the teacher spoke Spanish at times to clarify certain points of her lessons, the class was primarily conducted in English.

Betania felt lost. When her classmates left to eat lunch, she obediently followed them to the school cafeteria. Once in the line, she mimicked their actions. When students darted in front of her to grab food, however, she stopped. She looked in all directions, feeling overwhelmed by the rapid movement and the noise level. Finally, after receiving her food, Betania had the unenviable task of finding a place to sit. Standing in the middle of the large building, she scanned the many tables in search of an empty space.

"Look out!" cried out a deep husky voice.

Betania felt a hard object poking her in the back. She turned around to see a very large girl holding her lunch tray in front of her as if it were some sort of shield. Betania stared at her with innocent, questioning eyes. The girl had long sandy blonde hair that fell limp to her shoulders. Her white cheeks were covered with acne, and her T-shirt and blue jeans were stained. Standing next to her, Betania could smell the foul stench wafting from her body.

"What are you looking at?" shouted the girl.

Betania did not answer.

"Do you have a problem?"

Betania shrugged her shoulders and replied timidly, "Sorry. *No hablo inglés.*"

The girl frowned, shook her head at Betania in a demeaning fashion, and wandered off. Underneath her breath, she mumbled, "Great. Just what we need. Another dumb wetback."

A few students from Betania's class passed by, so she quickly followed them. As she passed the first row of long rectangular tables, a girl with long black hair and deep brown eyes seemed to be observing her. Betania made eye contact. As she did so, the girl's face broke into a mischievous smile.

"Hey, watch this! Looks like we got some new immigrants!"

Betania turned away, following two of her classmates. Suddenly, she tripped, falling to the floor. As she did so, her tray flew high into the air. When it finally landed, the food splattered across a nearby table, prompting more than a few students to be struck with apple sauce and an array of vegetables.

"What the...?" shouted one boy as he was struck with baby carrots.

"Hey!" screamed a girl as she wiped apple sauce from her face.

Betania felt dazed. Her eyes turned slightly to see a group of students pointing down at her. Some were openly laughing. Others were glowering. Slowly, she rose to her feet.

"You really need to be careful," said the dark haired girl to the laughter of her friends. She playfully dangled her foot to the outside of the table.

"*Cómo?*" asked Betania, still stunned. "*Lo siento, no hablo inglés.*"

"Oh no? Well, that's too bad. I feel so sorry for you."

The dark haired girl frowned. With both index fingers, she slowly touched her eyes and slid her fingers down, mimicking the tracks of tears. The girls next to her once again burst into laughter. As Betania stared at her, the dark haired girl suddenly turned serious. Her face changed, even menacingly so. "*Oye! Limpia esta mugre porque eso es el trabajo de los mexicanos!*"

Betania looked at the girl, stunned at her cruelty.

"*Pero…no eres mexicana?*" asked Betania. Her eyes began to well up with moisture.

"No!" she replied. "At least not like you! I'm Mexican American!"

"Tex-Mex, baby!" added another girl.

Betania stared at the group of girls, and then quickly left the cafeteria with tears rolling down her cheeks.

8

IN HIGH SCHOOL Betania was reunited with her sister, Pamela, and though they did not share a single class, it was a comfort just to know Pamela was there. Betania was slowly recuperating her confidence. One teacher in particular, Mr. López, served as great inspiration for her. He was short, possessed a very dark complexion, and dressed formally in slacks, collared shirt and tie, and polished shoes. Betania felt as though she could relate to him. Originally from a state called Nuevo León, he often shared personal stories about his upbringing in Mexico.

Mr. López reminded Betania of her teachers in La Antigua. She enjoyed listening to him speak Spanish. It was different than the Spanish in Texas. His English was also impeccable, and though he spoke with a slight accent, he displayed a **lexicon** that demonstrated mastery far superior to the other teachers.

"People will judge you by the way you speak," said Mr. López. "They will respect you or disrespect you based on your diction. Some of you have been in these remedial classes too long! A few years are enough, and then it's time to struggle in the advanced classes. Don't worry if you make mistakes, or if you speak with an accent, because everybody in Texas has an accent! Trust me, it's not a **stigma**; it's just a sign that you are bilingual, which demonstrates that you are an educated individual." He paused to smile. "Besides, a soft Spanish accent is very sexy."

The students broke into laughter.

9

THE DISSEMBLANCE BETWEEN the two Solíz sisters seemed to widen with each passing day. Whereas Betania was studious and quiet, Pamela was rarely seen kwith a book in her hand. Unlike Betania, she seemed to think of school as little more than a social gathering. This did not make her parents very happy, but if Pamela cared, she never showed it. As far as Betania could decipher, Pamela thought the daily fights with her parents were amusing.

"Eres una ingrata!" Betania's father would shout. *"Qué rebelde eres, Pamela! Si no me obedeces, te prometo que te voy a castigar!"*

When threatened, Pamela would simply shrug her shoulders and reply, *"A mi no me importa!"*

Despite the obvious problems Pamela was causing her family, Betania still admired her. Secretly, she even wished that she were more like her older sister. Pamela was aggressive. She was fearless. She never hesitated. Even in their childhood, Pamela had played the role of protector.

Betania recalled a time when the two girls were in *la escuela primaria* in La Antigua. Betania was only six years old. During the *recreo*, a girl had taken cookies from her that her mother had baked. When Betania informed Pamela of this injustice, she insisted that Betania point the girl out to her. Betania complied with her request, and Pamela immediately approached the girl and began to pull her hair. She then slapped the girl on the head. As if that were not enough, Pamela shoved her face in the dirt.

Afterwards, Pamela was taken to the *directora*. Inside her office, she pulled out a wooden paddle. The woman then explained to Pamela that she would stop as soon as Pamela apologized for her actions. But Pamela refused. After several *nalgadas*, the principal had to pause to catch her breath. Pamela remained slightly bent over. Once again, the principal began to hit her with renewed force. After several spankings, she stopped.

Pamela squinted. She tightened her jaw but refused to apologize. It was then that the principal understood that she would never be victorious. Seeing no other remedy, she shook her head, gently stroked her hair back, and finally released Pamela.

10

BY THE TIME Betania reached the age of sixteen, she had been promoted to college preparatory classes, excelling especially in mathematics and science. She dreamt of being like her aunt, tía Lydia, who was a doctor in Veracruz. As a small girl, she had been given tours of the hospital. Once, tía Lydia had even allowed Betania to assist her with a patient. It made an **indelible** mark on her young mind, convincing Betania that being a medical doctor would be the best career in the world.

Pamela did not share Betania's success, nor did she share her ambition. Instead of graduating on schedule, Pamela was informed that her failing grades required her to repeat one more year of high school. Her parents were deeply disappointed, but Pamela did not seem too distressed. Nothing seemed to faze her. If her father scolded her too much, she simply left the house, sometimes for days at a time.

"*Uno de estos días no te voy a permitir volver!*" said Betania's father as Pamela walked away from him. "*Ya verás!*"

In front of the house was a tan, muscular young man waiting for her. He was seated comfortably in an old black truck wearing nothing more than loose fitting blue jeans and a white cotton shirt. "Whoa, Loca," he called out to her. "Your old man is really mad!"

"Yeah, whatever," said Pamela, opening the thick metal door of the passenger side.

Betania peered out from behind the white curtains of the large front windows of the living room. From this vantage point, she watched as her sister quickly slid over in the front bench seat and kissed her boyfriend firmly on the lips. Both had square jaws, and Betania watched with fascination as their cheekbones moved in synchronization, as if in a dance.

"*Por lo menos te tenemos a ti!*" said Betania's father.

Somewhat startled, Betania quickly withdrew.

443

"Nunca vas a cambiar, verdad, princesa?"

"No, papi," replied Betania, though deep down she could not help but feel a bit envious of her sister.

11

BELOW THE CLEAR Texan sky, Betania stood next to Pamela on the sidewalk in front of the house.

"Take me!" begged Betania.

"No!" replied her sister. "Now go back inside!"

"Come on, please!" said Betania.

"Forget it!"

"If you don't take me, I'll tell mom and dad all about you and Francisco."

Pamela furrowed her brow in anger. *"Eres una mosca muerta, sabes?* Anyway, I don't care. Do whatever you want."

"I know where Francisco lives," continued Betania. "How would you like papi to show up one day when you two are over there all alone when you're supposed to be at school?"

"Wow," said Pamela, shaking her head slowly. "You are not near as innocent as everyone thinks. Look, Beti, it's not that I don't want you to go. It's just that, these parties aren't for you, that's all."

"Why not?" asked Betania. "I want to dance and have some fun! All I do is study in the house every day! Papi doesn't even let boys talk to me on the phone!"

"Just drop it, okay?" said Pamela.

"Fine, I guess I'll tell papi *todo!*"

"All right, all right," said Pamela. She scowled at Betania, then added, "But don't say I didn't warn you."

Betania stared at her sister, a glint of confusion in her eyes.

"Here he is!" shouted Pamela, pointing to a familiar vehicle which had pulled in front of the house. A window quickly lowered. "Hey! *Hermanita!*" Francisco called out to Betania. "Are you coming?"

Betania shyly looked at her sister.

"Come on!" said Pamela with a disapproving smirk.

"Hurry!" said Francisco. "All the hot air's coming in!"

The two girls quickly got into the large truck, Pamela going first. She sat closely to Francisco to make room for Betania.

"Are we late?" asked Pamela.

"Yeah!" replied Francisco. "The party's already started!"

"It's all Beti's fault!" said Pamela, her voice full of contempt. "I told her not to come!"

"No, no, *tranquila*," said Francisco. "I got the *carnales* working hard. They're cooking *carne asada* and getting the speakers set up. Trust me, we'll be all right."

"*Gracias*, Francisco," said Betania in a sweet tone accompanied by a smile of triumph directed at her sister.

"*De nada*, Beti!" said Francisco. "I'm glad you finally decided to come!"

Pamela crossed her arms in front of her and scowled. In a matter of minutes, Francisco slowed down to park next to the sidewalk of a home that Betania had never seen before. She looked at the red paint around the front door. It was cracking and falling in tiny strips. Betania followed as her sister passed through an old, metal gate. One swift swing from Francisco and it clanged shut, startling her. Then, to add to her anxiety, a stodgy bulldog ran out to meet them, breathing heavily and salivating at the mouth.

"Oh, don't worry, Beti," said Francisco. "She's too fat and lazy to bite you."

As they made their way around the house through a side walkway of dirt, dry weeds, and loose rocks, the music grew louder. Emerging into the backyard, Betania looked with excitement upon seeing several people dancing and eating. Some stood with paper plates in their hands whereas others sat down in white plastic chairs under the shade of the trees. Although late in the evening, the hot Texan sun shone brightly, causing everyone to perspire from the combination of heat and humidity.

"Hey, you hungry?" asked Francisco.

Both girls nodded affirmatively.

Francisco hesitated for a moment. "Uh, should I get her a beer or…"

Pamela replied quickly, "Get her a soda, baby."

After eating several small tacos, Pamela and Francisco began to dance. Betania remained alone at the table and watched. A few boys approached, requesting a dance with her. Some could even be called men. Betania politely refused each time. Then, as she continued to observe with great curiosity, another boy walked up beside her.

"Hey, don't worry, I'm not going to ask you to dance because I already seen you turn those other guys down," he said quietly. "I just brought you a drink."

Betania looked up at him. He was holding three aluminum cans with both hands against his chest.

"My name's Jorge."

Betania nodded, granting him permission to sit in the chair next to her. She found him less intimidating than the other boys. He was, if anything, quite small, even frail.

"Which one do you like the best? I've got Sprite™· Coke™· and Fanta™."

Betania giggled. "Fanta™, please."

Jorge handed her an orange can. It was cold to her touch.

"I've seen you at school before," said Jorge. "You're Beti, right?"

"Yes. What year are you?"

"I'm a junior."

"Me too!" exclaimed Betania, happy to meet someone her age. "But I don't remember you. Sorry."

Jorge inclined his head. "It's okay. I remember you."

Betania smiled shyly.

"So who brought you here?" asked Jorge.

"My sister."

"Oh, good."

"Why is that good?"

"Because I was afraid you were going to say your boyfriend."

Betania once again released her shy, feminine smile.

"So, who's your sister?" asked Jorge.

"Pamela Solíz," said Betania.

Jorge laughed. "Crazy Pamela? Are you serious? Like a *real* sister?"

"Yes, she is. Why?" asked Betania.

"Oh, sorry, it's just that you don't really look like her. I mean, you have such pretty long brown hair, and your face…. Don't get me wrong, Pamela's all right. But you—you look like an angel!"

446

Betania blushed slightly and looked down at her plate on the table. It was empty except for a few bits of scattered meat, beans, and salsa. She paused to take a few sips of her drink. "I take after my father. My sister looks more like my mother."

"Oh, that's why," said Jorge, smiling slightly. "So, when did you join?"

Betania cocked her head back. She then furrowed her brow. "Join what?"

"The Texas Syndicate," replied Jorge. "You know, our gang."

Betania paused.

"Well, you're here," said Jorge, a puzzled look on his face.

"I thought this was a party."

"It is a party—a TS party," replied Jorge. "You should run with us."

Betania tilted her head and furrowed her brow.

"With the TS, you're family. Everyone treats you well. And we're big, too! We got back up in Houston, Dallas, Fort Worth. Everywhere, really."

Betania opened her mouth to speak, but Pamela then returned with Francisco. Betania liked him. He had always been nice to her, and besides that, he was handsome. With expressive brown eyes and a face that had a slight beard, Francisco possessed a slim but powerful frame. Around his right bicep was a large tattoo. Betania had never paid much attention to the large "S" that was interwoven into the "T." It was as if she saw it for the first time.

"Beti!" said Francisco. "What are you doing talking to *Flaco*?"

Before she could answer, Francisco smiled at Jorge, extending his hand so that Jorge was forced to raise his own hand high above his shoulder. As their hands clasped, Francisco yanked Jorge out of his chair. It was a *macho* hug, where the arms and shoulders of both boys bump. A soft breeze provided a slight relief respite, but there was no escaping the Texan heat, even with light clothing.

Facing Betania, Francisco asked, "So you liking it? You feeling good?"

Betania smiled and nodded.

"Yeah, this is the life," continued Francisco, settling into a chair. He leaned back and stretched his arms widely. "We're your *familia* now, Beti. You can count on us. It's not just *la Loca*, you know what I mean?" Francisco laughed as he pointed to Pamela. Smiling, she got on top of him, and the two began a mock wrestling match that ended with Pamela on Francisco's lap.

"Yeah, we're getting bigger and badder," he continued. "Pretty soon, we won't have to worry about nobody, you know? Pretty soon, we can all walk the streets safe like and just kick back." Francisco paused for a moment. He lifted his beer to his mouth.

"How did you...?" Betania paused.

"What?" asked Francisco.

"Oh, never mind," said Betania.

"No, go ahead. What do you want to know?"

"Well, how did you get involved in...?" Betania's voice trailed off before she could finish her thought.

"Beti!" interrupted Pamela, grimacing. Then, turning to Jorge, she continued, "*Mira*, Jorge, you gonna stare at my sister all day or what? Ask her to dance, *pendejo!*"

"*Tengo miedo*," Jorge replied. "I don't want her to reject me like those other dudes."

"Maybe later," said Betania, "I want to hear Francisco now."

"He doesn't want to talk about that!" said Pamela.

"No, it's cool," said Francisco.

"Fine! Whatever, Frankie," said Pamela, quickly moving off his lap and settling into her chair.

Francisco shook his head. At first, his lips were pressed closely together, but then they opened up into a wide smile. "Why are you so mad?"

"Because of you and *pinche* Flaco keep talking to my sister!" said Pamela.

"Well, you brought her!" said Francisco.

"Because I had to!" said Pamela.

A few people turned in their direction.

Pamela raised her hands demonstrably. "What the hell are you staring at?" she shouted.

They quickly turned away.

"*Híjole!* Don't you share a room with her?" Francisco asked Betania, a mischievous smile on his face.

Jorge, too, smiled, but he dared not express his amusement too much.

"Anyway," continued Francisco, shaking his head in feigned exhaustion, "I joined when I was only twelve. I didn't have much of a family, and going back and forth from Mexico…well, you know, sometimes other kids treated me kind of bad. I was kind of alone, you know, and then these older kids told me that the Texas Syndicate looks out for us—*los inmigrantes*."

"I know what you mean," said Betania, **empathizing** with Francisco. "I felt very alone when I first came here, too. *Los americanos no me trataron muy bien y tampoco los mexicanos-americanos.*"

Francisco nodded. "Yeah, but you got it better than me," he said. "*Tienes tu hermana, tus padres.* Growing up in Matamoros, *yo no tenía a nadie.* My old man…. He was never around. He was always coming here, looking for work. At least that's what he said. One day my mom and me came here to surprise him. Yeah, he was surprised all right—surprised when his *vieja* and his kid came to the door 'cause he had his *sancha* inside with him. My mom, she looked at him and said, 'here's your son.' After that, she left! I went back with her for a while, but she sent me to my dad after a few months. I don't know why she didn't want me. One of my *tías* said it was because I looked too much like my old man. I haven't seen her much."

Francisco stopped. He inclined his head. A serious expression took over his face. Pamela walked behind him and began to massage his shoulders. "Hell, I haven't told nobody…" he mumbled before his voice trailed off.

"It's okay, baby," said Pamela. "Forget about it. Come on, let's dance."

"Yeah. Sorry, bro. Sorry, Beti," said Francisco.

"Actually, I was very interested," said Betania. "If it's okay, I would like to hear more."

"*Ya*, Beti!" said Pamela. "I knew it was a mistake to bring you here!"

"Really?" replied Francisco, arching his eyebrows.

Betania nodded, as did Jorge. Pamela frowned, her eyes full of anger.

Francisco rubbed the soft patches of uneven black hair that sprouted from his cheeks. "I lived with my dad and his girlfriend for a while, went to school. All that stuff. Then he started disappearing again. After a while we found out that the *cabrón* went back to Mexico. I heard he was in Juárez where he had another woman. I stayed with his old lady, but I knew she didn't want me. I mean, she had her own kids, and it was my dad who

left her. But she let me stay. I guess she was the only parent I ever had."
Francisco paused once again to take a few sips of his beer.

"Then what?" asked Betania, anxiously. "I mean, what happened to
your dad?"

Francisco laughed, almost choking on his beer. He then turned toward
Pamela and said, "Damn! I've never heard your sister talk so much!"

Pamela curled her lips. Betania smiled, somewhat embarrassed.

"Hell, I don't know, Beti. I heard he got shot or something. There's
too much competition down there, so you know it's gonna happen sooner
or later."

"Competition?" repeated Betania.

"Drugs!" snarled Pamela in a condescending tone.

"Yeah, that's right. Wait. What was I saying?" asked Francisco. He
finished his beer, opened another, and began drinking heavily.

"How you got in, bro," said Jorge.

Francisco took a few more drinks. "Yeah, yeah, that's right," he
continued slowly. His eyes moved toward Jorge. His speech became slurred.
"Thanks, Flaco. What did I do? Let me see. I stole cars. I was good at that,
you know? I'd take a crew with me and we'd steal it, then chop it up and
leave it burning in the fields by the river. You make good money like that."

"You make money burning cars?" interrupted Betania.

Francisco laughed. Pamela scowled at Betania.

"No, Beti," said Jorge. Then, in a gentle, patient tone resembling that
of a professor explaining a difficult concept to a confused student, he
continued, "They chop them up. That means they take them apart first
so that they can sell the parts. Then they burn the rest so that nobody can
identify it. Sometimes they even dump stuff in the Río Grande."

Betania nodded and smiled.

"That's pretty much it, *hermanita*," said Francisco.

"So to be part of the gang you have to steal a car?" asked Betania.

"I think Francisco's done telling stories," said Pamela.

"No, no," interrupted Francisco. "It's not like that. There's lots of ways.
It kind of depends—depends on the person—the *barrio*—lots of things.
Look at Flaco, here." Francisco paused to put his arm around Jorge. "He
had to get jumped. He was so damn skinny, and way too nice. I was afraid

he'd get hurt if he did something too hard, so I told everyone to pound on him."

Betania's eyes widened. She turned to face Jorge, who merely grinned back at her. "Did they hurt you?" she asked him.

"To be honest, I don't really remember much," said Jorge. "I just remember Francisco slapping me to wake me up and then hugging me."

Francisco and Pamela both laughed loudly. Looking downward, Betania said, "I don't understand what's so funny."

"It ain't like that, Beti! If we wanted to hurt this little *carnal* then we would have," said Francisco. "No, it was just enough to make him feel it. Jorge is actually tougher than he looks."

"Thanks, bro," said Jorge.

Betania pressed her lips together tightly. After a brief silence, she ventured, "So, you've been involved in the Texas Syndicate for a long time?"

"Yeah, I guess so," replied Francisco, speaking ever more slowly. "I'm an officer. *Carnales* even consider me an OG 'cause I've been in so long." He lifted his beer, shook the few remaining drops into his mouth, and then threw the can to the ground. Pamela quickly handed him another. "*Gracias, Loca*," replied Francisco, his words beginning to slur slightly. He opened the fresh can of beer he had been given. After taking several gulps, his face took on a hard, serious expression. "But once you're in, you're in. If someone tries to leave us, we'll find him. And when we do, he's done. We don't let nobody betray us."

"Okay, Frankie," interrupted Pamela, "I think she's heard enough."

"*Somos los vatos más fuertes de todos!*" Francisco shouted proudly, holding up his beer. "*No hay una clika más mejor!*"

Several people in the backyard responded by raising their drinks and cheering. Francisco smiled. He then grabbed Pamela with his muscular right arm and hugged her tightly. "We're the strongest, and *cada día* we're just getting stronger! Fools all over want to join us. They know *Los Tejanos* will take care of them!"

Jorge extended his hand, which Francisco struck so forcefully that the contact made a loud thundering noise that rose above the casual chatter of the party.

"Okay, okay," said Pamela, removing Francisco's beer from his hand and setting it on the round plastic table.

12

WHEN BETANIA AND her sister returned home, it was almost midnight. Betania's mother opened the door while dressed in a white robe. "*Dónde andaban?*" she asked. Her eyes were red and dark. "*Es muy tarde.*"

"*Ma, ya te dije! Estábamos con unas amigas estudiando!*" said Pamela in a crass tone.

"*A esta hora?*" replied la señora Solíz. She furrowed her brow. Then, turning to Betania, she continued, "*Betania? Es cierto?*"

"Why do you have to ask her if I just told you?" said Pamela.

La señora Solíz repeated the question. Betania hesitated. She looked at her mother, then glanced at Pamela. A stern expression was on her face. Betania licked her upper lip. Finally, she replied, "*Sí, mami. Perdónenos. Tiene razón. Es muy tarde.*"

La señora Solíz shook her head. "*Bueno.*"

"*Sí, tienes razón, mamá, es muy tarde,*" repeated Pamela, covering her mouth and yawning. "*Ya nos vamos a acostar! Buenas noches!*"

Betania followed her sister to the one bedroom they shared. There, they changed into their nightgowns. Then, after taking turns in the bathroom, both girls plopped into their beds. Betania could not sleep, though. Try as she might, she constantly tossed and turned in her bed.

"Hey, what's with you?" asked Pamela.

Betania sat up and peered through the darkness. A little light, caused by the brightness of a large moon, cracked through the curtain of their window, providing just enough visibility for Betania to make out her sister's contour.

"What exactly is the Texas Syndicate?" asked Betania.

"What?"

"The TS," Betania continued.

"Don't worry about it!" replied Pamela, anger creeping into her voice.

"Please, Pamela, tell me," asked Betania in the sweetest tone she could muster.

"Hey, I'm not Francisco or Jorge, so don't try that little *voz de miel* on me!" said Pamela. "Now go to sleep!"

Betania became silent, but her mind remained filled with images of Francisco, of Jorge, and of burning cars. She wondered what Francisco was like as a little boy. She wondered how Jorge could be so nice and polite and yet be a dedicated member of the Texas Syndicate. Suddenly, a chill moved down her spine. Pamela. She, too, must have passed through some sort of initiation. Betania was tempted to ask her sister more questions, but she dared not do so. Pamela could be very stubborn. She would probably not tell her anything. But Betania knew someone who would.

13

LEAVING HER CLASSMATES, Betania headed toward a particular bathroom. She knew she could find Jorge there. As she walked closer, a group of boys nodded and greeted Betania with a chorus of shouts and whistles.

One of them walked toward her, asking, "You looking for me?"

As Betania scanned the boys in search of Jorge, she heard comments such as "*qué guapa*" and "she's fine." Nervously, she began to have second thoughts. She took a few steps in the opposite direction when suddenly a voice called out, "Hey, Beti! Over here!"

Betania turned to see Jorge walking toward her. She smiled at him shyly. "I was hoping we could have lunch together," she told him.

The eyes of the other boys flashed as they began to shout once again.

"Wouldn't you rather talk to me?" asked a boy with a shaved head and a tattoo of a cobra on his forearm.

"Hey, leave her alone, Jairo," said Jorge.

Ignoring Jorge, he walked toward Betania in confident strides. He then put his arm around her without the slightest hesitation. Smiling, he asked, "Why do you want to have lunch with this little boy when you could be with a real man?"

"She's Pamela's sister!" said Jorge. "And Francisco told me to watch out for her!"

Suddenly, Jairo stopped. His mouth fell open. His face flushed. "Francisco?"

"Yeah, man," said Jorge.

Removing his arm from Betania's shoulders, Jairo said in an apologetic tone, "Hey, I'm sorry. I didn't know."

To Betania's amazement, Jairo walked away and took the other boys with him.

"Sorry about that," said Jorge.

"Oh, it's okay." Betania looked down at the white cement. For some reason, she felt embarrassed. The unassuming, even respectful manner of Jorge pleased her. "So, do you want to eat lunch with me? We still have time."

"Sure," said Jorge. "I usually don't eat, but for you, of course!"

They entered the line in the cafeteria and took their trays among the clang and clatter of a throng of kids hustling quickly to the many tables. As they took their food, staff members were standing conspicuously throughout the building, continually barking orders and pointing. Betania searched for an open space. She was happy to see that one small table was practically empty. As soon as they sat down, she blurted, "Jorge, why do you hang around those boys?"

Jorge smiled slightly. "Oh, they're not so bad. They just like to show off to pretty girls."

Betania smiled. "But they're so mean and you.…. Well, you're different."

Jorge furrowed his brow. "What do you mean?"

"I mean that I think you are so nice, Jorge."

"I think you are nice, too, Beti. And you're so pretty. You look like an angel, or at least what I think an angel looks like."

Betania took a bite of her grilled cheese sandwich as she studied Jorge. He was small, just an inch or so taller than she, and slender. He had short black hair and light brown skin that was smooth, even childlike. His face was somewhat square, but small and narrow. His eyes, too, were small, and formed in the shape of almonds, giving the impression that he possessed Asian ancestry within his Latino blood. He dressed conservatively, with black shoes, dark jeans, and a checkered collared shirt that was unbuttoned at the very top, revealing a neatly pressed white T-shirt on the inside. Betania did not consider Jorge terribly handsome, but she liked his face. There was something attractive about it. It was gentle—kind, even. She also liked the slow, simple way in which he spoke. The tone of his voice was soothing. Jorge was safe. He was nonthreatening.

"Jorge, is it okay if I ask you something?"

"Yeah, go ahead," said Jorge with a large smile still on his face.

"I've been thinking about the Texas Syndicate…"

"About the TS?" asked Jorge. His eyes lit up. "Are you in?"

"I'm not sure," said Betania. "I want to, but I'm a little afraid. I don't know what to do."

"Beti, you shouldn't be afraid to be in," said Jorge, "you should be afraid *not* to be in. There's a lot of bad kids out there just waiting to mess with you, but if you're with us, you got protection."

Betania paused. Jorge then picked up a small milk carton and finished it with one movement.

"But I still don't understand," continued Betania. "Do you have to do bad things?"

Jorge furrowed his brow. Shaking his head, he said, "Not really. We're respectful. We take care of each other and we don't bother anyone. And if we do, it's because they deserve it. But others—like La Emi—yeah, they're bad. They're disrespectful. All they do is go around causing trouble."

"La Emi?"

"Yeah, the Mexikanemi. They're the ones you have to worry about. Sometimes we just want to have a party or have fun, and they'll come over and call us names for no reason. They're always trying to start something."

"That's terrible!" said Betania. She then became conscious of the volume of her voice. Smiling, she instinctively covered her mouth with her palm. "Why do they do that?" she asked more quietly.

"It's just always been like that. They hate us, so we have to fight back. There's others, too, but La Emi is the worst."

"Who are they?" asked Betania.

"Like I said, they're really bad. They think they're better than us 'cause we're *inmigrantes*. They call us *llegados*. They're trying to claim our territory right here even."

"You mean Brownsville?" asked Betania.

Jorge laughed. "Yeah, everywhere! Your neighborhood, my neighborhood, here in our school, Brownsville, Harlingen. That's why we have to stop them, and we'll do whatever it takes."

Betania frowned as she shook her head.

"Look, Beti," continued Jorge, "I know it ain't right, but they started it, so we can't just let them come into our neighborhood and start running things, you know."

"But why? Can't you just stay away from them?"

Jorge frowned. "It don't work like that. They look down at Mexicans like you and me." He then lifted his index finger and pointed it directly in Betania's face. "They'll hurt you, Beti."

"What?" asked Betania. She cocked her head back. Her eyes widened. "Jorge, what are you talking about? Nobody's trying to hurt me!"

"You're innocent." Jorge curled his lips and shook his head. "I used to be like you until some guys from La Emi stabbed me." He paused for a moment. His head swiveled in all directions. He then moved closer to Betania and pulled up his shirt, revealing a long, thick scar that ran between his stomach and his rib cage. "This is what they did to me, Beti. And all I was doing is just getting a *pinche* carton of *leche* for my mom."

Betania observed the rough darkened wound. She then frowned. "They did this to you because you're in the Texas Syndicate?"

"Naw, it was before!" said Jorge. His face soured as he tucked his shirt back into his pants. "As soon as I came out of the market, these guys—big guys—older—they came up to me and asked me if I bang. I said 'no' and kept walking, but they followed me and shoved me down to the ground."

"Nobody helped you?" asked Betania.

"There was some people around, but they didn't do nothing. So after these guys shoved me down, they started beating on me and then one of them pulls out a knife and stabs me!"

As Jorge inclined his head, Betania quietly reached out and gently grasped his hand and whispered, "I'm so sorry. I can only imagine."

"Yeah, it was bad. There was blood all over the place," continued Jorge. "But it's all right 'cause when I joined the TS, we got 'em back." Jorge raised his head, allowing Betania to look into his eyes. "The TS saved me, Beti. They treat me good. Francisco's like an older brother to me, and I even met Antonio once. He was cool with me."

Betania furrowed her brown. "Who is Antonio?"

"Antonio Castañeda!" said Jorge, his admiration clearly resonating in his voice. "He's the *mero mero*! Everyone listens to Antonio!"

"Even Francisco?"

Jorge broke into laugher. "Francisco's an officer, Beti, but Antonio... he's like over everyone. He can get back up from Houston or Dallas if he has to!"

"Was he at the party?" asked Betania.

Jorge cocked his head back and shook his head vigorously. "No, he don't come here much."

"Oh," said Betania.

"Once, though, when we had some big trouble with La Emi, yeah, he was here. He brought a lot of guys with him, too. He shook my hand, you know."

Betania bit her lower lip slightly as Jorge smiled and nodded. His face seemed to be glowing.

14

IT WAS THE end of the day and the air was warm and humid. Students rushed in all directions through the outside corridors of the school. As they did so, a few of Betania's classmates hovered around her.

"Hey, Betania," called out a voice, "can we talk with you?"

Betania hesitated. It was Elizabeth. Beside her were two other girls, Marisol and Amanda. Betania did not know them very well, but she knew *of* them. Each seemed quite popular in her own way. Elizabeth was known for her intellect, yet she completely neglected her appearance. Above her thick black rimmed glasses hung a dark unibrow, and her mass of brown hair, which resembled a mop, was never styled. Marisol, on the other hand, possessed a stunning appearance. Her black shoulder length hair lightly covered a large bold face that displayed beautiful, symmetrical features. Her square, prominent jawline qualified her for modeling, and her upper body tapered to a small waist before widening to thick, firm thighs, giving her an amazing figure. Amanda, the smallest of the three, was also very beautiful, though her features starkly contrasted with those of Marisol. She possessed white silky skin that was virtually radiant, long red hair, and bright hazel eyes. Her voice was succulent, and flowed from pink lips that created a smile that was seductively charming.

"Some of us couldn't help but notice that you hang out with some kids that—well—let's just say they're not the kind of people we think you should be with. How do you even know them, anyway?"

"They're my friends, Elizabeth," replied Betania.

"Aren't they gangsters?" asked Marisol in a tone full of contempt.

"No, it's not like that," said Betania as she turned away and continued toward a large metal gate.

"Hold on!" said Elizabeth. "We're not done!"

The girls hurried toward her.

"You think I don't know a gang member when I see one?" asked Marisol with indignation in her voice. "Come on, Betania, wake up! Those kids are just going to end up in jail! What are you thinking?"

"And who's that scrawny little kid you eat lunch with every day, anyway?" asked Elizabeth. "Please tell me he's not your boyfriend!"

Betania furrowed her brow. "Look, you girls wouldn't understand. You've always been in the top classes; you're in all the school activities..." Her voice trailed off as she passed through a gate that led outside the school. Once there, Betania headed toward a large white stone that lay proudly over a large area of the green grassy field that stood between the school entrance and the main street. The three girls followed her.

"Waiting for someone?" asked Elizabeth.

"Yes," said Betania. "Now, please, leave me alone."

"Look," said Marisol, "just 'cause I'm a cheerleader doesn't mean that I've had an easy life. I've had to fight for everything I've got! Anyway, we're just trying to help you!"

"Why are you telling me this?" replied Betania.

"Betania, we're your friends," interjected Amanda in her thick Spanish accent. "We are just trying to protect you."

Betania felt the heat rise in her face. "I don't need you to *protect me* and the truth is you couldn't even if you wanted to. You girls live in your own little world and don't even know what's happening."

"I know what's happening," said Elizabeth. "You're falling for some bad boy because you think it's cool when really he's just some stupid kid that probably won't even graduate!"

"He'll probably end up beating her!" added Marisol, causing the others to laugh.

"That boy you're talking about has a name," said Betania.

"What is it?" asked Marisol. "Little Dummy? *Tonto? Perdedor?*

Betania's beautiful dark eyes flashed. "It's Jorge, and he treats me really well!"

Elizabeth adjusted her glasses. "So he *is* your boyfriend."

"So what if he is?" Betania replied. "It doesn't concern you!"

Elizabeth wagged her head from side to side. Marisol rolled her eyes.

"Look, there he is," said Betania. "Please, just leave me alone."

"Is he a freshman?" asked Marisol. "I've never had a class with that little dude."

Amanda frowned. "Betania, really? You must be kidding. You are much too good for that boy. Did you know that Jim Molina said he thinks you are really cute and wants to ask you out?"

"Jim?" repeated Betania. "I hardly even know him. Anyway, what makes him any better than Jorge?"

Amanda arched her eyebrows and chuckled. "Um, have you seen him? First, he's got brown hair and blue eyes! Second, he is so nice. Third, he is smart. Fourth, he is so strong. Fifth, he is on the football team. Should I say more?"

"*Ya! Déjenme en paz!*" shouted Betania. "I'm not like you girls, okay?"

"What's that supposed to mean?" asked Elizabeth.

"Excuse us for trying to help you!" said Marisol.

"Betania, please! Think!" said Amanda. "You could be with Jim!"

Betania furrowed her brow. Her eyes narrowed. "*Mira, Amanda, eso no tiene nada que ver contigo y de todos modos Jim es como…medio gabacho!*"

"*Es cierto!*" replied Amanda. Her face broke into a large smile. "*Su mamá es americana! Y te digo una cosa. Jim es cien veces mejor que ese perdedor tuyo!*"

"*Entonces, por qué tú no estás con él?*" asked Betania.

"*Porque me dijo que le gustas!*" replied Amanda. "But now that I see you like little *cholo* boys I think I will get with him!"

"Quit calling him that!" said Betania, walking toward Amanda.

Amanda, though much smaller, stood her ground. Marisol stepped between them. At that moment, Jorge approached. "Hey, Beti," he said, "is everything okay?"

Betania turned away from Amanda. She looked at Jorge and managed a weak smile.

"We're just trying to help you, Betania," said Elizabeth. She then faced Jorge and frowned. "Just don't mess up your life." Elizabeth then promptly walked away.

"Come on, she's blind!" huffed Marisol.

"Yes, Elizabeth has glasses," said Amanda, shaking her head disapprovingly toward Betania. "But what's your excuse?"

Both girls then also walked away.

"What was that all about?" asked Jorge.

"Oh, nothing," Betania replied. "Come on, let's go."

15

PAMELA OPENED THE refrigerator door, grabbed a flour tortilla and some cheese, and then quickly made a quesadilla on the stove. She then wrapped it in a paper towel. "Hey, you want to go walking with us?"

Betania glanced at her and then at her books that were spread across the table. Pamela then poked at Betania's binder and notebooks. Curling her lips, she asked, "Man, what is all this, anyway?"

"One is for algebra and the other one's for chemistry," replied Betania. "Chemistry is my favorite! I was telling tía Lydia about—"

"Yeah, yeah, that's great," interrupted Pamela. "Now, are you coming or what?"

After a short pause, Betania pushed her books away and followed her sister out the door. They walked several blocks until they arrived at a small white house not so different than their own. Pamela knocked loudly on the door, pounding the thin wood until it vibrated. Betania smiled at her sister's aggressiveness.

"Hey," said Vanessa, a dark skinned girl with a triangular, small face who was the same age as Pamela.

"Let's go get everyone," said Pamela.

Vanessa nodded and joined the them. This pattern continued until Betania found herself walking with her sister and four other girls.

"Hey, look," said Vanessa. "I think those are Emi girls."

"Or maybe Barrio Azteca," said another girl named Vicki, who had large eyes that almost seemed to bulge within her oval shaped face.

"Yeah, come on!" said Pamela, smiling widely.

Betania watched her sister's eyes flash; she seemed to be exploding with excitement as they quickly approached the other girls and called them names. Their insults were then returned. At that moment, Pamela grabbed several rocks from the ground and began throwing them. Betania and the others followed her lead, stooping down and grabbing anything that they could find. As the other girls were pelted with sticks, rocks, and glass bottles, they offered no resistance, but instead began to run in the opposite direction. Seeing this, Pamela, Betania, and all of her friends began chasing after them. They followed the girls down several streets.

"If I ever see anyone of you here again I'll cut you up!" screamed Pamela.

"*Este barrio es de los Tejanos!*" said Vanessa.

"Look at them run," said Rosa, who like Betania, possessed a much softer countenance than rest of the girls.

16

THEY WERE EVERYWHERE, and they no longer remained in the shadows. Betania was aware of their existence, but had never truly seen them. Slowly, though, she was beginning to recognize certain boys and girls, and they recognized her as well. Her school was supposedly a neutral area, but students claimed little spots. A bathroom, a water fountain, a bench. Wandering into a claimed area could result in serious consequences.

Betania could no longer pretend. She was one of them, and as she walked with the other girls on a crisp Saturday morning, she made her intentions known. Pamela, however, immediately began to shout her down.

"I have the same right that you do!" said Betania.

"Yeah, come on, Pami, she's one of us," said Vanessa.

"No, Vanessa, she doesn't understand!" Pamela replied.

"Yes, I do!" insisted Betania.

"See!" said Vanessa. "Beti's cool! She's with us! It's time to make it official!"

Pamela grimaced. "Give us a second, huh?"

"Sure, whatever," said Vanessa.

Pamela motioned for the girls to walk a little further down the sidewalk. Once alone with Betania, she began, "Look, I really care about you and I don't want you to get mixed up in all this! You only see the fun stuff. You like the parties, the cute guys, the excitement of chasing a girl down..." Pamela paused for a moment. She stepped closer to Betania, practically bumping her in the forehead. "There's a lot of other stuff you don't see. Trust me, if you officially join the TS, you're going to have to do a lot of..." Once again Pamela stopped in mid-sentence. "Just trust me, okay?"

"Trust you for what?" asked Betania.

"You don't want to know."

The look in Pamela's eyes and the tone of her voice was something that Betania had neither seen nor heard.

17

BETANIA WAS TAKING notes and listening intently to her chemistry teacher when she was unexpectedly summoned to the office. She accepted the call slip and promptly walked out of the classroom, down one of the many corridors, and then entered a circular building to see Mr. Alvarez, the school guidance counselor. Though she had never spoken with him before, she knew who he was. Everyone did. His many tattoos, his salt and pepper hair slicked back with gel, and his bushy goatee made him stand apart from the other school officials. Betania had also heard the stories of his past—a violent past, a criminal past, a past of respect, of power, of fear.

Stopping by the desk of one of the many clerks and secretaries, she was told to pass through an extended hallway that led to his personal office. The door was open, and Mr. Alvarez was on the phone. Betania listened as he spoke in Spanish, explaining his actions regarding a student who had been suspended. As Betania lingered near the doorway, he turned to her and motioned with his right hand toward a chair in front of his desk. Betania nodded and sat down. Once the phone conversation had ended, he cheerfully greeted her. "Betania, how you doing, *mija*?"

"Fine," Betania replied tersely.

Mr. Alvarez got up from his chair. Walking past Betania, he closed his office door. "Your grades have been slipping this last semester."

Betania remained quiet. She tapped the armrest of her chair.

"Why do you think your grades have gone down so much?"

Betania looked at him, said nothing, and then inclined her head.

"I'm worried about you, *mija*. I seen you hanging around the bathrooms with those TS girls. You trying to be like your sister now?"

Betania furrowed her brow.

"Don't look so surprised. I know everything that happens in this school. It's my *barrio*. I also have this." Mr. Alvarez laid a large file on his desk. "You're a good girl, Betania. You've had good grades every year until now." He withdrew a print out. "AP chemistry—that's impressive. You're a very intelligent girl. What do you want to ruin your life for?"

Betania frowned disagreeably.

"Gangs are bad news, Betania. I mean really bad news. *Eso no es ningún juego, mija.*"

Betania flung her head back, causing her long, brown hair to flow backward. She then brushed her bangs out of her eyes. "I know."

Mr. Alvarez arched his eyebrows. "Do you?" He paused. He seemed to be studying Betania. "Do you really? What do you know?"

Betania moved uneasily in her chair.

"You're running straight in *con los ojos cerrados!*" Mr. Alvarez covered his eyes. "I'm from California, Betania. I used to live in East Los Angeles. We were sureños—southside. It was all I knew. My brothers were in the gang, my neighbors. I always knew that I would be a Sureño. It was just a matter of time."

Betania perked up a bit. "How old were you?" she asked.

"I was thirteen, and some kids were younger than me."

"How did you get in?"

Mr. Alvarez paused. It appeared as though he had second thoughts about the direction of the conversation. Finally, he replied, "I had to do a drive by—a drive by with a shot gun. We were a blood in blood out chapter."

Betania's eyes widened.

"To truly understand the gangs, you have to be aware of their origins. You kids don't even know the history of your own gangs, let alone the first ones. I can tell you one thing. It's not about your friends or your little neighborhood."

Betania crinkled her forehead.

"The most powerful gangs come from the prisons," continued Mr. Alvarez, "and from there it spills into the streets."

"The prisons?" asked Betania.

"Yes, in prison people are forced to choose sides, and whenever prisoners get beat up, they unite to defend themselves. That's the way it works."

"So you've been in…?"

Though Betania did not finish her question, Mr. Alvarez nodded. "That's the way it's always been," he continued. "You unite to survive. It's usually about color, but with our people, the Hispanics, it was a little different. They weren't so much into race as they were geography."

Betania gave Mr. Alvarez a quizzical look.

"Geography, Betania. Hispanics are different than whites and blacks. They don't claim a history in the United States that goes back hundreds of years. That's why it took longer for them to gain power. You had the Mexican Americans on one side and the Mexicans straight from Mexico on the other. The ones from here, the Chicanos, mostly spoke English and looked down on the Mexicans."

Betania nodded.

The phone rang. Mr. Alvarez turned his head for a brief moment, and then continued, "It started with La Eme, also known as the Mexican Mafia. They were the early Chicano inmates."

Betania suddenly blurted out, "La Emi! The Mexikanemi!"

Mr. Alvarez smiled. "So you do know a little. But let me correct you. I'm talking about the original Latino gang, the Mexican Mafia from California, not a local gang from Texas. There's La Eme and La Emi."

"So there's two of them?"

"Okay," said Mr. Alvarez. He paused for a moment, then bit his lower lip with his white, upper teeth. "Pay attention, Betania, I'm going to give you a little history lesson that I teach at the intervention clinics, okay? Look, nobody knows for sure, but people usually look at The Mexican Mafia as the oldest Latino gang here in the United States. They originated in the prisons in California. The Mexican Mafia became known as Sureños because they were mostly from cities in the southern parts of the state.

Supposedly, they started as a defense against the white and black inmates, but soon they became so big that they were ruling all the *pintas*."

Betania furrowed her brow.

Overlooking her confusion, Mr. Alvarez continued speaking, "On the outside, when inmates left, they continued to recruit. It didn't take long for the Mexican Mafia to become the most feared gang out there. They called all the shots. They had the prisons, they had the streets, they had the drugs, and they had the money. But just as they had united and rebelled against the whites and the blacks, others united against them."

Betania remained silent, her eyes a study in concentration.

"The biggest threat to the Mexican Mafia came from within. Members who were recent immigrants from Mexico, or who lived in the small farming towns, were tired of being looked down on and abused, so they formed their own gang and called it La Nuestra Familia. They became known as Norteños because they were mostly field workers from central and northern California."

Betania leaned forward in her chair, somewhat surprised by her counselor's professorial tone.

"At first, the Mexican Mafia did not take La Nuestra Familia very seriously, but as their membership grew, the Mexican Mafia openly declared war on them. These two gangs became bitter rivals in the prisons and all through California. Then, just as these two gangs were battling for control, a new wave of Hispanic immigrants poured into southern California—the Central Americans. They were fleeing from the wars and poverty of their countries, but when they settled in places like Los Angeles, they were easy prey. But that didn't last long. Those guys were tough. As their numbers grew, they united and fought back. They called themselves the Mara Salvatrucha, and they could be as vicious and merciless as any gang out there."

Betania nodded.

"Do you know what all this has to do with us over here?"

Betania shook her head.

"Gangs spread and splinter, and when you study them like I do, the pattern is obvious."

"What do you mean?"

"Guys who got incarcerated in California, but who were originally from Texas, talked a little differently. The inmates knew they weren't from around there. They singled them out, which led to anyone from Texas banding together. That's how the Texas Syndicate got started."

Betania began to rub her forehead. "I don't understand! I thought the Texas Syndicate was for the immigrants who came here from Mexico!"

Mr. Alvarez tightened his lips. His face then broke into a somewhat sympathetic smile. "Betania, that's what I'm trying to get through to you. It's not like that. In fact, when the Texas Syndicate was formed, they had white members, too. It wasn't until they got more established that they limited their membership to Mexicans."

"So the TS isn't for the immigrants?" asked Betania.

"In a way, yes. But they're no different than any other gang," replied Mr. Alvarez. "They start out defending themselves in prison, or on some street in a neighborhood, but then they end up doing the same things as all the rest. Sure, they all say they're about family and protection. They all promise to take care of you, but that's just how they recruit kids and convert them into criminals. Gangs like the Texas Syndicate and the Mexikanemi are not fighting over race or pride, they're fighting over control!"

"Control?" said Betania. "Control of what?"

"Control of the drug trades, control of the prostitution rings, control over guns. Whatever means they can find to gain power."

Betania turned away. She stared at the many plaques hanging on the wall. Most of them were comprised of various awards granted to Mr. Alvarez.

"It goes real deep, *mija*. Gangs, drug cartels, organized crime. It's a **conundrum** of hatred and violence that hasn't been solved by the police or even the armies of the United States and Mexico!"

A brief silence followed. Betania's eyes shifted before finally resting on the brown face of Mr. Alvarez.

"Now do you understand what I'm telling you? None of this has anything to do with you or your little neighborhood in Brownsville, or next door in Los Fresnos, or Harlingen. It all goes back to the prison system and the drug cartels."

Betania began to speak but was interrupted by the sound of the phone. Mr. Alvarez turned but once more allowed it to ring. "I think I'm taking too much of your time, Mr. Alvarez," said Betania. "I better leave."

"No, no," he replied. "This is important, and you're worth it. Anyway, I was about done. Is there anything you want to say?"

"Not really," said Betania, getting up out of her seat. She hesitated. Finally, she said, "Don't worry, Mr. Alvarez. I'm not into those things, and neither are my friends."

Mr. Alvarez held up his hand as Betania reached for the door. "*Mija*, wait! I want you to see this." He pulled up his right sleeve, revealing a tattoo of the number thirteen in roman numerals. "This is how we did it on 18th street." Then, turning his arm around, he displayed his elbow. "See those three dots? You know what they mean?"

Betania shook her head.

"They stand for *Mi Vida Loca*. They also stand for where you're going to end up if you're a gang member. The hospital, prison, or the grave."

Betania nodded, opened the door, and quietly slipped away.

18

THE RED NUMBERS of the digital clock glowed in the darkness of the bedroom Betania shared with her sister. It was almost midnight. Finally, the door opened. Betania, dressed in her nightgown, sat up in her bed. "Pamela! I've been waiting for you all night!"

Pamela nearly stumbled. "Damn! You scared me! Why aren't you asleep?"

"I need to talk to you!" continued Betania, her voice brimming with excitement. "Where have you been all day?"

"Out," said Pamela flatly. She opened a few drawers, threw her clothes on the floor, and then quickly changed. "What's your problem? You're so emotional!"

"It's about the TS!" said Betania.

"Oh, hell no!" Pamela replied. She then tore off the top blanket on her bed and noisily lay down, struggling to get inside the sheets. "Don't even start! I already told you that you can hang out with us, but nothing more!"

"No, no, it's not like that," said Betania.

"Then what are you talking about?"

A knock was heard on the door.

"*Qué?*" shouted Pamela loudly.

"*Soy yo,*" replied their father. "*Siempre has estado allí, Pamela?*"

"*Sí, por supuesto!*"

"*Bueno pues, buenas noches.*"

"Yeah! Yeah! *Buenas noches!*" shouted Pamela. Then, after a brief pause, she added, "Man! *Me cae tan mal ese viejo!*"

"Pamela!" said Betania. "You shouldn't talk like that! Papi's just concerned."

"Whatever," said Pamela. "Anyway, I'm really tired, so I'll talk to you tomorrow."

"No, wait," said Betania. "I have to tell you what Mr. Alvarez said!"

Pamela released a loud cackle. "That drop out! I can't stand that guy!"

"Listen!" said Betania. "He told me all about the gangs, the origins and everything!"

"The ori—the what?" asked Pamela.

"Origins!" said Betania. "If you would go to school you'd know that word."

"Whatever," said Pamela. "School's boring. Look, I'm tired, so say what you gotta say!"

"He told me all about the history of the gangs! He explained it all! It's not what you think! The gangs aren't about helping us; they're all tied to the prisons and drugs!" Betania paused. Then, in a serious tone, she continued, "I think I finally understand why *papi* brought us here. I've always resented him for doing it, but now I see. It was for us. It's always been for us. *Papi* sacrificed so we could go to a nice school in Veracruz. And he sacrificed so that he could bring us here and have a better life."

Pamela huffed. "Yeah, some better life! *Mira*, Beti, Alvarez can go to hell for all I care! He's nothing but a drop out that goes around preaching to everyone! He got all religious! He's old school. He doesn't know what's going on anymore. And *papá*, please, he's just a *pinche* cook."

"I think you should have more respect for *papi*," said Betania.

"I ain't trippin'."

"Then at least talk to Mr. Alvarez," said Betania.

"Don't you think I've talked with him?" growled Pamela, her voice tinged with anger. "That guy gets on my nerves."

"Why do you say that?" asked Betania.

"He just does, okay!"

"But if you don't like Mr. Alvarez, then why are you telling me not to get involved in the TS?"

"It's got nothing to do with him!" said Pamela.

"Then why?"

Pamela turned in her bed and put her pillow over her head. Silence ensued. Then, quietly, Betania heard her sister's voice. "Because maybe I don't want you to end up like me."

Removing her covers, Betania stood up and walked over to her sister's bed. She began to stroke Pamela's bare shoulder.

"What are you doing?" asked Pamela, removing her pillow.

Betania observed Pamela's face. There was moisture on her cheeks. Betania then attempted to hug her sister, but Pamela pushed her away so violently that Betania fell to the floor.

"Get away from me!" screamed Pamela.

Startled, Betania replied, "Okay, sorry."

"Now go to sleep! I mean it!"

Betania slowly returned to her bed.

19

SOMETHING HAD CHANGED. When Betania attempted to speak to her sister and her friends, they greeted her quickly and then proceeded to ignore her. As much as that hurt her, she felt the most pain when Jorge became distant as well.

Betania was an outsider. Her loneliness led her to befriend some of her classmates. Jim Molina, especially, appeared happy. A clean shaven boy with soft white cheeks, he was intelligent and even quite thoughtful, but Betania still found herself thinking of Jorge. Sometimes, she purposely walked past the bathroom where he stayed with his friends. On occasion, she accomplished eye contact, but nothing else. Jorge no longer waited for her after school. Betania missed him.

As the school year came to an end, Betania had raised her grades, easily passing her classes. Pamela, however, did not graduate. The school released her and informed her in no uncertain terms that she was not welcome to return.

During summer vacation, Betania usually thought of rest and relaxation. But this time she had her eyes set on something else. She deeply desired to return to Veracruz to see her grandmother and to visit her tía Lydia.

"*No hay problema, hija!*" said her father, delighted with her decision. "*Puedes trabajar conmigo en el restaurante!*"

"*Gracias, papi,*" said Betania, hugging his neck tightly.

"*Está muy bien. Siempre necesitamos una mesera linda como tú!*"

"*Ay, papi,*" said Betania, slightly blushing. "*Usted lo dice porque soy su hija.*"

"*No, Betania,*" said her father, "*te lo digo porque es cierto.*"

Betania instantly became very popular working with her father. Between her attractive appearance and sweet demeanor, customers adored her and showered her with tips. Her father had to remind some of them that she was his daughter when they became a little *too* friendly. At the end of each day, Betania carefully guarded her money in a small jewelry box that she kept inside her top dresser drawer.

20

THE SUMMER WAS waning and Betania had reached her goal. Sitting on her bed, she counted a pile of bills and loose coins with a marked glee on her face. She then carefully began to place the money into a large wooden jewelry box. Unexpectedly, Pamela entered the bedroom. Betania glanced at her, and something in her sister's eyes caused her to flinch. She quickly angled her body, giving her back to Pamela.

Peeking over Betania's shoulder, Pamela exclaimed, "Wow!" Her eyes darted back and forth. "You must have a lot of game!"

"Huh?"

"Forget it," said Pamela, laughing.

"Well, see you later," said Betania. "I want to tell papi that I did it!"

"Did what?"

Betania did not bother to explain. She quickly closed the lid of her jewelry box and carried it out of her bedroom and straight to the family room. There, both of her parents were sitting together on a black couch, facing the television in silence.

"*Papi, lo hice!*" exclaimed Betania in triumph.

Her father arched his eyebrows. "*Mande?*"

"*Guardé todo mi dinero que gané con usted! Y con las propinas, tengo más de lo que yo necesitaba para el boleto!* Voy a Veracruz!*"

"*Sí? Tan rápido?*" asked Betania's father.

Betania's mother stood and embraced her. "*Felicidades, hija! Pero tenemos que hablar! Nunca has viajado sola!*"

"*No se preocupe, mamá! Tengo diecisiete años y de todos modos, tía Lydia se va a encontrar conmigo en el aeropuerto.*"

As Betania and her parents began discussing the arrangements, Pamela suddenly appeared. "*Yo quiero ir!*"

The room became quiet.

"*Mande?*" replied el señor Solíz, a slight smile on his face.

"*Yo quiero ir a Veracruz también,*" repeated Pamela.

El señor Solíz laughed. La señora Solíz shook her head as she pressed her lips tightly together.

"*Qué? Qué les pasa?*" asked Pamela, lowering her brow.

"*Qué muchachita más necia!*" said el señor Solíz between laughter. "*Tú, que no trabajas, que no me haces caso, y que ni te graduaste de la escuela, y ahora crees que voy a permitir.... No, aún peor, esperas que yo pague por el viaje, verdad? Porque yo sé que no tienes ni un peso y tú crees que yo voy a permitir que vayas a Veracruz? Estás loca!*"

As el señor Solíz continued laughing, Pamela scowled, then quickly headed for the door, slamming it behind her.

"*Y no vuelvas!*" shouted el señor Solíz. "*Estoy harto de tí y todos los pandilleros que llamas tus amigos!*"

"*No digas eso,*" said la señora Solíz. She opened the door and turned on the porch light. Pamela had disappeared into the night.

21

FRANTICALLY THROWING CLOTHES from her dresser onto the floor, a terrible dread overwhelmed Betania. She touched the thin wood of the drawer, dreamily hoping that the box would magically appear. "It's gone! It's gone!" cried Betania. "My jewelry box is gone!"

"*Qué pasó, hija?*" asked Betania's mother, running into the bedroom.

"*Todo el dinero que guardé para mi viaje desapareció!*" screamed Betania.

Betania's mother shrugged her shoulders and winced. "*Tal vez tu padre lo cogió?*"

"*No, mami, él nunca entra nuestro cuarto,*" replied Betania.

La señora Solíz reached into each of Betania's drawers and began moving her hands through each one. Betania breathed heavily, watching her mother's every movement. Suddenly, she exclaimed, "Pamela!"

22

THE NEXT DAY arrived and still there was no sign of Pamela. Several days later, the Solíz family received a phone call from tía Lydia. "*Lo siento tanto, Betania,*" said tía Lydia. "*No sé todos los detalles, pero entiendo que Pamela anda por acá.*"

Betania tried to answer, but instead burst into tears.

"*No, no, mi niña, no llores. Nos vemos en otra ocasión cuando ustedes arreglen todo.*"

Betania ended the call. Her mother hugged her gently. "*Qué pena,*" she said softly while holding onto Betania. "*Si yo tuviera el dinero, te lo daría, pero es mucho y tú sabes que acabamos de comprar un coche nuevo.*"

23

WHILE PAMELA TRAVELED throughout Mexico, Betania remained restless within her home. Lying comfortably in a pink blouse, white shorts, and sandals while sprawled across the living room couch, she numbly watched television. With a large black remote control in her hand, she perpetually changed channels. After nearly an hour, she exhaled deeply and threw the remote down. Next, she walked over to a large metal stereo that stood close to the television. Turning various knobs, she went back and forth in search of something that reflected her mood. Fluctuating between English and Spanish, she could find nothing that held her attention for more than a few minutes.

Betania's mother walked out of the kitchen with a damp cloth in her hand. In a gentle tone, she asked, *"Qué te pasa, hija?"*

Without saying a word, Betania frowned, stood up, and left the house. She walked down the old cement sidewalk of her street, thoughts of anger racing through her head. *"How could Pamela have gotten away with it? After all my hard work! It's not fair! She's not so tough. I'll show her. I'll show everyone!"*

When Betania looked up, she was standing in front of Vanessa's house. She lingered, staring at the reddish walls of the old house. She took a few steps up the white path that led to the front door. Once again, she hesitated. Then, slowly, she reached up and knocked on the door. A small boy answered, followed quickly by Vanessa. Betania was ushered inside. After a brief conversation, the two girls embraced.

"Let me call some of the girls!" said Vanessa. "Wait here! My parents are working. It's just Tito and me, so we might as well get this over with. I'll put him in my room and turn on some cartoons. He won't bother us."

Betania nodded as Vanessa took her little brother by the hand and led him away. Within minutes, three other girls had arrived.

"Okay, Beti, this is how it works," said Vanessa. "You're going in our garage with Rosa, Vickie, and Claudia. They're going to jump you in. I'm going to count to ten. When I'm done, it's official."

Betania nodded. She knew the girls were her friends. She had also witnessed them, along with her sister, initiate another girl while inside the school bathroom. They had slapped her around a bit, but that was all. Betania was more than sure that she could handle it.

As the girls entered the empty garage, Betania could feel the extreme heat of the stale, dusty air. It was dark, and even after Vanessa flicked a light switch, Betania could still barely make out the images of tools on the side walls, a washer and dryer unit, and a pile of old boxes.

"Walk to the middle," said Vanessa. Each of the girls followed her command, quickly forming a circle around Betania. Vanessa then said, *"Listas? Okay, dale!"*

Without warning, they struck! At first, Betania did not protect herself because she thought that they would go easy on her. But she was wrong. She had expected a few shoves and slaps, but the girls were actually punching her with their fists, the blows landing from all angles. Betania could faintly hear the voice of Vanessa. "…five, four, three…"

As the jolt of real pain surged through her body, Betania covered her face and slumped to the ground. But instead of relenting, the girls began kicking her. It seemed as if the beating would last forever, but just when Betania thought that she had reached her limit, Vanessa shouted, *"Ya! Ya! Basta! Ya Paren!"*

The girls stopped. Betania could hear their heavy breathing. She was then aware of her own sniffling.

"Beti, it's okay," said Rosa. "You did it. We're done."

Scared and dazed, Betania was slow to respond. Tears freely rolled down her cheeks, blood trickled down her nose, and her mascara smeared across her face.

"From now on, you're our sister," said Vanessa as she put her arms around Betania and helped her to her feet. *"Somos familia.* If you ever need us, we'll be there for you. And if we ever need you, you have to be there for us, too."

Betania nodded.

"Come on, Beti," said Rosa, "let me help you clean up. You don't want to go home looking like that."

24

BETANIA FELT LIBERATED. Pamela's large shadow was no longer hovering around her. Betania was just as important as Pamela. She had a boyfriend just like Pamela. She was accepted just like Pamela. They were equals.

"Buenos días, señora Solíz," greeted Jorge as he got out of his car, a blackish gray sedan with patches of missing paint. *"Cómo está usted?"*

La señora Solíz, a dark wicker basket in one hand and metal clippers in the other, knelt down to clip roses from the small flower garden in front of the house. She continued her work as she replied, *"Muy bien, Jorge. No te he visto por mucho tiempo."*

"Sí, señora," replied Jorge. *"Estoy ayudando a mi papá. El lleva cosas en su troca."*

"El maneja un camión grande?"

"Sí, es grandísimo!" replied Jorge.

La señora Solíz nodded. She laid her basket, which was full of an array of colored roses, on the ground. *"Bueno, voy a decirle a Betania que la estás esperando."*

Jorge waited in silence as la señora Solíz entered the house. Soon thereafter, Betania appeared, casually dressed in tan shorts, sandals, and a white sleeveless blouse.

"Wow!" said Jorge. "You look so beautiful! Like an angel!"

Betania smiled shyly. "You always say that."

"Because it's true! Hey, I have a little money and thought we could grab something to eat."

"Sure, yeah," replied Betania.

Jorge held his car door open for Betania. She smiled, slipped into her seat, and then fastened her seatbelt. Jorge jogged around to the other side, sat down, and then dropped his right hand. He opened his palm, and Betania quickly placed her hand inside his.

"You hungry?" asked Jorge.

"A little bit."

"How does Dairy Queen™ sound?"

"Good."

Jorge continued until they arrived at the familiar white and red building. As they parked, Betania loosened her seatbelt and began to open the door. "No, let me," said Jorge. He walked around the car and opened her door for her.

"Gracias," said Betania.

"De nada," replied Jorge.

Once inside, they ordered hamburgers, sodas and fries. They then sat down, placing their food around them. "So, have you heard from Pamela?" asked Jorge.

Betania frowned. "No, but my father said she's in big trouble. I don't think he even wants her to live with us, but he always says that when he's angry."

"Yeah, that was really messed up what she did to you. Even Francisco said so."

Betania smiled. "What did he say?"

"Well, at first he laughed," replied Jorge. He then released a loud chuckle of his own. "Sorry, but Francisco laughed so hard that it makes me laugh when I think about it. Then he, uh, called her some stuff, and, uh, said that he was going to have a serious talk with her, especially now that you're a *carnala*."

"Is that all?" asked Betania.

"Uh, then he said he couldn't believe she took off like that. Then he called her some more names. Then he said he missed her."

"I don't miss her at all!" said Betania.

"Oh, you don't mean that," said Jorge.

"Yes, I do!"

"No, you don't."

Betania smiled. Jorge smiled as well. He then grabbed several of Betania's French fries.

"So, can you believe we only have one year left before graduation?" asked Betania.

"Yeah, I guess."

"Have you ever thought of what you are going to do after high school?" asked Betania.

"Not really," said Jorge. He continued to take Betania's French fries. "I might try to drive a truck like my old man. How 'bout you?"

"Yes, actually, I have. I want to be a doctor someday, so I may study here at one of the universities, or maybe even back in Veracruz so that I can work with my *tía*," replied Betania.

Jorge nodded. He reached for the few French fries that remained. Betania furrowed her brow and promptly slapped his hand.

"Who's your tía?" asked Jorge.

"Tía Lydia! She's a doctor!" gushed Betania. "And she's amazing! I want to be just like her!"

"Beti, that's great and all, but I don't know."

"Don't know what?"

"Well, you're with the TS now. You can't just make big plans like that and take off somewhere."

Betania frowned. "What are you talking about?"

"I don't know. Maybe it's okay. I guess it depends on what the others think."

Betania cocked her head back. "Are you saying that I need their permission?"

Jorge shrugged his shoulders. "Hey, there's a party tomorrow night. The *carnales* told me they got a really nice home."

"Really?"

"Yeah, some guy named Hilario. His parents are gone for the weekend. It's at six o'clock. Can I pick you up?"

"Yeah, sure," said Betania half-heartedly.

25

THE FIRST TIME Betania attended a party held by the Texas Syndicate, nothing had seemed out of the ordinary. In many ways, it resembled any one of the many gatherings she had shared with family and friends. There was food. There was music. There was dancing. Betania had seen the outside. When she excused herself from Jorge to use the restroom, she finally saw the inside. Throughout the large home, sprawled across the sofas and even the carpeted floors, were many of the local officers. Several girls surrounded them. Betania observed them carefully. Many appeared very young. A few of them were moving their heads slowly, dreamily, with glazed eyes. Bottles of alcohol lay on the floor, on top of counters, tables. Smoke filled the room, creating a hazy cloud. A stench emerged.

Inside was different than outside. Inside, Betania saw older men with girls younger than herself. Inside, people were openly drinking, smoking, and swallowing pills while half-naked. Outside was a fantasy; inside was reality. The thought of it made Betania sick to her stomach. As she quickly left the bathroom, she found Jorge, grabbed him by the arm and whispered, "Come on, let's go."

"What?" Jorge replied. "Come on, Beti, it's only, like, nine o'clock. What's the matter?"

"I just don't feel good."

"Yeah, you look a little sick," said Jorge. "I noticed you didn't eat much."

"I'm having second thoughts."

"What do you mean?"

"Take me home, please," replied Betania.

Jorge let out a sigh of resignation. "Okay, let's go."

They clasped hands and walked through a side patio to the front of the home. There, Betania saw a small group of boys and girls talking. In the middle of them was Francisco. She greeted him warmly.

Francisco turned slowly and smiled. "*Hola, Beti, que tal? Cuándo regresa mi Loca para atrás? La extraño!*"

Betania opened her mouth to answer, but stopped when a black Ford Expedition™ pulled up to the front of the curb. Dark tinted windows lowered and then a voice called out. "Hey! Which one of you is Francisco?"

The atmosphere suddenly became tense. A few boys turned to Francisco.

"Beti, walk slowly to me," whispered Jorge.

She looked at him, but hesitated.

"Who wants to know?" shouted Francisco, extending his arms.

"La Emi! That's who, fool!"

Gun shots filled the air. Jorge quickly ran in front of Betania, knocking her to the ground and falling on top of her. Betania strained to see Francisco. He was reaching into his pants. He then pulled out a black revolver. More shots were heard as Francisco fell to the ground. Then, the sound of screeching tires was replaced by the sound of screams. Amidst the chaos, people ran in all directions. Some pulled out guns and fired them at the black vehicle which sped quickly away. Others lay on the ground, covering their heads. Betania attempted to speak, but was unable to do so. Jorge, too, was quiet. He remained on top of her in a warm, protective embrace. Betania could feel the weight of his small frame and the soft skin of his cheek firmly planted on her own.

A boy whom Betania had never seen before ran toward her and Jorge. "*Todos bien?*"

"*Sí, gracias,*" Betania replied, barely able to release the words. "*Jorge me salvó.*"

"Okay, okay. I'm gonna check on Francisco. They got him!"

A shiver of fear tingled in Betania's face, neck, and shoulders. She opened her mouth, forcing herself to suck in the warm humid air. "Jorge, it's okay. I'm fine. You can let go now. Go check on Francisco!"

But Jorge did not answer. Betania shook him and repeated his name, but he remained still. It was then that Betania felt moisture on her breast and stomach. She rolled Jorge off of her. His body fell limply to the side. Betania screamed. A girl knelt down next to her. It was Rosa. Soon, others gathered to her side. A few of them touched Jorge. He did not move. Betania felt a huge knot form in her throat. Then, turning to her, a boy said, "*Jorge está muerto!*"

26

BETANIA COULD NOT sleep. She could not eat. When a funeral service was held for Jorge, it was the first time she had bathed in days. Held at a small church, there was standing room only.

Most members of the Texas Syndicate sat in the back pews and kept a respectful distance. At the end of the service, Betania was one of the few who approached the open casket. She looked at the small, gentle face. Jorge looked as if he were asleep. Even so, Betania knew that he was gone forever. She offered her condolences to his family. As she looked at their faces, seeing their grief, she felt something beyond pain; she felt guilt.

"*Lo siento mucho,*" said Betania, embracing Jorge's mother, a small woman with long black hair that fell to her hips. "*El era tan bueno, tan dulce.*"

"*Gracias, mija,*" she replied, dabbing her eyes with a black silk handkerchief.

Slowly, two boys dressed in khaki pants and white T-shirts approached Jorge's father. "*No se preocupe, señor,*" said one. "*La familia de usted va a tener justicia muy pronto.*"

The man's face twisted quickly. "*Vete al diablo!*"

The two boys took a step closer. "*Cuíde esa boca, viejo!*" said one, extending his index finger.

"*Venimos en paz!*" said the other.

"*Déjenlo!*" came forth a gravelly voice from within the crowd.

The two boys immediately walked away. As they did so, a man who appeared to be in his late twenties approached Betania and the parents of Jorge. Without an introduction, Betania knew who he was.

"Hello, Beti. I need to speak with you."

He spoke with such a deep calm that Betania felt fear creep up from inside her. Unlike most of the others, he was dressed well, wearing black slacks and an orange collared shirt. His head was shaved to the point that his hair was nothing more than a dark shadow. Betania tried to avoid eye contact, but could not help but peak at his face. She noticed the potholes and acne, appearing everywhere except for the places covered by his unkempt black goatee. On his neck was a large spider's web that Betania found particularly ominous.

"I'm Antonio Castañeda."

"Hello," said Betania. She tilted her head downward, over her right shoulder, staring at the tile floor of the little church.

"Please, come with me."

Betania nodded. They walked toward the front entrance. "After you," said Antonio, opening the door for her. Together, they descended the white cement steps of the church, passing a small statue of Saint Peter.

"We're hoping Francisco is going to come out of this," continued Antonio. "We put out a contract on the guys who shot him. They're hiding right now like the *cobardes que son*, but we'll find them. Don't worry. We won't forget Jorge. We take care of our own."

"How is Francisco?" asked Betania.

"He's okay. He took two bullets to the gut, but he'll make it. He'll be out soon and when he does, he'll be better than ever."

Betania dared to look directly into Antonio's eyes. They were brown like hers, yet different. They were cold. They were hard. They were made of steel.

"I know you were Jorge's girl, so I issued the order to let you have the honor to make things right. Vanessa will tell you what to do. After you've done this, you'll be advanced. I had plans for your sister, but I'll be honest with you; she's too emotional. Too reckless. We can't depend on her. I like you, Beti. I like your character. Francisco told me you're a smart girl, but he never told me how pretty you are."

Antonio bent over, moved Betania's long brown hair to the side, and gave her a kiss on the cheek. It repulsed her and sent a shiver down her spine. It felt evil, but Betania dared not resist. Antonio frightened her to death with his voice alone. As he left to enter a dark gray car with tinted windows, Vanessa approached.

"Hold out your hand," she said quietly.

Betania shrugged.

"I said hold out your hand," Vanessa repeated. "Come on, do it before people start looking."

Betania did so, and Vanessa promptly dropped a razor blade into her palm. "It's for the girlfriend of the boy who shot Jorge. Her name's Iris. We know where she lives."

Betania stood staring at Vanessa, dazed.

"The boys take care of the boys and the girls take care of the girls. That's the way it's done. Be at my house at one o'clock tomorrow."

Betania nodded, still holding the razor blade loosely in her hand.

27

A SMALL CIRCLE of girls gathered together on the edge of the front lawn. As they did so, they nodded to each other. A certain intensity added to the heat and humidity, causing small beads of sweat to form on their faces. Nobody spoke when an old burgundy colored van slowly came to a stop directly in front of them.

Poking her head out of the window, Vanessa said, "Get in. Beti, you sit in the front with me."

Betania nodded and opened the front door on the passenger side. As the other girls settled into the back, Vanessa continued, "We're going straight to her house. We'll be right behind you, so don't worry. She takes care of her little brothers and sisters, so nobody else will be in the house except for those little kids."

"Little kids?" repeated Betania.

"Yeah."

"But we're not going to…?"

"Of course not!" said Vanessa, shaking her head. "Damn, Beti!"

"So is this ours?" asked Rosa.

"It is today," replied Vanessa as she slowly drove off and headed down the street.

Leaning forward toward Betania, Rosa asked her, "Have you been in contact with Pamela?"

"No," replied Betania. "I tried, but my aunt said that she did not know where she was. I think she's still in Veracruz."

"Yeah, that's Pamela," said Vicki. "She's probably partying somewhere!"

"Does she even know about Francisco?" asked Claudia.

"*Quién sabe…*" replied Betania.

Claudia shook her head. "We could definitely use her right now."

"Look, Beti, Iris knows us," interrupted Vanessa, "so you have to knock on the door by yourself. We're going to wait until she opens it and then we'll all rush her. We'll hold her down, but don't worry, you'll get the first cut. We wouldn't take that away from you."

"Go for her throat," said Vicki.

Betania nodded, but her stomach churned to such an extent that she feared she would vomit. When they arrived at their destination, Vanessa calmly parked the van on the side of the road beneath the shade of a large tree. "Put the razor in your shoe," she ordered. "Her house is that white one with that crappy torn up brown grass in the front."

Some of the girls laughed. Betania looked at Vanessa, nodded, and proceeded out of the car. She slowly walked toward the small house. There was no fence, and just as the girls predicted, there were no cars parked in the driveway. As Betania walked closer, she looked around the quiet street. It was early in the afternoon and the horrible Texas heat had forced everyone indoors. It was quietoo quiet. Too quiet. Betania could hear her own breathing and the pounding of her heart. The others followed her at a slight distance. When Betania walked up the cement steps to the front door, Vanessa motioned with her right hand for the other girls to stand to the sides of the house. Betania looked back. Vanessa was holding a knife. "Go on!" she hissed.

Betania nodded. She reached down and felt the razor hidden within her shoe. Gently, she allowed her fingertips to grab the ends, careful not to touch the actual blade. She placed it in her left hand, rubbing the cold metal sides. Slowly, she lifted her right hand, extended her knuckles toward the wooden door, and stopped.

"No," said a voice.

Betania paused. She looked at Vanessa. Her mouth was closed. Betania looked at the other girls. They seemed tense, but no one had said a word. Once more, Betania raised her hand to knock, and once more, she heard the same voice vibrate deep within her. "No."

The sound of the word became so loud that Betania began repeating it over and over again. "No...no...no...no..." She walked down the steps and returned to the van with her head down. Each girl quickly followed her.

"What the hell are you doing?" growled Vanessa.

Betania said nothing, but instead looked down at the pavement.

"Hey!" Vanessa hissed, grabbing Betania by the shoulder. "I'm talking to you!"

Betania remained silent. She looked at the other girls. They looked confused as well.

"Beti, what happened?" Vicki asked.

Betania's eyes began to tear up. "I—I can't."

"*Ay Dios! Oye estúpida! Tienes que hacerlo!*" said Vanessa, grabbing Betania by the arm and yanking her back and forth sharply.

"Vanessa! Stop!" said Rosa. She put her hand on Betania's shoulder. "Is it too early?"

"*Cállate*, Rosa!" said Vanessa, her hand still placed firmly on Betania's bicep.

"I'm just saying that she's still thinking about Jorge!" said Rosa.

"Then she should be filled with hate for that girl!" replied Vanessa. "Do it, Beti! Do it for Jorge! Come on! You have to! You don't have a choice! If we fail Antonio..."

Vanessa stopped. Betania looked at her and saw the same expression of fear on her face that she had once seen on her sister.

"I'm sorry," said Betania, "but I can't."

"You guys are too loud!" said Vicki. "Let's go! Someone's gonna see us!"

Vanessa scowled. She pushed Betania away from her. "Okay, get in the back with Rosa. Claudia, you sit in the front. We'll tell Antonio that Iris wasn't home. Remember, Beti, this is for Jorge. If you really loved him then you'll kill this girl!"

"Vanessa," began Betania, "I don't know..."

"Antonio's here!" interrupted Vanessa. "Don't you get it? You don't have a choice. You have to at least try! If you don't, then we're still going to get her...and you."

28

BETANIA SPENT THE entire day in her room. The next day was more of the same. She left only to eat something and then returned quickly. She refused to speak to anyone or answer the phone. As she lay on her bed, alone in the darkness, the door slowly opened. A slight figure entered and sat on the side of her bed. "*No llores, hija,*" said her mother. "*No quiero verte tan triste.*"

Betania frowned. In an angry tone that sounded more like her sister than the typical sound of her own sweet voice, she replied, "*Por qué le importa, mamá?*"

"*Qué tipo de pregunta es esta? Te amo.*"

Wiping her tears, Betania muttered, "*Mami, no merezco tu amor.*"

Her mother stroked her forehead. Betania closed her eyes, and then scooted over to make room for her mother. La señora Solíz responded naturally, pulling the covers over her and lying down next to Betania. She then put her thick arms around Betania, and the two cuddled tightly under the sheets. "*Mija, yo sé que es duro. Jorge era muy bueno.*"

An overwhelming feeling of hopelessness consumed Betania. Her sadness only deepened with the mention of Jorge. "*Mami,*" began Betania, "*es cierto que me siento muy triste por lo que pasó, pero hay más.*"

"*Sí, como qué?*"

"*Mami, si le digo la verdad, me promete que no me va a odiar?*"

"*Betania,*" replied her mother. "*Siempre te voy a amar. Dime.*"

Taking a deep breath, Betania continued, "*Mami, me metí en una pandilla igual que Pamela.*"

La señora Solíz stopped caressing Betania's forehead. A brief silence followed. *"Betania, no! De Pamela, era de esperarse, pero tú?"*

"Espere mami, todavía no he terminado," continued Betania. *"Las amigas de Pamela querían que yo lastimara a otra muchacha—la novia del muchacho que mató a Jorge—y cuando les dije que no, me dijeron que iban a hacerme daño!"*

Betania's mother held her closely. *"No te preocupes, hija. Le diremos todo a tu papá. No vamos a permitir que ellas te toquen ni un pelo."*

"No, mami, no!" said Betania. Her tears began to flow more freely.

"Tenemos que hacerlo. Es por tu propio bien, hija."

29

As soon as her father had left for work, Betania and her mother walked carefully around the house. They locked each door and pulled together the window curtains. The lights were turned off and the phone was disconnected. The silence was deafening.

By midafternoon, Betania joined her mother in the kitchen. They exchanged glances, but said nothing. When Betania placed a glass of milk on the table, it seemed to echo throughout the kitchen. She stood still, watching her mother stir the soup she was preparing. She could hear the wooden spoon make contact with the metal pot. Suddenly, a knock was heard on the front door.

"We know you're in there, Beti!" called out a loud voice.

Betania made eye contact with her mother and shook her head. "Vanessa," she whispered.

"Come on, we just want to talk!" continued the shouting from outside.

Betania raised her index finger to her lips. Her mother refrained from moving the wooden spoon in her hand. Betania, barely able to breathe, nodded in approval. The sound of several girls pounding the door continued to resonate throughout the house. "Beti, it's me, Rosa, just let me in—only me—I promise."

Betania liked Rosa. Unlike the others, there was a certain tenderness about her eyes. Betania took a step toward the front door, but her mother shook her head forcefully. Several minutes passed, and the shouting continued.

"Beti, we're here to help you! You better answer before it's too late!"

"*Debemos llamar a la policía,*" whispered Betania's mother.

"*No, mami, ya te dije que no!*" said Betania. "*Son mis amigas y las amigas de Pamela. Tarde o temprano me van a dejar en paz.*"

"*Hija, estás segura?*"

"*Sí, mami.*"

30

EACH DAY BETANIA and her mother followed the same routine. Slowly, the knocking on the door came to a halt. But that did not give Betania any reassurance. She felt like a prisoner, unable to leave the house, unable to tell anyone how she felt, and unable to feel at ease.

Late in the evening, while sitting with her family on the black family love seat that lay in the living room, Betania strained under the dim light of a lamp to read a book on anatomy that her aunt had sent her for her seventeenth birthday. She could hear her father's car pull up to the sidewalk. Next was the sound of his footsteps and a key opening the door lock as well as the upper deadbolt. When he finally entered, he was accompanied by a young man.

"*Betania, hay alguien que quiere hablarte,*" announced el Señor Solíz.

Her eyes instantly widened as a young man in loose fitting blue jeans and a long sleeved brown collared shirt entered behind her father. "Francisco!" Betania quickly got up, threw her book down, and wrapped her arms around him. "You're here!"

"*Tranquila, hija,*" said Betania's father, frowning at her enthusiastic display of affection.

"Easy, Beti," said Francisco, "you're going to put me right back in the hospital."

"*Siéntate, hija, y cálmate, por favor,*" said Betania's mother.

"Oh, I'm so sorry," said Betania. She released Francisco, took a few steps backward, and then noticed how much thinner he was. Slowly, she sat down on the family couch next to her mother. Her father occupied a dark leather sofa positioned to the side while Francisco remained standing.

"Beti, I don't have a lot of time," said Francisco. "Nobody can see me here. You're in trouble. We all are."

"Francisco," said Betania, "What's happening? How did you convince my father to let you in? How are you even talking to him?"

"I went to the restaurant," replied Francisco. "He didn't want nothing to do with me, but I told him I love Pamela and that you're like a sister to me."

"*No confiaba en él*," said Betania's father, "*pero me convenció. Me parece sincero.*"

"So, have they stopped?" asked Betania. "Have they forgiven me? I want out, Francisco, I want out! It was a mistake! I never should have joined! I should have listened to Pamela! And now, when I need her the most, she's not even here."

"They haven't stopped," said Francisco. "They just decided to wait."

"Francisco," said Betania between sobs, "you're an officer! Can't you stop them?"

Francisco shook his head. "No, Beti, I can't. I'm not that high up and even if I was, it's against the rules."

Betania cried louder, covering her face. Her mother embraced her. Her father stood up and approached Francisco. "*Qué le hiciste a mis hijas? Qué has hecho?*"

Francisco pressed his lips together and inclined his head. "*Lo siento, señor Solíz.*"

Betania's father raised his hand and pointed his index finger menacingly at Francisco. "*Me dijiste que ibas a ayudarla! A lo mejor llamo a la policía y te lleva a la carcel!*"

"*Cálmate, Eduardo, él está aquí para ayudarnos*," said Betania's mother.

"You're not going to do anything?" asked Betania, wiping the tears from her eyes.

"I can't stop them," replied Francisco, "but that doesn't mean I want it to happen. I've been talking to Pamela. She was about to come back, but I told her to stay."

"But what does that have to do with me?" asked Betania.

"The reason nobody's come to your house is because I lied to them," said Francisco. "I convinced them to let me take you out myself. I told them it would serve as an example."

Betania's eyes widened. Her father understood enough to curse loudly.

"Mentí por ustedes!" said Francisco.

Betania stood up from the couch. "Francisco, *no te entiendo*! *No entiendo nada*!"

"Ni yo tampoco!" added Betania's mother.

"I lied to buy you time," said Francisco. His brow lowered, and his eyes seemed to be pleading with Betania. "It was all I could do. They were going to hurt you, and they weren't going to let your parents get in the way. They already killed two guys and some girl."

"Iris," whispered Betania.

Francisco nodded. "Yeah, that's her name."

"Malditos pandilleros!" said Betania's father. *"Son muchachitos que se creen hombres! Jugando con pistolas y cuchillos! Todos son malvados! Están malditos!"*

Francisco shook his head and curled his lips. "I'm leaving for Mexico in a few days, but you and your family have to watch yourselves. If I were you, I'd pack my bags and leave, too."

"Francisco, summer is almost over!" replied Betania. "What do I do? I can't stay in my house forever!"

"No vamos a huir!" interrupted Betania's father as he combed back the small brown patches of hair that remained on his balding head. Betania's mother stood up and embraced him. *"Venimos acá para escapar la violencia de México,"* he whispered in her ear.

Francisco nodded. *"No tiene que regresar a Veracruz, señor Solíz. Hay otras partes que son mejores. Y es así también en Tejas. Hay otras ciudades mejores."*

"El problema no es Brownsville!" replied Betania's father. He released his wife and shook his fist in Francisco's face. *"El problema es gente como tú que mete a los jóvenes inocentes en la maldad!"*

Francisco squinted. His jaw tightened. *"Si tuviera a una familia como la tuya tal vez yo sería diferente!"*

The room became quiet. Both men stood inches apart. Finally, Betania spoke up. "Please, don't argue! *Francisco no es malo, papi.*"

"Thanks, Beti," said Francisco. His countenance softened. Slowly, he began to walk toward the front door. At the entrance, he turned back to face Betania. "School may be the safest place for you right now. They might try to scare you a little, but they probably won't do much with all those kids and teachers around. Since they already got their revenge, they may forget about you." Francisco stopped. He exhaled deeply. "But I doubt it. Please, do what I said. You and your parents need to get the hell out of here."

"*Adiós*," said Betania's father, practically pushing Francisco out the door.

Betania immediately fell into her mother's arms. "*Todo por mi culpa, mami!*" she sobbed. "*Jorge. Ustedes. Yo. Todo por mi culpa!*"

31

THE WEATHER WAS a bit humid, but overall quite pleasant. None of that mattered to Betania. Led by her father and followed by her mother, she walked trepidly toward the family car.

"*Papi, por favor, no quiero ir a la escuela!*" cried Betania. "Please don't make me!"

"*Eduardo, déjala,*" said Betania's mother. "*No hay otra manera?*"

"*Ya nos fuimos corriendo una vez, Ernestina!*" said Betania's father. "*No voy a permitir que unos muchachitos nos hagan huir de nuevo. Qué quieres? Quieres que nos mudemos de nuevo? Que durmamos todos en el suelo? Que yo ruegue que alguien me de trabajo?*"

"*Pero Eduardo, ya amenazaron a Betania!*"

"*No son carteles, Ernestina!*" said Betania's father. "*No estamos hablando de los Zetas. Son unos mocosos!*"

"*No, papi, no,*" said Betania. "*No entiende!*

"*Sí, entiendo muy bien! Lo siento, hija, pero vas a ir!*" replied Betania's father. "*Sigamos con nuestras vidas! Métete en el coche, Betania. Ya hablé con la oficina de la esuela y la policía. Nada te va a pasar!*"

Reluctantly, Betania complied with her father's wishes. When they arrived at her school, her father escorted her to the front office and vowed to pick her up at the end of each day if necessary. "*Si tienes cualquier problema, ve a la oficina. Llámame y yo te recojo. Todo va a estar bien. Vas a ver.*"

His promises did little to calm Betania's fears. "*Sí, papi,*" she replied quietly.

Betania walked alone. When everything seemed ordinary, she let out a silent sigh of relief. But this did not last long; soon, her fears were realized. As she turned the corner of the science building, girls she had never seen before bumped into her and called her names.

"Please, just leave me alone," said Betania.

"Never," replied one girl.

Turning away, Betania quickened her pace. She looked nervously at the numbers above the doors until she found her classroom. Upon entering, she observed her classmates. Well-dressed, smiling, laughing. Their ignorance reminded her of earlier days when she had no knowledge of the dangers surrounding her.

"Hey, mind if I sit here before we get a seating chart?"

Betania looked behind her. It was Jim. She smiled upon seeing him.

"We're going to have a great football season this year," he continued. "I was hoping you would come and watch." He pointed to the red number on his chest. "Look, lucky number seven."

"Yes, of course," said Betania absentmindedly as she looked at the white football jersey.

"Already putting the moves on, Jim?" asked Marisol, sitting down next to them.

"Yeah, save those for the game," said Elizabeth.

"Just being friendly," said Jim.

"Number seven is my favorite number," said Amanda as she slowly moved her index finger around the border lines of the large number on Jim's jersey.

Jim smiled as his light complexion reddened slightly. "Coach said we could wear our jerseys the first day of school to promote team unity. Betania's going to come to our first game, right Betania?"

Betania opened her mouth, but no words came forth.

"I'll come to your first game," said Amanda, releasing a smile that seemed to unnerve Jim.

The two remained facing each other for a moment. Betania frowned at Amanda. Elizabeth shook her head.

"Anyway, it's good to see you, Betania," said Marisol. "How was your summer?"

"Oh, uh, fine," replied Betania.

As the class began, Betania could not help but stare at the clock. She knew that she was safe for the moment, but once the bell rang she would be thrust outside once again. Her best possibility of safety lay in staying close to her classmates.

As they walked through the hallways, from class to class, Betania could not help but feel envious of their carefree chatter. Marisol bragged about the college boy she was dating. Elizabeth stated she was sure to receive several scholarships and had not yet decided what university she would attend. Amanda talked about her family vacation in Cancún. They were oblivious to the others who stared at Betania.

"You better watch your back," called out a voice from within a crowd of girls.

Elizabeth turned toward Betania and furrowed her brow. "Was she talking to you?"

"Uh, I don't think so," said Betania. She clutched her notebook to her bosom, instinctively, as if it were a shield.

While walking to her final class before lunch, Betania felt a premonition deep within her. It was only a matter of time. They were watching. Waiting.

As her teacher spoke about the importance of democracy throughout the world, Betania was unable to maintain her concentration. Every few moments, she found herself staring at the large circular clock positioned on the side wall of the classroom. Though virtually silent, she felt as though she could hear the sound of the big hand advancing slowly, minute by minute, closer toward noon. When it finally reached the large twelve nestled at the top, a discordant buzzing sound rang forth, jolting Betania from her thoughts. She jumped from her seat, knocking her book to the floor.

"Hey, what's with you?" asked Marisol, giving Betania an odd look.

"Somebody's hungry," said Elizabeth.

Betania frowned nervously as she settled back into her desk. Jim approached her, bent down, and picked up her textbook. "Aren't you coming?"

"Oh, yes, I," Betania stuttered. "I just want to talk to the teacher for a minute."

"You want me to wait for you?" asked Jim.

"No, I'll be okay," replied Betania.

"Are you sure?"

"She said she's fine!" said Amanda, grabbing Jim by the arm and pulling him toward the door.

"Okay, we'll be at the senior table. It's ours now!" Jim replied as he and Amanda left the room. "Come and join us!"

"Yes, I will," replied Betania, knowing full well that they had not heard her.

Elizabeth hoisted a large green backpack onto her shoulder. "I hope you mean it this time."

As Betania watched her disappear out the door, she walked over to her teacher, an older man with thick gray hair. He was dressed in a collared shirt, a bow tie, and an old-fashioned cap. "So, this class seems very challenging."

"Yes, it is," he replied as he stacked a pile of loose papers.

"I prefer science, but it's interesting to learn about politics, too."

Her teacher rubbed his chin. "That's nice."

Betania remained standing.

"I'm happy to see your interest in the class, but, well, it's time for lunch." He held up an old brown paper bag. "Don't you want to eat? I think your friends are waiting for you."

Betania stared at the clock. It was five minutes past noon. With glazed eyes, she asked, "I'm sorry, could you repeat that?"

"I said I think they're waiting for you," he repeated.

Alarmed, Betania turned pale. Her dark almond shaped eyes flashed. Her teacher appeared startled by her reaction. "Don't worry, you have plenty of time."

"Time?" repeated Betania.

"Yes, to eat with your friends. You better hurry." He motioned toward the door with his hand.

"I'm really not that hungry. Could I just stay here and study? I would love to learn more about the class."

Her teacher inclined his head. "Gosh, I'm flattered, but this is my only time to myself. I don't even eat with the other teachers. In my old age I prefer to be alone. I'm sure you understand. Perhaps another time?"

Betania smiled half-heartedly. "Yes, well, thank you."

Reluctantly, Betania left the room. As she walked down the cement path that led to the cafeteria, the two girls who had approached her earlier suddenly appeared.

"So are you going to fight us or what?" asked one.

Betania looked at them. They were both heavily painted with thick makeup that caked against their foreheads. One of them had long black hair that was greasy and limp. She extended her fist, revealing a small tattoo of the letter M.

"Hey! Get away from her!" called out a voice. "That *leva* is ours!"

Betania turned quickly. Before her, accompanied by two other girls, was a familiar face. It was Marta, Vanessa's little sister. She was small and comely. Her black wavy hair and pretty bright eyes were misleading. Betania was fully aware that she was a tough girl. She was also smart, and like Vanessa, brazen. The girls next to her were older and bigger, but it was clear that they were mere followers.

"Hey, look at me when I'm talking to you, you little whore!" said the other girl, reverting Betania's attention to her. "The Mexikanemi ain't through with you!"

"*Cállate pendeja!*" said Marta. "We have a hit on her!"

Betania turned so that she stood horizontally in relation to the two groups of girls assembled against her. "Marta, you're just a freshman. Why are you doing this?"

Marta seemed unmoved. She scowled. Her eyes were full of hatred.

"I know you, Marta. You don't have to do this," said Betania.

"Why? Are you afraid?" asked Marta.

Betania attempted to walk past her, but both groups of girls collapsed together, forming a wall. Betania frowned. She looked around, hoping someone would pass by. There was no one. "Please, just leave me alone. I'm not part of the gang anymore. I—I want to go to college."

Laughter broke out from both groups of girls. "Let us have her! She's not with you anymore! Her sister beat my sister bloody and then ran off to Mexico!"

"No way!" replied Marta. "We're getting credit for this!"

"We're not going anywhere," replied the other girl. "Who knows? Maybe you're going to need our help."

Marta shook her head. "We hate you even more than this *leva*. Now get the hell out of here."

The two Mexikanemi girls spat on Betania. "Fine, we'll get her later," said one as she snarled at Marta.

"There won't be any *later*!" shouted Marta. She then nodded toward the girl standing to her left. "Sandra, get ready." The girl responded by reaching into her pocket. She placed several rings on her fingers. Marta nodded to the girl to her right. "Maggie, get behind her."

The three girls spread out, forming a circle. Betania began breathing heavily. Her eyes darted in all directions. "Please, Marta, we're friends."

"Not anymore."

"I have to go to the cafeteria," said Betania.

"The only place you're going is a hospital," said Sandra.

"Or a grave," added Maggie in a tone full of mockery.

Without warning, the three girls simultaneously rushed Betania. Maggie grabbed her by the hair, yanking it so hard that Betania immediately fell down onto the cement. Feeling the sting of the merciless concrete, Betania began to panic. All three girls swarmed her, kicking her with great force. Betania curled into a ball and covered her ears, protecting her face with her forearms. This proved successful at first, but then Maggie fell on top of her and began to choke her.

Betania thought of her sister. *Pamela would never go down without a fight.* Gasping for breath, an instinct to survive quickly took over. Betania thrashed about onto her side. She then reached for her shoes. After a brief struggle, she slipped off each one and gripped them by the ends so that the thick black heels stuck out like a weapon. She swung wildly, hitting Maggie in the cheek several times. With a cry of pain, Maggie relinquished her grip on Betania's throat.

Recognizing the opportunity to flee, Betania propped herself up to her knees, but a kick to the face quickly thwarted her intentions. The blow dazed her momentarily. As a small trickle of blood flowed from her nose, she looked up to see Marta smiling at her.

"You are so going to get it," said Marta. "This is what happens to traitors."

Betania then grabbed one of her shoes and slammed the heel into Marta's shin. Marta immediately clutched her leg, then fell to the ground screaming obscenities. Once again, Betania attempted to get up. She began to run but was tackled from behind.

"I got her!" said Sandra.

The impact hurt terribly. Both of Betania's elbows were scraped and bleeding. Squirming violently, she lay flat on her back. Sandra smiled down on Betania, flexing her right hand to expose a ring on each finger.

"You're dead."

A fist came down on Betania's face, immediately opening a large gash. Betania cried out in pain. Then came another and another and another. As Betania felt the skin on her cheeks ripping apart, she flailed helplessly, trying in vain to grab Sandra's arms.

Two girls, nicely dressed and with books in their hands, stopped not too far away. "I think they're hurting that girl," said one.

"I think you're right," said the other, nodding. She then shouted, "Hey! What are you doing?"

Sandra scowled at them. "Shut the hell up and keep walking!"

The two girls exchanged glances and disappeared down the cement walkway. Betania opened her eyes. Sandra was no longer alone.

"You didn't think you were going to get away, did you?" said Marta. "Stand her up!"

Sandra and Maggie promptly grabbed Betania and raised her to her feet. Marta then reached into her shoe. Raising her hand, a small shiny object sparkled in the sun.

Sandra smiled. "*Dale! Dale!*"

Betania, breathing heavily, looked at them. She had lost the will to resist. She could feel the warmth of blood on her cheeks, her head, and her hair. Her entire face ached and throbbed.

"Over there!" called out a high-pitched voice. "I told you! They're hurting that girl!"

More voices followed.

"Get the football players!"

"Call security!"

"Somebody find a teacher!"

Betania strained to make out the blurry image of students quickly gathering about her.

"This has nothing to do with you!" said Marta. "Get out of here! All of you!"

More students approached. "Let her go!" shouted a girl from within the crowd.

Marta held a knife to Betania's face.

"Do it!" said Sandra. "Cut her up!"

"Make her ugly!" said Maggie. "Permanently!"

"Please, no…" whispered Betania.

More students assembled. Betania recognized many of them. Some were members of the Texas Syndicate. Some were members of the Mexikanemi. Some were her classmates.

"Betania!" said Jim. He slowly began to approach the three girls.

"Stay back!" said Marta. "I'll cut her!"

"Like hell you will!" said Jim, grabbing Marta's wrist.

"Stay away from her, white boy!" said someone from within the crowd.

"*Cállate, pendejo!*" replied another.

Jim pushed Marta to the ground. Several shouts followed.

"Get him!"

"*Mátalos a todos!*"

A boy lunged toward Jim. He easily threw him down next to Marta. Others joined in. A slew of white football jerseys joined the ruckus. Within seconds, more than twenty boys had engaged in full battle. Punches flew. Boys wrestled each other to the ground. Some students cheered while others gasped in horror.

Several staff officials arrived upon the scene. "Break it up! Break it up!" They attempted in vain to control the many boys who refused to give in. One man raised a radio to his mouth. "We need back up! Send all security officials to the northeast building!"

Betania was slipping into unconsciousness. She stumbled forward, attempting to dodge the many bodies around her. Then, she collapsed.

"Betania! Come with me!" called a voice from within the thick cloud of violence.

Betania was just able to lift her head.

"Hurry!"

Two arms hoisted her up. She was in the air. Resting her face on his shoulder, Betania mumbled faintly, "Mr. Alvarez?"

"Don't worry, Betania, I've got you."

32

A PLUMP WOMAN with dark hair quietly sat at her desk. Suddenly, Mr. Alvarez burst into her office with Betania in his arms. "I got an emergency," he said.

"Oh my goodness!" What happened to her?"

"You don't want to know," replied Mr. Alvarez. He then plopped Betania onto a flat red pleather bed. "I just need you to patch her up. We may need to call the hospital."

The school nurse quickly grabbed a few packets and cotton swabs. She then began to rub Betania's many wounds. As she did so, Betania moaned in pain.

"I know, dear. This is going to hurt a little," said the nurse.

"Betania, I'm going to do everything I can to protect you," said Mr. Alvarez, "but you know as well as I do that it won't be easy."

Opening her swollen lips, Betania replied slowly, "You were right, Mr. Alvarez."

Mr. Alvarez nodded. "I know. Sometimes we have to go through some pretty bad shit until our eyes are opened to the truth."

The nurse turned and frowned.

"What?" asked Mr. Alvarez, furrowing his brow. "Just keep fixing her up!"

"What do you think I'm doing?" snapped the nurse.

"I didn't want to fight," interrupted Betania. "I told them!"

"I believe you," said Mr. Alvarez.

"When will they stop?" asked Betania as tears dropped from her eyes.

Mr. Alvarez was quiet. He turned to the nurse. "Can I take her to my office?"

"I need to put some butterfly bandages on a few of those cuts first."

Mr. Alvarez nodded. The nurse applied a number of white bandages that criss-crossed on Betania's face. As Betania winced in pain, the nurse said, "Okay, that ought to do it, but she's not returning to class, is she?"

"No," replied Mr. Alvarez. "I'll handle this."

"Are you going to call her parents?"

"Yeah, yeah, I'll take care of everything, thank you," replied Mr. Alvarez. Holding Betania by the hand and the elbow, he helped her to her feet and then guided her down a hallway to his office. Once there, he escorted her into a chair and closed the door behind him. Taking a seat behind his desk, he continued, "I wish I could tell you that everything will be all right, but I can't. Those kids might leave you alone for a little while, but really, as long as you are here, it won't ever stop. You're in too deep. And with what happened with little Jorge…"

Betania looked Mr. Alvarez directly in the eyes. "You know about that?"

"I already told you. I know everything that happens in my school. This is my *barrio*, remember?"

"Yes, yes," stammered Betania. "But, if they won't stop, what do I do? What *can* I do? Maybe—maybe if I change schools—"

"No," interrupted Mr. Alvarez. "I'm sorry, Betania, but I don't think that will help much. I recommend that you leave this area completely. You know I give it to you straight, right?"

Betania nodded, and then began to cry once again.

"As bad as today was, it's just going to get worse. If the Emi kids don't get you, the TS kids will. They know you're alone and to them, you're a *traidora*. And in their eyes, there's nothing worse."

Mr. Alvarez handed Betania some tissue. As her tears flowed more freely, she felt the pain from the open wounds on her face. "What am I going to do?" she moaned. "Where do I go? All of my relatives are either here or in Veracruz!"

"I want to help you," said Mr. Alvarez. "But you're going to have to trust me. And not just you, but your parents as well."

Betania swallowed deeply. "I trust you, Mr. Alvarez."

"I know some people. An older couple that live in Iowa. It's a nice place called Cedar Falls. It's far away from here and they don't have to deal with all of the gang activity. You'll be safe there."

Betania wiped her eyes. She slowly regained her composure. "I—I don't understand."

"They run a ranch for teenagers. They can help you. In fact, they've helped hundreds of kids over the years. Their names are Lance and Karen Williams."

"You're saying I should leave my family and go live with people I don't even know?"

"Yes, I am. They're good people."

"How do you know?"

"Because a long time ago they helped me."

33

LANCE AND KAREN Williams were in their late fifties, but they had more energy than most young adults. He was a large man, with thinning blonde hair and a large leathery tan face. She was much smaller, but sturdy, and besides the wrinkles around her eyes, showed little signs of aging.

"Over there you have the horses," said Mr. Williams, pointing to a trio of large beasts that were trotting behind a white wooden fence.

"Wow! They're incredible!" gushed Betania. "They're huge!"

"Yes," said Mr. Williams. "They're Clydesdales."

"*Muy lindos*," said la Señora Soliz.

"My mother says that they are very beautiful," said Betania. She then approached the white fence. "May I pet them?"

"Yes, you go right ahead," Mr. Williams replied.

"*Con cuidado, hija*," said Betania's father. He then turned to Mr. Williams. "It's okay? It's safe?"

"Sure! They love attention!" Mr. Williams replied.

Betania reached up and stroked the large white streak that ran from the animal's eyes to its nose. It huffed. Betania quickly removed her hand, which brought forth a chuckle from Mr. and Mrs. Williams.

"I thought he was going to bite me," said Betania, smiling widely.

"Oh, no, he's just being friendly," said Mr. Williams. He pointed to a large brown structure that was divided into two separate triangular sections. "Okay, folks, to your left you'll notice the barn. Got hay in the loft. Down below there's stables for the horses. On the other side we've got a hen house. Use it for storage, too—equipment and such."

Betania glanced at the barn. Her eyes then drifted toward a seemingly endless row of trees. Her father seemed to notice this. *"Son de manzana?"* he asked her.

Betania shrugged. She then looked up and made eye contact with Mr. Williams. "Are those apple trees?"

"They sure are. Karen makes some of the best pies you could ever taste," he replied.

"Some of the best?" asked Mrs. Williams, smiling somewhat mischievously.

"Oh, beg your pardon, my dear. I meant to say 'the best' apple pies." Mr. Williams led the group across a dirt lot. "Now, the newer buildings over there are the dorms."

"One is for the girls and one is for the boys," said Mrs. Williams.

"Excuse me," said Betania's father, "but how many?"

"How many kids?" replied Mrs. Williams.

"Yes."

"Well, we're currently almost at capacity. Each dormitory holds up to ten. Inside, you'll see a lot of bunk beds and desks for them to study. Each one's got its own bathroom with showers, too. We all eat together, sometimes with visitors, but other than that, boys and girls aren't to be fraternizing. I'm the only one allowed in the girls' dorm and Lance is the only one allowed in the boys' dorm. Other than us, and the children who sleep there, the dorms are off limits."

Betania's father furrowed his brow. *"Qué dijo de los límites?"*

"Dice que los muchachos no pueden visitar la residencia de las muchachas," said Betania.

Her father smiled at Mrs. Williams. "Oh, that's good."

She nodded. "Well, let's head on back to the house."

It was a large rustic home, resembling the type of lodge commonly seen in resorts that reside high in the mountains. Inside, complete with a huge dining room was a large kitchen. As the group entered, Betania noticed several young people who appeared to be her age. Some were cooking hamburgers on a grill while others stirred large pots.

"They're getting things ready for dinner," said Mrs. Williams. "The kids have to check the work schedule to see what chores they've been assigned. In the kitchen, we're blessed by a group of volunteers that come pretty much every night. I think I'll go in and help out." She paused to face Betania and her parents. "Don't you worry. Betania will be in good hands here. I know you're still undecided as to your plans."

"Yes," replied Betania's father. "We hope to come, or we move to other place with Betania."

"No matter what you decide," said Mrs. Williams, "Betania's welcome to stay as long as God intends her to be here."

"*Muchas gracias*," said Betania's mother. Her eyes had become moist.

"You're welcome—*de nada*," said Mrs. Williams. She then grabbed Betania's mother and hugged her. After a long embrace, she walked off toward the kitchen.

"This dining hall is also our chapel," said Mr. Williams, waving his thick hairy arm upward. "Now, the way we do things here are simple. See that plaque on the wall, Betania?"

Betania looked up as he pointed to a large wooden plaque. In large engraved letters were the following five rules.

> Rule #1 The Fear Of The Lord Is The Beginning Of Wisdom.[11]
> Rule #2 Honor Your Father And Mother.[12]
> Rule #3 Love Your Neighbor As Yourself.[13]
> Rule #4 Forgive And You Will Be Forgiven.[14]
> Rule #5 He Who Does Not Work Neither Shall He Eat.[15]

Mr. Williams began to read each one aloud. He did not bother to look at the wall as he did so. "That's it, Betania," he said. "You follow those simple rules given to us by the good Lord and I guarantee that you will do just fine while you're here and long after you've gone. My wife and I are committed to all of our children on the ranch. We will do all we can to ensure your success. Here, we're family."

Betania jolted forward. Her body became rigid and her eyes widened. Mr. Williams arched his brow. "Are you okay?"

Betania nodded.

"Are you sure?"

Betania inhaled deeply. Slowly, her body relaxed. *"Familia,"* she whispered.

"What was that?"

Betania smiled. "I said *familia*...family."

BEYOND THE ELITE PART I

1

THROUGHOUT HIS CHILDHOOD, Aaron Holmes had to live each day with the uncertainty of his father's whereabouts. He never knew if his father would be home or in prison. Each one had its advantages and disadvantages.

When his father was away, Aaron missed throwing a football with him or doing some light boxing. He wondered if he would have food to eat or if the electricity bill would be paid. But when his father was home, things could be even worse. Aaron lived in constant fear. He never knew when his father might lose his temper. He had seen him go on a rampage, punching walls and breaking furniture. He had personally witnessed times when his father had beaten other men down until they sunk to the ground in a bloody mess. Jerome Holmes was feared—admired even—but hated, too.

Whenever Aaron looked out his bedroom window, he wondered if the people waiting outside were friends or foes, so it was a welcome relief when he spotted his grandfather's old gray truck pulling up in front of his house. First, there was a knock on the door. Then, the sound of creaking hinges. Silence followed. And finally, there was the sound of voices.

Aaron walked into the living room dressed in blue shorts and a short sleeved white shirt. Splashed across his miniature chest was a stamped logo of various sports paraphernalia. His slightly round face, a little large for his small slender body, displayed closely razed black hair behind a high forehead. Though not fully smiling, his lips were slightly curved, expressing an inexplicably positive perspective on life. In one hand was a small brown suitcase; in the other, an old leather football.

"You ready?"

"Yes, Granddad," replied Aaron.

Granddad Bailey stood on the worn out green mat that lay next to the door on the tiled entrance. He was wearing his customary blue overalls. His brown working boots were crusted with dirt at the bottom—no doubt the reason he seemed hesitant to enter the house and walk on the carpeted floor. His dark broad face had splattered patches of black and gray hair, a perpetual state that wavered somewhere between an unshaven face and a full beard. He stood just under six feet, and though not a large man, his powerful hands gave others the impression that he was a towering figure. They were composed of thick palms and long fingers which were heavily calloused.

Aaron's mother bent down to hug him. Dressed in black sweat pants that were a size too small and a white cotton shirt, her svelte figure was apparent. Her tightly curled black hair, which was finely cut around the ears, tickled Aaron's cheek. Kissing him gently, she said, "Aaron, be a good boy and behave yourself. You're going to stay with your grandparents again. It might be a little longer this time." She paused to wipe her eyes. "But as soon as I can…. As soon as your daddy comes back, I'll come get you."

"Yes, Mommy," replied Aaron.

"Why don't you both come and live with us?" said Granddad Bailey. "You'll have to work, though, and I won't have anything to do with smoking or drinking or anything else."

"So in other words I'm not welcome," replied Aaron's mother. Without waiting for an answer, she turned and plopped down onto a white plaid couch. From there, she grabbed the small stub of a cigarette from a small black ashtray. She raised it to her lips and quickly began to exhale a cloud of smoke.

"Did I say that?" shouted Granddad Bailey, furrowing his brow. "Nobody forced you into marrying Jerome, you know!"

"Don't even start, Dad." Aaron's mother frowned. She took a deep breath. Her eyes floated upward. "Besides, he'll get out soon."

"Sure he will, Susie, and then he'll sell drugs or beat on someone and end up right back in prison!"

"He needs me. Please, just take Aaron."

Granddad Bailey pressed his lips together, puckered them slightly, and then frowned. "Well, all right, then. You know where we live, and, well, your mother would definitely like to see you more often."

"I know," she replied softly.

"Then let's go." Granddad Bailey stuck out his thumb and waved it in his direction several times. "I got plenty of work for you, and your cousins will all want to see you. Got them long legs from your mom, I see. How old are you now?"

"I'm eight, Granddad," replied Aaron.

"Eight years old. That's a good age to learn the value of hard work. Here, let me help you with that." Granddad Bailey grabbed the little suitcase out of Aaron's hand and hoisted it to the back of a truck that appeared to have been manufactured sometime in the fifties.

"I can work real good, Granddad!" said Aaron, holding up both arms and flexing his tiny biceps. "I'm strong like my daddy!"

Granddad Bailey smiled. He then opened the front door. "Well, all right, then. Get on in and we'll get started."

2

MAX AND MARY Bailey lived on a small farm that technically resided within the city limits of Avondale yet remained just as close to Phoenix. After working arduously for some of the largest ranches in Arizona, the Baileys were able to buy a place of their own. Their name, engraved on a metal plate that swung at the top of a faded wooden gate, served as a testimony to their diligent labor. And though there were a few neighboring farmers that seemed to begrudge their success, most were more than happy to offer a helping hand.

They had pigs and hogs, roosters and hens, and a few mules. At times a horse graced their stable. They also grew hay, cotton, and vegetables. Though overshadowed by the prominent farms and ranches in the area, the acres they did possess served to provide them with their livelihood as well as a safe haven for many of their scattered grandchildren and other loosely related relatives.

Aaron learned very quickly that visiting his grandparents was not the same as living with them. If he did not like the food that his grandmother had prepared, then he would not eat. If he did not finish his chores, he did not eat. If his room was not clean, he did not eat. The house rules were very strict and everyone, from the oldest down to the youngest, was expected to contribute. Aaron's grandmother was often heard saying, "Spare the rod, spoil the child."

The Baileys did have a few farmhands who worked not for money, but rather for traded services. A butcher came out regularly to cut and pack pork for a portion that he set aside for himself. A neighboring farm lent out their tractors to the Baileys for a share in their vegetable harvest. It was a humble way of life, but it sustained them and the surplus was distributed to larger, more established farms for a small profit.

Daily chores made each child **assimilate** quickly into the Bailey household. They fed the animals, they took care of the crops, they assisted in the kitchen, and they continually cleaned the house. Surrounded by so many other children, Aaron never thought of himself as an only child.

3

OF ALL THE many boys and girls who had been taken in by the Baileys over the years, Terry was the one with whom Aaron related to most. He was actually a third or fourth cousin, loosely related to Aaron's grandmother, but that mattered little. Terry had grown up under circumstances that obscured Aaron's own difficult upbringing, but despite that, he was a soft-spoken and thoughtful boy.

Aaron and Terry played every sport imaginable. If there was a ball involved, then so were they. There was one ball, however, that they treasured above all others. It was an old leather football. Whenever they gathered together with other boys, it was a given that Aaron would be the quarterback and Terry the running back.

"Joe, you and Hector block," said Aaron. "Robby, you go long. I'm going to roll out and see if I can hit you; if not, I'll pitch it to Terry or run it myself. Everybody understand?"

"Yeah, yeah, we get it!" replied one of the boys as he broke out of the huddle.

"Just do your best to block a little," said Aaron, giving one last order before the smaller boys next to him lined up against their larger opponents.

Aaron gave Terry a knowing look, to which he nodded.

"Come on, children," said Derrick, one of Aaron's older cousins. "Y'all better hurry 'cause any moment Granddad's gonna be out here yelling at us to get back to work!"

"Yeah, yeah," shouted Aaron. "You're just mad 'cause y'all losing!"

"You're going down this time little boy!" said one of Derrick's teammates who was facing up against Aaron's tiny blockers.

Aaron approached his two man line, looked to the side at his one wide receiver and quickly to the back where Terry was knelt down in anticipation.

"Ready!" Aaron began. "Down! Set!"

"Just hike the damn ball!" said Derrick, a large smirk on his face.

Ignoring him, Aaron continued his cadence. "Hut! Hut!"

On the second count, the ball was snapped. Aaron quickly rolled to his right as his blockers were easily knocked down and tossed aside. Two large boys chased Aaron, but just as one of them was about to tackle him, he pitched the ball to Terry. Like a shot from a rifle, he was off. Terry first dodged his older cousin, Derrick, by faking further right, and then going to his left. He did not get far before another boy attempted to tackle him. Terry stopped suddenly, and pivoted back to his right. Aaron then blocked for him. Derrick, who remained on the grassy field, reached out for Terry, but instead of slowing down, Terry merely hurdled him.

"Get him!" shouted Derrick.

Two other boys quickly joined in pursuit of Terry, but it was too late. He continued to sprint down the makeshift football field. One boy managed to touch his back with the tips of his fingers, but that was all. The other one gave up entirely. Terry raced into the end zone, marked by wooden sticks that stuck out from the ground on both sides of the field. While he shifted gears to a mere trot, his older opponents put their hands on their knees and gulped in heavy breaths of air.

"Dag, man!" said Derrick. "You let a little kid outrun y'all?"

"Sorry, man, but your little cousin is sick!" said one of the boys. "If he keeps growing, man, he's gonna be unstoppable."

"How big is his dad?" asked another.

Derrick scoffed. "Who knows, man. I don't even think he knows."

"Hey! Did you boys finish your chores?" There was no mistaking the edgy baritone voice of Granddad Bailey. He stood near an old grayish wooden fence in his blue overalls and white cotton shirt, waving his arms wildly like a madman. Each of the boys stopped in their tracks. "You boys better stop throwing the pigskin and start cleaning the pig's skin!" he called out.

Some of the boys laughed. A few of them crinkled their foreheads.

"What's that mean?" asked one of Aaron's teammates.

"Aw, it's just old school talk," replied Aaron. "Time to go 'cause we gotta finish our work."

Terry caught up to Aaron and Derrick. Upon doing so, he flicked the ball to Aaron.

"Way to go, cuz," said Aaron.

Terry smiled, allowing his square chiseled face a slight demonstration of emotion. "Thank you."

"Yeah, yeah, you guys only won 'cause my guys are no good!" said Derrick.

"That's what you always say," replied Aaron.

"'Cause it's true!" said Derrick.

The group of boys slowly gathered around Granddad Bailey. "Sorry to break up the game, fellas," he began, "but my grandkids here need to finish their work."

"No problem, Mr. Bailey," said a large, somewhat chubby boy. "Later, Derrick. Later, Aaron. Later, Mr. Washington."

Derrick cocked his head back and furrowed his brow. "Mr. Washington?" he repeated in a high-pitched voice.

"Yeah, man, your cousin's gonna be famous someday."

Smirking, Derrick replied, "Whatever."

"In that case, you better start calling me Mr. Holmes!" said Aaron, a large smile on his face.

"Yeah, right," said the boys in unison as they walked away.

4

AARON AND TERRY were inseparable. As other boys and girls passed through the Bailey farm, they alone remained, undertaking adolescence together. Both quickly established themselves in athletics, receiving accolades as a dynamic duo that possessed an uncanny combination of strength, speed, and skill. Their days were full. Waking at the crack of dawn to work on the farm, they then headed off to school and afterwards participated in athletics throughout the year. Football turned into basketball and basketball faded into track and field. Their lives settled into a routine; but even so, they could not escape the family shadows that constantly lingered, flickering about as unsolicited reminders.

While walking through the west side of downtown Phoenix, Aaron and Terry passed many buildings. Markets, hair salons, bargain stores. Walls painted with a single shade of white and windows covered by black protective bars made it difficult to tell them apart.

"Sup dawgs!" called out an older boy standing in front of a small liquor store. The dark afro which covered his slender diamond shaped face was thick, large and uneven. His oversized white shirt hung over his baggy blue jeans. Aaron could see both himself and Terry through the reflection of his sunglasses. "I heard y'all be tearing it up on varsity!"

"Yeah, we're doing all right," replied Aaron. Both he and Terry stopped. "Next year is when it's all gonna happen, though."

"I believe it! It's in your blood, homeboy." He paused and nodded his head vigorously. "Yeah, that's right. I know who your daddy is!"

Aaron smiled proudly whereas Terry inclined his head.

"You know my dad?" asked Aaron.

"Hell, yeah! Everyone this side of Phoenix knows him. Dude's a legend!" He walked closer, extending his hand to both Aaron and Terry. "Name's Calvin."

As Aaron began to mouth his name, Calvin waved him off. "No need for introductions!" he stated matter-of-factly.

"Yeah?" replied Aaron.

"Come on, young gun! Don't be playin' me like that! People be talkin'. Sayin' you both gonna end up playing for the Cardinals or the Suns or whatnot!"

"We're only sophomores," said Terry.

"That don't mean nothing, son!" replied Calvin. "Y'all superstars, right?"

"Our coaches have made it abundantly clear that we shouldn't try to eclipse the older students," said Terry.

Calvin furrowed his brow. He then scowled.

"Coaches don't want us showing people up, man," said Aaron.

"Can't be letting people hold you back like that, dawg! Anyway, if y'all need to earn a little extra cash, I could always use a little help, you know what I'm saying?" Calvin slid his sunglasses down slightly. "It looks like y'all could use some."

Aaron and Terry exchanged glances. They were well aware of the thick polyester work slacks and the striped buttoned down collared shirts provided to them. "Thanks, man," said Aaron, "but we better go."

"Yeah," added Terry, "I need to see if my mother needs any assistance, and we promised our grandfather we'd return to Avondale before dark."

Calvin wagged his head. "Damn! Do you always talk like a white boy?"

Terry's mouth slowly opened. After a slight pause, he replied, "English is spoken throughout the world. The fact that its origin can be traced to England does not mean that white people own the English language."

Calvin turned to Aaron and laughed. "Can you believe this dude?"

"Lay off, man," said Aaron. "Everyone knows Terry's smart. What's wrong with that?"

Calvin laughed once more, cursed, and then shook his head. "Nothing, man, nothing. It's cool. Hey, if you young bucks want to hang out, we're having a big meeting Saturday. Dude named Timothy's been talking to a lot of people, telling us we need to get more productive, or organized, or something like that. I didn't pay much attention at first, but the dude's real, has this funky voice." He turned to Terry. "So I guess you're right, dawg."

Terry furrowed his brow. "About what?"

"About black people coming from England."

"Excuse me?"

"Timothy. The dude's from England."

Terry raised his thick, straight brows. "Really?" After a short pause, he asked, "Where is this meeting?"

"At Knights Inn, where Timothy works. It's a big fancy hotel. Located on Camelback."

"I doubt if we'll be going to any meeting," said Aaron. "Like Terry said, we're just here to check on his mom and then we—"

"Oh, come on, now!" interrupted Calvin. "Y'all need to get with the program! You know what I'm saying?"

"Maybe," said Aaron.

"I swear, dawg, y'all be missing out!"

"What are you talking about, man?" asked Aaron.

"For starters, you need to change the way y'all dress!" said Calvin. A large grin broke out on his face. Then, pointing to himself, he continued, "Look at these jeans, son! Look at these boots! Look at this shirt!"

"It's just a white shirt that doesn't fit you," said Terry.

Calvin scowled as he motioned with his hands toward his shirt. "Feel this material, son! This here's style! Now look at your old raggedy clothes! Little punk-ass shoes. Floppy collars y'all wearing. Come on, now!" Calvin rubbed the limp cotton collar of Aaron's shirt between his thumb and forefinger. "You can't be wearing stuff like that playing varsity!"

Aaron could hear his grandfather's voice shouting inside his head. *You boys don't need to be dressing like no peacock! All that matters is that you look respectable, and only somebody downright stupid would pay a hundred dollars for a pair of sneakers that you can't even get dirty!* He motioned to Terry. Facing Calvin, Aaron muttered, "Okay, man, later. We gotta go."

The boys then continued down the sidewalk while Calvin leaned against the wall in the exact same spot that he had occupied earlier.

"You want to attend that meeting?" asked Terry.

"No, I'm going to visit my dad," said Aaron. "My mom's going to take me to see him. And anyways, what are you thinking?"

"I don't know," said Terry. "I'm just a little curious. I've heard of Timothy."

"So who is he?"

"I don't know, but I've heard he's different," said Terry.

Aaron furrowed his brow. "Different?"

"Yeah, in fact, I've heard people refer to him as Doctor Timothy or the Professor."

Aaron laughed. "Yeah, they probably call him 'doctor' because he writes them little notes to get drugs!"

"Prescribes," said Terry.

"What?"

"Doctors don't write little notes; they prescribe medicine."

"Whatever," said Aaron. He reached out and squeezed the nape of Terry's neck. "Anyway, you know better, Terry! And if Granddad found out, he'd kick your sorry ass to the curb before you knew what hit you."

Terry grabbed Aaron's wrist and firmly removed it from the back of his neck. Raising his brow, he asked, "Does the farm have a curb?"

"Shut up!" snarled Aaron. "You know what I mean!"

Terry's perpendicular jaw tightened, causing his muscular face to become even more rigid. "I can make my own decisions, Aaron. I don't have to follow everything Granddad says."

Aaron curled his lips. "Oh, really? That's big talk, man, but tell me something. If you don't listen to him, where would you go?"

Terry remained quiet.

Aaron shrugged. "Yeah, that's what I thought. Anyway, like I said, I'm gonna visit my dad on Saturday so you can count me out."

Terry frowned. "I guess you're right."

"Of course I'm right," said Aaron, "so don't even think about going 'cause you're not gonna find anything but trouble."

Terry looked at him. "You know who you sound like, right?"

Both of them laughed as they simultaneously shouted, "Granddad!"

5

AARON AND HIS mother waited for the tall metal gate to slide open. Both of them were dressed similarly. Aaron in black Dickies™ pants and a white collared shirt. His mother in dark slacks and a white blouse. In front of them was a large quadrangular sign. Posted in bright red letters were the words "Danger" and "High voltage." Aaron looked upward at the silvery barbed wire. In the distance he noted the green and white tower which hid the armed guards and their high powered rifles. A large buzzing sound shook his thoughts. Looking forward, he and his mother passed through the moving gate. They walked on the cement path toward the reception building as the gate clanged shut behind them. As they did so, his mother matched him stride for stride, her legs being as long as his own. If it were not for his much larger torso, they would probably be of the same height.

Aaron rubbed his pink visitor's badge nervously. Upon entering the building, a fully armed guard with large black boots and a green padded uniform nodded to them and pointed. They sat by a small table until a solidly built man of six feet came and joined them. His ears were small and folded, a fact made more conspicuous by his large face. His nose was wide—flat, even, by all appearances. Covering his cheeks, upper lip, chin, and neck was a bushy dark beard that was only able to slightly hide the scowl on his face. The man embraced Aaron's mother.

"No kissing, Holmes."

The scowl on the face of Aaron's father deepened. His large biceps flexed through his blue short sleeved prison uniform. "I didn't get to kiss my wife on the last visit!"

"That's right, Holmes, and you know why."

"That's bullshit."

The guard took a few steps toward Aaron's father. "Excuse me?"

The two men stood face to face.

"Jerome, please," said Aaron's mother, touching his shoulder gently.

After a brief stare down, Aaron's father muttered, "Do you mind? I want to talk to my wife and son."

The guard twisted his lips. "Yeah, well, just watch yourself, Holmes, or you'll be talking to them behind glass." He turned and walked several feet away, and then said loudly, "and keep your hands on your lap!"

Sitting down, Aaron's father gritted his teeth before asking, "How much money you making at the beauty shop?"

"I'm actually doing pretty good. Getting some good hours. It's enough to pay the rent and put some food in the house."

"That's good—not good enough—but it's something. Your parents helping out?"

Aaron's mother inclined her head, then swiveled in little jerking movements. She appeared embarrassed by the question. "They've done enough already," she whispered.

"Why he still living with them if you're paying the rent?" shouted Aaron's father.

"It's just better," she replied.

"Dad," interrupted Aaron. "Some guy named Calvin said he knows you."

Aaron's father curled his lips. His thick black eyebrows lowered. "Calvin? I don't know no Calvin. Why? Who is he? What does he want?"

"I don't know. He just said he knew you and then he invited us to some big meeting."

"Who's us?"

"Me and Terry," replied Aaron.

"Some big meeting, huh?" huffed Aaron's father. "I don't know nothing about no big meeting. These men or them kids?"

"I think Calvin's like, a little older, and I don't know about the other guy. His name's Timothy and Calvin said he's the leader. Terry said he heard of him."

"Look, lots of people say they know me but that don't mean nothing," replied Aaron's father in a stern voice. "You just stay away from them and do what I tell you, understand? Sounds like a bunch of young guns trying to muscle their way into my business. Bunch of kids thinking they've got a right to have something they never worked for." He paused and shook his head. "I'll check 'em out soon enough. Mark my words; I'll check 'em out. Just 'cause I'm in here don't mean nobody can take what's mine."

"What did they say about your parole, Jerome?" asked Aaron's mother.

"Real soon, baby, real soon. Been staying out of trouble—doing what they ask me." He broke into laughter. "Couple months ago they told me I could work outside or help out in the mail room. And you know what I chose! Anyways, they know I can work. My father worked in construction, you might recall. Best in all of Phoenix! Taught me everything he knew, too. I had to tell all the rest of these lazy good for nothings what to do. Made me a crew chief second day on the job. I'll be out soon."

Aaron's mother smiled. His father then leaned forward. "Look, son," he began. "Your mom told me you been getting all kinds of medals for football and basketball, even track. You're doing good, son. You doing real good. And it ain't no coincidence. It's in your blood, son. You know I was golden gloves, right?"

Aaron nodded.

"If I didn't have to take care of you and your mother, I would've been world champ. You know that, right?"

Aaron inclined his head.

"Nobody could stop me in my prime." Aaron's father raised his fists and moved them in a circular fashion. "You're a Holmes, son. You're a Holmes. Don't you ever forget it."

6

UNDERNEATH A BRIGHT sun and a clear blue sky, a stocky man dressed in black shorts, a yellow shirt, and a black cap paced the green grass of the practice field. Coach More was a proud Marine, and he made no secret of the fact that practices were boot camp and games were war battles. Football was a metaphor for life and the blistering heat only added to the richness of the metaphor.

"Men, to the end zone!" Coach More bellowed. His tan skin glistened in the sunlight as he shouted instructions, followed by plenty of whistles and the hollering of his assistant coaches. In response, a multitude of boys dressed in black and yellow uniforms lined up to run each drill with precision. On their black helmets was the emblem of the predatory wasp known as the yellow jacket. "Now form two horizontal lines at the cones! Twenty yards of squat jumps! After that, give me twenty sit-ups! I will personally make sure you do every one. Then, sprint to the next cone at the fifty yard line! There, Coach Morales will ensure you complete twenty push-ups! When you've finished, sprint to the next cone backwards! Once you've accomplished that, you will complete twenty mountain climbers for Coach Spriggs! Next, sprint to the next cone on the twenty yard line! Once there, you will perform ten up-downs and sprint to the goal line!"

A sixty second rest period ensued, but once over, two units set up on both sides of the twenty yard line.

"Okay, coaches, set up the offense!" barked Coach More.

"You heard Coach! Set up the Pistol!" replied Coach Morales, a man somewhat on the chubby side who possessed a kind brown face and thinning black hair that he constantly slicked back with his hand and the help of the beads of perspiration that formed on his forehead.

"Defense!" said Coach Spriggs, the other assistant coach. Built more like Coach More, his large biceps bulged under his tight yellow sleeves. His face was stocky and round and his short black hair was razed so that it was but a mere outline above the black skin of his skull. "Three-Three-Five Stack formation!"

"Offense! What are we?" shouted Coach More.

"Unstoppable!"

"Defense! What are we?"

"Aggressive!"

"Offense! We…" began Coach More.

"…call the shots!"

"Defense! We never let them know…"

"…what's coming!"

Coach More was unique. Unlike most coaches, he allowed his quarterbacks to call audibles and permitted his middle linebackers to spontaneously adjust the defensive stack formation. He believed the soldiers on the field should decide the action, not the generals standing on the sidelines. Another peculiarity of Coach More was his insistence on keeping the offense and defense apart. Whereas most of the other coaches played their best players both ways, and treated all units as one team, Coach More divided his teams into three separate units: offense, defense, and special teams. Players were sworn to secrecy. The offense was never to allow the defense to know their plays and the defense was never to discuss their schemes to stop them.

His eyes darting peripherally from behind his face mask, Aaron quickly analyzed the defensive stack formation. He always felt more confident going against rigid alignments in league games than he did of the ever changing movement of his own team's defense.

"Down!" said Aaron. "Down! Set! Green two hundred! Hut! Hut!"

Jeff Buckey, the team's huge center, snapped the ball. Aaron turned and rolled to his right, then he placed the ball in his halfback's hands, and Terry was off. He exploded through a hole in the line, dodged the strong side linebacker, and sprinted downfield until he was dragged down some twenty yards later by the cornerback with the help of the strong safety.

"Way to work, men, way to work!" shouted Coach More. "Stay focused. Tomorrow, we do battle!"

"Round up, players!" said Aaron.

Players from all over the field, as well as the sideline, made a circle around Aaron.

"Honor!" he said.

"Hoo-rah!"

"Courage!" Aaron said.

"Hoo-rah!"

"Commitment!" said Aaron.

"Hoo-rah!"

"Dismissed!" said Aaron.

The players broke from the circle and headed for the showers.

7

On the wall of the locker room hung four huge large square signs. The first one stood for responsibility.

> **This is the ultimate proving ground**
> **For those who are driven**
> **By purpose, guided by values,**
> **And aspire to earn the title of**
> **Avondale varsity football player**

The second sign stood for character.

> **Honor. Courage. Commitment.**

The third sign stood for commitment.

> **I do solemnly swear that I will Support and defend my brothers on The team against all opponents; That I will bear true faith and Allegiance to the same; and that I Will obey the orders of my coaches Appointed over me, according to Regulations and the uniform code Of justice. So help me God.**

The fourth and final sign stated the mission.

Semper Fidelis

A large group of dejected players assembled around Coach More in a cement area just below his office. Some of them sat on the long narrow yellow metal benches with their black helmets dangling from their hands. Others, like Aaron, stood proudly with their helmets still on, refusing to believe that their season had come to an end.

"Men," began Coach More, "each one of you played your heart out. I believe you did the best you could and that's all I've ever asked of you. Our goal this year was to make it to the county finals, and we did. So maybe we lost this battle, but we won the war." He paused. Raising his hand, he placed his forefinger close to his thumb. "We were this close to saying *mission accomplished*, but be proud of the way you all did battle. With heart, with commitment, with drive."

Several players as well as the assistant coaches nodded in agreement.

"Now, as we reflect on another fine season, I want to remind everyone that this is not the end. It's just the beginning. For some, it's the beginning of a new season. For others, it's the beginning of a new life."

As Coach More had done at the end of each previous season, he called the graduating seniors to stand before him. "Today, you have worn the Avondale uniform for the very last time, but even so, you will always be part of our team. Some of you will leave us to pursue higher learning. Others will join the military. And I am sure there are those who will immediately enter the work force. Maintain the principles you've learned as an Avondale soldier. Conduct yourself with honor at all times. Remember your oaths and you will find that the same sense of purpose and success you've found here on the field will stay with you for the rest of your lives. Semper fidelis."

"Semper Fidelis!" replied a chorus of young men.

There was a certain **solemnity** in the air. Nodding toward one of the assistant coaches, Coach More removed his hat, revealing the short light brown hair that edged around his blocky, stout face.

"Let's take a knee, everybody," said Coach Morales, the unofficial chaplain of the team. "Let's thank our Heavenly Father for another season and another year of life that we should all cherish."

Following his lead, each boy knelt to the floor and observed a moment of silence. Then, slowly, they broke off, congratulating as well as consoling one another. A few people spoke, but out of respect for the seniors, the room remained quiet for the most part. One by one each boy showered, changed, and left the locker room.

"Aaron, Terry—before you go—I want to have a word with you," called out Coach More.

"Yes, sir," they replied in unison.

Dressed in the black and yellow polyester sweat suits that marked them as football players, both Aaron and Terry sported matching gym bags strapped across their shoulders. They walked up the cement steps that led to a small office composed of little more than a few desks and bulletin boards across the walls. On the desk occupied by Coach More lay two picture frames, as well as several original drawings dedicated to him in the familiar markings of small children. Aaron and Terry had seen various family pictures, as well as the drawings formed in the unmistakable craftsmanship of children, come and go, constantly replaced by new ones.

There was, however, a single photograph that constantly remained on Coach More's desk. It displayed him standing with two other men in Marine dress blues. The man to Coach More's left was clearly African American, but the man to his right seemed to be of some other type of ethnicity, more difficult to ascertain. He had a dark angular face, with bright blue eyes and thick brown hair that was combed to the side. While Aaron never assigned any great importance to the photograph, Terry often stared at it. He found the aspect of the man to Coach More's right particularly **intriguing**.

"You men have done a great job this year," said Coach More. "I already have college recruiters contacting me."

Aaron and Terry smiled.

Coach More smirked. "Don't get too excited! These are small colleges. Wait till next year because it's going to get real interesting. That's when the big schools are going to start calling. But the reason I called you both here is to tell you that we've decided to attend the Arizona State football camp next summer. We think your class is special and so we want to invest in you. Once you guys graduate…. Well, I don't think Avondale is going to see a collection of men like yourselves for a long time. Maybe never."

Aaron's eyes became wide. "Coach, that's incredible! So how many guys are going?"

"About ten. That's all we can afford. Think of yourselves as our Special Ops."

"Sir, if it's expensive, how are we going to go?" asked Aaron.

"We have a strong booster club. After our success this season, everyone's in agreement. All you men have to do is commit yourselves to our fundraisers. So, can I count on you both?"

Both boys nodded their heads.

"Yes, sir!" added Aaron with great enthusiasm.

"Okay, then, I'll be in touch," said Coach More. As Aaron turned to walk away, Coach More patted him on the back. "This year our goal was to reach the county finals, and we almost made it. With you two leading the way next year, we believe we can go even further." Coach More paused. "I'm talking about a state championship."

Aaron smiled as he rubbed his hands together. "Coach, I can't wait."

8

NARROW RAYS OF the early morning sunlight peeked into the old faded wooden walls of the barn. Aaron and Terry, dressed in a combination of dark work boots, blue overalls and old cowhide gloves, worked in opposite corners. Aaron lifted bucket after bucket, dumping a soup composed of corn husks and unwanted meaty parts into a large white ceramic trough. His biceps tightened and his forearms ached. Every once in a while he would pause, take off one of his gloves, and rub his eyes. He would also glance at Terry, who did not seem to be working with the same passion and commitment.

Once Aaron had finished with the last bucket, he tossed it aside and opened a gate which allowed two large hogs to feast. They rushed over to the trough, snorting as they did so, and then took gulps of the disgusting concoction, splattering it around their snouts and eyes. Aaron frowned at them, somewhat amused, and then approached Terry.

"What's wrong, man?" asked Aaron. "You still upset about the loss?"

"No," replied Terry. Holding a long green garden hose, he filled an adjacent trough with water.

"You mad because nobody ever watches us play?"

"No, I'm used to that," Terry replied. "Besides, lots of people watch us play. I have people congratulating me every time I walk down the street."

Aaron looked at him. "You know what I mean. People we know."

"Yes," said Terry, "people like family."

"Yeah," said Aaron. He adjusted his crusty gray suede gloves.

The two boys walked over to another part of the barn. They each grabbed pitchforks which were leaning against a wall of the barn. Then, they walked over to a small hill of hay.

"Then what?" asked Aaron, scooping up a bale of straw. "You played a hell of a game! If it weren't for that last touchdown pass, we would've won! We would've been in the finals! Hell, maybe we would've went on to play Yuma!"

"Gone," whispered Terry.

"Huh?"

"Nothing," said Terry.

"Don't even sweat it, bro, 'cause next year we're going to take it all! You heard what Coach said. Our class is special! You, me, Buckey, Lucas and Leo. We're going to dominate! And I ain't just talking football! We're talking basketball, track, you and me in the relay, Jeff in the shot put and the discus, Leo in the high jump." Aaron began to sway his hips and move his arms rhythmically in the air. "I can't wait! I can't wait!"

He bumped Terry with the side of his hip, which drew an annoyed furrowing of the brow.

"Can it get any better?" sang Aaron. "Can it get any better?"

Terry shrugged, but said nothing as he continued to shovel bundles of hay into the two stables within the barn.

"Yes, it can!" said Aaron, smiling at Terry. "How can it? How can it, you ask?"

"Actually, I didn't say anything," replied Terry in a serious tone.

"I'll tell you how!" continued Aaron, shouting into the cool morning air. "Because next summer we are going to football camp! Hoo-rah!"

Terry continued to work in silence.

"Say something, man!" said Aaron. "Tell me what's going on in that bullet head of yours!"

"Well, don't get me wrong," replied Terry. "It's just that it's going to be a big commitment. We're going to have to be at all of those meetings, fundraisers…"

"Yeah, so?" said Aaron. "Sounds like fun to me!"

"You think everything is fun," said Terry. "Life's not always easy, you know."

"Well, it ain't as hard as you make it out either, cuz!"

"Isn't," said Terry.

"Huh?"

"Life *isn't* as hard," repeated Terry.

"That's what I said!" said Aaron.

"No, you said *ain't*."

"Same difference," said Aaron, scowling at Terry.

"No, it's not," said Terry, "and *same difference* is an **oxymoron**."

"Whatever, Terry," said Aaron, raising his voice. "It's just words."

"No, there is correct grammar and there is the **colloquial** expression of an ignorant fool."

Aaron stopped, dropped his pitchfork, and pushed Terry hard in the chest. Terry fell back a few steps, recovered gracefully, and then began to laugh.

"I ought to bust your head!" said Aaron.

Terry dropped his pitchfork and raised his hands in a boxing position. Both boys possessed impressive physiques and at the age of sixteen, already stood slightly above six feet. Aaron was in good shape, sporting a lean, athletic build; but Terry was actually chiseled. Even his visage, unlike the slightly round face of Aaron, was very square and muscular, with high cheek bones and a perpendicular jawline. Though the boys often traded clothes, Aaron could not help but notice that shirts hung on Terry a little differently. He had the fast twitch muscle fiber that could easily be seen with even the slightest of movement, and it did not appear that there was even an ounce of fat on his body.

"Fly like a butterfly, sting like a bee! If you had half of my brains, you'd know you're not in my league!" said Terry, still laughing.

The boys playfully boxed and began to wrestle. Aaron did his best to grapple Terry down to the ground, but Terry quickly moved behind him and hoisted him high into the air before laying him mercifully onto a pile of hay. Terry then put his brown leather boot on Aaron's chest. As Terry laughed and Aaron struggled, a voice interrupted them.

"You call this working? Look at you two! You done scattered hay all over the floor!"

Terry quickly removed his boot and stood at attention. Aaron rose to his feet, frowned, and then brushed the hay off his overalls.

Granddad Bailey scratched his salt and pepper hair. "All right, all right, you both had your fun. I need water and hay in them stables before I bring the horses, so let's get moving! I saved 'em and I promised them both that I'd take care of 'em!"

"You promised the horses?" asked Terry.

Granddad Bailey scowled. "Yes, I did as a matter of fact! You got a problem with that?"

Terry furrowed his brow and shook his head. "No."

Aaron inclined his head and began to laugh. He covered his mouth, but the laughter continued. Granddad Bailey shook his head, smiled slightly, and then muttered, "All right, then, back to work."

"Yes, Granddad," said the boys in unison.

9

"ARE YOU GOING to be okay?" asked Terry.

The woman responded with large, blank eyes that were dominated by a mixture of white and yellow shades around the deep inner brown.

"Mother, please," said Terry.

"What do you want me to say?" she asked.

Terry did not respond. Instead, he stared at her, this woman, curled on an old beige couch covered by a white bedsheet, dressed in nothing more than a flimsy dark nightgown with open lacing that exposed her cleavage. Her slender arms had the marks of a heroin addict. Her nostrils possessed pinkish areas of raw skin that contrasted with her black face. Her hair fell limply to an area just above her shoulders. The abuse on her body had taken its toll, and the small glimpses of what was once an attractive woman were fading; a gift of youth quickly coming to an end. As Terry contemplated the significance of this person, this woman, a loud knocking on the front door interrupted his thoughts.

"Sorry, son, but I've got company," she said, walking away from Terry.

A man in his mid-forties entered the small apartment. His eyes immediately flashed toward Terry. "Isn't he a little young?"

"Shut your mouth, Lonnie," she said in a firm voice. "That's my son."

"Oh, my bad," he replied. "He staying?"

"No, no, he was just leaving."

Terry grimaced upon eye contact. The man standing before him had a scraggly black beard which had white hairs poking out on all sides. His belly hung below his untucked shirt. Terry struggled with feelings of contempt, disgust, and even hatred.

"Are you staring at me, boy?" he asked.

"I'm not a 'boy,' " said Terry. "I'm a young man."

Lonnie laughed. "A man? A man? You don't even look like you've used your first razor, boy!"

"Facial hair does not make one a man," said Terry.

Lonnie squinted. He took a few steps toward Terry. As he got closer, Terry looked down at him, unflinching.

"Maybe not, but this does." Lonnie pulled out a semi-automatic pistol. Slowly, he stroked the hammer and then the barrel.

"Hold on, Lonnie," said Terry's mother. "That's my son. My son, Lonnie! He's just a boy. No more than..." She scratched her forehead. "How old are you?"

Terry frowned. "She was right. I was just leaving."

"Yeah, that's right," added Lonnie. "You was just leaving."

Outside his mother's apartment, Terry sidestepped a few carelessly tossed cans and bottles, scattered trash and discarded old clothes. He then walked down a familiar street to catch the bus from Phoenix to Avondale. On the way, he glanced quickly at several men who were sitting against a dirty cement wall, their faces and all but their shoes hidden by the small streak of shade provided by one of the many small markets. In loud voices, they made comments to random pedestrians, visibly annoying each one. To Terry's chagrin, one of them pointed a large glass bottle at him.

"That's the one!"

"He ain't neither!"

"I'm telling you even his momma says he's mine!"

Terry attempted to ignore them, walking several steps further to the bus stop where a few people were sitting on a public bench. Seeing that it was occupied, Terry stood impatiently. He glanced downward at his black plastic wrist watch, straining to see the digital numbers.

"Hey, boy," a voice called out.

Terry turned his head. In front of him stood one of the derelicts he had seen sitting along the sidewalk. A middle-aged man with dark skin, he possessed patches of gray hair that conspicuously contained dust and loose pieces of dirt. His old stained collared shirt was loosely buttoned in the middle. His eyes were reddened and his teeth badly stained. In his right hand was a large glass bottle of malt liquor.

"See that man sitting over there," he continued. "Look, over there, the one waving his hand. Is that your daddy?"

Terry exhaled deeply, choking on the pungent body odor that reeked of alcohol, urine, and cigarette smoke. "Please go away."

"What you say?"

Terry struggled to remain calm. He repeated once more, "I told you to leave."

Instead of granting Terry's request, the derelict instead took a few steps toward him. "You think you can talk to me like that, boy?" he asked in a loud voice, holding his bottle near Terry's face. "Maybe I ought to teach you a little respect."

A heavyset woman sitting at the bus stop clutched her purse tightly. An older man moved his gray hat and shifted on the bench. As if from nowhere, a voice rang out, "He already treated you with more respect than you deserve, you old fool!"

Terry's eyes widened. To his right was a young gentleman of almost the same height. His face was a dark brown, slightly angular, smooth and soft. His black hair was nicely trimmed, perhaps a centimeter in length. He possessed a slender build, yet not overly so as he displayed definite muscle tone. Dressed in a cream colored silk shirt and blue tie, along with dark slacks and polished black shoes, he presented quite a dashing figure. But what struck Terry was not his suave face or impeccable clothing, but rather his eyes. They were large, abnormally so, and they never seemed to blink. Standing next to him were two black men and one white man. All three were clean-shaven and dressed in formal attire. They stood erect, their eyes focused, but they did not speak.

"In fact, if you were not such an ignorant waste of the human mind you would have recognized that a long time ago and therefore would never have asked such an absurd question!" continued the young gentleman, his voice practically singing in the pitch of a sweet tenor. Terry marveled. He had never heard such a voice. It was new. It was foreign, somewhat British by nature, and consisted of a strange composite of both charm and authority.

"And who the hell are you?" asked the derelict, still holding his glass bottle high in the air.

The young gentleman raised his head. His long delicate fingers, displaying shiny manicured fingernails, deftly moved about, adjusting his tie. "Does it matter? If you knew my name, would that enrich your miserable little inconsequential life in the most minimal way?" Waving his hand slowly in front of the derelict's face, he continued, "Why, just look at you! You have no profession, no purpose. Here you remain, wasting away, peddling quarters and a few dollar bills from people who respond to you not out of charity, but fear. And yet you have the audacity to think you are important enough to disturb this gentleman when in reality you should have the common sense to know your self-worth does not entitle you to such a privilege!"

The derelict scowled. He raised his bottle menacingly in the air but then lowered it slightly when the three men who resembled bodyguards quickly approached. "I—I don't know what you're talking about."

"Of course you don't, you uneducated fool!" The young gentleman grabbed the bottle from the derelict's hand, walked to the curb, and poured out the content, allowing the golden colored liquid to bubble down alongside the gutter. "You are far too ignorant and stupid to understand, so let me tell you exactly what you are going to do. First, you are going to apologize to this young man for meddling in his personal business. Next, you will request forgiveness of the fine people sitting on this bench for disturbing them with your lack of manners, your pathetic sense of equality, and the physical pain you cause them each day by the mere fact that they have to look at you and suffer your unbearable stench!"

Terry's perpendicular jaw slackened. The people on the bench sat rigidly, apparently too stunned to act. The derelict inclined his head, and then slowly turned toward Terry. "Sorry, man. I didn't mean no harm. Just trying to figure out if—"

"Enough!" interrupted the young gentleman. "You've already destroyed the few brain cells you had remaining. It's clear you're incapable of uttering a **coherent** apology! Spare us all the agony of having to listen to your senseless jargon and leave this instance!"

The derelict inclined his head and walked away in silence.

"Thank you," said Terry, still staring with his mouth agape. Then, choosing his words carefully, he continued, "May I know your name, please?"

The young gentleman turned to his three companions. "Do you hear how this man speaks?" Then, facing Terry, he extended his forefinger. "This is a true man, an evolved man, a developed man, a capable man."

The others nodded.

"My name is Doctor Timothy Ajala, my young brother," he said, extending his hand.

Grasping it, Terry whispered, "You're Timothy. I'm Terry..." Suddenly, unconsciously, Terry corrected himself, saying "I mean, Terrence. Terrence Washington."

"Do you know why I called you 'brother,' Terrence Washington?"

Terry paused before answering, looking into the two large orbs that never seemed to close. Finally, he replied, "Because I'm black."

"No."

Terry thought for a moment before adding, "African American?"

Timothy laughed. The other men around him laughed as well. Rather **didactically**, he replied, "Africa? Africa, you say? And what do you know of Africa? From what country do you hail? What tribe do you claim?"

Terry remained staring. He swallowed slowly.

"No," continued Timothy. "The brotherhood we share has little to do with our color. It has nothing to do with this." Timothy reached out and touched Terry's high cheekbone, his lips, and his closely razed hair. "In some parts of the world our minute differences could cause a war, and in other parts these differences would unite us."

Terry flinched uncomfortably. He took a few steps back.

"This is a mere shadow," said Timothy. "Some people gaze upon the same shadow, giving them a commonality, a point of reference, and so they believe they are one and the same, but that is not so, is it?" Without shifting his gaze for even a fraction of a moment, he continued, "No, we must consider other aspects, equally important, and perhaps even more so. Intellect, education, socio-economic class, language, nationality, culture, religion…"

Terry continued to stare at Timothy. His large eyes created a hypnotic effect, making it impossible for Terry to turn away.

"I called you 'brother' because I respect who you are—who you truly are. I do not respect shadows. I respect what is beyond the shadow. I respect this." Timothy touched Terry's right temple. "Spirit, soul, and body." Timothy then reached into his trousers and pulled out a small golden cardholder. "Anytime you need me, please, do not hesitate to call."

Terry accepted a small white card, holding it between his thumb and index finger. At the top in large black letters was the inscription: The Standard. Below was the name Doctor Timothy Ajala. Located in smaller letters in the right corner was personal contact information. Terry studied the card intently.

"Don't miss your bus, my young brother," said Timothy.

Terry looked behind him. He had not even noticed the bus which had pulled up to the curb.

"Thank you, Doctor Ajala," said Terry.

Timothy nodded and smiled. "Please, call me Timothy."

"Yes, sir. I mean, yes, Timothy."

Terry slowly entered the bus. He searched for a seat next to a window, where he curiously watched four nicely dressed men walk down the street.

10

WALKING PAST AN old simple wooden dresser composed of three rectangular drawers, Aaron approached a bed supported by a rusty metal spring frame. "Get up, man!" he shouted, shaking Terry by the shoulder.

"What?" asked Terry, sleepily, turning slightly in his bed. "What time is it?"

"You're gonna be late!" replied Aaron with great excitement in his voice. "They're here!"

"Calm down, Aaron," whispered Terry as he rolled onto his side. "Who's here?"

"Terry, just get out of bed and hurry up or you're gonna miss the pancake breakfast!" said Aaron.

"Oh, that. I'm not going."

"What?" asked Aaron in disbelief.

Terry propped himself up on one elbow and actually made an effort to open his eyes. He rubbed away the sleepy dust. "I'm not going. I have a forensics contest in Phoenix this afternoon."

Aaron scowled. "A foreign contest?"

"Forensics," repeated Terry. "The debate team. I have to be at school at nine to meet the team and practice before we leave for Saint Mary."

"That's cutting it close, but I think you can make it," replied Aaron. "Do your part and then someone can give you a ride."

"Aaron, did you hear what I said?" replied Terry. "I'm not going to get hot and sweaty cooking and cleaning and then rush off to the school. I have to look nice. It's a big event! The last one of the year!"

"But you have to go!" said Aaron. "You can't miss this, Terry. It's probably your last chance!"

"My last chance?" repeated Terry. "For what?"

"For football camp," said Aaron. "Terry, this is important. We're the few. The chosen ones. The Booster Club's going to be there. Bunch of old players and all."

"There's more to life than football, Aaron," replied Terry, rolling back on his stomach and putting his face down on his pillow. "Now get out of my room. I need my rest to be alert for the competition."

Aaron shook his head in disgust. "You don't deserve to be part of the special ops this summer. You've gone AWOL."

Terry's laughter, which was muffled by his pillow, was still loud enough for Aaron to hear.

Aaron frowned. "Something funny?"

"Yeah, you," replied Terry, rolling over once more to face Aaron. "Listen to yourself, Aaron! You sound like a damn commercial for the Marines! You're not Coach, you know! You can think for yourself! We don't just play football! There are other sports and other activities in school that are equally important. More important, in fact!"

"Nothing's more important than football," said Aaron tersely.

"You have a brain, Aaron! I suggest you use it!"

"Whatever," said Aaron, "I'm out of here. I'm not going to be late because of your lazy ass." Once at the door of Terry's room, Aaron added, "And I'm tired of making excuses for you."

"That's fine with me," replied Terry, rolling aggressively to his side so that Aaron was left looking at the back of his head. "I never asked you to."

As the sound of the horn increased in frequency, Aaron left the house quickly and ran toward a large brown van. As he hopped into the front seat, his coach smiled. Aaron returned his smile and then turned back and greeted the other students sitting in the bench seats composed of three horizontal rows.

"Sorry to honk the horn," said Coach More.

"That's okay, Coach, everyone's up. The only thing my grandfather's mad about is the fact I'm not working right now," replied Aaron.

Coach More held up his watch. In a serious tone, he said, "It's five minutes past seven. That's some serious insubordination, soldier."

"Sorry, Coach," said Aaron once more. "I was trying to…. Oh, no excuses. It won't happen again."

Coach More smiled. "And Terry?"

Aaron hesitated, not able to hide his disappointment. "He's still asleep. I think he's going to some school debate. We can't count on him."

"It's okay, you're here," said Coach More. "Besides, with Jeff, we may not have had enough room for ten, anyway."

A chorus of laughter was heard throughout the van.

"Hey, it's not my fault Coach doesn't get us a bus!" shouted Jeff.

Jeff Buckey, part of Aaron's celebrated graduating class, lived on a ranch not too far away. He was a huge boy, standing six feet and five inches and weighing close to three hundred pounds. Aaron often teased him, saying that he was actually larger than any of the cows that grazed on the Buckey ranch. Jeff played center for the team and was capable of creating huge holes for both Aaron and Terry; but though a force on the field, he was actually a gentle giant when off it. With short brown hair that was combed to the side and a smooth boyish face, Jeff had a youthful aspect to him despite his girth. Coach More had to constantly motivate him and tell him it was okay to be aggressive, to use his full strength, but Jeff was such a good nature that he never seemed to hit opposing players too hard for fear of hurting them.

"So what's up with your cousin?" asked Jeff. "Don't he realize how much we need him?"

"I don't know, Jeff," replied Aaron. "To be honest with you, something's not right."

"What could be wrong with Terry?" asked Jeff. "He's got it made! He's smart, the girls are always after him, and he's a total stud! He runs the forty in under five seconds and the guy has a forty inch vertical! Remember that three-sixty dunk last year?"

Carson Mills, a boy with bright red hair and freckles, shouted, "Sounds like someone's in love!"

"The dude's awesome in everything!" added Leonel Reyes, the team's tight end who was almost as tall as Jeff but much more slenderly built. With his short spiky dark hair and clear ruddy complexion, he emanated the strange feeling that he had been under the sun the entire day but without having suffered any skin damage. "Next year we're going to dominate! Football, basketball—"

"It's going to be lob city, Aaron!" interrupted Jeff. He then made a downward motion, as if dunking a basketball.

A few of the other kids nodded.

"Jeff, even if I placed the ball perfectly for you, you'd have to get on a trampoline to dunk!" said Aaron.

A burst of laughter erupted in the back of the van.

"More like a crane!" said Leonel. "He'd break a trampoline!"

"Hey! I ain't a brotha! I got cursed with white man's syndrome!" said Jeff.

"Leo ain't a brotha neither and he's got hops," said Aaron between laughter.

Leonel smiled widely. He moved his hands up and down near his face and torso. "Golden brown, Aaron, so in a way, I'm half black."

Once again, laughter burst out throughout the van.

"You just might be, man," said Aaron. "But I think in your case it's more like golden red."

"If he's half black than Jeff's half human!" said Lucas Wright, the team's middle linebacker.

"You're just jealous," replied Jeff. "You can't get off the ground any better than I can."

"I guess you got white man's syndrome, too, bro!" said Aaron.

Lucas scowled, his large bald head showing a row of lines above his eyes. He then raised both arms in the air and flexed, displaying his large biceps that pulled at his tightly fitted T-shirt. "Hey, some black men were made to jump and some of us were made to be strong!"

"And some got neither one!" shouted Leonel, pointing to Terry's understudy, Larry Butler.

"That's cold, man," said Aaron, wagging his head.

Coach More let out a slight smile. The boys continued to talk loudly until the van pulled into the parking lot of the Veteran's Hall, a large, rather old wooden building that displayed white flakes of falling paint throughout its walls and roof.

"Okay, follow me, men," said Coach More. He led them quickly to the back where he unlocked the door and led them to the kitchen. "Aaron, you and Leo got the grill, right?"

"Yeah, Coach, we got it," replied Aaron. "I'm a fry cook legend."

Leonel smirked. "Dude, you sound like a cartoon character."

"Lucas," continued Coach More, "you and Jeff are taking care of the tables and everyone else is helping them. I'll be in and out."

"Yeah, some of us have to do the men's work," said Lucas.

"Yeah, yeah, now go roll out those tables," said Aaron, pointing his spatula toward the kitchen door.

Signaling the remaining boys, Coach More continued, "Hand them food, pancake batter, orange juice, coffee. Whatever they need."

"Yes, sir," replied a group of boys.

A few moments later, a tanned brunette accompanied by two young girls with shoulder length brown hair walked in the front entrance. "I'm here!" she announced, smiling broadly.

"Hi, honey!" replied Coach More. "And you have two lovely helpers, I see."

"Hi, Daddy," said the girls in unison.

Soon thereafter, Coach More's two assistant coaches arrived.

"Just tell us what to do, Coach," said Coach Spriggs.

"Coach Spriggs, why don't you help out in the kitchen, and Coach Morales, you can keep an eye on Jeff and the crew out here."

"You got it, Coach."

"Here you go, Mrs. More," said Jeff, setting down a rectangular table in front of the entrance.

"Thank you, Jeff."

"Wow! You're strong!" said one of Coach More's daughters.

Jeff smiled.

"Pick me up! Pick me up!" sang both girls in unison.

"Okay, okay," said Jeff, "put your hands in mine and hold on."

The girls did so and squealed in delight as Jeff lifted them both high off the ground. When Jeff put them down, they demanded that he do it again.

"One more time! One more time!" they chanted.

"Come on, you're gonna get me in trouble with your dad," said Jeff, smiling as he turned away.

"Leave him alone, girls," said Mrs. More. "I need you to help me with tickets."

"Uh, Jeff, are you going to work or what?" asked Lucas, pointing to a stack of chairs. "We need to put these around the tables. Quit playing around and give us a hand."

"I'm coming, I'm coming," said Jeff. "It's not my fault that girls find me irresistible!"

Lucas snorted. "Yeah, little girls that are still in kindergarten."

"That's because they have a lot in common!" said Carson, pointing to his forehead.

The main room was soon full to capacity with parents, booster club supporters, and several former players who had settled down to live in Avondale and nearby Phoenix. Throughout the hall, people could be heard teasing players, wishing the coaches good luck for next season, and **reminiscing** about former games and their greatest moments. But as positive as the atmosphere appeared to be, people seemed to notice who was absent more than who was present.

"Where's that star running back of yours, Jenz?" asked an older gentleman as he sipped some of his coffee.

"He wasn't able to make it."

"He's not going to camp?" asked another man as he stuffed his mouth with a large piece of his pancake.

Coach More turned to face a different table. "Not sure, but we'll be ready by the start of the season. We have a great group. Holmes, Buckey, Reyes and Wright. I think they'll be state picks next year. I'm really excited about our potential."

A third man joined the conversation. He had a large pinkish bald head and curly gray hair on the sides. Pointing his finger at Coach More, he began, "Look, Jenzen, that's fine and all, but without Washington the team's not going to go all the way. You know we have high hopes for next year. This is the kind of group that only comes around once, so you have to make the best of it."

Coach More's jaw tightened. "I totally agree."

"Without Terry we can't reach the finals," said a woman nearby, "and that's the goal next season, isn't it? Some of the boys told me he hasn't attended a single fundraiser, Coach. Is that right?"

Coach More swirled his tongue around his closed lips. "Yes, that's right. He probably won't be attending summer camp, but I'll talk to him as soon as it's over. He's a busy young man."

"I sure hope so," replied another, shaking his head, "or we can kiss that state title goodbye."

"Forget the state," added another, "we probably won't even get as far as we did this year."

Coach More rubbed the side of his head vigorously. "Excuse me, everyone, but I have to check on the men in the back." Quickly entering the kitchen, he asked, "How we doing in here?"

"Everything's smooth, Coach," said Aaron, smiling. He then frowned and furrowed his brow. "Why, did someone complain?"

Coach More paused. He then replied slowly, "No, everyone's happy. You men did a great job. I think it's time we start cleaning up. I'm going to go outside for a minute to get a breath of fresh air."

Aaron glanced at Leonel. Coach Spriggs then followed Coach More outside the door. As the boys began cleaning, Coach Morales walked into the kitchen, followed by Jeff.

"Only a few people out there," said Coach Morales. "We just need to throw away the trash and put the tables and chairs away."

The boys in the kitchen nodded.

"Same here," said Aaron.

"Hey, uh, where's Coach and Coach Spriggs?"

"They went outside," said Aaron. "Is something wrong with Coach?"

Coach Morales frowned. "I don't think so," he replied before heading out the back door.

Lucas and Jeff entered the kitchen. "What's going on?" asked Lucas. "Why y'all so quiet?"

"Something's wrong," replied Aaron.

"I think I may know," said Jeff in a very solemn tone.

Each boy in the kitchen leaned forward to listen to Jeff Buckey.

"Well, I never knew this, but..." Jeff paused and inclined his head.

"What?" asked Aaron impatiently.

"Well, I don't know if I should tell you guys," Jeff continued.

"Man, just say it," said Lucas.

Jeff raised his large boyish face. After a long pause, he spoke very slowly. "Well, I couldn't help but listen to people talking to Coach, and... well..."

Aaron motioned with his hand. "What?"

"I just learned that Coach's first name is Jenzen."

"Dude, shut up!" said Aaron.

Lucas scowled. "Man, I should throw that leftover bacon at you."

"He'd probably just eat it!" said Leonel.

The boys broke into laughter.

Outside, Coach More spoke with his assistants.

"But what's the problem, exactly?" asked Coach Morales. "I mean, isn't it a good thing that Terry's so well-rounded?"

Coach More scowled. "I think that's another way of saying he lacks focus. That's the first thing they taught us in the Marines."

"Coach," interrupted Coach Spriggs, "Terry's not your typical athlete. He has a full load of advanced placement classes. He's always been worried about balancing his studies and sports. And remember, he doesn't just play football. The kid's a star in basketball and track, too."

"Yeah, but those sports aren't as important," said Coach More.

Coach Spriggs shook his head and frowned. "Coach, with all due respect, you know I'm in charge of the track and field program; and Terry's got a real future there. The other boys are good, but he's phenomenal."

Coach More folded his tan muscular arms in front of his chest. "I don't get it. Isn't Jeff Buckey our county champion?"

Coach Spriggs nodded. "Yeah, Jeff's good. Real good. In fact, I'd say he's one of the top throwers in the state, but when we get to the national trials he gets overshadowed by other boys. Terry, on the other hand…" The eyes of Coach Spriggs widened greatly, the white orbs contrasting with his black skin. "He's already set records in the long jump, the triple jump, the two hundred. And once he ran the hundred in ten seconds!"

"Ten seconds!" exclaimed Coach Morales. He scratched his high forehead at the very tip of his thinning black hair. "Is that a record?"

"For a high school student it is," replied Coach Spriggs, "and I'm not talking just this year. I mean—ever."

"I don't remember hearing about all this," said Coach More.

"That's because he did it at a league meet," said Coach Spriggs. "It's not official. They didn't check for conditions."

"So you're telling me that this is why Terry hasn't been to any of our fundraisers? He's too focused on track?"

Coach Spriggs shook his head, sighed, and replied, "Actually, no. We're done, and Terry didn't even make it to the end of the season. He let a lot of people down, including Aaron."

"What do you mean?" asked Coach Morales.

"They run the relay together. We had some times that were right up there with the best teams in the state, but without Terry, we never advanced past county. He disappeared." Coach Spriggs scratched his razed black hair. "And to think, we had aspirations of a state title and maybe even more."

"Well, did he say why?" asked Coach More.

"No," replied Coach Spriggs. "I tried to talk to him about it, but all he said was that I wouldn't understand."

"Well, Aaron must know," said Coach More. "I'll talk to him. But no matter what Terry's going through, I have to submit names for camp next week, so it doesn't look like he's going. It just wouldn't be fair to the others who've been working so hard." After a slight pause, he added, "It's really a shame, you know. If Terry doesn't get his act together he's going to lose out on a lot of scholarships. I mean, with his talent, he could go anywhere."

The two assistant coaches nodded. They were only too aware that Terry was the kind of athlete that appeared once in a generation.

11

HUDDLED TOGETHER IN a large indoor atrium, Terry nervously scanned the many people seated behind him as well as the tables decorated with several ribbons of green and white. The room was festive and had a classical, dignified air about it. He observed his table located under a large Avondale sign.

"Well, are you guys ready?" asked Mrs. Baldwin, a tall thin woman with short blonde hair that curled down to her shoulders.

Terry, along with three other students, nodded affirmatively.

"Nervous?" she asked.

Terry loosened his white collar and black tie while the other members of the team simply shrugged their shoulders.

"You've prepped us well, Mrs. Baldwin," replied Monica. The intensity of her voice matched her facial expressions: sharp brown eyes and a strong prominent jaw. Her only aspect that did not express a sort of dominant energy was her hair, which was long and fluffy. It surrounded her dark face in thick, cascading waves.

"Well, it was my pleasure," replied Mrs. Baldwin. "I love teaching forensics, and of course, working with the final four. You guys have been one of my very favorite groups, and the good news is that everyone except for Dennis will be here next year. Well, I'm assuming you're all going to continue."

"Of course," said Monica. "Right, guys?"

Terry and the girl sitting next to him, Nancy, both responded with a somewhat half-hearted smile.

"If it weren't for the importance of maintaining my 4.0 grade point average, Mrs. Baldwin, I'd flunk just so I could return next year," said Dennis.

Terry shook his head. The two girls rolled their eyes, and even Mrs. Baldwin frowned. Dennis, however, smiled widely, showing off large dimples that made tiny indentures within his white, pudgy face.

"Terry, remember, it's okay to be aggressive," said Mrs. Baldwin.

"Yes, ma'am," replied Terry.

"Yeah, just follow my lead," said Dennis. "Try to pretend you're throwing a touchdown or shooting a basket or something."

"Yeah. Thanks, Dennis," said Terry, his voice dripping with sarcasm. "That clarifies everything."

"Okay, everyone, let's take our positions," said Mrs. Baldwin. "We've studied hard, so now it's just time to compete."

"We got this, Mrs. Baldwin," said Monica. She then smiled, which caused the small golden shaped heart embedded in her nose to wiggle.

"Look, I appreciate your confidence, Monica," replied Mrs. Baldwin, "and that winning smile. But Saint Mary is a private school and we're on their home turf. They're not in the finals every year for nothing."

As the Avondale team walked to their brown rectangular table, four students dressed in matching green berets, white blazers, and green collared shirts crossed their path. Each one was quite attractive and possessed a certain air of confidence. The two young men wore white slacks while the young ladies strode in white skirts that reached down to their thighs.

"Hi, there."

Terry looked up. He had seen his share of pretty girls, many of whom had flirted openly with him, but the young lady standing before him had a certain aspect that made him pause. She was not classically beautiful, as there was a certain blandness to her facial features. Still, he found himself, unwittingly, soaking in her entire semblance. She had long red hair that was pulled back against a white face free of blemishes yet sprinkled sporadically with freckles around the bridge of her nose and cheeks. Her eyes were an Indian green. Her teeth were very bright and nicely shaped, and her lips were a deep red, contrasting with her skin tone while simultaneously blending harmoniously with the red hair that fell behind her back in a single strand.

"You know, it's okay to fraternize with the enemy," she continued.

"Oh, don't mind him, he's our weak link," interrupted Dennis. "The only time he's really effective is if he loses his temper. Allow me to introduce myself. I'm Dennis Landen the 3rd."

Dennis adjusted his small blue bow tie with both hands. He then licked his fingertips and ran them over his long brown hair before extending his hand. The young lady hesitated, frowned, and then slowly touched his palm. "Nice to meet you," she replied, smiling courteously before quickly withdrawing her hand. Turning from Dennis to Terry, she continued, "And do you have a name?"

"Oh, I'm sorry. Terrence. Terrence Washington, but most of my friends call me Terry."

"So you do speak," she said, smiling. "That could come in handy today."

Terry laughed. "Yes, I suppose it could."

"I'm Emily. Emily Potter."

"My pleasure, Emily," said Terry. He, too, then offered his hand to her. Emily grasped it securely and then to Terry's surprise, she maintained her grip. "Is it okay if I call you Terrence?" she asked. "I mean, that wouldn't affect me negatively in any way, would it?"

Terry furrowed his brow. "I—I don't understand."

"Because I like the name 'Terrence,' " she replied, "and I want to call you that, but I want to be your friend even more."

Terry remained staring at her, his hand still encircled around her smaller, softer fingers.

"You said that your friends call you 'Terry,' " said Emily.

"You can call me 'Denny' if you want," interrupted Dennis.

Emily said nothing in reply but instead seemed fixated on Terry. Monica then approached, stepping between them. With an exaggerated smile, she faced Emily and began, "Hi, I'm Monica, and you can call me 'Monica.' I'm the Avondale team captain."

Emily slowly released Terry's hand.

Monica's eyes widened as she folded her arms in front of her white blouse which revealed the upper part of her cleavage. "I'm so sorry if I'm being too direct, but that's how our teacher taught us to speak in competition, and since we're here to take you guys down, I thought it to be the appropriate rhetorical strategy."

Emily smiled. "Well, yes, good luck to you, Avondale." She then winked at Terry. "And good luck to you, Terrence."

Terry smiled timidly before replying, "Thank you, Emily."

As Terry's eyes followed Emily's movements to the table located on the opposite side of the room, Monica slapped him hard on the chest. Upon doing so, she squealed in pain. "Ouch! Man, what's your chest made out of, rock?"

Terry furrowed his brow. "What was that for?"

"What was that for!" repeated Monica, attempting to mimic Terry's low, soft-spoken voice. "What do you think?" She raised her hands to both sides of her face. "We're here to win, not melt with googily eyes at the competition."

"I was just being polite," said Terry. "Besides, she came to me."

"Yeah, to distract you!" Monica replied. "Please! Don't flatter yourself! Trust me, she's not interested! Now get it together and sit down!"

Terry curled his lips and shook his head simultaneously. "I didn't see you chastising Dennis," whispered Terry as they settled into their assigned table and began to organize their note cards.

"Dennis is a senior!" hissed Monica. "He's done this before! Not to mention that he thinks so highly of himself that he never gets distracted, especially when he's talking in front of a captive audience!" Monica divided four stacks of cards evenly among the table. "You, on the other hand, I'm not so sure about."

"Ladies and gentlemen," interrupted a gentleman dressed in a formal black and white tuxedo. "I am Mr. Huxley, the official moderator of today's event." His voice, amplified by the microphone attached to his podium, echoed throughout the room. "Welcome to the Maricopa Forensics Competition. Before we begin, I would like everyone to take a moment and honor our two finalists. Saint Mary Prep School and Avondale High School."

The audience responded with enthusiastic applause.

"Also, seated at the very back of the room, please welcome our three judges."

A polite, somewhat reserved applause followed.

"As agreed, the two captains will now approach me and receive their sealed envelopes. Our topic today is Intelligence: Genetic or Environmental.

Monica smiled at the audience and then proceeded to the moderator's podium. Across from her, a tall young man did the same.

"Please take your envelopes," instructed Mr. Huxley. "Shake hands, and I compliment both teams for having made it this far. I also wish to remind both captains that you will have exactly one minute to prep your team for the four rounds that follow."

"*Hola, qué tal?*" greeted the captain from Saint Mary.

"You speak Spanish?" exclaimed Monica.

"*Por supuesto! Soy mexicano!*"

"You're Mexican?" Monica tilted her head back. "Sorry, I thought you were white."

"I am," replied the young man.

"*Pero dijiste que eres mexicano.*"

"Excuse me," interrupted Mr. Huxley. "You both need to return to your teams. We need to stay on schedule."

"My name is Daniel Castillo. Good luck to you and your team."

Monica giggled. Her face glowed. "*Mucho gusto. Soy Mónica Garza.*"

"*El gusto es mío, señorita Garza,*" said Daniel, shaking her hand before walking away.

Monica remained standing with a wide smile displayed across her face.

"Uh, Monica, we're over here," called out Dennis.

"Huh? Oh, sorry," said Monica, turning around to face her team.

"What was that lecture about not getting distracted?" asked Terry.

"Did you see him?" Monica asked. "He's so tall! And his brown hair? It's so long and wavy! And those sideburns? Hey, did you see his eyes?"

"Yeah, he's gorgeous!" replied Nancy.

"Something that works in our favor!" said Dennis.

Monica frowned. "What?"

"Good looking guys are always less intelligent," replied Dennis. "Anyway, let's get organized! Open the envelope already!"

Recovering her composure, Monica replied, "Oh, yeah, sorry." She then carefully opened the envelope, revealing a large blue card with the words: Intelligence is Environmental. Monica pumped her fist in the air. "Yes! That's the position I was hoping for."

"I feel more confident on the other side," whispered Nancy.

"Well, that's why we studied this topic inside out," replied Monica. "Now, come on, you can do it."

"Too late for a pep speech," interrupted Dennis. "It's time to strategize, people! We all know our roles. Get your environmental notes out and be ready! I'm going to dazzle them with my opening speech, so all you guys have to do is hold your own."

"Avondale will now begin round one," stated the moderator.

Dennis walked over to a podium. He cleared his voice loudly several times. "Ladies and gentlemen, colleagues, and my esteemed opponents, I bid you a wonderful afternoon and hope you will find today's debate both educational as well as entertaining." He paused. He held his hands up high, as if attempting to stop the nonexistent adulation of the audience. Then, opening his arms and gesturing toward himself, he continued, "Though this topic be controversial, we wish to convince you that clearly intelligence is based on our environment and is not the result of our DNA. Studies such as the ones carried out by respected neurologist John Eccles demonstrate that we use perhaps up to one percent of our brain, and though we often refer to people as being slow, or on the opposite spectrum, as being ingenious, the vast majority of all human beings are the same. What, then, causes one person, such as myself, to take the most challenging classes and to succeed with a perfect 4.0 average and above, mind you, while others struggle in the most remedial classes and often fail or pass with the minimum grade? The factors are numerous and have nothing to do with the most complicated organ we possess, the brain, but instead have much more to do with such factors as our family environment, the schools we attend, and our place of residence."

A light flashed, indicating that Dennis' allotted time was about to expire. He promptly made his last remarks and bowed to the crowd as they burst into applause. The moderator then motioned to Daniel, who smiled and began his team's opening speech. Unlike Dennis, who was short and pudgy, Daniel's tall svelte physique, wavy brown hair, and firm jawline gave him a commanding presence. "I, too, would like to thank everyone who is here today," began Daniel with a charming smile that seemed to present itself effortlessly. "Parents, teachers, administrators, our moderator, our worthy opponents, and anyone else I may have failed to mention. Though our team believes that our environment has some effect on our intelligence, we believe that our brains are formed genetically, just as the rest of our bodies. For example, what color are your eyes? What color is your skin? How tall are you? We believe these rhetorical questions are easily answered. We cannot separate our brains from any other organs of our body. Yes, we may develop these at different rates, but our limits, our potential, is given to us at birth. To deny this would be to deny the very science of Darwin's evolutionary theories."

Amidst much applause, Daniel continued to present several scientific facts in a tone exuding great confidence. Daniel waved to them appreciatively until his speech came to an end. The moderator then nodded to both boys and signaled for them to sit down. The second round began with more debate and more presentations of case studies and statistics. The third round followed in the same vein. Finally, after nearly thirty minutes of intense argumentation, Terry walked over to the podium. Reluctantly, he faced his opponent. It was Emily.

"Ladies and gentlemen, we are now ready for our final round," began Mr. Huxley to much applause. "In this round, each speaker will be able to restate his or her team's position, and then rebuttal from both sides will follow. Is the team from Avondale High School ready?"

Terry nodded.

"Is the team from Saint Mary Prep School ready?"

Emily smiled. The moderator then signaled for Terry to begin.

"Ladies and gentlemen, you have been presented with an overabundance of evidence from both sides, but I would like to point out the case study known as the Equal Opportunity Project. Doctor Richard Hebert held an unprecedented experiment in which he took forty children from the worst neighborhoods. From these forty small children, twenty were enrolled in an accelerated class and given after-school programs to assist them in their studies. The other twenty were enrolled in regular classes and given no assistance. The results were startling. The experimental group that received so many services had an average IQ of 120 by the end of elementary school, whereas the control group that received no services had an average IQ of 87."

Terry nodded to the moderator.

"I confess I am not familiar with the study presented by Mr. Washington," said Emily.

Terry smiled affectionately upon hearing her refer to him by his surname.

"I would like to rebut his argument, however, by making the following two statements." Emily held up one finger. "First, did this Doctor Hebert make studies of the parents of these children as well as the grandparents?" She raised two fingers. "And secondly, though an IQ score of thirty-three points seems extreme, it is not. An IQ of one hundred is considered average or a mean, and elementary children are often grossly underestimated or overestimated. It is hard to take this study seriously due to the many flaws it presents."

Emily took a deep breath. She shuffled a few of her cards before placing one on top of the podium. "Instead, I wish to redirect our audience to an article in the respected academic journal entitled 'Social Stratification.' It distinctly demonstrates that educated parents, that is, parents who have graduated from college and who commonly have more than a hundred books in their home, increase the possibility that their children will also attend college. This study, I may add, was conducted over twenty years and with case studies that occurred in more than twenty countries. We must also contemplate the other side of this study. Uneducated parents were fifty percent more likely to have children who will never pursue higher education. I think this clearly shows that intelligent, educated people produce children who will also be intelligent. Perhaps Mr. Washington misunderstood the depth of the argument? Perhaps he did not contemplate the resources available to all, such as public libraries, computer labs, and cellular phones? Intelligent people create an environment that will enhance intelligence. So, when you think about it, there is some truth to what our opponents are saying. Our environment does have some influence on our intelligence, but even so, that requires a source, and that source is intelligent people. Intelligent people create the environment."

Many members throughout the audience began to clap and cheer.

"Ladies and gentlemen, please withhold your applause until the end of the round," admonished Mr. Huxley.

"Do you wish me to address your question or merely your statement?" asked Terry.

"Excuse me, Terrence?" asked Emily.

Terry paused for a moment. His face broke into a large smile. "Yes, Emily, earlier you said that you wished to present two statements, but that very statement was false as you actually presented one interrogative, that is, a question, and one declarative, that is, a statement."

A few of the students from Saint Mary frowned. Monica smiled and banged her fist on the table. Emily paused briefly, and then her face also broke into a wide smile. "I stand corrected, Mr. Washington. I suppose I would like you to answer my question and address my statement."

"Certainly, Emily," replied Terry. "Doctor Hebert did study the parents of these forty toddlers. Most of the mothers possessed IQ scores below eighty, and many of the fathers were absent altogether. And, while it may be true that one hundred is an average score, no one can deny the huge difference between these two groups of students. If mathematical terms seem cold and uninspiring, I offer my opponent..." Terry paused and motioned toward Emily. "Excuse me, I offer Miss Emily Potter the evidence of real people, of real lives. The experimental group was not only doing better academically, but socially as well."

"Thank you, Terrence," replied Emily, "but once again you and your teammates fail to look at this issue from a broad perspective. It is easy to help elementary children improve because their level is so rudimentary. In fact, it is not uncommon at all for parents to declare their children geniuses, or the next Einstein, merely because they learn simple math or read basic passages from a picture book. My own mother told her friends I would be the next Mozart when I played 'Twinkle Twinkle Little Star'!"

The audience broke into laughter. Terry, too, released a small chuckle.

"Being able to decode language and the ability to actually comprehend language are two very different skills," continued Emily. "Studies suggest that any child can learn to *read*; even babies can learn to *read*. This is because they are not truly reading, but rather *decoding*. They have learned the sounds of the alphabet or they have memorized words as symbols or matched them to a picture. I am sure the lavish attention paid to the children in the study mentioned by Mr. Washington did show positive results, but later in life I imagine that those children turned out to be very average students, if that. Perhaps, Terrence, if your study had occurred with high school students, or college students, we might all be able to take your evidence more seriously."

Terry paused. He looked at Emily. He then looked at the audience. He opened his mouth, but then slowly closed it. He glanced toward his teammates. Dennis frowned. Monica waved her hand in the air, forming rapid little circles. The audience began to fidget.

"There is such a study—a case study," began Terry. "I have personal information of a high school student whose mother is a prostitute…" His voice trailed off for a moment. Terry reached up and loosened his collar and tie. "…and a person heavily addicted to illegal substances." He swallowed deeply. As he did so, the quiet whispering within the audience stopped completely. "She is not educated," he continued, "and I seriously doubt that anyone who knows her would consider her intelligent. Anyway, when this aforementioned high school student was a little boy, his mother often left him alone. Alone to figure things out, like, how to turn on the television, or the toaster, or to use the toilet."

Terry inclined his head. He paused to wipe the perspiration from his face. "This poor little boy had nothing to eat and inhaled marijuana on a daily basis. Sometimes, his mother even poured cheap beer in his cereal instead of milk. There were never any books in the home, and to this day, he does not know who his father is." Terry paused once again. His eyes had become moist. The room remained tensely still. "But, some relatives, an older couple, came into his life. They took him into their home when he was ten years old. The older man became like a grandfather to him, the older woman like a grandmother. They, too, were not highly educated people, but they made him feel safe. They instructed him to respect his elders and to do well in school. It did not take long for this young boy to go from the very lowest classes in elementary school to the very highest in secondary school. This young man was once so afraid, and shy, that people actually thought he was mentally disabled because he rarely spoke. Now, however, he can be quite eloquent when he chooses to be."

After a moment of silence, Emily replied, "That is a very moving anecdote, Mr. Washington, inspiring even, but you never referenced your case study."

"It's a true story," Terry replied. "I can assure you."

"What is your source, then?" asked Emily.

Terry stood with his mouth firmly closed.

"Excuse me," said Emily, "are you refusing to cite your source? If so, your case study cannot be considered credible."

Terry inclined his head. He clutched the podium in his large muscular hands.

"Your source, Mr. Washington," Emily repeated.

Terry looked directly into her eyes. "I am the source, I was that boy, and I am that young man. And I am not an **anomaly**."

Emily's mouth slowly opened. A collective gasp was heard deep from within the audience. The tables of both debate teams remained quiet. Mr. Huxley, the moderator, began to fidget. He seemed lost as to how he should proceed. Finally, he addressed Emily. "There are thirty seconds remaining in our final round. Does Saint Mary have further rebuttal?"

Emily slowly moved her tongue across the surface of her lips. "No, sir, I have nothing more to say."

"Then we will conclude our debate and wait for our judges to inform us of their decision," said Mr. Huxley.

Terry and Emily sat down at their respective tables. The entire room was silent. Then, a bulky man with thinning dark hair and a large mustache stood up and began to put his hands together. As if a sign granting the audience permission to do so as well, others followed until the entire room was filled with heavy applause. Soon, everyone was on their feet.

A single judge approached the moderator from the very back of the room. In her hand was a sealed envelope. The Avondale table sat rigidly. On the other side of the room, the team from Saint Mary sat with grasped hands, forming a link amongst them.

"Ladies and gentlemen," began Mr. Huxley, "if you could please retake your seats." Slowly, the room became quiet. "With a victory by the slimmest of margins, our winner, by a score of thirty-nine to thirty-eight, is Saint Mary Prep School."

Once again, the sound of applause and cheers was heard. However, a chorus of moans and boos emerged from within the audience. As several people made their way to the two tables, congratulating each team, Terry and Emily inched closer together.

"Terrence, I'm so sorry," began Emily. "I never would have asked…"

"No, no, it's okay," said Terry. "There was no way you could have known. I never planned on speaking about myself." He paused for a moment. Then, slowly, he offered, "It just kind of came out."

"Well, that was very brave of you," said Emily, "and, well, your team deserved to win." She then extended her hand.

Terry stared, enthralled by her red hair and the green eyes that seemed to glow in contrast. He grasped her delicate palm, wrapping his fingers around it, and did not release his grip. "You—that is, your team, was really exceptional."

"Thank you," said Emily.

After a brief silence, Terry continued, "They really treat us well. The food looks incredible. Would you like to get something to eat?"

"When am I going to see you again?" asked Emily.

"Excuse me?"

"Terrence, your team will leave soon," said Emily. "I'm not interested in the food. I want to know when I can see you again."

"I—I don't know," said Terry. "You're not a senior, are you?"

"No, I'm a junior," Emily replied. "Are you a senior?"

"No, I'm also a junior!" said Terry, his eyes brightening.

"Oh, wow, that's a first!"

"What is?"

"Falling for a boy my age," said Emily. "Usually, I date college boys." Emily blushed slightly. She put her hand to her mouth and giggled. "I can't believe I just said that."

"Well, if it makes you feel better, I've never fallen for a girl with beautiful red hair and green eyes," said Terry.

Emily smiled. She pulled out her mobile phone. "Why don't you call me and I'll save your number."

Terry hesitated. "Well, I couldn't do that."

Emily furrowed her brow. She inclined her head. "I'm so sorry. I thought…"

"No, it's not like that. It's just that…" Terry bit his lower lip. "I don't have one."

Emily furrowed her brow. "Have what?"

"My own phone."

"Oh," said Emily, a slight smile breaking across her face.

A member of the Saint Mary's team suddenly appeared. He was of medium height and had blonde hair that splashed across his forehead. Slipping his arm around Emily, he said, "Hey, uh, if you're done getting a thrill from visiting the ghetto, we're going out to celebrate."

Emily flinched and then released her hand from Terry's grasp. "Norm, what are you doing? And get your arm off me!"

Norm smirked. He then offered his free hand to Terry. "What's up, man?"

"Hello," said Terry.

"Hello?" repeated Norm. He laughed loudly. "Come on, dawg, the debate's over. You can stop acting."

Terry furrowed his brow. "Pardon me?"

Norm mimicked Terry's serious expression and repeated, "Pardon me?"

Emily peeled Norm's arm off of her shoulder. "Norm, please leave."

Norm smiled and turned to Terry. "Hey, man, I didn't offend you, did I?" He paused for a moment, and then continued, "Or how would you say it? Something like *yo, yo, it's all good, ya feel me!*"

Terry frowned. He could feel the heat in his face.

"What?" asked Norm. He then bobbed his head up and down and took a step closer to Terry. "Hey, man, personally, I was a little disappointed in your performance."

"My performance?"

"Yeah, dawg!" said Norm. "After your little story, I thought you were going to break into some sort of rap up there about surviving the hood!"

Terry inhaled deeply as the sound of Norm's laughter echoed in his ears. He then began to rub his thumbs and forefingers together. "Look, I've had about all I can take, maybe we should go outside and—"

"Hey, Norm," interrupted a tall young man, "if you're done giving our school a bad name, why don't you get us all some refreshments?"

Terry turned to see the captain of Saint Mary standing next to him.

"Relax, Daniel!" replied Norm, slapping him on the chest with the back of his hand. "I was just having a little fun with my new friend."

"Really? And all this time we thought you didn't have any friends," said Daniel. "I heard what you said, so why don't you just do us all a favor and leave."

"The competition's over, so stop giving orders," Norm replied. "Being team captain doesn't mean a damn thing anymore."

"Well, maybe I'll talk to the dean about your embarrassing behavior and have you escorted out, then."

With a smirk on his face, Norm brushed off a few pieces of lint from Daniel's white blazer. "All right, Daniel, have it your way." He inclined his head, pausing for a moment. Facing Daniel once again, he raised his hands and continued, "The big student body president with all of the connections. I guess that's the reward for constantly kissing ass, huh?"

"Well, I guess I'd rather kiss one than be one," Daniel replied.

Terry released a loud chuckle as Emily's mouth popped open. Norm scowled and slowly walked away.

Turning to Terry, Daniel continued, "Hey, uh, sorry about that. Please don't take that guy seriously. It's not like we wanted him on the team."

"No problem," said Terry. "We've got one like that, too." Then, with a slight twitch of the mouth, he added, "Well, actually, I take that back. Dennis is not nearly as bad as that guy."

"Yeah, I don't think Norm was ever disciplined as a child."

Terry laughed once again. Emily smiled and nodded.

"That was quite a final round between you two," continued Daniel. He gestured with his hands raised and smiled.

"Thank you," said Terry.

"I don't think I've ever heard such a personal testimony before in a debate. Isn't that right, Emily?"

"Yes, I was just telling Terrence that," said Emily. She blushed slightly. "I mean, that's what we were talking about."

Daniel nodded. "Yeah, well, changing the subject, is that team captain of yours taken?"

Terry's eyes widened. "Monica?"

"Yeah."

"I don't think so. Most guys are scared of her."

Daniel laughed. "Well, I like the feisty ones! *Una chica feroz! Una tigresa! Wow! Me emociona eso*! I'll see you guys later! I'm going tiger hunting!"

Terry shook his head as Daniel walked away, disappearing into the crowd. "Did you get all of that?"

"Not really, I take French, not Spanish," said Emily. Then, extending her hand, she added, "But I think he has the right idea."

"The right idea?" repeated Terry.

"Yes, the right idea," said Emily, smiling coyly at him. "We should pursue what interests us."

Terry stared at her. "I've never had a girl make me feel so…"

"So what?" asked Emily.

"So nervous," Terry continued. "I think I feel more confident facing two big linebackers than talking to you."

Emily stepped closer to Terry, putting the top of her forehead within inches of his chin. "I don't want to make you nervous, Terrence. I would much rather make you happy."

12

THE CLATTERING OF dishes, the strong aroma of coffee, and the voices of several people filled the small diner. The padded brown booth where Terry sat contained several cracks. He shuffled every few moments. He adjusted the silverware that lay on top of his napkin. He pretended to be interested in the large plastic menu filled with an array of pictures that appeared much more appetizing than the actual food.

"Hello."

Terry raised his head and smiled nervously. "Thank you for meeting with me. I suppose you're wondering why I called you."

"Not at all," replied Timothy in the sweet tenor voice that had never left Terry's mind. As he sat down, he continued. "I fully expected you to call." He then touched the black collar of his shirt and ran his fingers across the triangular sides. Puckering his lips, he added, "Though I would have suggested a different rendezvous."

"What can I get you fine looking gentlemen?"

The conversation stopped. Terry glanced from behind the menu in his hands at the middle-aged woman who stood mere inches from the small quadrangular wooden table where Terry sat across from Timothy. Her hair was a rich blonde, obviously dyed to achieve such a color, and her face was heavily painted. A pinkish lipstick coated her lips. She wore a dark green skirt and a tight cotton blouse made of a lighter shade of matching green.

Timothy did not make eye contact with the waitress. Instead, he spoke directly to Terry. "This woman is intelligent," he began. "I do not know the level of her sincerity, and I do not know if she truly respects us, but she is scrupulous enough to know that if she gives us the appearance of respect, we will be sure to reward her with a tip and return to this restaurant. Why is that so hard for some people to understand?"

Terry did not reply. Instead, he fidgeted once again in his booth. The waitress moved her head randomly in different directions.

"Did I say anything inaccurate?" Timothy asked her.

"Uh, no, sir," she replied. "I guess I just never thought of myself as, well, intelligent."

"You have had a hard life," said Timothy, his large eyes focused directly on her. "You never finished school. You have been through a divorce. Maybe two. You have children. Some of them you are still supporting. But though you lack education, you are an intelligent woman, a responsible woman, and someone I promise to tip generously because you deserve it."

The woman dropped the small notepad in her hand. Terry's mouth slowly opened.

"Oh, I…" began the waitress as she bent down to pick up the fallen notepad.

In a casual manner, Timothy laid down his menu and said, "I believe I will try the chicken salad. I do hope it is as good as the photograph indicates."

Upon standing, the waitress straightened her skirt. Her voice quivered as she asked, "Your dressing, sir?"

"Italian. Low calorie."

"Something to drink?"

"Water."

She turned to Terry. "And you?"

Terry hesitated.

"I'm paying," said Timothy, adjusting his celestial blue tie. "Please, order anything you desire."

"Are you sure?" asked Terry.

"I would not have said it if I were not sure."

Terry nodded, then quickly ordered a large double cheeseburger, French fries, and a large Pepsi Cola™.

"Thank you," said the woman. She hurriedly walked away.

Timothy frowned.

"What's wrong?" asked Terry.

"Your diet," said Timothy, pointing his index finger directly in Terry's face. "You are obviously an athlete. You are also quite capable of logical thought. But you either know nothing of nutrition, or you are too lazy to follow healthy eating habits."

"I—I ordered most of the food groups," said Terry.

"You have French fries which are cooked at a high temperature in hydrogenated oil, a hamburger that also I am sure is high in trans fat, and a soft drink that has at least thirty grams of sugar in a single glass; and I have no doubt that you will request at least one refill. Now, I am being generous. I could have mentioned your bun, which is made of white processed flour, has been stripped of all nutrients, and will never digest well in your stomach."

Terry nodded.

"Our bodies are temples, Terrence, and we should never fill them with toxins of any kind."

"So you don't...?" began Terry.

"Never," replied Timothy, "but we are not here to discuss your diet—or worse—the absorption of unnatural substances. Though I believe that to be a future topic, we are here for a different reason, aren't we?"

Terry bit his lower lip. He swallowed deeply. "I wanted to know you. I wanted to know why you helped me that day when that old bum was threatening me. And now I want to know how you knew.... I mean, why did you say those things to the waitress? She seemed frightened by you."

Timothy arched his eyebrows. "She is not frightened by me. She is frightened by the truth."

"You know her?" asked Terry.

Timothy smiled slightly as if amused by the question. "The waitress? Yes, in a manner of speaking. I suppose you could say I know her the way I knew that worthless drunk who was speaking to you by the bus stop."

"I don't understand," said Terry. He paused, waited, but Timothy offered no further explanation. Finally, Terry asked, "Had you met either one of those people before?"

"No."

"Then how could you say those things to them?"

Timothy raised his dark thin brows. "Isn't it obvious? You are going to sit here and tell me that when you see a man in his fifties sitting on the cement in front of a liquor store each day, reeking of cigarette smoke and inexpensive alcohol, and speaking in broken grammar, that you know nothing of this man?"

Terry remained quiet.

"Is he an educated man? A profound man?"

Terry remained still.

"Could he possibly be a productive member of society?"

Terry glanced downward.

"Come now, my brother, your timidity toward the truth in favor of some unspoken social etiquette is both appalling and offensive. I would expect more from you."

Terry folded his hands in front of him. "And the waitress? How did you know?"

"Call it an educated guess."

"An educated guess? I don't understand. What does that mean?"

Timothy sighed as if bored by the direction of the conversation. He clutched his smooth chin. "The waitress greeted us in a complimentary manner, but she was not overly friendly. She, being an older, white woman, did not show any reaction to serving two young black men. It seemed natural to her. She did not look at us condescendingly, nor did she try to overcompensate to hide any insecurity or nervousness. She wore no wedding ring, but there was a clear indention on her ring finger—an uneven one at that. She appears to be in her forties, maybe even fifties, yet invests in her appearance in order to earn as much money as she may at this menial position. If she had a husband at home, or even child support, she would not have to put forth so much effort into making a living at her stage in life. This woman is highly motivated, and nothing motivates a woman more than children."

The waitress returned. Suddenly, a bright, sparkling cascade flashed in Terry's mind. He observed the woman closely. He noticed the make-up that hid the wrinkles near her eyes and the edges of her mouth. He also saw the red nail polish that made her white hands, though displaying wrinkles and brown age spots, quite attractive. Behind her thick blonde hair were strands of hidden gray. She placed a soft drink in front of him and a glass of water next to Timothy.

"Thank you, ma'am," said Terry.

"You're very welcome, hon," she replied before smiling and walking away.

"Now *you* must provide *me* with an answer," said Timothy, again pointing his finger directly at Terry. "You are a top athlete. You are also a fine student. You live with your grandparents in Avondale, but you constantly visit Phoenix to see your mother, who only holds company with the most despicable men—something that causes you great embarrassment. You have no idea who your biological father is. You are searching for purpose—for identity—because you still are very uncertain of whom you are."

Terry furrowed his brow. "That's not possible," he mumbled. "How could you know so much about me?"

Timothy laughed. It was a joyful, melodious sound which reflected his charming tenor voice. "My brother, I cannot take too much credit this time. One of my associates mentioned you to me. I believe you have met him? Calvin Dodd?"

"Calvin?" repeated Terry. "He works with you?"

"In a matter of speaking," said Timothy. "He is a member of The Standard."

"I thought he was just a drug dealer," said Terry. He sipped slowly on his drink, and then abruptly stopped. "Wait! Calvin doesn't know me that well!"

"He does not, but I do," said Timothy. He paused, lifting his glass of water to his lips. "And to address your other statement, he did sell drugs, but we have redeemed him. His potential has very definable limits, but he has other attributes that I find useful. He is no longer on the streets selling illegal substances. He now has a purpose—a meager one—but one that is far more productive." Timothy lifted his head slightly. "That reminds me. Next time we see him, he owes you an apology."

Terry lowered his brow. "For what?"

"I think you know."

Terry smiled. "You seem to enjoy having people apologize to me."

Timothy released an endearing, childlike laughter that was every bit as foreign as the man himself. "It does seem that way, doesn't it?" His gaze suddenly sharpened. "Look, The Standard is a political organization. Our mission is to reshape the world and therefore we must begin with the leader of the world. And that would be America. We will transform this country into the great nation that its founding fathers and others once envisioned. Once this is accomplished, we will turn our focus on Europe and other parts of the world. But it all starts here." He paused briefly. "Does this interest you?"

Terry bit his lower lip. "Doctor Ajala, I—I just turned seventeen."

"Why did you address me as Doctor Ajala?"

"I don't know," stammered Terry. "I guess I suddenly realized how important you are."

Timothy nodded slowly. His large, penetrating eyes seemed to be studying Terry. "Let others call me Doctor Ajala, Terrence. I prefer we have a more personal relationship. To be frank, I do not have many people with your potential in my organization..." As Timothy's voice trailed off, he stroked the creamy dark skin of his cheek. "Perhaps Kyle Brenner," he mused. "I believe he attends classes at Maricopa Community College, but still, though older and with more means, he does not share your stature."

Terry smiled slightly. "Thank you for thinking so highly of me."

"I only speak the truth, Terrence," replied Timothy. He then raised his index finger and pointed it directly in Terry's face. "Look, we are a fledgling enterprise, and the more people—no, let me correct myself—the more *intelligent* people, the more *productive* people we gather into The Standard—the more able we become to impose our will on society. We need youth and energy and zeal. Most people simply do not understand how miserable the world has become, and misunderstanding leads to fear, and fear leads to opposition."

Terry rubbed his temples with both hands.

"Here you go, gentlemen," said the waitress, placing both plates on the table. Then, facing Timothy, she added, "And anything you need, you just let me know!"

Timothy smiled. *"Merci beaucoup, ma belle."*

The waitress lingered. She blushed slightly and then playfully touched a strand of her hair before slowly walking away.

"I hope I am not overwhelming you," continued Timothy, redirecting his attention to Terry. He took a few bites of his salad. "The only way for any nation to be great, Terrence, is for its strongest members to be in a place of empowerment. The most intelligent people must be in leadership positions. The ruling class must be composed of people who think clearly and possess knowledge based on factual evidence. As we purge our nation of its weaker elements, and of the parasites who seek to hurt us all, we transform our nation and uplift the **elite**."

Terry paused. He took a large bite of his hamburger but found chewing difficult.

Standing abruptly, Timothy wiped his face with his beige cloth napkin. He lifted a dark briefcase that Terry had not noticed lying at his feet. "I await your answer, my young brother, but in the meantime, I have business that I must attend to."

Terry began to stand as well, but Timothy raised his left hand in protest. "No, no, you have barely touched your food. This will cover it and the rest will serve as a tip." He laid two bills on the table. "Terrence, come to a meeting at the Knights Inn. I will be addressing the general public in the main conference room." He reached into his briefcase and pulled out a small white brochure. "Here, take this. Consider it a personal invitation."

13

THE ARIZONA STATE University campus was much larger than Aaron had imagined. He had never seen anything so immense and so beautiful in his life. As the bright morning sun shone on the black gated entrance, Aaron looked up in awe. With a large duffel bag hoisted over his shoulder, he exclaimed to his teammates, "It seems more like a city than a school!"

"You've never been here?" asked Jeff Buckey, raising his eyebrows.

"Not inside," replied Aaron.

"Man, and they call me a country bumpkin," muttered Jeff.

"Hey, man, I'm just glad my granddad actually let me come," said Aaron. "Most summers he just works us to the bone!"

"Yeah, it wasn't easy convincing him," interrupted Coach More. "He said something about farming being three hundred and sixty-five days a year."

Aaron nodded. "Yep, that's him all right."

Coach More raised both arms in the air as the last of the boys assembled around him. "Okay, men," he shouted in a loud voice, "get your gear and follow me to the dormitory. We have to get everyone settled before the tour. Then, we need to report to the field."

"You're gonna love the stadium," said Jeff as the group of boys began walking forward. "It's huge. I'm excited to actually play on the field."

"Tell me about it!" said Aaron. "Last night I could barely sleep."

"Yeah," said Jeff. Then, pausing briefly, he mused, "Too bad Terry's not here."

Aaron nodded, as did a few others, as they followed Coach More down a long cement path. They passed a number of large buildings, trees, and grassy areas until they reached their destination. Entering the lobby, Coach More said, "I'll be here on the first floor. You men will find your rooms on the second. Line up and let me give you your keys."

One by one, the boys accepted keys to their rooms. Each one had a number.

"Looks like we're roomies," said Jeff to Aaron.

"Yeah, let's go!" replied Aaron with excitement in his voice.

They walked up the burgundy colored carpeted stairs and found the door to their dormitory. Inside, Aaron saw a small, but orderly room with two beds and two joint desks. He threw his belongings at the far end. "I got the window section."

Jeff nodded. As they began to unpack, Carson came running into their room.

"Yo, where's the fire?" asked Aaron.

"On his head," said Jeff.

Aaron laughed as Carson rubbed his red hair and continued, "I just took a whiz and I couldn't believe the bathrooms!"

"What are you talking about?" asked Aaron.

"They're clean!" Carson replied. "No piss on the toilet seats, no writing on the walls, no soggy toilet paper."

Jeff threw himself onto his bed, landing with a large thud. His large body occupied the entire bed frame, and his feet dangled off the edge. He folded his arms behind his head. "That's because these people have class," said Jeff, "like me."

Aaron and Carson burst into laughter.

"Dirty blue jeans and a T-shirt with holes in it," said Aaron. "Real class."

Carson waved his hand by his nose. "And the holes are under his pits!"

"Let's roll, y'all!" said Lucas, suddenly appearing at the door. "Coach says the tour is starting."

Racing down the stairs, the boys went down to the quad area where they joined a host of other high school students. Most were dressed in jeans and T-shirts. Some wore their official school sweat suits, and few groups were dressed formally in trousers, white collared shirts and ties. Mixed in the crowd were coaches and college staff members. Coach More motioned for the boys to join him. "Over here, men," he shouted. "They're dividing us up."

"Boys, my name is Bill Taylor," said a muscular man with a black visor that blended with the black skin of his bald head. "I played for the Sun Devils ten years ago. I also played in the NFL for two years on special teams. Currently, I'm proud to be working in the athletic department for Arizona State. Welcome to our summer camp, where you will learn from the best. But before we begin, I have been given the pleasure to show you the most beautiful campus in all of Arizona! Would everyone like to see it?"

A throng of young men nodded their heads. Some of them, including Aaron, openly expressed their enthusiasm with loud shouts.

"Okay, then, follow me!"

As they began to walk, Aaron kept his eyes on a tall young man with razed black hair. He had a light brown tan and a tapered build. Aaron whispered to Lucas, "Hey, isn't that Scotty Parker behind us?"

"Yeah, that's him," said Lucas, "the golden boy himself."

"He was all over the news last year," continued Aaron. "They said he put Yuma on the map! Everyone says he's the best! And I mean, the best! Little schools, big schools, here, there…"

"Man, calm down!" interrupted Lucas. "I think he heard you!"

"His dad coaches at Arizona Western!" Aaron twisted his lips and shook his head. "Man, must be nice to have a dad like that!"

Lucas nodded.

"I read this one article that said he has his own cook!" continued Aaron. "His father hired him just to make special meals for Scotty!"

"Come on, Aaron!" said Lucas. "You're here to get better and compete, not to get all excited over other players."

"Holmes, right?" called out a voice.

Aaron turned quickly.

"I'm Scotty Parker."

Aaron looked up at him in awe. Scotty possessed a harmonious square face, and together with his sharp brown eyes and perfectly placed white teeth, he seemed to belong on a billboard more than behind a football helmet. If that were not enough, he stood about six feet four inches. Aaron understood. Scotty Parker was not just another athlete; he was a football player, and he had been raised from day one to be a quarterback.

"Hey, yeah, you're Scotty Parker," replied Aaron, "the top quarterback in the state, or, hell, the entire nation!"

"Well, I don't know about that," said Scotty, laughing. "From what I've seen, I've got plenty of competition right here."

"That's right," said Lucas, "and I'm always right. Lucas Wright. Middle linebacker. Strong side. Weak side. Any side."

"Good to meet you," replied Scotty. He held out his hand, which Lucas shook with a tight grip. "You guys played tough last year. We were actually hoping you'd lose."

"Really?" said Aaron. "You know about us?"

"Of course! Until we won state last year, the winner always came out of Phoenix or Tucson."

"Why'd you say you hoped we'd lose?" asked Lucas.

"Because our defense is tough against the pass, but we're only fair against the run." Scotty turned toward Aaron. "You're the most mobile quarterback I've seen and that tailback…" He paused to shake his head. "Washington, right? My dad showed me film on him. That kid's scary."

"Yeah, he's my cousin," said Aaron.

"Which one is he?" asked Scotty.

But before Aaron could answer, the voice of Bill Taylor rose above the chatter heard from the crowd. "This is our first stop, the arena, host of sports such as volleyball, basketball, and wrestling. Follow me, and we'll take a look inside. In fact, you'll get to see some real action because I think the Lady Sun Devils are practicing."

The boys, as well as a few coaches, followed him down a hallway and into a large stadium. Once inside, they were immediately captivated by the women's volleyball team. The boys watched intently as the girls shouted to each other, exchanging passes that ended with a beautiful spike. As the ball thundered down on the other side of the net, one of the girls dived, missing it by inches. The competing girls exploded in shouts of triumph, exchanging high slaps in the air. Many of the boys began to cheer. A few of the girls smiled and waved.

"Wow!" said Aaron.

As if in a trance, Leonel added, "Beautiful, athletic, all shapes, sizes, and colors…. I think I'm in heaven!"

Scotty, who stood roughly the same height, patted Leonel on the back. "Easy, man, play it cool and they'll be chasing you."

"You guys don't have a chance," said Jeff. "They were looking at me."

"Maybe if one of them has a thing for Godzilla!" said Aaron.

The boys broke into laughter. Coach More then approached them. "Something interesting, men?"

"Uh, nothing Coach," said Leonel.

With a wide grin on his face, Aaron interjected, "We just really love volleyball, sir." He then gave Leonel a fist bump.

"There's definitely a lot to see at ASU," said Bill Taylor, a statement which unintentionally caused the boys to laugh once again. "I hope some of you become Sun Devils!"

"It's not a free ride though, men," added Coach More.

"No, it's not," said Bill Taylor. "Tuition is costly, and you need to fulfill certain academic requirements."

"But an athletic scholarship can help with all of that," said Coach More.

Bill Taylor paused for a moment. "Yes, but our next destination is what university life is really all about."

"What's that, sir?" asked Aaron.

Bill Taylor smiled. "The school library."

A collective moan was heard amongst the boys as they left the arena.

14

"YOU ARE NOT here by mere coincidence!" said Timothy into the tiny microphone that was neatly attached just below his collar. Dressed meticulously in dark slacks, a glowing blue silk shirt and a black tie, he walked up and down the platform, speaking to the large group of people who had filled the hotel conference room to capacity. "Oh, no, my brothers and sisters. It is not mere chance. Neither is it a whim. But rather, it is fate."

Terry perused the audience. Over half of the people seated were young black men, but scattered throughout the audience were people of all colors and ages.

"You are here for the same reason as the person next to you. You are tired. Tired of the same sickening society that rudely greets you every morning. Tired of listening to the sound of a gunshot. Tired of reading about someone dying, the victim of senseless violence. Tired of seeing trash in the gutter. Tired of the juvenile delinquents who choose to vandalize your neighborhood instead of attending school!"

"That's right!" called out one man.

"I heard that!" said a woman sitting only a few seats down from Terry.

The audience burst into applause. Timothy stepped down from the platform and walked through the center passage between the seated rows of the large room.

"Tired of hearing your children cry because they stepped on broken glass at the city park! Tired of being harassed at the bus stop on your way to work! Tired of the corporate greed that delights not in your hard work but rather in an eviction notice!"

"Too true!" called out a stout woman from the middle of the audience.

"Tired of being ignored by the government! Or worse, dismissed entirely because you were born on the wrong side of some imaginary line drawn in the sand! Yes, while some of you have obtained one, two, or even three positions of employment, laboring under the sun for a pitiful wage; your very neighbors fill their subsidized lives each day with alcohol and illegal substances!"

"Yes! *Sí se puede*!" called out a man from the very back row.

"Brothers and sisters," continued Timothy at full pitch, practically overloading his small microphone, "I am here to tell you that I see your weariness! I hear your cries of desperation! You are tired of the deaf and the mute who claim to represent you! Tired of the incompetent void of leadership that guides you! That is why you are here! You wish not only to live, but to live abundantly, with purpose, with achievement!"

Timothy paused. The room was silent. He then raised both of his hands high into the air. "Brothers and sisters of the world, of all races and colors and languages, rest assured that you have not failed any government; your governments have failed you!"

Heads nodded vigorously. People applauded with great energy. A small group in the very front stood up and cheered. Terry observed them with great curiosity. The men had black shoes, gray dress pants, and blue collared shirts with an assortment of dark colored ties. The women were also dressed formally. Each one wore a tight fitting dark skirt that reached just above their knees. Their collared shirts were white. Their hair was long, falling below their shoulders. Together, they presented a peculiar, yet attractive spectacle.

"It's time, brothers and sisters! Time to reclaim the streets! Time to reclaim your neighborhoods! Time to reclaim this nation! Time to blot out injustice! Time to blot out racism! Time to blot out poverty!"

Once again, the audience began to cheer. Terry could not help but feel the energy in the room. There was a glow on the faces of several people, a reflection of excitement and eagerness and faith. Timothy walked briskly onto the platform and stood behind a glass podium. He moved his hands slowly in horizontal fashion. "Ladies and gentlemen, we are in the middle of a dark age. An age where ignorance is all too common. An age where people no longer seek the light. An age of fear, of dread, of damnation. So I say it's time!"

"It's time!" called out a young man from the very center of the audience.

"It's time for a Renaissance!" said Timothy. "I said it is time for a rebirth! Of light! Of knowledge! Of new discovery! Hear me, brothers and sisters! Our organization, The Standard, represents a society not based on color, not based on citizenship, not based on religion, nor age nor gender nor ancestry, but on individual capacity!"

The audience stood to their feet, shouting in a frenzy.

"Yes!" said Terry amidst the cheering.

His arms spread wide and palms facing downward, Timothy slowly moved his fingers up and down until every person in the room sat down and became silent.

"Young men, young ladies, people of middle and advanced ages, listen to me! Listen to me! Let there be no doubt as to the message. The Standard is not an organization for the weak. The Standard is not for the misinformed or the confused. The Standard is not for the timid!"

From the very front rows of chairs, an attractive woman called out, "No, no, no!"

Timothy pointed his index finger at various people in the crowd. "The Standard is an organization which requires of its members the utmost clarity and courage imaginable. Only with a complete and unbending commitment will we be able to usher in a new age!"

Terry fidgeted in his seat. A surge of restrained energy could be felt throughout the room.

"As a member of The Standard, you will be asked to serve; each according to his individual capacity. Thus, we are all part of the whole. We all find our purpose in creating and maintaining our society so that it reaches its true potential."

A nicely dressed young man who was seated near the front podium shouted, "We are with you, Professor Ajala!"

Timothy nodded. He then raised his index finger upward. "We must have the courage to lead according to…"

"…our capacity!" said the front row.

Holding a second finger, Timothy continued, "We must have the honesty to understand that our capacity…"

"…defines us!"

Timothy held up three fingers. "When the elite rule..."

"...all benefit!"

15

AARON COULD NOT help but compete with Scotty Parker. He tried to outdo him in every drill and in each scrimmage, but as the camp came to an end, Aaron found himself admiring Scotty's focus and work ethic. Early in the morning, along with a handful of others, the two walked onto the deserted Arizona State football field dressed in an array of shorts and T-shirts.

"You sure this is okay?" asked Aaron.

"Oh yeah, no problem," replied Scotty. "You know how these things work. The last day is mostly ceremonial."

"Actually, I don't," replied Aaron.

"Trust me; all camps are the same," said Scotty, "even the big ones."

"Like I said," replied Aaron, "I wouldn't know."

Scotty stopped walking. "You're telling me that this is your first camp?"

"Yep, sure is," said Aaron.

"Wow!" said Scotty. "My dad's been taking me to camps since the sixth grade." Turning toward the group of boys following him onto the field, Scotty continued, "All right, let's set up. Holmes and I are going to practice some play actions."

Scotty proceeded to organize the others like a field marshal. He and Aaron would alternate at the quarterback position. Jeff Buckey, the largest boy on the field, would be the center. Lucas Wright, a gifted combination of strength and speed, would act as the defensive end. Corey Maynard, a boy standing a little less than six feet with tan skin and cropped brown hair, possessed a lithe body. He carried a reputation as Yuba's top receiver. Gerald Henderson, slightly bigger but not quite as quick as his Yuba teammate, was a nice looking boy with dark skin, a perpendicular jaw, and thick lips.

"Why don't we just play three on three?" asked Lucas. "We might as well make it Avondale against Yuma."

"No, man, this is practice," said Scotty, "and we need everyone to fill a role. Anyway, we're teammates at this camp, okay? If we meet somewhere down the road, then you'll have your chance."

"I can't wait," replied Lucas, smiling, "Because the only place we'd ever meet is a state championship game."

"That's right," said Scotty.

"You serious?" asked Aaron.

"From what I've seen here—and if your man Washington shows up— I'd say it could happen."

Aaron nodded.

"Corey, set up on my right," continued Scotty. "Gerald, you cover him. Wright, just give moderate pressure to Buckey. Let's start with a simple drag route. Go out fifteen and cut, Corey. Okay, on one, man," said Scotty to Jeff. "Down, set, hut!"

Aaron watched as Scotty took the snap from Jeff. With great precision, Scotty turned and shuffled with quick steps while placing the ball snugly against his stomach. He then raised the ball to his shoulder and cocked it behind his head. With his elbow up several inches in front of his shoulder, he squared his chest and hips with his target. Then, in one fluid motion, his arm came thrusting forward with the tremendous power created from his entire body torque. His wrist ended in a pronated position. The result was a pass that seemed to have been fired from a rifle. Whistling through the air like a rocket, the ball hit the wide receiver's hands perfectly.

Aaron shook his head. He then whistled. "Man, that's impressive."

"It's all technique," said Scotty. Then, turning to Lucas, he added, "Where's the pressure, man?"

"You said not to go all out," said Lucas.

"I said moderate pressure," said Scotty.

Lucas smiled mischievously. "Sure, whatever you say."

"Okay, Holmes, follow me," said Scotty. Aaron grabbed another football. As Scotty held the ball in front of him and repeated his passing action, Aaron mimicked his movements. "Good. Now, cock your arm back more." Scotty paused to review Aaron's posture. "Okay, go ahead."

"Same route?" asked Aaron.

"Same route."

"Down! Set! Hut!" said Aaron. He quickly turned and shuffled, calculated Corey's speed, and threw the ball. It was slightly behind Corey, allowing Gerald to bat it down.

"Not bad," said Scotty, "but you're using too much arm strength, you know what I mean? Trust the technique. It's not enough to just get your elbow above your shoulder. You have to position it correctly."

Scotty held up his hand to Corey, who was about twenty yards downfield. He then grabbed Aaron's arm, placed another football in his palm, and positioned his elbow. "Now, it should feel comfortable. Throw it and shift your hips so that you use your entire body, not just your shoulder and arm."

Aaron did so, throwing a nice pass downfield to Corey.

"How did that feel?" asked Scotty.

"Good," said Aaron, smiling. "It was smoother on my elbow. How did it look?"

"Pretty good," replied Scotty. "Now we just have to work on your follow-through. Here, watch my wrist." Scotty gripped the ball in his right hand and demonstrated his picturesque throwing motion. He then shouted, "Okay, Corey, bring it in! Let's try a deeper route. Do a streak and I'll hit you on the fly."

"You got it," said Corey as he once more positioned himself at the imaginary line of scrimmage.

Scotty stood behind Jeff with Lucas opposing them. Gerald then matched up against Corey as Scotty went through a quick cadence. As the ball was snapped, however, a group of cheerleaders dressed in riddish shorts and yellow tank tops walked onto the sidelines.

"Hi, there!" said a deeply tanned girl who possessed long blonde hair. "You guys don't mind if we practice a routine here, do you?"

As the group gaped at them, Jeff stuttered, "Uh, sure."

Lucas then bolted past him and plunged into Scotty. The ball left his hand and wobbled into the air as the two boys landed hard onto the ground.

With a deep scowl on his face, Scotty shouted, "Hey! What the hell was that?"

"Moderate pressure!" Lucas replied, smiling down on him.

"Come on, man!" said Scotty. He shoved Lucas in the chest. "We don't even have pads on! Get off me!"

"No problem, all-American," said Lucas. He got up to his feet and extended his hand to Scotty.

Several of the girls laughed on the sidelines. Scotty then approached Jeff and slapped him on the back of his head. "Stay focused, Buckey!"

Aaron laughed. "Sorry, man, but you could have avoided that with a simple jab step and pivot."

"A what?" asked Scotty.

"Well, it's kind of a reverse pivot," said Aaron. "To be honest with you, I developed it in basketball. You know, sometimes you get a guy all up in your face and you got to try to get rid of him. I juke him like this, see?"

Aaron took one step forward, shook his hips, moved his front foot back and forth several times, and then reversed in the other direction.

Shaking his head, Scotty replied, "No wonder you're so light on your feet. I don't know, man. That's just not my style." He turned away, then added, "And I don't think my dad would ever approve."

Aaron shook his head and smiled. "Look, I'll show you." He cupped his hands to his mouth and hollered, "Hey! Bring it in! Yo! Corey Maynard, set up and run that fly route again. Jeff, just stay out of the way and let Lucas charge me."

Jeff furrowed his brow. "Are you sure you want to do that?"

"Yeah, I got this," said Aaron, waving him off.

Lucas put his hands on his hips and frowned. "All right, Aaron, if you want to show off in front of these guys, go right ahead; but don't start cryin' when I dump your ass on the ground."

Aaron held the football in front of him with both hands while Scotty stood to the side.

"Hut!" Aaron called out, stepping back and then rolling to his right. Lucas charged him. He reached for Aaron, wrapping his bulky arm around Aaron's left hip, but Aaron quickly stopped, spun to his right and began running to the left. As Lucas lost his balance, his arm slid off of Aaron, and he crashed to the ground. Aaron then took his time to throw a perfect spiral that landed softly in the hands of a streaking Corey Maynard.

"You've got both options," said Aaron to Scotty. "You can run or pass. Or, when Terry's with me, there's three options."

Scotty furrowed his brow. Lucas, spread out on the ground, began to spit grass out of his mouth.

"Here, man, let me help you up," said Jeff.

Scotty rubbed his square forehead. "Hmmmm, I don't like to run too often in the open field. It's too dangerous. And how do you spin like that without getting hit? I mean, your turning your back on rushers. Isn't that kind of asking for it?"

"It's a timing thing, man," said Aaron. "It's only for a split second and it allows me to change direction faster."

Scotty attempted the movement awkwardly, almost tripping. Aaron burst into laughter. "Hey, man, haven't you ever played basketball before?"

"I used to," Scotty replied, "but that all changed in high school. Football is year round now."

"How about dancing? Do you dance?"

"Um, not much."

"Look, come here!" said Aaron. He grabbed Scotty and squared him up, then grabbed his shoulders and made him squat a little. "Okay, now loosen up, man, and bust a move! You're just too stiff, man. You need to let your inner groove come out!"

Scotty grinned. "My what?"

"Look and learn, son," said Aaron. He then began to dance. He moved fluidly, allowing his entire body to pop and wave. "Learned this from the Boogaloos!"

The others stopped and laughed.

"Oh, come on, y'all, it's hip-hop," said Lucas, shaking his head. "Henderson, you've never heard of the Boogaloos?"

Gerald Henderson shook his head. He rubbed his cropped black hair. "No, man, I'm a church boy."

"Don't you dance in your church?" asked Lucas.

Gerald frowned. "My mom would slap me if I started gyrating my body like that."

"Man, y'all are too stiff!" said Aaron. "Now watch, I'm gliding." Aaron moved his feet effortlessly across the grass, as if he were floating. "Here we go!" He bent his arms in front of him with his elbows out and his hands placed together as if in prayer. Next, he raised his right arm. Then, he bent his wrist. Aaron continued this pattern of perpendicular motions. With a wide smile, he shouted, "Now, I'm tutting!"

While Scotty shook his head, Corey Maynard ran over and joined Aaron. He also began to pop and glide. Scotty threw a football at him, but Corey caught it easily and then passed it from hand to hand in a display of coordination and precision.

"There you go, Corey!" said Aaron.

Lucas joined in, moving his shoulders up and down and gliding his hips back and forth in rhythmic motion. Jeff Buckey also began dancing, clumsily bumping into Aaron and practically knocking him down.

Finally, with sweat coming down his cheeks, Aaron took a deep breath and said, "Whew! Scotty, man, I owe you an apology!"

Scotty furrowed his brow. "For what?"

"I thought you were having trouble because you're white, but Maynard just put that theory to rest!" said Aaron, laughing as he slapped Scotty on the chest.

"It must have something to do with basketball," said Scotty. "Corey's our school's point guard."

Aaron looked at Corey and nodded his head in approval. "Is that right? Guess I'm gonna see you in two state finals this year. Wait a minute, do you run track?"

"Yep," said Corey, "won county in the hundred and two hundred this year, and next year, I'm winnin' state. Our relay team's looking good, too."

Aaron scowled. He spit on the grass. "Not if my cousin's there. I run the relay with him and I know there's no way y'all are gonna beat us. Dude runs like the wind and never gets tired." Aaron suddenly scowled. "We would've won county if he hadn't bailed on us. Hell, probably would've won state."

"I guess we'll find out," said Corey.

"While y'all are arguing, the only champ we got is over there dancing," said Lucas.

"Huh?" Aaron turned to see Jeff Buckey moving his large, thick legs back and forth.

The boys burst into laughter.

Corey pointed toward Jeff. "Buckey needs to stick to the shot put and the discus. He just doesn't cut it as a ballerina."

Aaron laughed heartily. "Can you imagine Jeff in tights?"

"Look, Scotty, like this," said Jeff, moving heavily back and forth before spinning around.

Aaron smiled as he shook his head. "Man, you better stop before you fall down and cause an earthquake."

Corey moved in front of Jeff. Standing directly in front of Scotty, he began to glide. "Come on, Scotty, you can do it."

"No, I'll pass," said Scotty.

"Come on, man! If King Kong can do it, you can!" said Aaron, pointing to Jeff Buckey who was still dancing, albeit quite awkwardly.

Scotty smiled, nodded, and attempted to emulate Aaron as the two danced side by side.

"Am I doing it?" asked Scotty.

Aaron nodded as he continued his movements. He then began to clap. "Scotty! Scotty!"

The other boys joined in as well, clapping and shouting in unison. Finally, the stoic face of Scotty Parker broke into a large grin.

Novel 10

BEYOND THE ELITE PART II

I

Terry spoke with two representatives of The Standard at a rectangular shaped table placed in the back of the hotel conference room. In his hand he held a white plastic bag full of pens, notepads, and pamphlets.

"So you are interested in joining us?" asked Timothy.

Terry turned quickly. "Oh, Doctor Ajala, I didn't see you there."

"That's because I was not here." He laughed. It was a laughter that amazed Terry. Somehow, it did not seem fitting. The high pitch and joyful resonance seemed much too childlike and innocent. Once the laughter had ceased, he released a charming smile and said, "And remember, I am Timothy."

"Yes, Timothy. I did complete the questionnaire and I would definitely like to know more."

"Then follow me."

Timothy began to walk toward the exit. Terry hesitated a moment but then quickly strode after him. Passing through the double doors of the conference room, Timothy entered a narrow hallway with Terry following closely behind. While briskly walking forward, Timothy announced, "This is where the inner circle meets."

"The inner circle?" asked Terry.

"Yes, our leadership team," replied Timothy.

"But I just decided to become a member," said Terry. His eyes shifted downward toward his thick polyester pants and dark leather work boots. "Also, I'm not dressed properly. I don't feel it would be appropriate."

Timothy's large eyes widened even further. "I am the president and founder of The Standard. If I personally invite you to a leadership meeting, then you belong in the meeting. Besides, we're in need of one more member."

Terry responded with a weak smile. He proceeded to follow Timothy down an adjoining hallway. Finally, Timothy stopped. He pulled out a large golden key.

"After you," said Timothy with a wave of his hand.

Terry entered a small room. There was a large white board attached to the wall and several markers clipped to the outlining metal frame. Timothy pointed to a V-shaped formation of luxurious brown leather chairs where five men and six women were seated. Gesturing toward the lone empty seat, he continued, "And that is your place. You are the twelfth."

Sitting down cautiously, Terry observed that no one in the room appeared older than thirty. Curiously, the young man next to him looked familiar, but Terry could not recall where he had seen him before. He attempted to make eye contact, but the young man seemed to purposely lower his head.

Standing in front of the white board, Timothy raised his right hand. "Brothers and Sisters of The Standard, I would like to introduce to you Mr. Terrence Washington. Please, take a moment to welcome him."

Each person approached and greeted Terry personally. He smiled, somewhat overwhelmed by such a hospitable gesture. As they passed him one by one, a conspicuous pattern became evident. The men had closely cut hair and dressed formally in white collared shirts and black ties. Of the five, one young man was white, one was Hispanic, and the others were black. The women were dressed in dark skirts and light collared blouses, and wore their hair extended slightly past their shoulders. They were slightly more diverse, with two being black, two being Hispanic, one young lady being white, and one of Middle Eastern descent.

"And now, before we proceed to business, I believe Brother Calvin has something he would like to say," continued Timothy, motioning to the young man seated next to Terry.

Terry squinted and then blinked several times. The angular face of the young man standing before him was cleanly shaven, his black hair clean and razor thin.

"Terry...or...Terrence, when I first met you," began Calvin, "I made a very ignorant comment. I believe you are aware of the comment."

Terry nodded, willing his mind to adjust to the vastly changed voice and verbiage.

"I shouldn't have said that to you. I apologize if I offended you."

After a brief pause, Terry replied quietly, "None taken."

"That is a lie," said Timothy. He pointed his index finger directly at Terry. "Are you going to sit there and tell us that you were not offended by his remark that your educated speech somehow made you inferior? Could anything be more preposterous?"

Terry swallowed deeply.

"Choose your words carefully, young man. Say exactly what you mean and mean exactly what you say. Anything else is an insult to your intelligence and it certainly is an affront to mine!"

Terry looked at the large, penetrating eyes of Timothy. Slowly, he got out of his chair and stood next to Calvin. Though not small in stature, Calvin was still several inches shorter than Terry, his body not near as muscular. But the real contrast between the two lay in their faces. Unlike the large, powerfully shaped horizontal cranium possessed by Terry, Calvin possessed a rather small oval shaped head, which lacked the protection of his previously thick afro. Gone was the former bravado, replaced by an expression of doubt, of insecurity.

"I accept your apology, Calvin," said Terry. "What you said did offend me at the time. I don't think the way we speak categorizes us as a certain color. I think our speech categorizes our level of education, or perhaps, our culture, and it appears you, too, now believe this."

Timothy applauded. The others slowly joined in.

"You see?" asked Timothy. "Now, does anyone believe I was exaggerating when I told you that Terrence Washington is a future leader in our organization? Do not let his age fool you. This gentleman is gifted. Truly gifted."

Several people around the room smiled and nodded.

"Yes, our speech defines us," continued Timothy. "Being from Nigeria, I have encountered the very same **bigotry** from ignorant Americans on more than one occasion. Make no mistake! Most people are stuck in a morass of mediocrity, or worse, a pathetic inferiority; they resent anyone who dares to challenge their stupidity and unproductive ways." Timothy paused. His eyes seemed to be aimed at Terry alone. "Intelligence without courage, without a passion for the truth, achieves very little. It is the duty of the enlightened to pull these people out of their hopeless quagmire."

After a brief pause, Timothy motioned to Terry and Calvin. "Please, be seated."

The two nodded and sat down.

"Very well," he continued, "as you know, we are slowly gathering in more associates, such as Brother Kyle, whose father owns one of the largest flooring companies in the state. Speaking of Brother Kyle, are you recording our meeting?"

A young man with short brown hair, a thick neck, and a white oval shaped face quickly pulled out a computerized notebook from underneath his seat. "Yes, Brother Timothy," he replied.

"Splendid! Let it be known that our work has not been conducted in vain. Businessmen, educators, and political leaders in our community and beyond are beginning to join The Standard. Among them is none other than our very own state representative in Congress, the prominent Senator Richard Brawnchild."

Several people nodded. A few gleeful smiles appeared.

Walking over to the white board, Timothy took hold of a black marker and wrote in large letters the word "RENAISSANCE." He then drew one line below and the word "ELITE." Next, he wrote two connecting lines and the words "MEDIOCRITY" and "INFERIORITY." Finally, he unveiled a silvery tube that extended into a long metal pointer stick. With great authority, he pressed the end of the pointer to the center of each word.

"These people understand our vision," continued Timothy. "They support us. They await our leadership. They await a new Renaissance which The Standard shall create. The European Renaissance, under Queen Elizabeth, did not suddenly happen. It was not a mere result of chance. As people began to rediscover the beauty and wisdom of knowledge from the great philosophers and men of science, knowledge that had been imprisoned in books lying under the dust and cobwebs of ancient castles inhabited by monks, it was as if a great light suddenly flickered among them. Artists such as Leonardo Da Vinci and Michelangelo were thrust upon us. Mozart and Beethoven created music that the human ear had never experienced. Galileo fought the ignorance of the church. Christopher Columbus defied human convention and set upon a journey that led to the

New World. Shakespeare wrote dramatic epics that captured the human spirit. In sum, the spirit of the Greeks was reborn."

Terry glanced at a few of the others; they appeared fully concentrated on Timothy.

"The European Renaissance set a new standard. A man was to be intelligent, curious, genteel, acquainted with many languages and cultures, a man of science, a man of letters, gifted in speech." Timothy paused and motioned to the women of the group. With an enchanting smile, he said, "And to my sisters, hence it appears I have forgotten them or fail to recognize their equality; I assure you, nothing could be further from the truth. Queen Elizabeth herself, Gloriana, led the way. Now, we must ask ourselves: How do we implement such a Renaissance today, here, in America? How do we create a Renaissance man and a Renaissance woman? And perhaps more importantly, how do we sustain a new Renaissance?"

Several people nodded, but no one audibly responded.

Timothy extended the silvery pointer stick upward. "It begins with the elite. Leaders in their area of expertise must pave the way for others. Now, what is our first precept of leadership?"

A woman with long black hair that flowed around a wide, symmetrical face tilted her head slightly. Her bright, expressive eyes, somewhat upturned in form, radiated a certain forcefulness. "Let there be no pretense," she said in a soft, yet confident tone.

Timothy paused. His slender lips spread at the ends to form a smile that reflected a certain satisfaction. "Yes, Camilla. That is right." He then continued, "There can be no false pretense of our abilities. That is not how the elite conduct themselves. All must recognize that each human being is the possessor of different gifts and intelligences, and it is our duty toward society to live according to our capacity—nothing more and nothing less. This is how we learn contentment in life. This is how we fulfill ourselves individually. Business, politics, technology, enforcement, all overseen by wise men. This is how we bring about a Renaissance."

Terry found himself nodding in unison with the others.

"The elite, composed of the most intelligent and the most dedicated of society, must oversee the average man. This, unlike unjust societies of the past, has nothing to do with a person's birth, gender, race, color, or nationality. It is based on the simple truth that the elite must occupy a position of leadership in order to further society. Those that fall into mediocrity have an important task: complete the instruction of the elite, fulfill their vision, and obey their mandates. Does everyone agree?"

"Yes, Brother Timothy," replied the others in unison.

"Do you agree, Brother Terrence?" asked Timothy.

Terry paused. "I...am still learning."

Timothy took a few steps toward Terry. He smiled. "Well, we shall have to ensure that your learning is complete." He then returned to the white board and pointed to it with the metal instrument he held in his right hand. "And now, the most difficult task before us. The inferiors. They live to serve. They lack the initiative of the mediocrity and therefore must be given very confined labor to fulfill. However, their lack of intelligence, ironically, is often lost on them. They are unaware of their inferior status. Thus, the majority of them become unruly."

Timothy paused. With a steely gaze he continued in a much more serious tone. "One of the foundational duties of the elite is to redeem reprobates. We must confront the indolent, the perverse, the violent, the corrupt, the unjust. If they respond in a positive manner, they shall be redeemed. If not, their removal is the only safe haven to assure the survival of society."

A young man possessing a large square head and olive skin raised his hand in the air.

"Yes, Brother Osvaldo," said Timothy.

"Excuse me, Doctor Ajala, but could you define the word you used? 'Reprobates'?"

"Certainly," replied Timothy without the slightest hesitation, "the reprobates of society are people that fall under the category of the evil or lawbreakers. They can be defined simply as unproductive and at times, counterproductive. They are the destitute that are unable or refuse to contribute to society. There is no need of them. Their only function is to siphon off useful resources that otherwise would be used for the greater good. The reprobates of society have no purpose. They are simply an unwanted burden that we must refuse to bear if our society is to be successful."

"Thank you," said Osvaldo. He then nodded and smiled.

2

AARON STOOD IN front of a large mirror attached to the back wall of the locker room. He ws fully dressed in his uniform, an intimidating combination of solid black and yellow. In his left hand he held his helmet, and in his right hand he caressed the growth around his mouth. A reflection of a huge jersey then appeared behind him.

"Don't think that new goatee makes you special," said Jeff. "I'm still the best looking guy on the team."

Aaron laughed. "Yeah, right! Keep dreaming, Buckey!"

Suddenly, Jeff stepped aside as loud chants echoed throughout the locker room. "Terry! Terry! Terry!"

A second reflection appeared in the mirror. "It actually looks nice."

"Terry!" said Aaron. He turned and hugged him. "It's about time! You've missed the entire preseason!"

"Those games don't count," said Terry.

The three coaches walked out of their office wearing their typical combination of shorts, cotton knit shirts and matching black caps. Each one appeared happy except for Coach More. He was frowning deeply. "Coach Spriggs, Coach Morales, could you start without me?" he asked.

They nodded.

"Let's go, men!" said Coach Spriggs.

"Everyone to the field!" said Coach Morales.

"Good to see you, Terry," said Jeff, patting Terry on the back.

"Aaron, you better join them," said Coach More. "The troops need their captain."

"Yes, sir," said Aaron. He glanced at Terry and pumped his fist on his way out.

As the last of the Avondale football players exited the locker room, Coach More tapped his clipboard. "You want to tell me why you haven't shown up for a single practice?"

"Sorry, Coach, I've been busy with other endeavors."

Coach More huffed. "Well, I'm glad to see you haven't lost your smarts, but Terry, what were you thinking?"

"That's exactly what I've been doing—thinking."

"Does that include thinking of the impression you're making?" asked Coach More. "Where were you when we were putting in extra time at the weight room? Where were you when we were running two a day practices under the blazing sun?"

Terry frowned. "Everyone seems happy except for you."

Coach More shook his head. "That's because most of the guys on the team are in awe of you, Terry. You have more natural talent in your pinky than most of them have in their entire bodies! They're never going to say anything, but you can't just come waltzing in here like this."

"If you recognize my greater talents, then why are we having this conversation?" asked Terry.

Coach More frowned deeply. "Excuse me?"

"You're asking me unnecessary questions when we could be on the field," said Terry. "Our first league game is Friday. I'm here. I'm ready." Terry touched his blue T-shirt at chest level with both hands. "Now, why don't you let me get dressed, so we can start playing football?"

Coach More exhaled deeply. "What's gotten into you? You've never talked to me like that before."

Terry maintained his eye contact, but said nothing.

Coach More removed his cap and scratched his short brown hair with a type of nervous energy. He then readjusted his cap quite forcefully, and as he did so, his jaw began to visibly tighten. "Everyone may be excited that you finally decided to show up, but that's not how we run our program. You need to serve in the trenches like all of the other soldiers. Maybe some of your other coaches think you deserve special treatment, but not me."

Terry smiled and then broke into a deep laughter that echoed throughout the locker room.

Coach More furrowed his brow. He took a step closer toward Terry. Coach More was the stockier of the two, but Terry was several inches taller. The two stood face to face in silence. Finally, Coach More said, "Do you find this situation humourous? Because if you do, you'll have to break it down for me."

Terry shrugged. "Certainly. Allow me to enlighten you, Coach More. We are a high school football team; we are not in the Marines. I don't know if you're trying to live vicariously through us, but the simple truth of the matter is that you were never a high ranking officer in the past, and you definitely aren't one now! I, however, am an elite athlete, as well as an elite student, so yes, I am special and yes, I do deserve special treatment. That's just the way it is."

The face of Coach More reddened. He slowly gnashed his teeth. "You know what, Washington?" he began, practically spitting the words at Terry. "That's the most selfish, stupid, and asinine thing I've ever heard!"

As Coach More raced toward the exit, Terry called out, "I guess I shouldn't be surprised! Mediocrity should never be allowed to govern superiority!"

Coach More exited the locker room and stormed onto the field. He then blew his whistle loudly before shouting, "Butler! Get over here!"

Larry quickly ran to Coach More. "Yes, Coach?"

"We need to practice our running options," barked Coach More. "You're starting Friday night."

"Huh? I—I don't get it. I'm special teams, and Terry's here now."

"Yes, and he's been AWOL! And he's been insubordinate! Terry Washington is no longer part of this unit!"

A few players stopped in the middle of their drills.

"Coach, I can do punt returns," said Larry, "but I'm not strong enough or fast enough—"

"Larry Butler will be our running back this season!" bellowed Coach More, cutting Larry off in mid-sentence.

The field suddenly became deathly quiet. Not a single person moved. Aaron then saw Terry in the distance. Leaving the grassy field, he quickly ran after Terry. Once he reached the asphalt, his cleats began to slip. Turning and twisting, Aaron was just able to maintain his balance. "Hey! Hey! Wait up, cuz! What just happened between you and Coach?" he shouted.

"It's not your concern," said Terry as he continued to walk away.

Aaron reached out to him, grabbing him by the shoulder. "Terry! Stop! It is my concern! What's going on?"

"You wouldn't understand, Aaron," replied Terry.

"Since when?" said Aaron. "Since when wouldn't I understand? Come on, bro! Look who you're talking to! It's me, Aaron!"

Terry finally stopped. He reached out and grabbed the face mask of Aaron's black and yellow helmet. "Are you my brother, Aaron?"

"What?"

"I asked if you are truly my brother."

"Of course I am! You know I've always thought of you that way. What kind of stupid question is that?" asked Aaron.

"It's not a stupid question," said Terry. "Timothy says that a real brother has nothing to do with bloodlines. It's a spiritual connection—a connection that has to do with commitment, with perspective."

"What are you talking about?" asked Aaron.

"I'm asking if you are truly my brother," continued Terry. "Do you believe the way I believe? Do you support me? The fact that we're second cousins or something like that doesn't really mean much. Timothy's helped me come to realize the true nature of my relationship with my own mother, and I can do this with you, too."

Aaron's helmet moved from side to side. "Terry—or whoever the hell you are—you're losing it, man. You've changed. You're letting that dude Timothy fill your head with all kinds of crazy ideas."

"You think like that because you're blind like the rest of them," said Terry, tapping the top of Aaron's helmet with his knuckles.

"I'm blind?" repeated Aaron as he slapped at Terry's hand. "I'm not the one who doesn't even know who his family is!"

"A spiritual family is more genuine than a biological family, Aaron!"

"So what are you saying, Terry? You saying I'm not your family? You saying Granddad and Grandma's not your family? Or your own mother?"

"First of all, he's your grandfather, not mine," said Terry. "And I'm not even sure how I'm related to Grandma. And my mother, my mother..." Terry's voice trailed off. He inclined his head.

"Look at you!" said Aaron. "You always think you're so smart, but behind all of that thinking and those fancy words, you know that whatever you say, Granddad and Grandma have been the ones to raise you, the ones to take you in. And as much as you may hate the way she is, your mom's still your mom, and you love her."

Terry's brow fell. His eye lids fluttered and his lips began to quiver.

"Look, man," said Aaron, putting his hand on his shoulder. "I'm your brother. I've always been your brother, and I always will be. And Granddad, and Grandma, they've been like parents to us."

"Aaron, we need to get started," a voice called out.

Aaron turned to see Coach More standing at the edge of the field.

"We need you," he continued.

"Yes, Coach," replied Aaron.

Terry snorted as he began to walk away. As he did so, he mumbled, "Keep the status quo, Aaron."

3

THE RECEPTIONIST BEHIND the dark wooden counter of the hotel lobby was meticulously dressed in a blue blazer that covered her white collared shirt and red scarf. Her blonde hair was tightly wrapped behind the top of her head in a bun, and the purple rims of her glasses made an interesting contrast with her tan skin. "Which manager?" she asked. "There are several."

"Timothy Ajala," said Terry.

"Oh, I believe he's occupied in his office with a client or a..." She hesitated. "...personal friend."

"It's very important that I speak to him. He told me that I could do so."

The receptionist smirked slightly. "I'll see what I can do." She picked up the handset of the phone and began pressing buttons. As she did so, Terry looked at the large digital clock attached to the wall. It was nearly 6:00 pm and his stomach was growling.

"No answer," said the receptionist.

"If you don't mind, I'd like to wait."

"Suit yourself," she replied.

After several minutes, Terry saw the outline of a man dressed in a white suit approaching him.

"Brother Terrence!" greeted a warm voice in a clipped British accent. Timothy emerged from one of the many light granite corridors accompanied by a woman with long black hair and honey colored skin. Her face was large and round, and her almond shaped eyes were dark and alluring. Her black skirt and white blouse hugged her curvaceous body. Terry immediately recognized her as one of the women seated in the leadership team.

"Hello, Timothy," said Terry.

"You remember Sister Camilla?"

"Yes, hello."

She smiled. "Hello, Brother Terrence."

"And to what do I owe this pleasure?" asked Timothy.

"Well, I know we don't have any leadership meetings scheduled for a while, but I just wanted to talk to you—to ask you some questions."

Timothy nodded. "Camilla, I'm afraid I'm going to have to conclude our time together."

She furrowed her brow. Her fleshy lips puckered outwardly. "Really?"

"Yes, really," said Timothy.

Camilla turned toward Terry and frowned slightly, emitting an air of condescension. "Sometimes I wonder if you value me enough."

Timothy kissed her on the cheek. "Trust me, *ma chérie*, I value you very, very much. *Tu es un trésor.*"

Camilla smiled. "I want to be the one, Timothy. The only one."

Timothy softly touched her nose with his fingertip. "Now, now, my dear; we have already had this conversation."

Camilla shook her head and then walked slowly toward the exit of the lobby.

Turning to Terry, Timothy asked, "Have you eaten?"

"No, I originally went for a walk," said Terry. "I was trying to clear my head, and then I saw the bus stop, and somehow I ended up here."

Timothy smiled. "Come, follow me. We can grab a bite to eat in the dining room and after that, I have a gift for you."

"A gift?"

"Yes."

Terry followed Timothy through the large lobby, down an adjoining hallway, and into the elegant restaurant of the hotel.

"Hello, Doctor Ajala," greeted a young lady with a dark complexion and long black hair.

"Hello, Jennifer. I would like a table for two in a closed section, please."

"Of course, sir," she replied. "Please, follow me."

Terry was led past many people seated at booths and round tables. To the right was a bar with several people seated at a long polished circular counter. When they arrived at the very back of the restaurant, the young lady removed a red felt cord. "Should I bring you menus, sir?"

"No, that won't be necessary, Jennifer. Please bring us two Turkey salads with honey mustard dressing—non-fat—and water to drink."

Terry frowned.

"I am going to make sure you eat something nutritious," said Timothy. He motioned to Terry. "Please, sit down, my brother. Tell me, *how you dey?*"

Terry furrowed his brow. "Excuse me?"

Timothy laughed. "That is our patois."

Terry smiled and shrugged.

"Patois—from Nigeria—and unlike the vulgarity of common American English—which I detest—our vernacular serves only to demonstrate our affection."

"Oh," said Terry. "So, what did you say to me?

"I simply asked how you are doing."

Terry inclined his head. "How am I doing? I never know how to answer that question. I have conflicting emotions. I'm confused. I always feel confused. It's as if one answer only leads to another question."

"Remember, my brother, emotions are not reality," said Timothy. "They are merely undisciplined responses to social conditioning. The mind is the most powerful weapon known to mankind, but you are only beginning to tap its true potential. You must train your thought processes."

Terry nodded. "How do I do that?" he asked.

"Through deep meditation," stated Timothy. "Delve into your thoughts from the left hemisphere of the brain and then to the right. The left is order. The left is logic. The right may be beautiful, but it is chaotic, dangerous, and from what you have told me, you have a very artistic temperament. I'm afraid it will take great focus and concentration for you to truly master yourself. Then and only then will you be able to differentiate between fantasy and—"

"—reality," concluded Terry.

"Yes. If your thoughts are pure and just and logical, then the feelings that follow them are allowed; but if your thoughts are impure or unjust or illogical, then the emotions you are feeling will be toxic to your mind."

Terry inhaled and exhaled deeply through his nostrils. "I feel alienated from my grandparents, my friends, my coach, and there's this girl..."

"Explain yourself more clearly, Terrence."

"My coach—Coach More—he's very demanding—and I don't really want to devote so much time to football. It takes time away from my studies; and Emily, this girl I met, we've been spending more time together. She's so attractive."

Timothy smiled. "There are few pleasures comparable to those of a beautiful woman."

"Yes, but strangely, as I've grown closer to Emily, it seems I've drifted away from my cousin, Aaron. We've always been so close..."

"Your relationship with Emily has caused this distance?"

Terry paused. "Maybe, but I think it has more to do with football. I'm no longer on the team."

Timothy arched his eyebrows. "Really?"

Terry bit his lower lip. "Do you disapprove, Timothy? Am I being... superficial?"

Timothy shook his head. "No, not at all. Any activity, if conducted with a higher purpose, is noble and productive. I, myself, for example, am quite enamored of tennis and have found it quite invigorating."

Terry released a wide smile. "Okay, so you do understand. Basically, I missed some practices over the summer and a few meaningless preseason games, and Coach made it abundantly clear that I was no longer welcome." Terry rubbed his forehead. "It's very frustrating, Timothy. They just don't understand—even Emily—but at least she's supportive. The rest, like Coach, Aaron, my grandparents..."

"Terrence, did you expect them to understand?"

Terry shrugged his shoulders. "I guess so," he replied.

"Do not speak like that," said Timothy, pointing his index finger directly at Terry. "Never use words that are ambiguous. Be precise. Express yourself well, Terrence; otherwise, you are wasting your gifts. You have a wonderful vocabulary, so use it to the fullest."

Terry nodded.

"You attempted to reach them," said Timothy. "You believed they would embrace the truth. They did not. They rejected the truth. They rejected you. But this is to be expected, not unexpected. Jesus said that 'many are called, but few are chosen.' "[16]

Terry raised his brow. "I thought you weren't religious."

"I am not, but I am spiritual," said Timothy, "and all great leaders are spiritual leaders. My point is that truth is truth, Terrence, and the response of the unenlightened cannot change this. Your friends may accept our message someday, or perhaps they never will; but regardless, we must persevere." He then extended his index finger toward Terry. "It is no small task to change the world, my brother."

An older man with dark skin and short gray hair approached the table. "Two glasses of water and two salads as you requested them, sir."

"Thank you," said Timothy.

Terry immediately gulped down half of the water which had filled the large glass. He then took several bites of his salad. "Have you lost friends over your beliefs?" he asked Timothy. "Have you lost people you cared about because of The Standard?"

"Of course," Timothy replied, "but I have learned the truth of Friedrich Nietzsche when he proclaimed: 'That which does not kill us makes us stronger.' "[17]

"But Timothy, with all due respect, you're answering me with a **platitude**," said Terry.

Timothy finished chewing. He wiped his mouth with his napkin and smiled. "You really are a gifted young man, Terrence. You actually challenge me. Okay, *no wahala*, I'll give you specifics. Yes, I have lost family members, I have lost friendships, and I have lost promising career opportunities. Still, I would change nothing."

Terry nodded eagerly. "You're still young, but you're older than I. When did you develop your beliefs? And how did you know?"

Timothy paused to gently rub the clear soft skin of his chin. "When did I start forming my beliefs? And when did I discover that the world was in need of radical change?"

"Yes."

Timothy smiled. "It is impossible to say with any type of real accuracy, but I suppose I found a systematic approach to what I believed during my time in Cambridge, and later I expanded on those beliefs while at Berkeley."

Terry reached for his glass of water while his eyes remained fixed on Timothy.

"My father had established his own law firm in my hometown of Abuja, so he sent me to study in Cambridge in order to continue the tradition. I agreed as long as he would allow me a year to travel, which he did."

"For what purpose?" asked Terry.

"I wished to know my country. The entire continent, really. I was aware of my limited perspective due to the modernization of Abuja as well as my affluent family, so I embarked on my journey with nothing more than a few belongings that I kept in a small leather bag. I spent most of my time in Senegal and Rwanda, but I also explored Morocco, Egypt, Kenya, and South Africa. After my travels, I returned to Abuja for a short time before attending Cambridge. It was during this time that I deeply considered my history, or rather, the history of Africa. The many peoples divided over ancient tribal warfare; the rise of the ruling Arabs from the north; the unjust sequester of our people and our land at the hands of the white man; the struggle against apartheid to the south; the violence over religious squabbles; the sickening poverty brought on by uninterrupted nescience." Timothy paused for a moment. His face revealed a level of anger, even disgust. "I saw the horrors of the past, the present, and the future, Terrence." He lifted the glass of water to his lips. Then, his expression seemed to recapture the charm that so often emanated from his countenance. "Are you aware that there are over a thousand dialects spoken in Africa? In Nigeria alone there is easily half this amount."

Terry shook his head. "No, I didn't. That's amazing."

"Yes, isn't it?" continued Timothy. "Well, with such heavy thoughts, I sailed for England. After completing my studies, I practiced law for quite some time in the United Kingdom. Success followed, yet I felt disillusioned. I began to see that no matter the country, no matter the culture or form of government, each society was controlled by the wrong people."

"Controlled?" repeated Terry. "By whom?"

"It depends," replied Timothy. "There is the power of finance, the power of the aristocracy, the power of the military, and the power of religion. They are all forms of control. But what I did not see in all my travels was a political system that was controlled by the power of truth." His large eyes widened further, revealing flashing circles of brown centered in a sea of white energy. His voice filled with passion, he proclaimed, "Terrence, think clearly! Has there ever been a society in which the political system was established with the purpose of electing the wisest people to govern?"

Terry furrowed his brow.

"Imagine a place, Terrence, where the elite, the most brilliant people of the world, governed the rest of society! Imagine what we could accomplish if our leaders were chosen not by their color, nor their affiliations, but by their capacity and their virtue! My young brother, we could put a stop to genocide! We could cure the most lethal diseases that have plagued us for decades! We could eliminate world hunger! We could end all war!"

Terry remained still.

"But in order to accomplish this, we will have to reshape society—not improve it—but reshape it entirely! This will not happen with a simple change in the political process because all politicians are trapped in their own blind incompetence and injustice."

Timothy stopped to take a few bites of his food. Terry remained still, observing him.

"Terrence, The Standard is not just another political organization; it is a movement! The Standard represents a new society! Our goal is not merely to fix a broken model but to start over completely with a structure that actually works!" He pointed his index finger at Terry. "Are you familiar with Plato and his belief in the philosopher kings?"

"I haven't studied him extensively," Terry replied, "but I know he was one of the three great philosophers along with Socrates and Aristotle."

"Yes, that's right," said Timothy. "Plato was the greatest disciple of Socrates. He was also a brilliant man who had become dismayed with the various forms of government. He saw firsthand the corruption of the Sophists, who used their rhetorical skills to manipulate people. He saw the unfairness of the oligarchy, where a few wealthy families ruled the rest. And finally, as a witness to the death of his mentor, Plato experienced the disgraceful repercussions of democracy; namely, allowing uneducated, unintelligent people the right to take part in government."

"How so?" asked Terry.

"Why, by voting of course!" replied Timothy.

"Oh, yes…"

Timothy took several bites of his salad. He seemed subdued briefly, as if his mind had suddenly settled into neutral. Then, he faced Terry and once again, his eyes flashed brightly. "After experiencing such anguish, Plato wrote his treatise, *The Republic*, which explains how society must function. There must be philosopher kings who rule their kingdoms, and underneath them are those who are the guardians, the ones who keep the peace, and those who are productive to society, such as artists, or builders, people who work with their hands. But the greatest in society are those who have been trained to use their minds! Only the elite have the capacity to make just decisions for all. Only the elite can explore the invisible realm, the realm of forms, of concepts. Only the elite can solve difficult problems that plague society through a rigorous **dialectical** method. Only the elite are rational enough to have dominated their lustful natures. And that, my brother, is what we are trying to achieve! A just society, a controlled society, a society of light!"

Terry paused. He licked his lips slowly. A strange wave of power seemed to settle deep within him. "Timothy," he began, "I see the greatness of what you are trying to achieve, but why don't the others see it?"

"For the same reason they did not understand Socrates. But now, tell me. What was the difference between Socrates and his disciple, Plato?"

Terry raised his hands and then turned his palms upward. "I wouldn't know."

"The difference was that Socrates was content to speak with a mere passerby. He was not interested in creating a formal movement. To his detriment, he underestimated the depth of human stupidity and greed. Plato, however, learned from his mentor. He established his Academy in Athens, which is basically the model for our modern universities. It wasn't enough to merely speak to people at the corner market. Plato understood that the only way to realize his vision was to train people, to educate them."

"But isn't that what we're doing now?" asked Terry.

"Most educational systems, and I include America here, are quite pathetic. They are but mere institutions of archaic methodology and superficial exercises." Timothy shook his head as he deeply frowned. "What we need is an educational system which is aligned to our vision of society. This nonsense of all children attending the same school, being herded into the same grade level based on their age, learning the same subjects.... It is complete rubbish! I graduated from junior secondary school in two years and senior secondary school in one year! I passed all of my examinations quite easily. One knows if a child is gifted at an early age. One also is only too aware if a child lacks functional mental capacity."

Terry frowned. He then inclined his head slightly and halfheartedly picked at a few of the vegetables that remained untouched within his salad.

"We need to create separate schools, each with a distinct purpose. Superior children must be separated and relocated to remote places of beauty and tranquility where they may study unhindered. In these temples of learning, they will be instructed in philosophy, in critical thought, and in government. Children who belong to the masses of mediocrity must develop their limited capabilities to support society while attending various vocational schools. Training will be given in law enforcement, mechanical operation, construction, technology—even the arts." Timothy furrowed his brow. He paused for a moment, and then exclaimed, "Oh, yes, I had almost forgotten! The inferiors. They require only the most rudimentary education before releasing them to fulfill their true purpose."

"Which is?" asked Terry.

"Menial tasks. They cannot be trusted with much independence, mind you, but when guided properly they can prove to be quite productive."

Terry paused and waited, but Timothy appeared to have concluded his thoughts. He appeared focused on finishing the remains of his meal. Finally, Terry asked, "But what about those who cannot?"

"Cannot?" repeated Timothy.

"Yes, what about the people who are not productive?"

Timothy frowned. "Those who cannot—or will not—should never have been born, Terrence. They have no purpose. They must be dismissed from society. There is no other way."

Terry furrowed his brow deeply. He set down his fork.

"Oh, look at the time," said Timothy, holding up his gold plated watch. "I really should return to my office. Please, follow me." He paused. "You did not finish your meal. Did you not like it?"

Terry swallowed deeply. Quietly, he whispered, "Yes, it was delicious."

"Splendid! Okay, off we go!"

Terry followed Timothy out of the restaurant. They walked down one of the many hallways that led behind the large front desk area in the lobby.

Timothy pulled out a card and swiped it. A green light flashed several times. He opened the door and entered. "This is my private office."

"Wow," said Terry, observing the many cameras and monitors mounted on the walls. Technology was abundant. Computers, copy machines, and flat screen monitors dominated the desk areas. "It's incredible...and so large. You can see everything from here."

"Yes, when I took over the supervision of the hotel I had them remodel this room," said Timothy. He then grabbed a large rectangular purple box that lay on one of the two mahogany desks. "For you."

"What is it?" asked Terry.

"You are a fine looking young man, Terrence, so do not hide behind the clothing of a mere laborer."

"I think I know what's in the box," said Terry, smiling.

"Yes, you do. I spoke to my tailor and gave him your estimated measurements. You are, perhaps six feet and two inches? I'm guessing you have a thirty-two inch waist and weigh approximately one hundred and ninety pounds? I am much more acquainted with the metric system, but I hope I appraised your body type correctly."

"Yes, astonishingly so," said Terry, moving the box up and down slightly.

"Be proud to set a standard for the rest of society, Terrence. Be strong in every way. Intellectually. Physically. Emotionally. Be committed to our cause, our vision, and someday, you will be a king."

4

"DAMN!" SHOUTED COACH More above the noise of the stadium. He paced up and down the sidelines dressed in khaki pants, a black shirt that had the Avondale school emblem of a yellow jacket pasted on the chest, and a matching black cap. "Even with only three linemen, Butler still can't get a decent run!"

"Yeah, that zone defense is really hurting us," said Coach Morales. "Jeff's creating some big holes, but their corners are coming in from the sides. They're on to us, Coach. Each game's gotten harder. We're lucky to be undefeated at this point. Our spread offense just isn't as effective without Terry."

Coach More scowled. "Don't even mention his name! He abandoned us! He's not part of this team. We make decisions based on who's here, not who isn't! Larry's our running back now!"

Coach Morales raised his hands. "Okay, I got it, but Aaron's exhausted. They're just waiting for him. Even when he gets a little yardage they're making him pay for it. You know he'll never complain, but he's really getting banged up out there."

Coach Spriggs then joined the two men. "Coach, face it; our triple option has become a double option. They're covering the pass and wearing Aaron down and Larry, well, he's just too slow."

"And weak," added Coach Morales.

"Well, we have less than a minute on the clock and it's third down. We may not get the ball back. It's Aaron or nothing," replied Coach More.

"He's practically limping out there," said Coach Morales. "He's going to get hurt if you keep running him. Go with Larry."

"This game's over," added Coach Spriggs. "We'll have time to figure out something before the playoffs. Maybe Leo Reyes."

Coach More removed his black cap and rubbed his hand through the tight bristles of his brown hair. "He's a tight end."

"Yeah, but the kid's bigger, faster, and stronger than Larry," said Coach Morales. "We can teach him the running back position. I've even seen him throw. Leo's a great athlete. He could be the key in the absence of Washing…" His voice trailed off. "…in the absence of a better option at running back."

"Better act now, Coach, while they're in the huddle," said Coach Spriggs.

"All right," said Coach More. He walked to the edge of the white sideline and raised his hands. "Time!"

The referee crossed his hands high above his head and blew his whistle. Aaron jogged wearily to the sidelines. "Yeah, Coach?"

"No more quarterback options," said Coach More. "If someone is open, pass the ball. If not, throw it out of bounds, but no more scrambling and no more runs. Either pass the ball or pitch it to Butler."

"What? But why?" asked Aaron.

"That's an order, Aaron," added Coach Morales.

"But Larry hasn't done nothing all night!" said Aaron. "Even the home crowd is mocking him. They're yelling for me to give him the ball!"

Coach Morales shook his head. "I know, Aaron, I know, but you're getting beat up out there! I can't remember you ever getting hit like this. We're going to take a loss on this one if we have to. We can't afford you getting hurt. Don't worry, we'll figure this out."

Aaron turned to Coach More. Peering through his helmet, he shouted, "Coach, we can still win this one! A touchdown and a field goal will win the game!"

"Not tonight," replied Coach More rather mechanically. "Listen to Coach Morales, Aaron."

Aaron inclined his head, and then replied to Coach Morales, "Yes, sir."

Once inside the huddle, Aaron called the play. The team then set up on the line. Aaron called out his cadence, received the snap, and rolled to his right. Not a single receiver was open. Leonel Reyes was surrounded by a collection of defensive backs and safeties. Aaron continued to look downfield for one of his wide receivers, but found nothing. Reluctantly, he threw a screen pass to Larry Butler who caught the ball and was promptly tackled.

"Too much *agua fría*, Holmes!" said one of the opposing linemen.

"You guys ain't nothing without Washington!" said another.

As time ran out, the referee pointed to the center of the field and began blowing his whistle. Coach More shook hands with the opposing coaches before joining the team as they headed off the field.

"You think there's any way we can get Terry back?" asked Leonel.

"Doubt it," said Aaron.

"It's going to be tough without him."

"Yeah," said Aaron.

5

TERRY AND EMILY walked along the gray sidewalk, gingerly avoiding the large cracks in the cement and the discarded glass bottles. Both were dressed formally—Terry in dark slacks, a white shirt and black tie—and Emily in a tight fitting red skirt and white blouse. To each side of them were a number of small stores, the majority possessing thick glass windows and heavy doors reinforced with metal bars.

"Terrence, I'm nervous," said Emily. "It's bad enough that you dragged me to this neighborhood, on a Saturday morning I might add, but do you really need to cover my eyes?"

"Yes, I do," said Terry.

"But isn't it dangerous?" asked Emily.

"No, it's too early in the morning to be dangerous," said Terry.

"I'm worried. Why are we even here? And why did you tell me to wear a skirt and high heels just to come to this place? We just don't fit in, Terrence. None of this makes any sense!"

"You know something," replied Terry as he guided her around a street corner, "you complain too much."

"You do realize that my life is literally in your hands," said Emily. She raised her index finger in the air. "And my car better be safe!"

Terry laughed. "Nothing will happen to your car. I promise. Okay, we're almost there. It's time." He revealed a white cotton scarf. Emily puckered her lips. "No pouting," said Terry as he began to wrap the scarf around Emily's eyes. He then secured it in a knot behind her long red hair. "Okay, now wrap your arm around my waist."

Connected at the hip, the two entered a large apartment complex. They then walked to an open parking lot that extended from the two floors of the apartments to a supermarket. Removing the scarf, Terry announced, "Okay, now you can look!"

In front of them was an amazing mural that had been painted on a wall composed of large white cement blocks. The background was a light blue texture. On one side was a bright yellow sun, shining down on several people. A few of the figures were larger than others, standing as giants among a throng of others whose faces were marked by desperation, almost worship, and whose arms and hands stretched upward. To the right of the painting was a poem written in broad strokes of green with the title *Dreamer.*

Dreamer, sweet dreamer
Dream a dream for me
Close your eyes, now concentrate
And tell me what you see

Live your life so very pure
Till you will not belong
People will not understand
But the message must go on

Dreamer, sweet dreamer
Can you not see in saving lives
That you have lost your own?

I dwell upon your sacrifice
Look down below and moan

"I—I don't know what to say," said Emily. Her eyes lit up. Cautiously, she left Terry to approach the mural more closely.

"Do you like it?"

"Terrence, did you paint this?" asked Emily. "Did you write this?"

Terry smiled slightly. "Yes and yes."

A few people passed by and pointed to the wall.

"This is Martin Luther King, right?" asked Emily, touching a large face.

Terry nodded.

"And this one? Who is she? Some saint?"

Terry shook his head from side to side.

Emily raised her hands in front of her and jumped in the air. "Don't tell me!" She faced the figure for quite some time. "Oh, it's not a halo, but a crown. Red hair, the clothes of a ruler, powdery white skin, green eyes…" Emily turned to face Terry. Placing her hands on her hips, she shouted, "Terrence! This isn't—"

Terry laughed. "No, no, it's not you! It's Queen Elizabeth, you self-centered little…" Without finishing his thought, he approached Emily and embraced her.

"Well, now I feel embarrassed," said Emily. "Queen Elizabeth, of course. And, this third figure?"

"Guess!" said Terry.

Emily puckered her lips and shook her head slowly.

"Well, you're going to have to because I'm not going to tell you."

Emily arched her brow. "Oh, really? You mean, not even under torture?"

Terry smiled widely. "And how would a pretty little redhead torture me?"

"I could kiss you to death."

Emily pulled on Terry's neck and kissed him on the lips. She then kissed his cheeks and neck.

"Okay, okay, you're breaking me," said Terry amidst laughter.

Emily released him and once again began to study the mural, fixating her gaze on the third unnamed figure. "Okay, that's good enough for me. Now, Mr. Washington, I shall solve this riddle!"

"Damn, you're cute!" said Terry. He took a few steps until he stood behind her and then wrapped his arms around her waist. As Emily continued to ponder the mural, Terry began to rock her from side to side.

Emily raised her left hand and touched the corners of her mouth. "I believe he's Hispanic."

"Perhaps," said Terry as he rested his perpendicular jaw over the top of Emily's head.

"He has to be famous. His clothes seem a little out of date, but they're very formal. A President, maybe?"

Terry grinned.

"Yes, a former President of Mexico or Spain."

"I'm not going to tell you," said Terry.

"I never asked you to," replied Emily.

Terry tightened his grip on her. "Has anyone ever told you how attractive you are when you get competitive?"

Emily turned to face Terry. "You know, I could begin with my torture technique again."

"You'll never break me, Miss Potter."

The two kissed, warmly at first, and then quite passionately. Terry pulled her body closer to his own.

"That's the way to do it!" called out a voice amidst cackles of laughter.

"Hey, man, if you get tired, I'll take a turn!" called out a second voice.

Terry looked up to see two men in soiled white T-shirts and stained khaki pants. Each one had nearly identical tan skin, long greasy brown hair, and beards that sprouted from their cheeks in all directions. One exposed several missing teeth when he smiled.

"That won't be necessary," said Terry. "We are going to have a rally here shortly. You're welcome to stay and learn something. Who knows? It might change your lives."

The two men laughed.

"A rally? There gonna be food?" asked one of the men as he took a few steps closer toward Terry.

"Food for thought," said Terry.

The other man spat on the ground. "You got any spare change, man?"

"No," said Terry.

"You look like you got money." He then pointed a dirty calloused hand toward Emily. "So does she."

Terry maneuvered Emily so that she stood behind him with her arms clinging around his narrow waist. He then lifted his chin and expanded his shoulders. He furrowed his brow. His eyes squinted. "We don't have any money."

Both men lingered a bit and then slowly walked away.

"Emily," muttered Terry, "even though I'm enjoying this, you don't have to hug me so tightly."

"I'm sorry," replied Emily. "It's just that those men—they frightened me. They looked awful! And they smelled!"

Terry laughed as he lifted Emily's arms and positioned himself to face her.

"It's not funny!" said Emily. "I thought they were going to assault you!"

"Sorry, it's just the way that you said it. No, those kinds of bums are all talk. They spend their days digging through trash cans and drinking beer. Anyway, I'm here to protect you. I would never let anyone hurt you."

Emily released a reluctant smile.

Facing the mural once again, Terry pointed to the third figure of the mural and said, "Okay, so do you give up?"

Emily stared at Terry. "No," she replied.

After a long pause, Terry said, "You're not saying anything."

"I'm just going to keep staring into those beautiful brown eyes of yours until I can find the answer," replied Emily.

Terry wagged his head. "Well, you're not going to find the answer there."

"Windows of the soul?" asked Emily.

Terry smiled. "Wow, do you know how special you are?"

"No, tell me."

Terry gently put his hands on the sides of her soft white cheeks. He stroked her thick red hair behind her ears. Emily closed her eyes and let out a pleasant sigh.

"Don't close your eyes," said Terry. "I love those green eyes."

"What else do you love?".

"I love those pink lips."

As the two remained locked in a provocative connection of unspoken words, a pleasant voice suddenly rang out, interrupting them. "Benito Juárez!"

Terry turned quickly to see Timothy. He was dressed in a celestial blue shirt, silk white tie, and cream colored slacks. Behind him were two large white vans, each with a magic carpet emblem painted onto the sides. Several people quickly poured out of them carrying tables, sound equipment, cables, and several cases.

Terry quickly released Emily, practically pushing her away. "Timothy! I'm sorry. I didn't see you. I guess I was completely engrossed in the mural."

"*No wahala*, Brother Terrence," replied Timothy, extending his hand. Then, turning toward Emily, he asked, "And who might this be?"

Terry gently touched Emily on the shoulder. "Doctor Timothy Ajala, allow me to introduce you to Miss Emily Potter."

"Oh, yes. Emily…" His large eyes darted up and down, left and right, as if analyzing every component that was involved in the summation of her being. "Finally, we meet. If I'm not mistaken, you attend a private school, Saint Mary Prep School, is it not?"

Emily nodded her head. She gripped Terry's right bicep tightly with both hands.

"Not too long ago I met a real estate agent by the name of Sheila Potter. Attractive woman. Would you happen to be a relative of hers?"

"Yes, she's my mother," said Emily, still clinging to Terry.

"Of course," said Timothy. Once again, he began to study Emily. "Catholic, conservative family. Both parents work long hours. So long that they are often completely unaware of your personal life..." Timothy paused. Walking slowly around Terry and Emily, he created a tight imaginary circle around them. "Firstborn, bright, studious yet adventurous, and though strong-willed someone who has not truly suffered in life. University bound, planning originally to attend a school out of state, but now you are not so sure..." Timothy then pointed to Terry.

Emily's eyes widened. Terry remained still with his lips pressed firmly together.

Taking a few steps toward the mural, Timothy continued, "Queen Elizabeth—a personal favorite of mine. Martin Luther King Junior—a splendid choice—though I confess I possess a certain proclivity toward the great Nelson Mandela." He pivoted and faced Terry once again. "You have great talent, Brother Terrence, and this talent must be put to greater use. Remember, talents not contributed to the betterment of society..."

"...do not truly exist," said Terry.

"Yes, well, are you prepared to speak?" asked Timothy.

"I prepared a small speech on the necessity of leadership."

Timothy grasped his hands together. He smiled widely, displaying his evenly shaped white teeth. "Wonderful! I must ask. Were you able to finish Plato's *Phaedo*?"

Terry smiled and nodded. "I also read Aristotle's *On the Soul* and Hegel's *Science of Logic*."

"Splendid!" said Timothy. "Your speech will precede my own, Terrence. This will be an important event in which I will bring attention to the contrast between this part of Phoenix and the neighboring communities. You have noticed the difference, have you not?"

Terry furrowed his brow. Suddenly, he exclaimed, "Now that you mention it, it seems cleaner, and there are less homeless."

"Except for the two men that were bothering us," said Emily.

Timothy raised his brow. "Two indigents were bothering you?"

"Not really," said Terry, "just looking for a handout. They did us no harm."

"But they could have," said Emily.

Timothy twisted his lips. His eyes narrowed. "Calvin! Osvaldo!"

Two young men, dressed formally in dark slacks, white collared shirts, and black ties, quickly approached.

"This young lady and our own Brother Terrence were accosted with evil intent just moments ago," said Timothy.

Terry smiled slightly. "Well, I would hardly say they were evil."

"I believe the lovely Emily would disagree," said Timothy. He then turned toward Calvin and Osvaldo. "Perhaps these streets are not as safe as we believed. I think we will have to double our efforts."

"Yes, Timothy," said Calvin.

"Terrence, allowing inferiors to harass a person of Emily's beauty and intelligence is not the least bit teleological. What would happen if we continue to ignore the wickedness that surrounds us? Did you learn nothing from Plato? From Aristotle? From Hegel?"

Terry inclined his head.

"Remember, all of our decisions must be rooted in a just cause, and the determinants of a just cause are the final results and repercussions of our decisions. Thus and only thus does logic fill our beings, and logical beings alone are able to form a rational society."

"Of course, Timothy," replied Terry. "You are right, and I was mistaken."

Timothy's smug look of disgust quickly vanished, replaced by his more commonly seen smile. "Okay, then, I'm off to inquire of the others. Senator Brawnchild should be arriving shortly. I must speak with him and see to some logistics." Timothy took a few steps but then paused. He reached out and slightly adjusted Terry's tie. "That's better." Then, he bowed his head toward Emily, clutched her hand within his own, and kissed it. "Emily, *mon petit ange.*"

As Timothy walked away, Terry furrowed his brow. "What did he say to you?"

Blushing slightly, Emily replied, "He called me his little angel."

6

THE ANGRY VOICE of Granddad Bailey echoed throughout the barn. "After all you've been through, and all you've seen, I can't believe you don't have any common sense!" He grabbed a large metal rake from the side of one of the old wooden walls as Terry stood in silence. "You ain't finishing your chores, you keep coming home late."

Terry began to bite his lower lip.

"Well, I'm warning you, son! If you continue to hang out with those troublemakers, or if I have a police officer talking to me again about vandalism, then you're going to have to find another place to stay!"

Terry got up and silently walked away. As he approached the large front door of the barn, he and Aaron practically bumped into each other. They stood face to face briefly, and then Terry turned and said in a subdued tone, "It's not vandalism. It's art. I was embellishing the city, and it's not my fault if the police, or you, cannot understand my **aesthetic** endeavors. It's a mural dedicated to vision, a tribute to a new order."

Granddad Bailey pointed the head of the rake toward Terry and called out, "What did you say, boy? Are you back talking me?"

Ignoring him, Terry continued on his way.

"Hey!" said Aaron. "Where you going?"

"Timothy wants to meet with me."

"Timothy? So it's true? You're hanging with that fool?"

Terry stopped. He grimaced. "You wouldn't understand."

"Oh yeah?" replied Aaron. "And why's that? Because I'm not smart enough?"

Terry shook his head and briskly walked away. Aaron could not help but observe his stride. Each movement was more of a bounce off the top of his toes than a normal step, as if he were ready to launch for flight. Aaron was an athlete, a great one by most measures; and yet, he understood that Terry was in a completely different class. His legs and arms were full of fast-twitch muscles; his hands and feet were large. His fingers were extraordinarily long. It was as if Terry had been designed with superior materials, like a high-performance vehicle that had been handcrafted to perfection.

"We need to talk, cuz!" shouted Aaron.

Terry continued down the wide dirt path.

"Coach keeps asking me about you! And so are the guys! I think he still wants you on the team!"

Terry did not answer. Aaron watched his diminishing figure turn onto the main street that touched the long dirt path of the Bailey farm until he slowly disappeared.

"How long were you planning on staying out there?" shouted Granddad Bailey, peeping his head through the barn door.

"Oh, sorry, Granddad. I just got back from practice," said Aaron. "Grandma said you wanted to talk to me. Can it wait, though? I'm really hungry."

"No, it can't wait, so get in here!"

Aaron reluctantly walked into the barn. He knew his grandfather was a loving man, but he was also very aware that he was a hard man to please.

"What's going on with Terry?" asked Granddad Bailey as he picked at some hay on the barn floor with the large rake in his hands. Even at his ripe old age, he was incapable of sitting still.

"I don't know," Aaron replied. "Granddad, is he in some kind of trouble?"

"So you do know something?"

"No, I just heard stuff."

Granddad Bailey scowled. "Well, what did you hear? Speak up, boy!"

"I know he quit football."

"He have a girlfriend?"

"Maybe," said Aaron.

"Your grandmother said some white girl been picking him up and taking him places. Drives a real nice car. She must be buying him all those nice clothes he's been wearing lately."

Aaron pressed his lips together.

"The police said some strange things have been happening over there in Phoenix where his mother lives. He tell you anything about that?"

"No."

"So you don't know nothing about him vandalizing some of the walls over on the West Side, then, I suppose?"

"He was tagging?" asked Aaron.

Granddad Bailey furrowed his brow. "What's that?"

Aaron paused for a moment. "May I be excused?"

"No, you may not," said Granddad Bailey. "I got an axe to grind with you, too! You may not be as bad as Terry, but you've been neglecting your work around here, Aaron."

"Dante's ten," said Aaron, "and how old is Brandy?"

"Dante can't do the heavy work, and Brandy's only eight years old."

Aaron shrugged his shoulders. "That's how old I was when you put me to work."

Granddad Bailey scratched his unkempt salt and pepper hair. "Well, you were different, I suppose. Besides, Brandy just got here last month. She's still adjusting."

"Granddad, practice takes three hours most days," pleaded Aaron. "I get home, eat, and fall asleep. Sometimes I'm just too tired to get up in the morning, but once football's over—"

"—I can't wait until then!" interrupted Granddad Bailey. "When does farm work end?"

Aaron looked at his grandfather with defeat in his eyes.

"When?"

"Never," said Aaron.

"That's right! Never! So I suggest you get up nice and early!"

Aaron stared at him.

"Don't be giving me those sad eyes, boy!" said Granddad Bailey. "You're my right hand man, aren't ya? I can count on you, can't I?"

Aaron inclined his head.

"How many times have I told you that my own kids aren't interested? This farm's going to be yours someday, Aaron. You're my number one."

"Yeah, I know, it's just..."

"It's just what?"

"Coach says this is my year! He says colleges are going to be watching me. He really thinks I can make it all the way to the pros!"

"Your coach told you all that, did he? Filling your mind with all them dreams? Well, did he also tell you how much it costs to pay for those clothes you're wearing?"

Aaron tugged at his striped collared shirt and frowned slightly.

"Does he tell you how much time and effort goes into preparing your food each day?"

Aaron remained silent.

"Well, did he?" asked Granddad Bailey.

"No," he muttered.

"No, he didn't, and he didn't take you in when your parents were doing drugs and your father was thrown in jail, did he?"

Aaron remained with his head inclined. "No, sir."

Granddad Bailey lifted Aaron's face up by placing two rough, calloused fingers under his chin. In a softer, kinder tone, he continued, "Look, we've got the hogs to feed, vegetables to pick, hay to bale. I'm getting older, Aaron, and we can't afford to hire outside help. I need you, son. I need you."

Aaron smiled weakly. "I'm your man, Granddad. You can count on me."

"Well, all right, then. You, my man, are excused. Go get yourself some supper, and I'll be right here waiting for you."

7

THE SMALL OFFICE was located against a side wall in the largest open area of the Avondale High School locker room. On both sides were doors that could only be reached by scaling gray cement stairs. And though shared by several physical education teachers and coaches of all sports, everyone knew that it belonged to Coach More. It was his private sanctuary.

Aaron was surprised when Coach More had told him to stop by during lunch. With a peanut butter and jelly sandwich in his hand, he quickly scaled the steps and opened one of the side doors to the office. Inside, he found his coach talking on the phone.

"That would be fantastic, Walter," said Coach More. "And after you buy me lunch, then we'll set it up. Okay...okay...take care." He turned to face Aaron, his face beaming. "Guess who I just spoke with?"

Aaron looked at his coach, surprised by the expression on his face. It was a joy he had seen only when Coach More was recalling some past experience with the Marines or a former football game. "I have no idea, Coach."

"See this guy right here," said Coach More as he grabbed a picture frame from his desk and pointed to a young man with dark brown hair and blue eyes. "That's Walter Cane. He's in Phoenix for a conference. He usually stops by once a year. He's a congressman in Ohio; he splits his time between Columbus and Washington D.C. now. Can you believe that? My old buddy is a bona fide congressman!"

"That's great," said Aaron, "so, he used to be a Marine, too?"

"Good old Walter—ain't no one like him," continued Coach More, holding the picture in front of him. He appeared lost in thought. Then, suddenly, he scowled and said, "There's no such thing as a former Marine! Anyway, I need you to do two things for me."

"Of course, anything," Aaron replied as he took the last bite of his sandwich.

"First, what do you think of running some options with Reyes?"

Aaron arched his eyebrows. "Like what?"

"Well, we're thinking of creating some options where Leo would set up in his tight end position, but instead of merely receiving or blocking, he could go into motion and take some pitches from you. You could fake the handoff to Larry and pitch it to Leo instead."

Aaron rubbed the trimmed growth on his chin and nodded his head.

"Terry leaving us was completely unexpected," continued Coach More. "Truth is, many of the kids who might have served as his replacement tried out for different positions years ago. They knew they could never compete with Terry, and he never seems to get hurt or even winded, so playing his back up isn't too appealing. Larry isn't so bad on special teams, but as our main running back he's just not cutting it. He's a good kid, and I don't want to demote him, but we just can't win with him getting many carries. News is spreading that the way to beat us is to set a three man front and zone the pass, wear us down, and win in the fourth quarter."

"I'm with you," said Aaron. "Leo's a great athlete. He's our small forward in basketball; dude can jump. I bet he could even pass the ball as an option."

Coach More nodded. "Exactly."

"All right, Coach, I better go. Lunch is about over and my next class is way over on the other side."

"Okay, okay, you're dismissed," said Coach More. As Aaron reached the door, he suddenly blurted, "Aaron! Wait! I just remembered! Walter wants to talk with Terry."

Aaron furrowed his brow. "Your friend? Why would he want to talk to Terry?"

"Well, I asked him to. I think he may be able to reach him."

Aaron furrowed his brow. "Really? But how? He won't even listen to me. He's even starting to disobey our Granddad and nobody does that!"

"He may listen to Walter."

"Why would he? He doesn't even know him."

"Because he's just like Terry."

Aaron lowered his brow. "Huh?"

"Walter's the smartest person I know," said Coach More. "He can speak his language. Anyway, he'll be here tomorrow. Do you think you could bring Terry over around the same time?"

Aaron inclined his head. "I don't know, Coach, but I'll try."

"We'll meet in the practice gym."

"The gym?" repeated Aaron. "Wouldn't it be better to meet here in your office?"

"No, the steps."

Aaron frowned. "Okay, whatever you say, Coach. I'll do my best."

"You always do," replied Coach More.

Aaron smiled before leaving the office. Once outside the locker room, he passed a swarm of boys and girls racing to beat the tardy bell. Many of them smiled and waved to him. Aaron hugged a few girls and bumped fists with several boys as he casually made his way down one of the many cement hallways. Then, as he passed the corner of a small building, he saw a circle of smaller boys.

"Mason! Mason!" echoed the sound of several high-pitched voices.

Aaron, for some reason, felt compelled to stop. He observed one particular boy with great curiosity. He had short, sandy brown hair; freckles covered his white face; his teeth were crooked; and his buttoned collared shirt and corduroy pants were practically falling off of him due to his small frame.

"Wh—wh—what do you wa—wa—want?"

"What do we want?" repeated another boy. He then tilted his head to the side and with his eyes moving upward. "I mean, wh—wh—what do we want?" The others began to laugh. Then, with a more serious expression, he continued, "I was telling these guys how awesome you are."

Mason smiled in delight while the other boys burst into laughter.

"What a retard!" said one.

"Mason, I was trying to crow like a rooster but I couldn't do it. Can you show me?" asked another.

Mason smiled widely. "Yeah, I—I can do that!"

"Cool! Show us how, man!"

"Yeah, go for it!"

"Do it as loud as you can!"

Mason pulled back his arms, sticking his elbows out as if they were wings, shrugged his shoulders, and cocked back his head. "Okay," replied Mason. "You—you do it like th—th—this." He then let out a loud crowing sound that echoed throughout the halls.

The boys laughed loudly. As Mason smiled, basking in perceived admiration, several of the boys began to slap him on the head.

"Owww!" shrieked Mason, rubbing the back of his head.

"Hey, don't hit him, Ned!"

"I didn't hit him, it was Lucio!"

Mason turned around and another boy slapped him.

"I said to stop it, Brock!"

"It wasn't me! Tell him, Mason!"

Once more, Mason was slapped. Once more, he shrieked in pain; and once more, the boys around him roared in laughter. Aaron furrowed his brow and shook his head. His jaw tightened. He had seen enough. Charging toward the circle that had formed around Mason, Aaron shouted, "What the hell do y'all think you're doing?"

The boys continued laughing.

Looking down at them, Aaron barked, "Bunch of idiot freshmen! You think this is funny?"

A few boys nodded, others smirked, and one boy continued to laugh.

"Did you hear what I said?" asked Aaron, approaching one boy so closely that the two stood mere inches apart.

"I heard you," he replied.

Aaron arched his brow. "So all this is funny?"

The boy shrugged in response. "Yeah, I guess so. I mean, come on. Just look at him."

A few snickers were heard from within the group of boys.

Without warning, Aaron slapped the boy across the top of the head. He instantly cowered. The laughter stopped.

One of the boys whispered to another, "Do something, man."

"I ain't doing nothing," the other boy replied. "That's Aaron Holmes."

"Did y'all like that?" asked Aaron. "Huh? Was that funny?" He pushed one of the boys in the chest. "You said it was funny, right?" He turned and faced each of the boys. "Why aren't y'all laughing?"

"We were just having fun, Aaron," said another boy. "Tell him, Mason. Tell him it's cool. Tell him we're your friends."

"Shut up!" said Aaron. "You want to be my friend?" Aaron approached him and pushed him back with his right hand. "How 'bout I slap you upside your head so you can be my friend? Huh? You want that?"

The boy fell silent.

At that moment a more mature voice was heard. "What's going on here?"

Aaron turned to see a teacher approaching. He was short and thin. The black frames of his glasses contrasted with his brown mustache and pale face. His green sweater gave him an air of informality. "Well? Get to class!" he ordered.

While Mason remained standing, Aaron began to leave with the other boys.

"Hey! You!" he shouted.

Aaron stopped and faced him. "Yes, sir."

"Come here, please." He then turned toward Mason. "How many times have I told you not to talk to those boys?"

"I—I'm sorry, Mr. Doug—Mr. Douglass."

"It's okay. It's not your fault. Go to class. Mrs. Lara is there. She'll get you started on your work."

Mason smiled and then skipped away down the hallway.

Redirecting his attention toward Aaron, Mr. Douglass continued, "You're not in trouble. I just want to talk to you."

Hesitating momentarily, Aaron took a few steps toward the teacher.

"Aren't you the school's quarterback?" asked Mr. Douglass.

"Yes, sir."

"What's your name?"

"Aaron Holmes."

"I saw what you did, Aaron. I just didn't want to talk in front of Mason. He understands enough."

"Sir, I don't think I've ever seen that kid before," said Aaron. "Um, what's…"

"…wrong with him?"

Aaron nodded slightly.

"I could give you a lengthy diagnosis," said Mr. Douglass, "and then again, I could say nothing at all. You could have asked me what was wrong with those boys who were bullying him."

Aaron opened his mouth to say something but then decided to remain quiet.

"Mason spends most of his time here in special day class," continued Mr. Douglass. "He's actually one of our top students."

Aaron arched his eyebrows. "He's a top student?"

"In our class he is. We have students who are much lower functioning than Mason. Some have severe mental retardation, some are autistic, quadriplegic, and some are permanently bedridden. So, in comparison, Mason is very capable. He actually helps Mrs. Lara and me a lot. Sometimes, he hands out papers to other students or helps them with their assignments. But you want to know what's even more amazing?"

Aaron shrugged.

"Mason's a really kind, loving person."

"Wow," said Aaron. "That's good." Aaron paused, then added, "To be honest, I didn't know about that class."

"Most kids don't. Our kids have a different schedule. Their lunch is delivered and we have our own physical therapy time in an adjacent room in our building. Still, if you look hard enough, you'll see them."

Aaron glanced peripherally at the empty hallways. "Well, it's late. I better go."

"Why don't you come in my room and I'll write you a pass," said Mr. Douglass.

"That's okay. My teachers are cool with me," said Aaron.

"Must be nice," said Mr. Douglass. "Why don't you come anyway and let me write that pass."

Aaron began to bite his lower lip. Mr. Douglass reached out and touched Aaron on the shoulder. "Come, and I'll tell you about Mason."

The two began to walk toward a nearby rectangular building that stood apart from the other larger buildings which hosted several classrooms. "Mason has been homeschooled all his life," said Mr. Douglass. "This is his first year in a public school. Everything is new to him, and he's very naïve. And in many ways, defenseless."

"But why does he act like that?"

"Not every kid is as lucky as you, Aaron. I can't go into specifics, but I can tell you he has certain learning disabilities. Mason has special needs, but even so, he's what we call high functioning, and we're hoping next year we can mainstream him into a few classes."

"So he didn't even know that those kids were making fun of him?" asked Aaron.

"I doubt it," replied Mr. Douglass. "The sad truth is that he probably thinks they're his friends. Even sadder, they intentionally look for him. This time he was lucky—you were there. Next time it could be worse."

"Why aren't people looking out for him?"

"We try," said Mr. Douglass, "but we can't be everywhere. Kids like Mason are a magnet for bullies. The students who are severely disabled are outside their reach, but Mason is high enough that he responds to them. He's capable of interaction, just not at the same level." Mr. Douglass stopped in front of a classroom with the number seven painted above the door. "Here we are." He opened the door and motioned to Aaron. "After you."

Aaron entered and was immediately struck by an odd odor. The air seemed stale. Several strange noises could be heard. Aaron noticed a boy sitting in a wheelchair. He bobbed his head up and down and moaned loudly. Dried drool stuck to his cheeks. His black hair was short and thick and appeared as though it had not been washed for several days. Aaron cringed slightly at the sight of the boy's bony legs which poked out of his khaki shorts. He then turned toward another boy who was constantly laughing.

"Hi, I'm Carmen," a nasal voice called out, interrupting Aaron's thoughts. "I just put away my puzzle."

Aaron looked down to see a girl with a large round head. Batches of disheveled dark hair surrounded her brown face. She was short and plump, practically obese. Her eyes seemed somewhat slanted, almost cross-eyed.

Her voice was so monotone and nasal that Aaron frowned slightly upon hearing it. Swallowing deeply, Aaron paused momentarily before saying, "Hey, beautiful."

Carmen smiled.

"I think someone has a crush on you," said Mr. Douglass. He then handed Aaron a slip of paper.

Aaron remained standing. He observed Mason, who was sitting at a computer station wearing headphones. Every so often, he wiggled and threw his hands in the air. A heavyset woman approached Aaron. Unprompted, she began, "It's a reading program. When Mason selects the correct answer, the screen turns into a party celebration. It plays music when that happens."

Aaron smiled. "Cool."

"I can't thank you enough for what you did," said Mr. Douglass.

Aaron furrowed his brow. "What do you mean?"

"What you just did for Mason; these kids could use more heroes like you."

Puckering his lips, Aaron rubbed his trim goatee. "Hero, sir?"

Mr. Douglass nodded. "Yes, hero." He then removed his glasses and rubbed the bridge of his nose. His eyes had become moist. "Aaron, have you ever heard of Cardinal Mahony?"

"No, sir."

"Cardinal Mahony said that any society, or nation, will be judged on the basis of how it treats its weakest members; the last, the least, and the littlest." [18]

8

STANDING AMIDST A group of noisy people waiting outside the restaurant, Terry looked past Emily toward the smoky brown wooden walls of the entrance. The building was modern and chic, with open windows where customers could easily peer through to see an open bar, piano platform, and kitchen area where the chefs were only separated by long transparent glass walls and doors. Terry, dressed in a black tapered suit, white collared shirt, and a thin black tie, stood unusually erect. Emily, who was holding on to his left bicep, was dressed in equal elegance with a black sleeveless dress that reached down to hug her athletic white thighs. Her red hair was styled back into several long waves that curled against the sides of her face and down to her shoulders.

"Relax, Terrence," said Emily. She nudged him by pressing against his side with her shoulder. "It will be fun!"

"You don't know Monica," replied Terry.

"She can't be that bad; and besides, I do know Daniel, and he's incredible!"

Terry arched his eyebrows. "Oh, really?"

Emily smiled. She tugged on his arm. "Come on!" As they walked across the cement path that led to the main entrance of the restaurant, Emily continued, "Terrence, I can see you both becoming good friends."

"I wish I could say the same about you and Monica," said Terry. "I still say this is a mistake."

"She must have some good qualities if Daniel likes her," replied Emily. "Besides, it's too late to cancel now; we're here."

Terry stopped at the door. "Emily, are you sure? This place looks really expensive."

"Terrence, don't worry! I told you. I understand, and it's okay."

"Well, thank you. I just wish…"

Emily put her hands behind Terry's neck, pulled his face downward, and whispered, "I said it's okay."

Entering the main lobby, they were quickly greeted by Daniel and Monica, who were seated in a corner. Daniel was dressed in a blue blazer while Monica was adorned in a white blouse and a navy blue skirt.

"Hey, guys!" said Emily.

"Hi, Emily," said Daniel, kissing her on the cheek. He then extended his hand to Terry. "Good to see you again, Terrence."

"Thank you," said Terry as he grasped Daniel's hand.

"Hey, Terry," said Monica. "Hello, Emily."

"I have reservations, so we should be able to sit down," said Daniel.

"I'll tell the hostess," said Monica. "Come on, Emily."

The two girls approached a wooden podium where a young brunette stood dressed in black slacks and a white blouse. "Hi," said Monica, "I made a reservation for a party of four."

"What's the name?" asked the hostess.

"Garza," said Monica. "We're here with our boyfriends." She turned and pointed. "They're over there."

"Oh, you both make such great couples!" said the hostess. Her face beaming, she turned to Emily and said, "That tall one is perfect for you! He looks so familiar. Is he an actor? Or a model? I just love his wavy hair!" She then faced Monica. "And that big strong one..." She paused to lick her lips.

Monica frowned deeply. "Wait! You got it all wrong! I'm with the tall, dreamy one! She's with the other guy!"

The hostess smiled. "Oh, sorry. I just assumed..."

"Assumed what?" asked Emily.

"Oh, nothing." She lifted four menus. "Um, why don't you tell your boyfriends that I can seat you now?"

Monica scowled.

"Thank you," said Emily.

Once seated, Monica began to tap on the table. She then turned her head toward the hostess.

"Something wrong?" asked Daniel.

"Oh, just something that girl over there did," said Monica.

Terry rolled his eyes. "You got into an altercation with the hostess?"

"No!" said Monica.

"Not so loud, Monica," said Daniel. "What happened?"

"Nothing," interrupted Emily, "she just made an innocuous remark. Now, let's enjoy this place. Look, Terrence! See the piano player?"

"Yes, that's nice," replied Terry.

"Do you know what she said?" asked Monica.

"What?" asked Daniel.

Emily frowned. "Monica, wouldn't you rather order?"

Monica furrowed her brow and shook her head. "Oh, I know what I want. Daniel's brought me here before. I love their stuffed tomato stack! It tastes so good with the blue cheese!"

Terry laughed.

"What's your problem?" asked Monica.

"No problem," replied Terry, "it's just that I prefer food designed for human consumption."

Monica scowled. Turning to Daniel, she said, "Anyway, that girl thought you were Emily's boyfriend."

"What girl?" asked Daniel.

"That cute little hostess," replied Monica. "Don't pretend you didn't notice her."

Daniel smiled. "Really?"

"I don't know why she would say such a thing," added Emily.

Terry turned to Emily. Arching his eyebrows, he asked, "Have you two come here together?"

Daniel laughed.

Emily patted Terry on the hand. "Terrence, please."

"Terry, don't you get it?" interrupted Monica. "She said that because you're black, I'm brown, and they're both white!"

The table became quiet. Daniel then shook his head and chuckled.

"I don't think it's very funny," said Monica. Turning to Emily, she lamented, "Do you think it's easy having a boyfriend who's prettier than me? Everywhere we go I see girls checking him out. Consider yourself lucky."

Emily smiled widely. "Actually, I know exactly how you feel. Besides being incredibly smart and an incredible athlete, Terrence is also the most handsome boy I know. And I do notice all the girls who stare at him."

"Thank you, Emily," said Terry.

Monica shook her head. "Yeah, well, they might stare a little but that's about all they'll do. He doesn't have Daniel's charm. Or his cousin's for that matter. Have you met Aaron? He's the cool one."

"No, I haven't," said Emily, "but Terrence has told me a lot about him."

A young man appeared and quickly left water, bread and butter on the table. As soon as he left, Monica smiled and poked Daniel on the shoulder. "Okay, back to you. Why were you laughing? Do you know the hostess?"

"No, of course not," said Daniel. "My laughing has nothing to do with that."

"Then what?" asked Monica.

"It's just that I've dealt with the whole color issue ever since my family moved here," said Daniel. "When we first came to the U.S., we moved to Nogales. It was just temporary, but I hated it. The kids at school made fun of me. It was even worse for my two older sisters. They were threatened every day."

Emily's eyes widened as she slowly began to shake her head. "That's terrible," she said.

"Yeah, the kids called me *güero* and *gringo*," said Daniel. "We were so happy to move to Phoenix and attend Saint Mary."

Monica laughed. Daniel frowned at her.

"Sorry," said Monica, "but you can't blame them. You do look white."

"I am white," said Daniel.

"Well, I meant American."

"So only white people are American?" asked Emily.

"And you think it's okay for a bunch of American *pochos* to harass my family?" added Daniel.

"No, that's not what I meant!" said Monica. "Terry, help me! They're ganging up on me!"

Terry grinned as he reached for his water.

"What I meant is that you can't totally blame them," continued Monica. "Their lives are hard and then they see this rich Mexican come in with brown hair and colored eyes."

Terry furrowed his brow. Facing Daniel, he commented, "But you're not really Mexican, right? Or at least not like Monica."

"Actually, I'm *more* Mexican than Monica," said Daniel. "She's a *pocha* without any history. I come from a community in Monterrey. Through my father's lineage we can trace our family back to the war for our independence." Daniel raised his chin. With a great sense of pride in his voice, he added, "And before that, to Spain."

Monica crinkled her forehead. Shaking her head, she said, "You are so lucky you're cute."

"So both of your parents are Mexican?" asked Terry.

Daniel smiled. "Yes, of course. My mother is from a prestigious Jewish community. She comes from a very well-known family in Guadalajara, *los Carvajal*. Between *los Castillo y los Carvajal*, we own majority shares in some of the top corporations in Mexico."

Monica rolled her eyes. "Do you know how conceited you sound?"

"I'm just stating facts, Monica. Is it wrong for me to be proud of my family?" Daniel arched his eyebrows. "Would you rather me say we work on some *rancho, bailando todo el día, escuchando corridos?*"

"First of all," replied Monica, "there's nothing wrong with working on a ranch. I love hearing stories from my grandparents about growing up on a *rancho en Chihuahua.*" She paused for a moment, and then suddenly said, *"Y otra cosa, no soy una pocha!"*

Daniel laughed. *"Sí, eres pocha, Monica! Naciste aquí!"*

Monica scowled. "Okay, *pero no soy una pocha!*"

"English, please," said Emily, "or I'm going to speak to Terrence in French."

Daniel turned to Terry. "You speak French?"

Terry laughed. "No, not at all."

"I remember when Daniel came to our school," said Emily. "My friends and I were shocked when we first heard him speak Spanish."

Daniel frowned slightly. "Why?"

"Because..." Emily's voice trailed off.

"Oh, just say it," said Monica. "I thought he was a white boy, too, when I first met him at the debate!" Monica then ran her hand through Daniel's wavy brown hair. "A very cute white boy."

Daniel smiled. "Thanks, Monica, but that's exactly what I'm talking about. No one should be surprised when they hear someone speak Spanish fluently. Having brown skin or black hair doesn't enable someone to speak Spanish anymore than having white skin or blonde hair enables someone to speak English."

Terry nodded.

"In fact," added Daniel, "Monica doesn't even speak Spanish correctly."

Terry instantly burst into laughter. Monica pressed her lips together. She shook her fist at Daniel. "You are really asking for it."

"Daniel," said Emily, "I didn't mean to offend you. I guess you're right. It's just that you speak so well. Your Spanish is nothing like my French."

Daniel took a slice of his bread. As he spread butter on the center, he said, "Well, of course, Emily. I'm Mexican and Spanish is my first language."

Terry frowned. "You seem to have mastered English as well."

"That's because I attended a bilingual academy in Monterrey," replied Daniel.

Monica curled her lips. "Of course!" she exclaimed. "Private school there, private school here."

Emily smiled. "Well, this has been very interesting. I never knew Mexico was so similar to the United States."

"Yes, Mexico is much more diverse than most people realize," said Daniel. "Maybe not to the level of the United States, but it's also a land of equality."

"Sometimes I wonder," muttered Monica.

Emily's dark eyebrows lowered. "Monica?"

"Well, I don't think we're as accepted as much as white people—here or there. I mean, you don't see people like you and Daniel picking fruit or washing cars." She turned to Daniel. "Or working on a ranch!"

"Don't say that," said Daniel. "Look at us! We're the new generation. We don't care about color. It all comes down to education and the will to succeed in life."

Monica arched her eyebrows. "Maybe so, but after listening to you I'm pretty sure your Mexican family looks down on me; and here in the United States I'm still not convinced people think of me the same way they think of a girl like Emily."

"Monica!" said Emily. "That's not true! We're no different! It doesn't matter that I have German and Irish in me or that you're of Mexican descent. Or—or Daniel's Jewish or Terrence is black. We're Americans. Nothing else!"

Monica arched her brow. "Really, Emily? Then why am I considered Mexican, or Mexican American, and Terry over here is an African American? But you? You're just American."

Emily narrowed her eyes and made a purring sound.

"Terry, you're awfully quiet," said Monica. "Say something! Aren't you going to back me up? You know I'm right."

Terry nodded. "Yes, in a manner of speaking."

Emily quickly took a drink of water. With a tinge of anguish in her voice, she asked, "What do you mean, Terrence?"

"I mean that the very notion of all men being created equal under God in a democracy or the attempt to make everyone equal through the distribution of wealth under Marxism.... It doesn't work. We're all different—now—in the past—and in the future. People will never be equal. That's the way it's always been and that's the way it always will be."

"I'm not following you," said Daniel.

"Neither am I," said Monica.

"What I'm saying is that *inequality*—and not *equality*—begins at birth and continues as we grow according to our abilities and our dedication to develop our abilities." Terry paused for a moment. "It's really quite simple. Some people are highly intelligent, some are average, and some people have very little mental capacity. And there are those that strive to develop their gifts while others waste them entirely."

"Terrence, now I'm confused," said Emily. "Are you saying that you don't even believe that we should strive to attain equality?"

Terry shook his head. "It would be like striving after the wind. It doesn't exist, Emily. We must all have the courage to speak the truth. Skin color or race should never determine how people are treated. That ancient bigotry and ignorance has dominated the world long enough. So, yes, of course I resent prejudice, of any kind, but it's equally dishonest to claim that all of us are equal. A new order is coming where the true elite of the world must be recognized." Terry glanced at Monica. "And that elitism will have nothing to do with skin color." He then looked at Daniel and added, "Or family prominence."

Emily ran her fingers through the sides of her red hair. Monica began tapping the table. Daniel rubbed his chin.

9

"It's taken years, Walter, but we have a winning program now!"

Coach More's voice echoed throughout the gym, bouncing off the wooden floor and rising to the roof. The man beside him had brown, undulated hair, a dark face and bright blue eyes. He wore a red tie that blended well with his yellow, short sleeved shirt. He was sitting in a wheelchair.

"We're a perennial playoff contender," continued Coach More. "Last year, in fact, we made it to the county finals!"

Walter nodded.

"Everything is patterned after what we learned in the Corps!" continued Coach More. "Our system, our camaraderie, our loyalty, our respect for chain of command."

"Even if there's a weak link in that chain?"

Coach More frowned. "What's that supposed to mean?"

"You know what it means, Jenz. It means that sometimes soldiers die when they have to follow the orders of a complete idiot!"

"Are you still bitter?" asked Coach More. He shook his head and frowned. "You were decorated."

"I'm not bitter, but that doesn't mean I have to remain quiet, and no piece of medal is more important than the truth!"

Coach More raised his hands in protest. "Okay, okay, I didn't ask you to come here so that we could argue! Anyway, our cadence follows our mission of fighting battles in the air, on land, and sea. White is for clouds, so that's—"

"A pass."

Coach More smiled. "Yeah, exactly, our first option. And green is our second option, to fight by land, so that means we go to the tailback—that's Terry—who may just be the most amazing athlete I've ever seen. Well, once you help him to get his head on straight, anyway. And then there's blue, which means we fight by sea. That means that the quarterback— that's Aaron—greatest kid you'll ever meet—runs it himself!"

"That's wonderful, Jenz," said Walter dryly.

Aaron and Terry entered the building. While Aaron wore blue jeans and a simple plaid short-sleeved collared shirt, Terry was dressed in dark slacks, a purple collared shirt, and a matching striped tie. Crossing the thick boundary lines of the basketball court, they approached Coach More and Walter Cane near the brown wooden bleachers.

"Hello, men!" said Coach More. "I want you to meet Congressman Walter Cane!"

Aaron and Terry took a few steps toward Walter. As they did so, he grasped the armrests of his wheelchair. Gritting his teeth, he struggled to his feet.

"Don't feel sorry for him," said Coach More. "Walter is as tough as they come."

"I have a condition referred to by specialists as a classification D spinal injury," said Walter, who stood below the full height of Coach More due to his bent stance. "I can go a little on my own, but I usually use a walking stick or a mobile walker to help me. If I'm tired, or if I know I'm going to have to go a long distance, I'll use my wheelchair."

"It's a pleasure to meet you, sir," said Aaron, "but you don't have to get up on our account."

"No, no, I'm fine," replied Walter. "I've heard a lot about you both from Jenz. I mean, Coach More. He says you both are fine young men as well as star athletes."

"Thank you, sir," replied Aaron. "But there are no stars, just teammates."

Coach More smiled, Walter nodded, and Terry released a slight grin.

"Aaron, I believe Coach More said he wanted to talk to you about some plays," said Walter.

"That's right," added Coach More. "Follow me to my office, and we'll let Congressman Cane speak to Terry."

Aaron and Coach More walked out of the gym. Once gone, Terry arched his brow. "And now we're alone."

"Yes, we are," replied Walter. He smiled. "May I say I'm impressed by your stylish clothing?"

"Yes, you may," said Terry. "A mentor of mine convinced me that society often judges us by the way we present ourselves. So, if we are to lead society, we should dress accordingly."

Walter released a small chuckle. "Wow, Jenz wasn't exaggerating." He then sat in his wheelchair and pushed the wheels until his knees touched the long bench of the extended bleachers. "It's electronic, but I prefer to get by manually to keep up my muscle tone."

Terry took a few strides and sat down beside him on the wooden bench.

"So clothes are a uniform?" asked Walter.

"Excuse me?"

"You say people judge us by the clothes we wear, just like in the Marines or maybe a mailman."

"Something like that," said Terry. Motioning toward Walter, he added, "It appears you agree."

"Yes, I'm coming from a business conference to create more legislature to help employ the disabled," replied Walter.

Terry smirked.

"You don't think we should do more to help the disabled?"

"No," replied Terry, "they have their place in society. They're limited, but if they're capable, they have a place."

Walter arched his brow. "If they're capable? What if they're not? In my case, I can't do half the things I used to."

"But you're a congressman," said Terry. "You're still productive. Perhaps in some ways you're even more productive because you're forced to rely more on your mind. In today's world, intelligence and knowledge far outweigh the necessity of physical strength."

Walter nodded. He lifted his hand to his chin. "That's a good point. But I tell you, I'm much more compassionate to the disabled because of my injury. In my two terms in Congress I've worked hard to pass legislation in the business sector to aid the disabled, but that only came after a long period of soul searching, and I'm one of the fortunate ones. Most victims of spinal injuries can't move their legs at all and many suffer full quadriplegia. Some have neurological damage as well and lose much of their brain function. My accomplishments as a politician stem from my weakness, Terry, not from my strength."

Terry remained silent.

"Being in a position to help others has given me great purpose in life. My own personal journey hasn't been easy. But, thanks to some special therapists, family, and friends, I have peace."

Terry inclined his head.

"Do you have peace, young man?" asked Walter.

"I don't know," whispered Terry.

Walter reached out and put his hand on Terry's shoulder. "I can see your pain, Terry. What are you feeling?"

"You wouldn't understand."

"Maybe so, but that doesn't mean you can't share it with me."

Terry touched both sides of his head. His long fingers then began to make small circular motions around his temples. "It's just that I have so many questions."

"Nothing strange about that. In fact, I would say it's quite normal for a young man of your age."

"I don't know. It doesn't seem like it."

"Well, what are some of these questions of yours?"

Terry moved his jaw slightly from side to side. "I wonder...I wonder about life, about who I am, about where I belong. It's as if I can't turn my mind off. I feel..."

"Alone? Different?"

Terry nodded.

Walter sighed. "Those are feelings I understand quite well, actually."

Terry raised his head.

"It didn't take me long to realize that I was different," said Walter, "and it caused me a lot of pain."

"How were you different?" asked Terry.

"I don't know. Part of it was a feeling, an awareness, a constant searching. But a lot of it had to do with my mixed heritage."

Terry nodded. "You're one of the men in the picture Coach keeps on his desk. I always wondered about that."

"Yeah, my father was white, and I mean really white—blonde hair and blue eyes white. My mother, on the other hand, was black."

Terry lost the rigidity in his body and settled more comfortably on the wooden bench. He listened intently as Walter recounted his origins. Two very different people from two very different parts of the world had met and fallen in love at Ohio State University. It wasn't a popular notion at the time. Walter was the first child. A novelty of some sorts. Growing up, he often felt excluded. For some, he was not white enough and for others, he was not black enough. And then there was the time his grandparents had come from Sweden to visit. His grandfather referred to Walter as his little "darkie." Walter cringed every time he heard the term, and secretly he seethed with anger.

Once of age, Walter joined the Marine Corps. With his high marks, he qualified for military intelligence. After boot camp, he flew off to Germany, where he joined the cross-cultural communication program as part of the Marine Corps European Command. As he traveled throughout the continent and beyond, his eyes saw firsthand the wonders of the world. But they all paled in comparison to a little known country named Andorra.

Andorra, tucked away between France and Spain, was a land like no other. Modern, yet traditional. Possessing its own culture, yet sharing all the cultures of Europe. Breathtaking landscapes across unfolding hills, medieval castles; it was a land of history, a land of peace, a land of love. Walter felt welcome. He felt at home. People spoke to him in Catalan when he was out of uniform. They assumed he was one of their own. His dark skin, silky brown hair, and blue eyes were not so extraordinary in an extraordinary land.

For Walter, the sum of all the beauty of Andorra was not found in its ancient monasteries, or snow capped hills, or hot spring waters, but in a woman. Her name was Melissandre, *una dona increïble, una veritable princesa.*

"That's an incredible story, Mr. Cane," said Terry. "I hope some day I can visit Andorra."

Walter smiled. "Yes, I always tell people I liked it so much there that I had to keep a memory. A memory that would never fade."

"Your wife," said Terry.

"Exactly," said Walter. "Melissandre is the most wonderful person I know. She's been with me through the good times..." He paused, stroking the armrests of his wheelchair. "...and the bad."

"I met an incredible girl as well," said Terry, "and she's white. She has red hair and the prettiest green eyes. She's a deep thinker, yet she's practical. Even happy. I think that's what I like about her so much."

"You sound like you're in love," said Walter.

Before Terry could reply, the main door to the gym swung open noisily. He turned to see Coach More.

"I thought you two might still be here!"

"Hey, Jenz," said Walter.

"Coach," said Terry.

Coach More held up his wrist watch. "Well, time's up. So, Walter, did you get through to him?"

Walter fidgeted slightly in his wheelchair. "Jenz, please, we were just getting to know each other."

Terry furrowed his brow.

With a wide smile on his face, Coach More asked Terry, "So, are you going to suit up for us this Friday?"

"Excuse me?"

"The playoffs are approaching, so we have no time to lose," said Coach More. "We're currently the third seed." He huffed loudly. "I tell you, when we lost two in a row, I was really worried. Butler's a great kid, but he just wasn't getting it done. That's when we came up with the idea to run options with Leo. We've started to win again, but games have been close. Too close."

Walter shook his head. "Jenz, not now."

Coach More punched his palm. "With you back, Terry, I still think we have a chance to go all the way!"

Terry stood up quickly. He turned to Walter. "So this was all planned? You were just pretending to be my friend?"

Walter shook his head. "Terry, wait…"

"No, I've had enough of this little charade, Mr. Cane."

"Terry, show some respect for God's sake!" interjected Coach More.

Terry tightened his jaw. He extended his index finger. "Let me make this real clear, Coach. I'm not ever going to play for you. Not today, not Friday, not ever. Do you understand?" He exhaled deeply and chuckled. "Did you really think you could recruit some old friend to try to win me over so that I'd play football for you?"

Coach More's face reddened. "That's fine with me! You convinced me! I was wrong to give you a second chance! You're not worthy to be part of our team!"

Walter thrusted the wheels of his wheelchair forward, stopping between Coach More and Terry. "Hold on, you two!"

"Forget it, Mr. Cane!" said Terry. "I'm leaving! This entire experience has been rather pathetic." Terry curled his lips. He then scowled at Coach More before adding, "I should have known better."

Walter rubbed his forehead as Terry walked briskly toward the exit.

10

FOUR LARGE, ATHLETIC young men stood curiously in a small circle under the thin metal awning of one of the many long corridors of Avondale High School.

"Remember what I told you," said Aaron. "Nobody better freak out! And whatever you do, don't stare!"

Jeff, Lucas, and Leonel exchanged dubious glances, yet they obediently followed Aaron in silence toward a rectangular building that stood apart from the other larger classrooms. Suddenly, Aaron held up his hand. The other boys immediately stopped.

Aaron exhaled deeply. In a solemn tone, he said, "Okay, here we are. Room seven. Y'all ready?"

Leonel pointed to Jeff. "Aaron, you really think there's something in that room that's scarier than this?"

Aaron remained serious. "I'm just saying the first time I came here, I kind of, well, I wasn't expecting to see…" His voice trailed off.

"What?" asked Jeff.

"Just be cool, all right?" said Aaron.

"Damn, man, why are you tripping?" asked Lucas.

Ignoring Lucas, Aaron said calmly, "We're going in. Just be quiet and be nice to everyone, especially my main man, Mason. He's a little dude with brown hair and freckles. You'll see him. He's real friendly."

Lucas frowned. Jeff smiled, an expression which was somewhat perpetual, whereas the easy going Leonel merely shrugged. Aaron pointed at his friends and then opened the door. As soon as he had taken a few steps inside, Mason ran to him and quickly embraced him.

"Aaron!" shouted Mason.

"What's up, man?" replied Aaron. He patted Mason on the back of his head and then released him.

"Uh, I was—I was just helping Stephen with—with his food," said Mason. He pointed to a boy with a dark complexion and long black hair who was sitting in a heavily padded wheelchair.

Aaron smiled, displaying his straight white teeth. "Cool!"

Mr. Douglass approached the boys. "Hello, I'm glad you guys made it."

"Of course," said Aaron. "Hey, Mr. Douglass, I want you to meet some future pro ballers. This is Jeff Buckey, Lucas Wright, and Leo Reyes."

Mr. Douglass extended his hand. "We're happy to have you. Feel free to walk around and talk to any of the kids."

"Do they understand us?" asked Leonel.

Aaron elbowed him in the ribs. "Of course they do! What kind of a stupid question is that?"

Mr. Douglass chuckled. "No, it's okay. Some of the kids understand you very well, and others probably won't get much. They appreciate a smile, though, and any positive interaction you can give them."

"Okay, then," said Aaron. "Spread out and talk to them, and if they're playing some kind of game, help 'em out."

"Hi, Aaron. I missed you."

Aaron knelt down. He immediately recognized the nasal voice and the peculiar body odor. "Hi, Carmen, I'm sorry about that. I've been real busy."

"You didn't come," she said.

Aaron rubbed her shoulder and smiled once again. "Well, how 'bout I make it up to you. I'll bring you some cookies next week."

Carmen smiled. "What kind of cookies?"

"Whatever kind my grandma decides to make!" said Aaron before bursting into laughter. Carmen, too, began to laugh.

"Now I know the real reason Aaron's been hanging out here," said Jeff. "He has a girlfriend."

"That's right!" said Aaron. He put his arm around Carmen's shoulders. "Tell him, Carmen. Tell him you're my girl!"

"Yes," she said. Her large face seemed to glow.

"He's just jealous because he doesn't have one," said Leo.

Mason jumped up and down. He pointed to Jeff. "You—you're—you're really big!"

"Yep, I am," said Jeff. "Hey, you want me to show you a trick?"

"Sure!" replied Mason. He began to jump up and down and clap his hands.

Jeff quickly grabbed Mason under his arms and lifted him up above his shoulders. He then raised him up and down several times. A few other students approached them. Some of them laughed while others pointed.

Mr. Douglass rubbed his light mustache. "Um, you're not going to drop him, are you?"

"Heck, no!" said Jeff. He raised Mason in the air once more before placing him softly down on the carpeted floor. Jeff then raised his large, thick hands and moved his fingers quickly. "All right, I got it." He paused for a moment and scratched the back of his head. "You weigh a hundred and twenty-five pounds."

Mason smiled and laughed. "How—how did you do—do that?"

"It's magic," said Jeff.

"No, really, how did you do that?" asked Mr. Douglass.

"I carry animals on our farm," said Jeff. "Sheep, colts, calves, pigs. I got it down to a science. I bet I could guess your weight, too."

Mr. Douglass quickly stepped back a few steps. "No, no, that's okay."

Aaron and Leonel laughed.

A boy with small slanted eyes approached Lucas. "Can I touch your arm?"

Lucas opened his mouth slowly but said nothing.

"He's admiring your guns, man," said Aaron.

Lucas inclined his head and walked away.

"Aaron, you've met Mrs. Lara," said Mr. Douglass, pointing to a plump middle-aged woman dressed in jeans and a simple cotton shirt, "but I don't think you've met Miss Domínguez. She comes twice a week as part of her internship."

A young lady with long black hair that fell in curved waves to her shoulders slowly approached the boys. She had a light blue blouse, with sleeves that hugged her arms, and tight jeans that displayed her shapely legs. "Hi, I'm Minerva."

Aaron's face broke into a wide grin. "Wow! You're…"

Minerva smiled. "Yes?"

"You're a teacher?" asked Aaron.

"Not yet," replied Minerva. "I'm at ASU."

Aaron's eyes widened. "Oh, yeah! ASU! It's a great campus, isn't it?" said Aaron.

"And the student center is awesome!" added Leonel.

"Yeah, all of us were there for the high school football camp last summer," added Jeff.

Both Aaron and Leonel scowled at Jeff.

Minerva furrowed her brow. "Oh, so you were just visiting?"

"Miss Domínguez, these boys are students here at Avondale," said Mr. Douglass.

She nodded. "Oh, I see."

Aaron smiled. He rubbed his goatee. "I'll be at ASU next year. I'm pretty much guaranteed a football scholarship. I could go somewhere else, but I'd rather stay local 'cause of the people." Aaron stretched slightly, expanding his chest. "Might just be me, but I think the people here are real nice, and of course we have the most beautiful girls."

Minerva laughed. Then, with a slight smile, she added, "Well, I guess I'll be able to cheer you on next year. I go to all the games."

"You could cheer me on right now," said Aaron. "Playoffs are starting, and you're talking to the team captain." Aaron snapped his fingers as he added, "I can get you in free like that!"

Minerva nodded. "Thanks, that sounds nice."

"I'll be there, too," said Leonel, smiling widely.

Mrs. Lara suddenly tapped Minerva on the shoulder. "Miss Domínguez, could you give me a hand? Carol wants to say hello to the boys."

"Yes, Mrs. Lara."

Leonel slid his arm around Aaron and said mockingly, "Pretty smooth, man, but the whole time you were talking, she was looking at me."

"Come on, guys," said Jeff, "she's in college. She ain't gonna come see us play."

"Maybe not you," said Leonel, punching Jeff on the shoulder.

"What do you think, Lucas?" asked Jeff.

"I don't know," he muttered in response.

Aaron smiled. "Trust me, she'll come. We had a connection. I could feel it."

Leonel began to laugh when a large hospital bed was rolled out in front of the boys. Lying under the white sheets and a tan blanket was a small girl. Her brown eyes were large and expressed a certain unexpected emotion—one of joy. To the sides of her dark cheeks were thick black braids. A plastic tube was attached to her throat by white adhesive tape and placed next to her head was a white Teddy bear.

"Carol, say hello to the boys," said Mrs. Lara.

She smiled widely, exposing several unevenly shaped teeth.

Leonel swallowed deeply. Lucas turned his head.

"Hi, there," said Jeff.

Carol continued to smile.

"How ya doin', Carol?" said Aaron, waving at her. "Looks like you got a new toy."

She nodded.

"Aaron, come here," said Mr. Douglass.

The two walked over to a desk located in the far corner of the classroom.

"What's up, Mr. Douglass?"

"Nothing, I just wanted to thank you. You said you were going to come with some of your teammates…" Mr. Douglass removed his glasses and wiped his eyes. "…and you did."

"It's no big deal. It's kind of fun, really. Besides, you got us out of class."

Mr. Douglass chuckled as he adjusted his glasses. "Well, anyway, I'm glad you could come. And Mason tells me he's been going to the games to watch you."

"Yeah, Mason's cool! I met his parents—good people. I wish I had parents like that. My dad's doing time and I hardly ever see my mom."

Mr. Douglass pressed his lips together. He then patted Aaron on the shoulder. "I'm sorry to hear that."

"Yeah, well, it is what it is. But it's not all bad. I live with my grandparents and they treat me real good—except for all the work. Every day I have to get up early and do chores!"

"I never knew," said Mr. Douglass. "Well, if it's any consolation, you made the front page of the paper. They're saying a lot of nice things about you."

Mr. Douglass handed Aaron the newspaper lying on his desk.

"Cool," said Aaron. His eyes darted left to right. Suddenly, he exclaimed, "Hey, I know that dude!"

"What's that?" asked Mr. Douglass.

Aaron pointed to a small picture at the bottom of the page. "Right here where it says 'Unsolved Mystery.' I seen that guy before." Aaron stroked the soft patch of hairs on his chin. "Where was it? Oh, I know! He's one of them bums always hanging on the West Side."

"I wouldn't know," said Mr. Douglass. "I try to stay away from that part of the city. I read the article, though. The Mexican authorities found him. And then they reported the scant remains of several bodies." He tilted his head up. "Strange. Just that and some old scraps of carpet."

Aaron crinkled his forehead. "This was in Mexico?"

"Yeah," replied Mr. Douglass, "in the middle of the Sonoran Desert." He frowned and shook his head. "You say you know this man?"

Aaron continued to stare at the picture. "I thought I did. I don't know, maybe not."

"Hey, Aaron, I need to go, man."

Aaron turned to see Lucas. "Huh?"

Lucas furrowed his brow. He frowned deeply. "I said I'm going, man."

"No, we're good, Lucas. Mr. Douglass got us permission to stay all period."

"Sorry, man, I gotta go."

Lucas turned and walked toward the door.

"Is he okay?" asked Mr. Douglass.

Aaron shrugged his shoulders. He laid the newspaper on the desk. "I don't know. I've never seen him act like this before."

"Well, maybe you better talk to him."

Aaron nodded and quickly exited the classroom. He looked in all directions until he spotted Lucas already at the midpoint of the main outside corridor. Aaron whistled loudly, but Lucas continued to walk away. Aaron then put his hands to his mouth and shouted at him, but Lucas only quickened his pace. Finally, Aaron ran after him. He reached out and grabbed Lucas by the shoulder. "Hey, man, what's going on?"

Lucas turned away.

"What is it, bro?" asked Aaron.

"Go away, man."

Aaron moved in front of Lucas and faced him. His eyes were moist and his large cheeks displayed the smudges of tears that had been roughly wiped away.

"Talk to me," said Aaron.

Lucas inclined his head. "That was hard. I didn't know what to do. I looked at that little girl in the bed—with tubes hooked up to her—and she—she—"

"What?"

"She smiled at me, man."

Aaron bit his lip. "Yeah, she always smiles."

Lucas wiped his eyes. "Aaron, she's in high school and hooked up to tubes. It ain't right. It just ain't right, man. I don't like it."

Aaron remained quiet when suddenly his name echoed throughout the corridor. He turned to see Mason quickly approaching.

"I—I thought you—that you left without saying goodbye."

Aaron smiled. He gently put his arm around Mason. "No, buddy, I wouldn't do that to you."

"Hey, later, man. I gotta go," said Lucas.

Aaron nodded as Lucas walked away and quickly faded behind one of the many large buildings.

"I want to—to help you," said Mason.

Aaron reverted his attention to Mason.

"I'm going to tell—to tell my parents to take me to—to your house."

"To my house?"

"Yes, to help you."

Aaron curled his lips. "Help me with what, Mason?"

"With your work. Mr. Douglass said you get up early, so I want to help you. Help at your farm so—so you won't be tired for the big game."

Aaron cocked his head back. His eyes widened. He slid his arm off of Mason's shoulders and instead gripped both of his willowy biceps. "Mason, are you serious? You would do that for me?"

Mason smiled widely, revealing his stained crooked teeth. "Yes, I want to help."

"But why?" asked Aaron. "I don't get it. Why would you do that?"

Mason smiled. "Because you're my best friend."

11

TERRY FOLLOWED EMILY into her house with more than a shade of anxiety. The living room was large, with a brown leather sofa that could easily sit four people placed in the center. A mahogany coffee table separated it from a smaller matching sofa which was more suitable for two. Attached on the opposite wall was a very large flat screen, whereas the side walls were surrounded by pictures of family members. Terry began to pull at the white collar that tightly encircled his thick muscular neck. He consistently adjusted his black tie that felt increasingly like a noose. As he glanced at the vanilla colored walls of the living room, he noticed that not a single item seemed out of place.

"Where is everyone?" whispered Terry.

"They're here," said Emily. She combed her hands through her long red hair. "Do you think I'm dressed well enough?"

Terry observed her white skirt and yellow short sleeved blouse. "Of course. You always look nice."

"I didn't do anything with my hair. Maybe I should have styled it. It's just kind of hanging down."

Terry wagged his head. "Emily, I don't understand. Is something wrong? You're making me more nervous than I already am."

"Wrong? No, nothing is wrong."

Terry touched Emily on the shoulder. "Then where is everyone? I thought the purpose of this dinner was for me to meet your family."

Emily took in a deep breath. "Okay, Daddy's probably in the kitchen, my mom's probably in her office, and my little sister must be in her room lost in her world of virtual reality."

Terry chuckled lightly. "Okay. So, why is your father in the kitchen?"

"He's cooking, of course. Why else would he be in there?"

"Your father is cooking our meal?"

Emily crinkled her forehead. "Yes, why?"

"I don't know. It's just different, that's all."

"I like *different*," said Emily, smiling. "I thought you did, too."

Terry smiled. "You're right. I do."

"All right, then, follow me. And be prepared for *different*." Emily led Terry by the hand to the kitchen. Inside, there was a slightly pudgy man with thinning red hair. He was dressed casually in blue jeans and a white polo shirt. Wrapped around his waist was a large green apron and two large padded kitchen gloves covered his hands and forearms. As Terry and Emily stood near a large silver refrigerator, he took out a large glass container from the oven, placed it on a granite topped island, and faced the dish with a smile of deep satisfaction. Terry took a large sniff of the delicious cheesy aroma that filled the room.

"Pretty proud of yourself, huh, Daddy?" said Emily.

Her father jerked slightly. "Sweetheart," he said with great affection. Without the slightest hesitation, Emily walked over to give him a hug.

"Daddy," said Emily, "this is the boy I've been telling you about. Terrence Washington."

"Hello, Mr. Potter," said Terry as he extended his hand.

Emily's father held out his right glove. Terry smiled and hesitated. He could not help but notice the strands of red hair and face covered with freckles.

"Daddy, your gloves," said Emily, laughing.

"Oh, I'm so sorry," said Mr. Potter. "You'll have to forgive me. I get lost in the kitchen."

He quickly took off the large oven mitts on his hands, laid them on the counter, and shook Terry's hand with both of his own.

"Are you a professional chef?" asked Terry.

Mr. Potter laughed lightheartedly. "Me? Oh no! I mean, I wish I was! Well, who knows? After you eat the meal, tell me what you think."

Terry smiled once again. Emily's father had a deep baritone voice that seemed to vibrate with warmth. His mannerisms, too, were so gentle that they immediately put Terry at ease.

"Well, what do you have for us, Chef?" asked Emily.

"My famous scalloped potatoes. Come, come and look. Have you ever eaten this dish before, Terrence?"

Terry looked at the large rectangular glass container. It gave off a very pleasing aroma. "I don't believe so, sir. It looks like a lot of expertise went into its preparation. I know very little about the culinary arts but I admire those who do."

"Would you like to know more?" asked Mr. Potter with a gleam in his eye.

Terry smiled and nodded.

"Well, obviously there are sliced potato wedges," said Mr. Potter as he moved his hand over the rectangular glass dish. "But the secret to the succulent flavor is the melted cheeses! I combine Parmigiano Reggiano with an English Farmhouse Cheddar and not to be outdone, a little *Brie de Melun*! Then, for added flavor, I add chopped ham and bacon, bits of black pepper, onion, and cilantro."

Terry smiled as he looked at Emily, and then back at her father. "So... when do we eat?"

Emily and her father laughed.

"Yes, why don't you two help me set the table and we'll get started!" said Mr. Potter with real enthusiasm in his voice. "We have mixed vegetables—only the tasty ones, mind you—and sparkling cider as well and a little wine. And I have pies for dessert! Maybe you could call your mother and sister when the table is finished, Emily?"

Emily nodded before kissing her father on the cheek. She then led Terry to a large wooden cabinet that contained a complete wall of glass. Within the cabinet were a variety of fine dishes, glasses, and silverware. The two quickly set the table.

"Let's go get my mom and my little sister," said Emily. "We're pretty much done here."

"Okay," said Terry. "Is your mother anything like your father?"

Emily frowned. "If only, Terrence, if only…"

"What's wrong?"

"She's very opinionated. Maybe *overbearing* is a better word."

Terry noticed Emily biting her upper lip, as if to signal that she was preparing for battle. They walked a few steps down a hallway and then stopped in front of an office door that was composed of glass with thin, wooden crossbeams. Inside was a woman dressed in a business suit composed of a yellow jacket and matching skirt. Her eyes were fixed on a large computer screen. Emily waited, then after her mother failed to notice them, rapped her knuckles against the door. Her mother continued to face the screen in front of her. In a tone that expressed her exasperation, Emily shouted, "Mom! Didn't you hear me knocking?"

Without bothering to turn her head, her mother replied, "Yes, and before that, I noticed two shadows by the door, but that doesn't mean that I felt obligated to stop what I'm doing."

Emily rolled her eyes.

"I'm almost done," continued her mother, "but I need to look at a few more homes. Go ahead and start without me."

"Of course," said Emily, shaking her head. She then said to Terry, "Come on. I'll introduce you later. Why don't you join my dad while I get my little sister."

"As you wish," said Terry, grinning. He left and headed back toward the kitchen area, where he found Emily's father laying down large, white cloth napkins. A large wooden bowl of steamed vegetbles—sliced carrots, corn, and chopped esparagus—all laced with butter—lay on one side of the table.

"Would you like to give me a hand with the drinks?" asked Mr. Potter.

"Sure," replied Terry, following him into the kitchen area.

"Why don't you take this pitcher of water to the table, and I'll bring these bottles."

"Yes, sir," said Terry.

Once at the table, Emily introduced Terry to her sister, a young girl with long thick hair, more auburn than red. Her face was free of freckles, and in some ways she appeared to be a younger version of Emily. Yet, her features were slightly more harmonious and her brown eyes more shapely. In her hand was a small electronic device. Though she had done little to adorn herself and was wearing simple blue jeans and a white cotton T-shirt, her blooming beauty was evident.

"Terrence, this is my little sis, Paige, the female ruler of an alternate universe but a mere freshman in the real world!"

Terry smiled. He then extended his hand, but Paige did not bother to look up. Emily then snatched the electronic device from her hands.

"Hey!" shouted Paige. Her eyes flared toward Emily. "Give that back!"

"Pleased to meet you, Paige," said Terry, his hand still extended.

"Hi," she replied, her voice absent of enthusiasm. She held Terry's hand loosely for a brief moment before suddenly proclaiming, "Scalloped potatoes! My favorite!"

Mr. Potter appeared without his apron. "I thought the aroma might get your attention. I made it just for you, sweetheart. Well, actually, that's not entirely true. I also wanted to impress Emily's friend."

"You have, Mr. Potter," said Terry.

"But you haven't tasted it!"

"Trust me, if it tastes half as good as it smells, I'm going to have to resist the temptation to overindulge myself!"

Mr. Potter smiled. "Wow! Emily, it looks like you've met your match!"

"That was just one of the many things that attracted me to Terrence."

"Stop, Emily," said Terry. "You're embarrassing me."

"Well, at least nobody would know," another voice broke in.

"Mom!" squealed Emily. "Please!"

Emily's mother shrugged. "What? I think it's an advantage." Then, turning her attention to Terry, she continued, "Whenever Emily is embarrassed, or angry, her face lights up like a cherry! It's almost like playing dot to dot with her freckles. But with your skin tone no one would ever know, would they?"

Taken aback by her candor, Terry's mouth slowly opened. An unpleasant thickening of saliva formed in his mouth. He swallowed, attempted to maintain his composure, and said, "Mrs. Potter, it's a pleasure to meet you. I'm—"

"Terrence Washington. I know. My husband may have been oblivious to your presence at the forensics competition since he was preoccupied with the food, but I couldn't help but notice your flirtation with my daughter as well as your doppelgänger case study given during your closing arguments."

Terry remained quiet. He remained in a transitional state of feeling offended yet impressed by the keen mind demonstrated by Mrs. Potter. Her attractive appearance slightly blunted the obtuse form in which she spoke. Her thick brown hair hung just over her shoulders. Her face showed signs of a professional woman who may have been a model in her earlier years. Curved eyebrows, long eyelashes, and just the right amount of make-up and lipstick. Her neck and jawline lacked the firmness of a young girl such as Emily, but by all accounts she was a stunningly fashionable woman.

"Where's my wine?" asked Mrs. Potter as she seated herself at the table.

"Mom, Daddy's not one of your employees," said Emily. "And neither is Terrence."

Mrs. Potter frowned. "And you're not the mother, I am. By the way, has everyone washed their hands?"

"Have you?" replied Emily. "You probably have ink and dust all over them from working so much."

"Emily, please, just do what your mother says," interrupted her father. "Maybe Terrence could accompany you?"

Mrs. Potter arched her brow. "Together? Alone in our bathroom? I don't think so. He can wash his hands in the kitchen if he needs to."

Emily scowled deeply. Her face reddened slightly. "It's not like we're going to close the door and lock it."

Mr. Potter took a deep breath. "Emily, you and your sister go wash your hands and—"

"And I want my tablet back!" interrupted Paige.

"Yes, yes," said Mr. Potter. "Emily?"

Emily twisted her lips slightly. "Here!" she said as she thrust the device into her sister's hands.

"Terrence," continued Mr. Potter, "please sit down and make yourself comfortable while I check on the pies. I'll be right back."

"I'll be right back, too," said Emily to Terry. "Don't let her scare you away."

Emily's mother poured herself a glass of wine. With a mocking smile, she asked, "Why, whatever do you mean, Emily?" She quickly turned to face Terry. "Go ahead and sit down. We can get to know each other."

"Yes, ma'am," said Terry.

"So, I hear you're not only a great debater, but a star athlete as well."

Terry smiled. "Oh, thank you, Mrs. Potter. Did Emily tell you that?"

"Well, she did, but I also take pride in doing my own research. Besides, I found your closing remarks extremely interesting." She ran her hand lightly through one of the brown waves of her hair. After doing so, it immediately bounced back in place. "So, now that the debate is over, tell me. Was that fact or fiction?"

Terry paused and looked down at the table for a moment. "No, ma'am, no fiction whatsoever. I really did grow up in that environment. It was difficult. Even today my mother lives in the same low income apartments on the West Side. It's nothing like the gated communities over here."

"They're ready," said Mr. Potter, returning from the kitchen with a deeply crusted pie in each hand. "Cherry and apple."

Emily and Paige returned as well.

"Shall we say grace?" asked Mr. Potter, taking a seat between his wife and his youngest daughter.

As they bowed their heads and closed their eyes, Emily slyly reached under the round wooden table and grasped Terry's hand.

"Okay, our guest of honor gets the first portion," announced Mr. Potter, placing a large portion of the dish on Terry's plate. The melted cheese moved slightly, releasing a waft of steam from the baked ham and sliced white potatoes. After serving the rest of the family, he asked, "Well?"

Terry finished chewing. He pulled his napkin off his lap and wiped his mouth. "Mr. Potter, it's delicious. I really do think you should become a professional chef!"

"I've been telling him that for years!' said Mrs. Potter. "When we were first dating, he used to bake special goodies just for me. They were so delicious! That's what won me over. Well, that, and the fact he had a full head of hair back then!"

Mr. Potter, blushing slightly, inclined his head.

"I don't know what stops him," continued Mrs. Potter. She released a loud chuckle. "I suppose it's a lack of ambition. He could easily enroll in a culinary program. It's not like his income does us much good. Not to mention personal pride." She paused to sip her wine. "I mean, really, a typical chef at a local restaurant has more dignity than a glorified receptionist!"

Emily dropped her fork noisily onto her plate. "Mom, Daddy isn't a receptionist! He works for the government!"

"Really?" added Terry. "That must be very demanding."

"Well, no, but it is very pleasant—stress free—which is what I prefer," replied Mr. Potter. "I help coordinate events in Phoenix. Our office also provides tourist information."

"Can you believe my husband graduated from college only to work as a city host? I mean, we have our little unique traits that I appreciate as much as the next person, but it's not like we're a tourist attraction."

"I believe it to be a productive occupation, Mrs. Potter," replied Terry. He lifted a large spoonful of his dish toward his mouth. "And I think we're also enjoying the benefits of Mr. Potter's other talents right now."

Mrs. Potter sighed. The table then became quiet enough for a collection of electronic sounds to be heard. Each person slowly turned toward Paige, who had her head inclined.

"Paige, I told you no electronic gadgets while we're eating dinner," said Mr. Potter.

"Oh, let her be!" said Mrs. Potter. "She's probably going to be the most successful one of the family."

"And how do you define success, Mrs. Potter?" asked Terry.

"Like anyone else. Money, status, power."

"And have you achieved success as you define it?" Terry continued.

"I'm a partner at my real estate firm." Mrs. Potter released a haughty smile, paused, and then scooped a portion of vegetables onto her plate. "A firm which sells more luxury homes than any other agency in all of Phoenix!"

Emily rubbed Terry's shoulder. "Oh, please don't ask her about her work."

"No, let him ask," replied Mrs. Potter. "Maybe he will appreciate the fact that my income is the reason we have this house, and you and your sister are in the finest private school in the county."

"So you help people find homes?" asked Terry.

Mrs. Potter frowned. "That is a trifling definition of what I do, but yes, in a manner of speaking."

"I meant to clarify, to make a distinction," continued Terry. "Do you actually help people find homes, or do you merely show larger homes to people who already own homes?"

Mrs. Potter scowled slightly. "Is there a difference?"

"I'm merely pointing out that it doesn't seem to me at all that you actually help people. That would be a misnomer. What you do is cater to the rich and assist them in increasing their assets when they undoubtedly have more than they know what to do with. What you do is not necessarily a great skill that benefits society, but rather a service created by our current economic system that continues to benefit the very people who need the least assistance."

There was a moment of silence. Emily smiled. Her father, too, released a large grin as he helped himself to a second portion of scalloped potatoes. Paige, seemingly bored by the topic, left the table and promptly lay down on the smaller of the two living room sofas.

"Excuse me, young man," said Mrs. Potter, "but do you have something against the wealthy?"

"No, not at all," said Terry, "but I do feel a certain pity for people like you."

Mr. Potter practically dropped his glass of water. "Oh, excuse me," he said as he attempted to wipe the small puddle that had formed around his plate.

Mrs. Potter twisted her lips. With piercing eyes, she said, "Listen here, young man—"

"Terrence," said Emily. Her interruption immediately drew a scowl from her mother. But instead of becoming upset, Emily released an innocent smile.

"Listen, *Terrence*," said Mrs. Potter, "I don't need a young boy to take pity on me. I'll have you know that I'm very proud of my accomplishments. I've worked my ass off to get where I'm at today. Someday, when you've actually experienced life, you'll understand that."

"That may be true," said Terry. "But how does that help society? How are you helping society as a whole if the rich merely get richer and the poor become poorer? Throughout history we have seen over and over again that sad model which only leads to an inevitable implosion. It would be much wiser to preserve wealth through a more judicious distribution to prevent such a collapse."

The table became quiet once again as all eyes were on Mrs. Potter. Finally, after swallowing the rest of her wine, she licked her lips and pointed her index finger directly at Terry. "Well, I guess I'm not too worried about that. But I promise I'll look to you for answers when we sink into the next Great Depression because of people like me."

The conversation was abruptly interrupted by the sound of the television. On the large screen appeared the face of a man that Terry found vaguely familiar. Before he could react, however, Paige had turned the channel.

Getting up from his seat, Terry took a few steps toward the living room and asked her, "Excuse me, but could you go back to that channel?"

"Really?" said Paige. "But it's just boring news."

Emily crinkled her nose. "Terrence, what are you doing?"

"I'm sorry," said Terry, "but this is important. Please, Paige, just for a minute? I promise."

Paige shook her head and plopped backward onto the sofa. "Okay, fine," she huffed.

A man with a chiseled jaw and dark hair appeared on the screen. "The Police Department of Lukeville has identified the man to be a Mr. Thaddeus Jefferson, who was in his late fifties. It is being reported that he had been living in Phoenix, though his exact address could not be confirmed. Mexican law enforcement officers of Sonora stated that Jefferson was turned over to them by ranchers who found him wandering alone, slightly delirious. Though it is common for Mexican residents to brave the dangers of the desert in order to reach the Arizona border, local authorites are baffled by Jefferson's whereabouts. For the time being, his death is being attributed to overexposure to harsh weather conditions as well as dehydration."

"Emily, I have to leave," said Terry abruptly.

"What?" replied Emily. She quickly removed her napkin from her lap and stood up. "We haven't even had a piece of my father's pie, and I wanted to take a walk with you, show you the neighborhood."

"Maybe beautiful homes offend him," interjected Mrs. Potter.

"I promise I'll make it up to you," said Terry, "but I need you to take me somewhere."

"I don't understand. Where do you need to go?"

"Well, actually, I need you to take me to a hotel."

Mrs. Potter frowned deeply. "I beg your pardon?"

Terry touched Emily gently on the shoulder before returning to the table. "Mr. and Mrs. Potter, it's not what it seems. I only need Emily to drop me off at the entrance. I promise you she will be home in no time."

"Why does my daughter need to drive you anywhere?" asked Mrs. Potter.

Terry hesitated. He inclined his head. "Mrs. Potter, some day it will be different, but for now, I have no car. I don't even have a driver's license."

"So you aren't against exploiting the upper class, you just don't like them. Is that it?"

"Mrs. Potter, please, if you invite me back, I promise we can resume this discussion," said Terry.

Mrs. Potter turned to her husband. "Do you approve of this? Do you think it's appropriate for him to eat our food and then in the middle of the dinner ask that Emily serve as his private chauffeur?"

Mr. Potter stood up from the table and faced Terry. In a very serious tone, he said, "Yes, I approve, but under one condition. You must take a piece of my cherry pie with you."

Emily smiled while her mother fidgeted in her chair, her lips curled, her eyes filled with contempt.

12

THE SILVER HAIRED man standing next to the door appeared to be studying his manicured nails. From the golden watch on his wrist to his open white collared shirt, he appeared the epitome of elderly vitality. "You're positive that nobody can trace this back to us?"

Calvin nodded. His face as well as his disheveled clothes expressed his angst. Timothy smiled slightly, his lips firmly pressed together. He adjusted his golden tie, which contrasted with the dark suit he was wearing. "I assure you, Senator," replied Timothy, "my associates have taken all precautions to make sure that our missions proceed without the slightest infraction."

Senator Brawnchild smoothed back his slick gray hair with his right hand and nodded slightly. "Doctor Ajala, my approval ratings have never been higher since we've made good on our promise to clean up downtown Phoenix, especially the West Side. You know how much I appreciate your help, but I'm worried."

"The dude's all over the news, Timothy," said Calvin.

Timothy arched his eyebrows. "The dude?"

Calvin inclined his head slightly. "Thaddeus. Maybe somebody helped him."

"Senator, it's been a pleasure," said Timothy. He gripped the senator's white shirt at the shoulder. "Allow me to escort you to the lobby." He opened the door and with a quick sweeping motion of his hand, he continued, "After you."

As the two men left the office, Senator Brawnchild whispered, "Doctor Ajala, I'm counting on you. I've already spoken to the mayor and the chief of police. There are murmurings."

"We will have a leadership meeting and give this issue our highest priority," said Timothy.

At the lobby exit, the two men shook hands. Senator Brawnchild smiled, displaying his white porcelain teeth. "We have a great win-win situation here, you and me. It would be a shame to see it end."

"Understood, Senator, and rest assured that The Standard is an organization that you want as an ally and not as an adversary."

Senator Brawnchild quickly lost his smile. He nodded, turned, and walked away. Once he had exited the lobby, Timothy quickly returned to his office. Inside, Calvin remained, pacing the long, rectangular room.

"Tell me exactly what you did," said Timothy. "And please, tuck in your shirt and straighten your tie."

"Yes, Timothy," replied Calvin. As he quickly adjusted his clothing, he began, "I did what we always do. We picked him up late at night—"

"Alone?" interrupted Timothy.

"Yeah, of course," said Calvin, still pacing. He paused for a moment and rubbed his small, square forehead just below his razed hairline. "He was sleeping on the sidewalk."

"Alone?" repeated Timothy.

"Yeah, sort of, I mean, you know how it is."

Timothy approached Calvin. "No, I do not know *how it is*. Now, why don't you explain to me what occurred, and despite your obvious shortcomings, I urge you to recall the most minute detail."

Calvin frowned. "There might've been a few people out there. There's always a few. Anyway, when we grabbed him, he started to holler a little, so we taped his mouth shut. Then we put him in Kyle's van and rolled him up in the carpet like we always do. Kyle can tell you."

"You applied the chloroform?"

"Yeah! He never moved. He was either dead or asleep by the time we put him outside."

Timothy arched his brow. "Obviously we know which one. You took Osvaldo with you, correct?"

"Of course."

"At what time did you enter Mexico?"

"Around two in the morning," said Calvin. He threw his arms into the air. "Timothy, this went down just like all the others! Come on, man! You're gonna stand there and give me the third degree after all I've done for you?"

Timothy furrowed his brow. His large eyes widened further. "*Abeg*! Let me remind you that you were an anonymous drug dealer on a quick path to prison or death when I redeemed you." Taking a few steps closer toward Calvin, he continued, "Do you not appreciate the apartment you now occupy? Are you not being properly compensated for your services?"

"I know, I know," replied Calvin. Once again, he began to pace back and forth within the office. As he did so, beads of sweat began to appear on his forehead and the upper parts of his angular cheeks. "I didn't mean no disrespect. It's just that I feel like you're blaming me."

"No one is blaming you for anything," replied Timothy, "but that does not alter the present situation. We must use **inductive** reasoning to understand how this man was able to reach others."

"Timothy, I'm telling you, I don't know!" said Calvin. "Thaddeus was bound and dumped in the desert like all the rest of them!"

"Are you insane?" asked Timothy. "Keep your voice down! Just because the door is closed does not mean that the walls are soundproof!"

Calvin wiped the perspiration off his brow. "Sorry," he said.

"Sit down!" said Timothy. He pointed to one of the padded leather chairs in his spacious office. "Your nervous pacing is beginning to annoy me! Now, do me the honor of restraining your words to the simplest of answers. I do not want your inferiority to interfere with my reasoning process."

Calvin sat down with his head inclined toward the carpeted floor. He then placed his elbows on his knees and rested his face in both hands.

Timothy closed his eyes. He inhaled and exhaled deeply. He then placed his soft hands together, as if in prayer, and then his long fingers began to slowly vibrate, rhythmically touching each other. "To the mind that is still, the universe surrenders."[19]

Calvin, his head buried in his hands, raised his eyes slightly. "What— what was that?"

"Lao Tsu," replied Timothy, "but that does not concern you. Remain quiet."

Calvin lowered his head once again.

"In the future, we will need to go further into the desert," said Timothy. "Obviously, you did not go far enough." He paused, puckering his lips to breathe in and to breathe out. "This man, starved and dehydrated, was somehow able to free himself. He must have stumbled upon someone. Perhaps he reached one of the small ranches in the area. I am aware they exist, though few and far between. I am also aware that there are several native tribes that lay claim to various parts of the Sonora region. They are not always friendly to trespassers, partly due to their fear of Mexican law enforcement and partly due to their own illegal activities. Arizona police officers, and perhaps other federal agencies, would never consider a drunken indigent capable of credible testimony. Also, we have the language barrier in our favor. Hopefully, he died quickly and was unable to utter a single word to anyone." Once again, Timothy rhythmically tapped his fingers. Hovering over Calvin, he asked, "You did remember to cover the emblem on the van?"

Remaining in his inclined position, Calvin replied, "Yes, Timothy."

"And you used plastic hygienic gloves?"

"Yes, Timothy."

"Then we will allow the authorities to draw their own conclusions. This time we were fortunate, but on our next mission we must assure that whatever dreg of society we place out there is left for dead. Besides the mountain lions and coyotes, no other contact must be allowed."

The distinct sound of the turning of the door handle was heard. Hesitantly, Terry entered the office. "Brother Timothy? Brother Calvin?"

Timothy turned quickly. "Terrence!" he exclaimed. His large eyes widened. "How did you enter?"

Terry remained standing next to the open door. "I just opened the door. The receptionist—she said that you were in here."

Timothy frowned deeply. "In my haste I must not have closed the door securely!"

Terry licked his lips. "Am I interrupting?"

"You look nice, Brother Terrence," said Timothy, the tension in his face slowly dissipating. He smiled slightly. "May I inquire as to how much of our conversation you overheard?"

Terry remained quiet.

Timothy approached him at the doorway. "Terrence, step outside with me. Let's get a breath of fresh air. Brother Calvin, thank you so much for stopping by. I'll be in touch."

Calvin passed by with his head inclined. "Yes, Timothy," he whispered.

Walking across the lobby, Timothy began to speak in the sweet tenor that characterized his voice. "Let's walk to the east side of the hotel. There is a lovely botanical garden there with quite an array of exotic birds. We can sit on one of the benches together."

Terry followed silently as the two men exited the building and entered a confined outside space. It was lit up with various light posts which possessed large, global domes. They passed through several trees, large leafy green plants, and close cropped shrubs. Timothy then pointed downward. "Come, sit with me."

Almost simultaneously, the two sat down upon a metal bench that had a certain burgundy shine to it. Terry glanced at Timothy's large, penetrating eyes. They appeared as focused and serene as always. Timothy opened his mouth, but then two young ladies in tight fitting skirts and long dark heels approached. As they walked by, one of them smiled and said to the other. "Now those are two fine looking men!"

"*Bonsoir mesdames*," Timothy called out.

The two women stopped. One of them, possessing a long black mane of thick frizzy hair, asked, "Do you work here?"

Timothy pointed to the small golden nameplate on his blazer. "Yes, I am the manager of this fine establishment."

The two women giggled.

"Do you think you could show us around?" asked the same woman. "I mean, it's such a large hotel."

"*Tout le plaisir était pour moi*," Timothy replied. "At the moment, however, I must finish an issue of some urgency with my associate, but if you leave your names with one of our receptionists, I shall come to your room and be your personal host."

"Okay, don't be long," said the young lady with the thick black mane.

The woman standing next to her, a young lady with brown skin and dark hair that fell across her shoulders in harmonious waves, winked at Terry. "And we would need two chaperones."

"Of course," said Timothy.

The two ladies giggled once again as they continued down the cobblestone path. After a brief pause, Timothy said, "Terrence, I planned on communicating this information with you in due time, but not now. You are still too young, too *naïf*."

"I don't understand," said Terry.

"Are you still playing that game?" asked Timothy, his jaw tightening. "Be truthful, my young brother. Yes, you do understand. But you are hoping that what you understand is not true, but it is. Now, tell me. What is to be done regarding the inferiors?"

Terry inclined his head. Slowly, he whispered, "There is either redemption or disposal."

"Yes!" said Timothy. His eyes lit up. "The time has come, Terrence! My seed, buried and put to death, is now beginning to bear fruit!"

Terry narrowed his brow.

Timothy raised his arms upwards. "Even as we speak, The Standard is becoming more and more powerful. Our organization has spread throughout Arizona and is beginning to extend beyond our Grand Canyon State. Yes, throughout the United States, I am engaged in multiple discussions with a host of politicians and corporate businessmen! If we are to redeem the world, we must influence people of power!"

Terry raised his head and looked directly into Timothy's eyes. "You didn't redeem those men."

"Excuse me?"

"The men you refer to as inferiors."

Timothy frowned. "Terrence, you must not preoccupy yourself with lesser beings."

"Yes, I must," said Terry.

Timothy's large eyes darted in both directions. "Very well, let us speak openly."

"Yes, let's," said Terry. "The inferiors. You did not redeem them."

"Indeed, but we did attempt to do so," said Timothy. "You have to understand that a society is a great organism, but if there exists disease, then the entire organism will die unless that particular disease is dealt with."

"You killed that man. The man who was threatening me when I first met you."

"Me? No, I did no such thing" said Timothy.

"Then Calvin killed him," said Terry.

"Nobody killed him, Terrence," said Timothy. "We merely allowed nature to take its course more expeditiously."

Terry shook his head slowly. "No, Timothy. What you are saying. What you are doing. It's wrong."

"Terrence!" said Timothy. "Do you still not understand? These people die of self-inflicted wounds! Even worse, they take productive citizens to the grave along with them! We're talking about the very worst dregs of society. Alcoholics, drug addicts, thieves, prostitutes—"

"Like my mother?" interrupted Terry.

Timothy paused. Scowling, he huffed, "*Abeg*! Your mother? Your mother? After all of our conversations, you still refer to that woman as your mother?" Timothy waved his index finger in Terry's face. "You disappoint me, Brother Terrence! It is as if you are taking a step backward! Have you forgotten how to properly judge between right and wrong? Do you actually believe that because an uneducated foolish girl allowed some stranger to mount her, she earned the right to be called your mother? Do you have the slightest idea as to what you are saying?"

Terry promptly stood up. Peering through the darkness, he gazed at the leafy branches of the trees. He listened to the discordant yet musical sounds of the various imported birds that occupied the hotel garden. "I understand your words, but that doesn't change the way I feel. I still care for her."

Timothy stood and faced Terry. "One thing I have learned is that a wise ruler cannot allow his emotions to cloud his mind. Wisdom is based on truth, on **empirical** data, on finding the essence, the forms of life, and not on some vague, indefinable emotion."

Terry closed his eyes for a moment. He exhaled profoundly. "I don't know if I can do that."

"You must," said Timothy, "for the unexamined life is not worth living."[20]

Terry rubbed his eyes with his thumb and forefinger. In a quiet tone of desperation, he muttered, "So many questions."

"Such as?"

"Such as what happens to the innocent?"

"The innocent?" repeated Timothy.

"Yes, what if someone serves in the military and then becomes paralyzed? Or what happens when a person is born with a mental disability? What then, Timothy? What then?"

Timothy arched his brow. "The elite would have to render judgment. If he or she is productive, even in a limited capacity, then that individual would still be capable of living a life full of purpose."

"But what if the person can't?" asked Terry. "What if someone needs assistance just to make it through the day? Or what if a baby is born with birth defects? Where would such a person go?"

"Go?" repeated Timothy. "Explain."

"What kind of facility would care for such a person?"

Timothy frowned. "Terrence, there are no *facilities* in a society dedicated to the whole. There is redemption of inferiority or there is removal."

"You mean death," said Terry.

"We all die eventually. But death is not important. Life is what is important!" Timothy lifted his hands and formed an imaginary circle, as if emphasizing the beauty of the garden that surrounded them. "Do you have eyes but do not see, Brother Terrence? Do you have ears but do not hear? People like you, people like me—we are the elite! And as such, we have an obligation to lead lives of the highest order! We must study, learn, and evolve! And as we do, we will be able to redeem more and more people! Terrence, the harvest is plentiful but the laborers are few!"[21]

Terry shook his head. "No, Timothy, no."

"Listen to me!" Timothy placed his hand on Terry's shoulder. "I believe with all my heart that a **utopian** society is within our grasp! And when it is, we will be able to save the *innocent* as you put it. We will heal the paralyzed warrior! We will restore those who suffer from mental disabilities! And there will be no birth defects as we usher in a new world order and unlock the mysteries of science!"

Terry took a few steps back. As he did so, Timothy's hand slid off of him. "But when, Timothy? When?" he shouted. "How long will it take to find those cures? And what will you do in the meantime? What if someone refuses you? What if someone refuses the elite? Are you describing a dictatorial society without freedom?"

"There is no such thing as absolute freedom," said Timothy. "Every nation that has ever existed established rules to govern society. The only difference with our society is that it will be based on truth and productivity. It will be based on what is best for the whole. I hear the urgency in your voice, brother, and that is why you must use all of your strength to help build The Standard, to help create the society that we all yearn for!"

"I don't know if I share your vision."

"You are struggling. I understand. I have passed through many struggles, my young brother. But you must trust me. Allow me to guide you! Allow me to be your eyes!"

"I'm not blind," said Terry.

Timothy laughed. "You are not blind? I propose that not only are you blind, but deaf as well!"

Terry turned away from the large penetrating eyes that seemed to siphon his strength.

"Tell me, Terrence! Tell me what you see! Tell me what you hear!"

Terry remained still with his lips firmly pressed.

"When I look upon this world, I see that most of its inhabitants spend their each passing day hurting each other, abusing each other, torturing and murdering each other! I see entire villages blotted out from the face of the earth because of a petty difference of religion!"

Terry placed his large hands over the crown of his head.

"I hear the sound of prison doors clanging shut! I hear the cries of entire multitudes—men, women and children—dying from starvation while others live in complete luxury!"

Terry attempted to walk away, but Timothy stepped in front of him. "Confucius taught that if we do not know life then we are incapable of knowing death![22] Those that refuse to be redeemed are not dying because they never truly lived!"

Terry pushed Timothy away. "I'm done, Timothy! I'm done!"

Terry took large, graceful strides down the walking path. As he did so, Timothy called out to him, "Do not attempt to escape your destiny, Brother Terrence!"

13

WITH BOTH HANDS firmly placed on the handles of his four-wheel mobile walker, Walter Cane slowly made his way past the dirt path toward the cement steps that led to the old wooden door of the Bailey residence. Once there, he unhooked a bright red metal walking stick that had four rubber prongs at the end. Measuring each step, he put his left foot forward then followed with his right foot. The strain on his face revealed the effort necessary to reach the small patio. He knocked on the front door. After a brief wait, Grandma Bailey appeared. Her medium length gray hair was weaved behind her head in a bun, and she was dressed in a simple white and blue gown that hung down upon her stout frame.

"Hello."

Walter smiled. "Hello, ma'am."

"May I help you?"

"Yes. As a matter of fact, I'm here to see Terry."

"Are you that Timothy fellow?"

"Oh, no, ma'am. My name's Walter Cane. I'm a friend of Coach More."

Grandma Bailey smiled. "Oh, I see. Terry's not playing football. Are you sure you have the right boy? Aaron, my other grandson, plays quarterback."

"No, ma'am, I've met Aaron. He's a fine young man, but I'm here to see Terry. To be honest with you, I'm not too interested in football. I'm a congressman from Ohio—Columbus, Ohio. I came to Phoenix for a conference and to visit Coach More. When we had lunch, he asked me to talk to Terry. I'm afraid it didn't quite work out the way I had hoped, so I was wondering if I could have one more opportunity before I leave."

Grandma Bailey nodded vigorously. "Is that right? Well, Lord knows he needs it. Would you like to come in?"

"Yes, ma'am."

"Please, call me Mary."

Walter slowly made his way into the living room, an average sized space with two couches, a rocking chair, and a television set. On the left side of the wall was a large wooden structure with several picture frames of various family members, both old and young.

"Please, sit down. I'll get Terry. He's in his room studying. Aaron still hasn't gotten home from football practice."

Walter nodded and slowly sat down on a white vinyl couch. Within a short time Grandma Bailey returned with Terry. She sat down next to Walter while Terry sat on an opposing gray sofa.

"Well, Walter," began Grandma Bailey, "I hope you can help these boys. They're getting to be men, and as such don't listen to us as much as they used to. Terry here is always off with some girl, or even worse, fooling around with a bunch of rabble rousers."

"Grandma, please!" said Terry.

"And Aaron, well, he minds us well enough but all he thinks about is football. He seems happy, but I know these calls from his mother—my daughter, Susie—are making him fret. His father's about to get out of prison, you know."

Terry frowned deeply. "Do you have to be so indiscrete?"

Grandma Bailey scowled. "Excuse me?"

"You sure have a lovely farm, here, Mary," said Walter.

"Oh, thank you," replied Grandma Bailey.

"I have a flight to catch later this evening, and I was hoping I could have a word with Terry before I leave. I don't think I'll be back till next year."

"Oh, yes, of course! You go right ahead!"

"Grandma," said Terry, "I think Mr. Cane would like to speak to me alone."

"See what I mean? This boy is asking me to leave my own living room." Terry shook his head.

"You're absolutely right, Mary," said Walter. "This is your home, and you have every right to do as you please. I do, however, have some personal information for Terry." Walter clutched his walking stick. "Perhaps it would be better if we speak outside."

"Oh, no! You stay right here. I'll just go back to the kitchen. Plenty of work to do. Will you be staying for dinner?"

"Thank you. That's very kind of you, but no, there won't be time."

Grandma Bailey slowly rose from the couch. "Well, it was a pleasure meeting you, and I do hope you can talk some sense into this boy."

Terry rolled his eyes as his grandmother walked away. Once she was gone, he looked directly at Walter. "Mr. Cane, what are you doing here?"

"I didn't like the way our initial conversation ended. I felt I owed you another visit."

Terry frowned. "You don't owe me anything. You're a member of the House of Representatives."

"And that's exactly why I *do* owe you. I'm a public servant."

"But you're from Ohio! I'm not even one of your constituents!"

Walter smiled. "My, oh, my. Jenz was right. No wonder he could never relate to you."

Terry arched his eyebrows.

"Your **elocution** is far beyond him, but that doesn't mean you can't learn from him."

Terry frowned. "With all due respect, Mr. Cane, I believe I made myself perfectly clear. I'm not playing football for Coach More." He paused for a moment. "I'm not going to lie. I miss it. Miss the competition, the challenge, the camaraderie; but there's no way I'm going to subject myself to Coach More."

Walter shook his head. "I'm not here to convince you to play football, Terry. That is your decision and your decision alone, but if it's just a matter of putting up with your coach, well, let me tell you. If I can do it, you can!"

Terry released a weak smile.

Walter inclined his head. "I had to take orders from him, too, you know."

Terry's eyes widened. "You were under Coach More?"

"Yeah, he outranked me."

Terry leaned forward. "How did you deal with that? You're obviously much more intelligent than he."

Walter exhaled deeply. "Well, it wasn't easy. But despite his rough exterior, I can assure you that Jenz is a good man."

"Why do you say that?"

"Because he took a bullet for me."

Terry's mouth slowly opened.

"We were both stationed in the Middle East," began Walter. "During a routine patrol our Humvee was hit. We lost control and drove directly into a wall. As I ran for cover, I felt a pop in my back. I collapsed instantly. I vaguely remember seeing shadows. And that's when I heard Jenz yelling at me. He didn't hesitate. He lifted me up, but he took a bullet to the shoulder. He fell down with me on top of him, but Jenz is the most stubborn son of a bitch I've ever met! He got right back up, hoisted me over his other shoulder, and carried me behind a building." Walter inclined his head for a moment. "While the rest of my troop covered their asses, Jenz came back for me. He was the only one. I guess that's why I keep looking for conferences here in Arizona."

Terry folded his hands in front of him. "I guess intelligence and education do not necessarily make one superior to others."

Walter nodded. "Knowledge is important, Terry, and wisdom even more so, but they're not the most important."

"Then what is?" asked Terry.

"Love."

Terry lowered his brow. "Love?"

"Yes, love," said Walter. "You see, I mentioned to you that I traveled the world as a young man. Like you, I was seeking answers. Answers I felt I could not find from my family, from my friends, from Ohio. Being in military intelligence, I studied various types of government and the cultural communication systems used to establish them. I had the opportunity to meet and listen to some of the most intellectual and educated people throughout all of Europe. But as impressive as their accomplishments, as impressive as the incredible structures they built, I found that their personal lives fell far short. Most of them were actually quite empty. I guess you could say that all of this kind of brought me full circle."

Terry leaned forward on the sofa. "Full circle?"

"Yes, after years of searching, I came back to my roots. I came back to the simple lessons I learned when my mother used to drag me to Sunday School. Namely, that God is love and I am to love my fellow man."

Terry shook his head. "I wish it were that simple, but being a nice person isn't going to set the world straight. We need leadership. We need intelligent people, and good people, to be in control of the nation—of the world for that matter. Only then can we set things right." Terry paused. He inclined his head. Lowering his voice, he added, "I'm just wondering if the right people exists."

Walter rubbed his chin. "Terry, you seem like a fine young man, and I admire your search for truth, but I fear you won't find the answer in any particular form of government. Whether it's a republic or a democracy, a form of socialism, communism, a dictatorship, or even a monarchy of kings and queens; they all fall short because they fail to factor in the human heart. And that, young man, leads us right back to a democracy. It's not foolproof, but it's the best we got! That's why Winston Churchill said that it's the worst form of government except for all the others that have been tried!"[23]

Terry chuckled. Then, suddenly, his face seemed to crumble. He put his large hands around the back of his head. Leaning forward, he cried out, "Then what is? What is the answer?"

"I already told you. Love."

"But how can that be?" asked Terry.

Walter's eyes narrowed. He raised his hand and made a fist. "Because I am convinced that love—true selfless love—is the foundation for everything in life. If you love your fellow man, then you will seek knowledge, you will want truth, and you will fight for justice."

Terry's eyes reflected his desperation. "How do you even define love?"

Walter smiled. "I think the Apostle Paul said it much better than I ever could. It goes something like this: 'If I speak in the tongues of men or of angels, but I do not have love, then I am only a resounding gong or a clanging cymbal. If I have the gift of prophecy and am able to fathom all mysteries and all knowledge, and if I have a faith that can move mountains, but do not have love, then I am nothing. If I give all I possess to the poor and give over my body to hardship so that I may boast, but do not have love, I gain nothing. Love is patient, love is kind. It does not envy, it does not boast, and it is not proud. It does not dishonor others, it is not self-seeking, it is not easily angered, it keeps no record of wrongs. Love does not delight in evil but rejoices in the truth. Love always protects, always trusts, always hopes, always perseveres. Love never fails.' "[24]

Terry exhaled deeply. "I don't know what to do," he whispered. "I thought I had the answers. I thought I'd met someone who could give them to me, but now I'm not so sure. I'm not sure of anything anymore."

"Some of the answers will come in due time, and some of them will not. Only God has all the answers. In the meantime, pursue love." Walter held up his watch. "I have to catch a flight, but maybe you could assist me down the stairs?"

"Of course," said Terry.

Walter grabbed his walking stick and struggled to his feet. Terry walked over to him and gripped his elbow. Slowly, they made their way toward the door.

"You don't know how long it has taken for me to do this," said Walter, grimacing slightly.

"Do what?"

"Swallow my pride."

"I understand," said Terry. "But you served your country. And you continue to do so. There's no shame in that."

Terry grabbed the metal walker that remained on the patio. With one hand he carried it, and with the other he assisted Walter. As the two made their way down the steps, a gruff voice called out, "Hello, there!"

"Granddad!" said Terry. His body immediately stiffened. "I was studying when Mr. Cane came to visit. He's a congressman from Ohio and a friend of Coach More's."

Granddad Bailey scowled slightly. "Well, I figured you were studying since you weren't out here helping me." Turning to Walter, he rubbed his dirty, calloused hands on his blue jeans and his untucked plaid shirt. "I hope I don't seem too strict with my grandson, Mr. Cane, but he hasn't been contributing like he knows he should. I can excuse him for studying, but not for socializing—present company excepted, of course. So you're a friend of Coach More's, huh?"

"Yes, sir," replied Walter. "Served in the Marines with him."

"Yeah, these kids really follow Coach More. I've had quite a few play for him over the years, but no one like Aaron or Terry. Well, before this one quit, anyway. At first, I was happy about it. Thought he'd help out more. But seeing the way he's never around I'd rather he play. Keep him out of trouble."

"I didn't quit, Granddad," said Terry. "Coach More removed me from the team."

"With the right attitude, you know he'd welcome you back," said Walter. "Remember, love is not proud."

Terry nodded his head. "I'll think about it. You know how Coach is. If he were a government, he'd be a dictatorship."

Walter laughed. "Terry, it was great talking to you. You're a very special young man, and I see great things in your future. If you need anything, and I mean anything, I'm here for you. Look me up or talk to Coach More. I'm at your service."

"Thank you, Mr. Cane," said Terry.

"Mr. Bailey, it's been a pleasure. Please tell your wife I hope to enjoy her cooking the next time I stop by."

Granddad Bailey nodded. Terry then assisted Walter to his car and watched in silence as he drove away, down the long dirt road that led to the main street.

"I don't like politicians much," said Granddad Bailey, "but I would vote for that young man."

"You can't. He doesn't represent our state," said Terry.

"I'm just saying that he ain't a bullshitter. Looks you in the eye when he speaks. Not too many politicians like that anymore."

Terry frowned. "No offense, Granddad, but what do you know about politics?"

Granddad Bailey cleared his throat. " 'Let America be the dream the dreamers dreamed. Let it be that great strong land of love. Where never kings connive nor tyrants scheme. That any man be crushed by one above.' "[25]

"Granddad!" exclaimed Terry, his eyes widening. "Was that Langston Hughes?"

"Yeah, so? What did you think? That I'm some **illiterate** farmer?"

"No, I—I just wasn't expecting…" stuttered Terry.

Granddad Bailey huffed. "Well, all right, then." He then turned and walked toward the barn.

14

TERRY STOPPED IN front of the entrance of the high school football stadium. Instead of slacks, a collared shirt and tie, he was dressed casually in loose jeans, a T-shirt, and a blue hoodie jacket. Emily, too, was dressed comfortably in a white cotton exercise suit which displayed vertical pink lines throughout the pants and top. Beyond them were a host of cars in the sparsely lit parking lot. Cheering could be heard in the distance.

"Now what?" asked Emily.

"I'm having second thoughts."

"Terrence, you told me you wanted to come!"

"I know," said Terry, "but I feel so indecisive."

"Really? Do you think maybe that's because you are?"

Terry inclined his head.

"I was just kidding…at least a little bit."

"Maybe you'd be better off without me," Terry mumbled.

Emily furrowed her brow. "Terrence, why would you say such a thing?"

"Because it's true. I feel so unstable, and we're so different."

Emily frowned. "Different? How so?"

Terry curled his lips. "Emily, please, don't patronize me. In practically every way!"

"You mean because of this." Emily stroked her white cheek. She then touched her thin red lips. She slowly ran her fingers through her long red hair. "And this." She reached out and touched Terry's dark cheek, his thick lips, and his short razed black hair.

"It's more than that."

Emily released a broad smile. "I could continue, but I'm warning you that the other parts of our bodies are *really* different."

Terry smiled. He then broke into a deep laughter. Emily, too, began to laugh.

"Come here!" said Terry. He embraced her tightly. "How do you do it? How are you not afraid?"

"Afraid?" whispered Emily.

"Yes, afraid of life, of us, of the future?"

"Terrence, you think too much," said Emily, caressing his shoulders. "It's easy, really. I love you."

The words seemed to jolt Terry. He paused to study Emily's face. It was symmetrical, composed of fine bone structure, and yet in some strange way it was bland. There was something missing that he had seen in both her mother and sister. The eyes were a bit dull. But this characteristic made her special, unique. He gently began to caress her temples. As he did so, Emily closed her eyes. The two kissed. Slowly. Lingering. And then tears formed, moistening Terry's cheeks first, and then Emily's.

"Love," whispered Terry. "It seems as though that word is following me."

"Yes. Following us both."

"What did I ever do to deserve you, Emily?"

"I don't know." Emily wiped the tears from Terry's face. "I guess I just like the dark, handsome, brooding type."

Terry released a large grin. "Emily, you're one of the few people that makes me..." His voice trailed off.

"Happy?"

Terry nodded.

Emily interlocked her hands around the nape of Terry's neck. "It's not a sin to be happy, Terrence. In fact, it's your right."

Terry remained still. "My right?" he mumbled.

Emily smiled and nodded. "We hold these truths to be self-evident, that all *people* are created equal, that they are endowed by their creator with certain unalienable rights, that among these are life, liberty—"[26]

"—And the pursuit of happiness," interrupted Terry. "Emily, you're right. You are so right. Everyone—not just the few—everyone. Thank you, Emily, thank you for that!"

"Terrence," said Emily, grinning widely, "I would love to take credit, but there were some old guys that said something very similar." She raised her wrist and then pressed a button on her watch, causing it to glow in the evening darkness. "Look at the time."

Terry nodded. "I know. The game's probably almost over by now." Grabbing Emily by the hand, he practically lifted her off her feet. "Come on, we better hurry! Maybe they'll let us in without paying."

They ran to a gate where they stopped in front of a middle-aged man who sat behind a small table. He was wearing a windbreaker and an old green cap. His grayish beard covered his reddish cheeks and neck. "Little late, don't you think?"

"Yes, we're aware of that," said Emily.

"You guys from Highland?"

"No," said Emily.

"But you're students, right?"

"Yes," said Emily. "I'm from Saint Mary and he's from Avondale."

The man curled his lips. "Well, you, sweetheart, I'll give the home team price, but this guy's going to have to pay double!" He released a high-pitched cackle. Then, squinting at Terry through the cool night air, he added, "Wait. You look familiar. Don't you play for Avondale?"

Terry replied, "No, sir, I'm not on the team."

"According to this you are." He held up a white pamphlet. "Isn't that you? Washington?"

Terry stared at his picture. "Wow. I suppose it is. Imagine that."

"Yeah, imagine that! So what happened? You get injured? Or you got smart and decide not to embarrass yourself like the rest of them?"

As the man cackled loudly once more, Terry did not reply. Instead, he looked up at the scoreboard. It was the fourth quarter and Avondale was down by seven points.

"Well, I guess this is your lucky day! Go ahead and go in, my treat!"

Emily frowned. "Thank you! You're so kind!"

Terry grabbed Emily's hand. As they walked toward the visiting section, he said, "Did I note a hint of sarcasm in your voice, Miss Potter?"

"Yeah, just a little," said Emily. "What a jerk!"

"Tell me about it," said Terry. "These guys take their football very seriously."

They walked up the thin metal stairs, and Terry promptly sat down at the first bench located in the lower corner of the bleachers.

Emily furrowed her brow "Why are we sitting here all alone? Don't you want to go to the middle?"

"No, too many people," said Terry.

"How about a little higher?"

"No, we're fine here."

Emily leaned forward. "I can't see much."

Terry remained quiet.

"I guess we're in the perfect spot to see Highland score," said Emily.

Terry turned to Emily and crinkled his nose.

On the field below, Avondale had the ball on their own thirty yard line. The large digital game clock was counting down from five minutes.

"All right, we're gonna start with a draw play!" said Aaron from within the huddle.

Larry Butler inclined his head.

"What's wrong?"

"Aaron, I've been getting stuffed all day," said Larry.

"I know, that's why I'm going to hesitate for a second and look downfield." Then, slapping Larry's black helmet, Aaron added, "You haven't gotten the ball since the second quarter. They're not expecting it.

Leo, you're blocking, but the rest of you guys are streaking long. Take them as far as you can. Trust me! Everybody ready?"

"Break!"

As the team set up, Aaron looked at the defensive line. He then stared at his receivers. The opposing linebackers took a few steps back.

"Down! Set! Green two hundred! Hut! Hut!"

Jeff snapped the ball to Aaron. He took a few steps back, wound his arm, gave one pump fake, and then placed the ball in Larry's hands. Larry, with helmet down, lumbered slowly through a huge hole. At one point he hesitated, as if surprised not to have been tackled. The crowd erupted in cheers. Coach More could be heard screaming from the sidelines for him to continue. A green uniform rushed toward Larry and tackled him to the ground.

In the stands, Terry fidgeted. He raised his hands behind his head.

"What's wrong?" asked Emily. "Wasn't that a good play?"

"Yeah, the play was fine," said Terry, "but the run was awful. If I would have been out there—"

"—But you're not," interrupted Emily.

Terry curled his lips and glared at her. Emily smiled.

Within the huddle, Larry said, "Aaron, I'm feeling it! I almost got a first down! Call another play for me!"

"No, man, you did your job. We can only pull those off once in a while. We're passing or I'm taking this one."

As the offense set up, Aaron called out, "White one hundred! Hut!"

Aaron stepped back, looked downfield but saw no one. He quickly glanced toward Leonel Reyes, but he was surrounded by the green jerseys of the Highland players.

"You're going down!" said a defensive tackle as he grabbed Aaron around the waist.

Aaron quickly pivoted and shook him off. He then rolled to his right, where a strong side linebacker was bearing down on him. Turning back to his left, he attempted to run to the other side of the field, but was quickly met by a defensive end who had penetrated the line. Aaron then felt two thick arms around his leg. Refusing to be taken down, Aaron began to hop on one foot. He looked downfield to throw the ball. As he continued to search, he was blindsided by a weak side linebacker. Aaron immediately felt a sharp pain rip through his side as he fell hard to the ground. Two other green jerseys piled on top of him. Aaron gasped for breath but found breathing difficult.

As the officials blew their whistles, the Highland players slowly rose to their feet.

"If you know what's good for you, you'll stay down there!" said one.

"Hell, yeah!" shouted another. "This game's over!"

"Get off him!" called out Jeff Buckey as he began to tug on a number of green uniforms.

Several Highland players quickly surrounded him. "You can't stop all of us!" shouted the linebacker who had hit Aaron.

Jeff shoved him hard in the chest. "Shut up and get to your side! I've been stopping you all night!"

"Oh, yeah? Tell that to your quarterback! I think I just heard his ribs crack!"

Two officials approached the boys with their whistles blaring. "All right, all right! That's enough! Break it up!" shouted one.

Jeff turned to Aaron and lifted him up. As he did so, Aaron released a load moan.

"Dude, you're hurt!" said Jeff.

"No, I'm good!" said Aaron. "Let's do it again, but this time Leo's going to stay and block. Butler missed his man. He got through."

Once more, Avondale set up at the line. Aaron looked to his right and then to his left. He then barked, "Down! Set! White one hundred! Hut!"

Rolling back, he cocked his arm and in one fluid movement brought his entire body forward. The ball flew through the air in a perfect spiral toward a streaking wide receiver, converting into a gain of twenty yards. The Avondale side of the stadium burst into applause.

Inside the huddle, Aaron looked directly at Jeff. "All right, we're at midfield. We're making them nervous. I want everyone to go long, but I'm taking this one myself."

"Break!"

On the line, Aaron said, "Down! Set! Blue three hundred! Hut! Hut! Hut!"

He stepped back, thrusted his arm forward with a pump fake, and then ran through a hole created by Jeff Buckey. With each stride, Aaron felt as if his side would burst. After a large gain, the strong side linebacker began to pursue him. Not wanting to risk further injury, Aaron moved to his right, cutting toward the sideline. As he did so, a safety came zooming forward. Aaron slipped out of bounds near the Highland team. Upon doing so, the safety smashed into him, throwing him down. The Highland players standing on the sidelines began to shout and cheer.

The officials quickly blew their whistles, waving their arms for players to back away. Coach More then began to cross the field. "That was a late hit! A late hit!" He shouted as he extended his arm and pointed to the line judge.

The head coach of the Highland team smirked. "Boys can't stop in mid-air. Now get back to your side!"

Coach More scowled. "You shut your mouth! You know that's not what happened!"

One of the Highland players approached Coach More. "You don't talk to our coach like that!"

"Why don't you teach your boys to not be afraid to take a hit?" said an assistant coach from Highland.

"Go back to your side, Coach, or we'll have to flag you," warned the referee. "Your player is fine."

"So you're not going to call a late hit? Or unnecessary roughness?" asked Coach More.

The referee shook his head as several Avondale players began to join them on the sideline. A few stood by Coach More while others assisted Aaron.

"You're raising a ruckus, Coach," said the line judge, "so get back to your side before things get out of hand."

"You weren't even in position!" said Coach More.

"You want that penalty, coach?"

Accompanied by two other players, Aaron limped past Coach More. Holding onto his side, he said, "It's okay, Coach, I got this."

Coach More turned to the referee. "Time out!"

The side judge blew his whistle.

"This is Highland football, Coach. This is how we do it over here!" said the Highland head coach.

Coach More snarled as he and a handful of players walked across the field. As they approached the Avondale sidelines, Coach Spriggs shouted, "Coach, what's going on? That was our last time out!"

"I know, but we got our first down. Aaron gets a breather and we're in position to score."

Aaron removed his helmet and quickly accepted some water. He then sat down on a small bench where his three coaches quickly surrounded him.

"Aaron, are you sure you can still play?" asked Coach Morales.

Swallowing his water, Aaron nodded. Coach More then reached out and put his arms around both assistant coaches. Stepping away from Aaron, the three men huddled together.

"I don't know, Coach, he was limping pretty badly out there," said Coach Spriggs.

"He's been taking a lot of hits," added Coach Morales. "All season, really."

"I know, but it's up to him," replied Coach More. "Aaron's a soldier."

"But he's hurt," said Coach Morales. "For his own good, we may have to tell him to give up the ball—and I mean fast. Let someone else make the play."

"It's his call," replied Coach More. "Aaron reads the defense and he decides."

"No, Coach," said Coach Morales. "It's not his call; it's yours."

Coach More inclined his head. He rubbed his forehead. Slowly, he made his way toward Aaron. "Aaron, you're our leader, but we have to do what's best for you. I don't want you to risk getting hurt. They're gunning for you and it doesn't look like the officials are going to help us much. Maybe we should play it safe with the next play...even if that means handing off to Leo or Larry."

Aaron took one last drink, stood up, and walked toward the field. As he did so, the face of Coach More beamed with pride.

"Huddle up!" said Aaron. "All right, time for some razzle dazzle. Leo, are you ready?"

Leonel nodded.

"Okay, just like we did in practice."

Standing in the lower section of the bleachers, Terry clasped his hands together and shouted loudly, "Aaron, you can do it! You can do it, bro!"

Not too far away, at the very top of the bleachers, a high-pitched voice pierced through the noise of the crowd "Yeah! Aaron! You can—you can—do it!"

Terry turned to see Mason.

"Who's that little boy?" asked Emily.

Shrugging his shoulders, Terry replied, "I don't know. He's kind of strange."

"Cheering for your brother is strange?"

"No, Emily, it's not that. It's just the way he said it." Terry pointed toward Mason. "Look at him, rocking up and down and swinging his arms in the air. And he's so..."

"So what?" asked Emily.

Terry's perpendicular jaw moved up and down slightly. "So emotionally involved in the game."

Terry began to walk upward in the bleachers.

"Terrence, where are you going?" asked Emily.

"I want to find out who he is."

"I'll go with you," said Emily, grabbing Terry's arm.

As they made their way across the metal stands, several people began to call out to Terry.

"You should be out there, Washington!"

Terry nodded.

"Looks like we're doing just fine without you!"

Terry frowned.

"Hey, Washington, having fun watching the game while your cousin puts his body on the line for us?"

Terry shook his head.

"Gosh, Terrence," whispered Emily, "you're like a celebrity. A rather infamous one, but a celebrity nonetheless."

"Thanks," Terry mumbled.

On the field, Aaron called a no huddle offense. As he began the audible, Leonel went into motion. The Highland defense began shouting and pointing. Two linebackers shifted to their right.

"Down! Set! Blue three hundred! Hut! Hut! Hut!"

Aaron rolled back, faked a pitch to Larry, and instead appeared to give the ball to Leo, who reached out and cupped the imaginary ball close to his stomach with both hands as he continued toward the left sideline. The defensive line immediately reacted as Aaron stopped to watch the action unfold. Then, suddenly, Aaron revealed the ball which had remained hidden behind his back. He stormed down the right side of the field as fast as he could.

"It was a fake!"

"Fake handoff!"

Through the corner of his eye, Aaron saw a green uniform quickly approaching him. It was a Highland free safety. Aaron stretched out his left hand and stiff armed him. The Highland player clawed at Aaron. A struggle ensued before Aaron was finally pushed out of bounds.

In the upper section of the bleachers, Terry raised his fist in the air. "Yes!" he shouted.

Mason, standing a few feet away, jumped into the air and also said, "Yes!"

Terry approached him carefully. "Hey, little guy, enjoying the game?"

Mason rocked back and forth on his heels, but said nothing in reply. Emily then smiled at him and introduced herself.

"Hi," said Mason before quickly turning toward the action on the field.

Emily frowned as Terry released a wide smile. "I guess your charms don't work on everyone," he said.

Suddenly, the people around them burst into a collective moan. Mason fell back. He put both hands on his head and said, "Oh no! Oh no!" He then ran to a man and woman who were sitting a few feet away at the edge of the bleachers. "Aaron got hit. He got hit hard!"

"Don't worry, Mason, Aaron's tough. He'll be okay," said the woman.

"Excuse me," said Terry, "but how do you know Aaron?"

"He's my best friend," said Mason.

Terry furrowed his brow deeply. He then whispered to Emily, "Did you hear that? He said he's Aaron's best friend."

"How can you not know your cousin's best friend?" asked Emily.

Terry shook his head. "I don't know. We haven't talked much lately, but this is bizarre."

On the field, Aaron threw a short screen pass to Larry, who stood alone near the right sideline. He ran several yards before being pulled down.

Terry jumped to his feet. "Damn it! Thirty seconds left and Butler can't get his bony ass into the end zone!"

Emily's green eyes twinkled in the night air. "Terrence! I've never heard you talk like that before!" She paused a moment before adding, "I kind of like it."

Terry arched his brow. "Oh, trust me, a couple more plays like that and you're going to hear a lot more! If Aaron had run that screen pass with me, I would have—"

"No, you wouldn't," interrupted Emily.

Terry turned to look down at her. "Excuse me?"

"I said you *wouldn't*, but actually I meant you *couldn't*."

Terry ran his upper lip against his bottom teeth. "Emily, have you ever seen me play?"

Emily shook her head. "No, I haven't, and that's precisely the point. You wouldn't—and couldn't—because while he's playing down there you're up here watching with me."

Terry scowled. "Would you quit doing that?"

Emily released an innocent smile. "Doing what?"

"Never mind, let's just watch the damn game. It could be over soon."

Emily folded her arms in front of her. "Fine with me, but could you at least sit down? I'm cold."

Terry sat down and put his arm around her.

On the field, Coach More paced up and down the sidelines. He turned in all directions. There was something about his body language that made him appear helpless. Inside the huddle, Aaron had called his own number. "Hey! It's real simple! The crowd's against us! The refs are against us! But we got one thing those guys don't!"

Silence followed.

"Jeff Buckey," said Aaron.

"What's that supposed to mean?" asked Leonel between heavy breaths.

"It means he ain't any good," said Aaron.

"Gee, thanks," muttered Jeff.

"You know why you ain't any good?" asked Aaron. Before Jeff could answer, he continued, "Because you're great! And right now..." Aaron paused to catch his breath. "Right now, good ain't gonna do it. We need great—not good—great. So listen up! I'm faking a pitch to Larry and then

I'm taking this ball all the way to the end zone, so that means you have to get there first. You understand me?"

"I guess," replied Jeff.

Aaron slapped Jeff's dark helmet with his right hand, followed by his left. "We didn't get this far for you to be guessing! Do you hear me? You ain't no good! You're great! Great! Great!"

"I'm great?" asked Jeff.

"Great!" snarled Aaron.

"Great!" said Leonel, also hitting Jeff on the side of the helmet.

"Great!" repeated a host of players, slapping Jeff hard on the helmet.

"All right! All right! I get it!" shouted Jeff.

"What are they doing?" shouted Coach More from the sidelines. "They're not even going to get the play off in time!"

The seconds ticked off. Five…four…three…two…one…. The ball was snapped to Aaron, who extended one hand toward Larry before charging behind Jeff. With a loud shout, Jeff pushed people aside, clearing a huge hole. Together, he and Aaron burst into the end zone.

As cheers erupted throughout the visitor's side of the stadium, the line judge ran over to Coach More. "This doesn't happen much, Coach, but you're allowed one play."

Coach More nodded, turned, and motioned to Carson. "You ready?"

"Yes, sir."

"Okay, then, get that extra point and tie it up!"

"Yes, sir."

In the huddle, eleven weary players squatted with their hands on their knees. "No! No! No!" shouted Aaron, his helmet moving from side to side.

"Come on, Aaron, I'm here to tie it up," said Carson.

"We'll never make it in overtime."

"It's an order!" said Carson. "Coach said!"

"If only Terry were here," said Leonel.

"He's not here!" growled Aaron. "But I remember one thing that fool said to me. He said I can think for myself. Coach doesn't understand. We'll never win in overtime. It's now or never, so block like hell because we're taking this right now! Be ready, Leo, 'cause one of us is getting to that end zone! Break!"

Both sides of the stadium were on their feet. The noise was deafening. Avondale set up in formation with Aaron and Carson in the backfield. Aaron shouted the cadence. Jeff Buckey snapped the ball high into the air. Aaron grabbed it and immediately knelt down, placing it for Carson to kick the extra point. Suddenly, Aaron rose to his feet. He ran to his right. He avoided one Highland defensive lineman and jumped over another. He then looked ahead. A large green image emerged. Aaron clenched his teeth as the Highland linebacker bore down on him. He quickly assessed his location. He was still behind the line of scrimmage. Doubts emerged. He was too far away to run, and Leonel was still in motion. But then a black and yellow uniform suddenly appeared in front of him. It was Larry Butler. Throwing himself at the Highland linebacker, Larry caused him to stumble. It was not a solid block, but it was enough. Aaron could see Leonel curl to the right corner of the end zone. He zipped a rocket pass high into the air. As Leonel leaped with outstretched hands, Aaron felt a powerful thud as he was knocked to the ground. A roar was heard on one side of the field, a deep moan emerged from the other.

Deep within the stands, Terry shook his head in disbelief. "I don't believe it."

He then leaped down several benches, acrobatically skipping two at a time. He landed at the bottom of the metal stands and in one single movement grabbed the rail and hurdled it, landing softly onto the dirt below. From there, he sprinted toward the field.

Emily's eyes widened. "Wow!"

The referees tried in vain to control the bedlam. Avondale players surrounded Leonel. Highland players fell to the ground. Terry made his way to Aaron. His helmet was marked badly. Stains of green and red were smeared against his uniform. His body, somewhat limp, leaned against the solid figure of Lucas Wright.

"Aaron!"

"Terry?"

The two stared at each other in silence. Finally, Terry said, "You're strong, bro. You're strong." He then turned to Lucas. "Here, let me."

Lucas nodded as Terry ducked under Aaron's arm and helped him off the field.

15

IT WAS A beautiful Saturday morning. The sun shone brightly in the clear blue sky, but even so, the winter air was cool and pleasant—and appreciated for as long as it would last. The smaller pigs and the larger hogs were busy snorting. Roosters could be heard crowing and chickens clucking. Aaron and Terry, dressed in their overalls and dark work boots, scattered feed among the fenced chickens. While they worked slowly and without a hint of enthusiasm, Mason, was a flux of activity.

"I—I finished, Mr. Bailey. I beat Dan—Dan—Dante."

Max Bailey ran his fingers through the brown eggs that Mason had gathered into a wired egg basket. He then smiled, removed Mason's black baseball cap, and ruffled Mason's sandy brown hair. "That's good work, Mason. These boys just can't keep up with you. Why don't you leave them eggs with Mrs. Bailey and help Dante clean all that chicken poop out of the nest boxes."

"Yes, I—I will."

Granddad Bailey pointed to Aaron and Terry. "You put these two right here to shame!" As Mason ran off toward the house, Granddad Bailey continued, "Now that's what I call a hard worker! No questioning! No whining! I'm going to have to pay that boy real good at the end of the day!"

Aaron cocked his head back and furrowed his brow. "You're gonna pay Mason? Granddad, I should be sleeping right now! It was almost midnight when Coach dropped me off!" Then, stretching a bit, he added, "Every bone in my body aches!"

"Not to mention you get free labor out of us!" added Terry.

Aaron and Terry exchanged fist bumps.

"Free? Boys, take a look at those clothes you're wearing! Take a look at that house where you sleep! And I'm not even going to talk about the money I'm paying on shoes!"

"Granddad, Coach More bought my cleats through the Booster Club!" said Aaron.

"Well, what about those fancy high top basketball shoes you both wear?"

"Jeff Buckey's dad," said Terry.

Granddad Bailey smiled. "Well, I guess it's a good thing you both have so many friends because after I pay Mason there ain't gonna be much left!"

A loud moan emerged from both Aaron and Terry.

"All right, you've cleaned enough. Go and check on the shallots and garlic. Take the gardening hoes with you."

"Yes, Granddad," they replied in unison.

Walking to the middle of the vegetable garden, Terry began, "Mason's a pretty cool little kid."

"Yeah," said Aaron, "I really like him."

"Really?"

Aaron frowned. "Yeah, why?"

"Oh, nothing. It's just, I mean, I think it's nice of you to help him."

"I'm not helping him. He's helping me!" said Aaron.

Terry raised his brow.

"That kid doesn't have a bad bone in his body," continued Aaron. "All he does is tell me how great I am, or ask me if I want to come to his house and see his comic book collection. I wish all my friends were like him. He doesn't lie. He doesn't cheat. He'd do anything for me! Mason's a great person!"

Terry raised the gardening hoe in the air. "Okay, okay, you convinced me." After a short pause, he added, "I didn't expect such a passionate rebuke."

"Sorry," said Aaron, "it's just the way you said it."

Terry nodded. "You're right. I apologize."

"All right, then," said Aaron.

Terry smiled. "You know who you sounded like just then."

Aaron scowled. "Don't even say it."

They continued working. Then, slowly, Terry continued, "Hey, you were incredible against Highland last night. I didn't think you guys were going to pull it off."

Two gardening hoes flew through the air, clutching at several weeds and unearthing them from the ground.

"Yeah," said Aaron, "everyone played tough. Leo came through when we needed him, and Jeff and me was able to do the rest."

"*Jeff and I were* able to do the rest," said Terry.

"That's what I said!"

"No, you said—"

"Whatever!" interrupted Aaron. "Anyway, I was kind of glad we got the win for Larry's sake, too."

"Larry Butler?"

"Yeah, he's been taking flak all year for not being you."

Terry nodded. "That's not right, especially because I'm not the one who can't be replaced."

Aaron nodded. "Thanks, bro." After a brief silence, he inclined his head and said, "Man, look at all these weeds. I ain't feeling this."

"Neither am I," said Terry.

Aaron smirked, "Yeah, but you ain't the one suffering; every muscle in my body aches." Aaron threw the hoe down, digging the metal head deep into the soil. "I wouldn't have to work so hard if you were there. It's exhausting both physically and mentally."

Terry arched his brow before yanking a particularly stubborn weed. "Physically and mentally?"

"I can use big words if I want to!"

Terry's square face broke into a slight smile.

"We wouldn't have so many options if you was there," continued Aaron.

Terry began to open his mouth when Aaron pointed his index finger at him and said, "Don't. Anyway, what I was saying was that Coach designed all these plays where Leo acts as a tailback, or Larry pitches the ball back to me. Bootlegs, flea flickers, double reverses, five receivers off the shotgun." Aaron shook his head and blew out a puff of air. "Man, we've never done that stuff before, and most of the time it don't even work. And now look at us. We're going to the state finals, up against Scotty, everyone saying we don't have a chance."

Aaron dug his gardening hoe deep into the ground with great force.

"I know, I know," said Terry.

"This row looks pretty clear," said Aaron.

Terry dipped down to the ground and moved a small hose to allow water down a narrow burrow. "That's why I want to come back."

Aaron stopped suddenly. "What did you say?"

"I want to play."

Aaron threw down his gardening hoe and wrapped his arms around Terry in a bear hug. Lifting Terry off the ground, he asked, "Are you serious?"

"Yes, I am," said Terry. "Now put me down."

Aaron smiled widely. "Sorry, cuz, I'm just so excited!"

"What happened to being exhausted 'both physically and mentally'?"

Aaron smiled. He rubbed his right side of this ribcage. "You're right. I guess I couldn't help myself."

Terry grinned as he shook his head. Then, suddenly, his face took on a serious expression. "It will be my last opportunity. After that I'm leaving."

Aaron crinkled his forehead. "Huh? Leaving?"

"Yes." Terry paused for a moment. He bit his lower lip. "Aaron, I'm going to tell you a secret. A secret that nobody else can know."

Aaron furrowed his brow.

"Everyone has been singing the praises of Senator Brawnchild and how he's cleaned up the West Side of Phoenix. No more transients, no more drug dealers, no more prostitutes, no more drunks. It's just the tip of the iceberg."

"What are you talking about?" asked Aaron.

"I'm talking about the unsolved mysteries reported in the news."

Aaron rubbed his goatee. "Yeah!" he shouted. "Those dudes who've been disappearing! But what do you gotta do with all that?"

"Shhhhhhhh!" Terry hissed. "Keep your voice down. It echoes in these fields. Nobody can know about this, Aaron. Nobody. Granddad, Grandma, Coach More. Nobody. It's Timothy, Aaron. He's the real leader, and I know enough to incriminate him."

Aaron shook his head. "I don't get you. Break it down for me, bro. You always make things so complicated. Just say what you mean."

Terry turned in all directions. "I can't tell you everything. It's not safe. That's why Mr. Cane has invited me to live with his family in Ohio. I'm leaving after Christmas. I'm going to testify against him. He needs to be stopped."

Aaron placed his hands on the back of his head. "Terry, hold on! Forget the team! What's to stop Timothy from coming after you?"

"He won't," said Terry. "I mean, at least not now."

"How do you know?"

"I just do. I know Timothy; I know how he thinks; he values my life... as I value his. Part of me still admires him. Part of me wants to follow him." Terry turned away. "I need support, Aaron. I need to be with Mr. Cane."

Aaron placed his hand on Terry's shoulder. "I don't know. Are you sure about all this?"

"I'm sure," replied Terry. "Now, how am I going to get Coach to allow me to play?"

Aaron smiled widely. "Easy, I'll plant the seed and you water."

16

As several members of the extended Bailey family ate dinner, a knock was heard on the door. Since no one indicated that they were prepared to move, Grandma Bailey got up from the table. "Kind of late for visitors," she mumbled.

Underneath the porch light, a dark figure was seen with arms folded. Her hair darker and shorter, the face younger and without wrinkles, the legs longer. Still, the resemblance was apparent.

"Susie? Is that you?" asked Grandma Bailey.

"I'm sorry I didn't call first. I know it's late. It's just that..."

"Susie, come inside," said Grandma Bailey. "What's wrong? What happened?"

The two women walked into the living room.

"I didn't know where else to go. It's Jerome. He got out. We were going to come visit, see Aaron, but then he said he had to settle a score."

The others quickly assembled around Aaron's mother.

"How many times have we told you that Jerome's no good?" said Granddad Bailey.

Susie Bailey lowered her face into her hands. "I know! I know! He said he would be right back, but that was two hours ago!"

"Max, please!" pleaded Grandma Bailey. "She's here. She needs our help."

"She doesn't want our help!" replied Granddad Bailey. "We've been offering her help all her life!"

Aaron knelt beside his mother. "Mom, what's going on?"

His mother raised her head. "Aaron, we were going to come talk to you, convince you to come back, spend Christmas with us, but your father told me to wait until he took care of someone in Phoenix. Some foreign guy's been meddling in his affairs."

Terry's eyes flashed. He then quickly left the room. Inside the kitchen, he lightly pressed the square buttons of the telephone. After a brief conversation, he returned and immediately went to Aaron. "Come on, we need to go."

Aaron glared at him. "Can't you see my mom's not doing well?"

"Come here!" said Terry. He grabbed Aaron by the arm and began to pull him away.

"What in God's name?" shouted Grandma Bailey.

"Terry!" shouted Granddad Bailey. "Have you lost your mind?"

"Sorry, Grandma. Sorry, Granddad. No time to explain," said Terry as he pulled Aaron toward the front door. "We're going for a run."

Aaron struggled to release himself from Terry's tight grip. "Are you crazy? Why would we go jogging right now?"

"It's Timothy. I know it. Your dad went to confront Timothy."

Aaron was finally able to free himself. "What?"

"Aaron, just come outside with me and I'll explain."

Aaron pressed his lips together and shook his head, but complied all the same. Once outside, Terry began, "Timothy's not some little lackey your dad's going to intimidate! He's smart. Incredibly so. And he's dangerous. He always has people around him. Your father doesn't know what he's getting into."

Aaron scowled. "My dad's not afraid of anybody, Terry. It's more like people are afraid of him!"

"Not Timothy." replied Terry. "Trust me, we have to go now!"

"Go where?"

"To school," said Terry.

Aaron furrowed his brow. "What? To school? This is getting crazier and crazier!"

Terry gripped Aaron's sweatsuit with both hands and pulled him closely. "You said you're my brother, right?"

Aaron scowled. "Yeah! So what of it?"

"Then trust me, my brother!"

Aaron stared at Terry. "Fine. I don't know what's going on in that bullet head of yours, but I'm with you."

Without another word, Terry began to sprint down the dirt path of the Bailey farm. Aaron quickly followed him. They turned onto the main street and continued to run, passing field after field until Aaron could no longer keep pace. As they made their way past country roads and into residential neighborhoods, Terry slowed down to allow Aaron to reach him. Soon, they were at the main entrance of Avondale High School.

Aaron bent over and put his hands on his knees. Panting, he said, "Okay, we're here. Now what?"

Terry furrowed his brow. "Don't worry. She will come."

Aaron slowly stood erectly. "Who?"

A light blue sedan slowly approached. "Emily!" said Terry. "Come on!"

Terry pointed to the back door while he jumped into the front.

"Terrence!" said Emily. "I hope you know what you're doing! I had to lie to my parents!"

"Terrence?" repeated Aaron, smirking.

"Emily, this is my cousin, Aaron." Terry paused. "Excuse me, I mean, my brother."

Emily reached behind her shoulder and extended her hand. Aaron scooted forward and gently squeezed it.

"Pleased to meet you, Aaron," said Emily.

"Yeah, I've been wondering where Terry's been hiding you," Aaron replied.

"Okay, formalities are over. We need to go," said Terry. Turning to Emily, he continued, "You remember how to get there?"

Emily nodded as she proceeded down the street. "What's going on, Terrence? You couldn't have chosen a worse night. It's dark and windy. I wouldn't be surprised if it rains and you..." Emily's voice trailed off.

"It's better that you don't know. I apologize for asking you to do this for us, but I couldn't think of anyone else."

"You know I'd do anything for you," said Emily as she extended her hand.

Terry caressed her shoulder. "I'm sorry, but please, both hands on the wheel."

"So she doesn't know what's going on, but she does know where we're going?" asked Aaron.

"That's right," said Terry.

"So tell me!" said Aaron.

"Phoenix. Knight's Inn, to be exact."

Aaron shook his head. "And why's that?"

"Because that's where your father is," said Terry.

When they finally arrived at the hotel parking lot, they were greeted with the noisy sound of several ambulances and the flashing lights of police cars.

"Terrence, what is happening?" Emily shrieked. "Please, tell me!"

"Just stop here and let us off," said Terry. He unbuckled his seatbelt and kissed her on the lips. "Emily, please drive straight home."

"I'm frightened," Emily replied. "I'm frightened for you."

"I'll be okay. I promise. In the meantime, I want you to do some research on Ohio State University."

Emily crinkled her forehead. "What?"

Terry smiled. "I have to go!" He kissed her once more. "I love you."

Emily smiled widely. "You said it! I knew you would!"

Terry paused for a moment. He nodded at Emily.

"Come on, bro," said Aaron.

Leaving the car, they quickly walked toward the main entrance of the hotel. They had not gotten far when a pair of paramedics crossed their path. Aaron stared at the first gurney. Underneath a dark gray blanket was a man with a thick dark beard. Attached to his face was an oxygen mask. Terry put his hand on Aaron's shoulder. "Aaron, I'm sorry."

The second gurney passed. The body was completely covered. One of the paramedics muttered, "There's no way this one's gonna make it. Might as well put him in a body bag."

His partner nodded. A cold breeze passed through, causing Aaron and Terry to shiver. The blanket on the gurney moved, falling slightly to the side. Terry's eyes widened. "Calvin," he whispered.

Aaron stood motionless. His eyes followed the paramedics hoisting his father into the back of the ambulance. Terry slowly left him, walking toward the outside patio of the hotel lobby where an unmistakable figure dressed in a golden suit remained standing.

"And remember, if you need any further corroboration," said Timothy, "please contact Senator Brawnchild."

After the officer had left, Terry approached more closely. Standing next to Timothy were two men, formally dressed in a manner that marked them as members of The Standard.

"Brother Terrence?" said Timothy.

Terry swallowed deeply. "I was informed that you might be involved in a confrontation."

Timothy smiled. "So you haven't abandoned us after all. I knew you would come back. That makes me very happy, Terrence."

"Timothy, I'm sorry."

"*No wahala.* All is forgiven. We suffered a slight amount of collateral damage, but nothing substantial. We did lose one of our guardians, but such people are easily replaced." Curling his lips condescendingly, Timothy suddenly reached out and touched Terry's cotton jacket. "Brother Terrence, are you in need of proper clothing?"

"No, I—we—rushed over here."

"I see."

Aaron appeared, but was quickly intercepted by the two men who accompanied Timothy.

"Brothers, he's with me," said Terry.

Timothy nodded and the two men quickly stepped aside, allowing Aaron to pass.

"As I have often instructed," continued Timothy in his usual self-assured tone, "we must always be prepared for opposition. In this case, our encounter involved little more than a common thug. He proved to be less than adversarial, and I have been assured that he will remain behind bars for the rest of his life. That is, if he survives." Suddenly, Timothy paused. He turned toward Aaron. "And who is this strong young man? I'm guessing you are Aaron, the cousin I have heard so much about."

Aaron nodded. "Yeah, how did you know?"

"I know Brother Terrence would not choose just anyone to accompany him during such a moment as this. Besides, I think I recall seeing you before. Perhaps it was in a newspaper." Upon saying the words, Timothy recoiled. "Aaron…Aaron. Remove twenty years. Replace the beard with a light goatee, the scowl with a much more pleasant expression." Timothy smiled. "I do not recall your surname, Aaron."

Terry stepped forward. "Timothy, it's not like that."

"Really? I believe your words would grant me more assurance if your allegiance were not so questionable at the moment." Timothy then addressed Aaron. "Will you excuse us? I would like to speak to Brother Terrence in private."

Aaron shook his head. "No. He ain't going nowhere."

Timothy arched his brow. His large eyes wandered throughout Aaron's face. "Interesting. Such loyalty. Such instant reaction. So **visceral**. I believe you would lay your life down for Brother Terrence."

Aaron raised his chin. He furrowed his brow in a steely gaze.

"Timothy, please," said Terry, "there's no reason to involve Aaron."

"Your place is with me, Terrence," said Timothy. "You belong at my right hand."

Terry exhaled deeply. He shook his head. "I admire you, Timothy. I admire you greatly, but you have to change. You have to stop hurting people."

Timothy huffed. "You poor misguided soul. You continue to see the world from a narrow lens. I fear I may not be able to convert you from the tiny path of the deontologist."

"No, Timothy, I am not looking at morality from some isolated incident," said Terry.

"Really? And how is that?"

"I am looking at the end, Timothy. And the end of your world is destruction."

Timothy furrowed his brow deeply. His jaw tightened.

"Yes, a world where people do not value the weak. A world where people no longer care, no longer feel. Timothy, your world is a world without love, without happiness. The world you propose is a world where we lose our humanity."

Timothy remained still.

Terry put his hand on Aaron's shoulder. "Come, Aaron, it's time to go home."

17

THE STATE CHAMPIONSHIP would be decided at Arizona State University. On the front page of every media outlet throughout the state were pictures of Aaron and Scotty. Both boys were interviewed and contrasted in the press. Scotty Parker, the defending champion; and Aaron Holmes, the challenger. Scotty, the quarterback with the golden arm; and Aaron, the most athletic quarterback in the state. Scotty, the son of a highly successful college football coach; and Aaron, the grandson of a simple farmer.

In the spacious collegiate locker room, the entire Avondale team assembled, their helmets lying on the floor next to their bended knees. Coach More took a few steps in front of his assisted coaches and addressed the team. "Don't be intimidated by the stadium. Don't be intimidated by the noise. Don't be intimidated by Yuma. You earned the right to be here, and I don't mean our last game. You earned the right to be here all season. You earned it with your sweat and your sacrifice. You earned it with honor. You earned it with courage. You earned it with commitment."

Aaron stood up. "Honor! Courage! Commitment!" he bellowed.

Jeff Buckey followed and joined in. "Honor! Courage! Commitment!"

Soon, the entire team was standing and chanting. Several players put their helmets on and began to strike each other like two dominant rams. Then, as the yelling reached a feverish pitch, Aaron raised both arms high into the air.

"Coach More, Coach Spriggs, and Coach Morales. My fellow soldiers, I have an announcement. Before we go to battle, and give Yuma a serious asswhoopin'—."

Once more, the locker room exploded with shouts. "Hoo-rah!"

"—I would like permission for two new players to join our team."

Leonel Reyes, who was standing next to Aaron, lowered his brow. "Two players?"

"Yeah, two," whispered Aaron.

The room suddenly became quiet. Coach More adjusted his black cap. "Aaron? What are you doing, son?"

"I know I disobeyed orders last week, Coach, and here I am doing it again; but I've been talking with the guys, and we made a decision."

Aaron paused and motioned to Leonel, who nodded before walking to the main entrance. As all eyes remained fixed on the opening of the large door, Terry entered along with Granddad Bailey.

"Your grandfather's gonna play for us, too?" asked Jeff Buckey.

Aaron scowled at him. A few others snickered. "The first new player I would like to announce is Mr. Aaron Bailey."

Several quizzical expressions could be seen throughout the room. Coach More, in particular, furrowed his brow deeply.

"Yes, Aaron Holmes will not be available today. He will be replaced by Aaron Bailey. I've given this a lot of thought, and it's something I'd like to do. My father was never there for me, and probably never will be." Aaron made direct eye contact with his grandfather. "It's always been you, Granddad. You raised me, you taught me right from wrong, and it was you who taught me the value of hard work." Aaron embraced his grandfather. "If it weren't for you, Granddad, I don't know where I'd be right now."

Granddad Bailey nodded and smiled. A slight amount of moisture had gathered in the corner of his eyes. "Aaron Bailey. I like the sound of that."

The Avondale players put their hands together. They then shouted, "Hoo-rah!"

Aaron waved his arms. As he did so, his teammates fell silent. He then motioned toward Terry.

"Thank you, Aaron," said Terry. "A lot of you know I've struggled this year. I abandoned you. I abandoned my coaches. And for that, I am truly, truly sorry. I wasn't right inside. I had to find answers. Answers to questions that I had held deep inside for a long time. I still may not have them, but I'm here. Here, where I belong."

"Hoo-rah!"

Terry nodded. "I will join you today if you will have me. I am ready to do anything to help you—to help us—win. If that means playing with you, I will run with everything that is in me. But if it means standing alongside you, then I will proudly cheer for you. Semper fidelis."

"Hoo-rah!"

Coach More approached Terry and extended his hand. Terry grasped it eagerly.

"Semper fidelis, Terry," said Coach More. "We're glad to have you back. You can wear your uniform and support your brothers on the sidelines."

"I understand, sir," said Terry.

Larry Butler walked forward. "Coach, I've been doing my best to fill in, but that's all I've done. Terry's our running back."

"No, Larry, Coach is right," replied Terry. "You've been here. I haven't. It's your position now."

Larry shook his head. "Listen up!" he shouted. "I'm volunteering to give up my position to Terry! I took an oath at the beginning of the year that I would support and defend my brothers against all opponents. The best way for me to do this is for Terry to play!"

Several players nodded. A few began to clap.

"Hold on, everyone," said Terry. He turned to Larry. "That wouldn't be right. This is our last game. You have to play."

"He will play," said Coach More. "Larry will be reactivated to the special teams unit."

"Everybody hear that?" shouted Aaron. "It's settled! Hoo-rah!"

"Hoo-rah!"

Jeff Buckey led everyone onto the field. The cheers sounded like thunder. Aaron stared in all directions, observing the thousands of faces in the crowd. As he marched past the cheerleaders and toward the sidelines, Coach More waved to him. "Aaron! You know what to call!"

"Heads!" Aaron replied, "Always heads."

"And protect those ribs!" said Coach More.

"Yes, sir!" replied Aaron as he backpedaled toward the middle of the field.

"Hey, watch where you're going or you're going to fall over," called out a familiar voice.

Aaron quickly turned around. "Scotty! How you doing, man?"

The two quickly grasped hands and bumped shoulders.

"I'm good," said Scotty. "I've been working on those dance moves. How about you?"

"Been working on my throwing motion," said Aaron.

"So I've heard. Well, whatever happens, just remember, this isn't our last game," said Scotty.

Aaron furrowed his brow. "What do you mean?"

"I've made up my mind. I'm not going to play for my father. I'm going to USC, Aaron. Word has it that you're going to end up here at ASU. So this is just the beginning for us, man. We're going to be rivals for a long time."

Aaron released a wide smile. "Sounds good to me, man."

The referee cleared his throat loudly. "Hey, uh, sorry to break up this tender moment, but we have a game to play."

Aaron called the coin flip, but lost. Even so, Scotty elected to kick the ball. As Aaron rushed back to the sideline, he continued to soak in the immensity of the entire stadium, marveling at the deafening roar of the crowd. "They won, Coach, but we're still going to get the ball."

"They're trying to ice us," said Coach More. "They don't think we're ready for all this. They don't think we can handle the pressure! But you men are going to prove them wrong! Special teams unit! Assemble!"

The assistant coaches shouted and pushed various players onto the field. Larry Butler was placed in the very back near the end zone. As the ball was kicked high into the air, and the players charged forward, Larry caught the ball. He took off downfield until he was stopped just beyond the twenty yard line.

"Okay, okay! Set up the pistol!" said Coach Morales.

As Yuma set up their defense, Coach Spriggs said to Coach More, "Can you believe it? They're playing us with a three man front!"

"Yeah!" said Coach More, who was grinning from ear to ear.

Aaron, eyeing the defense, called out, "Down! Set! Green two hundred! Hut! Hut!"

He rolled back a few steps and handed the ball to Terry, who immediately plunged forward through a large gap created by Jeff Buckey. Once he had passed the defending linemen, he dodged a strong side linebacker and then overpowered a cornerback who had converged upon him from the right side of the field. As more defenders swarmed toward him, Terry moved from left to right like a gazelle. His legs churned like fine pistons.

Coaches from both teams stood in awe as defenders hopelessly tried to bring Terry down. It was breathtaking. Next to Terry, everyone else appeared to be running in slow motion. A few defenders were able to lightly touch his jersey or get a hand on his knee, but they knew what everyone else in the stadium knew. It was over. They had never seen anyone like Terry.

As he cut sharply to the middle, he ran past the lone safety that stood between him and his destination. He then danced untouched into the end zone, where he gently tossed the ball to the line judge. The crowd erupted in pandemonium as Aaron and his teammates rushed to catch up with Terry. Led by Jeff and Leonel, they hoisted Terry on top of their shoulders. And, to the dismay of the officials, they began to parade him around the goal post.

Meanwhile, at the very center of the stadium, lost between the myriad of faces, a charming man in a brown checkered coat and celestial tie stood and applauded. He turned to the formally dressed man on his right, and then to the one at his left. A pleasant smile appeared on his handsome face. "Terrence, my dear Brother Terrence," came forth the words with a melody so pleasant that they resembled a song. "So much talent, so much potential. *Maintenant la question s'impose. Seras-tu mon Pierre? Et moi, je te dis que tu es Pierre et que sur ce rocher je construirai mon Eglise, et les portes du séjour des morts ne l'emporteront pas sur elle.*"[27] He then paused. His eyes narrowed. His smile disappeared completely. In an ominous tone, he continued, *"Ou seras-tu mon Judas Iscariot? N'est-ce pas moi qui vous ai choisis, vous les douze? Et l'un de vous est un diable!"*[28]

Endnotes

1   *BibleGateway.com.* Mark 8:36. KJV. n.p. n.d.

2   *"Make Me an Instrument of Your Peace, Saint Francis Prayer."* Catholic Online. N.p., n.d. Web. 7 Sep 2013. <http://www.catholic.org/prayers/prayer.php?p=134>.

3   *"Library."* The Walden Woods Project. N.p.. Web. 7 Sep 2013. <www.walden.org>.

4   *"Knowledge is Power Quote."* Brainy Quote. Bookrags Media Network, n.d. Web. 7 Sep 2013. <http://www.brainyquote.com/quotes/keywords/knowledge_is_power.html>.

5   *"Wikipedia contributors. "A journey of a thousand li starts beneath one's feet." Wikipedia, The Free Encyclopedia. Wikipedia, The Free Encyclopedia, 19 Aug. 2013. Web. 3 Nov. 2013.*

6   "Ronald Reagan Quotes." Ronald Reagan Quotes (Author of The Reagan Diaries) (page 2 of 7). N.p., n.d. Web. 15 Apr. 2014.

7   *Quotation 28715."* Quotation Page. QuotationsPage.com and Michael Moncur, 2013. Web. 7 Sep 2013. <http://www.quotationspage.com/quote/28715.html>.

8   *IU School of Liberal Arts.* The Santayana Edition: The Critical Edition of the Works of George Santayana. IU: 2011. http://iat.iupui.edu/santayana/content/santayana-quotations.

9   *Transcript of Martin Luther King Jr.'s 'I have a dream' speech.* Foxnews.com. Aug. 27, 2013.

10 *"Michael Jackson Lyrics:* "We're The World (USA For Africa)"." . AZYLyrics.com, 2013. Web. 7 Sep 2013. <http://www.azlyrics.com/lyrics/michaeljackson/weretheworldusaforafrica.html>.

11 "Bible Hub." Proverbs 9:10. Biblios.com, n.d. Web. 21 Dec 2013.

12 "Bible Hub." Deuteronomy 5:16. Biblios.com, n.d. Web. 21 Dec 2013.

13 "Bible Hub." Mark 12:31. Biblios.com, n.d. Web. 21 Dec 2013.

14 "Bible Hub." Luke 6:37. Biblios.com, n.d. Web. 21 Dec 2013.

15 "Bible Hub." 2 Thessalonians 3:10. Biblios.com, n.d. Web. 21 Dec 2013.

16 "Bible Hub." Matthew 22:14. Biblios.com, n.d. Web. 19 Jan 2014.

17 *"That which does not kill us makes us stronger."* Brainy Quote. Bookrags Media Network, n.d. Web. 21 Jan 2014. <http://www.brainyquote.com/quotes/quotes/f/friedrichn101616.html >.

18 Cardinal Roger Mahony in a 1998 letter entitled "Creating a Culture of Life."

19 Brainy Quote. Bookrags Media Network, n.d. Web. 16 Feb 2014. http://www.brainyquote.com/quotes/authors/c/Lao Tsu_3.html

20 *"The unexamined life is not worth living."* Brainy Quote. Bookrags Media Network, n.d. Web. 21 Jan 2014. <http://www.brainyquote.com/quotes/quotes/s/socrates101168.html#q6XrkfJZMAqtRuGu.99>

21 "Bible Hub." Luke 10:2. Biblios.com, n.d. Web. 16 Feb 2014.

22 Brainy Quote. Bookrags Media Network, n.d. Web. 16 Feb 2014. http://www.brainyquote.com/quotes/authors/c/confucius_3.html

23 "Quotation #364 from Michael Moncur's (Cynical) Quotations." Quotation Page. QuotationsPage.com and Michael Moncur, 2013. Web. 16 Feb 2014. < http://www.quotationspage.com/quote/364.html>

24 "Bible Hub." 1 Corinthians 13: 1-8. Biblios.com, n.d. Web. 16 Feb 2014.

25 Hughes, Langston. "Let America Be America Again." Poet's.Org. Academy of American Poets, n.d. Web. 17 Feb 2014. <http://www.poets.org/viewmedia.php/prmMID/15609>.

26 "The Declaration of Independence." *ushistory.org.* Independence Hall Association, n.d. Web. 18 Feb 2014. <http://www.ushistory.org/declaration/document/>.

27 *BibleGateway.com* Matthew 16: 18. Segond 21 (SG21). n.p. n.d.

28 *BibleGateway.com.* John 6:70. Segond 21 (SG21). n.p. n.d.

CPSIA information can be obtained at www.ICGtesting.com
Printed in the USA
BVOW05s1913110416

443824BV00003B/128/P